Isobel **of Glenmoriston Series of Books**

Wolves and the Curse

This is a MacAlpin Story

Zaynab El-Fatah

Dedication

To all
victims of domestic violence,
male and female,
past and present.

Contents

Main Characters

Book 1

"The Tragedy That is Zahra"

Book 2

"Shapeshifting, Haunting & Depravity"

Book 3

"Misty Mountain Ranch"

Illustrations by Brisbane Artist Claire Karger, Contributions by Jonathon Grant,

Localised Highlands

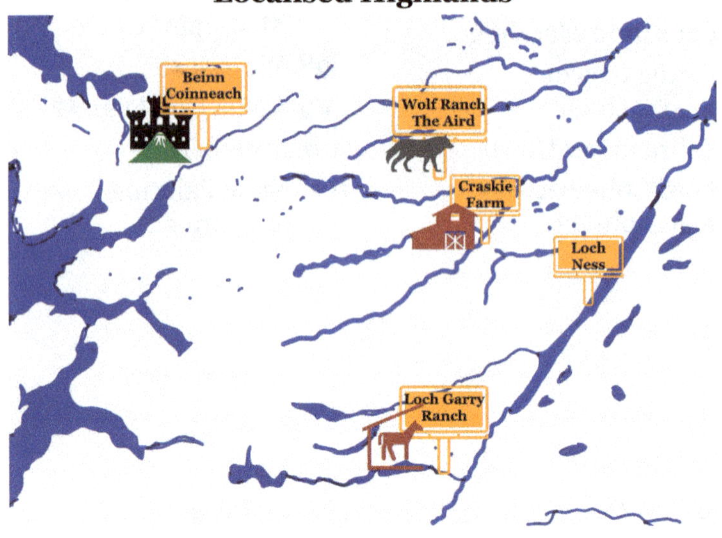

Clan Maps 1700s

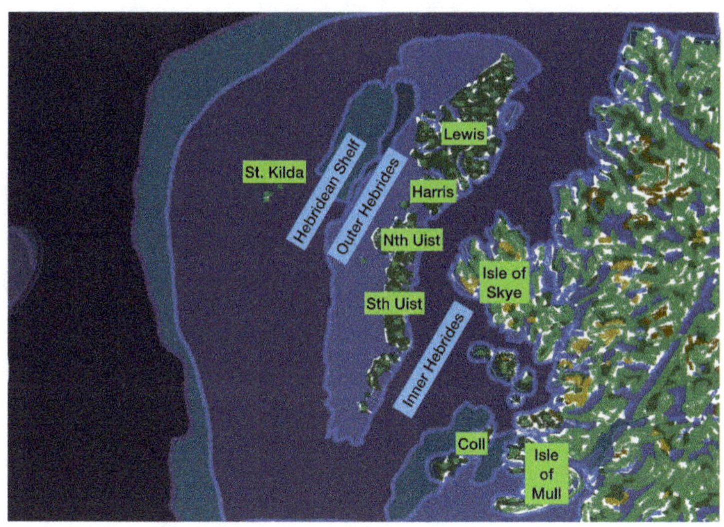

The Hebridean Islands

Introduction

"May your cattle wander off at night,
May your chickens cease to lay,
May the wolves eat your sheep,
And your wife's face turn to mush...
by your violent hand....
Lost be your horses, your bairns and your life
Never again will love return to your marriage bed
Only a wolf like stranger can ....
Her face restore.
But love for you will be....
Never more — A Druidic Curse.

She didn't see his fist coming, it was too quick. It knocked her off her feet and she hit her head on the corner of the dining table on the way down to the stone floor, unconscious landing hard, flat on her face. She awoke through blurred vision, to see the familiar face of the old man from the Crohn's house, Coinneach MacAlpin.

"Hello Zahra, my dear child. You are coming home with me for a wee while, with your two youngest bairns, Causantin and wee Dihaoine. Your daughter, Isobel has packed your belongings, as well as the bairns' belongings. You've taken a nasty hit to the head and face, so you have a concussion, so don't try to talk. I'll take good care of you. I'll bring those books over there with us too, and when you are well enough, you can read to me," the kindly gentleman said. Despite his age, he lifted Zahra up effortlessly with Dihaoine, while Causantin was following close behind him, holding onto his legs, beneath his kilt.

Grigor was nowhere to be seen, but apparently, he had granted permission to this man, whom he had never met before, to take Zahra to his home of an unknown location. They were all mounted on his horse, with Dihaoine strapped to Zahra's front and Causantin holding onto the gentleman from behind. His belt added extra safety to secure him, at Zahra's suggestion in case he fell off. He was still a wee lad. Zahra had no re-call of what had happened to her, after she had been struck, because she had been unconscious, so she didn't know, when the older man had arrived, or what had transpired between the men. She was glad of it though, as his horse took them higher and higher up the snow-covered, misty mountain and time seemed to have lost its meaning.

Forward

Padruig Dubh Grant asked himself what a woman from another time, was doing amongst them and asking probing questions. It was for a book, she had said, as she came and went, gathering information. She hadn't met spectres before, and was wary of him and he had never met someone, who could come and go from another time, wearing strange blue trousers, but it was Samhain. She conceals her identity and goes by the name of Zahra.

From the farm in the Aird, Cannich in Glenmoriston, down to the Glengarry farms and across to the magnificent Highlands of Scotland, Zahra navigates the 18th and early 19th Centuries. Meeting spectres from across time, she is accidentally killed and marries two of the Seven Glenmoriston Men, and divorces them both, only to remarry them while miraculously being able to give birth to many children, despite living in what was now her Otherworld. No-one else in that world was able to produce new life, once deceased. She and her spectre husbands and friends, live a hidden and secretive life, whilst intermingling with the living but her ability to procreate, doesn't go unnoticed.

Violence being a way of life, she unexpectedly meets Coinneach. None of this was meant to happen, but she was dead now and could never return then, to her first family. Her husband Grigor reactively punches her then contemplates her destruction, when Coinneach MacAlpin then tells her that he had been expecting her to come into his life. Living atop a magnificent mountain in ancient, palatial surroundings, her journey throughout life and her own death, was to encounter him, he tells her. Battling her own inadequacies of learning how to live in that time, she overcomes most battles, except who to trust, or for how long, as well as the physical abuse towards her and then that of her own precious son.

Coinneach brings peace to her for only a while, as well as much needed protection. A handsome man of royal descent, his identity is mysterious and mythological but it's all in his name, Coinneach MacAlpin, which meant nothing to her in not coming from that part of the world, or that century. This is a story of love, lust and longing for intimacy for people who needed each other for different reasons, where her children are never forgotten and some of our favourite characters move in and out of the story line. Zahra's introduction to the world of wolves takes on many forms, both physical and spiritual.

A royal baby is needed to complete Zahra's life and Coinneach is the father. How long then did she have in a marriage that she thought would endure? Contemplating her own end, she then rekindles an unlikely, old friendship and Inverness in the Highlands becomes her safe haven, but only for a while. And yet, another child is born to Zahra.

The tragedies that befall Zahra seem endless, until Grigor returns.

Book 1

"The Tragedy That is Zahra"

1. Herbs, the old Man, and a Pup

Zahra asked her son, Hector to accompany her to the old Crohn's place. She thought that she remembered the way there and John Fraser wrote down the directions on a piece of paper, indicating any landmarks along the way for the two of them. Satisfied, that herbs were truly the purpose of the journey, her husband, Grigor Mohr MacGregor, eventually approved, with wee Dihaoine on Zahra's back and her son, Hector as her bodyguard. After asking her many questions first, as to the nature of her journey, concerning herbs, Zahra explained to her husband that although she had been given samples of all the herbs from Cannich, she was unsure of what some of them were intended for.

The wee book that had been passed from Old Isobel of Glenmoriston, down to her daughter Helen, had mysteriously disappeared after Helen's suicide, so for Zahra, there was a combination of guess work, knowledge, and complete ignorance with her herb garden. She took samples with her, to show to the old Crohn to identify their uses, whether they were just for flavouring food, medicinal purposes or downright poisonous.

"What I am seeking, Grigor is a herb that I know exists, for the prevention of any further pregnancies, so we can have more sex, without the concern of my being with child afterwards," Zahra explained. Grigor went a little red in the face, not expecting such a candid reply over the

dinner table, with their whole eccentric family listening.

"Will it affect your lactation for wee Dihaoine?" Grigor asked.

"I hadn't thought of that, but I will ask her. So, do you want me to go the full two years breast feeding Dihaoine, without any interference, if it does affect lactation?" Zahra asked.

"Aye, of course, I do," Grigor replied.

Grigor was a bit snippy over the entire issue with balancing both his needs from Zahra and the wee bairn's needs from Zahra.

"Do you want to come Grigor?" she asked.

"Nae, the old Crohn doesna like me," Grigor replied. "You could ask her what she meant though, about knowing who you were. She might learn of the gaps in your family tree," he suggested.

Quite frankly, Zahra was tired of the whole matter concerning her family tree, which seemed so important to everyone else. She knew she could never produce acceptable Clan credentials in the land in which she now found herself, the Scottish Highlands, before the turn of the eighteenth century.

Hector started to cheer up, with his new responsibility of taking care of both his Mither, Zahra and his wee sister, Dihaoine.

Hector had everything prepared, early the following morning, while her oldest daughter, Isobel packed up food for them both into their saddle bags. Zahra suddenly felt a pang of longing to be parting with her husband, so she dismounted and went to him once again, to reassure him that they would be home before dark, as the days were becoming shorter. Zahra was unaccustomed to Scottish weather and short daylight hours as wintertime approached, so her husband didn't altogether trust that she would be home before it became dark. She told him how much she loved him and tried to make him feel confident, but he knew it was a risk allowing his wife this much freedom, even with their trustworthy son, Hector.

"Are there really herbs that can prevent pregnancy?" Grigor asked again.

"Aye apparently, but I don't know which plant it is, darling. I have my sketch book with me as well, to identify all the other plants, or even mushrooms that might be helpful too, medicinally. I might already have it here, but I don't know that yet. Helen must have destroyed her Mither's book before she killed herself, or someone stole it afterwards," Zahra said sadly. Grigor helped his wife back onto the horse and told her to take care of herself and their wee bairn.

"Well, there was no cure for whatever ailed Helen, that was for sure," Grigor remarked.

Poor Helen was still a topic of conversation, long after she had hung herself from the banister in Glenmoriston and had left poor Hamish and the staff, to find her like that, God forbid.

It wasn't too hard to find the old Crohn's house again, if one had full daylight and if it wasn't snowing. The small old house just seemed to appear out of nowhere and the wrinkled old lady, was standing there at her front door, waiting for her, it seemed.

"Zahra," she called. "We have been waiting for you," the old Crohn said.

The horses were carefully stabled and fed first and Zahra introduced her handsome son, Hector who towered over her now, as he had grown so tall suddenly. Upon entering the wee stone home, the old lady introduced an older man present also, who was seated in one dark corner, with a shadow that was cast across his face, in the poor candlelight. His name was Coinneach, or today that would be Kenneth she said, disgusted at how her language was altered to suit the English.

"I am pleased to meet you Master Coinneach," Zahra said. She was more than just surprised to find that there was company.

"The Master wants to see you clearly Zahra, so sit on the floor closer to Himself. His eyes are not as they once were," explained the old Crohn. She indicated for Hector to take a seat by the fire.

Zahra hesitated for a moment wondering who the gentleman was but followed her instructions and sat in front of him, on the floor where he could see her clearly.

"He will touch your face," the old Crohn said, "So allow it," she commanded. Zahra allowed the older man to touch her face as he ran his fingers all along her jawline as he felt her high cheek bones and her fine nose. Then his fingers ran across her eye sockets to her brow, and he measured the length of her forehead. He spoke a language unknown to her, but the old lady understood it and replied in that same odd, sounding language. It wasn't Gaelic or Erse. She was starting to wish that she had chosen another time to come because of the strange man but felt that she had to co-operate and get it over with.

He confirmed Zahra's eye colour, hair, and skin. After learning her story, he asked other questions that were physical once again and asked for Zahra to lean forward, while he felt her neck, spine and ear shape. He asked for her to stand up then, which the old lady translated. "He will now feel your body shape, so allow it," she said. The old man's hands felt Zahra's shape from her shoulders to her waist to her hips, as well as her arms and when he wanted to explore her thighs, Zahra stopped it.

"That's enough. My husband would disapprove," Zahra stated becoming disturbed. She then asked why he needed all the physical and visual information about her.

"I have been summonsed here by the old Crohn, who believes a certain thing of you, and I am here to verify or deny that. That is to say my dear that, I am here to identify who you are," Master Coinneach replied.

"I have told you who I am. I am not from here. I am not Scottish," Zahra said. "I wasn't meant to be dead, but I am," she explained. She was starting to become annoyed with this man.

"That's what we are here to help you with. I was expecting a visitor from a far-off land, who would come to me with knowledge, not of our time and it appears that it's you, as this woman was of the early MacGregors, related directly to Griogar, brother to King Coinneach. I have identified you as Clan Gregor of our early royalty. Your features are as they should be." Coinneach said.

"Your husband gave you a brooch from Culloden Field, is that right?" he asked.

"I'm not giving it to you, if that's what you want. It's mine," Zahra declared.

Smiling, the older man leaned forward into the light, revealing more of his features.

"You look similar to my husband, just older and much fairer than him," she added thoughtfully.

"Aye, you need to tell him that he can do no better than with the woman he married. I will give you charts to indicate your family tree, but it ends there, at Culloden with your ancestors who died there," he said. He took Zahra's hand, feeling her body temerature and looked deep into her green eyes. "You want a herb to keep your husband from straying, by preventing a pregnancy, but there is at least one more bairn to come from you, before your role ends. You cannot take that herb or discourage him from being with child again, unless you marry another, of course. He fears that he might lose you, and maybe he will," Coinneach stated.

Zahra felt as if she had just been cursed and pulled her hand away.

With that, the older man, stood up and Zahra saw that he was surprisingly, very broad and tall, and his back was as straight as an arrow. He then said that he would see her again, very soon, then he departed.

Zahra hadn't heard the whimpering sound until then and looked to hear where it came from. A dark grey puppy was underneath one of the old Crohn's chairs.

"Oh, it's a sweet little puppy," Zahra exclaimed. The puppy licked her face vigorously and sniffed at her breasts.

"What is he doing Mistress?" Zahra asked.

"He is hungry lass, is all and he can smell your breast milk. He came to my door just yesterday emaciated and starving hungry and thirsty. He must have lost his Mither. There was a big shoot here a while ago, maybe his Mither was shot? I gave him everything I had. Can you give him some of your breast milk?" she asked.

"But he has sharp wee teeth. He may bite me Mistress," she responded.

"Then don't let him suck lass, just squirt it into his mouth somehow," the old Crohn said.

Zahra took out her breast to feed the young pup when he tried to suckle directly from her. Zahra automatically slapped his muzzle.

"Bad dog. Don't," she said, and the puppy obeyed her, and she took his mouth and opened it up, avoiding his teeth and she squirted her milk into the thirsty animal's mouth. Then wee Dihaoine wanted to be fed too and suckled on Zahra's other breast. The pup looked at his sibling, it seemed, and Dihaoine patted him on his head. They both enjoyed all of the milk that Zahra had, looking across at one another, all the while.

The remainder of the time spent there, was identifying the plants that Zahra had taken for identification and was pleased to learn of the many qualities that they imbued, including preventing pregnancy. She was indeed already growing that herb in large quantities, as it had never been used. On her way home, she was informed where to obtain mushrooms of many varieties. One type that could heal infections, so they stopped briefly to collect those, before continuing on their way back home.

The air was fast becoming colder and there was a flurry of snow, as they were approaching familiar territory, and they were both pleased that the snow had held off, until then. Hector, Zahra and wee Dihaoine arrived home, as they had promised, before it was too dark. Hector advised his Ma to go inside with the wee bairn, while he attended to the horses and Grigor was waiting at their front door, looking unhappy with his wife's lateness, it seemed.

"You are a bit late wife," Grigor stated. Zahra apologised but passed the wee bairn to her father and thanked him for his patience, as there was much to tell him. Grigor responded to her tone and was understandably curious about everything that had transpired at the home of the old Crohn, whose name was unpronounceable, so she was just the old lady, or the old Crohn.

The entire family were all seated at the table, waiting to eat.

"Come on Ma. We are hungry," lamented Fatma.

Isobel and Fatma, with the help of Padruig, had cooked the dinner, which was delicious. Padruig had even made Zahra a cup of Turkish coffee.

"You can do this well now Padruig. You won't need me at all soon," Zahra commented.

"Aye, we do. I made the bread and the coffee to help the lassies, but that's your job," Padruig said.

"Tell us all what happened then," Grigor demanded.

Hector then walked in, having achieved his task with the horses.

"Here's the mushrooms Ma," he said and placed them in front of her.

"Both Hector and I have achieved a lot today and he has been a wonderful companion and protector," Zahra said.

"There was a strange man there Da," Hector divulged, ahead of time.

"What man?" asked Grigor, looking instantly worried and jealous.

"Ask Ma," Hector said.

"His name was Coinneach or something like Kenneth," Zahra said. She explained his appearance and approximate age and that seemed to calm down her husband, but strangely he had similarities to Grigor, only an older and fairer haired version of him. She showed her husband the charts, given to her by the older man, which were on old parchment, or something similar, detailing her family tree from King Cinaed MacAlpin and Prince Griogar of the Picts, right up until the time of the Battle of Culloden when the brooch was worn by her direct ancestor. After that, the records are lost, he had said.

"He said I am related to early Pictish royalty, like you Grigor," commented Zahra. "He said to tell you that you could do no better than me," she added. "He said other stuff about waiting for someone from a far-away land to come with knowledge, but I didn't follow all of that," Zahra said. "Also, he said that I would have one more, wee bairn, so as not to take the medicine to prevent pregnancy," added Zahra and she showed them all, the strong-smelling herb that would be used for that.

"I'm glad you are not drinking this as a tea Ma," echoed the sentiment around the table from her bairns, as well as Padruig who examined the smelly herb up closely.

"Smells like poison Zahra. Don't drink this and keep it away from the bairns. If it's in the garden here, cover it over so not even the birds, can eat it," Padruig added seriously.

"I don't want another bairn Zahra, have you forgotten that?" Grigor said, sounding annoyed.

"I didn't agree to anything, but that was his prediction. He was like a Seer. I am sorry if it upsets you. Do you want me to leave out things that he said, that might upset you?" Zahra asked.

"Nae, what else?" Grigor asked.

Hector told the attentive family that the older man, whose eyesight was poor, felt his Mither's face and all over her body, just to be certain that Zahra was of Clan Gregor.

"I did not let him feel all over my body, Hector," Zahra corrected. "When he wanted to feel my thighs and legs, I told him that he couldn't. I told him it was the domain of my husband," Zahra said, correcting any misunderstanding.

"That's right Da. Ma said that, so he didn't touch her there," Hector said, hoping to please his father. Grigor was becoming obviously enraged.

"You were just supposed to get herbs Zahra, not all of this," Grigor said angrily.

The family all knew then that the conversation was going to deteriorate from there and hurriedly finished up their meals and Isobel collected up their plates and bowls.

"But Ma, the wee wolf pup. You didn't tell Da that you breast fed a wolf pup," Hector said, hoping to gain maximum attention, and it worked.

"Wolf pup? Hector, it was just a wee puppy dog that was hungry, and I didn't breast feed it. I was asked to give it milk, so I squirted milk into his mouth. Don't make your father upset," she demanded.

"Zahra, did you or didn't you feed a wolf pup?" asked Grigor.

"I thought it was a cute little puppy dog, not a wolf, but aye, I gave him my breast milk. He was starving hungry, poor wee thing," Zahra answered.

Padruig and Alex both held their heads into their hands.

"Go to bed family," said Isobel. "Come on wee bairns, off to bed now," she said as she ushered everyone from the room, except John, Padruig, Alex and Grigor, while Fatma finished cleaning up and left the room too. Zahra had Dihaoine on her breast once again, while she answered a barrage of questions for the next half hour, which was exhausting.

"I need to change her nappy, Grigor and put her to sleep and take a bath myself. I feel dirty after that journey out there. That older gentleman also said he would see me again soon. I didn't know he would be there Grigor. I am so sorry that he was there too. The old lady called him there, without my knowledge," Zahra explained looking a bit upset.

Realising then that he had been too harsh, he held out his hand to his wife and kissed her gently on the face.

"I know it wasn't your fault, but you will not go there again," he ordered. Zahra agreed and she hadn't planned to go there again anyway. It was all a bit too weird, even for her.

"Hug me," Grigor said, and Zahra warmly hugged her husband and was relieved he still loved her. "After all, you might be a Princess," he said lightly.

"You keep the papers my love," she said. "If it displeases you, burn them. My relationship with you is more important than knowing any of this," Zahra said.

"He's not burning them. That's historical documentation," said Padruig. "Keep it Grigor, but it won't change anything with Zahra, other than now you know that she is better than that woman from Inverness. The baby thing is another matter, but maybe I can help. If you don't want to sire a new bairn, I can be its father, if you like?" Padruig suggested.

"What? That's unbelievable Padruig. You are so opportunistic. Nae, never. I'll not do that with you. That's disgusting and disrespectful to even verbalise. Grigor, you would never agree to that, would you?" begged Zahra. "I thought you didn't want to see me suffer again, no matter who the father was. There is suffering in childbirth, and that man didn't say that I would survive it next time," she added.

"Go to your bath Zahra and put the bairn to sleep and wait in bed for me. We men will talk further," Grigor ordered, bringing her conversation with him to an abrupt end.

Alex declined and went to bed with his wife, Isobel who had been tired and needed some comforting. John sat listening in for a time but was awkward, after all it was him who had introduced Zahra to the old lady, and it wasn't supposed to end like this. Zahra would never agree to having a bairn with Padruig.

It would be sad to see their friendships end, but inevitably it would, John concluded.

◇

Zahra was in one of the three most fertile days of her cycle when Padruig entered her bedroom the following morning as she was making their bed. Grigor was out working, as were most of the family engaged in farm work of one kind or another. He was the only man in the house and other than her two youngest bairns, Zahra was alone. She knew immediately what was on his mind as he looked directly at her. Despite her protestations, he claimed he had the permission from her husband to engage sexually with her, to make him that baby.

Zahra continuously refused, but to no avail and she was raped by her one-time good friend, now of many years. Crying as he left the room, she didn't know what to do. Her heart was shattered, and she would most likely be with Padruig's child. Then she remembered that poisonous herb, up in the kitchen cupboard. She went quickly to get the herb and steep it, as soon as possible to prevent a pregnancy. It was a horrible smelling herb and it tasted as strong, as it smelled. She gulped down an entire cup of herbal tea, then another until she felt nauseous, when Grigor came inside.

"What are you doing Zahra?" Grigor asked.

"You should know. You arranged the rape with Padruig last night, didn't you?" she said gulping back tears of heart break. "We are husband and wife Grigor. How could you do that to your own wife, without even a good reason or consent with me?" she said accusingly to a guilty looking Grigor.

"So, what were you just doing?" Grigor asked.

"Do you have to know every little thing I do from one hour to the next, when you are noticeably absent when your best friend Padruig, was raping me in our bedroom?" she asked.

"It wasn't rape, I gave him permission," Grigor said.

"I am sorry but that's not how this works. This is my body, and my permission is required. You arranged for him to rape your wife. What have I ever done to you Grigor, that could equal that kind of betrayal within our marriage? You call yourself a Catholic. What a load of rubbish. You have no morals. You cannot prostitute your wife. I am not for sale. Do you understand me, Mr MacGregor?" Zahra exploded in a manner, unlike her in character. She'd had enough of the ill treatment towards her.

"You drank that tea, didn't you?" Grigor asked angrily.

"Aye, I did, so there will be no bairn from that rape, you monsters, all of you who were in agreement to that despicable act," Zahra retorted.

2. Didn't See it Coming.

She didn't see his fist coming, it was too quick. It knocked her off her feet and she hit her head on the corner of the table, on the way down to the floor, landing hard on her face. She awoke through blurred vision to see the familiar face of the man from the old Crohn's house, Coinneach MacAlpin.

"Hello Zahra, my dear child. You are coming home with me for a wee while, with your two youngest bairns, Causantin and Dihaoine. Your daughter, Isobel has packed your things, as well as the bairns' things. She was kind enough also to pack up a lot of beef, vegetables and honey and Turkish coffee as well. You've had a nasty blow to the head and face, so you'll have a concussion. Don't try to talk. I'll take good care of you. I'll bring those books over there with us too and when you are well enough, you can read to me," the kindly gent said.

Despite his age, he lifted Zahra up effortlessly, with wee Dihaoine. Causantin was following close behind him, clinging onto his legs, beneath his kilt.

Grigor was nowhere to be seen, but apparently, he had granted permission to this older man, whom he had never met before, to take Zahra to his home of an unknown address. They both mounted on his horse with wee Dihaoine strapped to Zahra's front and Causantin was holding onto him, from behind. His belt added extra security to secure him onto the horse, at Zahra's suggestion, in case he fell off because Causantin was still just a wee lad.

Zahra had no idea what had happened to her, after she had been struck, because she had been unconscious, so she didn't know when the older man had arrived, or what had transpired between the men. She was glad of it though, as his horse took them higher and higher up the snow and fog covered mountain and time seemed to lose its meaning. When they arrived at the top, he carefully took his passengers down from his horse and a worried looking groom took his horse, while another servant took their belongings.

Inside was a beautiful warm mansion with very high ceilings, different to what she was accustomed, and it overlooked the braes and glens. It was palatial, with Turkish and Persian rugs on the floor and many large portrait paintings on the walls, that appeared extremely old. He handed the food parcel from Isobel to a middle-aged woman, who must have been the cook, and she called him Master, as did they all, very respectfully. The cook looked very worried about the injured guest, with two bairns.

"Make up the biggest room overlooking the glen," he instructed, "Two smaller beds for the bairns in the same room as their Mither," Coinneach instructed.

"Master, can I attend to the Mistress's face first, or later?" she asked.

"I'll take care of my guest," he said and placed Zahra, gently on an enormous purple, velvet covered, lounge with lion's feet, carved at the base, in front of the big roaring fireplace. Then Zahra closed her eyes and began to drift off.

Knowing every inch of her face fortunately, Coinneach first felt where there was swelling, broken bones or skin and found all three.

"Poor lass," he said compassionately to himself. Dihaoine wanted to be fed, and she climbed up over her Mither's body to her breasts to be fed.

"Ma, Ma," Dihaoine cried.

"It's okay my darling, just take a drink when my blouse is undone. Master Coinneach, can you please unbutton my blouse for my wee bairn," Zahra asked with her speech making it difficult to understand and painful for Zahra.

The kind gentleman obliged, not daring to do more than what was asked of him, to avail the child of her Mither's breast. He couldn't help but notice, what beautiful breasts Zahra had, as she gave her bairn her brown nipple to suckle on. Putting another pillow under Zahra's head, he went to get a bowl of warm water to wash Zahra's face from the last of the dried blood that had been left behind, from Isobel's hasty clean up job, as Zahra's nose and mouth continued to bleed. It was then that she thought she felt the presence of someone or something else and her jaw felt miraculously healed. She had bitten her own tongue at some stage that kept bleeding. He washed her ever so gently, catching any more blood from her mouth from loosened teeth that miraculously were no longer loose.

Her nose and jaw had both been broken, as well as both of her eye sockets, but that was easy for him to repair, or so it seemed. She felt grateful to the healer, after all she had a new wee bairn who relied on her continuing to feed her breast milk. It felt like a miraculous healing taking place each time he turned around, her broken nose was no longer broken, her eye sockets were no longer broken, nor shattered in parts, just horribly bruised and both of her eyes were filled with haemorrhaging blood. Who was this miracle man who could heal her when moments before her body was all but a lifeless corpse?

"Can I please remove your arisaid?" Coinneach asked. He hadn't yet seen her hair, nor felt its sticky texture and in removing her arisaid, it made everything more visible for him. There was drying blood in her very long brown, curly hair, so he searched for the source. Her brunette ringlets had long been a source of ridicule for her, as a child because nobody else had hair like hers. Defiantly in adulthood she had allowed her hair to just keep on growing and it was now down to her knees, but on this day, it was soaked in blood, on one side. Zahra had an open, gaping wound on her skull behind her right ear, around two inches long or longer, that required stitching and sterilising. She just hoped that no-one would shave off her hair that she loved more than her health, it seemed.

He would need the eyes of his cook after all, he thought. Healer he may have been, but he had his limitations. When Mairi came back, after preparing their room, Coinneach asked her to bring him his stitching kit. Coinneach used to do all of his own stitching, but his eyes weren't good enough now and he was too vain to wear eyeglasses.

"Mairi, I need your eyes for this wound please," he asked, as Dihaoine kept on suckling on her Mither's breast.

All of Zahra's bairns had been breast fed for a minimum of two years each, or until she was with child again and the breast milk maintained their children's health throughout their lives she had always claimed, and so had Grigor. Zahra's eyes continued to close, while she drifted off to sleep, but Coinneach had to keep her awake intentionally, fearing that she may not wake up again. "Zahra, do you have another name, so you will respond to me better?" Coinneach asked. How he knew that Zahra wasn't her real name, was indeed a mystery to her. But he was a man of many mysteries, she was fast learning.

No one there had known that Zahra wasn't her real name, and it was whispered to him in both surprise and secrecy. Both Mairi and Coinneach worked on the wound, aided with a pain relief given to her in a herbal tea. Despite it being a strong herb, she could still feel and hear every stitch, as it went in. Her whole face, then felt like it was throbbing with pain. She was just only now beginning to feel how bad the damage was or had been. She thought she felt a butterfly like motion along her nose and jaw line when Coinneach turned his head just for a moment. Then it ceased as did the bleeding when her jaw on both sides seemed to be back in place and no longer broken, if that was at all possible. So too was her flattened nose and both of her eye sockets, leaving her eyes that were both haemorrhaged, and just how this was achieved she never knew. But he refused to give her a looking glass.

The bairns were both very tired, but Causantin wanted to eat first, before his bath. He didn't even notice that his Ma looked any different, he only knew her still to be his Ma and was extra clingy and loving.

"I'm hun'ry," he complained.

"Aye, you must be. You have been a brave lad today. Wait a little longer for Ma to have her wounds fixed, then cook here, will give you a meal, then both you and your wee sister will have a bath," Coinneach said.

"Aye Master," Mairi responded. She did as she was told, with no argument or questions asked as to who or why these guests were there on their mountain. The Master always knew best, and the servants knew, never to doubt or question him was Zahra's immediate observation of their household. Mairi's shift would end that day, but only after the bairns were attended to and asleep, as well as the Mistress, who needed help in the bath. Mairi knew she wouldn't be able to lift her into or out of the bath.

"Master, can you please help me when I bathe the Mistress?" Mairi asked. "There may be other injuries that we can't yet see," Mairi said. Zahra was pleased when the stitching was over finally and Coinneach gently wiped her face, as a tear rolled down her cheek remembering some of what had happened to her, on the farm.

"I upset my husband, I think," Zahra said, then began to sob.

"It's alright my dear. Don't try to remember what happened to you or to speak, it's too soon. Time will confuse you, so just relax and allow us to heal you," Coinneach said.

"Padruig raped me," she continued, while weeping, still in disbelief. Mairi then took the bairn and went to bathe her, as Zahra wrapped her arms around Coinneach's waist, and he held her gently in his arms.

"I guessed as much. Did you drink the tea that I gave you to prevent pregnancy?" he asked.

"Aye, two cups of it. It made me feel nauseous. Was that enough? I don't want Padruig's wee bairn, please Master

Coinneach," Zahra asked. "It's enough, dear lass," Coinneach answered. "Why did he rape you?" Coinneach asked.

"My husband gave him permission to do it, so my husband wouldn't be the father of my last bairn," Zahra cried into his side.

"So, there is already permission from your husband to have your next bairn with someone, other than himself?" he stated incredulously, almost talking to himself.

"Zahra, we need to handfast for the sake of decency. I wish you were my wife, but handfasting for now will make us decent, don't you think, or the servants may gossip?" Coinneach said.

"Aye," she answered, and the cook tied their hands together with a ribbon to make a small ceremony and it was official, before God anyway. He looked emotional momentarily but now, this was her and her issues once again, because of Grigor letting her down continuously. She had always thought so highly of him, but bit by bit, his character had changed, and he was becoming more violent. So many people had helped her each time that she was injured, or he had gone to another. It was a humiliating life.

She adored her bairns and was so proud of them all, but her marriage was a mess.

She decided to keep in touch by mail with her other bairns, especially Isobel, her oldest daughter, to reassure them of her well-being and to learn of what their activities were, such as Fatma meeting the lad, Simon Fraser, as well as a friend of Ali's from the farm. She was keen to see her daughter married, especially now, but worried about Isobel, if Alex decided to leave the farm with Padruig, which she worried may have happened already. Padruig had predicted that they would all leave, one by one, if she left and this time, she was in no hurry to return to the farm in the Aird, if she ever did, but she couldn't stop thinking of her other bairns now stuck on the farm, without her.

Zahra missed her hero Hector, and her heart ached for them all.

Coinneach and Mairi had succeeded in feeding, bathing, and putting the bairns to bed and it was now time for her to be bathed, with their assistance. Mairi removed all her clothing, as her arms were both uncoordinated, as were her fingers. She would take a while this time, to overcome the brain injury, if that was the accurate diagnosis. Each time Grigor injured her, it was worse than the time before. Zahra was ashamed of herself and felt her life was never going to be normal, as she searched for solutions in her limited understanding of Grigor MacGregor.

Zahra had fallen in love with Hugh Chisholm and love had seemed like it was enough, but of course it wasn't and now his body was somewhere at the bottom of the waterfall in bits, as her son, would say. Then she was in love with her current husband, Grigor Mohr MacGregor and that seemed like it was enough, despite knowing how hard it was to please him. However, she had always adored him, so coming to terms with what he had done to her was confusing. Why did she deserve such an awful blow? He had been her 'sweet Grigor', until now.

Love was not enough in the Otherworld, in Scotland's Highlands, where she was now living, for a very long time to endure, until the Day of Judgment. She solemnly wished once again that Hugh had never accidentally killed her, that day in Glenmoriston, which was a blur, just like the details of this awful day in the Aird, but with Grigor. Accepting death was one thing, but her life wasn't as she thought it would be, after you died.

This life after death was much harder than life itself, she thought.

3. Master Coinneach

As Coinneach lifted her gently into the bath, naked as the day she was born, she felt no embarrassment. Was that because he was too old to be embarrassed in front of, or was her brain injury much worse than she had realised? Unsure of why she was comfortable, being naked around the caring persona of Coinneach, she cooperated with the wash and thanked God that there were only masses of bruising, but no open wounds or broken bones, this time, only the ones on her face and head.

Mairi wanted to ask what had happened but refrained from asking, out of respect. Washing her very long hair of ringlets was a little more difficult than her body but was achieved with Mairi removing any traces of the sticky blood. Being lifted from the bath was a little more difficult as Zahra herself tried to climb out but was stopped by 'Himself'.

Mairi thankfully, then dried her off, while she sat on a milking stool, feeling dizzy and afraid that she would fall off the stool.

"I am dizzy Coinneach," she said reaching out for him. He took her hand and they both dressed her.

"Master, will she be alright on her own with the bairns?" Mairi asked.

"I hope so Mairi, but she can call me, and I will help her if there is a problem. She won't stay like this, we hope. It's just the concussion," Coinneach said hopefully, aware that Mairi would leave soon with her husband, one of the Farm Managers whom he employed. They lived in a house on the farm, further down the mountain, where there was adequate grazing for the cattle.

Zahra hadn't noticed the plump, dark grey pup that had grown since she first saw him at the old Crohn's house. He was now

Coinneach's pet dog, and he was obviously well fed as he had grown a lot in just a short time, it seemed.

"When you come tomorrow Mairi, there will be letters for you to post in the village, if you are up to it, as well as cooking beef stew, which is what the family are all accustomed to eating. The bairns may like scones too, with jam and cream," he added. He went on to give instructions to his cook.

"You will need to plan your meals differently for some time, I think. Ask the wash lady to wash out all the blood from the arisaid, as it is a nice-looking garment too," Coinneach asked and bade her good night.

Coinneach took both of Zahra's hands and asked her to stand up very slowly and he assisted her awkwardly walking in the direction of her bedroom, then he carried her the rest of the way. He had selfish thoughts of taking advantage of such a vulnerable and trusting woman, as his manhood stirred, but chose the high ground. He wanted her to trust him. There was a warmth between them, and he liked that. He hadn't had feminine company in a very long time, in fact he couldn't recall the last time he had a woman in his house other than staff.

"Here you are Zahra. This is your room with the fire just keeping the room warm. Your bairns are safe, as are you. We have security outside every night," he said. He took her to her bed and pulled back the bedclothes.

"Enjoy your sleep my lovely. There is a chamber pot under your bed, as well as under wee Causantin's bed. There is also a wash jug over there to wash your hands, should the need arise. If you want to open the window you may, but it will be too cold, in my opinion. It's best to keep it closed," Coinneach added. He kissed her gently on the forehead, but she automatically wrapped her arms around him to say goodnight.

He enjoyed the physical touch of this woman, and he then found it hard to get to sleep. Zahra was unaccustomed to not having all of her bairns hovering around her and there being a lot of physical touch in all her relationships.

It was lonely, as Zahra too tried to fall to sleep in the enormous, ancient, and creaking old house, with strange new smells and complete uncertainty of what the morrow would bring.

Finally getting some rest, Zahra was woken up by her two small bairns. Causantin was on top of her telling her that wee Dihaoine was hungry, and he wanted to pish. She told him where the chamber pot was under his bed, and she went to get out of bed herself when her head then began throbbing with the sudden movement of sitting up and she then had a massive headache that was going to be hard to be rid of. She heard Coinneach at her door softly rapping on it and asking if she needed any assistance.

"Aye, I do please. Can you bring Dihaoine to me to feed, I have a throbbing headache after I moved to get up," she explained. Coinneach was already washed up and dressed well for the new day, as was his habit, she thought of the kindly and very clean older gentleman.

"Come on wee Dihaoine, you are a bit smelly. I'll change her first, if that's alright," he said. "You really know how to smell out the whole room, don't you wee one?" Coinneach said, as he humoured her.

"I've pished too, Mr. Coinneach, so I am smelly too," Causantin said, not about to be beaten by who was the smelliest bairn, at the start of the day.

"Zahra, you have the most adorable wee bairns. I love them both. They are such characters," he commented. "Do you want to bathe them both before you feed Dihaoine or after?" Coinneach asked. Cleanliness, or maybe the hot water, was obviously a high priority for this man.

"She will need feeding now, my friend or she will be upset, but Causantin can have his hot bath, if that's how you do things," Zahra replied. He handed Dihaoine to Zahra looking concerned as he saw her appearance.

"How do you feel today?" Coinneach asked.

"My whole head and face are throbbing, and I have an awful headache," Zahra answered. The cook was already there, so he called out to her to bathe Causantin and to dress him before breakfast.

He was objecting to another bath and was hungry, but it was the rules, apparently and his hair was dirty, it had missed out on being washed the night before, because it had been all a bit hasty.

"Take your time cook," Coinneach said.

"Ma, I don't want to bathe again, it's too cold," Causantin pleaded.

Zahra encouraged the lad so his hair could be washed.

"Aye lad, we might have to cut it off if it's dirty," Mairi the cook said. He then cooperated, because he loved his hair, as did most of Zahra's bairns. Dihaoine was happily feeding when he asked Zahra if her headache was abating, which it wasn't. He took a cool wet cloth and wiped her forehead, to see if it helped. Then dabbed her forehead with lavender oil.

"Apply this as often as you need Zahra" he said giving her a wee bottle of lavender oil.

"Anything will help, thank you. I think I just sat up too quickly, is all," Zahra said.

Zahra's health over the coming days was slowly improving from headache to headache or from her attempts to walk from her door to the other rooms. She was wobbly on her feet and didn't want to fall again and so was aided by Coinneach intensely, for a full week. His cook removed the stitches finally, as that wound healed, but the headaches were still frequent.

"Does your husband often hit you like this?" Coinneach asked one day.

"He didn't use to hit me at all, other than strapping me for a punishment, of course," Zahra answered honestly.

"He would strap you. What for?" he asked.

"I can't remember all of the things now, but I may have said something that displeased him, or the food wasn't ready on time, that kind of thing, but as I became a better wife, that stopped and the bairns also asked him to stop doing it," Zahra said. "That all changed recently after he began seeing that MacGregor, widow woman in Inverness. When we were in Loch Garry, he tried to choke me, then there was this punch to my face, which he has never done before, despite signing a contract with his friends that he wouldn't do me harm, like the choking again, but he has done. In my opinion, it is inevitable that eventually, I would be disposed of completely," Zahra said.

"He doesn't like me anymore. He might still love me, on some level, but he hated what I did, which drew attention to him and his infidelity with that MacGregor woman. Not that I can prove that there was infidelity, but I am certain of it." she explained.

"Do you have her address?" Coinneach asked.

"Aye, I do." Zahra said and wrote it down with difficulty.

"I'll have someone look into that for you," he said.

"When a man starts to hit his wife and gets away with it, by her submission to him, the violence increases. Eventually, he will, as you say, dispose of you. After Dihaoine has been weaned from breast feeding, is a guess at the time frame. He would already have a woman already planned to replace you, but I will investigate it to see if it's the same one, or a different one, unknown to you yet. If you were to go back to him, you may not survive it, the next time, and the concern I have is, that he will then turn onto one of your older lassies, like Isobel, who is loyal to you, as well as being another man's bairn," Coinneach conjectured.

Zahra couldn't stop the flow of her tears, knowing that her marriage was not only finished, but that Grigor was now a threat, to not only herself, but could be to Isobel too.

"Is my marriage over then?" Zahra asked, stating the obvious.

"I have lived for a long time Zahra, and I have committed many sins, as well as killing the families who were married to the armies who we were fighting against, here in Scotland. They were bringing their wives into Scotland, and it was my job to deter them from doing that and I was very successful at it, and I am not proud of what my role was, only that we were saving Scotland. Nowadays, I cannot bear the suffering of women, in the slightest. That is what I live with every day and why I will do everything I can to help you Zahra, because in my opinion, your marriage is over. Aye, but I am so sorry about that and with so many lovely bairns," Coinneach said.

"Zahra, on another topic, I have a confession to make, or maybe you could call it a declaration, so you can either accept or reject my friendship and my protection. I may be falling in love with you and like any man would, I find you sexually appealing to me. If you were to divorce your husband, although older than you as I am, I will not get any older, being like you, of the Otherworld. I would therefore like to marry you legally if it was what you wanted also," Coinneach said.

"I would pay for all of your expenses and clothes as well as any of your bairns who chose to live with you, or who are yet unmarried, like Fatma. If the adult children remained on the farm in the Aird, Grigor should pass it on to the oldest son and depart from you all," Coinneach said. "You said Ali earns a wage at Cannich, how long will his course last and what is the duration of his commitment to them?" he asked.

"Ali is committed for two years, he has completed more than one but not quite two years, then he was to take that knowl-edge to the Aird, to grow the oat crops," Zahra replied. "Hamish Chisholm takes care of him there, at Cannich," she added.

"If he has other needs, just let me know and I will pay for it," he said. "Sounds like a responsible lad," Coinneach added.

"Aye, he is Fatma's twin, so she misses him a lot. I was hoping to marry her this weekend to a Fraser lad, but there are two lads to choose from. One lad of the living and one of the Otherworld," she added.

"Can I have something to vomit into please, I feel sick?" Zahra asked.

He only just got it to her on time when Zahra vomited up all that she had eaten the previous night. "I'm sorry Zahra, it was my fault. Too much information. Please forgive me?" he asked. Resting his hand on her thigh, he gently squeezed her in a familiar way, and she didn't mind now that his intentions were made clear and there was no guess work.

"So, you care for me Coinneach?" she asked as she wiped her face. "I can't imagine anyone liking me with a vomit bucket in front of me, not yet washed and I suppose my skin colour is greyish. Additionally, I have dependent bairns and half of the gang of the Glenmoriston Men hate you now, because of me," Zahra said.

"That's without even mentioning all of my injuries," she said.

He then laughed, which surprised her.

"You have painted an accurate picture for a lady who has a brain injury," he commented. "You are going to be just fine Zahra, my love and yes I do care for you," Coinneach answered quite boldly.

"The instant you sat in front of me in the old Crohn's house, you owned my heart. Now let's get you to the bath, but you'll know now that I am looking upon you in your nudity, as a normal man would, with what I have declared," Coinneach said. "Do you accept my assistance?" he asked.

"Aye. I do. You use posh words and use no Gaelic, to me anyway. Thankyou. I can at least understand everything you say," Zahra said and smiled at her friend and touched his face gently in a new and gentle way, as if to search for God to give her the answer to his declaration.

"I won't kiss you, because I smell of vomit," Zahra said, attempting a smile, as she went to bathe with his assistance. He decided to lift her bodily as he was an exceptionally strong man, despite his age and it was easy to carry her along the corridor to bathe her, leaving the bairns with the cook.

Zahra was still uncoordinated, with unbuttoning or buttoning her clothes, so Coinneach loaned her one of his woolly jumpers to avoid using buttons, all the time. He undressed her with them both, now knowing that there was an attraction between themselves.

When he saw that she was not wearing underwear, he asked her if she normally did and she said she didn't, which he approved of. His hand fell across her female anatomy, and he wanted to stimulate her, but he asked first as she herself felt the longing and the desire when his hand fell onto her private parts. Carefully moving his fingers, he searched for her clitoris which he found, and she held him around his neck, which he wasn't expecting. Her longing was more extreme than his, he thought as he gently rubbed her clitoris and held her firmly in his hands. He felt the tiny organ slowly grow under his fingers. She couldn't stop the moan that came from deep within her soul and she wept for love lost and love gained but most of all, love lost. Her husband of so many years was to be no more, as she gave herself over to this new-found love. She wept into his big and manly arms, as his hand explored further, bringing her ecstatic joy at the same time as relief and sorrow.

When Coinneach removed his kilt, it exposed a very large member, bigger than her husband's.

"Do I need to go slowly?" Coinneach asked.

"Aye, I think so," she said.

"Are you sure you want me?" Coinneach asked. Her body ached for him, but her heart ached for Grigor.

"Please can we wait a little longer? Maybe, I'm not yet ready," Zahra asked.

"Of course. Because when you do decide, you will belong to me," he said. "And I am a jealous and possessive man. Wait until you are certain," Coinneach added.

He lifted her gently into her bath still naked himself. He was a beautiful man of perfect proportions and unusual muscular strength. His chest hair was a mixture of fair hair and silver that grew all the way to his shoulders and down to his stomach. His pubic hair was prolific and thick, with only a few blonde hairs, the rest were still fair. His male member was unusually wide, and he was circumcised.

"Can I ask you if you are circumcised?" she asked.

"I am. Do you like that? It makes for a more handsome cock, don't you think?" he asked.

Zahra then giggled at his description of his own cock as handsome. She covered over her mouth in glee.

"You can look, it won't bite you until you say so," Coinneach said, looking pleased with his impression that he had created for her.

"It is beautiful," she confessed. "I have never seen one look quite like that before," Zahra said.

"How many cocks have you seen then, sweet lady Zahra?" he asked.

"There was my husband Grigor, then there was my husband here before him, Hugh Chisholm, Isobel's father. And in my other life before coming here, I had been married and divorced twice with three lassies to my first husband. I saw my father's once if that counts, so in total, five cocks. Is that considered too many for a lady to have seen?" Zahra asked.

"Nae, if you were married to them all and I presume your father's cock was a mistaken appearance?" he asked.

"Oh aye, it was. I was only four years old, and it seemed huge and scary at the time," Zahra said.

"You didn't have brothers to look at then?" Coinneach asked.

"Nae, no brothers," Zahra replied.

"So out of all of those five cocks, is mine the most handsome one?" Coinneach asked as he posed erect to display it in all its glory. As Zahra peeked at his cock, she became a little shy, but then said it was the most beautiful cock that she had ever seen and would ever see again, she was sure of that. The effect it had on his cock was astonishing, as it became hard, and it rose to its magnificent strength.

"You will enjoy this one day, but I have no control over him at the moment," Coinneach said totally accepting of his erection.

He began to shampoo her hair, still walking around the tub naked and she enjoyed watching him and it gave her a kind of peace that she had never felt before. A man's cock could be used as a veritable weapon, or one of love and lust, or just a natural way of being.

"Do you wear underclothes under your kilt then?" Zahra asked.

"Nae, never," he answered. "My hand can go there to pish and now another hand can go there to meet her new companion, whenever she likes," he replied. "How's the head now?" he asked.

"The headache is going away," Zahra answered. He scrubbed her body from her feet and up to her private parts carefully washing that area gently.

"I am an artist you know my dear Zahra," Coinneach said. "I'll show you my Art Studio later," he said.

"Can I paint you naked today? You are rather lovely, and I don't need to paint on the bruises, or your blood shot eyes," Coinneach said smiling.

"Aye", she replied. This made her feel even more aroused. Zahra reached out her hand to touch his male member, asking "May I?"

"You may," he replied. Zahra felt for his beautiful large member to see how it felt in her hand and to know the texture of his skin. His member began to rise again, and his skin was surprisingly softly textured, pure and unblemished.

"You two have met each other now," Coinneach said. His manner of speech was interesting to her, but always non-threatening.

"Would you like me to join you in the bath?" Coinneach asked.

"Aye, I would," she said, and he slid underneath her into the tub, holding her over his body. It was so comforting to her. She could feel his hard penis beneath her, as it became more aroused. He held his arms across her breasts and felt them both.

"Your wee one is lucky to have these beauties. But now she can't have them all to herself, I want to squeeze them. May I?" he asked. Coinneach spent time feeling both breasts, squeezing and then when milk came forth, he just put his hand over them both, measuring each breast in proportion to his hands. "These breasts are so beautiful for a woman who has had so many bairns. I love them. When you make up your mind, they will be shared between me and Dihaoine, until we have our own bairn of course," he said.

"Do you want a wee bairn with me?" Zahra asked.

"I do," he replied. "You see my dear, I died a very long time ago. One of my wives died in childbirth, leaving me without an heir, and my other two lovely big sons were killed in battle. As I am royalty, it is expected, not that that means much now, but it will mean a lot to me, if you and I can bring a royal baby into this time. What a miracle that would be. You are not of this time, are you?" Coinneach asked.

"Nae, I am not," Zahra replied. "It's better that people do not know that my friend," she said.

"I don't think I am just your friend anymore, do you? Unless you bathe nude with all of your male friends," he stated.

"I have only once bathed with my husband, let alone a friend," Zahra said. "But you are right, we are no longer just friends, are we?" Zahra rolled herself carefully over on top of him in the bath so that she was facing the man that she was falling in love with. "May I kiss you? I think the vomit smell has gone now," she asked.

"Yes, you may," Coinneach said smiling.

Leaning towards his face, she first felt all the contours of his jawline and lips and looking into his eyes, she saw that they were a dreamy blue, with a ring of unusual yellow and her heart melted. She kissed his lips gently and he responded. He sat up holding onto her carefully and passionately kissed the woman he wanted to marry and to have a family with and he had chosen her. They embraced in their watery love bed.

"Zahra, have you decided yet?" Coinneach asked. She thought he must have been bursting to make love to her.

"Aye, I would like us to be together, and you may enter me slowly, but not here. Maybe on a bed, do you agree?" Zahra asked.

He helped her out of the bath, feeling a lot better and dried her, with the emphasis being on her private parts, which aroused her again. He kissed her vagina, then he asked her to dry him, which she did with her emphasis being on his beautiful big cock.

Coinneach then carried her effortlessly to his bedroom up a flight of stairs, onto the top floor above that one. It was a huge

Master bedroom with an enormous soft bed. The windows were long and wide, extending down from the very high ceiling, right down to the floor, so the view of the mountains and the glens could be seen clearly. There was an enormous carved stone fireplace, with the fire already raging. The stones were of a different type to the rest of the house she thought, and the carvings were mysterious but they meant nothing to her. It was lovely and warm in there, as he held her bottom and squeezed it.

"I love your bottom. I want to kiss it," he expressed and kissed it. He had many unusual methods of foreplay, all of which were maddening, waiting on that moment of entry. He took his cock and reminded her of its size. "Now you know for sure of its size," he said. Zahra was totally overcome with shyness laying on his bed, as he entered her slowly, looking her in her big green eyes for any change of heart.

"Coinneach, Coinneach I want you please now," she said, and he went in full thrust as she reached her peak and he held back with such self-control, as only an older man could have. Gently rocking back and forth inside her warm and wet interior, she knew she was now with her new husband. They both gave up loud joyful sounds at the pleasure of it.

"Is it good for you? My cock's size I mean?" he asked.

"Oh aye, I can feel him on every side of me like it fills me up completely," she replied.

"You are all mine now Zahra." Coinneach said.

"I am yours Coinneach," she responded, then with hearing those words, he thrusted faster and more vigorously and then he moaned from deeper down in his soul and the man she was with, was hers forever, hopefully. He was as emotional as she was with his own tears, intermingled with hers.

"I was worried that you would not accept me, and I needed you, from the moment I saw you. I love you Zahra," he exclaimed. "I will paint you naked in every position and put them on my walls here. Will you please join me now to sleep together in our room with me, as husband and wife?" Coinneach asked.

"Aye, I will. Can you also paint one of me and the puppy dog? I really love him. He is so cute," she asked.

"Of course. I can paint an enormously big canvas of just you and the grey wolf," he stated.

"It's not really a wolf, is it?" Zahra asked.

"Aye my precious, he is and because you fed him your breast milk, the Crohn said, he will be loyal to you and guard you. The benefit to me, however, is he will always know where you are," Coinneach added. "So, wolf or dog, he stays. Tell the bairns not to antagonise him, especially Dihaoine," he added. "In my observation of you all, he thinks of your bairns, as his siblings, but that might change, as he matures," he said. "Now my dearest, you must write to your other bairns on the farm," Coinneach said.

Zahra wrote several letters with difficulty. One was to Isobel who liked to hear how much she was loved. Zahra also asked her if she could pick up the rest of her belongings from the house, as she wouldn't be returning to the Aird this time. She informed her that she was handfast with Lord Coinneach and was divorcing Grigor MacGregor when she could arrange it.

She wanted to know how many of the men were still there on the farm, as she thought she had seen Padruig leave on the same day that she had. Most importantly what was happening with Alex and whether he had followed Padruig or stayed with her and John. The biggest question was, where Grigor was and if she knew his current address, if he had moved away. Of course, she wanted to ask if he was with that woman in Inverness. How she hated that woman.

Zahra hoped Fatma would marry the red-haired Fraser lad whose name was Simon. Of course, his name had to be Simon, what else? She asked if Isobel could spare her two nanny goats, so she could start to wean Dihaoine and if Fatma could spare her one beehive, so she could have honey at her new home. She also asked which lad she liked for Fatma and how Ali was with his Mither not being there. She gave them her address which wasn't to be given to Padruig, Grigor or Alex and hoped Isobel would write back to arrange a date to go there and pick up the nanny goats.

The second letter to Fatma was more cheerful and less worrisome for her and Zahra re-assured her that she was in a safe place with a good man whom she had fallen in love with and wished to marry. She even described how beautiful her surroundings were, high up on a cloud covered, misty mountain. However, she wanted to know which lad Fatma had chosen. She had liked the sound of John's relative, the sixteen-year-old. If they handfast, she told her to give him the job with the potatoes, if Alex had gone and to help her finish off the building of the kiln. She hoped that Fatma could take over making the pottery and sell some of it at the Glenmoriston Markets.

The third letter was to Ali, informing him now of her circumstances, what had happened and how well she was being cared for and where she would remain and to notify Hamish, of her current address. She mentioned divorce to all four of them, including Hector, in his letter. She prayed that they would all receive her news well, but she missed them all terribly. She hadn't lived like this, without them all, with no plan to return, and it was new territory for all of them. Hector's letter was one that was the hardest to write because she ached to be with her big and loveable son, and she knew Causantin missed him too.

Coinneach said to his new wife of only a few days that one of his rules was to read her outgoing mail and to let her know if he disagreed with anything contained, therein. She agreed to his rules. He was, as he said, a jealous, possessive, and a protective man and had to know if Zahra had compromised herself in any way. The only comment he made was the nanny goats.

"Leave out the nanny goats my dear. I can buy those for you. It will be better to leave them with your sweet lassies," he said.

Zahra re-wrote that letter to Isobel, excluding the nanny goats.

"My handwriting is poor now Coinneach. Will it improve as I get better, do you think?" she asked.

"Aye, my love. But you must be patient with yourself. I will always be here to help you," Coinneach said.

"Don't you leave or work? I must be taking up so much of your time. Why, do you care for me so much, I don't quite understand it. I feel afraid that it will suddenly stop. Will it Coinneach?" Zahra asked.

He commenced his answer in a rather complex way.

"The "why" part is the hardest to answer, because there is a natural attraction between us that any man could feel with someone as beautiful and as sexy as you are my love, even with injuries and bruises, you are still beautiful. I had the advantage of knowing that you were coming into my life, so when I saw you, I think I was shocked, as well as in adoration of you. You were prophesied to be here from another time, with knowledge that I would need and what that is, even I do not know. Then there is the bairn that must be born of you and me and as you know, there are no other women who can re-produce in our Otherworlds.

That's good enough don't you think? As for not understanding it, I too will not understand much of your previous life, so we need to include God in that too. You do understand grace, don't you? Then you say that you feel afraid of it suddenly ending. This is your own insecurities talking, based on your previous relationships, like this last one, whom you thought you could trust. You can believe in us and trust me. Lastly, nae I do not go out to work, other people work for me and you are not taking up my time my lovely." Coinneach responded.

"I am not an ordinary person, as you must have realised by now, and I would not invest my time or money in anyone other than one given to me by God, and I will never release you. You will have me until the end of time. Can you trust in that? Can you trust in me because I do need you as my Lady to trust and believe in everything I say or do, whether it is for you, your bairns, or another?" he explained in such detail that Zahra felt bad for having voiced what she had worried about.

"That having been said, I need to know what you are thinking all of the time, so I can correct any misunderstandings you may have, like now," Coinneach added.

"I am sorry Coinneach, have I offended you? I am truly sorry for that. I do trust you and all your decisions," Zahra said. "I agree it's just my insecurity that doubted your love for me. I am unaccustomed to being able to really trust, even though I have given all my trust to two men, and it was betrayed," she said. Zahra took his hand and kissed it and apologised.

"Nae, please do not feel you were wrong to speak up about what you were thinking. It is all a process. I understand that, and I will always be here for you day and night for the rest of our lives. You are mine Zahra. You belong to me now," Coinneach stated again.

"You will be Lady Zahra Coinneach of Beinn Coinneach, as soon as the wedding papers are official," he added.

"Lady Coinneach?" Zahra queried.

"Aye, Lady Coinneach. You would have been my Queen at one time, but that time has passed. Do you like the title?" Coinneach asked.

"Aye, it sounds pretty but who would call me that?" she asked.

"Everyone except me and your bairns but in company, even the bairns need to defer to you. I don't of course," he explained. "Now my dear, enough of the serious chatter. Cook is posting the letters to the bairns, so how about you come and pose naked for me to paint?" Coinneach asked.

The Art Studio was enormous. It almost took up an entire floor.

"Do you see what's over there?" he asked. Looking into the direction that he was pointing, Zahra was amazed to see her fairy art. The very first one called 'the Incomplete Work of a Fairy'. "That artwork told me that you were nearby, but I couldn't get your name or address from them. They said you were too shy," he said, "I paid a small fortune for it as I knew it was my lady love coming to me soon," Coinneach said in his quaint way. Zahra ran her hand up his arms and kissed him passionately. He took her hand and placed it under his kilt onto his erect member and it felt good.

"The great thing about kilts is a man can hide his passion," Coinneach said. "There is a couch over there my dear, can we make love again?" he asked as he took Zahra across to a velvet covered couch and took off all her clothes in the heated room.

"This is where you will lay when I paint you," Coinneach said, then he made love to her again and again. It was magnificent as he entered her, this time full thrust immediately which made her squeal with the elation. Zahra couldn't stop grabbing at his arms and digging into his skin with her fingernails and even grabbed at his thick hair, like a wild cat, she was let loose, set free. He similarly responded to the wildness and bit at her neck and sucked her breasts ferociously, needing all of her to be his, as she also wanted him to belong to her, as she wrapped both of her legs around him giving herself over to him. He held her arms above her head at one time to suck under both of her arm pits and held both her wrists tightly, so she could not escape his grasp. She bit his ears too, equalling the biting and sucked the trickle of blood that came from there. When he ejaculated it was like an explosion into both their brains and the room was spinning momentarily and Zahra went quiet.

"Zahra are you alright, my darling. Are you alright?" Coinneach asked looking upon the temporary silence and vagueness in her face.

"It's ok, my love, I was somewhere else, I don't know quite where," Zahra said. "But it was heavenly, I never knew sex could be so heavenly," Zahra added.

"You had me worried for a moment. I thought you were gone. Oh God don't ever be gone Zahra" he pleaded.

"Who is insecure now?" Zahra jested. "It happens sometimes when an entity calls on me", she said.

"What entity?" Coinneach asked.

"I'm not sure yet, but they are tall and bluish but lovely" Zahra replied.

"Can I paint you like this? I want to capture this moment," he asked, noticeably ignoring what she had said.

"Aye," she added. "Maybe one day it will be in a museum somewhere," Zahra jested.

"It is for my pleasure, not others," Coinneach said and began to instruct her how to lie and position herself and look at him.

Nude Painting

"So, you won't sell it?" Zahra asked.

"Do you want me to sell it?" he asked.

"I've never been in a painting before. You can if you want to like to one of those sexy places where aristocratic men go and pretend, that they are not having love affairs with their poor wives at home eating cucumber sandwiches, with other posh ladies," Zahra said.

"You mean an exclusive men's club with Zahra on the wall overlooking them all?" he asked.

"Hmmm. Now that you say it like that. Nae, not really. I think I would like to be more appreciated than that," Zahra said thoughtfully.

"I know just the place where it would be considered that one's wife naked in a painting could be revered and not a dirty joke, where other men just want to take off your clothes. They would respect you as my wife and I would gain status. Do you want your bush to be fully shown in all its glory?" Coinneach asked.

"Of course," Zahra replied.

"Can you part your legs a little then and if you don't mind put one of your fingers onto your lovely woman hood with the other arm above your head revealing the fullness of your breasts. Then turn your head towards me. That's good," he instructed. "There's a young artist in Glengarry who has a nice Art Gallery. Would you like it on show or for sale there first?" he asked.

"You don't mean Kenneth MacNachten?" Zahra asked.

"Aye, the lad who sold me your Fairy Art," Coinneach said.

"Oh, I'm not sure. I know Kenneth and his wife Ivy. What would they think? And there's his brother Malcolm and their Mither Marion MacDonald," Zahra said as she sat up, looking worried. "What do you think Coinneach? Wouldn't they judge me as a woman of low morals?" Zahra asked.

"Are you a woman of low morals?" Coinneach asked.

"Nae," Zahra replied.

"Then it doesn't matter who you know in Glengarry. What is important is that it is talked about to get the highest price," Coinneach said, as he walked across to her again, smiling with an enormous erection.

"Take care of him my darling, I have paint on my hands, and he is so demanding," he said. Zahra massaged his beautiful cock, before taking his member into herself once more as she lay down, enjoying the heights of her newfound love.

He had decided on at least five paintings on canvas of her naked body in various positions, including one from behind as her bottom was a very beautiful feature. He asked her to squat on the couch facing in the opposite direction with a full view of her lovely derrière with her face turned around with only a side view of her face, to suggest never really having known her.

"Just ignore the scarring from the stitching you may see from a previous rape," she said almost casually.

She didn't notice the expression on Coinneach's face at first, but coffee time was his suggestion to take that news in.

"I think it's coffee time my darling when you can tell me all about that previous rape. Scones and cream today," he said as he helped Zahra dress and kissed her breasts as he did so. "You are so beautiful my lady love, I could eat you," Coinneach said.

"Then, I'm glad you are not a vampire," she jested.

"You have a bite on you, and you sucked my blood," he laughed. She hadn't seen him laugh before and he was so handsome when he laughed.

"When you were young Coinneach, were you especially, handsome?" Zahra asked.

"Och, aye, I was. But I still am, aren't I?" he asked. "I was then, and I am now," Coinneach said, confident of his manhood.

"Oh aye, you are gorgeous," she replied. He then kissed her like there would never be another opportunity to kiss her again. He was so desperate to take her into himself with his tongue exploring her mouth and tasting her from every cavity when the pup pushed the door open and came in to visit and went straight up to Zahra.

"I want a painting of Wolfie and I with me fully clothed, holding onto my puppy in the painting," she said.

"Nae that is not in the least bit artistic Zahra. You must be naked with the puppy but let's talk about it over that coffee," he said.

"Can I make it?" she asked. The cook looked to her boss to get his permission before allowing it. Zahra made the coffee as she had always done at home for cook as well, as for her new husband.

"I can make the stew tonight Mairi too if you like, so long as my bairn is fed, do you have a herb garden?" she asked. It seemed unheard of for the lady of the house to make the coffee or do any cooking.

"You are avoiding that other rape story. Mairi, please leave us in privacy," Coinneach ordered.

Zahra had not wanted to reveal those disgusting details of Grigor's relative, demanding rights over her and in the ensuing struggle, as he was so enormous, she was injured badly. Grigor had permitted it, as he said it was their custom, but she had disagreed and so she left him, taking two of the youngest bairns with her, until the relative was gone. That was the first time she had left home and obtained a job, unknowingly with Grigor's oldest son, from her husband's previous life. A nice man who helped her and allowed her to commence the 'Fairy Art.'

"So, there is another Grigor MacGregor, but of the living?" Coinneach asked.

"Aye. His wife, Helen committed suicide a while back now. Grigor is a very caring man," Zahra added.

"Who was his wife?" Coinneach asked.

"Helen Grant MacGregor," she responded, "She was also an artist, but she mostly painted Culloden," she said.

"I have one of those paintings," he added.

"She wasn't bad and technically correct, but they all lacked heart and soul, except one, which I was unable to procure, called "Fraser of Inverallochy," Coinneach said.

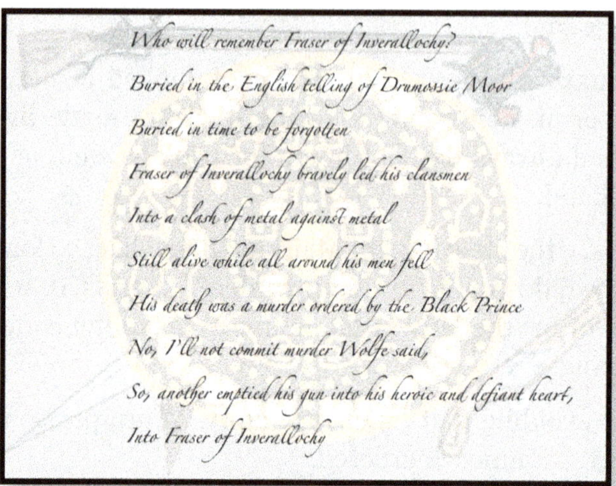

"Coinneach, you know the books you bought with us from the farm?" Zahra said.

"Aye," he replied curiously.

"You may like me to start reading them to you. That painting is mentioned in one of those books, as well as its poem." Zahra said. "Lord Simon Fraser inherited it from Old John Fraser of Stratherick, but he won't part with it either, I think," she added.

"See that was what I meant about what I would learn from you?" he said.

"Did you like the poem too?" Zahra asked.

"Och, aye, why do you ask?" Coinneach asked.

"How much did you like it?" Zahra asked.

"You are going to tell me something that's unbelievable, aren't you?" Coinneach enquired.

"How much did you like it?" Zahra asked again.

"The poem gave the painting its entire meaning, otherwise you may not understand it," Coinneach said.

"I wrote that poem" Zahra said proudly. "At that time, I was able to zap in and out of both worlds, unlike now because Hugh Chisholm accidentally killed me, but at that time, I was able to leave the poem beside Helen's work, and then leave and go home again. It was sold with the painting. I'm glad you liked it," Zahra said a bit shyly.

Suddenly, Coinneach wanted Padruig's books to see the reference to her poem, which naturally Zahra said that someone else had written.

"Where are those books Mairi?" Coinneach shouted. "Where are those two books?" he demanded again. Relieved once they were both in his hands, he saw the name of the author as being the same name that she had whispered to him quietly. Zahra's actual real name was on the front covers of both books.

"You wrote these books?" Coinneach asked incredulously.

"Aye, that's why I was here in Scotland talking to the 'Seven Glenmoriston Men,' as research for the first book. I wanted to know if they were happy with it and they were," she said feeling sadness coming over her of better days with all seven of the men. Two of whom, she later married and had adored. Zahra finished the last of her coffee, unsure where to look, feeling Coinneach's eyes boring into her.

"How did you communicate with them?" Coinneach asked.

"As soon as my family and I began talking about them, they appeared to me, but in different ways," Zahra said, then was reluctant to talk any further.

"You mean as spectres?" Coinneach asked.

"I really don't know how to label them anymore, but ghosts, spirits or spectres will do. They were very real. I am tired now Coinneach can I please go and lay down?" Zahra said.

"Of course, my love. Lie down on the couch and I will stay with you," he said feeling sorry, he had exhausted her.

The life within her seemed to drain right out of her at their mention. Padruig and Grigor had deeply hurt his new woman on an entirely different level, beyond his understanding. Padruig, even more so than her husband. For once, he felt he had no answer to alleviating that problem. It also meant that they could continue to communicate, no matter their state of being, dead or alive. Probably Grigor, too as well as Hugh. This was a different kind of problem, to which he was unaccustomed, and delicacy was obviously required, or it would only hurt her. The thought of them all making up however, terrified him. And they must have all been very close for her to have married two of them, in the first place. Highlanders always had a way of surprising him, but this was different. He decided to start reading the books, as she had suggested.

Shopping trips were always something that cheered up women. So, he decided to take her into Invermoriston to a nice lady's wear shop that he knew of, to buy her some much-needed new clothing. Maybe buy her lunch there and visit Kenneth in that Art Gallery in Glengarry in his fine coach. Meeting up with Kenneth again might be nice for her and break the ice about nude paintings. Maybe take a completed one with them? Either way, he knew he had to act.

The very next morning the coach was outside of their enormous front doors of the mansion on the cloud covered mountain, with a driver dressed nicely and two lovely matching horses. Coinneach hadn't told Zahra the night before what their plans were, but Mairi was busier than usual, preparing her bairns for a journey and then he told her.

"Darling, I am taking you shopping in Invermoriston to a nice lady's shop, then we can all have lunch there. I want to buy you nice dresses, skirts, blouses, boots, and coats and gloves for the cold weather. Of course, you may wear your family tartan, but I must approve of your choices. You may like to buy your wedding dress also?" Coinneach suggested.

"The bairns will get new clothes and boots too, what do you think Causantin?" he asked. Causantin was delighted and wanted to get in the coach right away. "Wait for your Mither, lad," Coinneach said. Zahra had to bathe quickly then and was able now to wash herself but couldn't climb out yet and called for Coinneach to help her out. He rubbed her dry, while not missing the opportunity to rub her private area.

"Do you want me?" Coinneach asked.

"I do but we don't have time, do we?" she said.

"There's always time for sexual gratification," he replied, and they went back to the bedroom and had wonderful oral sex first driving her wild, then pulling his hair demanded he enter, which he did.

"Oh my God in heaven Zahra, you drive me crazy," Coinneach said.

"If we weren't going out shopping, I would have sex with you all day long, I am so needy of you 'my fairy lady,'" he admitted. He couldn't resist her, whenever the opportunity arose.

The shopping trip was exciting, and Zahra's co-ordination was improving, although she couldn't walk too far in one go. She would need to rest in between shops. Her husband was patient, but her wee Causantin was anxious to get moving and of course Dihaoine wanted to be fed at the most inconvenient of times, but that was life with wee ones, and she was a wonderful Mither to them both and obviously adored them. The Bridal Shop looked very expensive, and she reacted to the prices and wanted to leave.

"Nae Coinneach, it's too expensive," she pleaded.

"Of course, it is, my dear because it is pure French silk. Now try it on please just let me see it on you," he begged. Zahra tried it on to please him, but she did love it. She really wanted it but could not ever imagine herself in such a glorious gown.

She came out shyly to show Coinneach, who melted at the sight of his wife in the lovely ivory coloured gown, with tiny pearls, decorating the low neckline.

"This is perfect my wife. May I now name you Anleta Thora MacAlpin, Lady Coinneach of Beinn Coinneach?" he asked. Shocked on many fronts, she didn't know what to say.

"Will you accept my gift Anleta?" he asked again.

"Aye, I do," she answered.

"Do you accept your new name Anleta Thora" Coinneach asked.

"I do," Zahra said just following her new man's need to change her name. Besides which Zahra wasn't her real name anyway, so it didn't really matter what anyone called her.

"It might take me a while to get accustomed to," Zahra added.

"It is fitting for someone of your station now Anleta," Coinneach declared boldly. The shop workers were all wide eyed with their mouths open. She heard one of them say. "Who are they?"

"Servants, please allow me to pay," Coinneach demanded. The Manageress was rubbing her hands together for the cost of the wedding dress and didn't mind being called a servant by the handsome, rich man and recommended a nice tea shop for their lunch. He bought clothes and shoes for the wee bairns too and a complete wardrobe for Anleta. He told them to deliver them at first, but Causantin wouldn't part with his new boots and tartan trouse and so all the shopping was piled into the carriage.

The young family began happily walking back to their carriage, after enjoying their big lunch.

4. Enter, James Grant

James Grant had been shopping that day too and Malcolm was supposed to have been with him, but one of his coos had begun to calve and so he stayed behind to help the calving process and trusted James to buy him a new shirt, for an upcoming occasion. James loved shopping and catching up with the gossip from Malcolm, so he had been disappointed, until he saw a familiar face walking towards him. He had only met Zahra once in Glengarry, but she was unmistakeable. Her beautiful long flowing, brown hair with those incredible ringlets, was even longer than he remembered. There was no-one else in the Highlands with hair like Zahra, let alone those huge green eyes. But she walked straight past him, without even noticing him, so she can't have remembered him.

Zahra was with only two of her many bairns, one of which she was carrying, with difficulty and so her male companion who was unknown to him, carried them both. James had never seen the like of that man before in their district and he wondered who he was. Tall, fair, strong, very straight backed and positively regal looking.

What was Zahra doing with him, he wondered and where was the bairns' father?

The big box that the man was carrying, was from a bridal shop, gave it away. Zahra was getting re-married. Had he missed the divorce?

She walked a little awkwardly, but he couldn't

quite put his finger on what was different. Was she a little unco-ordinated? The gentleman did need to assist her up into the lovely, very expensive looking carriage.

James just had to go and talk to that Bridal Shoppe to confirm their names. Was it Zahra to be certain, so he could tell Malcolm? The ladies were all very happy to tell him every little detail of the elegant couple, revealing both names that she had been known by in the shop. First, they said she was Zahra MacAlpin, but he changed her name, when he saw her in the wedding gown and so he named her Anleta Thora MacAlpin, Lady Coinneach of Beinn Coinneach.

They all laughed at being called servants by the handsome, older man.

The Manageress of the Bridal Shoppe said quite honestly, "That gorgeous man can call me whatever he likes, so long as I can look into his dreamy eyes. They are positively hypnotic," she remarked.

"Are they getting married then?" James asked.

"Son, what rain shower did you come down in?" she asked. "You don't shop in a Bridal Shoppe if you are not getting married and the Mistress carried it all away with her, fully paid for, by Mr Handsome, who is already her new husband. She is one lucky lass for sure," the Manageress added. James thanked the informative ladies but asked one last question.

"Was she a little unco-ordinated did you think?" James asked.

"Och aye, I had to help her dress and undress," said one of the workers and James couldn't wait to tell Malcolm the latest gossip.

◇

I was pleased to see my cousin James arrive back, after having completed a difficult calving for one of my youngest Highland Coos. I never wanted to lose even one of my precious coos.

"I wonder about you sometimes Malcolm with your arm right up that lady coo, but your secret is safe with me," Cousin James jested.

I was accustomed to being criticized for being overly caring of my precious coos, even reading books or poetry to them all and brushing their coats. I believed it helped them relax and become impregnated.

"Each to his own," James said. "But you missed out on some big gossip by having your hand up that lady coo," James said.

"James, I can rely on you to tell me every detail correctly, as you love gossip more than you love sex and I can't make that claim. At least I do love sex with my wife, more than any other activity," I claimed.

"So, cousin, I could walk away now mentioning 'Zahra in Invermoriston', and then leave, and it wouldn't drive you mad, until you knew the whole story?" James said very cleverly.

"Alright cousin, you have my full attention," I said and turned to face my cousin.

I always wanted to know what Zahra was doing since she had been to Glengarry for assistance to save her marriage with Grigor Mohr MacGregor. So, what James had seen was a real curiosity. James told me every detail of the man he saw her with, who was of some standing, being a regal and dignified looking, very handsome but older man. Not from around here or Glenmoriston and older than her. James described him in so much detail that I am sure that he missed his vocation as a private detective, I thought.

"And guess what she was carrying?" said James.

"Not the guessing games, please James. What was she carrying?" I responded.

"A shopping box from a Bridal Shoppe," James said.

"The shop confirmed it with me and who she was and guess what? She has had her name changed too by that man who she is marrying," James said.

"I can't believe you left that until last that she was marrying someone else, other than Grigor Mohr MacGregor. When did they divorce?" I asked, now very interested. I hadn't been told of a breakup with them, in the Aird. To my knowledge she had never left the farm, after they had returned.

"I don't know. You can do some of the heavy lifting cousin, I have done mine and you haven't even asked what he named her," James said.

"What do you mean? He changed her first name?" I asked.

"Aye, it's now Anleta Thora MacAlpin, Lady Coinneach of Beinn Coinneach," James recited proudly.

"Good God, I didn't even know you could change your wife's name. Is that even an option?" I asked.

"He seemed to think the whole world was at his feet, so of course he can, but the likes of us wouldn't dare," James said.

"It makes my father look ridiculous trying to assume the gentleman role. Now that man, whom I saw today was a true gentleman," James added.

"How is your father, James? Still unwell?" I asked.

"In all honesty Malcolm, I don't think he has too much longer to live. Then I'll be stuck with Ma, who is well, even though she never gets out of bed. Da has been ill since young Simon, my nephew, passed away. It was quite the sight, the poor lad with a broken neck and frozen solid too in the snow, by the time we found him," James said.

"Not much of a horseman then, young Simon Fraser, eh? Unlike both you and Beth. What a shame, poor lad. Anyway, you will own the business, on your own when your Da, Patrick passes away. Do you have a Trainee Manager to assist you?" I asked sincerely.

"I do now. Simon was supposed to come and work for me, but I don't think we all had enough bairns, unlike you Malcolm," James answered.

The Hart of the Highlands Manor, built by our grandfather, Padruig Dubh Grant, was soon to change its direction.

"You should write to that man, Coinneach and offer up your business for their wedding party if they are having one," I suggested. "You might need to pursue business more than your Da has done to ensure continued business," I said.

"You are right Malcolm. Is it afternoon smoko time around here yet Malcolm? I'm thirsty," James asked.

James joined Kenneth, Ivy, wee April, Islay, Angus, Ailsa, Hugh Og and security, Duncan Mohr MacDonnell, inside my house. Meredith had baked bread and scones with jam and cream, with coffee or tea. We all caught up with our respective days. Hugh Og was with my twins, Malcolm Og and Hamish-Hugh Og, learning to be Teamsters from him. They were telling me of the day's excitement as the lads walked in loud and boisterous, but lovingly hugged me and their step Mither, Ailsa. The table was both loud and happy with all the joys of family exchanged, as well as the condition of each section of the farm businesses reported.

Kenneth shared some interesting news too from a client wanting to meet with him again, by appointment, to discuss a nude painting on canvas of a beautiful woman, who was his wife and asked if we thought that Glengarry could take on a nude painting. It drew a few giggles and a few gasps, but mostly agreement to the idea. Meredith especially thought that it was progressive, and Kenneth needed to keep his art relevant to maintain people's interest.

The consensus was that if his wife had agreed to it, then why not? It was a large canvas, he said, so he would need to move a few of his older paintings for it to fit.

"Och Kenneth, you could become a really outrageous Art Gallery," said his wife, Ivy.

"The new generation making changes," added James. "Sounds wonderful, I wonder if that type of painting would be suitable in our Manor House. Like above my front desk?" he asked.

"Do you have many families staying there, Uncle James, with bairns?" asked Islay.

"Och, aye we do. So maybe certain rooms then for adults only would be a better location, do you think Islay?" James asked.

"I don't. The front desk, in reception, is my vote. Bairns won't care about that painting being a nude lady, unless it was their Mither. I think you should come and buy it when Kenneth has it on display but allow time for everyone to see it first, while being held for you," I said, "I like the idea of a nude painting, so long as my wife allows me to see it without becoming jealous," I added smiling at Ailsa.

"Och Malcolm, I am the real thing. She will be just some unknown nude," Ailsa added.

Duncan, however, seemed to think security might need to be increased when it arrived.

"Any chances of an offsider Malcolm?" he asked seriously.

"I'm still looking Duncan, I'll get you a good offsider, not just any old trigger happy or violent, odd bod," I added lamenting the loss of Hamish, my dear friend who had taken to managing Cannich.

"I heard that Zahra had asked Hamish to employ her second son, Hector and he had agreed, if Grigor allowed both her sons to live in Charlotte House," Hugh Og said.

"Have you seen Zahra too then?" I asked.

"Nae it was by mail, Hamish said. She informed him that she had moved from the Aird to a place called Beinn something," Hugh added.

"Will you tell them Malcolm, or shall I?" James said with glee in his voice, dying to repeat his gossip from the morning in Invermoriston. Who could have thought that Invermoriston could be the centre of gossip in Glengarry I wondered, of such a wee village?

"Go ahead cousin," I said, smiling at my humorous cousin who I had always liked, despite him being one of the Grant family but, so was I.

"Zahra now goes by the name of Anleta Thora MacAlpin, Lady Coinneach of Beinn Coinneach," James said.

"That's it. Beinn Coinneach," interrupted Hugh Og, feeling pleased with himself.

"Zahra or Anleta must have divorced Grigor Mohr MacGregor, or is divorcing him, because she is now getting properly married to a handsome, older man of some mysterious, high station, named Coinneach. They must be hand fast at present, as she referred to him as, her husband. She was buying a bridal gown in Invermoriston this very morning and I passed her on the street with two of her bairns and that gentleman must be wealthy, because his coach was expensive and so was the gown that he paid for, and they had a footman too. I think he would have servants too," James added.

"I'm seeing Grigor Og this afternoon about a delivery to Cannich. I'll ask him if his deceased father, has divorced Zahra or Anleta. I'll find out what's going on," Hugh Og said with certainty. "Sounds fishy to me, but maybe if you are already dead you don't need a divorce. I mean how can you take a divorce to court if you are already dead?" Hugh added.

"Good point Hugh didn't think of that. Are you up to fishing this weekend? If so, can you let Hamish know and tell him I think he's a bastard for not working for me," I jested.

"I'll leave the last bit off but maybe he knows someone in security, for us here Malcolm?" Hugh added.

"It sounds to me like Zahra or Anleta is offloading her older lads, so my guess is they have all broken up there, in the Aird and gone their separate ways, like Padruig, Alex and Grigor. Grigor must have run off to that other woman in Inverness after all," Meredith concluded.

"Oh, sorry Ailsa, it was with your Mither, wasn't it?" Meredith added knowingly.

"Aye he was with my Mither, just that once but they both promised not to do that again. I am disappointed in my Mither," Ailsa said, feeling embarrassed.

"Don't be Ailsa," said James. "Zahra was happy with her new man. I would go so far as to say as I think that she was in love with him, and he with her," James said.

"Happy endings?" I added.

"Hmmm. Sounds too good to be true. Anyway, back to work everyone or nothing will get done around here," I said.

"Malcolm, your shirt," said James. "It was 10pounds Scots" he said with his hand out waiting to be re-imbursed.

"Really? Daylight robbery, but here it is James. Thankyou cousin and give my regards to both of your parents and I hope your father gets well again soon," I added.

"Kenneth, can you let me know when that sexy painting comes. I want to peek at it?" I said out of earshot of Ailsa.

They all then went their own ways on MacNachten Farms in Glengarry including Islay, Malcolm's oldest daughter who was now the Manageress of the 'Islay Goat Farm', except for the slaughtering and Bruce still did that but eventually, her husband Angus would have to do the slaughtering when needed.

◇

5. The Priest is Coming

Anleta was exhausted after the big day out shopping but was pleased at least that she had enough milk to satisfy, wee Dihaoine. She would need those nanny goats soon.

"I know what you are thinking my precious. The nanny goats. My Farm Manager does all that kind of thing, and he was going into Inverness to get you two nanny goats, as well as a new horse and saddlery for you and a whole variety of herbs that I heard you talking to Mairi about. Your poor old horse was left behind in the Aird and I thought I'd get the yardman to make a nice garden for all those herbs and make up wee labels for them all." Coinneach said.

"I am so grateful to you for everything my darling, but I still want my horse and saddle back, unless the men have stolen it," Zahra said.

"They most likely did, so just in case, I have bought you a new horse with all the gear, so you won't stress then, if your old horse isn't there when we visit, but if he is, then we can pick him up too, if you still want him back," Coinneach said.

"I suppose it will depend on if Fatma's new husband of choice, has a horse or not. I am sure the lad from Cannich would already have a horse, but I'm not sure if Simon has one. Then again, he might be afraid of horses, seeing as how that is how he died from falling from a horse," Zahra added.

"Now my dear, I am worried about you. Please come and lie down with me and we can both rest while the bairns are resting, before we all eat tea," Coinneach said.

"Do you want to bathe first my love, Mairi has the water ready?" she asked.

"Aye of course I do, come in the tub with me then and I'll rub you all over. I am such a lucky man to have you. By the way I have arranged for the Priest to come here to save our legs, tomorrow morning ten o'clock," he stated.

"You know I am not a Catholic sweetheart," Zahra said.

"Just don't tell him and it'll all be good. The divorce papers went through already. I signed for you. I hope you don't mind," Coinneach said.

Somehow, she knew she should have minded, but instead she felt a stirring in her desire for him.

"I love you Coinneach, so much. You are a wonderful man and perfect for me. Can we make love before we sleep, I need you," she said "When we are one, it is perfectly heavenly? Can I please ask you something too darling?" she asked.

"Aye always, my precious, ask me anything," Coinneach said.

"Do you think, my condition is permanent or am I going to get better?" Zahra asked.

"What condition is that my love. You are perfection itself?" Coinneach answered.

"I am still unco-ordinated, and my handwriting isn't improv-ing," Zahra said.

"My darling, you have a wee brain injury. While you slept a few days ago, the Doctor informed me that it may well be per-manent, in small ways, like fine motor skills. That's why your handwriting isn't as good as it was. My plan is to teach you calligraphy which will be easier to complete and even more beautiful than before. Would you like that my beloved?" Coinneach asked.

"Aye Coinneach. But husband, will you still love me if I am still a bit wobbly?" she asked fearing his answer.

"I will love you more and more, especially if you need me. I love being needed by you. I will carry you on my back if I must.

I love you so much and tomorrow I will take you on my horse, after we are married and show you around this property and introduce you to the staff who need to know they have a Lady Coinneach now," Coinneach said. "I will not allow you to ride by yourself until you can manage a horse again, which I will teach you, all over again if I need to. Can we agree that you will not just get on any horse without my permission?" he asked.

"Aye of course my love, it sounds like you have it all in hand. I am glad I don't need to feel embarrassed," Zahra said.

"Why would you anyway, it was a violent attack on a wee beautiful woman and I must say, that I have had to restrain myself from doing him harm, out of respect for you my dear, now let's make love, I am needing you too much please," Coinneach asked and she smiled as he lifted her out of the bath, dried her carefullyand carried her to his room up a flight of stairs.

"Coinneach, we need a tub nearer our room don't you think?" Zahra asked.

"Don't spoil my male ego's need to show off my power and strength to carry you up these stairs," he said.

"My dear, I tasted you only once and you are delicious, I have to say. Will you allow my tongue to explore you inside and suck your delicious juices that your body gives of itself to her husband, the animal that I am?" Coinneach asked. Giggling as he placed her on their bed, he pressed open her lovely, shapely legs and began to explore her vagina with his tongue and licked her as he opened her up to himself hearing her sounds of delicious enjoyment. She came suddenly and became even wetter than before. He was ravenous for the juices that her body gave to him. Having the appearance of one consuming her, he was maddened by her taste, making grunting sounds, as he was sucking all of the fluid coming from her. She repeatedly called his name, but he resisted the temptation to enter his wife. He wanted to hear her joy for much longer until she was pulling on his hair and pleading.

"Wildcat, my little wildcat you are. Keep on asking for it my wife," he repeatedly said until she reached her peek screaming as he then knew to enter her and taking his own pleasure thrusting hard holding her down by her shoulders, so her body would take the full thrust of his large member. Coinneach moaned an almighty moan from his diaphragm upwards to his throat sounding more like a growl, releasing years of built-up need for this woman. The noise came out from him like a roar.

"We will make a bairn soon. Not immediately but it is soon," he said as he felt her rounded stomach, imagining his bairn being in there one day. "Oh, my wonderful woman, hold me darling and wrap your legs around your husband," Coinneach said. They slept like that in absolute bliss, until morning when erect again, he entered her while she slept and watched her face transition from sleepiness to glorious pleasure to start their day when they would marry in front of a Priest.

6. To Dream and to Vanish

"Coinneach. I had a strange dream last night. Can I tell you about it?" Zahra asked.

"Aye, I would love to hear what you dream about my dearest," Coinneach replied.

"I was in a strange place, that I do not recognise at all. There was a lot of thick forest and animals around, and then I saw you, but you were much younger with a wee pointed beard. You were mounted on a beautiful horse that was all dressed up, as were you also, in fine robes, but with armour too that covered your shoulders. I called out to you saying 'Coinneach, Coinneach' and ran towards you, but I was stopped by men guarding you who said to bow to you, so I did. Then I said, 'It's just me Coinneach can't you see me?' You looked puzzled, not knowing who I was, and you just rode off and I wasn't allowed to follow you and I was crying, as you left me. You turned to look at me again, as if to try to remember me, but then I was just left all alone in the forest once again. Then, there was a chubby wee bairn, a fair-haired bairn in my arms and I was seated on the top of a high, misty mountain with him. 'Coinneach' I called out again, but this time you came, and you knew me. The bairn was ours," Zahra said.

"My dearest when I was a young man, there was a beautiful woman like that which you have described, whom I saw calling out to me. So, I went to my Seer who said you were to be my wife in the far distant future, from a faraway land and I knew to wait for you from that day forward and to seek out the signs for your reappearance and here you are. The bairn is a sign that you may already be carrying our child," he said gently rubbing her stomach again and again. It is indeed a miracle you have been sent to me by God my wife. No-one but you and Isobel can have bairns in this world but how many do you have? So many? How have you hidden it so well?" Coinneach asked.

"Through fear of being caught and practicing vanishing well and all the bairns are taught to vanish from two years old onwards, except Dihaoine who vanished just before all this recent trouble happened. Hector, my son taught her how to, so she has achieved it much quicker than us all. It's too dangerous for her to do that, so please keep the front door always closed, because she went outside in the snow, invisible until her father found her there crying, and he blamed me. He thought I had left her outside in the snow. Hector had to admit to teaching her how to vanish ahead of time," she explained.

"I haven't had to vanish in a long while. I had better practise. Have you tried since your wee accident if we can call it that?" Coinneach asked.

"Nae but I can try now, however please close the door because I don't know my way around these parts," Zahra answered.

And she was gone before he got to the door.

"Zahra, where are you? You can come back now," he said with panic in his voice.

There was a knock on the door, and she was outside of their room. It had been too quick for him to have reached it on time.

"Well, you certainly haven't lost that skill, my dearest," Coinneach said.

"You called me Zahra," she said.

"Aye it came more naturally to me. Are you thinking what I am thinking?" he asked.

"We should keep Zahra. I have hidden behind that name successfully now for a long time, so maybe it should stay. Are you offended Coinneach?" Zahra asked.

"Nae, so long as I can find you if you vanish on me again," Coinneach said.

"We should only do that together when we see a problem coming my love, such as hiding from authorities or curiosity seekers. There were a few of them after the newspaper published the advertisement for the Fairy Art, so we had to make the whole house invisible too. That wasn't easy," she said. "We made it appear as an old ruin that you see from the Clearances," Zahra added. "So, they lost interest." she said.

"One thing those Glenmoriston Men were very good at, was survival. They taught you that well, at least," he added. "Now we had best prepare for our wedding day. I have a surprise for you too my love, so go and bathe now," Coinneach added.

"What surprise?" she begged to know.

"Nae, I'll not tell you until you are ready after breakfast and only if Dihaoine has been fed," he answered with all the power on his side, so bathe she did with his assistance getting out of the tub. She was getting better at washing herself, at least there was that small achievement.

"My dear, would you agree to Zahra Shushannah MacAlpin, Lady Coinneach of Beinn Coinneach, for the marriage papers?" he asked, as he dried her legs.

"That sounds nice," Zahra said.

"Good, Zahra Shushannah it is then, and I can find you if you vanish on me," Coinneach said.

"I won't do that to you again my love. You asked me if I could still do it, but we would do that together in the future," she said to reassure him. "For example, in Invermoriston after shopping for my wedding gown, there was a man whom I recognised, but I had to ignore him. Ordinarily you and I would have vanished together when we knew he was there, but we hadn't had this conversation, so he saw me with you. I hope you don't mind that I was recognised. He is a Grant. I am trying to remember his first name. Anyway, there may be folk who already know about us because he is known as a gossip. I remember now. His name is James Grant, husband to

Susan, whom I do not know at all. He lives up at the Hart of the Highland Manor with other Grant family members. He is a member of Padruig's family. He must be a grandson. But he is also a good friend and cousin to Malcolm MacNachten from Glengarry," Zahra explained.

Coinneach took out a letter from his bureau and asked. "Do you mean this place?" he asked. The letter was addressed to Coinneach asking if he wished to hold a wedding party in the Hart of the Highland Manor House. "I wondered how they got our names and the connection and now I understand. I hope you won't mind not having a party up at that place my dear. I couldn't think of anything worse, could you?" he stated as a matter of fact.

"Your lovely mansion is all we need, my dearest and each other with my wee bairns," Zahra said.

"Hmmm. Come for breakfast dearest so we can get ready for this Priest and so you can practise looking Catholic," he jested. "What religion are you, by the way," Coinneach asked as they carefully walked down the stairs.

"I'm Muslim" Zahra said, so are my daughters Isobel and Fatma. Ali was, but with the influence of others over there in Cannich, I am unsure presently," she said.

"How interesting and you won't mind marrying a Catholic?" he asked.

"I don't mind," Zahra replied.

"So, will you convert to my religion?" Coinneach asked.

"Nae, I will not do that. We can accept each other as we are, can't we? I don't want anything to change," Zahra added.

"If and when we have a bairn, I want him to be Catholic, are you alright with that?" he asked.

"Yes, I am," Zahra answered.

After breakfast with the whole family well fed, Mairi drew back the enormous drapes, revealing tables outside on the huge patio, overlooking the magnificent valley below and the mountains beyond, as well as the tiny village of Fraser Ville.

"That's a lot of tables. Are we inviting the staff?" Zahra asked innocently.

"Nae it's a surprise, you will see," he said cheekily with his secret up his sleeve.

"Can you make sure my wee bairns can't get out there, unless we are there, my love?" she asked. "I will have to wear something warm under the wedding gown then, don't you think?" Zahra asked.

"Nae the fires haven't been lit yet to keep us all as warm as toast. Mairi, is the food nearly ready?" Coinneach asked the cook, and the food was ready.

"Good, then dress your Mistress's bairns and we will go up and dress now before they all come," Coinneach said.

"Tell me who's coming Coinneach. Is it people I know?" she asked. "I won't get shy, will I? Are strangers coming?" Zahra asked.

"No strangers are coming, my dearest heart. I will tell you soon enough," he said as he helped her up the stairs once again. "You are getting stronger Zahra with all of the walking we have done, that's wonderful," he observed. Coinneach helped her lift the gown up over her head and buttoned it up for her.

"I love buttons on you now because I have to undress you my sexy wife," he said. "It's driving me mad being so close to you and feeling the warmth of your skin and feeling your sweet breath on me. I must hold your breasts first, may I?" Coinneach asked.

"Aye of course you can my husband. You can have me anytime, anyhow, anywhere and you don't need to ask anymore," Zahra said. Coinneach caressed each breast and kissed them both and then kissed her neck and her face and mouth, savouring each moment.

"I want you again. May I?" he asked.

"Aye of course anytime. You can write it in the marriage contract if it would make you feel better, so you don't have to ask. I love that you want me," Zahra stated honestly. Lifting the billowing layers, he had to enter her immediately at the very suggestion of it being written into the contract. He couldn't hold back and ejaculated with little foreplay and apologised for it.

"Please don't apologise, I am happy. I love everything you do. If I orgasm or not, is not the issue. I want to satisfy my husband," Zahra said sincerely.

"Zahra, you are crying. Have I upset you?" Coinneach asked.

"Nae, I am happy. It's happy tears Coinneach. We are getting married, and you love me," Zahra said. "What could be more magnificent than that?" she asked.

"I am going to paint another portrait of you for our sitting room to stand over anyone who enters our home, Lady Coinneach," he said.

"Are you really a Scottish Peer?" Zahra asked.

"Not just a Peer my dear but I will explain it all one day. So, I just send the papers in every year, and they must think that there is one son after another inheriting the title, but it's been only me for centuries now. Our son, however, will inherit the title and vast lands on this estate. It pays to keep them confused down there. They are easy to confuse, especially with our names repeating over and over like Coinneach, Alexander, Simon, Aonghus and so on," he explained with just a little mystery.

"Our son will be Coinneach too then?" Zahra asked.

"He will," he said with certainty.

"I wonder what he will look like. Fairer hair than my other bairns, except Isobel who has blonde hair, but your hair is a lovely colour, not blonde, not brown, just fair. I love your hair," Zahra said.

When carefully navigating the stairs again in her gown, Coinneach said, "Oh God, I have to have you again," with an emergent sound in his voice. She felt his beautiful, large member underneath his kilt to be hard and erect, so soon after already making love just minutes before and suggested they go to the bairn's room, where he could relieve that tension.

"It must be nerves darling, come on. We will fix that?" Zahra didn't have time to lay on one of the beds as he entered her from the rear as she leaned over the bed, and he ejaculated once more.

"Oh, Zahra you make me want things I never imagined of a woman," he said.

They were both smiling as they entered the very large room when the Priest who had entered, was seated on a couch. Upon seeing them both, he stood then kneeled.

"Lord Coinneach, Lady Coinneach, it is a pleasure indeed," the Priest said, as he bowed down to them both.

"Come on father, your knees won't take all that," Coinneach said, very comfortable with the Priest who was well known to him.

"My wife, Lady Zahra Shushannah MacAlpin, Lady Coinneach of Beinn Coinneach," he said introducing her to the Priest who took her hand momentarily. Zahra didn't ordinarily shake hands, with men anyway. You never know what that hand just did, she always thought, especially a Papist Priest who probably had to do himself a service every day. What a terribly unnatural life, she thought.

"Father Michael," he said introducing himself. What else would it be between Patrick and Michael and a few other names. She had only met Michaels and Patricks.

7. Wedding Day Surprise

"Now your surprise, my sweetheart. I do think, I can hear the carriage coming," Coinneach said.

They both went to the enormous front door, and he ushered her outside. When the carriage pulled up, the door opened, Causantin was clutching onto his Mither's legs while Dihaoine was sleeping peacefully in Coinneach's arms. The first face that Zahra saw, from the carriage, was her oldest daughter, Isobel and she was ecstatic to see her, and they both reached out for each other and embraced.

"Ma oh Ma, I've missed you so much," Isobel expressed as both women cried and held on tightly to one another. She was followed by her sister, Fatma with her red-haired friend, Simon Fraser. Fatma also was emotional at being reunited.

"Ma, this is Simon," she announced. "We are hand fast," Fatma said. Young Simon looked awfully shy, especially when he was hugged by his new Mither in law.

"Welcome to the family my lad. This is my new husband, Lord Coinneach," Zahra said.

"You may call me father, lad," Coinneach said.

"Father," repeated the lad, looking upon the man with awe only seen on the faces of young lads who admired their fathers, so it was a good sign for young Simon Fraser. Following behind Simon was Isobel's husband, John Fraser with the matching red hair and obviously related to Simon.

"Ma", John said for the first time ever and dropped his head down, in the memory of what had transpired that terrible day in the Aird. He was about to cry when Zahra held him closely and re-assured him that she was alright, not perfect but much better than when he last saw her.

"I thought you were dead and gone from us Ma," John said as he continued to cry.

"I'm already dead John, but I know what you mean. Coinneach has taken good care of me here and we are getting married. Do you approve?" she asked.

"Aye Ma. Are you divorced as well from Grigor then?" John asked.

"Aye Lord Coinneach took care of that," Zahra replied.

"Grigor has just disappeared now Ma. Maybe to America, we think, with that gold you gave him, accompanied by that woman from Inverness," John explained with deep sadness.

"The other two men?" she asked quietly.

"They have gone too, but I don't know where to," John said.

"I am glad of the help from my nephew, Simon, here. He has taken over the potato patch as you suggested," he explained, keen for her to be caught up with everything.

Zahra introduced him also to Lord Coinneach who once again said "Call me father," John seemed happy to co-operate with the new member of the family, as the family waited for Hector and Ali to alight.

Hector bounced down, trying to appear confident, but the pain was close beneath his confident façade.

"Hamish is taking good care of me Ma and I am working hard to make you proud of me. I am sorry Ma. I should have protected you," Hector said, then he too wept, unable to hold it in any longer.

"My hero, my Hector, you will always be my hero. You couldn't have stopped any of it, my love," Zahra said. "Please know that you are not guilty of anything. I didn't see his fist coming and so I don't remember most of what happened to me. I was bought here to safety and protection, to recover and I fell in love. He is a wonderful man. Would you like to make him your new Da?" Zahra asked as the poor lad filled up with emotion went across to her husband and threw his arms around Coinneach asking.

"Are you my new Da then?" he asked.

"Aye lad, I am. Call me father," Coinneach replied.

"Can't I say Da. Our Da has gone?" Hector asked.

"Alright then son. Just you, mind," he said.

Ali was last to alight, which made Zahra increasingly nervous. She hadn't seen her oldest son for a while now and he wasn't there in the Aird when the violence had occurred. Thank God one of them was spared, she had thought. Coinneach hadn't expected the emotional reunion and looked upon his newfound family with deep concern for them all.

"Ma, what happened to you? One minute you were there and so was Da, then suddenly, no parents at all. Did you place me at Cannich because you knew that it could happen?" Ali asked.

"Aye lad, I did. I am glad that you were spared. Did your father put the land in your name with John, like I asked?" Zahra asked.

"Aye Ma, reluctantly he did that, just before he left for America, to live with that Mrs MacGregor. I wanted to kill her Ma. She was evil for breaking us all up," Ali said.

"Your father made his choice son. He has always had choice and he must have stopped loving me. Would you please accept my new husband as your new father?" Zahra asked gently.

"Aye Ma, for you I would do anything to make it up to you," Ali said and shook the hand of his new father, first saying,

"Father, my name is Ali. I am pleased to meet you," he said. But his emotions got the better of him too and Coinneach held Ali to himself caringly and lovingly. The compassion he felt for this wounded little family was obvious and Zahra was so pleased that her husband cared for her children.

"You're a good lad Ali. Call me father if you like. My name is Lord Coinneach of Beinn Coinneach. This mountain is Beinn

Coinneach. Come inside now out of this cold wind. We don't want your Mither to get sick, do we?" Coinneach asked.

Ali was satisfied that his Mither's new husband did care for her and therefore he respected him, that was obvious. John looked the worse affected by Grigor's actions, after both Hector and Isobel. John felt the responsibility weighed heavily on him for the entire family in the interim period, until now. He began to relax a bit but never completely. He hadn't realised how much Zahra had done, until she was gone. This time he knew that it was permanent and the sadness of it was hard to reconcile for the entire family, including for his own bairns with young Isobel.

Zahra stood before the Priest with her new husband and they both recited their marriage vows. She wasn't asked if she was Catholic, but he didn't dare to ask anyway. The whole family and the cook, as well as her husband, were present as witnesses to the occasion. Coinneach gave his new wife two gifts. One expected and one that was totally unexpected. Mairi called her Mistress aside and put a necklace around her neck and explained it was an heirloom from her husbands' family, the MacAlpins. It contained multiple large, precious gems and diamonds. On her lovely neck, the necklace was beautiful, like something one would see in a portrait from olden times.

At the time of her vows, her wee son Causantin slowly approached the two of them, wearing his tiny kilt and carrying a wee pillow. On top of the silken pillow were their wedding rings. Two for her and one for him. His ring was a large gem of some age set into a wide gold band. Hers were one ring, being a large solitary diamond surrounded by tiny rubies set into 24 carat gold as well as a matching plain gold band that was engraved on the inside. Zahra was astounded, as she hadn't seen rings of this quality before, let alone get to wear them as her betrothal and wedding rings, that she wept with happiness as he slipped them both onto her wedding finger.

She kept wearing her ring from Grigor for having their last bairn, Dihaoine together.

8. Hector's Hero Story

The wedding feast was held outside, as there was little wind that day, with the open fire pits lit, overlooking glorious views on all sides, it was warm, and the feast was enormous. All the bairns were hungry, too hungry Zahra observed. Over dinner, as they ate, conversation loosened up a little and Coinneach took the opportunity to learn a little more about his new big family.

"Hector, my son, how did you earn the title of hero in the eyes of your Mither?" Coinneach asked.

Only too pleased to be the centre of attention, Hector began his story.

"I was coming out of the shed one day when I saw that Ma was jumping out from her bedroom window onto the soft snow below and before I could warn her not to jump onto the soft snow that swallows you up, she jumped. Of course, she sank deep into the snow, and I couldn't see her. Then I saw her hand just waving up out of the wee hole at the top and so I crawled up to her on the surface of the compacted snow and ice nearby, then reached out to take her hand. Then I pulled her hand, but it was hard to get her out. Then her other hand came out, luckily so I pulled and pulled until she was coming out gradually. If not, the snow would have swallowed her up and closed over completely. So that's why she calls me her hero. What do you think?" Hector asked.

"Was it a normal thing for a son to do or heroic? I think it was normal, but you see Da, Ma and I hadn't had a great relationship, and I always wanted to make her cry, until that moment. She always said it was like that story of 'Mac Fie and the Black Dog', where it says, 'the black dog's day will come'. So, you see Da, even though I was always mean to her, she had always

"

believed in me the whole time, like that story from the Isles. It's folklore you know?" Hector explained.

Coinneach was amazed at the horrible story, as he could have lost his wife had it not been for young Hector.

"My son, you are as your Mither has described a hero. I would like to offer you a job here on my mountain, as a horseman of your choosing, knowing you could take care of your Mither too, if ever the need arose. I know you work for the good man Hamish, but he won't mind if he wants to see you re-united with your Mither. I will pay you well lad and you could live here in our home, if you liked and if your Mither agreed," Coinneach announced with his plans in his head unravelling. "Your wee brother Causantin misses you too and so does Dihaoine, whom I heard learned a trick or two from you lad? What do you say then?" Coinneach asked.

"Ma?" he asked Zahra cautiously, "Do you want me here in this nice palace?" Hector asked, doubting his own worth.

"Och aye, my son. I miss you so much. I miss all of you, but if that was possible and if Ali and your sisters didn't mind, then please, my hero, come and live with us here. Coinneach is an artist you know, and he is painting me in the nude," Zahra declared. "Would you like to see one of the paintings?" she asked.

"Can they see the paintings of me Coinneach please?" Zahra asked.

"Would you like to see your Mither on canvas in the nude. She is beautiful, isn't she?" Coinneach stated. The family hadn't thought of her as beautiful and they all looked at her like it was the first time they had ever really done so, especially John after having seen her face so badly damaged on that awful day. He was surprised at how quickly the healing had taken place.

"Aye, she is," said young Simon Fraser, without hesitation.

"What is your answer, my son?" Coinneach asked.

"I would like to then, please father," Hector said then reverting to the more respectful title of father.

"I will organise it then. Pack when you go home lad and my Farm Manager will go with you and collect all that you need and speak to Hamish with a letter from us both, explaining things," Coinneach said. "My dearest, does that all sound alright with you? Mairi will sort out Hector's room, so he is comfortable. Maybe I will open the wing that hasn't even been lived in yet, for cleaning," he added.

"Of course, I agree darling and thank you so much, that would be wonderful," Zahra said. She secretly wanted all of them with her, but she had to be realistic.

Ali MacGregor

"John and Ali. Can I please speak to you privately by the fireside, after desert?" Coinneach announced, then desert came with an enormous cake. The cake was so popular that it raised everyone's spirits and when Hector spoke some incidental Gaelic to his brother Ali, Coinneach asked him where he had learned that style of speaking old Gaelic.

"From Uncle Padruig," Hector admitted. "Alex and Da too, but mostly Padruig with the obscenities and curses, so Ali and I compete with each other, like in a duel, as to who can say as many Gaelic obscenities as possible, at the same time, like Highland dancing, and whoever wins, then doesn't have to wash the dishes after teatime," Hector explained.

Ali was smiling broadly at his brother, remembering those days.

"Let me see it then, this Highland dance with duelling Gaelic." Coinneach said. Both lads were so excited to show off their skills, of no renown and began with the Gaelic going back and forth, while they danced. It was hilarious, but very serious, at the same time. This excited wee Causantin who hopped up on top of the table to do his version of a Highland dance and lifting his kilt with revealing his wee manhood at the age of two and a half. Zahra's daughters were enthused by the rhythmic beat, tapping the table and performed their version of Highland dancing.

Instead of withdrawing from the fun, Coinneach reached underneath the table, to fetch out his bagpipes and began to pipe along with the rhythm. Simon had a flute in his pocket, which he carried with him to entertain the coos, he said and began to play in tune with the sound of the pipes. Mairi bought out a bodhran and handed it to John who didn't know how to use it, so he passed it to Zahra who tried, and it sounded quite good but most importantly, in time. It sounded more like a Celtic war rhythm, than a happy dancing tune, so after the girls finished their dance, Isobel took it and played it much better than her Mither, who was still learning. Ali and Hector completed their duel with Hector as the victor when a song was asked of Zahra, unexpectedly, who was shocked at the request made of her, but she complied.

Grigor Og MacGregor had taught her one MacGregor Gaelic song, when she worked for him. It had a haunting sadness to it, lamenting the death of a loved one, named Grigor, so it may not have been the best choice of song, but being the only one she knew, she began to sing it, with her husband on the pipes playing along with his wife. The mood altered dramatically with tears running down the family's faces, mourning the loss of a father and a husband, which was a very real and honest feeling to be acknowledged. Their whole way of life had vanished in an instant. No-one was pretending that they were mourning his loss and felt the real damage left behind in his wake.

It was a hard song for Zahra to sing at the best of times, let alone when it had real meaning. Zahra was praying hard that her family would slowly recover and strengthen, despite the recent events, but she prayed also for Grigor, who was never far from her mind, nor his children's minds and hearts, that was evident, as well as her stepson Grigor Og.

Coinneach announced the winner of the duel, as Hector but both lads were given prizes of gifts of substantial coin prizes from Coinneach. Wee Causantin received coin as pocket money for his efforts to dazzle and it went into a wee box to save up for one day when he might need it. The lassies were awarded both as equal winners for their lovely dance with monetary gifts too and Simon was awarded coin for his flute playing.

 Zahra was given the best gift of all, her husbands' acknowledgement that she sang 'Griogal Cridhe', very well surprisingly, given that she spoke no Gaelic, and it can't have been easy to achieve. He positively raved about her effort, and it gave her hope that one day perhaps, that she could master the difficult language of her adopted country. He kissed her softly on the cheek and thanked her.

Isobel and John shyly then gave the wedding presents to the married couple, who were not expecting anything. Isobel and John had carved a wooden statue of a Mither holding a wee bairn, representing Zahra and Motherhood for Zahra to keep. John had an ancient antique sword from his Clan of the Frasers of Lovat, an heirloom of an unknown age, and presented it to Coinneach.

"Oh, my darlings John and Isobel, this is so beautiful. Look Coinneach this is our wee bairn," she said pointing to the wee bairn in the carving.

"Aye, it is my love. John, my son, I cannot accept your gift. Surely you should keep this as a Fraser heirloom," he said to John.

"Nae, father we have all decided to give it to you. Please accept our humble gratitude, appreciation, and love for making our Ma well again," John said feeling emotional again. Coinneach knew its value, because no-one else would know what era that sword came from, but Coinneach certainly did and agreed to hang it high up on the wall, in pride of place.

"Then, thankyou my son," Coinneach said. "It will be much admired by anyone who enters our home," he said.

"Now let's have that chat with young Ali, the new landowner," Coinneach said.

9. The Plans for the Aird

Coinneach had a few proposals to put to both men, who now jointly owned the Aird property. Firstly, ascertaining the duration of Ali's course, he suggested as their father, and at his cost, a plan lasting for a period of two years.

Initially Coinneach would have a nice, substantial stone home built, suitable for a husband-and-wife Farm Manager and his wife. After the two years, of paying the wages of both of those two people, who would assist them to get back on their feet, the home would then pass to Fatma and her husband and her children, should there be any. The Farm Manager and his wife would then leave. In the two years, the farm manager's wife would cook, clean, wash, iron and deliver smokos to all the workers on the property. She would act as the 'Farm Mother' of sorts, but a paid employee, just the same and at the end of the day, she goes back into her own cottage with her husband, without disturbing the privacy of the couples, living in the main house. Her husband would manage the finances, the animals, and the preparation for the crops in the second year, in conjunction with Ali, as well as oversee the whole building process.

"This is also when Hugh Og, Teamster, will plough for you as well as deliver multiple loads of manure and kelp, under the direction of Ali here with all his acquired knowledge. In the meantime, start a manure pile and don't waste any manure, even from the chickens. You will need to increase your fold of coos to reach sixty head, at my cost, so long as you can take them to winter pasture and that would be your responsibility, John.

Beyond the new stables, I will pay for the construction of three additional buildings. A grain storage shed, goat farm and large cattle shed for the bad weather or for calving. The goat shed that you have presently, is not big enough, and you will need a herd of thirty goats and the lassies will milk them each morning, separate the milk, make the butter and the cream, make the yoghurt too and most importantly the cheese, if you are very good by then at raising goats. I will pay for the additional goats, as well as the coos. Any bills in these two years, including your own personal medical costs, clothing and footwear, will come directly to me. Any questions?" Coinneach asked.

"Who will the employees be father?" asked John.

"Their names are Rose and George MacKenzie. They will return here, after the two years is over and you can show me your farm's books to ascertain if the farm is starting to make a profit. I will also send an accountant to go over the books to ensure that you are up to date with taxation and so on. He will visit you every six months and his name is David Robert Menzies. So, starting from tomorrow, I will send those two-management people with Hector, who is to collect his belongings, as well as the building team of six MacKenzie men for the new house, the storage shed and the goat house. They can temporarily stay in your main farmhouse, but Rose will do all their cooking and cleaning," Coinneach added. "Their leader is Kalien MacKenzie with five of his brothers and sons".

"In addition, the main house will have its roof replaced and a lightning rod attached to each of the buildings and outbuildings. You don't need to know all those details. Do you agree and will you accept my assistance? My men will also be armed, in case of any unwanted guests. You, John will also need to ensure that the Law Courts are aware that there is also a risk to your two bairns, born of the Fraser marriage, who could be kidnapped by Alexander MacDonald, and they will issue you with the necessary papers, if you provide them with their original birth papers. They are the children of the Fraser marriage, no matter who sired them. Do you understand me, John? They are MacDonalds but of your marriage," Coinneach said.

"There will also be a six-foot high, front wall built from

Caledonian stone and a perimeter fence with a wrought iron gate out the front and rear on the borders, thereby preventing entry from others who are uninvited. There will also be pole lights to light up the place, as it is currently in utter darkness. Do you have any requests?" Coinneach asked.

"Aye, father. Can I please have an ox or two Clydesdale horses for deep ploughing?" Ali requested.

"You may. Good lad anything else?" Coinneach asked.

"Och, aye. A water wheel to pump water to where we need it from the burn," Ali said. "The lassies especially will need water to the houses into the kitchens, bathing rooms and the laundries but I also need accessible points for water on the land for the crops and vegetable gardens," Ali explained. Coinneach was thrilled to have the requests and to avail the farm of whatever they needed, including all new furniture and drapes when the time came for the second home's completion.

"When you leave this afternoon, pack up Hector's things, as well as my wife's things and they can all come back with him, as well as his horse," he added. "Did you build the kiln yet?" Coinneach asked. "Is your Mither's old horse still there?" he asked doubtfully.

"Not the new horse father, but the old one, aye," John replied.

"Does Simon have a horse then?" Coinneach asked.

"Nae, he doesn't," John said.

"Then he can have that old horse. Your Ma has already agreed to that," Coinneach said. "You can let young Simon know that John," he added. "John, I will expect a written monthly report from you for two years while this is all taking place. Can you accomplish that, do you think?" Coinneach asked.

"Aye, of course father, thank you so much. I was just so overwhelmed. We had twenty coos stolen. Ma's horse was stolen too, with all of its saddlery and I felt like I couldn't cope, but now you have given me confidence," John said and was visibly relieved. A weight had been lifted from John's shoulders.

"Tell Fatma that when the stone home is being built, that she should ask for anything that she likes, as it may be hers one day, such as her preferred type of wood stove," Coinneach added.

"Ali, are there any lassies on your horizon?" Coinneach enquired.

"I am too busy working, currently father. When the farm is earning enough money and I can afford to educate bairns, then I will marry, but not before then," Ali added.

Both Ali and John could not believe that this man had not only saved their Mither, but the entire family also. It was going to cost a small fortune.

"Out of interest Ali, what education would you seek for them?" Coinneach asked.

"I thought of Architectural engineering for a lad, so more bridges or roads could be built, God willing, if my wife and child both survived childbirth," Ali answered.

Ali was even too candid for Coinneach's comfort who was wanting his new wife, Zahra to be with child and had not factored in the possibility that it could end her life, as she currently knew it. Coinneach felt Ali was a very old soul like him, but in a young man's body and felt an immediate and deep connection with him.

"Now there is only just enough time to see the painting of your Mither, but you will love it and we don't want to disappoint Mummy," Coinneach said.

When they all went upstairs to see the painting, Zahra was assisted by her new husband, who carried her the last part of the way up the stairs. Astonished by his strength, Ali stood gaping, but then walked on. When he saw his beautiful, but naked Mither on canvas, so tastefully painted by her husband, he understood her strange and new relationship and prayed it would all work out, for everyone's sakes. He was still coming to terms with his father's departure from them all and would naturally continue to miss him.

"Ma, you are indeed beautiful. I love this painting," Ali said.

Maybe Ali said it to make his Mither, feel better. Her bruises were still visible beneath her thick make-up and were a reminder that day of what lay just beneath the surface. Was her marriage even real, Ali asked himself? Everything on that mountain had the effect of making everything seem unreal, Ali felt.

The carriage rattled off down the mountain finally, with Zahra's family on board, after the huge day, that saw Zahra re-married. Her grief was immediate, as her family departed the mansion, leaving only her youngest two bairns behind, who were also crying for their siblings. They were all accustomed to being one big family, all together and confusion, still plagued Causantin and wee Dihaoine. Mairi began to prepare a room for Hector, who was returning to Beinn Coinneach to live on the same floor as the two wee ones and the day had come to its end, finally.

Each member of the family took with him or her, their impressions of the day that they had met Coinneach MacAlpin and had seen their Ma again, almost but not quite, well. Zahra wept as her bairns departed and her new husband understood how deeply they were all connected to one another. It was going to be necessary for him to impress them all and to work much harder at getting these poor wee orphaned bairns into more successful and happier lives.

But he was a MacAlpin after all, so to him, everything was achievable.

The reports that Coinneach had received back from his scouts in Inverness, were that Grigor Mohr MacGregor had indeed left Scotland from Leith, to live in the Americas and it made him feel sick at the reality of it. He was accompanied by a Mrs

Belle MacGregor from Inverness, and he couldn't help but feel ashamed of Grigor MacGregor, who felt nothing of the damage that he had caused, even to his best friends, doubting that even Alex MacDonald would ever feel the same about him again, after having lost his only wee family, Domnall and Anndra.

It worried John that Alexander could easily re-emerge someday, to visit the bairns that he had sired, or worse than that, he feared that they could be kidnapped, as easily as was the horse and the cattle.

◊

10. Enter. Kenneth MacNachten

Both Kenneth and his wife Ivy, were in the Art Gallery on the farm in Glengarry to meet a client with whom Kenneth had made an appointment, to view his collection of paintings of his wife, posing in the nude.

He couldn't remember who the gentleman was, only that he had purchased the first of the 'Fairy Art' collection that he had sold on commission for Zahra, after convincing Peter Heath to part with it. He never did know how much Peter was paid and suspected that he and Zahra may have been ripped off.

But today was another day and it was buzzing with excitement on the Glengarry farms, awaiting the naked lady on Kenneth's walls. Kenneth hadn't yet told his Mither, who may not have approved, but she was presently at Loch Garry and wouldn't see it, he had hoped. I was anxious to see it however, being a man who loved a woman's body, if only just to look at. Our cousin Alex, from Loch Garry Ranch knew about it also and had asked to peek too and if he could give an opinion, being of the artistic type himself.

The lovely old-fashioned coach arrived and pulled into my farm, halting right in front of the Art Gallery. The footman opened the door for the occupants within, whom I now realised must be of some standing and wealth, to have their own footman.

Alighting from the carriage was a refined looking gentleman, positively regal, Kenneth thought, and he assisted his wife by carrying her down from within the carriage and gently placing her onto the ground, disallowing the footman any contact with her.

Her hair was unforgettable, with its lovely long curly brown locks and ringlets, but her eyes were cast down, concentrating on walking to Kenneth's gallery. Was she a little unsteady on her feet I wondered? They were followed by a tall, dark haired and handsome young man, carrying a sweet looking wee lad held on his hip and a wee lass, strapped to his back.

The young man gave the wee lad instructions not to touch anything, in Kenneth's Art Gallery and their likeness to each other, made me surmise that they were both brothers. Kenneth was watching the gentleman, who was fussing over his wife, ensuring that she could safely climb the few stairs into the gallery. He was unusual looking for Glengarry and quite appealing, even though he was an older man. His features were sharp with an aquiline nose and his hair was fair, but not blonde.

He stood out in the countryside, because he was wearing a beautiful, expensive black jacket with gold buttons and an obviously well-worn kilt of some importance and hose to the knee with the traditional skein dubh in one of his hose. His black leather shiny shoes had gold buckles to match his jacket. Overall, Kenneth assessed that his outfit looked very expensive.

The gentleman then approached my brother, striding confidently with a very straight back. It was true what was said about his eyes, even from a distance. They were dreamy.

"Kenneth MacNachten, is it? My name is Lord Coinneach MacAlpin and this is my wife, Lady Zahra Coinneach MacAlpin. We are here about the art, expressing nudity, are you still interested?" he asked very directly. Kenneth took note that her name was still Zahra, not Anleta but his client was just adding the 'Lady' part.

"Aye, Lord Coinneach, pleased to meet you. This is my wife, Ivy Fraser MacNachten," Kenneth said, making Ivy's name extra-long to impress, with her Clan credentials. It was then that he turned, and Zahra looked straight up at him.

"Hello Kenneth and Ivy, do you remember me? You gave me some advice when I was here a while ago, when I was staying in the wee house by the Loch. I am married now to Lord Coinneach," Zahra added.

"Zahra, is it really you?" Kenneth exclaimed. "You look even more beautiful than I remember," Kenneth said, hoping not to offend his client.

"Would you like to see the paintings, my fellow artist friend?" Coinneach asked. Kenneth obviously liked this gentleman and was pleased for Zahra that she had found love in his arms. What a huge change from Grigor MacGregor, he thought.

"I would, Lord Coinneach," Kenneth said carefully addressing him 'Lord' each time, so as not to lose this business. Coinneach opened the first large canvas, but first apologised for not introducing his two stepsons and his wee stepdaughter first.

"These are my two sons, Hector and wee Causantin and my daughter wee Dihaoine, asleep in my son's arms," he said proudly. Hector then shook Kenneth by the hand, and they appeared to like each other.

Looking upon the canvas, not yet framed, Kenneth gasped.

"It's you Zahra. It's so beautiful. Ivy come and look at this," he asked. Ivy was impressed, if not a little surprised, but she wasn't one to lose her composure, even though she did look underdressed compared with their new clients' expensive attire.

"I like it, Kenneth. It won't be too much, even for your Mither, because it's so tasteful and so well done and beautiful. How much are you asking for it Lord Coinneach?" Ivy asked.

"I think, with a frame, it should just be displayed on your wall first for a while, to get public opinion and to see what people are willing to pay. I was thinking around two thousand pounds, or the highest bidder, when you invite people here," Coinneach expressed.

At that moment, both myself and our cousin, Alex Grant had arrived and introduced ourselves to Kenneth's exclusive clients and most importantly to see that nude painting. Feeling embarrassed, Zahra had moved away from my vision and had vanished into thin air, as she was loathe to answer the questions surrounding the obvious enquiries that there would be, concerning Grigor Mohr MacGregor. When Kenneth turned to introduce her to us, he couldn't locate her.

"She has just gone to the privy," said Hector, covering up for his Mither, but Coinneach knew that she had vanished.

I was a sore spot, and that was going to be obvious to him, so there was shame attached to her previous marriage ending, her husband deduced, as did I.

"Can we both see the painting too please, Lord Coinneach?" I asked.

"Oh my God in heaven. Isn't that? No, it isn't. For a moment there, I thought it was Zahra MacGregor," I exclaimed.

Coinneach ignored him and glanced across to Kenneth and asked if there was a market for the nude male body also.

Alex answered for him and said, "Aye there is. Can we see it too please?" Gazing upon the glorious male bodies, Alex said he would buy it and pay whatever Coinneach asked.

"How much?" Alex asked.

Coinneach said he wanted the nude male painting to be exhibited only for a time to obtain public opinions, attitudes, the value of the work and so on. After time, a value could be placed on it more accurately, as it would most definitely be a timely piece, possibly ahead of its time. Alex was disappointed to learn that he couldn't just walk away with it and take it home, which was not the artists' intention.

Ivy informed Lord Coinneach that she also did the framing there on site, if he trusted her to frame his work, which he did. Kenneth found his family to be a distraction to his appointment, if not even a bit embarrassing, but continued to ask if Lord Coinneach had more works of nude art to reveal.

I then saw the lovely Zahra, re-entering the Art Gallery with her son, Hector, who had talked her into returning, after having vanished. Zahra knew that I would ask her what had happened to Grigor Mohr MacGregor, and this was what she had wanted to avoid, but Hector told her to just say it how it was, that Grigor had abandoned the farm, his children, and his wife and now she was happily married to Lord Coinneach.

"Zahra, is it you?" I exclaimed at the sight of her looking more beautiful than I had remembered.

"Lady Zahra Coinneach," corrected Zahra's husband.

"I'm sorry, Lady Zahra Coinneach," I then added.

"What happened to Grigor then? Where is he?" I asked unashamedly.

Kenneth was now regretting permitting me in to view the paintings and he hoped it wouldn't put off his valued clients. Zahra responded to me, just the same.

"Mr MacGregor is on his way to the Americas, Malcolm. You may wish to let your wife, Ailsa, know that her Mither is no longer in Inverness, she is with him, on board the same ship, I am told. Grigor abandoned us all a while back and my husband now is the gentleman you see here, Lord Coinneach," Zahra said, trying to remain dignified and composed.

Zahra then held onto her husband, both for companionship and to steady herself, while Hector's steadying arm remained in the centre of her back also.

"Will you explain to me what happened Zahra?" I asked her.

"Nae lad, my wife will not explain her life to you, unless she feels it necessary and is it necessary to put my wife through anguish and pain, when we are here by appointment, concerning art and not the antics of a man who abandoned his children, his wife and his farm?" Coinneach said angrily.

Kenneth then asked if Alex and I could both leave and closed the Art Gallery door behind us both.

"I apologise my Lord, but my brother is a good man, if only a little abrasive and now he has to tell his wife, Ailsa about her Mither, so please forgive us all here in Glengarry," asked Kenneth.

"Certainly, lad but from now on, you will come to me on Beinn Coinneach, for my art and we will not return here. Will that suit you?" Coinneach asked firmly.

"It will my Lord, aye if you show me on the map where that is," replied Kenneth.

From then onwards Kenneth went to Beinn Coinneach to view Lord Coinneach's art and selected many of his works, especially the series of nude paintings of his wife, Zahra. Her demise with Grigor Mohr MacGregor was now a topic that was out of bounds for them all in Lord Coinneach's presence, but it had only caused more reasons to speculate and gossip amongst us, in Glengarry and all the way to Glenmoriston and even the gossipy Frasers' Trading Post, concerning Zahra's lost and found marriages.

They were no longer the hidden family of the Aird.

Kenneth discovered through various other sources, like Hugh Og, Hamish and James Grant, a tale that shocked us all. We were then aware that Zahra's condition, with her lack of co-ordination, was probably due to a brain injury, that could have only been sustained by a serious incident with her former husband. She was most fortunate to have met a man of Lord

Coinneach's standing by her side, who seemed to adore her. It made Kenneth feel a deep sadness of a peculiar quality. Her marriage with Grigor MacGregor, even if it was in his 'in between life after death', his Otherworld, had been very real and his children were what worried him the most, as well as what that man had been capable of.

There was a degree of guilt on all their parts in Glengarry, of waving Zahra off with Grigor MacGregor to return to the Aird that day, only for her to end up disabled. Could they have prevented it? He dared not use that word 'disabled' in front of Ivy, or it would be repeated, after all Zahra covered it up quite well. Her beauty in the paintings was going to offset any downside to her physical abilities, he felt, so it was important to display the art and sell the nude works of such a beautiful woman and get the money rolling in, he had thought, before Zahra could feel ugly, which is what could happen, in a psychological way. Kenneth still felt that he was helping her in that way without needing to ask her, to her face, what had taken place.

Domestic violence is every man's shame.

After they had all left, Kenneth had to then deal with me, his brother. And I was very upset at being removed from the Art Gallery.

"Thanks a lot for kicking me out brother," I said, upon seeing Kenneth.

Both of us men were not bairns anymore and as grown men, we were now facing off for the first time, since Kenneth had moved onto my farm.

"I am sorry brother, but I cannot afford to lose a client, and you can find out what Hamish and Hugh Og know about the end of her marriage with Grigor, when we all go fishing. What do you say? I had to choose brother. It is no different to you making choices with your coos when James was here, and you chose the lady coo over James. Please brother, I do love you. But gossip is secondary to business, and I have to go to his home from now on, every second weekend. He won't come back here with his wife. Zahra seems disabled and she needs assistance walking from both her son, Hector, as well as her husband.

Whatever Grigor did to her, was obviously shocking" Kenneth stated.

"Alright Kenneth, I understand. Your arty clients are a little bit touchy," I said.

"I was deeply involved, that's all and I expected to be filled in. A divorce as the result, is a disaster. Who knows what Zahra and her family have all suffered? I feel lousy because its Ailsa's Mither too. Sorry brother, can you please let me know what happens with her in your dealings with them and I won't bother them personally?" I asked genuinely concerned and disappointed for both Zahra and my wife.

Kenneth already had one of the paintings that Coinneach left behind for Ivy to frame beautifully with a golden edged, double frame. It was fully supported by a wooden support structure, pulled tightly from corner to corner and once it was on the wall, it looked incredible. They decided to advertise it that weekend to test the market, for nude art and sent out invitations too to view it. The painting was of Zahra laying naked on a purple velvet covered, single couch, with her beautiful long brown hair in locks and ringlets, all the way down to her knees. Some of her hair covered her face a little but her big green eyes looked out at you, in the most haunting of ways. She was both alluring and inviting, yet sad as well.

There was a power surrounding her, in not smiling, yet questioning. Her body was captured in the artistry beautifully, of that there was no doubt with her shapely legs being a feature. You could almost feel those legs wrapped around you. Even though she had beautiful breasts in full view, the painting didn't take you to her bedroom or to thoughts of sex, it took you to what was on her mind. What was she saying with those big green eyes? What had she seen with those sad eyes?

That was the takeaway for almost everyone I spoke to. I suppose it made people want to buy it as well, so they could sit and ponder what was on the lady's mind.

Most people put the value at under one thousand pounds, then many others valued it between two and ten thousand pounds. There were three offers of purchase of over five thousand pounds even though, strictly speaking, it was only on display until the artist decided whether he would accept an offer. Much like buying a house, rather than art.

The next piece on display, also on the following weekend, would be the male body. Kenneth needed to go to Beinn Coinneach to pick that one up once it was completed. It was bound to cause a stir.

◇

11. Art of the Male Body

Upon arrival, finally on Beinn Coinneach, Kenneth looked around at the stunning surroundings and he couldn't blame them for not wanting to leave such a beautiful place. It was a heavenly location. The top of the mountain was inside of a cloud. His horse didn't much like the trek up the tall mountain, and he decided next time to bring the carriage. The surface of the long winding track was slippery and wet and partially covered in snow and ice and the higher he went the more snow he encountered, until it was barely a track at all. He was relieved to finally arrive there and look out over the view, misty though it was.

'An artist's dream', he thought and quite magical in a way.

"Kenneth lad, welcome. Good to see you made it up here to see Zahra and me. The groom will take your horse," Coinneach said, which he did.

"Come and warm yourself by the fire lad. Tea or coffee? I am having coffee," he asked in a noticeably friendlier mood in his own home. Still wearing his kilt, Kenneth assumed then that it must be his traditional way of dressing.

When the cook delivered their coffee and sandwiches by the fire, with still no sign of Zahra, Coinneach said, "We need to get to know each other young Kenneth. Your Clan name MacNachten is an old name, but you must know all your history son?" Coinneach asked.

"Not really, nae," Kenneth answered candidly.

"What is your father's name then lad," Coinneach asked.

"Nachtain MacNachten, my Lord," Kenneth replied.

"Is that so, and from where then?" he asked.

"I am from Loch Insh, my Lord, as was my father and his too I think," Kenneth replied.

"Loch Insh, I am surprised. I would not have guessed that, with you living in Glengarry," Coinneach said.

"It's a long story my Lord," Kenneth said, thinking of the long road that they had all travelled to get to where they were now.

"Where is your father now then son?" Coinneach asked.

"He passed away my Lord, when I was just two years old, and Malcolm was four years old," Kenneth answered.

"I am sorry son. I thought you were all part of that Cannich crowd. The Grants," Coinneach said.

"It is true to say that my Ma was born a Grant, but not part of Cannich, as she was one of twins, a boy Alexander and a girl Marion, who were both under some threat by a neighbour, so my grandmother and her father, John Grant, decided to hide one of the bairns in Loch Insh," he explained.

"Who was your grandmother then?" Coinneach asked.

"Isobel Grant of Glenmoriston," Kenneth replied. "She tried to have us all returned to them when she came to Loch Insh, when I was in my teens. Up until then, they had lost everything on their farm, so she could not see my Mither beyond my Ma's age of ten years. As a result, my grandfather arranged a marriage between my Mither with my father, Nachtain MacNachten, his fellow Clansman and nephew. Our childhood was very good there in Loch Insh," Kenneth said.

"So, you were raised by whom?" Coinneach asked.

"My foster Grandfather, Gillcrest MacNachten and my Mither Marion MacNachten, after our Da passed away," he recalled.

"Well, my lad. You do have a tale to tell, that is for sure. I am pleased that you somehow made it back home to your family and I understand then that you must have chased up your inheritance from the Grant family then?" Coinneach asked.

"I couldn't have achieved anything with them, without Malcolm, my Lord. He dealt with all of that. Ma and I both owe him our lives and livelihoods. I became an alcoholic, my Lord and nearly died and if it wasn't for Malcolm, I would be dead and while I was in hospital, he built me the Art Gallery and my solid stone home on his farm. Please forgive him my Lord. I love him with all my heart," Kenneth said, becoming emotional with tears in his eyes.

"Och, my dear lad. I am so sorry I am intolerant where my wife is concerned. Of course, tell Malcolm to come here with you next time, so we can all talk together and get to know one another. I am also related to the MacNachtens which was why I asked you about your Clan credentials. We are distantly related, you see. My brother married a lady who was Clan Nachtain, a long time ago now, but their offspring are forever connected to us MacAlpins," Coinneach explained.

"Why did your father, name you Kenneth and not Coinneach like me?" he then asked.

"I was named Cinaed upon my birth, my Lord. My school in Loch Insh changed my name to Kenneth," he explained. "Malcolm also had his name changed. His name was Mael Collum. We were disallowed any Gaelic language usage, including our names and I was made to wear a sign about my neck with Kenneth written on it and was punished by the English teacher, if I spoke my language," Kenneth explained.

"I want you to consider using your real name again lad. My

languages are two, Pictish and Gaelic and I have lived to see the loss of my Pictish language, so it is only my family, the MacAlpins now who speak it in our Otherworld," Coinneach said.

"Now a personal question if you don't mind Kenneth. What is your manhood like? Large, small, average?" he asked, "I need a good male member for one of my paintings and you look like a healthy lad, are you interested in featuring in one of my nude paintings with my wife Zahra? Can I see it?" Coinneach asked boldly. Shocked and yet tempted too at the question, Kenneth glanced around to see if they were alone, which they were, and opened his breeks to show him, hoping it was what he needed for a painting.

"Pull them down lad, my eyes aren't that good. You should wear a kilt. Much more convenient don't you think?" Coinneach asked. As Kenneth struggled with his breeks to reveal his male member, he began to see the merits of the kilt. Once Kenneth's member was finally revealed, Coinneach took a good close look.

"Do you mind if I measure its size for suitability son?" Coinneach asked. Feeling like he should object to the personal touching upon his member, he allowed it, just the same and unfortunately his member began to harden. He was aroused by being touched by the older gentleman.

"It's alright son. This is a normal reaction. You are a healthy lad. Perfect for my painting," he said, taking a chamber pot, for Kenneth who ejaculated into the chamber pot provided for him.

"Och, I am not sure. I am no marvellous specimen and that might happen again. Can I just see the painting I came to see?" Kenneth nervously asked, feeling very embarrassed.

"Of course, you can lad, but I would love that member of yours in my next painting. You'd be surprised, lad at how many men have rather poor looking cocks. Look at mine. It's magnificent, isn't it?" he said, showing young Kenneth.

"My wife thinks it's the best cock that she has ever seen. You can ask her. But my wife can't paint. Come on upstairs to my art room lad," he said. Impressed by Coinneach's large member and the palatial surroundings, Kenneth was eager to see the art room and that other painting that was to go on display. He was still feeling a little aroused by his surroundings and being fondled in that way, so he put it down to sexual frustration. Ivy wasn't always keen to have sex, as often as he would like, so that was probably it. When they both walked in, so did a naked Zahra, moving with her awkward gait.

"Hello Kenneth, so you are our male member, are you? How lovely. Best take off all your clothes then my dear friend, and I'll just lie here and await my husband's instructions for us both. I hope you are not shy. Just do what he says, and you'll be alright," she said reassuringly. He was then aware of the expectation upon him and just did what Zahra said and took off all his clothes quickly and moved in her direction.

"Good lad," said Coinneach, "You will not regret this decision, and I pay my sitters ten pounds, except my wife because she has the benefit of making love to me throughout the whole process," he said and smiled to her. They were in love, he thought, and it was a relief to see Zahra smiling, finally.

"After three ejaculations and a lot of embarrassment later, Kenneth's sitting was complete with squatting above Zahra's legs spread wide open with one of his hands upon her inner right thigh and the other on her left knee, feigning the act of love making, which almost became a reality, three times. Her leg nearest the artist was lower down, so that Kenneth's member was fully visible and truly memorable. Zahra was happy for him. She knew Malcolm would be a bit envious of him. Her face was turned facing Coinneach in her alluring way and thinking of his cock.

Coinneach explained the process with this type of artwork and to get that moment, he had to paint fast to get the outlines, then go over it all again to deal with the finer details and colour it later. He took a separate drawing of Kenneth's member, so that exact details could not be lost.

"Now lad, you will be motivated to sell this one because you get commission for your Art Gallery, and you will get royalties as one of those sitters in the painting. I get the lion's share of course," he added.

"Now my son, after you take the 'male nudes' painting, do you have any regrets or questions?" Coinneach asked.

"No regrets, Lord Coinneach, none and thank you for this wonderful experience. It beats drawing beetles for my wife," Kenneth said.

"Why beetles?" Coinneach asked.

"My wife is an entomologist who wrote a book on all of the insects and beetles of the Highlands of Scotland, and I did all of the illustrations," Kenneth said.

"Is that so? May I have a copy of that book?" he asked. "My wife is an author also," Coinneach added proudly, momentarily forgetting into which century Zahra was published.

"Aye, you may. Ivy would like that," Kenneth said.

The afternoon was becoming darker, and a rainstorm had set in, so Kenneth was invited to sleep the night, so it would be safer for his return to Glengarry the next day, which he happily accepted.

"You can sleep with us, if you like, or in Hector's bed," Zahra said spontaneously.

"Aye, you can," Coinneach added. They all had dinner together, happily chatting and it was decided they would all sleep in the one bed, provided Kenneth didn't mind the noise they made when making love. Kenneth reassured them both that he wouldn't mind, he wanted to get into the higher-level, artist mindset. Not sure what that was exactly, Zahra asked for help with her bath, and they all went to bed together happily, and she was looking forward to making love, as she had longed for her husband, all day long.

He spoke to her in his usual sexy way, wanting her to open to her husband, which she did. His hand went there immediately and fondled her vigorously and upon finding her clitoris, he made sure she was driven mad by his foreplay with his tongue and asked Kenneth if he was comfortable with them making love up against his warm body.

The three of them felt at ease with each other in the same bed and in no time, Coinneach was inside his wife thrusting hard and she was responding with joyous squeals. It was nice to share the experience with each other, as they all felt their friendship grow stronger. Kenneth cuddled up to them during the night. At one time hugging Coinneach and at one time hugging Zahra, but they all slept beautifully until her husband made love again with his wife in the earliest part of the morning, sucking his wife's face it seemed, as he showed his love and adoration and need for his woman. Forever the gentleman, he took her to the bathroom for toilet needs and another bath.

Kenneth watched Coinneach move around their room, naked as he dressed his wife who was still unable to do most of the difficult small things. He did admire his beautiful body and his compassion for Zahra.

"Kenneth can you please put on Zahra's boots and socks while I bathe?" Coinneach asked. Holding onto Kenneth's head and his lovely hair, to balance herself, Zahra thanked him and gently kissed his forehead.

"You are such a lovely friend Kenneth," Zahra said. He hoped he would be invited back, as often as possible, as it was creating a depth of feeling that he had never known. He loved them both in a new and strange way. She was so gentle, and he was lovely.

"Kenneth, dear lad, you have been so helpful. Those boots are a curse to get on and off again for a wee lady. They should design these things better," Coinneach expressed.

"It was my pleasure my Lord," Kenneth answered.

"Are you needing your wife today son, if you know what I mean?" he asked.

"Aye. I do have a need," he answered truthfully. Kenneth bathed and when he was about to dress, Coinneach entered the bathing room and said he could have one of his kilts.

"Do you want me to relieve you now son?" Coinneach asked, but before he could reply to him, Coinneach's hand had quickly reached for Kenneth's member.

"Good lad," Coinneach said. Kenneth enjoyed the experience, and ejaculated, moaning in pleasure.

"Maybe we won't wear the kilt today on the horse but for the next visit we should, in case we both need quick access," he said grinning at the young Kenneth. The two men held each other, and Kenneth felt for Coinneach's member underneath his kilt, which they both enjoyed. Coinneach kissed him passionately, while holding Kenneth's head tightly in place and Kenneth was shocked at his pleasure of the whole experience with the older man. He could also feel the strength of the man when he was held so tightly in his grip.

"I should have that painting finished soon, but I do have five unfinished works of the nude paintings of my dear Zahra. Make it two weeks from now for the weekend when you and Malcolm come over unless you are going fishing. Mairi can make up two rooms for you and your brother too and stay in in the new wing," Coinneach said.

As Kenneth was departing Beinn Coinneach, he looked out over the beautiful scenery, once more and breathed in the fresh mountain air, before he asked his horse to take him home.

12. Where's Grandda?

"Grandda, where are you?" I asked, becoming frustrated at how many times I had tried to find Grandda.

"What do you want now Malcolm?" Grandda, finally replied.

"I have been worried about you all. James said he saw Zahra in Invermoriston, with a new man, buying a wedding dress. What's going on? Where's Grigor Mohr? What happened? Did they get divorced, after all that effort to save their marriage then?" I asked.

"Look Malcolm you nosey wee shite, it's none of your business. Why do you want to know? What's it to you?" he asked rudely.

"Zahra came to my doorstep, followed by her entire family, including you, so I think I have the right to know. Where is Grigor Mohr?" I asked.

"I was the first one to leave, so how would I know?" Grandda snapped.

"Why did you leave?" I asked.

Reluctantly answering, Grandda said, *"Grigor offered Zahra to me, and it all went to hell. Of course, she didn't want me, never has, never will. Are you satisfied now? Good luck to her if she has a better bloke than me. I'm surprised she survived that."*

"Survived what and why would she want you?" I persisted.

"Grigor punched her in the face for drinking a deadly herb to kill my unborn bairn, Zahra hit the table, losing her

balance, then she landed flat on her face on the stone floor," Grandda said.

"Good God. Grigor punched Zahra in the face and what bairn of yours are you talking about, Grandda?" I asked.

"Grigor gave her to me. Zahra didn't want me and I'm regretting every minute of this darn conversation with you Malcolm," Grandda said.

"Where are you then, if not in the Aird?" I asked.

"Why should I tell you? You seem to be able to pester me without even knowing where I am, physically," Grandda said.

"Where are you, Grandda?" I once again insisted on knowing.

"I'm haunting my own hotel Room 203, alright? Good luck to any guests who try to come into this room. I'll scare the life out of them. James told you all about Zahra, did he? That wee shite. Nosey wee gossip. Who's the bloke Zahra's marrying then?" Grandda asked.

"Don't know his name. Some older posh fella, with a nice carriage. You're overlooking Craskie Farm waiting to see if Zahra turns up there, aren't you?" I asked.

"Might be. What's it to you?" Grandda said.

"Well, she's not there, Grandda. She's on some big mountain with that posh arty fella, who paints her in the nude. But where's Grigor? You haven't answered my question," I asked once more.

"What? Well, this might affect your wife, so don't blame me now for you being too nosey. Grigor Mohr MacGregor is on a ship with Mrs Belle MacGregor, Ailsa's Mither, heading for the Americas with the gold in his pocket, that Zahra gave to him. Are you satisfied now? And where's that art showing?" Grandda asked.

"James Grant might be buying one. Could be right downstairs from you, Grandda, in your own hotel," I replied.

And he was gone.

How was I going to tell Ailsa? This was even worse than I had expected. I didn't think that I would come off damaged by that cursed Grigor Mohr's MacGregor's lust for women with huge bosoms and an equally huge bottom. What on earth could he see in that worn out old trollop? Compared to Zahra, no-one rated, let alone a worn-out widow, of questionable morals. Grigor had abandoned his entire family and all those lovely bairns, one of them, still on the breast.

Poor Zahra must have suffered a lot, by the sounds of it.

What did Grandda do? Did he rape her? Is that what he meant? I was considering not ever contacting my grandfather again, after that unpleasant conversation. I heard Kenneth arrive home and go straight into his house and slam his front door shut, so that didn't seem too friendly either.

Can't wait to go fishing. Hmmmm.

"Ailsa, did I tell you that I was going fishing tomorrow afternoon with the usual crowd, unless Bruce doesn't come. Have you seen him?" I asked.

"Aye he was slaughtering a goat, just now. He might still be in the goat shed," Ailsa said "And nae, you forgot to tell me about the fishing trip, but I don't mind darling. Some fish would be nice, but stay out of trouble, eh?" Ailsa said.

"Bruce, are you coming fishing tomorrow with us all?" I yelled out.

"Aye thanks son, I'll tell Grigor Og. What time and where do you want to meet up?" Bruce asked.

"Two o'clock, my house, then Hugh Og is meeting us there and we are all meeting up with Hamish in the boatshed," I replied and then started to wonder about this combination of people, given the recent happenings. There would be Grigor Og, who doesn't know that his father has run off with the trollop to America, leaving behind Zahra, who was now disabled. That will be a fun conversation to have in a boat, in the middle of the loch, I thought sarcastically to myself. Hamish will know more from Zahra's bairns, who worked for him and could even know where she now lived. Then there's Kenneth who was still in a peculiar mood because I upset his arty clients, one of whom was Zahra's husband. What a balls-up. It might even spoil our fishing trip, and I was hoping to escape from all of that, for a while, at least.

All we needed now was for James to want to come fishing too and complain about the haunted Room 203, on the top floor of his hotel.

13. Fishing for Gossip or Fish?

Hamish had already arrived at the boat shed, waiting for us all, beaming his big friendly smile, that only Hamish could smile. God bless his heart and soul. The world needed more souls like Hamish. I hoped he knew what he was in for, if conversation started to deteriorate, out on the loch.

We all decided where to go on the loch, because Hamish and Hugh Og knew where there were fish today and we always knew to follow them. That was a skill they would die with and the rest of us could only learn how to fish and not where the bloody things were, at any given time.

That was a mystery known only by the brothers Chisholm.

"So, I'm a bastard, am I Malcolm, for not working with you?" Hamish said, still smiling and so was Hugh, who said he would not repeat what I had said, but brothers are brothers at the end of each day.

"Sorry Hamish my good friend. I didn't mean it. I'm still looking for a suitable security man to work with Duncan Mohr, especially when the Art Gallery is open, with those nude paintings on display," I said.

"I heard about that. You will see me on that day, perving on the painting," Hamish said and laughed at the idea of himself perving.

"You do know that it's Zahra MacGregor in the painting, don't you?" I asked.

"Don't spoil the effect, Malcolm," Kenneth quipped, in a cranky mood.

The first fish was caught by Grigor Og, who was minding his own business at the top end of the boat, hoping not to get involved with anything concerning his former cook and step-mother, Zahra MacGregor.

That didn't last for long.

"Have you seen those paintings, Grigor?" asked Bruce, who he had known since boyhood.

"This is the first I have heard of any nude paintings," Grigor Og said innocently.

"Surely Zahra wouldn't pose nude? Such a sweet lady like that. Surely not?" Bruce added, totally bemused.

"Kenneth son, does your Mither know that you are going to display nude paintings of some lady?" Bruce asked his stepson.

"Thanks a lot Malcolm. Now Ma knows, when Bruce goes back home," Kenneth said.

"Bruce, it's nothing to worry about. It's only Zahra, and the paintings are beautiful and tasteful. I am in one of the nude paintings now, so prepare Ma for that one, when the artist has finished it," Kenneth declared, proudly.

"Fully clothed son?" Bruce naively asked a vehement Kenneth.

"Nae. My manhood is good enough for a painting," Kenneth replied. "So, it's one of myself and Zahra," Kenneth added.

Hugh Og was so shocked that he dropped his fishing line.

Hamish and Hugh Og Chisholm

Hamish and Hugh Og Chisholm

"Oh shite," Hugh Og spat as he prepared another line. Hamish was shocked too but decided to make no comment now that it was a family issue, between Kenneth and Bruce. I was pulling the fish in one by one, which was an amazing distraction from any involvement in their argument, other than being blamed for Bruce now knowing.

I decided to leave it, until we were on dry land.

Grigor Og then answered Bruce, "All I know Bruce, is that Zahra was wanting two of her sons to work on Craskie, then she changed her mind and has taken Hector to live with her and her new husband, as he has explained in his letter to Hamish."

"She has a new husband now then, does she Grigor?" Bruce asked.

"Aye, she does. He must be well off. The paper was home-made, and he had his own title atop the letter. Lord Coinneach MacAlpin of Beinn Coinneach. Zahra and my father have divorced, and he has disappeared. I can't locate him any-where," said Grigor Og sadly.

"I know where he is," I declared, in between unhooking a fish and baiting the hook for the next one.

"Oh, you do? If you don't mind Malcolm, I would like to know his new address, so I can see how he is. Can you give it to me?" Grigor Og asked.

"I would give it to you my friend, if it was anywhere on dry land in Scotland, but he is somewhere out at sea, on his way to the Americas, with that trollop you met, Ailsa's Mither and I haven't told Ailsa yet, so don't say anything to her yet either," I said.

"Da didn't say goodbye to me," Grigor Og lamented.

"You may be one of the lucky ones then," I said. "He left a lot of damage in his wake, Grigor. I am sorry to say, but he caused his wife a lot of harm. Punched her in the face he did, she lost her balance, hit the corner of the dining table, leaving her unconscious, then she landed face down on the stone floor. They thought she was dead, so Padruig cleared off, as did Grigor soon after, then Alex did too. All the family were then abandoned, leaving John Fraser and Isobel in charge, and Zahra was rescued by Mr Handsome, as he has been called in Invermoriston, according to James," I said.

"They are very much in love and are a nice enough, couple. Zahra is a little handicapped now though. I had to assist her putting her boots on. She has to be helped to get around and wobbles a bit when she walks. I think she may have a wee brain injury, that affects her fine and gross motor skills, but nothing else, thank God. Lord Coinneach has been a God send, literally to her on that awful day.

Malcolm my brother, you would be pleased to know that Lord Coinneach has invited you as well as me, the next time I go there. I think we might need a carriage to safely get up that mountain. It's as slippery as hell and steep and it just keeps going up. God only knows how they built that palatial place on top of that mountain," Kenneth explained.

"Am I invited too?" I asked. "I thought he didn't like me?" I remarked.

"He does now, and he might even paint your cock too," Kenneth said chuckling to himself.

"I'll be bringing my dirk then, if anyone goes near my cock," I said.

"Sons, I don't think a carriage would get up that mountain, better than horses could. You'd be better off taking Highland Ponies, that are built for that terrain," Bruce said, ignoring comments about cocks and dirks.

"What if I need to carry his paintings on the way home?" Kenneth asked.

"Carry them as canvasses son, not yet in their frames and enclose them in a waterproof covering and then attach them to your saddle, like a saddle bag. You could carry several paintings, depending on their length. Keeping them dry is your main concern," Bruce added. Bruce had stopped fishing, wishing to solve his stepsons' issues, before he went home to his wife, Marion, whom he would have to explain this all to. She sometimes still thought of her adult sons as wee bairns, Bruce thought, most especially Kenneth.

Both Hamish and Hugh Og had gone noticeably silent, and it wasn't because of the fish. They were serious about what had befallen Zahra, after she had left Glengarry. Hugh Og was reminiscing about the night that Zahra asked him to take her to Glengarry on his team of horses. She had two wee bairns with her. One was still on the breast.

"She really fought hard for your father, Grigor. I am sad about that. What a pig he turned out to be. I know he is your Da, but maybe in death, people change? Zahra was a bit naïve. I hope to God this new man looks after her, now that she is also disabled. God what a horrible ending to that story and Grigor just took off to the Americas, with another woman, leaving all those lovely bairns, fatherless," Hugh Og said.

"That must be why Zahra wanted to leave her lads with me, on their way home to the Aird. The very next day Grigor fetched back Hector, but luckily, I had already enrolled Ali in the soil course, because Grigor wanted them both back and he was hard to negotiate with, over Ali," Hamish added.

"So, you must be the last one of us all, that my Da spoke to Hamish?" Grigor Og sadly realised. "I think you can have more autonomy with decision making from now on Hamish. It slows down the process if you have to get word to me in Glengarry. How about you have sole decision-making rights, and we can still talk it all over when we meet monthly?" Grigor asked.

"That would be much better," said a greatly relieved Hamish.

"Is anyone in your house in Cannich then Grigor?" I asked. I was thinking of Grandda watching over that farm, at who was coming and going.

"Nae. The two lads were going to move in there, but his father fetched Hector back again, so Ali is still in Hamish's house, right Hamish?" Grigor asked.

"Aye, he's a good lad. Helps Cora clean up after teatime. Lovely well-mannered lad. Zahra has raised him well. He even makes up his own bed," Hamish added. "Then he works hard, non-stop. He had one family day off for a wedding. So now that I have learned more about this, I assume, it was his Mither's wedding to Lord what's his name?" Hamish added.

"Lord Coinneach MacAlpin of Beinn Coinneach," I added.

"Really? That name was the name of the first King of Alba. What a co-incidence. His Mither was Pictish. His half-brother was named Griogar, of all things, one of the Kings of the Picts. Uniting Dal Riada and Pictland must have been tricky. I read somewhere that MacAlpin just had all the other Pictish Kings and Princes bumped off, so there was no opposition. Ruthless fella that MacAlpin," Bruce said innocently touching on that Pictish topic once again.

"Your name was Coinneach at birth, Kenneth. I still remember calling you that, before the school changed it, in Loch Insh, to Kenneth," I said. "So, you have something in common with your arty client, as well as comparing cocks. Does he have a big one then?" I asked.

"Aye and he's circumcised. Coinneach's cock is much bigger than ours," Kenneth admitted, suddenly feeling shy at how the painting would reveal the size of his cock too.

"I wonder if people would like to look at men's cocks as much as they would like to look at women's breasts," said Hugh. "Let me know when you are going to be on display Kenneth and I'll let you know how you rate amongst all of us fellas, like me and Hamish," he said teasing his brother.

"Hamish here has a big one, don't you, big fella?" Hugh Og stated.

"I do," said Hamish a little red faced.

I confess to never having thought of the size of my friends' cocks, especially Hamish. It was evening and approaching that time when I should have already been home, but our lengthy conversations had added to the fishing time, none of which was regrettable, with all of the accumulated information. Fishing trips were great like that, even though the women folk would frequently accuse us men of being bigger gossips than themselves. Maybe they were right.

I still had to tell Ailsa about her Mither but I had more confidence now than I had earlier. The very idea of even approaching the topic of her Mither was sensitive. I hadn't known Ailsa at all much before we married, but one thing I did credit her widowed Mither with, was that she had married off all her daughters to good men and saw them into secure environments, before she unleashed herself and her needs, onto the world of men once again.

She hadn't hurt or abandoned any of her own bairns and so I decided to come in on a positive angle about her character, compared with Grigor, who had abandoned the family farm, the family and had beaten up his beautiful wife, left her for dead and cleared off, without saying goodbye to his oldest son, Grigor Og who was now clearly mourning his loss. Losing his father twice, would be hard to come to terms with and I liked Grigor Og, these days.

My worries were nothing compared to Kenneth's, however who had to tell Ivy that his cock had been a feature in one of the nudey paintings. Ivy was conservative and wore neck to ankles coverage clothing, every single day of her life, on the farm. She had been positive for Kenneth to include nude paintings in his gallery, which all galleries must decide on eventually, and this was a turning point for Kenneth's Art

Gallery, but hopefully a good one and not one that could disturb their stable marriage.

That sleazy artist wasn't getting anywhere near my cock, that was for certain, but I did want to go there to that bloody mountain. My twins had Highland Ponies that they could lend us, I hoped, but if not, I would buy two Highland Ponies, just to achieve it. I was desperately curious to see this mysterious man with Zahra, in her new surroundings. James was right, it was driving me a bit mad.

I prayed she was alright.

Riding my old mare home, eventually with Kenneth, Bruce, and Hugh, I thanked them all for the enjoyable fishing trip. I did appreciate their input, and I wished them all well. Bruce had problems too, now. He had to tell my Ma and fill her in about the whole nudey art thing, but she didn't go to Church, so I hoped she would accept Kenneth's decision to be a feature in one of the nudist paintings. Some folks would feel flattered, I suppose and there was the money he would make too. Ma may not see it that way, because she mollycoddled Kenneth, especially since he had been ill. At least she didn't baby me, because she had hidden behind me for years, until she was confident enough to face up to the whole Glenmoriston mob.

I was relieved for both Ma and I, once that Bruce was established as a trusted new husband for her, and she adored him now.

14. All Three Wives

After I stabled my horse, I went over to my lads' Highland Ponies, to try and imagine riding one of them and called Kenneth over. They were much smaller than what I was accustomed to. Kenneth and I both had long and lanky legs, so it would be different riding on one of those wee but wild ponies.

"We could borrow these ponies, brother? What do you think?" I asked.

"Great idea, but will your lads mind?" Kenneth asked.

"I'll ask them and if they mind, I'll buy two more," I said.

I bade him goodnight and wished him a lot of luck with his wife, Ivy, and he wished me luck with my wife, Ailsa.

My lovely wife had already prepared dinner but wanted me to wash off the fishy smell first, before we ate. She took my fish and handed them to Meredith, who was going home and just said plainly that she wasn't cleaning the fish, she was knocking off. And she left to go home to her mighty man, Hugh. So, I thought it better to depart from the women, briefly having a disagreement. I took the bath water myself from over the fire and walked to the bathing room, and wished it had water plumbed to it by now.

I was going to investigate the cost again.

Ailsa wasn't always ready with the bath water, like Cherry always had been. It was a thing that Cherry had been fixated over, but I had taken that for granted. It took a couple of trips for the bath water, leaving more water on, cooking each time and then went into a shallow bath, that always made me shiver and become cold, when it was too shallow. I scrubbed myself and washed my hair and hoped that would wash off the smell and got out sooner than I would have liked. There was no sexy talk over bath times anymore and I missed that part from my first marriage with Cherry, but overall, I was very happy with Ailsa.

I needed to get indoor plumbing and not expect a wife to do so much heavy lifting with the water.

After I was dressed and ready to face Ailsa, unfortunately she was in a bad mood over Meredith having left, without cleaning the fish.

"I'll make an outdoor area where I can clean them before I come inside, next time and maybe the twins would like to clean the fish. I then noticed their absence. Where are the lads?" I asked.

"They're upstairs doing their lessons, like I told them to," Ailsa said grumpily.

"Have they already eaten then? I want to see my lads. I've missed the wee rascals. Lads," I called. "Come and see your Da," I called out.

They then came running to me gleefully and hugged me.

"Have you already eaten? Come and eat with me, my good lads," I said. I needed something from them with hooves and obviously, they also needed something from me.

"The twins were not well-behaved Malcolm, so they were not to eat, until they were well behaved," my wife complained.

"Nae Ailsa, you will not punish them with food. They work hard and they need to eat," I rebuked.

"Do you understand Ailsa? Never do that again," I demanded.

She then broke down in tears.

"I do my best when you're not here, Malcolm," Ailsa said, sobbing.

"Alright, now lads eat up until you are full, okay? Do you have desert for them Ailsa?" I asked.

"I told them they couldn't have desert either," Ailsa said.

"Where is it Ailsa? They can have desert too," I said.

Reluctantly, she went into the kitchen and got my lads their deserts.

"Lads I have a request of you. Can Uncle Kenneth and I borrow your wee ponies next week for the weekend," I asked.

"Och, aye Da, but it will cost you," they both said, laughing.

"Pony rental fee of two pounds per day," Malcolm Og said.

"Per pony," Hamish Og, then added.

"That sounds cheap. Can we all shake on it then?" I said, knowing full well that I was being ripped off, but it might make up for their evening, being a lousy one, with Ailsa.

"We might even clean the fish now for you Da, so Ailsa will stop complaining," Hamish Og said.

"Okay then, eat your desert, then clean the fish for me and you can finish the lessons tomorrow," I said.

I didn't correct them from calling my wife by her first name, as that was how I addressed Bruce on and off, depending on my mood. Sometimes he was Da, most often I called him Bruce, so I allowed the lads the same rights to choose, because Ailsa wasn't their natural Mither, either.

"Where are you going next weekend, Malcolm?" Ailsa asked.

"It's just for two days for Kenneth's artwork to be collected from a mountain in the MacKenzie lands, I think or if not, it's on the border, called, Beinn Coinneach," I replied.

"Kenneth said it was real tricky going up that slippery mountain track on his horse and was going to use a carriage next time, but Bruce advised against it, given that it's so slippery and partially covered in snow and ice. He suggested that we use Highland Ponies, that are built for those conditions," I explained.

"Will the twins be working, or will they be with me?" Ailsa asked.

"Both, I imagine. They do have to eat love," I said. "If we had four ponies, I would take them, but we only have two and what's going on anyway? Why are you unhappy with my lads? They are the best lads in the whole district. Everyone loves them, don't they lads?" I stated.

"Aye Da, if the lassies know we are coming with a delivery, they all hang out of their windows and call out our names and Malcolm here, flashed his ass to a few of them, eh Malcolm?" Hamish Og said.

I was so proud of my lads, they were just like me and Kenneth, growing up in Loch Insh. Soon they would be peeking through the lassies' windows and then they'll be having sex with married women, all in days' work with the Team. I never had one complaint from Hugh or Meredith, who adored my lads. It was normal behaviour, in my opinion.

"Ailsa love, if the lads spank you on the bottom, don't worry, that's a normal laddie thing to do, so don't punish them for that," I said, merely as a precaution.

"That's what they did Malcolm. They both spanked me on my bottom and then ran off laughing," Ailsa said.

"Ailsa darling, it just means that they like you and they are not attracted to their own gender. Just laugh it off next time, or try and enjoy it, they must like your ass," I suggested.

"Why do they call me Ailsa? It's disrespectful," Ailsa added, red-faced.

By then I had had enough of the complaining, and it wasn't how I planned it to be, but I got angry, knowing what I knew of her disgusting Mither, stealing Zahra's husband and leaving the wee bairns, fatherless.

"At least my lads didn't break up a good marriage, then cause the man to abandon his farm, his bairns and beat up his wife to be with your Mither, sailing away to the Americas, with his gold bars in his hands, leaving disaster in their wakes, because your Mither chose to flirt with a married man in the first place. Ailsa, your Mither has left Inverness, without saying goodbye or good luck to you and so don't tell me that my lads are worse than your Mither," I said.

I wished I hadn't said it so harshly, and it all came out so badly, as Ailsa crumbled into a weeping mess and I never spoke to her again like that.

The lads cleaned the fish as they had promised, but quietly now as the scene had deteriorated too badly and they felt partly to blame, and they didn't enjoy seeing Ailsa crying. When they had finished and cleaned up after themselves, they left the fish in plain sight for her to cook or store and came and kissed me goodnight.

"Sorry Da," they both said.

"Lads it wasn't your fault, now off to bed. I love you both, now here is that money for the ponies," I said and that cheered them up a lot, as they planned what to spend their newfound wealth on.

"Are you talking about Grigor Mohr MacGregor then, Zahra's husband, with my Mither?" Ailsa asked through her tears. "It's not my fault what she did Malcolm. I cannot excuse what my Mither has done at all, but I am so sorry. Is Zahra alright now then?" Ailsa asked.

"Nae, she isn't, and neither are her bairns, nor her old farm, she has a brain injury, but she has found herself a good husband, by some miracle of God and he has saved her life, I believe," I replied.

"Is that where you are going then, next weekend, for that nude artwork?" Ailsa asked.

"It is," I replied. "He is very protective of her now and she is limited with what she can do, so it is better that we go up there, until that whole series of nude art is completed. It will cause a bit of a stir around here, especially with one of them, but others won't. Either way it will make Kenneth a big name for himself, as well as for his Art Gallery business," I explained.

"Look love, this issue has affected, so many people, most especially her poor and sad bairns. Three of them are now living with her and her new husband, but the farm in the Aird, is now undergoing some new re-development, at Zahra's husband's expense, according to Hamish. Poor John Fraser just couldn't cope on his own. The three Glenmoriston men, all just left the farm. First my Grandda, then Grigor Mohr, then Alex, so John was alone with all that heavy responsibility, without Zahra there, whom he thought was dead. If that wasn't bad enough, the men then snuck back that night to steal Zahra's horse and her saddlery and twenty of John's coos. It's lucky that Zahra has married a very wealthy man. I want to know what their plans are and to see if I can help in any way.

After all, it did involve your Mither and that fact will never be overlooked," I said.

"You personally won't have to worry, but don't overdo the 'disrespectful' label, or it will not go down well, until this all blows over. People will eventually forget that his lover was your Mither and don't tell those who have forgotten or didn't know in the first place. One thing you can feel better about, is that at least your Mither didn't abandon you, or your sisters. She waited until you were all married, before she went fishing for a new fellow," I said.

"Sadly, your Mither stole a married man whose wee bairn was only a few weeks old and still on the breast," I added.

"Grigor punched Zahra in the face you know, breaking both her jaw and her nose?" I said and then I could not contain it any longer and blubbed at the very thought of a man doing that to such a delicate and beautiful woman like Zahra.

"Oh, Malcolm, I am so sorry," Ailsa said, and she put her arms around me.

Zahra was special in so many ways and I prayed for her that night and every night thereafter.

"I am sorry I did the wrong thing with our lads Malcolm," Ailsa said.

"They can call me Ailsa if they like, I don't mind, really," she added, and I hoped my life with Ailsa was back on track. After all, she too had lost her Mither and she had loved her Mither, despite her strange change in behaviour after Ailsa had left the family home, in Inverness.

"Do you think they will like living over there? I mean the war is over now, isn't it? They are no longer colonies of Britain, so it must be a bit disorganised there, I imagine. I haven't kept up with it, being so busy as we are," Ailsa said.

"I don't want to think about them. They have chosen that life, Ailsa. They are both adults," I said. "Leave them now to their own devices. God will take care of them both," I said, knowing what I meant in hoping what God would do to them both.

I was hoping that Kenneth was doing better with Ivy than I had been with Ailsa, when he was to tell Ivy of the nude painting, displaying his cock in a very compromising position, but he wouldn't tell me what that was exactly. I found out later when Bruce wasn't around. I was also hoping Bruce fared better with Ma, than us both and expected Ma at my door first thing in the morning, at breakfast time, and I was right.

A knock on my door, while we all ate breakfast, was predictably, my Mither, looking very unhappy with me.

"Malcolm, what's this I hear about nude paintings, one of them featuring my son Kenneth. Why didn't you prevent that from happening?" Ma demanded to know, thinking that I could have stopped any of the whole nude painting's evolution.

"That's right Ma, Kenneth is selling art now, featuring a nudist theme, although very tasteful, I am told," I answered.

"And the one with Kenneth posing in it?" Ma asked. "Did my son need to take his pants off for a client?" Ma ranted.

Marion MacDonald

"Ma, I wasn't there, and I know as much as Bruce and yourself, so we would need to ask Kenneth to get those details, if you really think, that you want details," I responded. "It will launch the Art Gallery into the wider art world. He will make a pretty penny Ma," I said. "I want his business to succeed, and I want to support him, as he is treading new ground. Now is not the time to make him feel unloved, or unsupported by his own family".

"There will be people who will disapprove of this form of art, like the Church or competing Art Galleries. You are neither one of those. You are his Mither. Please support him Ma. He needs you. I am even going to that man's place with Kenneth next time, so I promise that I will look after him, Ma, you hear Ma, I promise," I emphasised.

"That is true Marion, my darling, sweetheart, love," said Bruce, "I gave our lads advice to take Highland Ponies travelling up that slippery mountain track".

"My twins have agreed to lend us their ponies Bruce, so we can take them," I said.

"That's bonny lad, bonny," Bruce said. "Our son might be rich one day darling," Bruce said, hopefully.

Something we said convinced Ma to calm down and support Kenneth with his new business direction, so when he walked in, looking much worse for the wear, Ma was ready to accept the new direction for his art gallery. His appearance worried her more than anything else and she forgot the whole nude art issue.

"Are you feeling alright, my darling son?" Ma asked.

"Ivy won't support my new venture Ma. I suppose you don't either?" Kenneth asked, as he sat down, about to cry.

"Not at all my darling son. You will always have Bruce's and my support, as well as your big brother Malcolm, now tell me how we can help you with Ivy," Ma said. I looked across at Da and was relieved and left Ivy to Ma, as she marched off to speak to her daughter in law, while Ailsa sat Kenneth down to eat a big breakfast, as he hadn't yet eaten.

"Here Kenneth, my dearest brother, eat up," Ailsa kindly said.

Islay was aware of all sides of the argument and kissed her Uncle Kenneth on the cheek and said, "Good luck Uncle Kenneth, I am on your side," and she went to work with her goats. She was a good lass, and her husband Angus followed her and shook his hand.

"You can count on me too, Uncle" Angus said.

This really lifted Kenneth's spirits and then he ate his huge breakfast of three fried eggs, two sausages, two fried tomatoes and toasted eggy bread and then his face started to return to his normal, healthy colour. I felt for my brother. He couldn't be pushed, or he may become sick again. I dreaded a return to those bad old days when I found Kenneth near death, from alcohol poisoning.

"I have the ponies sorted brother, thanks to my lads," I said, hoping to cheer him up.

My lads then went over to their Uncle Kenneth, feeling proud to have helped him, even if they were overcharging me and they kissed him, as they always did. They really loved my brother, and he had always loved them, from the moment that they were born, and he had even named one of my lads. They had always climbed all over him and even now, as big as they had grown, still loved to climb onto his lap, competing for his attention and love. Kenneth forgot his troubles with them arguing over who could sit on top of him. I was sure that Ma would sort Ivy out and I told Ailsa that I was off to my beloved coos and told her that I loved her and kissed her gently on the forehead.

"I love you Ailsa" I said.

◇

15. A Stinky Woman

Grigor Mohr MacGregor arrived in Philadelphia in Pennsylvania, via New York, after two months at sea, with Mrs Belle MacGregor. The pair of them were both exhausted and had lost weight from sea sickness and poor rations, on board the ship. Grigor knew that ship life would be bad, because he had listened to Padruig's stories, but had never thought it could be quite that bad. Grigor had dysentery and lice, as did Mrs MacGregor, so the thought of sex, was far from both of their minds, until they could bring those conditions, under some semblance of control.

Belle stank like nothing else, and if there was one thing that Grigor Mohr MacGregor could not stand, was a woman who stank.

Reluctantly, he paid for a rented room for the two of them, saying it would be her turn to pay, next time. This was met with immediate opposition, as she had expected that the man with the gold bars, was going to pay for all her expenses. She didn't know him well enough to have thought that. Even poor Zahra had to pay for his cup of tea in Inverness, when she had sold her 'Fairy Art' and she paid entirely for Hector's new horse and his saddlery. Grigor didn't like debt, and he didn't like to spend, if there was another who could pay willingly.

"Go and wash woman", Grigor demanded. "You stink like all hell," Grigor said to his new woman, Belle MacGregor, Ailsa's Mither of Inverness, in Scotland.

They were a very long way from home and very unhappy.

On the ship across the sea to this God forsaken place, he thought that Belle appeared very happy as to where their journey would take them. On the other hand, Grigor was only able to look over the side of the ship at the churning waters below and felt that it was representative of his life and the horrible mess that he had made of everything. His life had been good, and he hated to admit that, because he had convinced himself that he would be happier without them all, even Zahra. He thought that freedom from all that responsibility and cost would release him from a lingering unhappiness, which he blamed on Zahra, even though, she did everything he asked of her. It was her perfection that niggled at him. He couldn't even say what a lousy wife she was, because she wasn't, other than when she left home to protect herself.

Grigor just couldn't stick it out long term, in a normal, family way of life, always afraid that he could lose self-control at any moment. He had self-control but he was a part of that group of seven men, for a good reason and it was his sheer brutality and ruthlessness that had made him a welcome part of that group, when they were fighting against the Redcoats, as well as his knowledge of the Unseen and the mountainous terrain. The 'family man' façade may have worked out if Padruig and Alex hadn't moved onto John's farm as well. Those two men were a constant reminder of Grigor's true nature and Padruig worked on his every weakness, to move in on his wife Zahra, still desperate to replace Isobel Grant, his late wife.

Padruig was never going to overcome what Hugh and Isobel had done to him, while he was away in Quebec.

Grigor already knew that he had made the wrong decision in leaving Scotland under the cloud of a curse, with Belle MacGregor and was already planning on his return to the Highlands, well before they had even started to settle down, or getting to know other Scots in the Americas. He heard Belle returning from the bathing room, complaining about how cold the water was to other residents. Totally naked, she strolled into their room having washed out her clothing, not caring if other residents had seen her nudity, which infuriated him, partly because in the raw flesh, Belle MacGregor was ugly, as well as immoral.

His anger drove him, and he hit her for displaying herself, in that way.

But this wasn't Scotland, and things weren't the same in this new country. The neighbouring Quakers, upon hearing the altercation, knocked on his door, objecting to the violence, to which he responded, once again, with violence. He thought better of staying there with her then and made his way silently and invisible to all, to the docks, to find a ship to take him back, upriver to New York. Back to Scotland. He wasn't going to pay a fare this time.

Belle MacGregor could take care of herself.

16. Zahra Meets Coinneach's Family

Zahra woke up, aware of the bairn that she was carrying within and the love she felt now for her new husband, Coinneach. He was still peacefully sleeping, and she wanted to declare her love to him as she hadn't really, if at all, but she couldn't remember. She also wanted him to know of the stirring within her womb. She thought she was with child.

"Coinneach," she whispered quietly to him. "Coinneach, I want to tell you something". Coinneach stirred and rolled over to look at his wife looking right at him with her big green eyes.

"What is it my love?" he asked, sleepily.

"Coinneach, I want to tell you that I love you more," Zahra said.

"So, you now love me more than your last husband. Is that why you have woken me up?" he asked with a smile in his eyes.

"Oh, it came out all wrong," she lamented.

"So, if I said, 'Zahra I now know that I love you more than all the other women I have had in my life', it would be a romantic moment, would it?" Coinneach asked cheekily, knowing it wouldn't. She suddenly felt jealous of every other woman that he had ever looked at, let alone married over the many centuries.

"Nae, that's just awful, it wasn't supposed to sound like that, and I don't want to share you with all of those others," she said jealously.

"Jealousy is what I see, my precious little wildcat. You are truly jealous, aren't you?" Coinneach said so cheekily, it was infuriating.

"Aye, I am jealous of any memory you have of other women, of course," Zahra said.

He rolled over to be right over the top of her, looking deeply into her eyes, with his strong arms and knees, supporting him, either side of her.

"Is there something else then that you want to tell me, my jealous wife?" Coinneach asked smiling from ear to ear.

"Aye, there is. I might be with child Coinneach. Our child," Zahra declared.

"Exhilarated, Coinneach then sat up suddenly and felt her stomach and his hand just rested there gently while he took it all in. Momentarily in disbelief, he was emotional.

"Our bairn?" Coinneach asked.

"Aye," she replied, "I think so. I am getting fat you, see? And I am nauseous too as I usually am if I am with child. I just couldn't keep it to myself, I just had to tell you," Zahra said. "I used to tell Isobel first, but she is not here. Do you mind, are you pleased?" she asked.

"Pleased? I am overjoyed. This will be the first royal bairn, born of us MacAlpins in centuries," he added.

"If it's a boy, will he be named Coinneach or Cinaed like your Da?" Zahra asked.

"Coinneach, of course and if it's a wee lass it can be Erin," Coinneach added.

"But it will be a boy, I know it will," Coinneach added and then made love to her.

"My wonderful wife, let me make you joyously happy," he said. Coinneach always knew how to bring Zahra to orgasm which he took pride in as he would watch her face, observing his efforts come to fruition.

"I love it when you lose yourself completely to me, my love," Coinneach said.

"Och Coinneach," she cried out in pleasure with his dreamy, hypnotic eyes boring into hers and his large member gently entering her, she began to weep, both in pleasure and the expectation of their wee bairn, as a married couple.

17. The MacAlpins

That day, Coinneach showed her where he kept all of his pigeons, beside the mansion in a circular, cemented housing structure, for them all, called a doocot. At one end, he explained were over five hundred pigeons which were for eating in the winter months but at the other end, there were the little houses for a different type of pigeon, kept for messaging to his father and his brothers. One of the MacKenzie staff always cared for them all and it had been his job for centuries, it seemed. He knew them all by name.

"Your father and brothers?" Zahra asked. "I didn't know that you had family here too. Why weren't they at our wedding?" Zahra asked.

"They had to be certain of who I was with and now that there is a bairn coming, they will come and assess you. Don't worry my love. Nothing they say can undo us, but we would be complete, as a family if they were involved too, don't you think?" he replied. "We will need them," Coinneach said. "It's just my four brothers, their wives and my father, Lord Cinaed," he declared.

"Oh aye, I want to meet them, I would have a father then too and brothers," Zahra answered.

Just then, she recalled what Grigor's father did to her, resulting in the first time that she ran away from her home in the Aird, injured, escaping to Grigor Og's house to work as a cook, with one broken bone in her lower right leg.

"Coinneach, I had one bad experience with Grigor's father. It doesn't involve a particular tradition, involving his need for sexual gratification too, does it?" Zahra asked.

"Nae, my dear. They do assess you, there is that, but you are already with child, so no-one but I can have intercourse with you. Did that happen to you with Grigor's father?" Coinneach asked.

"Oh, aye and I fought hard against his advances and was badly injured in the process. He was a huge man of unnatural proportions. Like a giant really and to hold me down, he bodily leaned on my right leg and one bone was fractured, beneath his weight, but I didn't know that it was broken, although I had pain and difficulty getting about. I eventually saw Doctor Heath in Inverness, who put it in a splint. It took a while to heal," Zahra said.

"And your feminine area? Were you raped by him too?" Coinneach asked.

"Aye, I was. I was split and a midwife stitched it up for me and luckily it split side to side and not lengthways. Grigor didn't stop him. He said it was a tradition," Zahra explained. "Do you have that custom too?" she asked.

"It's an ancient Irish tradition that does exist, that is true, but in this case, you are already married to me, and you are with my child. What is the normal way for royal families to determine who is right for the family is assessment. You will not be subjected to rape. I can guarantee that. Will you agree to an assessment, so we can have my family involved in our lives?" he asked.

"Who will be present at this assessment?" Zahra asked.

"Myself, my father and my four brothers Padraig, Anndra, Cinaed Og and Prince Griogar. Their wives will be in another room at the time. It may be a bit embarrassing, however it will be worthwhile in the long run, if you are dignified, to have our family relations, back on track. It will only take fifteen minutes, at the most, then we will have their support, which I have a strong feeling, we will need. I dreamed that your ex-husband was returning to Scotland. My brothers, especially Prince Griogar and I together, have an army to combat anything that might come our way. In addition to that, the MacKenzies form a fortress around us all, when there is trouble," Coinneach explained.

"Were you supposed to have consulted with your family first, before you married me?" Zahra asked.

"Aye, I was of course, but I knew you were the one that I had been waiting for and my father had long given up on my belief that you were coming to me. But here you are, and I wanted to ensure that our bairn was mine and not my father's," Coinneach replied.

"So, if you had consulted with them first, then I would have been raped by your father?" Zahra asked.

"We don't call it that. It's the right of the father to have the first act with the bride from days of old but that would only apply if you were a virgin anyway," Coinneach said. "It's an ancient custom but we are an ancient people, and I hope you are understanding of that by now," Coinneach said.

"Will they object to my not being a virgin then, before marrying you?" Zahra asked.

"There may be those discussions, and we need only to tell them the truth of what has occurred. They may wish harm to come to your ex-husband. Do you have a problem with that?" Coinneach asked.

"I don't want any harm to come to him, no matter what he has done to us all. The betrayal still hurts me, as is natural for anyone with dependent bairns. He didn't have concern for any one of us, not even Hector whom he used to adore, when he was wee. He was even hitting Hector over the head, but I still want no harm to come to Grigor, or else I am no better than he," Zahra said.

Wiping away tears, she said she'd consider Coinneach's family peculiar requirements. He held her closely to himself and thanked her.

"I know it is a sacrifice for you, because you love me and for that, I love you even more that you have quizzed me like this," Coinneach said, without fully comprehending the depth of his wife's pain and what he was asking of her.

"Now the pigeons. They are to send messages to my family. Are you ready? Say that little prayer thingy I hear you say before things happen," Coinneach asked.

"Do you mean "Bismillah ir Rahman ir Raheem?" Zahra asked.

"That's it," Coinneach said.

And the pigeons flew high up into the sky and Coinneach's family were expected to respond within the same day. She was nervous, still trying to take in that Coinneach even had a family, let alone one that was influential.

Zahra was given beautiful silken robes to wear for when they would all meet, but the plan was first to meet them all as a family together with their wives in the larger of the two sitting rooms, overlooking the glens. Staff were extremely nervous at the presence of all the MacAlpins, especially one of the brothers, of whom they were terribly afraid, and he spoke harshly to all of the servants.

Zahra was initially dressed in the finest of gowns on this occasion, allowing for expansion in the stomach area. It was accompanied by the ruby necklace worn on her wedding day and it was all approved of first by her pedantic husband, who had impeccable taste. Her slippers were a soft golden texture, where she could look elegant, but not cause her to trip over, with her awkward gait, which she endeavoured to conceal, as much as possible. In herself, she felt somehow removed from the event about to occur.

Of course, wee Dihaoine was there too, and was all dressed up like little lassies enjoy doing, as were her handsome brothers, wee Causantin and Hector, who loved these exciting moments. Hector had been given a lovely new Clan Gregor plaid, with a matching waist coat and a beautiful linen shirt. His long black hair was clean and shiny, and he now carried his own comb, which he frequently used to comb his hair encouraged by his Mither. Both wee ones looked all dressed up, without a hair out of place and both were wearing sweet new shoes that Coinneach had bought them on the day that they had all been shopping. Dihaoine was especially thrilled to be wearing two matching butterfly shaped combs in her curly hair.

"Ma, I can't wait to tell everyone about this," Hector exclaimed. The thrill of the occasion was still in telling the rest of his siblings. Zahra felt no such thrill.

The three coaches rambled up the mountain track, carrying the ever-important father, Lord Cinaed, alone in the first carriage, the four brothers were in the second one and the four pretentious wives were in the last one. The household staff had been increased by more than twenty, all MacKenzies to attend to any of the needs of the MacAlpins. Some may have been security in disguise too, Zahra thought. It was a huge occasion. The staff knew it was an important moment in time, and they hadn't seen this display of MacAlpin family force, in this generation, or more.

Watching on, as the MacAlpins alighted, they were greeted by the staff who were all dressed in uniform, standing outside of the mansion in two lines, as if they were meeting someone of immense importance, Zahra still hadn't quite grasped that they were important, most especially her husband, Lord Coinneach and his father Lord Cinaed whom she didn't like from the outset.

The wing of the mansion, that was normally closed, had been re-opened and cleaned impeccably and fires were lit all over the entire mansion, ensuring its warmth. His family might be staying the night, but they weren't certain of that, and no-one hoped that they would, by the nervous tension felt upon their arrival.

Coinneach's father, the very stout, Lord Cinaed was first to start the walk to the mansion's, huge front door, where

Coinneach stepped out first to greet his aged father, with great reverence and kissed an enormous ring, that he was wearing on his right hand. He was an elderly and portly old gentleman with a very long, grey beard that hadn't been trimmed for a very long time. Zahra stood behind Coinneach, waiting on instructions from Mairi, who was to tell her what to do next and at what stage.

"Father," Coinneach said, "Welcome to my home, this is my lovely wife Lady Zahra Coinneach," he said bravely to his unsmiling, bearded, and portly father. Zahra thought he looked like a fat teddy bear, if you got to know him, otherwise he would be a hard task master with having raised all of those big sons. She was instructed to bow to him, but as she told Coinneach, she can't bow her head to a human, only to God in her religion. So, he had to be content with an awkward curtsy, with Mairi concealing, that she was supporting her from behind to ensure that she didn't fall over.

The grumpy old man stopped for a brief moment and looked at Zahra with a curious expression.

"So, you are what this fuss is all about lass, is it?" the old man asked, still unsmiling.

"I suppose so, Sir," she replied. "What should I call you?" Zahra asked.

"Foreword lass, aren't you? Well, Father is better than Sir, so call me Father," Lord Cinaed said and offered his arm and told her to walk with him into the warmth of the mansion.

"You don't need to get cold out here, greeting the others," the old man remarked. She was hoping that this would not happen, because then he would notice her wobbly walk, but she did her best to walk with him, or rather he walked her, to the nicely arranged seating beside the big, ornate fireplace.

"You have an awkward gait, Lady Zahra, why is that?" Lord Cinaed asked directly.

Zahra was feeling insecure without her husband and looked in his direction first before replying, but the old man disapproved.

"Don't look to him first. Answer me lass," Lord Cinaed demanded.

"I have been told that I have a wee brain injury father. It's much improved now, thanks to your son, Coinneach but what remains is a bit of a wobble when I walk and my handwriting is still rather poor, although Coinneach is teaching me calligraphy now," Zahra answered.

"Indeed, but why my dear?" Lord Cinaed asked, just as Coinneach entered with his four brothers, who were all large men, like him but not as tall as her Glenmoriston men, of fine stature, with very straight backs and handsome in an Irish/Nordic kind of way she thought. Their father was the only one who was sporting a long grey beard and moustache, and he wore a great kilt, wrapped all around himself, it seemed, but it didn't suit him, Zahra thought and neither did its tartan colours that clashed with his grey beard and brown boots that he wore inside the mansion. He needed a stylist, Zahra thought and Mairi wouldn't be pleased with those boots inside the house.

"I was knocked out a while back and hit the edge of a table, then being unconscious, I fell face down onto the hard stone floor, breaking my nose in the process. They didn't think I would recover at all, and I don't remember any of what happened then, other than seeing Coinneach's face. Your son said he was bringing me here to recover which he has done miraculously," Zahra said to the senior MacAlpin.

"Sorry Coinneach, your Da asked me about my wobble," Zahra said to her frowning husband who was wondering why she was telling his father that story.

"Don't judge your wife son. She obeyed me and I got the truth, so now tell me son, why was she knocked out and by whom, in order to hit a table in the first place? Please, explain it to us all," Lord Cinaed demanded.

"I will father. May I introduce everyone first?" Coinneach said.

"My dear, stand up please, these are my brothers, Prince Griogar, Cinaed Og, Padraig and Anndra MacAlpin and their lovely wives, Ladies Eschina, Annabel, Ealasaid and Siobhan," Coinneach said.

The wives looked awfully snobby, who were also expensively dressed and made remarks in Irish Gaelige, that she could not understand a single word of. She wasn't getting approval from them, of that she was quite sure. One of the brothers looked especially harsh and his name was Prince Griogar, which wasn't surprising, but she wasn't put off by his attempts to intimidate her. The others were so similar in appearance, she hoped she could remember how to tell them apart.

None of them congratulated them on their nuptials nor did they bring gifts of any kind.

The servants all scurried nervously around with coffees and teas and other refreshments, while Lord Cinaed, persisted on his line of questioning.

"The story my son, please retell it, to us all," Lord Cinaed demanded.

"I first met Zahra at the home of an old Crohn in the Aird, who had requested my presence to identify Zahra, because she answered the description of the woman, who I had been waiting for over the centuries of whom you are all aware. Zahra then walked in, with one of her beautiful sons, Hector here," Coinneach replied.

"Pleased to meet you all," Hector said cheerfully. Zahra asked Hector to sit down beside her, and she kissed him. Slowly the brothers all took a seat to be more comfortable, while they looked upon the reason that they had all been summonsed there. Only one of the brothers seemed to smile a little and his name was Cinaed Og, the same name as his father. He was very fair haired and quite handsome. He must have died quite young Zahra was thinking.

"My eyesight isn't as good as it was when I was a young man, so I asked for Lady Zahra to sit in front of me, so I could identify her by feeling all of her facial features and her body shape, to be certain that she was indeed of Clan Gregor. At that, Prince Griogar himself looked seriously upon Zahra.

"You are a MacGregor then?" one brother asked.

"I don't know. Is that correct, Coinneach?" Zahra answered.

"Aye, that is true, my love. Show him your brooch," Zahra showed him the brooch that she always wore from Culloden field.

"Where did you get this? This is one of our ancient ones," Prince Griogar asked, looking angry.

"I was researching a book, my Lord Griogar and entered the world of the Seven Glenmoriston Men in the 18th century, while I was in 2023 and that brooch was given to me on Culloden Field, by one of them, Grigor Mohr MacGregor, as from the Otherworld, when I was still alive. He said that I wouldn't be able to complete my family tree, due to all of the missing information, one reason of which was due to proscription, but that I was indeed a MacGregor and the man who had worn this brooch was under the ground there, on Culloden field.

At that time, I was still alive but far into the future with my family still at home, but in this time, I married Hugh Chisholm, the youngest of the Seven Glenmoriston Men, who then, during an altercation with his friends, I was accidentally killed in Glenmoriston, Scotland. I was then unable to return to my previous life, as I had known it," Zahra explained.

"My question still has not been answered," their stout father said.

"Zahra has lived here in Scotland for a long time now father, most often happily, but successfully learning how to live here and after her marriage with Hugh Chisholm ended, due to the death of her bairn, Grigor MacGregor rescued her from that situation, and they started a new life together in the Aird, with her daughter, Isobel from Hugh," Coinneach explained with difficulty, as the brothers kept interrupting each other at one part of the story that interested them.

"How did it come about that you had a child with Hugh Chisholm and exactly how many children, in total do you have and from whom?" Prince Griogar asked, being very nosy.

"I thought that I was able to give birth to a wee bairn, because I was still a live spirit at the time of conception and as I lay dying, the child lived and so Grigor MacGregor remained with me, due to Clan obligation and he delivered the wee bairn. Hugh named her Isobel later, when I had been sent back to him. Isobel has blonde hair, just like her father, Hugh Chisholm. When we were both well enough, Grigor sent us on our way, with a map, to return us both to the bairn's father, so Hugh would know that he had a wee bairn. However, initially upon meeting us both, we were rejected by him when he saw us and I also found out that he had another wife living in Chisholm country anyway, with many children and grandchildren.

So, Hugh Chisholm had deceived me, and a neighbouring widower farmer took us both in then for me to be his cook," Zahra said when interrupted once more.

"Zahra, I am sorry to interrupt, and we will return to that story later. Please answer my question," Lord Cinaed asked once more, and he was growing impatient.

"My husband and I lived in the up until Aird recently and he was Gregor Mohr MacGregor, my Lord, but one morning he punched me in the face whereby I lost my balance, hit the dining table, then landed on the floor unconscious, face down." Zahra said.

"Coinneach, please help me, I can't explain it better than that, because I actually don't remember it all," Zahra asked.

"I was there," said Hector. "You were drinking that tea that prevents a pregnancy from occurring, because Padruig Dubh Grant had raped you, that morning, when we were all out working. Da then walked in and saw that you were drinking that tea, and he became angry with you, because he and Padruig had arranged something between themselves, so you that you would have a bairn with Padruig Grant and not with my Da.

My father was shamefully having a love affair with a Mrs Belle MacGregor from Inverness and wanted you to be seen as also being unfaithful to him, when in fact he had wanted to offload us all, not just you Ma. He asked you if you had drunk that tea and when you said you had, he punched you in the face, in a blind rage. Padruig was going to dispose of your body, but I threw my body over you, disallowing what they had done to the Chisholm's," Hector said and broke down into tears, because he had kept it all to himself for all that time, so as not to further worry his Mither.

"Hector. You stayed with me?" asked Zahra. "My hero Hector".

"Aye, they said that you were dead Ma, and you needed to be disposed of into the burn and I wouldn't let them Ma, but then Coinneach arrived, thank God," Hector said emotively.

"Were they going to chop me up into bits?" Zahra asked in disbelief.

"Aye Ma, they were, and you weren't even, really dead," Hector said.

"Who wanted to chop me up exactly?" Zahra asked.

"Da, Padruig and reluctantly, Alex as well," Hector added.

"After Lord Coinneach arrived and ascertained that you were still alive, he said he could take you to heal with your two youngest bairns and then Padruig became afraid of what they had all done and rapidly departed on his horse, then Da too, and eventually Alex. John was the only adult left to care for the rest of us and the farm.

Then to make things worse, that night, your horse and twenty coos were stolen, so it wasn't looking good, for any of us. We didn't know if we would ever see you again Ma, until you invited us all here to your wedding. I have never been so scared in my life, Ma, thinking you could be gone forever from us," Hector's story was so emotional that the snobbish wives even took on a serious and compassionate demeanour.

"I'm sorry Lord Cinaed, I am flawed, I know. I hope you can still accept me into your family," Zahra expressed with tears in her eyes.

"I'm sorry Hector, my precious son," Zahra said.

Coinneach had moved to hold onto his son Hector and wee Causantin sat on his lap too, holding onto him tightly.

"Don't cry too Dada," he said. Mairi then bought Dihaoine over to be fed and Zahra automatically went to feed her, but her dress could not be undone.

"Father, can you please undo it. I can't do that either," Zahra asked.

Her new father-in-law carefully undid her dress to reveal her breast for the bairn and was unable to stop staring at the loveliness of her breasts, as the wee bairn suckled. Hector was needing comforting as he had kept it all inside, as Coinneach held onto him and spoke kindly to him in Gaelic, mixed with a few curses then a few more which finally bought a smile to Hector's face. He responded with another curse, then the duel began with the two of them engaging in the Gaelic duelling competition that he and Ali had always engaged in.

The MacAlpin brothers looked on and listened in amazement, possibly learning a few new curses. It took their eyes and minds off Zahra's breasts.

"You know why we are here dear, don't you?" Lord MacAlpin

asked quietly.

"My husband explained it as an assessment for an approval my Lord to belong to your very respectable family. Do you wish to explain it further?" Zahra asked.

"It's not like we can undo what has already been done in terms of your marriage to my son. He knows our system and despite that, he went ahead of us to prevent me from rejecting you. It could affect family relations and inheritance, going forward, if we had found you unsuitable in any way, then my son would be cut adrift from us, which is serious, if he finds himself with enemies and I believe he will, if your ex-husband returns for you, for example. He needs us to assist him, I believe which is why we are also here. After this gathering today, we can let him know what we can or can't do for him. He must really love you to have put his inheritance at risk. He will not lose this house though, so you can put your mind at rest," Lord Cinaed said.

"In the old days, we would have dealt with him differently, but these are modern times, so we move with the times, as everyone must. The ladies will go and eat now, without us," Lord Cinaed said.

Zahra's heart was pounding so hard, she hadn't even known that he had family, so it was a shock to even be in the company of his odd family, who didn't even like her, it seemed. Her customs had been ignored in expecting a wedding gift or congratulations, like her own bairns had extended to Coinneach. These were heartless people whom she couldn't understand. Women's rights were a very long way off, Zahra concluded.

"After hardship cometh ease," she quoted to herself repeatedly.

Their ways would never be normal for her, and she disliked them all and they all knew that in that moment. The only brother who was obviously bothered that she might hate them, was Cinaed Og, for some unknown reason.

The old man would love to have had enjoyed a sexual rendezvous with Zahra, but he wasn't going to say so, in front of his sons. These were men of the 10th century and Zahra had already told them her flaws and the hidden brain injury, but the old man was very observant, so if there was a devious woman, of which there were a few too many, they would certainly weed them out after the continued questioning of Zahra's life.

"It will be hard for me to ever look them all in the face again Coinneach, but if it helps you, that is good," Zahra said.

"Father announced he would stay overnight but the rest of my family are leaving, once we have had our talk," Coinneach said.

"I want to go home with the bairns, now Coinneach, so we can get there before nightfall," Zahra said.

"You are home, what do you mean?" said a confused looking Coinneach.

"I mean my home in the Aird to see all of my bairns. To be with people who are not looking at me like I am something that the cat just vomited up," Zahra said.

"Just for a while. I'll ride my new horse, or I'll double with Hector. I need to see Isobel. I miss them all, can't you understand?" Zahra expressed, on the verge of breaking down.

Did she pass their test? She wasn't told. Did she receive wedding congratulations or a wedding gift of any type? No. The MacAlpins were, in her books, completely primitive.

Coinneach reluctantly agreed to Zahra visiting her family and waved her off with Dihaoine strapped to her back and wee Causantin strapped to Hector's. He wondered if in achieving one momentous task, that he had created another and was deeply saddened, as he discussed all the arrangements with his family, which all seemed a little less important now if his wife could never look upon their faces again. He hadn't thought that she would react like that. Hector was a lad he trusted and at the farm in the Aird was also one of Coinneach's Farm Managers, with his wife. It wasn't as if the two places were totally unknown to each other, but she wanted to feel herself once again and that was the only place where it could be achieved, especially now that Coinneach's father was staying overnight with him on Beinn Coinneach.

Even with the enjoyment his father would get from being with Coinneach, it had been too much for Zahra and she didn't trust him. Coinneach didn't want to believe it, but it was clear to him now that he hadn't taken into consideration that Zahra was also emotionally too damaged, and she couldn't take any more blows. She may require support for the rest of her life, or it could end her completely, was his worry, as he ate dinner with his talkative father, Coinneach felt unhappy and lonely.

The big house already seemed so empty, without Zahra's spirit enlivening it. He had taken her for granted already, in such a short time and he berated himself for his idiocy. It had been too soon for her, but Grigor Mohr MacGregor was on his way, and he could feel him getting closer.

"Are you going to tell me where your wife has gone, while I am here, or was it a pre-planned visit to see her family?" his father asked. He decided to lie to him rather than reveal any more truths.

"Pre-planned father. She misses Isobel, her daughter, especially now that she is with child," Coinneach said.

"You overlooked telling us that part, son. She is already

expecting your bairn which is surprising. Was the questioning harder for her, being with child? I must admit I have never had to assess a lass so much who was already with child," father said.

"It is your way father, and she comes from another time, where your ways don't even exist. She only answered your questions for me," Coinneach said. "I wished for my family to be a part of our lives, but now I may have ruined my relationship with her and both our futures possibly?" Coinneach declared. "You didn't even tell Zahra that you approved of her. Why not? That may have helped. Welcome to the family, might have helped too," Coinneach complained.

"Are you complaining to me son, is that it?" Lord Cinaed asked.

"Her bairns and sons in law came here, without knowing me and gave me treasured gifts for our wedding, when you all refused to come. So yes, why not complain a bit, if you have caused me loss or pain?" Coinneach expressed.

"See that sword up there on the wall? That was given to me by her son in law, on our wedding day and he had nothing, other than that to give to me. It is a valued Fraser family heirloom. I really love that rusty old thing, because I was welcomed into their beautiful family," he said emotively and felt himself about to weep, if he had lost his wife. "Have any of you welcomed her into our family, or have you alienated her for the rest of her life?" Coinneach asked.

"Where were the wedding presents from you all?" Coinneach added. "Not one wedding gift was had this day and I am ashamed of you all," Coinneach said.

"Do you think you have lost your wife son?" Lord Cinaed asked. "Nae you have not. She loves you as you love her, but it is true to say that we have not yet gained a family member and I will have to make that up to her, I promise you that son. You will see," he said. "Her son Hector is an amazing lad, I became fond of him, in that short time," Lord Cinaed added.

"But not Zahra?" Coinneach asked.

"Not Zahra, that is true. I am too afraid of bad women, and I took it from that viewpoint. How could you have fallen for such a strange one as this?" Lord Cinaed asked. "Cinaed Og liked her the most out of your brothers and Prince Griogar too, I believe," he said.

"Of course, they did. She is a MacGregor. You saw his face at the sight of that MacGregor brooch," Coinneach said. "And Zahra is not strange. Did you think for one minute that it could be you that is strange?" Coinneach said emotionally.

"Aye, I had considered that," Lord Cinaed said. "If she has won Prince Griogar over, then you have no problems. There's not another who could have succeeded in achieving that, I am certain. He is much harsher than I am, son," father said.

"You said she's from another time. What time?" Lord Cinaed asked.

"The future. Like she was trying to tell you. She was a novelist, still is and you might end up in her next book in a bad light," Coinneach added. "If she can make the Seven Glenmoriston Men look like heroes, she can equally make you look like a barbarian and I hope she does," he added.

"What books has she written then?" Lord Cinaed asked curiously and a little worried.

"I only have two of them here by sheer luck because Padruig Grant left them behind on the other farm and I didn't realise they were his," Coinneach said. "They are nicely illustrated by one of her daughters with drawings of Isobel of Glenmoriston and Padruig Dubh Grant. All seven of them are named. Poor Zahra thought that they were all heroes, and they were, when it was appropriate to do what they were best at and no one denies their skills, especially Padruig Grant and Alex MacDonald," Coinneach said.

"I will show you her novels, if you like later, or tomorrow. My concern right now, is my wife," he added. "Zahra wants Isobel here, I think. Isobel is loyal to my wife and has helped her with delivering all her other bairns. When it is time for our bairn to be born, we will need her, or I'll lose Zahra to the Aird again," Coinneach concluded.

"Then have Isobel here lad, what's the problem with that?" Lord Cinaed asked.

"Isobel is married, like I said to John Fraser and has two bairns, Anndra and Domhnall but there is a story behind their paternity, so even though they are born of the 'Fraser marriage', being with John, the man who enabled her to have any bairns at all, was Alexander MacDonald, one of the Seven Glenmoriston Men. So, Isobel had the second bairn while married with Alex and was handfast with him also, so in effect, she has two husbands, despite being the most conservative of them all, in appearance.

That was what worked for them, until the recent disaster," Coinneach said.

"Alex loved his bairns but chose to follow Padruig and Grigor that day. The decisions made that day would affect them all, for the rest of their lives," Coinneach added. Coinneach wanted to ensure that Isobel would never lose any of her children.

"I have advised both Isobel and John to seek legal counsel to ensure the bairn's security as children of the 'Fraser marriage', which I believe they were going to do with some urgency," Coinneach explained.

"So, in addition to all of the other issues that you have discussed with your brothers and I, there is also a possibility of kidnapping those two bairns?" Lord Cinaed asked.

"You should bring Isobel and the two bairns back here immediately, until the farm upgrades are completed. Your brothers can offer all the security you need here in this fortress, but there in the Aird, it would be very hard to guarantee the bairns' safety. The wall is incomplete, right?" he asked.

"That is right father" he replied. "I want to go there tomorrow and bring them back home. Do you think I should go there tomorrow to see my wife and bring them all back?" Coinneach asked.

"I do son. Bring her back home. Now where are your latest paintings that you have worked on. I want to keep up with your artwork too," Lord Cinaed asked.

Coinneach hadn't told his father about the nude paintings, let alone that his wife featured in them and other males, as well as the Art Gallery owner, himself.

"You may not like my new style of work, father," he commented.

"Take me to them and I will tell you if I like them or not," Lord Cinaed said bluntly.

"Father they are nude paintings of both a woman and a younger man," Coinneach warned.

"That sounds very French or Italian. Well, show me," he insisted.

"Father, the lady featured in all of my nude paintings, is my wife Zahra," Coinneach said.

"Zahra. Your wife Zahra?" he exclaimed. "How did you talk that sweet thing into doing a thing like that?" Lord Cinaed asked.

"Sweet thing now, is she?" he teased. "Come and see them and tell me what you think, then don't blame me if you feel faint father," Coinneach said.

The walk up the stairs alone, was enough to give the older man difficulty, but it hadn't prepared him for the first painting that he saw, upon walking in, which was the latest of his unfinished work. The first painting he saw was of Kenneth MacNachten, feigning the art of love making with Coinneach's wife, Zahra MacAlpin.

Coinneach had fond memories always of that day as the poor young man struggled with his modesty and had to be moved away from his wife to ejaculate three times. It wasn't an easy sit, then out of fondness for him and the late hour, Kenneth had slept in their bed, alongside them in harmony. His favourite memory, however, was when they were alone in the bathing room. Pretty young men used to be always available to him in the old days when he was the proxy King, and no-one thought anything of it.

"Oh my God, what have you done to this woman's decency? Have you corrupted her son?" Lord Cinaed asked.

"Nae father. It isn't as it seems. It is only intended to appear as if the two of them are making love, but I can guarantee, that that they were not. I was there for the entire duration, and I had to help the lad with himself, if you know what I mean," Coinneach said.

"Well, I suppose I did ask. What else do you have to shock an old man?" he said with good humour. He then looked upon the lovely one of Zahra, outstretched naked but not indecent, with only one half of a breast showing, as well as her beautiful round, milky skinned, bottom. "She is rather lovely, isn't she? It is well-done son, not indecent at all," he commented.

"Incidentally, have you adopted Zahra's bairns yet, son? You need to adopt them all if their father is on his way back to Scotland," Lord Cinaed advised.

"Alright father, I would love to adopt them all," Coinneach added. "Thank you for the advice," he said. "I will see my lawyer first thing, then go to the Aird. I think, Ali will need to give his permission, due to his age as well as his twin Fatma, but permission isn't required from all the others, except Isobel of course," Coinneach said.

"You can compromise by naming the oldest lad, Ali Gregor MacAlpin, retaining Clan Gregor but losing his actual father's name," Lord Cinaed suggested.

"That's a good idea," responded Coinneach.

"These other paintings over here are just of Zahra, so no terrible shocks, just different lovely poses, but they are all unfinished. I wanted to finish them all before Saturday when the owner of the Art Gallery comes to pick them all up, with his brother, Malcolm," Coinneach said.

"See this one son of your wife, may I buy it?" Lord Cinaed asked. "How much will this cost. I suppose a small fortune, knowing you?" he asked.

"Aye you can, but it's not going to be cheap, when it's finished father," Coinneach replied

"Don't send that one to the Art Gallery son, how much?" Lord Cinaed asked.

"Five thousand pounds father," Coinneach replied.

"Well, I must have it, so I will give it to you when you finish it. Deal?" Lord Cinaed stated.

"Deal father," he replied. Coinneach felt better that his father was paying for Zahra's discomfort, as well as the cost of the adoptions which would not be cheap, knowing his lawyer.

18. The Adoptions

The lawyer had to work faster than he had ever had to do before in drawing up all the adoption papers, including three that were requiring signatures, to finalise them, being of Ali and his twin sister Fatma, both named with Gregor as a middle name. Ali Gregor and Fatma Gregor MacAlpin.

Concerning Isobel, he also adopted her named as, Isobel Chisholm MacAlpin Fraser, because she was married to a Fraser but honouring her father, Hugh Chisholm, as well. Isobel's two sons, Anndra and Domhnall, would then both be, Alpin MacDonald Frasers. He considered leaving off the Fraser name but the lawyer forgot it anyway.

Coinneach's adoption list was:

Zahra's bairns:

Dihaoine Zahra Gregor MacAlpin

Causantin Gregor MacAlpin

Hector Cinaed Gregor MacAlpin

Fatma Zahra Gregor MacAlpin

Ali Gregor MacAlpin

Isobel Chisholm MacAlpin Fraser

Being of the MacAlpin marriage between Lady Zahra and Lord Coinneach MacAlpin of Beinn Coinneach.

Isobel Fraser's bairns:

Anndra Alpin MacDonald Fraser

Domhnall Alpin MacDonald Fraser

Being of the Fraser marriage between Isobel and John Fraser of Wolf Ranch in the Aird.

Arriving exhausted in the Aird, with his paperwork in hand, Coinneach had a mixture of nervous emotions. He was afraid that his beloved wife was still upset, but at the same time, he was excited to be able to see her and produce the adoption papers. He had barely slept the night before. He knew that Zahra completed him, and he could not go on without her. In such a short time, she had owned him completely and he would have done anything for her and her bairns, whether they were of him, or of any other man.

The paperwork he was carrying also was both an achievement and a scary proposal now to present to them all. He prayed, as he approached them, that all of his and his father's plans, would be accepted.

Upon arrival, he was pleased at last that the front stone wall and heavy iron gate, with a sign above the gate, was completed and it looked completely secure. The stone wall was six feet high, and the gate was made of black wrought iron in a pleasant pattern. The family had named the farm, 'Wolf Ranch', in memory of the wolf hunt.

To his absolute pleasure, his wife saw him and ran to him awkwardly and before he could dismount from his horse, she had opened the gate and was emotionally holding onto one of his legs and wanting him to hold her. She had missed him like nothing else, as did he.

"I am sorry Coinneach, I really am. I could not bear the night without you," she said through tears.

When his horse was taken to the stable, he too became emotional, and they both held each other in a locking embrace that surprised even the family and workers who all stopped their work to watch on.

"My dear wife. My father will make it up to you. Our son, Hector is going to receive a business venture proposal, all at my father's expense, on my land, if Hector wishes it," Coinneach said.

"Really?" Zahra asked. "I am so pleased my darling. I do want us all to be one big happy family, as you do," Zahra said.

"I have news also that I will need to talk to you all about, as well as a request of Isobel, can we go inside out of the cold, my lovely one?" Coinneach asked.

"My family, I am so pleased to see you all," he greeted them all, as John embraced him. Hector ran up to him, "Da, I missed you too, not only Ma. So did wee Dihaoine and wee Causantin," Hector said. Coinneach was happy to learn that and picked up both wee ones and kissed them profusely in turn.

"Isobel, dear child, I hope to speak to you too, after I have spoken to everyone else," Coinneach said, which took her attention. The cook, who was paid by 'Himself' prepared him coffee and cooked up cakes for everyone, nervous that her big boss was there. "Master," she said and curtsied to him. Isobel watched on in confusion at the curtsy and thought maybe they were all supposed to do that too, but didn't know why.

Coinneach presented the adoption papers and asked all present, including John, Fatma and Isobel, Hector, Anndra and Domnall, previously named Andrew and Donald, to hear him out. The wee ones climbed all over him as he tried to speak, so Dihaoine was put on Zahra's breast, but Causantin remained on his lap, as if to own his new father. So, he spoke to wee Causantin first and asked him if he would like to be legally adopted by him, so that forever, he would be his son.

"What's adopted?" Causantin asked.

"It means you will be mine from now on," he replied as he showed the lad the paperwork.

"Look Ma," Causantin said.

"So, son you will take my name. Would you like that?" Coinneach asked. "In this paperwork you will be Causantin Anndra Gregor MacAlpin, to honour my brother Anndra as well," he explained. "Do you like your new name?" he asked.

Other family members began to peer over his shoulder to read the adoption of Causantin.

"Look Ma, it still includes Clan Gregor," said Isobel. "He doesn't lose the clan connection, while also taking on father's name," she said proudly.

"Can I see it?" asked Zahra.

"Aye you can. Give it to Mummy," Coinneach said saying Mummy accidentally.

"Mummy, am I now?" Zahra asked with a smile on her face.

"Sorry my darling, it was automatic, I used to call my Mither, Mummy well into my older years. You can still be Ma, I don't mind," Coinneach said.

"Am I yours now already, father?" Causantin asked.

"Aye, you are mine now and you will live in my house on Beinn Coinneach in your own room, but you can still visit Wolf Ranch when we all come here together," he explained. Fatma was looking a bit sad, so he explained to her that they were all adopted, but he required her permission as well as Ali's, due to their ages.

"What about me father?" said a worried Hector.

"Here son, read the paperwork, you are mine too. You are Hector Cinaed Gregor MacAlpin. Cinaed is my father's name, and he gave you his name because he loves you. He wants to buy you a business, breeding Highland Ponies and is building the stables and yards, as we speak. He is arranging the pure stock from Beth Fraser, four stallions and thirty mares to begin with and you will sell them as their numbers increase and of course break them all in. They are vital in our part of the world, on that mountain. Do you accept my adoption of you, my father's name, and his offer of your new business venture? He really loved you when he met you and heard you have saved your Mither twice, and so now deserving of reward, he believes," Coinneach explained.

"Aye. Where do I sign then father?" asked Hector.

"Fatma lass," he said. "You are Fatma Zahra Gregor MacAlpin and when if you marry in the Kirk, you add Fraser to that, if you marry Simon or whatever husband it is that you chose," he explained. But you need to sign in agreement. Young Simon was relieved that he wasn't left out of the family story. "John, I will have to leave Ali's paperwork with you for him to sign. Can you do that, or do you think we should visit him?" Coinneach asked.

"This is important my love and we don't want a misunderstanding. I think we should go to Cannich, to see him personally, even if we must stay there overnight, on our way home," Zahra advised.

"Alright my love. Whatever you think is best," he said, wishing to co-operate.

"Isobel, you are also mine my dearest, as are your wee lads, I have named you Isobel Chisholm MacAlpin Fraser and your bairns with John are, Anndra Alpin MacDonald and Domhnall Alpin MacDonald. We might have forgotten to add Fraser. I require your signature if you would like me to adopt you all into my family. You too John." Coinneach said.

"I have been adopted before by Da and that didn't last. Neither father lasted. Will you be my forever, father, and grandfather to my sons?" Isobel asked, seriously wanting him to be and sad too at how she had been let down.

"I understand what has happened to you Isobel and how confusing it must be, and I can't excuse what the other men folk have done to both you and your Mither. I will be here forever for you, if you want that, because I think the world of you Isobel and how much you have done for your Mither," Coinneach said. The atmosphere in the room was dropping from happiness to recalling all the sadness's cumulatively.

Isobel had suffered silently and was the unnoticed, wounded one of the family. Her wounds included Hugh Chisholm, and she was often seen praying over the waterfall, where his bones lay below.

"I didn't agree with what happened to my biological father and now I can never see him again. That should have been my choice to see him again or not, in my lifetime, not Grigor MacGregor chopping him up into bits," Isobel said.

"None of us knew that was going to happen Isobel. I too miss your father. All John and I knew, was there would be a fight and an attempt to kidnap both me and you, so that was why we all left to hide in Cannich, until it was over, for our own safety. I only found out what was done to your Da and his two brothers, when Hector taught wee Causantin that poem," Zahra said.

"I know that you didn't have a hand in it, Ma but even Alex shouldn't have done that," she expressed sadly.

"It isn't the end of him, my dear Isobel. He is still here with us. You can't kill someone, who is already dead, only disposal which delays contact with them, that is all. You can try to communicate with him, if you really need to and if he wishes to return, he can piece himself back together, with difficulty. The old Crohn has had to do it twice for herself, having been disposed of by unhappy clients," Coinneach said.

"I had another reason for talking to you too my dear. My wife needs assistance leading up to and during the birth of our new wee bairn. Has your Mither told you yet?" Coinneach asked.

"Nae, are you with child, Ma?" Isobel asked.

"Aye, I am but I wanted us to be together when we told you all as a family. Our bairn is due in around five months' time. We are both very happy about this wee bairn aren't we, my darling?" Zahra asked.

"Aye, but I need your assistance, Isobel. I know its sudden, but can you come with us today and move into our house for the duration of your Mither's confinement, until your Mither is well again, after the birth? This includes both your lads,

Anndra and Domhnall of course and John you are most welcome to visit, as often as you need, but it would be good if you completed this work here on the farm, without distraction, as I want the perimeter fence also worked on, at the same time, so I will be sending more fence builders to complete that. It will also be safer for Isobel and the bairns on Beinn Coinneach. My brother, Prince Griogar has an army, who are going to patrol my property day and night, dressed up as farmers," Coinneach added.

"Why do we need so much security Da?" asked Hector.

"That reminds me son, Uncle Griogar asked if he could train you also in weaponry, including guns and swords and fighting tactics, so you can assist too, should the need arise," he asked.

"Da, is there something you are not telling us, because I'd rather not be trained to be a killer like Da was?" Hector said decisively.

"Very perceptive my son. Aye there is, but it might amount to nothing, and you are not compelled to do anything you don't wish to do," he answered. "I dreamed that your biological father was on his way back from the America's and posing a significant threat to all of us and wanting the farm back. So, today I will take your Mither home of course, you too Hector, Causantin, wee Dihaoine, Isobel, Anndra and Domhnall, until after my wife delivers our bairn safely, God willing.

If there are no threats at that time, and the fences and lighting are all completed, with security increased on Wolf Ranch, then Isobel and her two bairns can return here to Wolf Ranch. Do you agree with that plan, John?" Coinneach asked.

"Aye I do. Thankyou that would be a load off my mind, then I can walk the coos again," John replied.

"Now Isobel we have to go via Cannich today, so will you please pack your things and sign this document?" Coinneach asked with some urgency.

It was with some relief that Ali completely understood the need for the adoptions, especially if his father, Grigor Mohr MacGregor, turned up unexpectedly, laying claims on the farm and so he quickly signed it and gave his new father a kiss, and even though they were all invited to stay with Hamish, they all decided to ride on to Beinn Coinneach, before darkness fell and to scale that mountain in safety.

The family group rode steadily for a long time, before taking a small break to allow the horses to drink at a fast-flowing burn and for the women folk to relieve themselves. Coinneach went with his wife to steady her and to ensure that no harm came to her. Now that he had her back, he never wanted her to be gone again from him, it was too agonising. Finally, Beinn Coinneach appeared from out of the mist and cloud, surrounding the top half of the mountain and Isobel gasped at its magnificence.

"Ride slowly sister," advised Hector.

It could be said that there was a degree of nervous tension, as they slowly rode further up the mountain track, and the mist surrounded them all, as they disappeared into it. Luckily for them, Coinneach knew the old track so well, that he could ride it blind, and they all followed behind him closely, in single file. There was a collective sigh of relief, as the huge, palatial mansion appeared out of the thick fog and a servant woman appeared out of the mist, also welcoming them all, then a groom appeared as well. Visibility wasn't always the best when up that high.

"Master Coinneach, Lady Coinneach are you both well?" Mairi asked.

"Aye, but pleased to be home Mairi, you have two more bairns to care for, our grandchildren Anndra and Domnall, so tomorrow please employ two more women from your family for extra cleaning, caring and cooking," he ordered. "Take my wife first to warm up by the fire," Coinneach commanded.

"Hector, can you help with the horses, then when you come

back inside, show Isobel to the room nearest you, and her sons next to her, until we work it out better tomorrow," Coinneach asked.

Coinneach felt tired after the long day and after bathing, they all ate altogether as one family. The big beef stew was prepared for them all, followed by chocolate pudding and they all agreed that they were tired, and sleep was their next plan. Coinneach and Zahra slowly climbed their stairs and were finally together once more, in their bedroom and melted into each other's arms.

"My wife," he expressed, like it made him feel relieved and loved at the same time.

Zahra had ridden her horse well, he had thought but he had organised a Doctor from Inverness, who had treated her broken bone once before, to come to the mountain and check out her right side and see if something more could be done for her, even if it was exercises to keep her more balanced. He also wanted to get another professional opinion, if her condition could affect her ability to give birth to his bairn, as easily as before. If he was a good doctor and Zahra liked him, he would get him to stay over in the latter stage of her confinement up until the bairn was born, as well as their own midwife. He had forgotten to mention this to his wife.

Zahra had said she would need two men to aid her walking around in labour and that would be two of his brothers, now that Padruig and Alex were no longer worthy to be in that role. It was hard to even imagine that they ever once were, especially Alex who had been especially helpful and was constantly hit over the head, by Zahra in the process and sworn at with language that angels wouldn't care to hear.

Zahra leaned over to Coinneach and kissed him gently and ran her hand along his beautiful lean body. He didn't think he had enough strength left in him to respond to her gentle touch, but immediately her fingers began to explore him, he wanted her, and his body responded.

"Oh, my precious Zahra, it was agony being apart from you, even just that one night. I cannot be parted from you anymore," Coinneach declared.

"I made a necessary decision when I felt so emotional. It was better than having an outburst in front of your family, however I too cannot be apart from you either. It was pure suffering my love. I just couldn't look at your family again. Did your father say if I had passed their test?" Zahra asked, about to cry all over again.

"Of course, you did my poor darling, and he will make it up to you. I have spoken to him about it all and I even threatened him with you writing about him as a barbarian in your next book, so he is trying hard and so are my brothers, Prince Griogar and Cinaed Og who have expressed concern and offered assistance too. We do have their support now, so thank you. We will need it. My father was annoyed with me for getting married, without consultation, even at this age. My father is also purchasing one of your nude paintings for five thousand pounds, once it is completed," Coinneach said.

"And I do believe that Grigor MacGregor is on his way back to Scotland. He has left that ghastly woman behind in the Americas apparently, according to my sources," Coinneach said.

19. Enter. Dr Peter Heath

Dr Peter Heath was an effeminate Doctor who'd had brief sexual relations with Alexander MacDonald, but had somehow ended up with the younger, Alexander Grant, after his father's death, on Loch Garry Ranch in Glengarry. Matilda was still living there at that time.

Alexander MacDonald was devastated when he saw the two of them together and had contemplated his own disposal, one very wet night by the side of the burn in the Aird, when no-one was able to locate him at first, until Padruig finally found him.

Alex was talked into turning his life around and that was vaguely when he became handfast with Isobel Fraser and had a bairn with her, making Isobel a two-husband woman, which seemed to suit them all, until that dreadful day when Grigor knocked Zahra to the floor, breaking her jaw, her nose, and both of her eye sockets, leaving her bloodied, bruised and unconscious.

Zahra saw that very same Dr Peter Heath, Alex's former lover, walk through the enormous front door of their mansion on Beinn Coinneach, the next day upon their arrival back home from the Aird, just after the rush and bustle of breakfast was over. Isobel and her two sons, Anndra and Domnhall had slept in the rooms allocated to them in the new wing of the mansion. That wing was equipped with an enormous library and a huge school room for home schooling, to which Isobel was now devoted, as she now had more time than she had on Wolf Ranch. Other than milking the two nanny goats, that Coinneach had bought for her Mither, she was free, when Dr Heath first walked in, as well as Zahra, both equally shocked to see him once again.

Wee Dihaoine was being weaned now that Zahra's milk flow had reduced, due to being with child once more and Dihaoine was not only drinking the goat's milk, but she was also able to hold a wee cup and was eating parritch with a wooden spoon, like everyone else, in the mornings. She made a mess, but it was worth it to see her being weaned, thought her Mither.

Isobel only remembered Dr Heath because he had assisted with the delivery of wee Causantin in the Aird and was asked to leave the Ranch by Grigor's ghastly father, who had evicted another 'Unalive' man as well, who had been staying there, while he was adjusting to being dead. It was just as well, Isobel thought, because her Mither was making that man pay for board and lodgings by taking his very expensive watch, as payment for his accommodation and meals.

Isobel had wondered about Dr Heath's interest in men in general, and even his interest in her Mither as she watched on in interest.

Standing about one inch taller now than her Mither, Isobel stood side by side with Zahra, mouths wide open, wondering what Dr Peter Heath was doing up on Beinn Coinneach. After all, it wasn't an easy place to get to. Mairi seemed to know that he had been expected and welcomed him in, to sit by the fireside, beside them both. She went on to introduce him to both Zahra and Isobel.

"Mistresses, this is Dr Peter Heath from Inverness. Dr Heath, this is my Lady Zahra Coinneach MacAlpin and her daughter,

Mistress Isobel," she said and left to make the tea and coffee. There was still a lot more staff, all over the mansion, in the kitchen, cleaning, cooking, replacing and making candles, bringing in firewood, stoking fires and who knows what else?

"Hello Peter, what are you doing all the way up here?" asked Zahra politely.

"I could ask the same question of you, Lady Coinneach," Peter said sarcastically. "What happened to your last husband? That's three now, isn't it? Hope this fellow is more resilient," Peter said.

"How many bairns do you have now, Lady Coinneach?" Peter asked.

"I have six bairns and expecting my seventh, is that why you are here?" Zahra replied, noting his sarcasm.

"That is if you still have your Licence to practice Medicine. Do you?" Zahra asked.

"You heard about that I see," Peter asked.

"It was in all of the newspapers, I could hardly miss it on the front-page news," Zahra replied. "Matilda did a good job on you, didn't she?" Zahra stated, to clarify the gossip and to wound him.

"She most certainly did," Peter agreed with his posh English accent. "All my dirty linen was there, for all the world to read about, but it wasn't dirty enough to lose a doctor here in Scotland, so long as I didn't go back to England, I was informed," Peter said.

"I have sons, Dr Heath. Please stay away from them, just the same, unless there is a medical emergency, of course," Zahra demanded.

"Fair enough, Lady Coinneach. So, my task here then was to speak to Lord Coinneach about you, his wife, concerning a disability? Now what disability would that be?" Peter asked.

"I think Lord Coinneach must have known or remembered your name from when I told him that you had treated my broken leg very well, so he may have thought that it was connected, in some way, to my current circumstances, but you would have to ask him, because I was unaware, that he had called upon you," Zahra said.

She asked Isobel to speak to Lord Coinneach and notify him that Dr Heath had arrived.

"I would also ask of you not to appear in any of my husband's works of art, in the nude, or I will not agree to this consultation," Zahra added, speaking quietly in private, thinking it would throw the wrong light over all the other paintings expressing the naked body.

"Agreed," Peter said, although somewhat surprised, awaiting Lord Coinneach.

"What happened to Grigor then?" Peter asked.

"No idea. The Americas was the last I heard, with a buxom trollop," Zahra said.

Zahra knew how busy her husband was in trying to complete the last five paintings, six of which were to be collected the next day by Malcolm and Kenneth MacNachten, as well as another two. It was a small fortune in artistic terms. Her Father-in-Law, Lord Cinead was also buying one painting of her, in the nude for five thousand pounds and he had hinted that three of his sons were interested in buying one each as well, which surprised her. Coinneach came down rag in hand, wiping off the paint, as he walked.

"Dr Heath, is it?" Coinneach asked as Peter stood up, in obvious respect of the man, whom he must have heard of, in artistic circles, Zahra presumed.

"My dear, I am sorry I forgot to warn you, but with so much going on, you can't blame me can you my precious love," Coinneach said, as he amorously kissed his equally adoring wife. Isobel felt it time to leave the group to their privacy, but Coinneach insisted that she stay, so she was fully informed of every detail, especially as he was busy completing the artwork.

"Do you mind staying, my child?" he asked Isobel.

"Nae, I don't mind. I will stay. We are acquainted. I met Doctor Heath once before when he assisted delivering wee Causantin. Mither's broken leg was also treated later by him and she was pleased with his work," Isobel replied.

"Alright, please be seated, Peter and I will explain. My wife was recently abused by her former husband, Grigor Mohr MacGregor, whom you must have already met, from your previous association with them both. Lady Coinneach may have a wee brain injury now, because of the blow she received from him. At first, I believed it to be only a concussion and that it would all rectify itself, in good time, but her gait is still affected.

This is where you come in. You are familiar with her legs, I am told and that bone that was previously broken, I want you to assess whether her 'walking wobbles', we call it, is due to a brain injury, or if her leg has been re-broken, or something entirely different. Either way, it will require a complete examination on your part, or she may just require some exercises to strengthen that right hand side of her body," Coinneach said seriously.

"In addition, Dr Heath, she is with child, our child, and if she likes you, and you like her, or however it works, you may consider sleeping here for a few weeks during her confinement, until she is in labour, with the assistance of her midwife and Isobel. Two of my brothers, along with Zahra's daughter, Isobel will also assist the Midwife. Your main role then, would be to assess the bairn for any abnormalities, his eyesight, hearing, and general health, the delivery of the placenta of course, as well as the presence of any blood clots in my wife," Coinneach said.

"The midwife will be the main deliverer, I am told, so my wife can deliver in the old way, not the new ways, using gas, ether or chloroform," Coinneach added.

"How does all of that sound Peter and what, if any of it are you prepared to engage in, and how much will it all cost?" Coinneach asked.

"I should add that I know too of your tarnished reputation, and I heard my wife asking you to stay away from our sons, which I too re-iterate, and I am not interested in you as a subject for my art, just so that my wife is at ease tonight. I am only interested in what you, as a healer can do for my wife and to assist her when she eventually goes into labour."

"So, what is your reply then Dr Heath?" Coinneach asked.

"As you say Lord Coinneach, my reputation was tarnished, somewhat, despite being a good doctor, but I do not deny any of it. My business has suffered as a result, so I can't afford to refuse business, even if it is uncomfortable, like this is. Your wife, however, would have to agree too, or I will be on my way. Do you agree Zahra, to any or part or the whole of what your husband proposes?" Peter asked in his educated English accent.

Zahra felt her husband knew best and after all she was once friends with Peter, until Alex and he were sexually engaged and then they weren't, and it was all a little awkward. Overall, however he was a good Doctor, even with his peculiar English mannerisms, at times.

"I agree to all of what my husband has proposed. Thankyou Coinneach for caring so much for my wobbly walk. It would be nice to walk normally eventually. I heard someone say that I walked like a cross between a Scots dumpy chicken and a duck," she said with humour.

"Well then, I will go back to work after you tell me how much it will cost, Peter," Coinneach said.

"The treatment to her leg and her delivery with staying here will cost you around two hundred pounds per day with food provided, unless something untoward occurs," Peter added. "I would like to start today on Zahra's leg, if you all agree. Where can we do a full body examination?" Peter asked.

"Mairi, can you please arrange the small guest room on the lower ground floor for this treatment?" asked Coinneach then Mairi ran off to prepare the room.

"May I be excused then my dear and I can leave you with Isobel and Peter?" Coinneach asked.

"Isobel, dear can you leave all four bairns with Mairi when she comes back. Just ensure that the front door is always locked please. Dihaoine likes to escape I heard," Coinneach asked, remembering the vanishing possibility of any one of Zahra's bairns.

Zahra had wanted her husband close to her as he walked away and was worried what Peter might find.

"It'll be alright my love. He won't hurt you. At least I hope he won't," Coinneach added.

"Later, after Peter has left, come and get me for our meal together and you can tell me all about it," Coinneach said as he embraced her completely.

Peter watched on the loving couple, in admiration of the obviously genuine relationship that Zahra had fortunately become involved in. On one level, he was jealous of her success, but on another with the back story, he was determined to get her walking normally again after her obvious suffering, but being the gossip that he was, he was dying to learn the whole story.

As the three of them walked into the first aid room, set up for them, Isobel instructed Mairi regarding her bairns and then took a seat to observe, ready to assist if needed. Isobel had no difficulty instructing staff, unlike Zahra who was loathe to ask anything of them.

Dr Peter Heath had his medical bag with him and examined Zahra on many levels, not only involving her leg. Asking to watch his finger moving about and so on. Then the leg, finally. He examined where his previous work had repaired her broken bone and asked if there was pain and there wasn't any pain there. With lifting and moving her leg about, his focus moved to her right hip and then her spine. Then when walking, she favoured her right hip.

"One problem is your hip and the full length of your spine, my old friend. Was it painful riding your horse?" Peter asked.

"Aye it was, but I ignored it," Zahra replied.

"Can you tolerate it if I work on your spine for a while?" Peter asked.

The crunch, followed by a loud scream, reached the ears of Lord Coinneach, who dropped his paintbrush and ran to his wife who was lying on the bed crying in agony, with Isobel consoling her and the Doctor standing back, waiting for her to settle down.

"What happened to my wife? Have you harmed her?" Coinneach demanded.

"My darling, are you alright?" he asked with Zahra weeping.

"I don't know. It hurt Coinneach," she replied.

"Let me please explain, Lord Coinneach. Her spine was dreadfully out of position, and it still is. Please let me finish my work. I believe I have located her problems," Peter explained by demonstrating it on Coinneach's spine, which he said was affecting multiple nerves, in various areas, affecting handwriting and fine motor skills.

"It is the worst that I have seen, I admit, and she will require a hot bath and a walk, when I have finished. Her neck, however, is by far, the worse problem. May we please speak in private, outside?" Peter asked.

Coinneach and Peter returned in a short while, looking serious and they had both come to an agreement. Peter would put her head back to where it was supposed to be, and it would hurt. Coinneach had agreed to the treatment and was staying to comfort his wife, or delivering a bairn would be too agonising and possibly cause her death.

Firstly, he completed her spinal work, then asked Coinneach to hold her feet and speak to her to comfort her, all the way through. Peter discovered that this manipulation was very serious, and it could fail, but it had to be done. Peter was horrified at what force had caused it, and he began with her head held firmly in his hands, while Isobel began to pray on a floor mat, unable to watch.

They all heard the crunch, then Zahra fell silent. Only tears flowed down her face.

Surprisingly, she then uttered, "Oh Grigor, why?"

Isobel was seated on the floor where she had been praying for her Mither and then held herself in the foetal position, crying along with her Mither. Both the Doctor and Coinneach, despite the success, knew they were both looking upon the dreadful damage that only domestic violence can do, and they both wiped away their own tears.

Peter put his own face close to Zahra's, saying, "Are you going to be alright Zahra?" he asked, and she was still silent.

"We will both help you up slowly and you will need a hot bath then a walk, okay?" Peter said gently. Coinneach called out to Mairi to prepare the hot bath. Soaking in the hot water, Zahra heard her husband talking to Peter asking him to stay overnight to perform it again perhaps, the following day, in case her spine fell out of place, once more.

"That's not the biggest problem my Lord, the betrayal is," Peter added.

"It will take a long time to recover from that. When I knew them both, I could never imagine them apart. So, like she has exclaimed, why? I too have that same question. Why? I heard the trollop story, but he had six bairns. Take that in for a moment when no one else in your realm can have bairns. I am sorry my Lord, but I just assumed that you are of the Otherworld too. They were so lucky or chosen by God, I don't know? But he loved her and she loved him.

I thought I was the only one with relationship issues, but her friend Alex also had no one, until he and I became friends for a wee while and Padruig had no one either. He may be the reason for their breakdown, because he was attracted to Zahra, I thought and was envious of his friend," Peter said.

"Although they all seemed like very close friends, Grigor was different. What he was saying and what he was thinking were not always one and the same, if you know what I mean. I was never close to him for that reason. You would never know where you stood with him and I am not talking about a close man to man relationship, just a human-to-human relationship, but he did love Zahra. How did he stop loving her? Do you know?" Peter asked.

"It bothers me. Where is Grigor? Are you sure that he is in the Americas?" Peter asked.

"Doctor Heath, I agree you should stay overnight and treat my wife again tomorrow, but she is my wife now and Grigor MacGregor had better not come and try to retrieve that which he has abused, repeatedly. He was sleeping with another woman. Isn't that enough of a reason and he obviously wasn't coping with his large family? You are witness to the abuse. That is not love." Coinneach said.

"Grigor and his friend Padruig were going to chop her up into little bits and throw her into the burn, but for her son Hector, he may well have succeeded. When I arrived to visit her, what I encountered was utter chaos on that farm, with Zahra still lying face down, on the stone floor and bleeding, so I decided then and there to rescue her, with her youngest two bairns and the rest is none of your business. Just do your job please," Coinneach said, but felt disturbed that Peter too had guessed that Grigor was on his way back to Scotland.

"I will my Lord, but please also consider that those Glenmoriston Men had a creed or something to fight to the death. He will be back and maybe with his friends and may fight to the death for her. I am just warning you, for your own sakes. He will not give up, once he gets it into his head, if he wants her back," Peter added.

The mood on Beinn Coinneach altered drastically, with just one visit from Dr Peter Heath from Inverness and it almost frightened Coinneach.

Zahra took her walk as instructed with Isobel on one side and Coinneach on the other. Fresh air was as much for Isobel as it was for Zahra's spinal work. Isobel felt shattered all over again and her father's departure from them all became fresh in her mind once more. Zahra's wobble was improving, as was her level of pain, which she had never complained about and for that, Isobel felt grateful, but deeply saddened and miserable.

"Do you think I might stop wobbling, Coinneach?" Zahra asked.

"Aye, my love, I do," he answered feeling worried now about his wee bairn.

"Can I sleep in your art room with you after lunch my love. I want to be near you and poor Isobel needs to take a rest too," Zahra said.

"Aye, you may. I would love your company. I am finishing the canvas for my father of you. He loves it. I am so proud of you," Coinneach added.

For the duration of her confinement, she slept alongside him on a couch, while he worked. Wee Dihaoine took delight in terrorising everyone and was constantly threatening to vanish, if ever the front door was left open. Mairi was always a target for Dihaoine, whom she knew would fall for her every antic. Coinneach's house had never been so lively in so many years, but now with Hector too, they all filled up the mansion with their energy, as well as Causantin who followed in his brother's footsteps, pretending to be Hector.

Their cousins, both Anndra and Domhnall with Isobel, their Mither added a different dimension to the overall character, describing Zahra's bairns. They insisted on book learning, as well as outdoor work with the horses and were fluent in Gaelic, as was Hector but they could read and write and spell it accurately. So, despite Hector's bragging about his Gaelic obscenities, his spelling wasn't as good as was theirs, so there was some friction over mealtimes where spelling Gaelic was concerned and Coinneach was fascinated that bairns could be so serious about their native language, with no chance that it would be taken away from them.

They all spoke English fluently also, as well as French. It wouldn't have surprised Coinneach how many languages they could all speak, and he made a few suggestions of his own, such as Greek, Latin and his own native language of the Picts.

Dr Heath stayed over for three days to repeat some of his work, followed by hot baths and walks listening in to the families' day to day chatter and grew fond of them all. He would return to Beinn Coinneach closer to the birth. He felt a deep connection to this problem for some reason and his compassion and concern for Zahra, knew no boundaries. He hadn't yet asked the delicate question of why her face didn't appear injured or scarred, considering the blow that she had endured.

There was no evidence of disfigurement on her cheek bones or her nose. He assumed the healer must have been an expert in restructuring her face. He had heard of such people in London but wondered how that expert just happened to be there on Beinn Coinneach at that precise time.

He decided he would ask that delicate question when they became closer.

20. Enter. Malcolm and Kenneth

The ponies were all saddled up early Friday morning and with farewells said, both wives had packed their husbands' food and had waved them off, ensuring that they had warm berets, gloves, and waterproof coats with layers of undergarments for added warmth and dryness.

"You'll owe me for this Kenneth, if that man comes anywhere near my cock," I said, before we left Glengarry.

Us two brothers looked up in awe at the cloud, covered mountain range and Misty Mountain stood out and so we brothers then began the slow climb upwards, to be met frequently by men, who appeared to be farmers for Lord Coinneach, who ushered them onwards in a friendly and welcoming manner. Passing by large folds of highland coos, we were temporarily stopped to allow them to pass, as another farmer, carrying a big stick with deer's horns atop it, came meandering on down, also greeted us with a salute in Gaelic.

Malcolm MacNachten

Kenneth MacNachten

"You didn't tell me they were so friendly here," I said.

"I hadn't noticed all these farmers here before," Kenneth remarked, but was pleased that they weren't unfriendly at least.

It gave the appearance of a busy Highland farming community, I thought, and I liked it. Finally, reaching the top of the mountain, where the clouds blanketed the mansion, we were both met by two polite groomsmen and Hector, who also confirmed with us, that we were the MacNachten brothers, Kenneth and Malcolm MacNachten from Glengarry.

"I've met you before," Hector said. "In Glengarry at the Art Gallery. I hope you don't upset my stepfather this time," he added. "My sister, Isobel and her bairns, Anndra and Domhnall are staying here too now, for a while anyway, while the farm in the Aird is being upgraded. They've called it 'Wolf Ranch' now after all those wolves that you killed, Malcolm. Watch out for the wolf that survived that big kill. It's inside this mansion. He's Ma's pet dog. His name is Wolfie. Ma doesn't believe he's a wolf, but he loves her, so just don't kill it, okay Malcolm?" Hector asked.

"Okay, but does he attack people?" I asked.

"Not yet," Hector replied in jest, smiling with a cheeky grin, as he opened the huge front carved wooden doors, for them both.

We were greeted by a growling, Wolfie with nasty big sharp teeth showing. A big, young dark grey wolf, of the same family of wolves that I had killed, in the Aird was staring right at me. That wolf knew and recognised me, as one of the shooters that day, who had killed his Mither wolf and all his brothers and sisters. Wolves never seemed to forget anything or anyone, even if they were pups at the time. It gave me the creeps.

"Wolfie darling," Zahra called, and the wolf immediately ran to Zahra's side.

"Welcome to Beinn Coinneach, Malcolm and the lovely Kenneth," said Zahra and she kissed us both on our cheeks.

"Is it the lads?" called Coinneach cheerfully.

"Aye darling, they are both here," Zahra said. "Please sit down by the fireside to warm up and Mairi will get you something hot. Tea or coffee?" Zahra asked. "Your bedrooms are prepared for the night. Thank you for coming out this far," Zahra said.

I needed to know what had happened to Zahra for her to be here on Beinn Coinneach, and no longer in the Aird, with all its many gruesome details, and where Grigor Mohr MacGregor was, if she knew, so I asked her directly what had happened for them all to be sent to the four winds.

"Malcolm, my dear friend, I'll answer all of your questions, after you both finish up with my husband and the art, is that alright?" Zahra said. Coinneach approached us to shake both our hands in a much friendlier manner to how he had been in Glengarry.

"Malcolm lad, I acknowledge my previous rudeness to you and no further conflict is necessary between us both. Your brother, dear Kenneth, has explained, so I am grateful to you both for coming up here to my mountain. Drink up your coffee. I can't wait to show you the finished work. There is one you have missed out on lads, as my father bought it for five thousand pounds," Coinneach said. "Then when we are all finished with the business of my artwork, the prices and so on, we can all eat. You must be starving hungry. Do you all eat that same beef stew as well?" he asked.

"Aye we do," we said in unison.

"Mairi, beef stew, with tomatoes, all round for dinner in about an hour," Coinneach ordered.

We all then went upstairs to the huge art room, accompanied by Zahra and Wolfie. I kept the wolf in the corner of my eye, holding my dirk, wondering who to be the most afraid of, the wolf or the artist.

"Malcolm, you are paying more attention to the wolf this

time and not at all worried about the nudity in my paintings. I should be pleased, I suppose. Glengarry is already becoming accustomed to the idea of nudity in art. Now let me show you the finished product of your dear brother and my wife. He was very cooperative, lending his lovely cock to the cause, shall we say Kenneth?" Coinneach said humorously.

Nothing had quite prepared me for the painting of my brother Kenneth, naked with his cock appearing to enter, the lovely Zahra. I felt faint.

"Oh, God. Kenneth, you didn't, did you?" I exclaimed. "Did you feck Zahra?" I asked. I couldn't stop myself from cursing and I apologised profusely for my bad language in front of the Lady Coinneach.

Zahra was giggling as she sat on her couch with her wolf, stroking his head and often kissing him.

"Nae, nae, dear Malcolm, it's all pretend. Poor dear Kenneth. Well, he did have an erection, several times, didn't you, you poor darling? But Coinneach helped him to the chamber pot, before it went all over me," Zahra said, like it was a normal, daily occurrence.

"Aye, it wasn't easy, I can tell you," Kenneth answered.

Placing his hand on Kenneth's shoulder, Coinneach said, "You're a good lad Kenneth. I am so proud of you," and kissed my brother, as was their MacAlpin custom apparently, but Kenneth seemed to enjoy the kiss, which I thought was revolting but each to his own, I thought at that stage.

"I hope your Mither will be proud too, when she knows how much effort went into achieving it without 'fecking', as you say, dear Malcolm lad. Kenneth has a lovely cock, don't you think? Yours must be as nice as his, but don't worry, I'll not strip you naked to have a look, or whatever it is on your poor, tortured mind, presently," Coinneach jested.

"Mine is as good as Kenneth's, maybe even bigger, I think and better," I stated confidently.

"Show him then Malcolm if you think yours is better than mine. I don't think so," Kenneth stated.

"So long as that wolf is out of the room, I might. He makes me nervous," I replied, I was keen to prove my manhood suddenly and I was certain that Kenneth's cock was smaller than mine. It can't have changed that much since we were lads in Loch Insh.

With Wolfie out of the room, I said, "See bigger and better and I can outperform you just like I did in Loch Insh when I had five married women on the go and you only had two," remembering those carefree days in Loch Insh.

"It's a fine cock indeed Malcolm and a very healthy lad you are too. Five at one time, eh? That's some record," Coinneach stated.

"Do you want to be in one of Coinneach's paintings too, Malcolm my dear friend?" asked Zahra.

"It doesn't have to go to Glengarry, I can keep it to look at, on my bedroom wall," Zahra said.

"Oh, you are a clever darling. You are not perving on Malcolm," Coinneach said.

"See, even the artist is too afraid to put one as fine as mine, on canvas," I bragged with my brother smiling at the whole humorous scene.

Zahra seemed happy too that I hadn't succumbed to the temptation of being in one of Coinneachs' paintings, and she loved making her husband jealous. She hadn't seen her husband jealous before, I thought and she was keen to make him jealous again, with such a nice cock as mine, in the house.

"Let's have lunch darling and we can all talk about who has the best cock of all. Coinneach has the best cock that I have ever seen," Zahra said.

Coinneach then couldn't resist the temptation and revealed

his glorious manhood hanging long and wide and even I was astounded at the big man's obvious win on that front. He had the biggest cock in the house.

"Looks like you win, Lord Coinneach," Kenneth said smiling happily.

"I think all three of you should stand together with cocks revealed and I can be the cock judge," Zahra declared. "I do have a measuring tape with me." she added.

All three men stood with cocks revealed for Zahra to make the judgement, but the measuring tape was refused by them all. As Kenneth had said, Coinneach was the official winner, but Zahra got a kick out of perving on all three of them. Coinneach knew what his wife was up to and smacked her bottom as they left for the dining room. She was aroused, there was little doubt Coinneach's wife had desire for her husband.

Kenneth felt a fondness for the older man and was keen to be closer to him, so at lunch, surprisingly he sat next to him. "Here is your list then, my young Kenneth and the prices. Your commission comes out of that and in the painting wherein you appear, you also get paid, but my wife doesn't of course," Coinneach explained.

"Why doesn't Zahra get a commission too?" I asked.

"I am a kept woman, and my husband pays all of my bills and buys me beautiful things and he is even renovating my bairns' farm, so that is my payment, my dear Malcolm," Zahra explained.

The beef stew wasn't bad. Mairi had cooked it much better with all the improvements to the recipe that Zahra had suggested, but Meredith's was far better.

"This is nice stew," I complimented, just the same and both Mairi and Zahra smiled at their achievement.

"Lord Coinneach, there were a lot of farmers on the road coming up the mountain. How many tenants do you have on this land? It must be enormous?" I enquired.

"Aye, it is huge, too huge to walk in two or even three days. Maybe on horseback you could do it in two, but it incorporates part of the old MacKenzie lands, mostly and a smaller part of Fraser land too, but owned now by MacAlpins. All legal but how many tenants you ask? I am not sure. My Farm Manager deals with all of that and collects the rents and so on, dotted all over the place. He will come and go from here and don't bother about him, it's his job to know what's going on and he's Mairi's husband. For all I know the pair of them are probably having a bit of nooky on my time," he answered.

Coinneach had a sense of humour, that could not be denied, but he used a lot of vocabulary that sometimes went over our heads, but Zahra seemed to always understand him, unlike when she was with Grigor Mohr MacGregor, whom she had trouble understanding, at times due to his continued use of the Gaelic language and her lack of knowledge of that language. I'm not that fluent in Gaelic myself, so I had sent her some books to learn from, that I had found helpful.

"Malcolm wanted to know how I was recovering darling. Would you like to inform him for me, as I don't remember it all," Zahra said.

"Zahra is much better now Malcolm, thank you for asking, but it has taken a while to get her better, after what had happened to her in the Aird. Luckily, I had already met her the day before at the old Crohn's house and had then chosen to visit her on that day, when I encountered the most horrific scene and so here, we are, married and with child," Coinneach said.

"And Grigor Mohr MacGregor?" I asked, still wanting to know about him.

"They are divorced, we are married, his children are now mine, legally adopted, the farm was signed over by Himself, before he left for the Americas with the trollop, but it is in my opinion that he is coming back, so we must be on the lookout for trouble from now on in. We have additional security and Isobel, and her two bairns are safe here with me now. Nasty piece of work is that Grigor MacGregor to punch his wife like that," he added.

"My brothers are assisting me now, as is my father and all of the MacAlpins lad, so don't worry, but we do hope you don't read about a massacre on Beinn Coinneach," jested Lord Coinneach.

"That's not funny father," said Isobel.

"You are right my dear, poor taste," Coinneach replied.

Their huge oak front doors opened wide, allowing a cold draft to enter the enormous space and Mairi hastened to greet Lord Cinaed, Lord Coinneach's father. She curtsied, as had all the staff at the farm, Isobel noticed, and she was as perplexed as I was. His big voice filled the empty spaces of every room that he entered.

"Son, I am joining your family to eat. What is left?" Lord Cinaed asked.

Lord Coinneach stood out of respect for his father, bowed, then kissed his ring, and gave him his seat at the head of the dining room table, while he then went and sat at the other end. He had obvious respect for his father. My brother and I then were either side of the very stout, older gentleman with the big, long, grey beard and we both looked on at him, staring a little, as if he was indeed a curiosity. We had never seen anyone who looked quite like him. He looked like someone from one of our old school textbooks from Loch Insh, I thought.

"Who are you lads? Surely not more of Zahra's bairns? How many did you say you had, my dear?" he asked, referring to us. How odd it was to think we could be one of her bairns. He was of the Otherworld, so it was beginning to make more sense.

"Nae, my Lord, they are not my bairns. They are our very good friends from Glengarry, Malcolm and Kenneth MacNachten.

I only have six bairns, my Lord," Zahra replied, as Mairi placed food in front of the old and strange looking man.

"Come here lass. I have something for you," Lord Cinaed said to Zahra. Looking to her husband for approval, who nodded in agreement, Zahra went along the table, to where he was seated near us, and the old man asked her to sit on the floor directly in front of him. It was becoming strange, so if it didn't improve soon, I was going to leave my seat.

"Kiss my ring, my dear," Lord Cinaed asked, so Zahra awkwardly kissed an enormous family heirloom-looking ring on his right hand.

"This is for you," Lord Cinaed said, as he handed her a strange looking, pale pinkish coloured rock. She thanked him for it with a frown, thinking it an odd gift too, but a gift just the same and better than nothing.

"Now my dear, where you come from and in your time, how would you greet a family member such as I, ordinarily?" Lord Cinaed asked, and her facial expression altered completely, and it was one of sadness at the loss of her family back in her home country, wherever that was, with their warm greetings, which she had obviously almost forgotten. I didn't know what to expect next.

Zahra missed her old life, that was clear and none of us were a part of those memories, which felt peculiar.

"Are you sure my Lord, as it involves touching you?" Zahra asked, gaining composure.

"Aye, I am sure. Show me," he asked again.

"Can you please stand up my Lord, as if you had just entered our home?" Zahra asked. Both Zahra and the old man stood, while he was looking curiously upon his new daughter in law, of whom he was growing fond, but she gave little away of herself, he had noticed, and it appeared only Coinneach enjoyed a closeness to Zahra, apart from us MacNachten brothers and her own bairns. It looked like he too wanted that closeness, as that too would make his son happy or himself, I wasn't sure.

"I would hug you my Lord and you would hug me in response," Zahra said, which she demonstrated by hugging him lightly and he then held her awkwardly with his fat stomach hindering the exercise.

"Like this?" Lord Cinaed asked.

"Hold onto me more, like in a bear hug and then we would kiss," she added. He held her tightly, enjoying it immensely, as I saw his manhood was responding and then she kissed him on the cheek, but he insisted on kissing her on the lips and wouldn't stop, until Coinneach had to interject.

"Father, you've got it now, you can stop," Coinneach said jealously.

"Och well my dear, you can do that each time I visit, if you like," Lord Cinaed suggested.

"Also, when you leave Lord Cinaed," Zahra added.

"Well, that's a nice enough custom for us all to have. What do you think son?" Lord Cinaed asked Coinneach, who was visibly annoyed, but agreed anyhow.

"Yes, father, but there is to be no kissing of my wife on the lips, just the cheeks," Coinneach added. I wouldn't have allowed that old man anywhere near my wife, Ailsa but it was humorous to watch.

Isobel was laughing at how it had all happened and so were we, the two MacNachten brothers.

"Well, I see we have entertained a few of you anyhow like you, pretty lass. What's your name lass, with the blonde hair? Surely, you're not one of Zahra's bairns?" Lord Cinaed asked.

He just couldn't get it right.

"Aye, Lord Cinaed, I am Isobel, the oldest here of Lady Zahra's bairns, with her first husband, Hugh Chisholm, hence the blonde hair," Isobel replied, pointing to her blonde hair.

"Come here then lass and give me one of those nice greetings that you were laughing so much at," Lord Cinaed asked.

Isobel then went across to him and wasn't at all accustomed to those types of greetings and he grabbed a hold of her and kissed her passionately, which she enjoyed, unexpectedly.

"You are the lass who had two husbands then? You are missing one now my dear, I have heard. How about you make an old man happy, just until you go back to that farm in the Aird?" Lord Cinaed asked. Isobel liked the creepy old man a lot and decided that she would like that. She had been lonely since Alex had left her and poor John Fraser had never fulfilled her, no matter how much she loved him, and he loved her.

"Alright then," Isobel said, much to everyone's shock. Coinneach asked Zahra if she was allowing it, and she was.

"Isobel always knows what she wants and just goes for it. She wants your father," she replied.

"Well then, we might take our leave just for tonight and return tomorrow. Will that suit everyone?" Lord Cinaed asked.

"Ma, can I leave Anndra and Domhnall with you please?" Isobel asked.

"Of course, darling, you have fun," Zahra replied. Mairi was hastily handfasting the couple as they left, forever trying to keep couples decent. Then the old man came back briefly.

"Hector my lad, the ponies are here, thirty mares and four stallions are ready for you to run your new business. Good luck son. I'll leave the papers with Mairi," he said and was gone again.

The papers read 'Hector's Highland Ponies, MacAlpin Industries, Beinn Coinneach, Scotland.'

"Ma look at this," Hector said. "It has my name on it. 'Hector's Highland Ponies,' he added. Zahra had never seen her son look so happy in his life and went to him and hugged him and congratulated him. Everyone then congratulated him. He was now a businessman.

"Oh son. You're now a businessman. I am so proud of you," Zahra said and kept hugging her biggest lad, her hero. Zahra loved Hector dearly.

"You had better spell correctly now then Hector," said Anndra seriously. "I can help you if you need help with the spelling," he said.

"It's mathematics he will need most of all Anndra, not spelling. I can help you with mathematics," Domhnall offered.

Lord Cinaed MacAlpin

"Maybe both of you can be my offsiders then, but I'm not paying you much, mind," Hector added.

All three of them wandered down to where the ponies had arrived and Zahra watched on from their front porch, as did her husband, who put his arm around his wife.

"Well done darling," Zahra said and turned and kissed him. "Och, Coinneach, thank you so much for all of this. My bairns are happy and that means so much to me and I know you worry about Isobel, but please don't worry. She's not like me. I am a little fragile and shy too sometimes, but she is bolder and stronger than me, I think it's the Viking blood from Hugh's family, the Chisholm's," Zahra said.

"He wasn't much of a Viking if he got himself all chopped up like that. How gruesome is that?" Coinneach added.

"Oh, he had that blood though, through the Norman Vikings, I thought, and I see it in Isobel," Zahra said.

"So, Ali and Fatma, the twins are MacGregors and appear different then?" Coinneach asked.

"Oh aye, very different but they are unlike most MacGregors, because they are twins and they've always relied on each other," Zahra said.

Kenneth and I went outside to look at the beautiful view.

"Keep in good with my brother Griogar by the way" I heard Coinneach say. "Now we had best get back to our guests, Malcolm and Kenneth," he said. Kenneth and I had moved out onto the patio, overlooking the glorious view, from atop the mountain, at the rear of the mansion.

Scottish Hare

"Malcolm, I have a request of you. Your brother told us how you would dream where a hare could be hiding in Loch Insh, so he could paint it. Also, you located a rare beetle for his wife, Ivy to go into her book. Is that correct?" Coinneach asked.

"Thanks brother," I said. "Aye, that is true," I replied.

"Can you locate a person for me, do you think or is that harder?" Coinneach asked.

"Who might that be then?" I asked.

"Grigor Mohr MacGregor, I fear he is here, or near the Scottish coast and I would appreciate your assistance in protecting my family," Coinneach asked.

"I already know where my Grandda is located," I said.

"Grandda. Who is that then?" Coinneach asked.

"Padruig Dubh Grant," I replied.

"Is that so? Where is he then?" he asked.

"He's haunting a room in his own hotel above Craskie Farm in Cannich, Room 203, waiting for you Zahra. He expected you to go there, but I told him you weren't there," I said.

"What do you mean exactly? How did you tell him Malcolm?" asked Coinneach.

"Well, that's hard to explain really. It's a kind of 'cosmic connection', where we can communicate, but he was rude to me the last time, so I thought I wouldn't try again. I was just worried about Zahra," I tried to explain.

"This is an amazing skill that you have. I assume that it's only you two who know of it?" Coinneach asked.

"Aye, it was, until now. My ex-wife saw him once, when there was a wolf in our house, and Grandda had no choice but to make himself visible to her, so she would close the front door, but she is long gone now," I explained.

"In my opinion, if Grigor Mohr MacGregor returns to Scotland, he will seek out my Grandda in Cannich, as well as Alexander MacDonald, who will want his two bairns back.

Then there's John Campbell MacDonald, otherwise known as Oss 'Ian, who was originally from Cannich, before he left for Canada, where he died, then returned as a spectre, so he might join them also, to assist.

They would have food from Cousin James's kitchen and live in the empty hotel rooms. My guess is on Grandda's hotel in Glenmoriston, but I will try and locate them tonight for you and see what happens," I said.

◊

"*Grandda, where are you? It's Malcolm. I need to know something. Are you still at your hotel?*" I asked.

"*Grandda, Grandda,*" I said.

"*Oh, shut up Malcolm, you pesky wee shite. What do you want now?*" Grandda answered.

"*Glad to hear your voice too Grandda. Just wanted to know if you knew if Grigor was back in Scotland. Heard some whispers he might be. Is he then?*" I asked.

"*Might be, might not be. What's it to you? You are the peskiest of humans that I have ever met, and you are related to me, unfortunately,*" Grandda said.

"*Well, you sound worn out, so you must have company. Which company might that be? Alex, Grigor, John MacDonald or has Hugh put himself together again from the bottom of the waterfall?*" I asked.

"*He can't do that can he?*" Grandda asked.

"*He can, according to my sources. His brothers all can too, so you'd all be one big happy family again, haunting that hotel, until it loses so much money, it'll have to close because of you,*" I chided.

"*We're only using two rooms. That won't put Patrick out of business,*" he said defensively.

"*Is John getting your food from James's kitchen too?*" I asked.

"*Aye, but not enough to make them go broke, you little stirrer. He has enough money to spend on nude paintings you said,*" Grandda added.

"*Aye, I did but it might be that he doesn't have to pay for it and just recommend the Glengarry Art Gallery to his clients,*" I added.

"Glengarry, is it?" Grandda asked.

"Aye, so will you take Grigor there to see his ex-wife, posing nude with my brother Kenneth?" I asked.

"Might do, but Alex wants his bairns first. Problem is they're putting walls up all around that whole place, the feckin rats. Where did they get the money?" he asked.

"Zahra's new husband, of course. Nice fella with special artistic talents and buckets of money," I said.

"Real wimp then?" Grandda stated.

"Nae, not a wimp at all. If you do have Grigor with you and I assume you do, with Alex too, then they should all know that the MacAlpins go a long way back, if you get my drift Grandda, a real long way back and his brother is Prince Griogar. Tell Grigor MacGregor, not to go to where Zahra is, or he will come across extreme opposition, so if you too don't want to end up at the bottom of a waterfall somewhere, leave him to his own fate, at least," I cautioned.

"I told him that already and I'll not join in, so piss off Malcolm," Grandda said.

And he was gone.

Kenneth had decided to share the bed with both Zahra and Lord Coinneach, leaving me to my own thoughts, beside the crackling fireside in my room, and so I then went to the kitchen alone, looking to make a hot chocolate drink for myself, after lighting a candle. Coinneach became aware that there was light coming from the kitchen and decided to investigate, quietly leaving both his wife and Kenneth. He found me searching for the hot chocolate and offered to make it for us both and I didn't object.

"I wanted to take a wee look at your library too, if you wanted to bring your hot chocolate with you Coinneach," I said dropping the formalities of the day. The two men both knew there was more to this conversation, but both took their hot chocolates there to the library and sat on low purple velvet covered couches, near a low old oak table. I glanced through a few books, until I found what I was looking for.

"This language Coinneach, I have this at home, in a book that belonged to my foster Grandfather, Gillcrest MacNachten. I asked my linguist cousin, Jean what language it was, and she said it was similar to Egyptian hieroglyphics, but it wasn't. Do you know what this language is?" I asked.

"Aye that is my language, the language of the Picts. Not spoken anymore, except amongst us," Coinneach added.

"Can I bring that book here sometime and get you to translate it for me then?" I asked. "Aye it sounds like a good trade for the information that I have requested. Do you have it then lad?" Coinneach asked.

"I do. As you suspected, Grigor MacGregor is already here in Scotland, to be precise, in Glenmoriston with three of their old gang, trying to urge them to retrieve back your wife. My Grandda has refused him, but their main occupation presently has been in trying to retrieve back Alex's bairns, so it was most fortunate that you bought them here, when you did. He mentioned having been to the Aird already. I don't think he knows yet that Zahra is here on Beinn Coinneach, but I have warned him off, because of Prince Griogar and he has said that he will not be joining in any fight to retrieve Zahra. Along with expletives of course," I said.

"Well done lad. I will inform my brother," said Coinneach.

We both then drank our hot chocolates together and then went back to bed. Coinneach made no attempt to make more of our relationship other than man to man, and I ceased feeling so fearful of his intentions. I wondered about Kenneth, but I thought his interests were in Zahra, however as he is married to Ivy, I didn't want to discuss that any further.

We had plans to leave early the next morning with all the art carefully packed up and weatherproof, but the weather was not conducive to going down that mountain on Highland Ponies. We were on the inside of a heavy rain cloud and then it began to rain and then rain some more, until it was obvious that taking ponies with art loaded on board, was not going to become a reality, on such a slippery, wet, and steep mountainous track on ponies who were unaccustomed to the route.

Both Kenneth and I were concerned about our families, but there was nothing that we could do about the weather, until Coinneach suggested using his coach, which would provide us with comfort and keep us both dry as well as his precious art and apparently the horses he had, were well accustomed to the trip up and down that mountain, in all kinds of weather. Our two ponies would be tied to the back of the carriage. Coinneach offered us his two drivers, free of charge and his coach, all the way to Glengarry via Cannich to check on Ali, as his father was watching his every move from the hotel, above the oat fields. He asked us to take Ali home with us, if the situation was at all threatening and he would later go to Glengarry to pick Ali up, with Prince Grigor's, carriage in no less than three days.

Both of us were only too happy to take care of Ali, so time wasn't a factor, Ali's safety was, and I knew firsthand that Grigor Mohr MacGregor was overlooking those oat fields.

I received a message from Grandda as we were about to leave.

"Malcolm are you there?" Grandda asked. *"Malcolm, it's me Grandda, I don't know where the hell you are, but I need to tell you something,"* he said.

"What is it Grandda, I am busy right now," I said.

"It's your Uncle Patrick. He died last night from a heart attack, it seems. Some guests were complaining about the noise we were making, so they

left their belongings in their room and went downstairs to complain to Patrick about it, so when Patrick came up, to the room next door to check it out, John had stolen the ladies' jewels and money. So, the guests had a fit, realising then that they couldn't pay their bills and so I returned their money to Patrick and when he saw me, he dropped down dead, instantly, right on the spot," Grandda said.

"It's okay Grandda, Patrick was sick anyhow. James told me, he didn't expect him to live long, so it wasn't your fault, but I would clear out your friends, if I was you. Is Grigor giving Ali any trouble on the oat fields?" I asked.

"He was watching him like a hawk, until Patrick dropped dead and then he did a runner. Don't know where he is now. The funeral is the day after tomorrow," Grandda said.

"Thanks for telling me, Grandda. Sorry for your loss." I said

And he was gone.

Coinneach was informed that Grigor MacGregor had moved on from the hotel and was alone and no longer a serious threat to Ali. We still however all decided to take Ali on to MacNachten Farms in Glengarry. The carriage was amazingly comfortable, loaded up with food for the journey and blankets to sleep with. That precious art collection was the main concern, and it was carefully packed on board and would be framed upon arrival with Ivy's skilful hands assisted by her daughter, April.

I had a funeral to attend to now, on the following day, after I returned. Poor James. It would still be a shock. I felt sorry for my cousin. Fortunately, he didn't really know how poor Uncle Patrick had really died.

When our carriage arrived outside of the Craskie Farm gates, we contemplated what to say to Ali and I was feeling watched, as Kenneth and I entered. Ordinarily, entering that farm these days, I would only be looking forward to seeing my good old friend, Hamish, but Ali clouded my thinking, because I couldn't remember having met him. I remembered that he was in my house, or Hamish's house by the Loch, but I couldn't place his face, or which of the houses he had stayed in, when Zahra stayed in Loch Garry.

Ali wasn't a family member who was spoken of a lot, because his twin and himself were often referred to as 'the twinnies,' like as if they had no separate identities, but having twins of my own, that is a ridiculous concept, even if the twins are identical as mine are. Zahra's twins were not identical and here we were to negotiate with his boss, Hamish, accompanied with a letter from Ali's parents to release him with an unproven threat which was now under the cloud of Uncle Patrick's funeral.

I had never felt nervous knocking on that big oak door before at Craskie Farm, but it was widely known to have been built by Grigor MacGregor, in his better days, assisting Isobel of Glenmoriston, who was my grandmother and his half-sister. Grigor had good in him, that was undeniable, but the dual personalities of a man doing good and doing evil, has always been a mystery to me, dead or alive. I was knocking on the door of that which was a part of Grigor, that was good, and it felt confusing. So much love had obviously gone into the work to make that beautiful door.

Our good friend Hamish answered that door, not a maid or home help of some description. I loved this big man, but he was looking drawn and a little pale.

"Hamish my friend, can we both speak to you, and I am not here concerning Uncle Patrick's funeral, but I will be here tomorrow to attend. My condolences to you all," I said.

"Malcolm, Kenneth, thank you for coming. I have had trouble getting Priests to even come here as they were asking about his grave and if it had a cover on it yet and so on," Hamish said, stressed by Patrick's sudden death.

"Just get the Episcopalian Reverand then. Uncle Patrick was never a serious Catholic, was he?" I explained.

"I'll do that then," Hamish said, looking relieved. "So, what are you here for, if not the funeral arrangements?" he asked quizzically.

"I have a letter here from Ali MacAlpin's parents, Lord and Lady Coinneach. They are concerned for his welfare, currently because it has been reported that Grigor Mohr MacGregor is back on Scottish soil, and he may try to convince Ali to sign the farm back over to him. Have you noticed anything going on around here, out of the ordinary?" I asked.

"Actually, I noticed that young Ali was looking uncomfortable and kept looking up at the Manor House, but surely Grigor wasn't up there?" Hamish commented. "Was he?" Hamish asked.

"He was there apparently, for a time but he has left, according to my sources. This letter requests of you that you release Ali into our care to stay with me in Glengarry, until his stepfather comes to collect him in a few days' time," I said.

Hamish read the letter carefully and clearly recognised his handwriting.

"I have no problem with allowing him to go with you Malcolm, of course, I am just concerned it will affect the completion of his course, so I will explain it to Gilcrest, and he should understand," Hamish said.

"What are the chances of bringing the course to a close and passing him, despite not finishing the last few months?" I asked.

"He is top of his class of course, brilliant lad is Ali," Hamish added. "So, you may take him today and I might never see him again, is that possible?" Hamish asked.

"Not never, my friend but all of us need to co-operate with his parents, as they do have real concerns," I added. "Can you please release him to us. I am sorry to disrupt the farm," I added.

Finally in agreement, we all went up to the fields where Ali was working, and I was relieved to have him pointed out to us. He was so tall and very handsome, with dark hair, growing long, not unlike my own. At first glance, he was working and chatting with his friends. He then beamed a big smile, upon seeing Hamish and I thought he was one of the most handsome young men that I had ever seen, locally. Only Zahra could have a son, that handsome, I thought and with beautiful teeth too.

Hamish hugged the lad warmly and it was obvious that he didn't want to leave Hamish, whom he had grown so fond of, as a surrogate father. Could I replace Hamish? Not likely, Hamish had qualities, unlike anyone else that created trust and Ali trusted him. I felt bad about taking him away from this kind of security and I hoped it was the right move, and my home was secure enough, until Coinneach came to fetch Zahra's handsome son.

Ali came over to me and asked directly and respectfully, "Uncle Malcolm, will my course be recognised, if I leave Uncle Hamish now?" Ali enquired.

"I think Uncle Gilcrest will do the right thing lad, and I will talk to him," I said.

"Are you certain that there is a threat against me, Uncle Malcolm?" Ali asked politely.

"Let me ask you this, lad. Have you felt the presence of either your father or Uncle Padruig or Uncle Alex nearby here?" I asked.

"Aye, I have. There was the strangest feeling that they were all up there in that hotel. But how could that be?" Ali asked.

"That's correct lad, they were all there, until Uncle Patrick died and then your father, who was trying to get his friends' support, left alone, as far as I know. He left Belle MacGregor in America incidentally," I added.

"So, will you trust me and Kenneth to care for you in Glengarry? One of us has to come back to the funeral tomorrow, but you will be safe, as I do have a good security guard and your Stepfather, Lord Coinneach will be there in Glengarry, soon to pick you up. Apparently, Grigor Mohr MacGregor wants you to sign the farmland back over to him, especially now with all the renovations paid for. You won't do that will you, under any circumstances, unless you were paid I suppose?" I asked.

"Nae, I will not relinquish my ownership rights to my father. I'll come with you Uncle, but I want you to guarantee me that you will talk to Uncle Gilcrest to pass me on the soil course and give me my certificate please," Ali added. "I have all of the knowledge I need now for cropping in the Aird, but we need the plough that's here and we need to ask Uncle Hugh Og to deliver many loads of manure to the Aird as well as kelp, at Lord Coinneach's expense also," Ali added.

"Sounds good lad, so there is only Uncle Hamish and Aunty Cora to say goodbye to and to collect your belongings, because we do have to get going now," I said.

Ali and Hamish were hugging one another, and I felt emotional, seeing the bond that they had formed.

"Thank you, Hamish old friend. See you tomorrow for Patrick's funeral," I said.

All of Ali's few possessions were put into the carriage and Ali and Hamish hugged once again, and Ali was given the last of his pay, owed to him. I heard them both saying they would miss each other.

"We farewelled Hamish and I told Ali that the paintings of his Mither in Glengarry are all completed and will be framed this week and go on display on Saturday. Did you want to stay in Glengarry for the opening of the Art Gallery with the display of the new paintings of your Mither, or leave immediately your Stepfather comes?" I asked.

"I will follow Lord Coinneach. Hopefully with my certificate, Uncle Malcolm," Ali persisted.

He was certainly a persistent lad and that was starting to irritate me.

Kenneth asked me if we should stop in Invermoriston and get that certificate, while on our way home, so we did and thank God, Gilcrest co-operated with the situation, given Ali was the top student and had nothing further to learn. Gilcrest reminded him that he was entitled to free students to work with him, after he started cropping, and he himself would come out to the Aird, if it was both safe and prepared. The complete perimeter fence was the ultimate safety net for the family, he had thought and wonderful renovations.

He also mentioned to Ali that he will not be available the following year, as he was moving back to Loch Fyne in Argyle, with his reluctant wife, Morag- Freya, as he was their Laird and his Mither had sadly passed away. Gilcrest was also attending the funeral the following day for Patrick Grant, leaving only one child remaining alive, of the infamous, Padruig Dubh Grant, and that child was *our Mither, Marion MacDonald.* We were the first to learn of Gilcrest's plans to leave our district and he would be sorely missed. His replacement was a young woman scientist, he said. Alicia MacKinnon was her name. I was glad of the time spent with Gilcrest over the years, but I never planned to visit them in Loch Fyne. Too many Campbells down that way.

We had to stop once, to water the horses, as well as to feed them a little, before we were on our way once again, so it was quite late at night, when we finally saw the gates of MacNachten Farms in the distance, nicely lit up by the two big pole lights. There was an immediate reaction to a fancy coach approaching, let alone opening the rattling gates with both Duncan Mohr and Duncan Og there. One man with his rifle, aimed at the coach to shoot someone and the other just ready to care for the very tired horses.

The carriage was parked at one end of my newish stables, and it did look rather grand. The horses and ponies had been taken and rubbed down and fed and fussed over finally with admiration of what we had arrived in.

"You've done alright for yourself Malcolm, I wondered what royalty could be honouring us with their presence at this hour of the night," Duncan Mohr jested.

"How are the lads' Highland ponies then?" he asked.

"They were great on the way up there Duncan, but the weather was not suitable for the return journey with our valuable cargo on the way home. Poor wee things. This is Ali, by the way. Ali this is Uncle Duncan. Duncan I am entrusting Ali to you as a security task until his father, Lord Coinneach comes to collect him in a few days' time. His life has been threatened, so I will pay you to guard him, around the clock, up until he leaves, I will give you my home by the loch for you and your wife to spend a few days off, after Ali has left. Can you live in my house here to guard him as a bodyguard would?" I asked. Duncan looked grave but agreed, and asked Duncan Og to inform his wife that he wouldn't be coming home for a few days, but she would still benefit, after it was all over, with her holiday by the loch.

"You will both have to sleep in the same room, on the first floor, in my house. Will you both agree to that, before we go inside to inform my wife, Ailsa?" I asked.

Kenneth carried the paintings inside with my assistance, and we decided that they would be safer in my office, locked up well, until Ivy was to frame them all. Ailsa was awoken, as we all entered lighting up candles, lamps, and torches. It looked like the plumbers had been and finally, we had water plumbed to the kitchen, the bathing room, and the laundry. Kenneth was too tired to wake Ivy, so he just went to the room always put aside for him and slept soundly, glad to be finally home. I showed both Ali and Duncan where they would be sleeping and asked if Ali wanted to bathe, but due to the lateness of the hour, he didn't wish to disturb the whole house, so he also went to sleep, and Duncan and I had coffee, thankfully made by Ailsa.

"Ailsa love, I have worried about you a lot, in my absence, and I have news that will not please you. Your Mither was left behind in the Americas, by her lover and he has returned to Scotland, without her. I hope she may write to you one day, but I am sincerely sorry," I said.

"We also have a guest too, Ali MacGregor, as you can see, who must be watched over, 24 hours of each day, until his parents come to get him, so please care for him, as you would your own son. I need to attend a funeral in the morning in Glenmoriston for my uncle, Patrick Grant and I'm going with Hugh and Angus, for Cousin James's sake," I explained.

Looking miserable at all the bad news, especially concerning her Mither, Ailsa agreed to do what was needed for Ali and kissed me goodnight, said welcome home and went back to bed.

"How has everything been my good friend?" I asked Duncan, who was worried about what the background was on Ali.

"Ali is Zahra MacAlpin's son, one of unidentical twins. He was working for Hamish in Cannich, until his father, Grigor Mohr MacGregor returned to Scotland and was watching his every move from the hotel rooms, with the intention of getting him to sign back the farm in the Aird to him, so I am told," I explained.

"Grigor had a change of heart did he, by returning to Scotland without his Mistress? So, he wants his wife back now too, I suppose and his bairns as well as his farm?" Duncan Mohr asked.

"Aye I suppose he does, but I have just spent time with Zahra and her new husband, as you know, and they are a happily married couple now. There is nothing he wouldn't do for her. He really is a gift from God for Zahra, after all her suffering. I sincerely hope Zahra herself doesn't fall for any of Grigor's attempts to win her back. She was always so forgiving and that's what worries me, that she may forgive him," I said.

"Let her forgive him, if that is her way, my friend, so long as she remains loyal now to her new husband. Does she love him, as much as he loves her?" Duncan asked.

"I think so, on the surface anyway. She had a problem with his family, but I think that was all sorted while we were there. Her daughter, Isobel has gone off with his father, who is old enough to be her great grandfather, but she totally fancied the old bloke. He was quaint and got everyone, even his son, to kiss his ring. What's that all about?" I asked.

"Kings and Popes and the like do that, don't they Malcolm?" Duncan asked.

"Never met a King or the Pope. I wouldn't know. Maybe Islay knows from one of her books on Scottish Kings. I'll ask her when I have the time. Goodnight my friend. Thank you for this at such late notice," I said.

"Always a pleasure and I'll hold you to your promise of your wee house by the loch. My wife will love that," Duncan said, and they both went to bed, tired after a long day.

"Duncan, I forgot to mention, that I have to attend a funeral tomorrow at Craskie farm leaving early," I added.

"Och aye. Who died?" Duncan asked.

"Patrick Grant, my uncle. I'm going to support my cousin, James," I said.

21. Prince Griogar

Zahra had forgotten her own midwife's name, who had delivered Dihaoine, but after the treatments to her spine, the Midwife's name just popped back into her head. Her name was Lillian Ross.

"Coinneach, darling, I remember my Midwife's name now. It was Lillian Ross. Can you please find her in Inverness, and can we have her come for the birth to deliver wee Coinneach Og?" Zahra asked.

"Of course, we can my precious one, if it's to deliver our wee Coinneach Og," Coinneach replied with a smile and held her warmly and wanted her then and there on the couch and just as he was about to enter, his brother Prince Griogar opened their front door and walked in, without knocking. Fortunately, Zahra had most of her clothes still on, but her breasts were bare, and her brother-in-law would have seen them, before she had the chance to dress herself once again.

Coinneach's manhood was still standing erect, so it couldn't have been a worse time for a visitor to barge in, but it put a smile on Prince Griogar's face, which was indeed rare. Zahra noticed how handsome he was, when he smiled. And he noticed how lovely her breasts were.

"She's my wife, brother, of your lineage, she may well be, but Zahra's my wife now, so you cannot covert her," Coinneach stated very possessively.

"Live with the facts brother, go ahead if you want to finish making love on the couch," he teased. "I'm here to tell you that Grigor Mohr MacGregor is on the move. He is no longer in Cannich, or that hotel in Glenmoriston" his brother said

Both men had been in this situation before, she thought, and

Zahra was the only one who didn't know who would lead but Coinneach did. His brother Prince Griogar, whom he had upset centuries ago, was still bitter about an old issue and was going to try and upset Coinneach's cosy relationship now, centuries on.

Coinneach's hand then fell across Zahra's big belly claiming his wee bairn inside of her.

They were indeed a very odd family with traditions that Zahra had never known nor even read about in history books. It seemed that she was now the property of the MacAlpins. Coinneach and Prince Griogar, being the main players in this game of power, love, and lust.

"Let's not invite Prince Griogar around for dinner tonight darling," Zahra said as a precaution.

"I agree. God help Grigor MacGregor if he comes to Beinn Coinneach," Coinneach said.

"I really don't need this much protection from Grigor and how would he find us here anyhow?" Zahra said.

"Those Glenmoriston Men knew their way around the mountains, like no-one else, but not here. However, I do think he will find us," Coinneach replied. "Prince Griogar is prepared. It may be time now to keep the bairns inside during daylight hours, except Hector of course, as he is running his new business venture. Griogar told me that Hector has significant skill with the rifle already and just needs some practice." Coinneach said.

"Really?" Zahra said. "I hope he doesn't get hurt darling," said Zahra.

"A natural sentiment for a Mither to have my love," Coinneach said, evasively.

Hector continued working with his horses the next day with Domhnall, but Anndra was tired of assisting Hector with the spelling on all of the documents, pertaining to each and every

Highland pony and he didn't really understand the meaning of blood lines anyhow. He decided to leave his brother, Domnhall with Hector, so he could whittle one end of a strong stick into a sharp spear, to catch a fish in the burn, not far from them. He had never made one before, but it was briefly sunny, so he was enjoying sitting on a small rock by himself, contemplating a fish at the end of his spear. He wanted to be a big man too one day, when he grew up, like Hector whom he admired so much.

"Anndra, Anndra" a voice spoke quietly. "Anndra it's your Grandda, I have a sweet for you," he heard a voice say as he turned his head. Then he saw his Grandda, Grigor Mohr MacGregor, hiding in the heather and his heart began to race.

"Grandda what are you doing here? You are not supposed to be here," Anndra said.

Standing up, Anndra found then that his Great Uncle Griogar was standing right

behind him, with his hand held firmly onto his skinny shoulders and neck.

"Who are you talking to lad?" Prince Griogar demanded to know, holding the fearful wee lad by the neck.

"Grandda's in the heather, Great Uncle," Anndra declared as Griogar took him then by the shoulder and told him to run back to Grandma.

"Grigor, come out. You can't stay there all night long trying to tempt wee bairns," he said, and Grigor Mohr MacGregor stood up, having been camouflaged well, by his old plaid in the heather.

"I am here for my wife, Zahra MacGregor. I want her back. She's mine, not some arty fella from here and I want all of my bairns back too," Grigor stated to the unsmiling face of Coinneach's brother.

At one signal, the entire mountain top was covered, shoulder to shoulder by the army of the MacAlpins, not known to have ever lost a fight or a battle. Grigor Mohr MacGregor was alone in the heather. No-one had accompanied him to support his baseless claims, and he gasped at the sight of an army big enough to have defeated the Redcoats and he knew that he was defeated. That didn't stop his desire to achieve his foolish endeavour. He was going to run into a volley of fire, rather than lose his one man show, when he saw his ex-wife, also standing atop that ridge.

She was more beautiful now than he had remembered. She was healthy again and especially beautiful, but how? He saw her silken robes flowing out into the breeze that captured the scene of some kind of 'dream-like' figure, or a fairy. Had he been married to the Sidhe all along, Grigor wondered? Zahra then casually strolled down the mountain with ease, to stand beside Prince Griogar. As she walked, the breeze caught her robes in all their fine layers. The ringlets of her hair were so long, as to reach to her knees, flowed out also, catching the wind.

But Zahra wasn't alone. Following her, was a huge dark grey wolf, who then stood beside her as she patted his large, lupine head.

No one knows what was going through Grigor's mind exactly. We will never know as Grigor Mohr then went as white as a ghost, perhaps thinking that she was of another world entirely and he only knew to escape, as quickly as he could, leaving only flattened heather as he ran, until he reached his horse, at the bottom of Beinn Coinneach.

No one has heard from him since.

Prince Griogar turned to his sister-in-law, Zahra and witnessed only her beauty standing in amongst the heather, accompanied by her big wolf. He approached her on the opposite side to her wolf and offered her his arm to return her to Coinneach, waiting atop the ridge. He escorted Zahra slowly up the hillside, aware that it was her alone that had put the fear of God into Grigor Mohr MacGregor and not himself, nor his entire army. Standing beside Coinneach was wee Anndra holding his Grandda's hand and on his other side stood Hector.

Looking upon Coinneach's new family, he returned Zahra to her husband Coinneach, respectfully.

"Brother, your wife, Lady Coinneach," he said as he passed her to Coinneach, and they both melted into each other's arms. Zahra finally allowed herself to feel the anxiety of the moment drift away, as her kindly and protective husband held her close, while at the same time, wishing she'd had the opportunity to speak with her ex-husband. The sight of him running away in sheer terror, confounded her.

Each of them was left with their own thoughts as Grigor galloped away, leaving Coinneach with the firm belief that she really was the woman that the Seers had spoken of centuries ago.

◊

22. Patrick's Funeral

I barely had three hours sleep, before I was awoken by Hugh Og telling me to wake up and dress for the funeral and suggested that I sleep in the cart on the way to Glenmoriston. The quickest breakfast ever, consisted of a mouth full of toasted bread, washed down hurriedly, with coffee. Hugh Og kept hurrying me up, as I put on the new shirt that James had bought for me, for another occasion, as well as a warm waist coat and a warm overcoat, long pants, not a kilt and long leather boots, gloves and hose. I kissed my wife, Ailsa farewell and reminded her about caring for Ali and then left and hopped into the pre prepared cart, driven by my son in law, Angus MacKenzie and Hugh Og, who were both also wearing warm coats, beanies and gloves.

I lay down in the back of the cart, hoping to sleep some more, but with the back, bumpy tracks that Hugh had chosen, there was no chance of sleep, so I carefully made my way back to their front seat, to join them both. They had a thick woollen blanket over their knees, and they included me under their blanket.

"How did Uncle Patrick die Da?" asked Angus.

I valued my relationship with my son in law and considered lying and had dreaded that very question. I chose to tell them both that there were two stories concerning that matter.

The truth and the lie.

"We only repeat the lie, if I tell you the truth, is that a deal?" I asked them both in my half sleep.

"First there's the lie. Patrick was ill already and responding to guests' complaints, he climbed to the top of the stairs, with the guests and he became short of breath, then had a heart attack, and died instantly.

Then there's the truth. Patrick was ill already and responding to guests' complaints about noise in the room, they entered the room to find that the client's jewels and money had been stolen by John Campbell MacDonald, Grandda's friend. Upon hearing that, they then were unable to pay their bill, so Grandda Grant, returned the money to Patrick, who was alone at that time. Patrick reacted upon seeing the spectre of his dead father and dropped dead on the spot," I said, in my half sleep but hoped it did the job.

I hadn't noticed the looks on both of their faces, after all, it was still dark and freezing cold.

"Bloody hell Malcolm, you can sure tell some weird stories. So, which is the true story really?" Hugh Og asked, not believing either one.

"I just told you. Patrick was shocked to see Grandda alive if you like, as a spectre and dropped dead on the spot. Grandda told me so," I said, as I was rapidly waking up.

"Grandda told you so, eh?" Hugh Og asked "I'm getting worried about you Malcolm and the company you are keeping. Now tell us how Zahra is. That might be a more interesting topic?" Hugh Og asked curiously.

"Thank God my cock wasn't needed that's all I can say," I replied.

"What does your cock have to do with Zahra?" he asked worried that Zahra had been compromised in some way.

"The nudey paintings. He didn't need my cock, only Kenneth's. The artist had the biggest cock in the house anyway," I said.

"I think I should wait until you are fully awake before your fantasy dream world takes over your reality, my friend. Just rest on Angus's shoulder for a while," Hugh Og said, which I did.

"Don't take any heed of what he was just saying Angus lad, he's overtired and possibly in shock over his Uncle's sudden passing," Hugh Og said.

'It's an odd thing when you tell the truth, people are less inclined to believe you', I thought as I drifted off to sleep on, Angus's shoulder. Hugh will see Kenneth's cock on the wall in his gallery soon enough. I thought he had known about his cock in the painting, but maybe he hadn't believed that either. 'He's going to get a big shock then' I thought.

"Who are the pole bearers?" I asked, as an afterthought, coming out of sleep.

"Don't know Malcolm. Poor Hamish was left with it all to organise, because James and Henrietta fell in a heap. I doubt there's any food afterwards either," Hugh answered.

"Aye he was having trouble getting a Priest. I suggested he get an Episcopalian Minister because he wasn't a strict Catholic anyway," I said.

"When did you see Hamish?" he asked.

"Yesterday. He looked awful mind, that's when I suggested that he ask for an Episcopalian fella," I answered.

"Why were you there in Cannich, if not to organise the funeral?" Hugh asked.

"That's not my job. I was only there to pick up young Ali, Zahra's, son to keep him at my place, until his stepfather comes to collect him," I said.

"He's at your place now then?" Hugh asked.

"Aye he is. We picked up his certificate in Invermoriston on the way, so he wouldn't lose recognition for all of that learning. Did you know that Gilcrest MacLachlan is leaving next year for Argyle?" I asked.

"I didn't, but he is their Laird, so it is about time," Hugh said.

"He is being replaced by a scientist woman, name of Dr Alicia MacKinnon," I said.

"Ali wants to speak with you too about multiple loads of manure and kelp, as well as taking the plough from Cannich and delivering it to the farm in the Aird, at Lord Coinneach's expense. Its name now is Wolf Ranch," I added. "Lord Coinneach is at Beinn Coinneach presently, but you might want to meet him yourself, when he picks up Ali, unless you are too busy?"

"Why the name change?" Hugh asked.

"The farm is undergoing extensive refurbishment, at Lord Coinneach's expense, to set up Zahra's bairns but I hope young Isobel does go back to her husband, John Fraser. She fancied an old gentleman, who is Lord Coinneach's father, Lord Cinaed. They went home together for at least the one night that I was there," I said.

"I learn a lot about life, listening to you Da," Angus said out of nowhere.

"Well lad, young Isobel had herself two husbands for a time, one legal, one not and that has created a problem, because the bairns were both sired by the second one, because John Fraser was unable to impregnate her," I added. "With the second husband, Alex MacDonald, now re-united with the old gang, she's lonely and turned to a grey haired, grey bearded, fat bellied, ancient old man, who fancied her right back. Gross, if you ask me," I said.

"If the bairns were sired by the second fella, who wasn't the legal husband you say, does he have any rights to see his bairns?" asked an innocent Angus.

"If it's taken to Court, they would decide that, I expect, but they are the bairns of John Fraser's marriage, so I doubt he has any rights. Additionally, Lord Coinneach has adopted the lot of them, so he is the only male parental figure to speak for Zahra's grandchildren, Anndra and Domhnall," I explained.

"What if Alex MacDonald asks his father to speak for him in Court? Will that make a difference?" Angus asked.

"Whose side are you on lad?" Hugh Og asked.

"No one's side, just justice for both sides. It seems unfair if he can't ever see them again," Angus added.

"Lad, he ran out on them on that day, they were all going to chop up Zahra and put her in the burn," I said a little angry at the thought that Alex could get the law on his side.

Angus MacKenzie

"I am sorry about Zahra, there is no doubt. But can I ask about the wee bairns of Alex MacDonald and how they would feel, if they never saw their real father ever again? Had he been a good father until that day? Had he been guilty to any of the planning to what happened to Zahra? Do they have another father who has replaced him, equal in love and care? That's all Da. Both sides and all that," Angus said.

"That's disturbing Angus. You have missed your vocation," I said.

Quite relieved to arrive at the funeral with it still unsure who was pole bearing, I sought out my cousin James, who was thrilled to see me.

"Oh cousin Malcolm, Da has gone. It was so sudden. I don't know if I can manage the business alone. Ma has fallen in a heap. My assistant is useless. Thank you for coming. Can you help me carry the coffin, I might drop it Malcolm," James lamented as he then held tightly onto me and cried.

"It's sad that not many people liked him, so there won't be a big crowd at least," James added.

Even Hugh and Hamish had to be pole bearers, along with James but they needed two more, so Angus volunteered and looked about for another volunteer, who ended up being just one of the grooms, who had no say in it. Patrick was heavy in that coffin. 'I hadn't cursed Grandda until then, trying to carry that heavy coffin, all the way up to his hole in the wee Chapel's floor, that was intended for Grigor Og MacGregor. It was still covered with only the privy door. The lovely grave covers, I had made for both Helen and Grigor, were removed as well as Helen's body, at the insistence of both Henrietta and Patrick who had informed the Catholic Priests of Helen's suicide. He deserved what he got, 'a privy door' I thought. I wasn't going to offer up my skills to make one for him after he did that.

"Is there any food James?" I asked.

"I went to the kitchen and all the stores were missing. I think we have a food thief, Malcolm," James stated.

"Really?" I said, thinking of Grandda's friends, helping themselves to all his food.

"Oh, Cousin James. Have you ever thought of getting in one of those Priests who do exorcisms?" I asked. "Especially to empty out rooms like Room 203 and that kitchen, you never know, maybe because of opening Helen's grave up, you have a haunting there? Get that done on the quiet and I'll help you with a nudey painting, I hope and that will attract business, so long as you send clients back to my brother's Art Gallery. Is that a deal?" I asked.

"I never would have thought of all that Malcolm. I'll ask this Priest fella about who does exorcisms then," James said, and off James went to arrange an exorcism.

"Let's go home now while we have the opportunity Hugh," I said hastily. Hugh and Angus readied the horse and cart and we quickly left, before our absence could be noticed and I shot one last glance up at Room 203, in the hotel and hoped Grandda could see me. I waved goodbye, then all three of us hurriedly left for Glengarry, to hopefully arrive before midnight, this time. At least there were blankets in the back of the cart, so any one of the three of us could try and sleep, despite the bumpy tracks.

"Why didn't Ma come, do you know why Hugh? Patrick was her brother after all?" I asked.

"Oh God, Malcolm. I forgot your Mither. She was waiting for me to pick her up, but with getting you up, I completely forgot. Tell her I'm sorry, will you?" Hugh Og asked.

I imagined Ma dressed all in black, standing outside of her wee house on Loch Garry, waiting for hours, until she finally gave up hope that Hugh was ever coming to get her.

"I'll tell her that she didn't miss much, Hugh," I said.

The day started and ended in disarray with a touch of hilarity, imagining Grandda and an exorcist facing off against each other. I was looking forward to when he contacted me again. Grandda's going to be mighty annoyed, and he deserved it, after eating all of James's stores of food.

23. Picture Frames and Spectres

While Malcolm was at Patrick's funeral, Duncan Mohr hadn't left Ali's side. At least Ali could not complain that he didn't have adequate security. Ali hadn't met the other members of the household, including Islay, who hadn't known of his arrival during the night and was pleased to see that they had a house guest, and she introduced herself to him.

"I'm Islay," she said. "My father is Malcolm, and I manage the goat farm. What's your name and what are you here to do?" she asked.

Duncan Mohr answered for him before he had a chance. "This is Ali lass, he is under your father's protection, until his family come to fetch him home," he explained.

"Sounds worrisome. Do you want to see my goats, Ali?" Islay asked.

"Aye I would," Ali said, as he was getting bored with Duncan.

"Then follow me Ali," Islay said.

Just then Ivy and her daughter, April arrived to frame the paintings.

"Morning all. Is my husband asleep here somewhere?" Ivy asked.

"Aye in there," said Duncan. Ivy found her husband still sound asleep.

"Poor baby, wake up my darling. I need those paintings to start framing them," Ivy said. Kenneth wasn't ready to start the day at all. The trip had exhausted him, and he could only imagine how tired Malcolm would be, after a funeral too.

"Is Malcolm back yet?" he asked sleepily.

"Of course, not," said Ailsa.

"He won't be home until tonight, so we had better cook up a storm for the three of them Meredith, what do you think, with Ali here too?" she said cheerfully enough.

"Ali do you like beef stew?" she asked.

"Oh aye, my favourite, with tomatoes added mind. I hope you can cook better than Cora," he said smiling. "Do you make deserts too Aunty Ailsa?" Ali asked.

"I do. Would you like chocolate pudding?" Ailsa asked.

"Oh aye, sounds delicious," Ali responded.

"Islay, I will have to come with you and Ali to watch over him, okay? Wait until I get my rifle," Duncan said and then they had to wait until it was loaded and watch as he added all of his knives to his belts.

"Right, I'm ready for the goathouse," said Duncan, clinking as he walked with all of his weaponry. Glancing all around as if he was expecting 'the army of the bastards' to appear any moment, with their weapons, Duncan Mohr stealthily followed closely behind both Islay and Ali, who both giggled to each other at the silliness of it, in their minds. Islay had never really witnessed violence up close, even though she was aware of poor young Dougal, who was accidentally shot by one of Old John MacDonnell's men, trying to shoot Cherry. That didn't count and she couldn't imagine anyone trying to harm this handsome young man.

"Can you milk a goat, Ali?" Islay asked.

"Nae, but I've seen Ma do it," Ali replied.

"Who is your Ma?" she asked.

"Used to be Zahra MacGregor but now she is Zahra MacAlpin, known as Lady Coinneach from Beinn Coinneach. And can you teach me how to milk a goat?" Ali asked.

"Aye, it's easy," she answered. "Is your Ma the pretty lady who tried to save her marriage with Grigor MacGregor and stayed here for a while?" Islay asked.

"Aye that's right, but now she has re-married a nice man, Lord Coinneach," Ali answered.

"So, do you like your new Da then?" Islay asked.

"Aye, I do," he takes care of Ma and all of us too. He is renovating our farm to make it more viable, in a business sense and safer too with a wall out the front, so cattle thieves can't just wander in and steal our coos again," Ali said.

"You married yet Ali?" Islay asked.

"Not yet but I want to be established on Wolf Ranch first and be earning enough to care for a wife and to put the bairn through university maybe, if he liked that idea. That's not stopping me from looking at what I like," Ali added.

"You are a funny fella, Ali. Tell me what you like to look at then, I'm curious," Islay asked. "But just so you know, I am married to Angus," she added. "I've loved him since I was wee. I used to peek through his window when he was undressing at the staff house over there, until I was caught by Da's stepfather," she said quite openly with Duncan listening. "You don't have to listen Uncle Duncan," Islay said. "So, tell me what you like to look at?" she asked again as they were both milking the goats.

"I would like a sweet looking lass, hopefully with brown curly hair like my Mither, or even black hair, like mine, not blonde like my sister, Isobel. My Mither is the best-looking woman in the world and so I would like my wife to be like her. Also, a kind lass who makes a good stew and keeps herself very clean and works hard and likes to please me," Ali answered.

"Well Ali, I'll keep a look out for you with that criteria in mind and if you give me your address, I can tell you if I find someone. How about that?" she asked.

Islay MacKenzie

"Sounds good, but not until I am back on the ranch, I have to establish growing oats in the Aird and its hard work for a long while and that's no life for a lass. I'll wait until I can say, 'I planted that crop and it's growing well, and we are going to make money this year my dear,'" he said and laughed at himself. They were both enjoying each other's company as Ali had a way with everyone, even Kenneth's young bairn, April liked him, as did anyone who met him at MacNachten Farms.

"Do you want to meet our other relatives too, down at Loch Garry Ranch?" Islay asked.

"Siobhan grows bees and her sister-in-law Jean, my second cousin, makes pottery to put the honey in and all other manner of things like bowls and so on. It's nice pottery now. My Grandmother and her husband, Bruce used to run this goat farm, but they have retired to the Loch, unless I need Bruce to slaughter a goat for me. I can't do that," she added.

"Do you make the cheese then too?" Ali asked.

"Och, aye. Do you want to see it? You must put protective covers on your shoes and wash your hands before you enter that area, as it is sterile. Uncle Duncan can't follow us in there, can you Uncle Duncan?" Islay teased.

"That's right lass, be quick," Duncan said. Islay showed Ali the cheese factory where she was the sole manageress and was making a small fortune out of cheeses of many varieties now.

"I am good at this. It's the first thing in my life that I was good at that wasn't easy and could make us all some money. I get people asking for my cheese all the time," Islay bragged. "Do you want to take some for your Ma?" she asked.

"Och, aye if you can spare it," Ali answered. "You don't want coin for this?" he asked.

"Nae, it's my gift to you Ali. What's your last name?" she asked.

"It was MacGregor and now it's MacAlpin, like Ma. My full name is Ali Gregor MacAlpin, so I don't lose Clan Gregor," he explained.

"Why did your name change too?" Islay asked.

"Lord Coinneach, my new father, adopted me and my twin Fatma, as well as the wee ones," he answered thoughtfully.

"That's amazing, he must have been sent by God to you all. I have loved that name MacAlpin, since I was wee, reading about all the Kings of Scotland and I especially loved King Kenneth MacAlpin who was King of Alba," Islay said.

"Och, was he?" Ali asked.

"Aye, I'll show you the book tonight. Now come to meet Siobhan and Jean," Islay said. Islay locked up the sterile area and Ali carried the cheese for his Mither, who he was missing a lot for some reason.

Meeting Siobhan and Jean was lovely, and they were both given smoko there. They gave him a wee pot to keep things in and a large pot of honey for his Ma and passed on their regards to her. Duncan Mohr said that was enough socialising and wanted Ali back inside Malcolm's house, as it was close to lunch time, and he was feeling uneasy. He took Ali back and all the ladies went back to work with the criteria list also for a nice lass, when Ali was ready.

Kenneth's wife, Ivy was busy in the Art Gallery framing paintings, after having retrieved them all from Malcolm's office in his house. They had already completed two large paintings, elaborately framed, and were hanging them up and taking down some of Ivy's paintings of beetles. Ali asked if he could briefly look into the Art Gallery, before going back to Malcolm's house. Duncan Mohr reluctantly agreed and stood guard at its entrance, feeling concerned at the unseen threat.

"Well done Aunty Ivy," Ali said.

"Just Ivy lad and this is my daughter, April," she said.

"Hello Uncle Ali," the sweet lass said. She was all of five or six years old and not shocked by the nudity in the paintings at all.

"Will you be staying here long Uncle? I hope so. I like you," April said, and Ali remembered Islay's story of peeking through the window at Angus when she was wee. These Glengarry lassies were indeed forward. He thought of their age differences for a moment. She was five or six and he was seventeen years old. Only twelve years difference. It seems a lot when the bairn is wee, but the lass at ten or twelve years wouldn't seem too young. He felt indecent momentarily, thinking that way but asked Ivy if young April was betrothed to anyone yet, just the same.

"Betrothed? Good God, no Ali," Ivy replied.

"Do you still follow those old traditions, Ivy?" Ali asked.

"Are you serious lad?" Ivy asked.

"Aye, I am. Would you and Uncle Kenneth please consider it, if my father and Mither both approved? It would be many years of betrothal, maybe until April was twelve and then marriage, if all parties agreed," Ali said seriously as the sweet innocent lass looked lovingly upon him. She made him feel like a God.

All the talk of marriage had made him feel a need he had never felt before.

"I'll ask my husband and when your parents come, we can discuss it all together. We don't yet have enough dowery, so we need a lot more time to accumulate that," Ivy said now thinking along practical lines. Life without her only child would be miserable too. She had left it too late to have any more bairns and she didn't want that to happen to April.

"Leave it with me concerning Kenneth's approval, and you ask your parents when they come. Okay?" Ivy asked.

"Ali," Duncan called. "We have to go now," he demanded. He took Ali by the arm, closed the gallery door and hastily rushed him back to the security of Malcolm's house. Whatever the threat was, was close by and Duncan could feel it getting closer. Inside the safety of Malcolm's home, Duncan gave his instructions.

"Don't open the door now Ailsa," he commanded and closed any open windows and locked and bolted the rear door.

"Meredith don't go outside now for anything," Duncan Mohr impressed upon the household. Meredith took out her concealed pistol from the upper cupboards in the kitchen and loaded it.

Ailsa knew nothing about weapons but took Ali upstairs to the marriage room that had bars on the windows and overlooked one side of the house, onto the Drovers Road. Duncan blocked the top of the stairway and waited there, long rifle in hand, pointed in the direction of the front door.

Kenneth had finally woken up and wandered out of his bedroom, nearest the front door, wearing very little and walked into guns pointed at him from three directions. Meredith, Duncan Mohr and Islay, who had followed them home, seeing that something was amiss. She had been taking lessons with both the rifle and the pistol and she was a very good shot.

"I give up," said Kenneth with his hands held high in the air with his famous cock hanging freely.

"If Ivy could see you now lad," jested Duncan. "Go to your bath and get dressed will you, then arm yourself. We have a situation." Duncan demanded.

"Thank you, Meredith and Islay," Kenneth added with a smile and a bow.

"I'm a MacKenzie" Meredith added. "I Shine, not Burn" she added.

"Och," Ailsa exclaimed, "I don't even know my motto thingy," she said.

Ali called out "Royal is my Race," then a kind of peace descended upon the household.

"I think it may be going away," Duncan then observed. "Thank you, Ali. You can keep that up," he said.

"What was it or who was it, Uncle?" asked Islay.

"Ali's biological father, Grigor Mohr MacGregor, taking advantage of Malcolm being at Patrick's funeral. The ratbag," Duncan replied.

"I won't ask you how you sense these things, Uncle but thank you and I am sorry for making fun of you," Islay said hugging their bold security guard, who after all, was fighting an invisible threat at times and relied on his inherited sixth sense.

That family all had that sixth sense, even his son, who didn't want to become a security guard, but had invented the gate rattling tins, to alert them all, when Cherry had tried to return to MacNachten Farms. So, he too was aware when threats were nearby, even if he chose to stay with his precious horses. Duncan Mohr really needed additional security on this farm, and it had now reached a critical need, where lives were at risk.

Duncan suspected his enemy was not only elusive, but highly skilled and if he had chosen to, could have wiped them all out, but for Ali calling out the creed of Clan Gregor. He may have been named MacAlpin but he was indeed a MacGregor, Duncan believed. His father at birth had heard his son's voice, then left. They all felt a collective sigh of relief but still uncertain that they were all safe, so the family were all told to stay inside and when Ivy returned, she was to stay with wee April.

"Is April safe in the Art Gallery?" asked Ali.

"I think so son. He was after you, wasn't he?" Duncan asked.

"Aye, but I still think you should bring wee April in here with us," said Ali.

Duncan gave the orders for the family to remain inside, with the door locked, while he went to negotiate with Ivy, who would not like to lose her offsider, in the work that had a deadline for completion.

The atmosphere outside the home had changed. The horses were restless and were all moving around uneasily, in their stalls, Duncan too was then worried about Ivy and April. As he approached the Art Gallery, he felt the return of that threat and ran quickly to the front door, opened it up and both Ivy and wee April stared up at him, like as if to say,

"What?"

"Ivy and April, can you come with me to the house, now please?" Duncan asked.

"Nae Duncan, I'll nae come with ye, but take April, if it makes ye feel better because I can't leave this valuable artwork. Go April and talk with Ali, if you like," Ivy said but refused to abandon the artwork entrusted to her husband.

They stood to earn a lot of commission and Ivy had been responsible for sending out all of the invitations for the viewing and purchasing of all of Lord Coinneach's beautiful work, worth a small fortune. She had also put-up posters at the local post office to advertise the event, as well as an advertisement in the Inverness Times Newspaper. She was careful to mention that it was for 'adult viewing' and had also sent invitations to all sorts of clubs and government organisations, as well as hotels like James's in Glenmoriston.

Ivy wasn't going to leave the art for anything. Duncan was annoyed, but helpless against Ivy who was a true Fraser after all, and just locked up her windows and told her to lock the door behind him, as he departed with wee April.

Ivy felt that the Art Gallery was too stuffy with all of the windows closed and add to that, the strong smell of whatever was in her husband's paint, became suffocating, so she opened up a window once again, despite Duncan's dire warnings. After all, there were bars on every window, she justified to herself, but kept the big doors locked.

As Ivy continued to work on the precious art, stretching out each canvas onto their lovely frames, she felt a distinct uneasiness. Ivy had only ever felt a peace and happiness in her husband's Art Gallery, but this was different. There was a dark, ominous, and threatening presence inside the gallery. Ivy stopped her work momentarily and spoke to the spectre whom she realised, had joined her.

"Hey ghost, whoever you are. You are really making me angry. I have work to do, and you are just too lazy to do anything but haunt people. It's pathetic," Ivy said, and she meant it.

Ivy heard sounds like footsteps all about her gallery, but it stopped at the two paintings that she had already hung on the wall.

"Don't think about it ghost, I know nasty ghosts who might just get you and you will regret ever coming here to MacNachten Farms you, ratbag lazy ghost," Ivy said.

It could be humorous, if the ghost had a sense of humour, but Grigor Mohr MacGregor was not known to have one of those. He appeared out of nothing, right in front of her.

"Brave still now are you, lassie?" Grigor asked her, leaning over Ivy directly with his face up close to hers.

"You must be that poor lad Ali's, father? Now I know why he has lost respect for you," she replied, trying to be brave but shaking inwardly and hoping her husband, Kenneth, would appear to assist, but he didn't, of course.

"Are you displaying this artwork to the general public?" Grigor asked.

"Aye, we are. Why does it matter to you?" Ivy asked.

"My wife is naked in them, that's why little lassie," Grigor said angrily.

"Did you think that maybe by abandoning them, that they may have needed the money to survive, Mr ghost," Ivy added.

"I wasn't gone for that long," Grigor justified.

"You stole her horse too, I am told, as well as twenty coos. That was taking food from out of your bairn's mouths. On top of that, your wife, as you keep calling her, was half dead and needed intensive care, which was provided to her, but ordinarily that would cost a fortune, wouldn't it?" Ivy said.

She was pleased then that she had listened to the whole gruesome story.

"Hungry, were they?" he then asked thoughtfully.

"Aye, until Lord Coinneach assisted them all and married your wife, whom you had already divorced," Ivy reminded him.

"That half blind, old man?" Grigor asked.

"Aye, not that old, I am told and very handsome, with dreamy eyes, according to some," Ivy added.

"I've heard enough. I'll get her back. I am certain of it," Grigor said and was gone and left through the door.

Ivy Fraser was known to have grown up around her brutish brothers, George and Colin Fraser, so she had been toughened up by having lived with them, for most of her life, until she met with the gentle, sweet and kind, Kenneth MacNachten. However, an invisible brute was quite a different matter, altogether. She felt her hands trembling too much to continue her fine work. 'Time for lunch', she thought and locked up the precious art and meandered on down to the house with her legs feeling like jelly. Pleased at least, that she didn't need to run.

"Is it lunchtime yet everyone, I could eat?" Ivy asked, as she walked into Malcolm's secured home. They all agreed to bring lunch forward a bit, so she could tell them her tale of the encounter with the spectre of Grigor Mohr MacGregor.

24. Zahra & Wolfie

The families of Beinn Coinneach and Glengarry were now going over all their respective experiences with both the spectre, and in person of Grigor Mohr MacGregor.

Ali loved his stay in both Glengarry and Beinn Coinneach, but being with his Mither was the best time of all. He knew it was coming to an end, and he would be returning to the Aird to commence his work on his oat crops. Hugh Og had been organised to meet him there in two days' time with the plough and he would harness up the ox, already purchased by his adoptive father and ensure that it fitted the poor beast. Then he was going to be hand ploughing for days, before Hugh arrived with those loads of manure, followed by loads of kelp, from the coast.

The opening of the Art Gallery was an exciting topic of conversation because three of Coinneach's brothers had attended the opening and created a bidding war on the painting with Kenneth and Zahra, but didn't buy it themselves, they just drove up the price to an incredible five thousand pounds, which Old John MacDonnell of Glengarry, paid. He loved it.

Three of the MacAlpin brothers bought one painting each of Zahra, in various poses, but not Prince Griogar, while the other two paintings sold for two thousand pounds each. One was purchased by James Grant, to hang over the hotel's reception desk. He was told it was an especially cheap price just for him, so long as he recommended their Art Gallery.

There were a lot of people who missed out and even if there had been three times that many nude paintings, Kenneth could have sold them all. The gallery was happy, Coinneach was happy, and Zahra was happy. Coinneach's father, Lord Cinaed delighted in his painting above his mantle as his prized piece as he took down the portrait of his late wife. Isobel was happy too, because she wanted to be with child to the old, stout and bearded man, now that Alex was gone, and she kept the old man very busy.

When Prince Griogar was asked why he hadn't purchased one yet, he simply said he wanted one painted especially for him and he would discuss it with the artist. The painting, he had in his mind was of the beautiful woman, Zahra, who was clothed in silken flowing robes in pinks and apricot hues, walking down to him from the mountain, amidst the purple, flowering heather, accompanied by her dark grey wolf, with her long, brown hair flowing outwards in the breeze. He wanted that scene captured for eternity by his brother to remember the woman, who was Zahra, not just a nude and not just an ordinary person.

Could Coinneach capture the magic within her? That was what he wanted.

Coinneach was inspired by his request and went back to the scene with his brother, to have the exact location with its colours and light at that precise time of the day, with the heather flowering, as it had been before they started to die off to be that rust colour. He wanted the sun in its exact location and the ridge as it was on that day. Coinneach was so grateful to his brother for his army that there was no cost for the painting, provided he didn't tell their father. Wolfie was going to be harder to paint, as he never stood still, unless he was asleep when he could capture his body length, size, and height. While trying to sketch him sleeping, Zahra asked Coinneach,

"What are you doing with Wolfie my darling?"

"Just sketching him, my love for the painting I am doing for Griogar. I can't get him to pose, can I?" Coinneach remarked sarcastically.

"Och, aye you can. Wolfie darling. Come here to Mummy," Zahra said.

"Now sit for Daddy," she asked the big wolf who then just sat still on their bed. However, it was a great pose, and he was able to sketch him much better.

"Are you wanting him to be as he was on 'the' day that Grigor ran away?" Zahra asked, using the correct emphasis.

"Aye I do," Coinneach replied.

"Then Wolfie wasn't sitting, my darling, he was standing, and I was patting his head," she said.

Zahra then got off the bed and asked Wolfie to jump down and 'stay' beside her for a wee while," she commanded, as her artist husband quietly sketched Wolfie, in that position.

"Good boy," Zahra said and kissed him fondly and then took him downstairs for a reward from the kitchen, for doing so.

There were always bones left out for Wolfie on her instructions to Mairi and she took one and gave it to him, when he suddenly nudged her in the crotch and his large lupine appendage became visible.

"No, bad dog," Zahra exclaimed.

Coinneach heard her drastic change in tone from loving to 'bad dog' and went to investigate. He and Prince Griogar had already had lengthy conversations of what to look out for when Wolfie would mature, needing a wolf partner and would need therefore, to be returned to the wild. The only problem with that, was Zahra's attachment to him, as well as the obvious hunters who could shoot him on sight, Malcolm being of that calibre who would never trust a wolf. How Wolfie had stayed domesticated for this long was a miracle, but one that Zahra had needed, and she loved the animal and had always refused to believe that he really was a wolf.

If she had allowed herself to believe it, he didn't know what would happen. His wife was still fragile and Wolfie had been a great comfort to her.

"What has happened my darlings?" he asked. "Are you

alright, I heard you say, 'bad dog'. I never thought you would ever allow yourself to say he was ever a bad dog," he asked looking upon the face of an obviously thoughtful and very disappointed wife.

"Coinneach, Wolfie nudged me in my crotch and then I saw that he had a pink doggie, cock showing," she declared.

"Is he growing up, do you think, is that all it is, or should I be worried?" Zahra asked.

Coinneach knew it was time to have 'that conversation' with his wife and felt grateful to his brother for already searching for any existing wolf packs that Wolfie could possibly join, or any safe place, other than merely releasing him from their front door. However, he had had no luck in finding any other wolves at all, even going as far as Sutherland, but his advice to Coinneach was to eventually return him to the Aird, so he could search and howl for a partner himself, as they do, until he finds one, if there was one more wolf left, in the Highlands.

"He would be safe on their own farm, if no-one was told of his presence there, so long as the Manager kept his gun loaded, in case he did become a threat to anyone, or the livestock. They could feed him when he needed it, and he knew them, and they knew him, and it was his birthplace. There really wasn't a better location, unless Zahra was worried about Fatma, in which case, she also could live with them on Beinn Coinneach, at least until Wolfie found a wolf partner," the prince said.

Coinneach agreed, believing that Zahra would still have a loyal wolf for life, as they are like that and never seemed to forget anyone, especially their surrogate Mithers. Now the change had begun from surrogate Mither, where she could be thought of as his Alpha female which, in turn, meant Coinneach, himself may be in danger from attack from the wolf, in his own home. That was what Coinneach's concern had been all along.

With Wolfie munching on his bone, he sat his wife down to

have that dreaded conversation, which he knew would break her heart. He hated having to do this but explained that Wolfie was a wild animal and although she thought him to be a dog, he was indeed a wolf. He was now coming of age, where he needed a wolf partner, as every one of God's creatures' desires and needs. He explained that they would both need to release him into the land of his birth, being the only safe place with their family's co-operation. If he began to attack them, or their livestock, he would lose his life, but he hoped he would find another one of the puppies that had escaped the 'great cull' that had occurred there and survive.

At first Zahra was silent and couldn't take it all in.

"Do you mean that I will never see him again?" Zahra asked.

"Nae I do not. You will see him frequently because he can never forget you, as is the way of the wolf. He would still protect you, to the death, if the need arose, but you are not a wolf my darling and you cannot live in the wild, but the wild is calling him. Can you see that?" Coinneach asked.

"I can't part with him Coinneach please, not yet" Zahra pleaded.

"My darling wife, our baby is due soon and Wolfie will not like that the wee bairn has your love and attention and could easily kill our bairn, with one shake to break our wee bairn's tiny neck. I have seen it, with my own eyes, unfortunately. That was a long time ago now, when wolves were plentiful in number, in the Highlands, but we can't take that risk, can we, my love? I want him to be happy and to have his own wee family, so he too is fulfilled. Wouldn't you like to see that?" Coinneach asked.

His wife cried tears of grief from deep within her and lay over his lap crying, imagining life without her precious Wolfie. Maybe some of her grief was left over, unexpressed from her shocking life, until now. He hadn't quite expected how long she would weep for and how deep her feelings of sorrow could be with the knowledge now that she was losing her Wolfie. He hoped he had made the right decision for both his family and her wolf. He loved his wife dearly with her deep sensitivity, but it worried him, that which he admired and loved about her, could well be her own undoing.

25. Coinneach's Dilemma

Zahra's daughter, Isobel was unlike her Mither. Coinneach had put it down to having inherited her father, Hugh Chisholm. Isobel wouldn't have become attached to a dog or a cat, only her bairns and her Mither, with a brand of survival that was unique, given her attraction to Coinneach's own father. With no respect to the royal family of old, or any authority, she was taking care of herself and wanted something from his father, most likely a bairn, now that Alex had gone. He didn't know Fatma well yet, but she did appear sensitive, at least more than Isobel, who was often described by the men as, snippy, or bad tempered, so they left her alone, or in John Fraser's case, obeyed her.

Isobel had even inherited Hugh Chisholm's fluid morals and would shift them to suit herself, although praying regularly with her Mither. Despite all of that, her loyalty to Zahra was what he most admired about her, and their story was a long and harrowing one. He knew therefore, of Zahra's daughters, that Isobel could be relied upon for anything regarding her Mither, but nothing sentimental. Isobel certainly hadn't missed Grigor Mohr MacGregor and that was a relief to him, as their new father, who looked out for signs of sadness in his new family.

He was worried about Alex's bairns, Anndra and Domhnall, who had enjoyed a good relationship with their father. Alex had never hit them, nor neglected them, until the day he chose to abandon them both, to follow Padruig and Grigor MacGregor. He must regret having made that decision, but Coinneach and his father, Lord Cinaed had lengthy conversations about the law, concerning Alexander MacDonald and there was still more work to do, if they wanted to keep Alex away from Zahra's grandchildren.

Of all three men, Coinneach only felt sorry for Alex, for that hasty decision made on that fateful day. Alex hadn't harmed Zahra, nor was he a part of the plan to harm her, so the household breaking up, so completely, after Grigor punched his wife in the face, had left no time to contemplate the outcome for Alex and his two handsome and intelligent, young sons.

Polyandry being illegal, was not going to win any sympathy from a Presbyterian led court system, so in his opinion, it would be a private matter, decided upon by the people concerned. John Fraser, Isobel Fraser, and Alexander MacDonald of Aonach. Coinneach decided that when he was to visit Wolf Ranch with his wife and Wolfie, that he would check on how much of that fencing had been completed and how secure the rest of the property was, given that any one of that family could give in to Alex, if he ever turned up with flowers, toys, and the loving Daddy act, begging to see Anndra and Domhnall, formerly Andrew and Donald. Both lads seemed happy enough on Beinn Coinneach, but he had to try harder to replace Alex. Fusball was a thought, but his eyesight wasn't good enough to see that small ball. The library however was a huge win, as they all loved it. He could teach them advanced Gaelic, or old Irish with its characters and perhaps, his own language.

Ordinarily, Ali would be Coinneach's successor although not actually being born of him by blood. His new bairn would be, and he wondered how fair that was now, and if Ali would see it as unfair, given that he was the oldest son in Zahra's family. He decided to speak with Ali who was, after all, an intelligent lad, before he departed for the Aird.

Included in that conversation was the life of Wolfie on Ali's farm, now named Wolf Ranch, being half owner with John Fraser. Ali, co-incidentally was also wishing to speak with him about the ring that Lord Coinneach had paid for, to be betrothed to April Fraser MacNachten, with their total approval, especially Kenneth, who was delighted that his wee lass, April was betrothed to Zahra's handsome son. It then made Kenneth a relative, by marriage to Lord Coinneach and Lady Coinneach and Kenneth loved that idea.

Ali wanted to pay his father back, for the simple betrothal ring, when he had the money, but his father declined. Ali was saving up for April's wedding ring, so his response wasn't disappointing.

"You are my son now lad, there is no repayment in this relationship and furthermore, I have the cash for Hugh Og Chisholm, to pay for the delivery for all of the fertilizer to you, on Wolf Ranch and other items promised to you," he explained. He handed Ali a handful of notes for him to pay Hugh Og and if it wasn't enough, he was to send him the bill on Beinn Coinneach.

"Ali, as you know, I consider you to be my eldest son and ordinarily, you would be my successor. Unfortunately, due to MacAlpin royal bloodlines, that can't be the case within my family. How do you feel about your Mither's new wee bairn being my inheritor, if it is a lad?" Coinneach asked.

"I don't expect anything more from you father. I have already inherited Wolf Ranch from my biological father, Grigor Mohr MacGregor. What you have done for John's and my farm is more than I could have ever hoped for. I am more than happy for the new wee bairn to be your successor" Ali said.

"Father, I do have one more question if you don't mind. Is it a custom in your family, to kiss men on the lips too?" Ali asked.

"Oh, aye lad. I should have explained that to you all. Have you seen my father, Lord Cinaed, kiss me and my brothers Padraig,

Anndra and Cinaed Og?" he asked.

"Aye I have. I have never been kissed by a man, on the lips before and I thought that only effeminate men did that, with one another," Ali said.

"Like Alexander MacDonald, do you mean?" Coinneach asked. "He had a doctor boyfriend and lover for a time, but he was a good Doctor at least. I have employed Dr Heath to help deliver the new wee bairn," he said. "Doctor Heath has been told to stay away from all of our sons, including you my son, so don't worry when you meet him, he will not dare touch you, let alone kiss you, God forbid. If he ever did, however, then tell me immediately, son," Coinneach explained, planting the knowledge of Alex's previous liaison with Peter, into Ali's limited mind.

Ali would no doubt repeat it to all his brothers and sisters, especially Isobel if she hadn't known about that side to her 'husband.'

"His name is Peter Heath," he added. "You are safe with any of the MacAlpins kissing you lad, but not with your Uncle Alex or Dr Heath," Coinneach said.

26. MacAlpins on Wolf Ranch

"When you leave Ali, could we accompany you with Wolfie, in the carriage?" Coinneach asked.

"You must be aware by now that Wolfie is a wolf and not a dog, son? He has now reached maturity, whereby he needs to find his own wolf partner. Will you agree to him living in the Aird on Wolf Ranch, without notifying anyone, other than your immediate family, that he is there, or hunters will pursue and kill him? We want him to find a pack of his own, without harming any of you. If he looks like harming anyone, or the livestock, then he will have to lose his life. For your Mither's sake, we all want a good outcome for him.

Can you help us, sadly, without telling Uncle Malcolm and I will give you a long rifle with ammunition, if you must put him down?" Coinneach requested.

"Aye father, of course. Poor Ma. She will really miss him. Are you getting her a puppy to replace him?" Ali asked.

"Nae, she will reject it son. She is broken hearted, that's true, but I can't risk Wolfie killing the new wee bairn. I would appreciate your help lad," Coinneach said.

All of them travelled in the carriage, including Prince Griogar and Isobel, who was now returning to the Aird, with Wolfie.

Anndra and Domhnall stayed on the mountain and would follow, once all the work on Wolf Ranch was completed. It was possible that Isobel was with child, but she wasn't yet sharing that with anyone, not even her Mither. Isobel wanted enough time to have passed by, where some confusion could be achieved over the paternity of the bairn. Lord Cinaed would disallow his bairn to depart, if he had known, so he could not be told, was Isobel's rationale.

Zahra thought differently for the old gentleman and his right-ful bairn. Another royal bairn could be on its way, but Zahra's mind was only on her dog, Wolfie.

◇

The release of a beloved pet, who looked confused, was even more heart breaking than was expected. Zahra walked into the forest with him, away from the old farmhouse and the rest of the family and they all stayed patiently there, awaiting the out-come. Zahra told Wolfie, he could go. Eventually, by choice as the forest beckoned to him, Wolfie suddenly seemed to make up his mind and ran away, stopped momentarily, turned and looked at Zahra, as if to keep her as an imprint on his memory, then ran into the deeper forest and did not return.

He had chosen freedom by himself. The old Crohn would see him from time to time, then she saw his pack and knew them all by name, as she would throw meat to them all, given to her by John Fraser who monitored Wolfie's situation.

Zahra's walk back to the farmhouse seemed to take forever and it felt like she was in a bad dream. The snow underfoot, gave her senti-mental memories of her old life in the Aird and married to Grigor. It had been her home for so long. The after-noon was quickly becoming colder and dimmer, as she approached the small group waiting upon her. She didn't always want to appear to be the weak one, but she felt weak suddenly, without her wolf. Heavy with child, her legs were becoming heavier and heavier awkwardly approaching her new husband Coinneach and his brother, who were both wanting to know the details. She didn't feel like sharing it with anyone, but the closer she came to Coinneach, she could only feel his compassion from his wonderful big body. Both of her daughters, as well as Ali and John, watched on too, with young Simon behind them all.

"Wolfie has gone Coinneach," she said and wept, was all she could say, before she fell into his strong embrace. He was holding the woman he had waited for, as she sobbed sorrowfully. Eventually tiring, she sat on a stool in front of the house, in the cold air and Ali stood before her and began the prayers to which she, Fatma and Isobel joined. He then recited supplications that were unknown to the MacAlpins and the Frasers, with Coinneach watching on in amazement, as did his brother.

'This was the actual strength of Ali, in leading his family. Their mysterious faith concluded Coinneach.'

The cook called them all in, after enough time had passed, to the prepared meal and she told them their beds had been made up for the night and she was then leaving to go up to her husband in the small cottage, which was now completed, behind the old farmhouse.

The stew cooked by the woman lacked a few of the usual ingredients that Zahra would ordinarily include, so Zahra boldly put it all back into the pot and added salt, pepper and about three different kinds of herbs and more tomatoes, then re-heated it. It was then ready, and Zahra served it up again, much to the surprise of her husband and her brother-in-law, unaccustomed to seeing Zahra cooking or serving up food. Additionally, it tasted much better.

"That's nice Ma, thank you," Fatma said. "The poor cook can't cook as well as you can," she added.

John then proceeded to talk a lot about the farm with Coinneach, as this was his only opportunity and Hugh Og was expected, mid-morning, the following day, after they would all be gone.

"Please give my kind regards to Hugh," Zahra said. "And Malcolm's lovely twins. Please be careful not to mention Wolfie to the twins, or it will be repeated to Malcolm. I hate keeping it from him, but maybe we must, do you agree Coinneach?" she asked.

"Aye I do, sadly my love. He may understand it in time, but not yet," Coinneach added.

The humble surroundings of Wolf Ranch, surprised Prince Griogar as to how Zahra had lived for so many years and this was the improved and renovated version. "How did you all live here? It must have been so cold," he commented, trying not to sound like a snob.

"Ma did get cold often, didn't you Ma? Hypothermic even, at least three times, not including the time that you were nearly swallowed up, by the snow," Fatma said very innocently.

"Aye, I am prone to hypothermia, but luckily I had some help for that," Zahra said, not wishing now to mention how Padruig had helped her return to normal body temperature, after nearly freezing to death.

"That was one good thing that Uncle Padruig did Ma," Ali commented.

"Aye son, it was easy for him, because he always runs at a high body temperature, unlike your father who was quite cool to the touch," she remarked, shocking herself at the memory of his touch.

"How did you all end up here, living together in the first place?" asked a very curious brother-in-law.

John Fraser responded, "I had owned this property for a long time, while I was still alive and I retired here, but when I died, I became lost in the forest one day. By the time I found the house again, time had passed, and the house had been ransacked and many things were stolen. It took a while to adjust to being dead, but when I did, I noticed that family men were leaving their families down near the burn, under the big oak tree, to die. They were abandoning their wives and bairns there, who froze to death. That's how I would find them. Then one day, when I saw Zahra, I quickly went to her and Isobel, in case she was being abandoned too, but she and Isobel were leaning up against the big tree there and said they were just waiting for her husband, Grigor who was hunting food for them. They wouldn't come into my house, insisting that he would come," John said.

"Later that day, it was becoming much colder, and they were both still there, so I went down to them both again and then suddenly Grigor did appear, carrying a small deer, that he had caught on my land. I invited them all in and then they accepted, following Grigor's instructions. Zahra was a sad looking lady at that time," John recalled. "I thought then that Grigor was a good man, and I needed to take my coos to higher pasture and would be gone from the house, so I employed him to watch over it all, which they all did, and it worked. I wanted to marry Isobel later and so for the dowery, I offered Grigor my whole farm for her, but he accepted half and that's how it still is, except now half belongs to his son, Ali, when Grigor didn't need a dowery from me anyhow for Isobel. But I was determined, I just wanted Isobel," John explained.

"That explains John, Zahra, Grigor, Isobel and Ali, what about the rest of them, like Alex?" the prince asked, wanting to know everything.

"It's a very long story brother. We were in Inverness at the Doctor's house, Peter Heath. The Glenmoriston Men, Hugh, Padruig, Hugh's brothers and Alex were all laying siege to the Doctor's house, to get Grigor back into their gang. Grigor was refusing and I secretly went outside to negotiate with Padruig, who was leading them all and he tried to kidnap me, unsuccessfully and when Alex realised, that I was breast feeding, due to my breast milk leaking through my clothes, Alex decided to return me back to Grigor, given there were bairns involved," Zahra said.

"Grigor was naturally irate, but I passed out during the stressful process, requiring Alex to carry me back inside the Doctor's house. They were all still outside, and we were unable to leave, so that Doctor offered us all jobs, because he was new in the Inverness area and needed a cook, a cleaner and a gardener. When the men finally left, Alex then accompanied us all back to the Aird and remained there, with us, until recently.

Padruig and the Chisholm brothers would still stalk the Aird farm then, and I threw snowballs at him and his horse, but he wouldn't budge. Hugh would hide behind the big oak tree, but eventually all the Chisholm brothers gave up and went home. Padruig didn't because he blamed me for breaking them all up. I was also falsely blaming him for what had happened to my second bairn, wee Sakina, with Hugh but the person to blame was the oldest of the Chisholm brothers, Alexander.

Eventually Padruig was welcomed inside where he could tell his side of the story, in a nutshell," said Zahra. "Of course, there's more detail than that, but I am too tired now brother. May I go to sleep now, Coinneach?" Zahra asked.

"Aye of course, my love, but can you please tell me first who Sakina was? I haven't heard you mention that name before," Coinneach asked.

Taking a deep breath first, Zahra said, "My first child with Hugh Chisholm is Isobel, as you know Coinneach. I was with child a second time to Hugh, but his oldest brother, being a fanatic Papist, thought it could only be a demon, given that I should not be able to be with child again, considering that I had been accidentally killed, in this place. Our, Otherworld. The three of the brothers planned it, I thought at the time, with locking out my only Clansman, Grigor, to kill my unborn child, of over seven months, into the confinement," she explained.

"Isobel has a very strong memory of what happened to wee

Sakina, the blood, the screaming and with Grigor trying to bash down the door, because she was a witness to it all. It was too late to save wee Sakina, only me. By the time Grigor broke the door down, he saw what had occurred, packed up all our belongings, then packed up two horses and silently put us on the horses, after Sakina's wee burial. Only Alex attended that burial. Grigor took both Isobel and I and himself away permanently, from their home, in Glenmoriston. He just rode and rode, until we ended up here in the Aird, where we were handfast," Zahra said, feeling sad and miserable all over again.

Isobel began to cry and the two of them hugged each other, over their shared grief.

"Ma, I'm sorry. I will pray for wee Sakina," Ali said.

Fatma began weeping too, so Coinneach regretted having asked who Sakina was.

"You are an idiot sometimes Coinneach," Prince Griogar said and Coinneach, agreed and took his wife to bed, as she had requested.

Prince Griogar looked around at all their faces. John Fraser appeared to know the whole sad story and dropped his head in sorrow for both Zahra and Isobel and the pain of that wee bairn. Simon was new to all of it, and it made him feel ill. He started cleaning up the kitchen silently and planned to go to bed with Fatma afterwards. Prince Griogar thought there were many things yet to learn about his sister-in-law, not in the usual way you learn of hidden events.

Zahra hid what she couldn't bear to speak of, not an evil design of her own, but evil committed against her.

That explained why the rest of the men disposed of were, all of the Chisholm's and the prince agreed then with their actions and hoped Hugh would not re-appear, although he couldn't understand a man who would kill his own bairn. That left only questions.

Returning to Beinn Coinneach immediately may not be the right decision. Had they bought all the bairns with them, they probably should have stayed longer in the Aird, but all four, as well as Hector, were back on Beinn Coinneach. The family felt wrongly split up in that very moment, he thought. Even he missed the presence of Zahra's son, Hector, and her grandchildren. She was indeed a unique woman amongst them.

Zahra slept for a while but then she awoke to the sound of her wolf, howling for a mate to appear.

"Oh Wolfie," Zahra lamented as she climbed out of bed. She cried looking out of the bedroom window. Would another wolf find him and respond? She was joined by Coinneach listening and holding his wife to keep her warm. Naked as they both stood there, he wrapped his big arms completely around her to keep her warm. His massive body was warm up against her bare skin and especially soothing, as he kissed her gently on her lovely bare neck.

"He will, my love," Coinneach said, as if he knew her thoughts. "Wolfie will find a mate in time".

He lifted her up gently and easily, kissing her big belly. He was aroused in these surroundings, with nature so close to them and he rubbed her body all along both her sides, as well as her belly placing her back comfortably on the bed and kneeled before her legs as he opened them both up to himself gently.

"Just relax my dear and I will do everything to bring you pleasure," Coinneach said.

Zahra was magical where sex was concerned, and he waited until she begged him to enter, which he did with his large appendage. He gently entered her, trying hard not to enter too fast, fearing for their bairn and with the backdrop of the sounds of the howling of the wolf and the crackling of the fire, the two of them both came to orgasm, with Coinneach groaning loudly. It was a powerful statement being in the marriage bed, of her previous husband, Grigor MacGregor, who at one time she could not ever have imagined living without. That hadn't stopped Zahra thinking of him, just the same.

"Can I ask you a delicate question my love?" Coinneach asked. "Should I purchase a small property for your former husband a long way from all of us, north of here, or even further," he asked.

"Why? His homelands are south I think, near Argyle?" Zahra asked.

"Because he saved you once, at least and he is the biological father of the bairns," Coinneach replied.

"That's true but ask your brother just the same and give the task to the two of them, to achieve together if they both agreed to it, which I doubt. However, if they both did, please give the task to the prince. Our bairn is coming soon, and we will be too busy," Zahra opined.

"You must stay with me now please Coinneach. Doctor Heath is due on the mountain soon," Zahra remembered.

"So is Lillian, the Midwife. We are getting busy, aren't we?" Coinneach agreed.

"Will you finish the paintings of me and Wolfie, as well as your brother's paintings?" Zahra asked.

"Of course, in the morning I will talk to the farm manager here and get the overall understanding of how the work is all coming along here and when Ali is starting the ploughing and then we can all leave. On the way home, we need to stop in Inverness, is that okay with you my dear?" he asked.

"What for?" Zahra asked again.

"I need some new tartan. Do you need anything new too?" Coinneach asked.

"Can I have a new tartan arisaid. Nothing fits me anymore and I am so fat. I need a thick woollen MacGregor arisaid," she asked.

"Of course, my sexy one, we will choose a nice one, won't we?" Coinneach said.

After the business was over at 'Wolf Ranch' and all the emotional farewells said. En route to Inverness, her brother-in-law was asked his opinion concerning purchasing land for Grigor MacGregor and he was horrified at the idea but said he would think about it. His plan, however, was quite the opposite. The fate of the Chisholm brothers was far more appealing to him, rather than a reward for Grigor Mohr MacGregor.

After the work his army had done, it felt like a slap in the face for his work, which he took very seriously. Grigor Mohr MacGregor might have to be disposed of was what he was thinking. He hoped that Zahra would not miss her ex-husband and father to most of her bairns and so, this was what he set out to do and only the most trusted chiefs of his army, would be aware of his plan.

Grigor Mohr MacGregor however, had disappeared and no one knew where he was, so that made his disposal, difficult to achieve. That man was so elusive to the likes of the prince. His loyal friends would never give up his location either.

Grigor seemed to always be able to disappear into the mist, thought Prince Griogar.

27. Lust and Love

Tidying herself up, Zahra alighted from the carriage to go shopping, as did the two men.

The shopping was nice enough, but it hadn't been serious, and she bought herself a beautiful arisaid in a red MacGregor tartan. Just one year previous she couldn't have afforded such luxuries and would have appreciated them more. She bought wee kilts for all the bairns, including Anndra, Domhnall and wee Causantin and a tiny wee tartan dress for Dihaoine. She had missed her youngest wee lassie and Causantin so much. They had never spent time without her and hoped they were happy in the loving care of Mairi and her daughter.

Coinneach asked to visit a jewellery shop in Inverness too, where he was browsing the necklaces. He asked her if she liked a particular ruby stone that was enormous, set in pure gold, on a pure gold chain.

"Aye, I like it darling, but that price is too high. You could buy a farm for that price, or ten horses. It's too much," she complained. The worried jeweller didn't want to lose the sale and whispered a sweeter price to Coinneach, who was very surprised. Zahra didn't even want the jewel, but he seemed intent on getting it for her.

"Yes, we will have it Master jeweller," he said happily. Rather than boxing it up, he hung it around his beautiful wife's neck. "It has a matching ring too, Lord Coinneach," he added, "And bracelet too, if your good lady wife is interested," the jeweller said, as he presented the lovely ruby ring with diamonds set all along its band. The bracelet consisted of rubies set in yellow gold, except at the catch, where the safety had diamonds also.

"Nae Coinneach, please, the price is far too high," Zahra complained once again. The jeweller whispered a sweeter price into

Coinneach's ear once again. Zahra really did mean, nae on this occasion. Maybe it was her mood that disallowed her to show even a little appreciation and felt a positive dislike, given it could have bought that farm for Grigor, after all.

"I will buy them for you my dear, for after our wee bairn is born. Will that please you at a much better price?" Coinneach asked lovingly.

"How much better?" Zahra asked patiently. The jeweller once again whispered an even better price to her husband.

"Much better my dear," he said, and he bought them without disclosing the price. "They are a gift for my lovely wife," Coinneach said and proudly put them into his sporran. "Well done my dear. I am never given a discount. If anything, they put the price up whenever they see me coming," Coinneach added.

"I think they do," his brother said. "It's lucky your wife is astute," he added.

When they arrived home later that evening, they were all tired, but food had been prepared for them and servants came to serve them immediately, once the carriage was attended to.

"How are my sweet bairns?" Zahra enquired.

"Bonny Mistress, just bonny. They waited up for you but fell asleep, sweet wee things," Mairi said. "Master, can I sleep here now for the night, due to the lateness of the hour?" Mairi asked.

"Aye Mairi, you can but first prepare a room for my brother before you retire," he ordered.

Her brother-in-law was hungry and tired and went straight to bed after the long day, for which she was very relieved. Coinneach's bath was prepared for him, as was his habit before they all went to bed, and Zahra joined him. It was so relaxing in the hot water, after being in the chilly air of the Aird, it felt like she was defrosting. Their luxurious big bed, with its feather down pillows and doona too was a luxury she was now enjoying in her new life. Mairi had even placed the bed warmer in between the sheets. The luxury of it all should be making her happy, but it wasn't.

She thought she needed to talk to Peter when he arrived, which was coming up very soon. He understood things that most other people didn't. Her bairn was due any day and there would be another big new personality, to get to know and his legs kicked continuously inside of her, letting her know, that he wanted to get out soon.

It could be exciting, beyond the pain, but she just had to get there, beyond that terrible pain and fear of childbirth. She prayed that this was her last.

This new bairn would be her first without the soothing presence of her former husband and it scared her to be without him.

Malcolm kept coming into her mind, like when you see a tree as you are riding past on a horse and then it has gone, and you can't quite capture its image once again. Was he coming to Beinn Coinneach soon, was all she could think it might be or maybe she just needed a friend to talk to?

Zahra missed Grigor, after being in her old home in the Aird, but she couldn't tell anyone that.

She concluded it was a friend she needed or just wished she had been born as someone else, like Malcolm. She liked him, even more than Kenneth and thought he was luckier than her to have been born in Loch Insh as a carefree lad, even free of the Grants, for most of his life.

'Oh, Grigor,' was her nighttime silent sigh, just feeling utterly lonely now in that enormous house, without her pet wolf and nothing left to look forward to. She wondered if Grigor ever thought of her. There was no point in going over the past and wishing that she was back home in the future either, where she wasn't ever exploited or abused. She hadn't been anyone of consequence, other than her humble writing, but she had felt like a normal person, felt herself and in this place, she could rarely, if ever, feel normal in freezing cold Scotland, in the 18th century.

Maybe she would never adjust to life in the Highlands, as she slipped finally into sleep, but the bairn kicked on.

Book 2

"Shapeshifting, Haunting & Depravity"

Malcolm MacNachten

Dr Alex MacNachten

Ailsa MacNachten

1. -Enter. Dr Alexander MacNachten

"Malcolm, did you know that Ruth Beaton's old house has gone down in sale price? It's been reduced from five hundred pounds to two hundred pounds. No one wants it because of what she did in there. Do you think we should buy it?" Ailsa asked.

"Why would we need that old house, Ailsa?" I asked curiously.

"For Alex, my love. You always said that you wanted him to be the local Glengarry Doctor, not at that hospital. It could be refurbished by us to make him a proper Medical Practice. What do you think? Please at least come and look at it.

He and his wife, Mairi could live there too," she said excitedly.

I always wanted Ailsa to care for my bairns, as much as her own, born with me and maybe she was trying to show me that she cared for my oldest son, Alex, so I relented, despite knowing Ruth's house too well, while she was alive. That was where I learned of how many of my bairns that my ex-wife had terminated, in that very same house, and she tried to have my precious twins terminated too. If Ruth hadn't fallen in love with Hugh Mohr Chisholm, at that time, with him living there, giving his opinion on everything, my twins would not have taken their first breaths.

I never forgave Cherry MacLean for that and never will. And I might be a little overprotective of my boisterous twin lads. Nothing could ever bring back the lives of my other three wee bairns, that Cherry killed, without my knowledge. That was a deep sadness that I had had to learn to live with.

Ruth's old stone cottage was a mess and totally overgrown, with its garden. The back yard was equally overgrown, and the old wooden stables were all collapsing and now only good for demolition and firewood. The stone home, however, was of good solid quality, but musty smelling and filthy. The old furniture was still in there, as well as Ruth's old implements. No-one had had even stolen Ruth's old tea pot. It wouldn't have been surprising if we had found skeletal remains of her old cat. The entire interior would need to be gutted and thrown onto an enormous bonfire.

To please Ailsa, I offered the family member one hundred pounds, believing they would reject it, but it was immediately accepted, and the ownership went through to my son in less than one week, in lightning speed, in case I changed my mind. Alex was even more shocked than I was, so I told him to relax, while we gutted it all, as well as the garden and its broken-down stables, only good now for firewood.

Firewood first, I had reasoned. My stable hands could deal with that, and I would need volunteers for the rest of the mess.

If Alex liked it, after we had completely renovated it, he could do what he liked with it, whether he decided to be the local Doctor, although a wonderful idea, he may prefer the certainty of a regular wage from the hospital. Islay offered her assistance, as did cousins, Jean, Siobhan and Cousin Alex, my brother Kenneth, Ivy, and Ailsa. Hugh was busy with work in the Aird with my lads, he said for some time and was staying there. My cousin Gilcrest was asked for his advice on design, and he told me to rip up all the flooring too and remove the ceiling.

I asked him why we needed to remove the ceiling too and Gilcrest simply said, "Everything goes up Cousin Malcolm and what happened in there with Ruth, went up," I still didn't know what he meant, but followed his advice anyway and ripped out that ceiling.

I replaced it with ornate pressed tin, which was quite modern at the time.

There were insects that Ivy would have been thrilled to have had access to, for her book on insects up there, but we got rid of every creeping, crawling creature that had moved in since poor old Ruth had passed away. I discovered that there was enjoyment in destroying some things and carting it off to burn. Cousin Gilcrest designed the rooms needed for a small Medical Practice with a birthing room for women included. His wife, Morag-Freya came to look too, but she was looking miserable to be leaving our area, to live in Argyle soon. I left her to herself but wished her good luck with it all.

Even Old John MacDonnell came down to snoop. He always wanted to know everybody's business.

"What are you up to now Malcolm?" Old John asked, curiously.

"I hope my son, Alex might need it one day," was all I said.

"Alex. Do you mean the, Dr Alexander MacNachten?" the cunning old man said.

"Aye, that's my son, Alex," I replied. I'd paid all my son's university fees for years and suffered my first wife, Cherry complaining continuously, because of the cost of it.

"Medical Practice then?" Old John persisted.

"Not necessarily. Rental maybe?" I answered.

It was all around Glengarry, after Old John had visited, that a

Medical Practice was opening soon in Glengarry. The pressure had begun.

The back yard was cleaned up of any debris and I asked a local gardener to lay down green turf only with a line installed for clothes drying and I employed a builder to put in a new stable for two horses, complete with a tackle and feed room.

Two new privies were added as well, alongside the stables, one for patients and one for residents. The rear of the house had some direct sunlight and was quite pleasant. The front yard would be cleared but paved in stone, last of all, after all the renovations on the interior were completed. Ailsa designed the neat kitchen, complete with plumbed water and a lovely big wood stove, bought from Frasers. The back veranda became the laundry with a fireplace under a large copper, as per usual. Ailsa bought a nice round dining table for their kitchen, with four padded chairs.

Ma and Bruce came up to look, after most of the work had already been completed to remind me of the need for metal bars on all the windows and solid front and rear doors, if Alex ever kept dangerous medicines in there. In addition, they suggested that a high rock wall was built all around the perimeter of the Practice, with a big, solid metal gate installed that could be closed and locked up securely at night. Bruce also suggested evenly spaced torches, for excellent lighting,

Ailsa MacNachten

both inside and out of the building, as well as additional overhead lighting and to ensure that each office space had a large enough window for adequate lighting too.

"A big guard dog out the back too," Bruce suggested.

"Son, get Alex back to ask him now how he would like it designed, whether it's a rental or if he decides to use it as a Medical Practice," Ma advised. I was exhausted just listening to their list of demands but agreed.

Gilcrest's design for him was close enough, but Alex did make some alterations that were still possible to achieve, including a waiting room and improvements on his office space. That meant he was keen to start it up as his own Medical Practise. Jean had offered up three sketches from her ex-husband's former waiting room in Glenmoriston, of a lamb, a hare, and some chickens, all completed by Helen and Padruig Grant, to decorate Alex's waiting room. So, with a waiting room, sketches, and a beautiful new pressed tin ceiling, it was complete, so Alex's wife then had to design how she wanted the three bedrooms.

Once that was complete with the furniture, including a nice big mahogany desk for Alex. My son went and registered the business name, after all of his doubts had passed.

He named it 'Dr Alexander MacNachten, Medical Practitioner'. He made up two signs. One on the heavy iron gate and one on the building wall, nearer the door buzzer.

They moved in after giving his notice at the hospital. Glengarry didn't need any advertising, as more and more people wandered past, asking questions, and were pleased to know that Glengarry would be getting its very own local Doctor.

Dr Alexander MacNachten with his wife, Nurse Mairi MacNachten.

There was a queue even before Alex officially opened the doors, as a business. His poor wife Mairi was exasperated with the people who were demanding immediate treatment, when she realised, that they needed to employ another person to deal with people control, as well as a pharmacist. My son then asked if my wife Ailsa was available to work again, as she was a qualified pharmacist, then his wife could deal with appointments and assist her husband, while leaving the medicine up to Nurse Ailsa MacNachten. In time they would also need a security guard."I think your son needs security," Duncan Mohr, my security said. That was easier said than done. I still hadn't achieved an additional security guard for the farms, so I put an advertisement in the newspaper for both jobs.

These men were increasingly hard to find, despite a course being available for them in Inverness.

2. Cherry's Grisly End

I thought I had some spare time to do my own work in my office for a while, as Alex's business was starting up, when Ailsa came to my office door, looking pale, grim and worried.

"Malcolm love, you have a visitor with Duncan Mohr. It's a Constable from Fort William," Ailsa said, with dread in her voice.

"Can you take them into the sitting room and start coffees or tea please Ailsa? I'll be there in a moment," I responded. I closed my books to contain my heart rate that shot up rapidly and I then locked the office door behind me. As I walked in, the two men were still standing and were both looking grave. The uniformed officer looked like he held a superior rank, and the kilted Duncan Mohr looked like someone from a Highland poster, not smiling or speaking, with his eyes cast down.

"Please be seated Gentlemen," I said.

"Mr Malcolm MacNachten?" the Officer clarified.

"That's correct, and you Sir?" I asked, feeling grief coming on. This was bad news.

"Lieutenant Campbell from Fort William, Sir," he responded.

"Do you wish your wife to hear unpleasant news, Sir?" he asked. "If not, please ask her to leave the room," Lieutenant Campbell advised. Ailsa delivered the coffee, and I asked her politely to leave the room.

"The cook?" the officer enquired.

"I'm a MacKenzie. I'm staying," Meredith said plainly.

The officer of the law didn't question Meredith's reasoning and so he commenced his story.

"Some young lads were walking through the back way to Glenmoriston, on a short cut in a forest, called 'Donald's Den,' for some reason," he said. "They came across a predated, obviously deceased, female human body, about forty years of age. Cause of death was a shot to the head, by a single shot. Her body wasn't found until birds had eaten both of her eyes, and foxes had eaten part of the corpse, as well as ants and maggots," he added rather descriptively. "A hunter's accidental shot to her head is thought to be the cause of death, that being where many deer still roam and other wildlife, like foxes," Lieutenant Campbell added.

"What does this have to do with me Officer?" I asked.

"We have a number of deceased people who are awaiting a pauper's burial, and we wondered if you would agree," he asked. "The homeless freeze to death most often, sometimes from starvation, but this is the first shot to the head, that I've come across," he said, starting to ramble.

"Officer, why am I concerned with this unfortunate soul?" I asked, becoming impatient.

"We realised, Sir that she had been in custody before, at Fort William for one night, after a complaint of trespassing had taken place here, on your farm in Glengarry and there was enough to identify the corpse with, as well as her wedding ring," the Officer said.

"Can you please identify this wedding ring, Mr MacNachten?" the Officer asked.

The officer passed me Cherry's wedding ring. It was Cherry MacLean. My ex-wife.

That was how Cherry died, and she was in our area still, at her time of death.

"Nae, do not bury her in a pauper's grave. I will send Duncan to retrieve her body," I responded to the officer.

"Can you please arrange a coffin, Duncan?" I asked.

"It's all ready to go Malcolm, with the horse and cart and I can take her to Cannich and stay the night there and bury her there in the family graveyard, if you like. I'll deal with Hamish. You can arrange the headstone later," Duncan answered. I was so grateful to Duncan in that moment. I couldn't have dealt with Cherry's body or her burial. The headstone was easy enough and I had to consult with my bairns to ask if they wanted to be mentioned, or not on it. She was, after all, their birth Mither. Alex, Islay, Malcolm Og and Hamish Og were all born from her.

There was no funeral to the Mither who had abandoned them and who had three of my wee bairns terminated, nearly the twins too. It was odd, coincidental timing with us cleaning out Ruth's old house and Cherry's death. I wondered if she had been living there, until we all turned up to gut the house. Despite all her MacKenzie boldness, Meredith was crying into her hands. Ailsa, despite telling her to leave, stayed within earshot and returned when the two men left then came, and hugged me.

"What a horrible way for her to go Malcolm. I am so sorry," she sympathised.

"I feel sorry for the bairns who found her, don't you?" I said holding onto my wife who I was so grateful for.

The twins were in the Aird with Hugh, so I could only complete part of the headstone anyway, with her name upon death, being MacNachten. It read simply, Cherry MacNachten of Islay with her birth and death dates, until I spoke to all her bairns together. Alex and Islay were informed first and hadn't wanted their names on there, as such but Alex suggested, 'Accidental death. Mother of four,' to be added in which case I decided to go ahead and engrave it like that and take it to Cannich with my wife, and Alex and Islay, after the twins returned from their work in the Aird.

When they returned, they were full of stories and were hyperactive as usual, until finally Meredith said something.

"Lads, your Da has something to tell you, so be silent for a moment please!" she commanded, and they always obeyed her tone when it sounded like that.

Dressed in black or our kilts, we took the cart out again, with both Kenneth and Ivy, to erect the headstone for their now, deceased Mither, 'Cherry of the Isles'. How beautiful she had been, when I first saw her. How ugly she was, upon death and that was how God had decided her fate. The identity of the shooter took one guess. One of Old John MacDonnell's men or Himself. I was going to ask him to put my mind at rest, that we didn't have a murderer in our midst.

As we all stood in front of the grave, there was a sadness naturally, of a Mither who had let them all down but who died, so horribly. I also engraved her name on the black marble plaque too, on the interior wall of the wee Chapel.

"You know Malcolm, when you were married to Cherry, I was jealous of you and your happiness and your success. I am truly sorry brother. How wrong was I?" Kenneth admitted. "I know you were," I said smiling, hugging my brother, remembering how it had all been.

"Are you worried that she'll haunt the place?" Ivy asked.

"If she tries to haunt the place, she has strong competition and might regret trying to be top ghost. Padruig scared that exorcist Priest, nearly to death, so she would be a piece of cake, I imagine," I answered.

James wandered on down casually from his hotel, hugged his cousins and asked who had died. Then looked and read the headstone.

"Oh, dear. Malcolm, how did she die?" James asked sympathetically.

"Shot apparently," I replied.

"How's your hotel now Cousin James, Room 203?" I enquired.

"I gave up trying to clear him out after what happened to that poor Priest. So instead, now I have dedicated the room to my grandfather, Padruig Dubh Grant and it's cleaned daily, with the sheets and towels changed and two meals a day are delivered up there and there's only the two of them now and no food is stolen anymore from the kitchen. The other guests are all much happier, especially with that nude painting of the lovely Zahra. Isn't she gorgeous?" James added.

"Well, our grandfather has company now with my ex-wife and aye, Lady Zahra is lovely," I said.

James kindly invited us all to the hotel for a free meal, which we gladly accepted. My twins loved it, and we all ate three courses, including soup, an enormous main meal of fried chicken and corn, followed by chocolate pudding. Uncle Alex would have loved that meal, it was his favourite dish. I was very grateful for that food, as were we all, especially Ailsa who was pleased having the night off cooking. We were very late getting home again that night, as we declined the offer to stay in the haunted hotel.

If I'm honest, I also wanted to get away from Cherry's grave too. She was present, I could feel it and I needed to get home to Glengarry, to our home. Ailsa had been so supportive and understanding, all throughout this period and I was looking forward to just sleeping alongside my wife. Before we left, Hamish told me he was sending me a suitable security guard for my farm but would look out for another for my son, Alex. Hamish said he was a sharp shooting MacKenzie, name of Colm, about forty years old, so would need to live on site, in the staff house with my students and my grandson Padraig, if possible, because he was separated from his wife and his family, back in Kinlochewe.

I liked the bravado of the MacKenzie's, so long as he got along with Duncan, and if not, he could be relegated to Alex. However, I was curious about MacKenzie lands now, since I had been there myself and wanted to ask him about what he knew about Beinn Coinneach.

Our rattling cans on the gates woke up the sleeping groom, who ran out to us to take the tired wee pony.

"Where's Duncan Mohr?" I asked.

"Don't know Malcolm. I just woke up. He was just here doing his rounds with his dog tonight," he added. By the time we reached the front door he was upon us, rubbing his tired face.

"Sorry Malcolm. I fell asleep. I've been tired ever since taking that body to Cannich to bury," Duncan said.

"Good timing for an offsider then? Hamish is sending him up tomorrow. Take the rest of the night off Duncan and get some sleep before you meet him at ten o'clock in the morning," I said. He was grateful and went home to his wife, leaving his dog behind to scare anyone off.

3. The New Security Man

Colm MacKenzie was a broad shouldered, tall man who appeared to be physically fit, at first glance. He introduced himself politely enough, but he was unaccustomed to face-to-face pleasantries, it seemed as I explained to him that we had a dry farm, as well as the neighbouring farm, which he would have to agree to and sign a document to that end, and not only that, would have to ensure that the farm remained that way, by enforcing the rule of strictly no alcohol.

If he agreed to frisking staff and visitors alike, for concealed flasks as well, then we could continue the conversation, otherwise I told him that he may as well leave. I had wasted too much time before on interviewing people, only to find that they were heavy drinkers themselves. However, Colm MacKenzie was pleased with the rule and appeared relieved and wished that more farms would introduce the 'dry' policy.

Colm was a hunter of some high level with all his own weaponry, who was known as a crack shot, could use all his many knives effectively, was an accomplished boxer and could knock out anyone who posed a threat. He didn't have a criminal record, that he declared, and he had the certificate from the security course, so they would have checked that.

He wasn't happily married, that was no secret and was pleased to live a long way from his wife in Kinlochewe, whom he planned to be legally separated from. He jogged several miles every day to keep himself fit as well, but he couldn't swim. He was familiar with farming, because he had grown up on a farming croft and knew his farm animals well and crops, seasonally. He didn't know what issues we had in Glengarry but asked and needed to know what to look out for.

Duncan Mohr arrived then, and I introduced the two men who

both shook hands. Duncan was pleased he would have help to cut down some of his working hours, so they talked about when they would work together and when they would work alone, giving each other mealtimes and adequate sleep.

"Our people here are accustomed to seeing Duncan wearing a kilt, so to everyone, that means you represent security, so can you wear your kilt on the job," I asked.

"Oh aye. I have it with me. MacKenzie colours though?" he said.

"Also, our cook is one of your Clan, Meredith Chisholm. Do you want to meet her?" I asked. I called Meredith in to meet Colm MacKenzie, and she stopped dead in her tracks.

"Colm?" she said unsmiling, without being introduced. "Why are you here?" Meredith asked becoming agitated.

"Meredith. It's you. I'm applying for the security job," Colm said.

"Well don't you go botherin' me again, Colm MacKenzie," she declared. And walked out.

"Not popular with Meredith then?" I asked, seriously.

"I bothered her for a while aye, but she didna' like me," Colm replied.

"Well don't you go botherin' any of the women folk here, is that clear?" I said, "You'll be packed off quick smart, or her husband will beat you to a pulp," I added. "One month on probation. Will that suit you?" I asked.

"Aye," he said looking disappointed that he had made a poor impression.

"By the way, what can you tell me about Beinn Coinneach in MacKenzie country," I asked.

"Nothing much. It's like Fort Knox up there, no one can get in, to even know what the owner even looks like. They had a funeral there, just the other day on my way here, is all I can tell you." Colm said.

Ailsa was now working three days per week, with my son Alex, in a compounding laboratory room that he had set aside for her, so Meredith was back to her old routine of cooking and cleaning, which suited us all, as did the extra wage for Meredith, small though it was.

Ailsa was enjoying working with my son, and it gave them all an opportunity to get to know and respect each other better and they both agreed that they needed a security guard.

Ailsa had some dangerous looking chemicals there, that she was loathe to mention and would hate it if the Practise was ever broken into. For the interim, we borrowed one of Duncan's hounds which he picked up each morning. Alex paid for that service. He was a particularly nasty looking, Irish Wolf Hound.

I decided to ride my horse that day up to Old John MacDonnell's farm to ask him who the shooter might have been, regarding the death of my late wife, Cherry MacLean.

"Cherry MacLean. You are asking me about your ex-wife? Aren't you more likely to have shot her, than me Malcolm?" Old John asked.

"Nae, I'm not a murderer, but your men have tried to shoot her before. All I need to know is if we have a murderer in our midst, or if it was still the result of your vendetta against Cherry MacLean, for terminating your wee bairn," I asked. By the look on his face, I had hit a raw nerve. I may have forgotten that the information concerning his bairn with my wife, was meant to have been private. I put my foot in it, I think.

"We do not have a murderer in our midst, Malcolm, so go on home and rest peacefully tonight," he answered sternly.

It was indeed Old John who shot Cherry MacLean, and I put the matter to rest. There was an acceptance of his vigilante tactics around about Glengarry, as there wasn't the law to deal with the minor crimes that mattered to folk. No wonder Glengarry had a reputation, despite the influx of the English since the '45/46. There were quite a few of us in Glengarry who were all competent marksmen.

"How's your son's business going then?" Old John asked with that tone that meant if I took it any further, my son's business would suddenly dry up.

"He needs a security guard, but a qualified one," I added as I was leaving. Alex had one within the day, who he not only liked, but who did his job well.

He was a powerful fella, was Old John.

4. Cosmic Connection with Grandda

"Malcolm, Malcolm, where are you? You little gob shite?" asked Grandda.

"I'm here, Grandda. What can I do for you?" I asked. "I've seen you twice now and you've avoided me.

I even saw you wave at my room on the day of Patrick's funeral, you cheeky wee shite. Why didn't you visit me, instead of sending up that exorcist Priest? I sorted him out. I've got James where I want him now,

delivering meals to me and Alex. Who were you burying then, with all of your family there? There's a bunch of you now. So, who?" Grandda asked.

"My ex-wife, Cherry MacLean. She was shot in the head by Old John MacDonnell. He cautioned me when I asked, if it was him who shot her, with a veiled threat of ruining my son's Medical Practice in Glengarry," I answered.

"He's the old pervert who paid a fortune for one of those nudey paintings isn't he?" asked Grandda.

"Och aye, that one with my brother in it, feigning love making with Zahra. I saw it when I was over at his house in his office, behind his desk. Locked up at night I suppose," I added.

"Well, he did better than me, did young Kenneth. I couldn't get Zahra to open her legs for me, voluntarily," lamented Grandda.

"Above his desk in Glengarry, is it?" Grandda asked.

And then he was gone.

Ailsa wasn't due home for a while, now that she was working, so I had left my office door open while I was talking with Grandda, but she came home unexpectedly early.

"Malcolm, who were you just talking to?" she asked at my office door.

"Ailsa, it's just my Grandda, we talk on and off, nothing to worry about," I answered. Ailsa had no spirituality or even religion, so explaining away the presence of a spectre was one thing but a ghost who could also contact you from a distance and appear as if he was just sitting in your office for a coffee, was another. I decided not to try. But she went on.

"Your Grandda is dead Malcolm. Isn't he the one that's haunting James's hotel?" she asked.

"Aye, that's the one," I answered lamely, not looking at her in the eye.

"Malcolm, look at me. How are you talking to him or are just talking to yourself?" Ailsa asked.

"You're home early love. I was just reminiscing. I'm just lonely now without you. How about we have a coffee, and you tell me all about your day?" I said.

She was happy enough that I was missing her.

The next day was chaotic in Glengarry with Old John MacDonnell and his *'army of bastards'* going from farm to farm, door to door, seeking a valuable, stolen artwork. None other than the one with my brother, Kenneth, and Zahra, feigning the art of love making and I knew immediately what had happened. *'Oh Grandda. You didn't steal that artwork from Old John by being invisible, did you?'* I asked myself. The security men at my farm were both very disturbed by their insistence to enter my property.

"Let them in," I said.

They searched my house, Kenneth's house, the goat farm, and the Art Gallery itself. To no avail of course. Kenneth managed to sell a painting to one of the lesser intelligences, of a beetle, saying it was a rare beetle, which it might have been. It sold for forty pounds for the trouble they put us all through.

"It was your cock, was it youngster?" Old John's farm-hand asked.

"Aye, it must be a popular cock, don't you think, for someone to want to steal it?" Kenneth said in response.

"I never saw it," he replied, revolted at the idea. "Who would steal a cock and a sheila like that? Disgusting if you ask me?" said the farmhand.

"Maybe then, it was the Presbyterians?" Kenneth said to stir them all up. Then they left, having purchased overpriced honey, a painting, pottery and a lot of cheese and promised not to return to disturb the family again.

I was later told by Grandda that it was on his wall in Room 203, and they had painted over Kenneth's face and tried to paint on an impression of Grandda, as a handsome, virile, young man and had lengthened his appendage, so it appeared to be genuine love making. It really was pornographic now. The maid who cleaned their room refused to go back in there to clean, so James asked a male waiter to clean their room instead and he loved the new artwork but had to sign a document saying that he had never seen it. James was really getting into the whole 'bad ghost' thing.

Alexander MacDonald still had hope that Isobel would allow him back one day to be with his lads. Unknown to him, Isobel was with child again and starting to show and congratulating her current husband, John Fraser for their 'little miracle', forgetting poor old Lord Cinaed. Isobel could be ruthless when she wanted something. Her two bairns with Alex, Domhnall and Anndra were due back in the Aird any day now that all the work was completed, as well as the ploughing and Hugh's team had left, with Angus and my twins.

According to Hugh, Ali had turned useless soil, into nutritious soil and was seeding now. He literally prayed over his crops, not unlike Grigor Og as a young man and was a fanatic, soil perfecter. The fencing and the wall were both completed, as well as extensive lighting, be it on poles, the gate, or attached to all of its outbuildings and the house. The lights were all run on whale oil for now and Coinneach had provided a huge drum of it to keep them all going for at least six months.

The cottage was supposed to only be a small construction, but due to the depth of snow during the winter months, they built the foundations of the cottage out of rock, up five feet being higher at one end to the other, due to the lay of the land. The space wasn't wasted as there was room allowed at one end for a Priest hole and the higher end nearer the old house, allowed for a larger area, under the house for the storage of corn. The house was larger overall, with a stairway entry at the front, which led into a small room where all coats, boots, hats, and umbrellas were kept. In turn, this led through an additional heavy door into the house. The sitting room was at the front end of the home, overlooking the roof of the old house, with an outlook all the way to the front gate.

The kitchen had water plumbed into it from the burn, as did the laundry and the large bathing room. There were three bedrooms, instead of two. The large master bedroom consisted of a large double bed with all new bedding and cupboards. It had a lovely outlook over the forest as well as the coos, meandering past. The other two rooms had two single beds in each one, so in effect it could house five people, or parents and four children. No expense was spared for this neat farmhouse to keep the family warm as well, with its many fireplaces.

It was going to belong any day soon to Fatma, who was still hand fast with Simon Fraser. The roof of the cottage was a very high, slated A frame, for the snow to slide off easily. The front sitting room had enormous, long sitting room windows, with coloured lead light glass across the tops and at the bottom. All the windows had white decorative steel bars on them and a lightning rod on the roof to cater for the many storms there were, in the Aird. Wolf Ranch was looking beautiful, functional, productive and most importantly, ready for work.

Both Anndra and Domhnall had been returned home in the carriage, to the old farmhouse with a new room each, because Fatma and Simon moved out into the new house. Isobel had received a love letter that same week from Alex, asking if he could visit his lads, enclosing money that he had stolen from Old John MacDonnell's safe. But she was too obviously with child and due to return to be by her Mither's side on Beinn Coinneach, so she pocketed the money and considered how to reply to Alex. She was showing now, and she didn't want Alex to know that she had been sleeping with another man.

Zahra's bairn was going to come early, were Peter's predictions. Her Mither was huge, apparently and carrying high and it wasn't twins. Just a very big baby.

Alex was going to have to wait.

◇

"Da, can we tell you about the Aird now, when we were working there?" asked Hamish Og and Malcolm Og during smoko one day, with Cherry's death was well behind them all, as well as the furious MacDonnell's seeking the stolen artwork.

"Aye lads," I said, curious now as there was obviously something they needed to impart.

"Out there in the Aird, we heard the howling of a wolf Da, and another one responded to it, so there were heaps of wolves howling one night," Malcolm Og said.

"Was there? Maybe it was Zahra's dog. She calls it a pet dog but it's a domesticated wolf. She might have released him back into his birthplace, as he matured lads and maybe he has found a mate," I responded.

"So, he is a tame wolf then?" Hamish Og asked.

"To her he is, aye but not to others, like wee bairns that

he doesna' know. He knows her bairns, like Dihaoine and Causantin, to be his siblings. His loyalty is to her, because she fed him her breast milk when he was a wee wolf pup. Zahra was his stepmother, I suppose but as wolves mature and need their own partners, they change and then I have heard stories of the wolf attacking the husband of their human stepmother, so it could have become dangerous for Lord Coinneach, eventually and even Aunty Zahra would be seen differently by her wolf, as he matured and may have tried to mate with her.

So, all wolves must be returned to the wild. I think this is what has happened.

It is better amongst Glengarry folk, especially those who went on that last wolf hunt, that they don't know anything of what you heard in the Aird, lads. If I am needed, Aunty Zahra will contact me, if ever Wolfie needs to lose his life, whether due to livestock losses, or an attack on a human. Has Hugh told anyone yet?" I asked.

"I don't know Da, we got busy with what happened here," Malcolm Og said.

"Thanks for telling me. You are both good lads," I said.

"Da can we practise with the rifles now that we are old enough?" they both asked.

"Aye you can. It's good to be accurate in your shooting. One day you might be as good as me. Just don't kill any wild birds or my coos. Ask young Duncan Og for some of his Mither's jam tins, if he has any to spare," I said.

Hugh Og had been overdue to do my ploughing, with being gone for so long in the Aird, but he had bought back a load of kelp, in preparation for my crops.

"What's all that firewood over there?" Hugh Og asked.

"Ruth Beaton's old stables. Don't worry. I've saved you all the knobs, latches, screws, and nails," I said, as I handed him the large bag of things that I had salvaged from Ruth's house for Hugh.

"Well then, we will call it a good trade. No charge on the kelp," Hugh said.

"Thanks Hugh. I do need more manure. Can you access any? I don't have enough this year," I asked.

"Aye, No problem. I'll bring it tomorrow and plough it in right away, then you can get to work on it with your students," Hugh said happily.

I told him that I had bought Ruth's house for a very low price and my son was now the local Doctor. He was very pleased about that, with the many farm accidents around Glengarry, especially now that he could access cheaper rates at the doctor.

It was a very busy week with being behind on everything and I felt I was catching up all the time and never getting ahead, so I worked harder, earlier, and longer to improve my situation, just in case something else went wrong. Another funeral, a death, or just unavailability of my main man Hugh.

I was saving up for my own Team of Clydesdale horses for my lads, after they had learned all the ropes from Hugh, but I only had enough money for four horses, so far because I was also putting away money for Eschina's dowery. One more year was the plan, with bigger stables. Once I had finished with the seeding, I started on the bigger stables that Hugh and I had designed that could house two Teams at the one time. So, we also needed more grooms.

At least with my wife's wages, Ailsa was buying her own clothes and shoes and that helped the budget a lot. Grooms were easier to come by than security men.

I introduced Hugh to Colm MacKenzie and informed him that he was on one month's probation due to the uncertainty with the lassies, Meredith in particular, which sent him flying into Meredith to ask of their background. It was an old story from

Kinlochewe, when they were both only seventeen and he kept bothering her and she didn't like him. She kept him at a distance and refused all of his advances, so there was no history, other than that, but just the same, Hugh scowled at Colm, every time he walked past him and told him to his face to stay away from his wife, or he'd kill him.

If I didn't know him better, I'd think he was joking, but he wasn't. He really would kill him if Colm bothered his wife. Sometimes he reminded me a bit of Hugh Mohr Chisholm, when he was like that, although unrelated, other than by Clan association. He really could be a bit primitive at times, but his wife loved that about him, and their sex life was active, judging by when they both lived in our house.

Meredith loved her dirty, smelly, horsey bloke Hugh, and everyone trusted him and that's an amazing character and reputation to have, especially in Glengarry.

5. The Birth

I received an unexpected letter with a fancy letterhead on homemade paper, reading Lord Coinneach of Beinn Coinneach but the letter was from Zahra, Lady Coinneach.

She was letting me, and Kenneth know how much she had appreciated our efforts with their art and the money they had received but also that she was now coming to the end of her confinement, and could I please be there to assist, because her brother-in-law, was no longer available. She said she would explain that to me in person but if I could write back to let her know if I was available to assist her in the birthing process.

I was aware of how it was all done and had assisted for both of my wives, so it would require my wife's consent. I also wondered if Alex should come, as childbirth was one of his areas of expertise. It would mean being unavailable to Glengarry patients for over four days or more, so he may not agree to that, but I asked anyway.

I asked both Ailsa and Alex. Ailsa was fine with me going, but Alex had misgivings because of his current patients, but closer to the time that I was going, then he would decide. Zahra told us that a Dr Peter Heath, also would be there just for the end, but not for the delivery, which was up to the midwife. Her unborn bairn was unusually large, and she had concerns as to how difficult her labour might be. Wolfie was no longer on Beinn Coinneach, so not to worry about him, she had added.

I was ready to go on my horse when both of my lads ran out to express their concern and almost begged me to not go. I hugged them both and told them how much I loved them and to try and be good for Ailsa and Hugh and to keep an eye on my crops as they sprouted. Then my son Alex arrived suddenly on his horse with his saddle bags filled with his doctor needs. I was so glad of his company, even if he wasn't needed.

"Och, well son, let's go, shall we?" I said and my twins were left standing there embracing each other and I think they were crying. Maybe they had heard the whole 'Fairy Dun Theory' of that mountain, but I don't quite understand why they were so upset, so I planned to bring them back something. Alex was a great horseman, despite being an academic and we rode for a long time before we stopped to give the horses a drink at a fast-flowing burn.

The scenery was becoming magnificent, and Alex was enjoying the ride, and we stopped at a wee bothy for one night, where Kenneth and I had stayed previously, and we ate all of our prepared food.

The last leg of the journey to Beinn Coinneach was stunning, as I had remembered it, and the majestic mountains seemed to reach up high to the heavens. Unbelievably huge, majestic mountains, one after the other, as we wove our way in between them, feeling as small as God had intended us to be, I suppose.

Alex was worried that we would get lost in the thick fog, but I was certain that we were going the right way. As we arrived at the base of Beinn Coinneach, there were fewer farmers than there was the last time, but coos were being driven down, who we had to give way to, and then we proceeded slowly upwards. I knew we would be welcomed once we arrived at their beautiful front door, but it was quite a climb, as the mist became thicker towards the top.

They heard us coming and it was quite late, so we were feeling hungry, thirsty, cold, and tired. The servants welcomed us, and the grooms took both of our horses. Alex took his saddle bags when we were greeted by Lord Coinneach who was looking quite different to how I had seen him on our last visit. He looked worried and pale. Zahra's confinement had aged him, which I thought impossible, given he wasn't of the living, but I hadn't yet mentioned that fact yet to my son.

"Lord Coinneach, may I introduce my son, Dr Alexander MacNachten. He is here to help in response to Lady Coinneach's letter to me, asking for assistance with the delivery," I said.

"Welcome Malcolm and Alexander. Thank you both for coming," he said politely but quietly. There wasn't his usual boldness and flair. As I went to shake his hand, he embraced me instead.

"Malcolm, lad, I am worried about my wife. The bairn is large for her, I think, and she looks like she may go into labour much earlier than we thought. I really appreciate you both coming. I didn't know your son was a doctor. I have sadly underestimated you, Malcolm, my son. Alex, I am so grateful to you. I am terrified that she may not make it, despite not being alive already. She has been so unhappy since giving up her Wolfie, so she isn't getting on top of it," Coinneach said.

"What do you mean, she's not alive," asked Alex.

"You haven't told him?" Coinneach asked.

"Nae, I thought it would come up naturally, as it has," I said.

"Thanks, Da," Alex said. "What are we dealing with?" Alex asked.

I had to explain Zahra's story which horrified him and worried him even more. A stroke was what he was worried about, given the possibility that clots could have been on her brain, since the incident with her ex-husband, Grigor, in the Aird.

"If a blood clot moves, that could spell disaster, even though she appears alive, but in an Otherworldly sense," Alex said trying to get his mind around it.

"Now you will need baths and dinner before you meet my wife," Coinneach said.

Baths for us both was a wonderful idea and being so hungry, we dressed quickly to eat. Zahra was at the dining table ready to meet us both. I was starting to understand why bathing was so routine on the mountain. If you didn't bathe in hot water, you froze or succumbed to hypothermia.

"Och Malcolm darling, I am not doing so well. Thank you for coming, and you have such a big grown-up son, who is a doctor. How wonderful. Welcome to our home, Alex," she said. "Dinner is your favourite stew. I hope Mairi has cooked it well enough. We are expecting Isobel too soon. She is with child as well, did you know?" she asked.

"I guessed as much when I was here last," I said.

"Och, really?" Zahra asked. "So, do you think it is Lord Cinaed's bairn then?" she asked.

"Aye, John can't have bairns and Alex hasn't yet been with Isobel. He is in Glenmoriston with Grandda," I declared.

"Really, is that where he is?" Zahra asked.

"Aye. He is haunting Room 203 with Grandda," I replied.

Alex, by this time had decided to take the 'other worldliness' of the conversation in his stride.

"Ailsa doesn't need to know that Alex," I added.

Lord Coinneach was quiet over dinner which was unlike him.

"Are you well, Lord Coinneach?" I asked.

"Och, in my body lad, aye but not in my mind. I am over-wrought with my wife's suffering," he said sincerely.

"Did you hear that the painting of Zahra and my brother Kenneth was stolen from the MacDonnell farm?" I asked, hoping to change the subject.

"Nae, I hadn't heard. I hope it was retrieved son," Coinneach said.

"Nae, but I know where it is. Room 203. The haunted room of the 'Hart of the Highland Manor House', James Grant's hotel, above Craskie farm," I said. "They have painted over the face of my brother and replaced it with my Grandda's image and added length to his member, so I do apologise for that. It's quite pornographic now. Grandda was very jealous of Kenneth," I added. "We had to tolerate our farms being turned inside out with the MacDonnell's searching for it, but I didn't tell them where it was," I said.

 Zahra was amused but Coinneach didn't approve of the painting being altered in any way.

"I am sorry my dear. You have ended up with Padruig," Coinneach said.

"It's not me, my love. It is only an image of me. Anyway, you have now completed the lovely artwork with me and Wolfie as your masterpiece," she said.

Their enormous mansion was much quieter without Anndra, Domhnall and Hector, who were all in the Aird because Hector was picking up his sister, Isobel. Dihaoine was already asleep, as was Causantin.

"Tomorrow, we are expecting Dr Heath, as well as Lillian, the Midwife," Coinneach added. "My brothers, Cinaed Og and

Padraig will arrive in the late afternoon," Coinneach said without consultation with Zahra.

"Zahra, may I examine you now then, before we all go to bed?" Alex asked.

"Of course, Alex, if I can call you that, or do I call you Doctor?" Zahra asked.

"Call me Alex. We are friends," Alex replied.

"Oh, how lovely," Zahra said and the two of them walked off, arm in arm to her bedroom to be examined. I waited for Alex in the large guest suite, allocated to us with the fire crackling, having said goodnight already to Lord Coinneach. When Alex returned, I was already curled up in bed, nice and warm, when he sat on my bed.

"Da, you owe me. Dead people. Honestly?" Alex said and went to his bed.

"What will you do son, to deliver the wee bairn? I asked.

"I will have to cut her to ensure that she doesn't split. I have the instruments with me, just no pain relief but pure alcohol for infection. I think she will find walking around more difficult than she has before, due to the bairn's size. He is maybe a ten pounder or possibly more, poor wee lass," Alex added. "There is a healthy heartbeat for both Mither and bairn. I do, however, anticipate a period, once he is born, when Zahra may go into shock, so it is important that the other Doctor doesn't influence Coinneach too much or panic, and just concentrate on the health of the bairn?" Alex added.

The day and the people all arrived too soon, and Zahra was in labour by mid-afternoon with the room already set up with sterilised instruments, boiled sheets, and an enema pre-arranged before she came in, just as her waters broke. I was needed immediately to walk her around, with Coinneach. Lillian, the midwife was waiting on the floor, that was covered in a soft blanketing to break the fall if she slipped. Isobel had her station already prepared to clean up the wee bairn, so Dr Peter Heath was the only one looking like he wasn't sure what his role was.

"Sit and wait outside until we need you," Isobel said.

Alex was in charge, that was obvious, and no-one challenged his authority. He had cut her as he had planned to do. It was amazing to see my son in action and I was so proud of him and all that money that I had spent on him had been worth it, in that very moment. Each agonising step for Zahra, once in labour was obviously too gruelling for Lord Coinneach, so one of his brothers took over from him and continued and he went outside briefly, listening to his wife's agonising screams, which was too much for him. He wept and prayed in some unknown language that Peter had never heard before.

Lord Cinaed came over to the house quietly and went to his son. "Come and have a coffee son or maybe something stronger for this occasion," he said, and they left briefly.

Zahra's sounds altered and he ran back and went back inside to be with her. The bairn was coming at last. He had to hold his wife now and his brother allowed it as the midwife skilfully took the wee bairn from his Mither, while she screamed her final scream, as the bairn left the birth canal and Alex carefully and gently took him from the Midwife and passed him to Isobel while calling Peter in as they cut the umbilical cord.

The wee bairn with chubby cheeks and fair hair, was in good health, but Alex was worried about Zahra, as he placed her then on the bed to birth the placenta and any blood clots. Her screaming was silenced. She wasn't even asking if her bairn was a boy or a girl and then he saw her eyes slowly closing. He felt for a pulse and there wasn't one. Technically she really was now dead.

"Zahra wake up," Alex kept on saying, repeatedly. My heart began to pound in a panic state when I remembered my sons' words, not to panic.

"Da, where is she from originally and does she have any other name or language that she goes by?" Alex calmly asked. Lord Coinneach came and whispered her real name to my son and said where she was from and who her three other daughters were and their names, from that era.

"She has left us then for a time," Alex opined. "I will perform cardiopulmonary resuscitation to bring her back, but she may just be visiting her other family," Alex hoped, which he performed for over a period of twenty minutes. Everyone there held their breaths, waiting for Zahra to breathe again. Zahra suddenly then awoke, with her green eyes, wide open, and her pulse was felt. He wasn't sure if she had suffered a brain haemorrhage and so he performed those tests first, to see if she had normal brain function. Mairi had then prepared a bath and her brother-in-law, Padraig, carried her to her bath. He too, was visibly affected by the heightened emotion of the whole birthing process.

Coinneach was too emotional over both his bairn and his wife, to assist, although once she was in the bath, he was able to gently bathe her, as he had often done before, when she was ill. She spoke then for the first time.

"Coinneach," was her first word to him. "I saw my other three daughters from the future. They told me all about their lives now in their marriages, with bairns too. I have more grandchildren, Coinneach," she said. "I gave them the third book to publish called 'Wolves and the Curse'. There was enough money from book sales to pay for more publications of the second book too, called 'Secrets of the Braes and Glens.' All in the 'Isobel of Glenmoriston' Series of books. Isn't that good news?" Zahra said. Then like an afterthought, she asked about her new bairn.

"Where is our wee bairn? Is it a boy?" Zahra asked.

"Aye my darling, Coinneach Cinaed Griogar MacAlpin was born today of Lady Zahra and Lord Coinneach MacAlpin of

Beinn Coinneach. The first royal baby to be born in nine centuries. A notice has been placed on the front door and at the base of Beinn Coinneach," Coinneach said proudly.

"Come now and feed him," he asked as he lifted her from the bath, dried then dressed her and carried her gently to their room, giving instructions to bring the bairn to her. Alex examined the bairn, as thoroughly as Peter had done, and they both agreed that the new bairn was in good health. Alex carried the wee bairn to her and placed him onto Zahra's breast. Coinneach Og immediately started to suck strongly.

"He will need a supplement to go on with now and you will need rest. Lord Coinneach, please stay with your wife and get me if you need me tonight," Alex instructed.

"I leave for Glengarry tomorrow morning," Alex added.

"Thank you, Alex my son," Coinneach said. And it was all over but I couldn't wait to leave with my ingenious son Alex and quite honestly, I don't know how he does it, week after week with such high levels of stress, emotion, and responsibility.

6. My Ordinary Life

Life wasn't quite the same with my son Alex, once we arrived back home with having kept secrets of my 'Otherworldly' connections from him. It was better. I had brought back presents for my twin sons of waterproof warm coats for their Teamster work, as well as knee high leather work boots in tough leather and waterproof pants. They really looked handsome in their new clothing. Lord Coinneach gifted them a beautiful new rifle each and so their identities were sealed. They were tough, strong teamsters who could handle a rifle, the Clydesdales and all the ladies that loved them.

I bought my long-suffering wife, an eternity ring. Alex bought his wife Mairi an eternity ring too. We were both feeling grateful for our wives after the harrowing weekend on that mountain and Alex's wife was with child, he said.

Zahra was given those two ruby items, a ring, and a bracelet for giving her husband his heir, finally. Alex came home to a surprise in the mail that arrived in Glengarry before we did. It was two thousand pounds for delivering wee Prince Coinneach, but he would never assume that title. Once Alex understood who Coinneach really was, his life changed. Having an association with Coinneach MacAlpin was an unforgettable experience. He was a kind human being with a big heart who had raised Zahra up from the impossible pit, into which she had fallen. Now she was his wife and Mither of his bairn.

We all hoped it would stay like that, but life has a way of throwing other challenges in our paths, in my experience of life so far. Just the same, I was grateful for my ordinary life, waiting for my oats to grow into a fine crop, once again in this difficult terrain for oats and walking my cattle up to higher pastures and meandering on back home with them. There was beauty in the simplicity of hard work in our lives, collectively. My sons and daughters were all earning their hard-earned income, except Gordon who was still too young. He was aiming to be an engineer one day, but he always helped on the farm during the busy seasons, as did Alex, despite being a doctor. The twins could always be relied upon and kept our spirits up at the same time, with their antics.

By the age of fourteen, my twins were already having love affairs all over the braes and glens, competing as Kenneth and I once had, as lads. My wife was worried that a lassie may become with child with their sexual prowess, as time went on, but they always chose married women, they said whose husbands were either incapable of procreating, absent or just too lazy.

"You'll be bitten by the love bug one day lads and when it bites you, just make sure, she's not a MacLean," I advised.

Alex's bairn was born healthy and Mairi, his wife had no difficulty. I must admit I feel nervous at every mention of a birthing since that emotive and almost disastrous day on Beinn Coinneach. It didn't detract however from my joy at having yet another grandson and I felt proud of us all. I presumed he'd grow up to be a doctor too, like his father.

Alex and Mairi bought the house next door to them too, which they renovated by themselves this time, but I paid for both homes to have new slate rooves. Essential for this climate. They named their wee laddie, Malcolm Kenneth MacNachten. I was silently pleased that another Malcolm had entered our family. They wanted a big family and Mairi being a qualified nurse, had all the answers, so along came the next wee laddie in no time. Alex had met the Old Lord Cinaed, Coinneach's father and so he named his second lad, Alexander Cinaed MacNachten. There were quite a few 'Alexanders' in our family, with my cousin as well and no-one ever confused him with any one of us.

James Grant always visited us with a gift when a wee one was born, as Susan and he only ever had the one wee bairn, like my brother Kenneth who only had wee April. Her time was ticking by, being betrothed already to Zahra's son, Ali Gregor MacAlpin.

April would be married soon and that's when regret begins, when deciding on a small family.

7. Kenneth's Gallery

Luckily Ivy, being an academic had already started her new illustrated entomology book and needed her husband to be the illustrator, once more. It was a nice wee income from her books as the universities became more aware of her work. My brother hadn't received any work from Lord Coinneach for years when a fancy carriage rattled onto our farm, delivering work from him to sell. They were a series of eight of Zahra in her pregnancy of each month, right up to the last month when we met up with her, before the delivery. They were tasteful of a woman with child, not sexual, just enlightening for any woman seeing herself in a beautiful light, instead of feeling ugly, as many women often did, when they were with child. I wasn't sure of those paintings' saleability at all, pleasant that they were, but Coinneach wasn't asking a fortune for them and left it up to Kenneth to see what the public would pay, or even if they would buy one at all.

Invitations went out in the usual way to obtain public opinion.

The opinions ranged from high prices to 'disgusting display of womanhood' comments, low prices, and everything in between, including disapproving church like remarks, obviously from the religious corner within our community.

The most interested individual was Old John MacDonnell, who had turned his office into Fort Knox, so nothing more could be stolen from him. He wanted all eight of them and made an offer up front, so he wouldn't be beaten on price, if they all went on sale. I confess I was surprised but only because I knew that Grandda could still steal them, no matter what Old John did to his office. Kenneth handled him beautifully, stating they would still need to be offered to the public, saying the artist wanted a small fortune for them, which he didn't of course, but Kenneth was the salesman now. From one thousand pounds per painting, the price then jumped up to double that, totalling sixteen thousand pounds for them all.

Kenneth said while it was a handsome offer and he would certainly tell the artist, he wanted more and would still offer them up to the public. He wrote to Lord Coinneach with all the public's comments and the price offered by Mr John MacDonnell, whom he reminded was the man who'd had his painting stolen previously.

Kenneth's advice to him was for Lord Coinneach to send family, like his brothers, to drive up the price again a wee bit, and see what it reached, on the following Saturday with all significant persons invited, as well as an advertisement in the newspaper and a poster at the local post office. The hospital board from Inverness was also invited for the maternity ward. Government money, Kenneth thought.

On the day, there was a queue almost to our gate from Kenneth's Art Gallery. They were getting in the way of our horses' entry and exit from my farm, so I hoped it wouldn't be for long. Hugh wasn't happy and stood guard over his Clydesdales. He didn't trust anyone. Duncan's guard dog had become a regular feature and sat with Hugh growling at them. Then the expensive and very identifiable, MacAlpin carriage appeared, needing entry passed all the people, who had to give way to the carriage, whose entitled occupants alighted, of course, right at the gallery doors.

Surprisingly, Zahra herself stepped out, beautifully dressed and bejewelled and waved to the crowd, like she was royalty, and the women all waved back and many cheered, others booed. She was allowed entry first, of course and sat beside Kenneth, while people filed past, either smiling or scowling, but at least they had the real person represented in the paintings with her son, Coinneach Og.

The Hospital Board Manager was there and introduced himself

to Zahra and thanked her for representing the stages of pregnancy to all women and Scottish government money would pay whatever the artist asked. It was a ridiculous sum of money, even more than Old John this time and all those workers walked away carrying one each, to hang in the halls of the Maternity Ward in Inverness. Old John was fuming, until Zahra spoke to him.

"Mr MacDonnell Sir, is it? I am Lady Zahra Coinneach MacAlpin," she said.

Old John was all but wetting his pants at the attention and Zahra gave him a miniature of herself to him to compensate for his loss, she told him. He bowed his head and kissed her hand. Old John's heart was won over by that one simple gesture. I think he might have even been in love with her. The unsmiling persona of Zahra's brother-in-law had accompanied her there and stood beside her frowning and John departed, fully aware of her protector. Zahra was also escorted back to her carriage, by her unsmiling escort and she waved to me as she left.

I was then even more grateful for my simple life and loved Ailsa more each day.

The crowd bought other paintings while they were there and gradually left, so a grateful Hugh and I could get back onto normal farm work. Hugh wondered if the Art Gallery should be moved eventually, given it gets in the way and it was no longer working for either party, on occasions like this, I had to agree. Some people did buy cheese or honey while they were there. I decided to ask Kenneth about the third house near Alex now, that was also up for sale. It would be big enough for an Art Gallery and he could still use his existing gallery to work in, if he wanted to. Security down there was the only concern, but Alex's security could cover it in the interim.

In the meantime, Lord Coinneach had finished translating my grandfather's book for me, from Pictish into English which he enclosed with some strict instructions for both me and Alex.

And to keep it always locked up in a safe. No eyes, other than mine and Alex's were to read it. My lads had written to him and thanked him for the rifles, and he was thrilled to get any news from my twins.

8. Malcolm Og & Hamish Og

I asked my brother Kenneth, to paint a portrait of my twins, before they grew any older, to capture that youthful mischievousness they portrayed. They had beautiful long, jet-black hair, like mine. No-one dared tell any one of us to cut our hair. It was just us.

The twins tied it back when they worked and that was all. They wore identical clothing each day, to one another and wore their hair the same as each other. They were identical twins, so to the untrained eye, it was hard to tell them apart. Only their family and Hugh knew, one from the other and Hugh always knew, if it was Malcolm Og or Hamish Og, when he worked with them.

Malcolm Og and Hamish Og MacNachten

Hugh adored my lads in that Hugh kind of way. He only had the one wee lassie Ferne and I knew he missed not having a son. I never asked why they didn't have more bairns, as it may have been too personal for Meredith.

Finally, I had saved enough money for my lads' Clydesdales and the stables were enormous now, but complete. Hugh came with me, as did the twins to buy the horses at a sale that was coming up in an equine market in Inverness. Our intention was to purchase all eight Clydesdales and to drove them back home to the big stables in Glengarry, already prepared for them. It was a wonderful day to purchase them, with magnificent horses put up for sale, but my plans may have been too ambitious.

Young horses as well as stallions and brood mares were all for sale.

I purchased a stallion, recommended by Hugh who said he was a beauty, a bit dangerous but a great, young stallion to breed from with a proven bloodline on paper. I chose two brood mares and the other five younger horses who were all needing training in Teamster work. They were not easy to drive home to Glengarry, especially the flighty stallion. The lads oversaw the younger horses, who were less dangerous, Hugh managed the stallion, and I managed the brood mares. I must admit that both riding and walking that far, wasn't an envious task, but we did stop by a burn for water and to eat and rest ourselves.

We contemplated sleeping in the heather and the lads loved that idea, but Hugh was worried we might lose either our own horses or the new ones. We rested long enough and ate enough to start again while people waved as they passed us on the way, making nice remarks and even offered us food and water, which was pleasant. Our journey took us through Glenmoriston and we had both thought of Cannich's big stables and Hamish in the house on Craskie Farm, who could feed us and so had my twins whose legs were tiring.

"Da, why don't we stop at Cannich and keep the new horses there for the rest of the night and eat with Uncle Hamish se we can all catch up?" Hamish Og said.

I couldn't argue and the horses were getting hungry. What a great idea. Sleep in a comfortable bed for the night, instead of this continuous walking and riding. I had underestimated just how much assistance that we had needed to cover. The grooms might have come too, if I'd thought of it. Hamish was thrilled to have visitors and glad to have the horses accommodated in his stables. He was looking older these days, but we all were, I suppose, it was only the Zahra's of this world who never aged anymore, in their state.

"I can come with you tomorrow too and help with the horses. Nothing's happening here that needs me, and I can ask Grigor Og for a day or two off, if Cora comes too and then we can stay at the Loch for a while. What do you think love?" Hamish asked.

"Bonny, I'd love to do a bit of droving and then we can all have a barbecue by the loch tomorrow evening with the families and catch fish and cook them too, so long as we take our midge nets?" Cora smiled. We all slept well after eating one of Cora's famous, but awful stews and left very early together with another of Hamish's grooms to assist. Then there were fewer horses, per person to drove.

They were big and strong horses, after all.

We all met at the loch with our families the next evening, as pre-arranged and my twins jumped into the loch wearing just shorts and as I was about to say, 'but you can't swim', when Hugh said "Don't worry I taught them how to swim," I was amazed to see them swimming strongly back and forth and still with energy to burn, while all of mine was spent. We cast our fishing lines in, and Hamish strolled down to tell Grigor Og that he wasn't at the farm, and asked if he could have a few days off, while Grigor Og minded his farm for a few days, to which he agreed.

We had all planned a fishing trip after I had had all of the new horses shod and checked by the farrier in the morning. The lads wanted to ride on them and were a little wild in getting to know them, but I reminded them of the stallion being potentially dangerous, so to be quiet around him and to speak in Erse, as I had taught them. They needed a little more self-control, I thought. But it was early days and the excitement was understandable. They argued over what they would name each horse, but they had decided on the stallion when I stopped listening.

They decided to name the stallion, Goliath.

Their business was called "Malcolm and Hamish Teamsters, MacNachten Farms, Glengarry." They were coming fishing with us this time, because we were short two men, Bruce, and Grigor Og.

Ailsa wasn't too pleased about me going out again, but I needed it and so did Hugh. We relaxed in the boat and for once the twins matured, realising the privilege and were silent. The only thing I heard one of them say to the other was did they believe there was a monster in the loch to which the reply was "I hope not". Maybe the silence was fear of the monster in the loch, that was alleged to be there. I never believed in that myth, but I think my poor twins did. Hugh and Hamish still had that magical knowledge of where the fish were, and we caught buckets of fish. More than usual.

"You must be good luck lads. We are catching heaps of fish today with you here," Hugh said.

Sometimes Hugh was superstitious like that. The weather had held out for us, then over it came and as those big grey clouds rolled on in, we decided to head on back. We had enough fish, after all. It was pouring down with rain, by the time we arrived home, and we were all soaking wet.

This time Ailsa did prepare me a hot bath and we enjoyed some husband-and-wife time together, finally. I had missed my beautiful wife.

9. Zahra's Life Beyond

On their way back home in the carriage from the Glengarry Art Gallery, headed back to Beinn Coinneach, Zahra was sitting opposite her brother-in-law, the prince.

"I'd like to live on Beinn Coinneach with you both. My wife hates me, so it would be perfect," he said.

It worried her that he had somehow staked a claim, and she was the object of that claim.

Prince Griogar felt that Zahra's unfortunate journey from the century and place into which she was born, ahead of their current time, made life in the Highlands of Scotland more dangerous for her, with her level of trust and it made him feel protective of her. In some ways, she was not unlike a child, at times was how he thought.

He was what she needed, he believed, and he believed that he was a lot more handsome than Coinneach ever was anyway, and it would only be a matter of time that Zahra would leave Coinneach for him, the handsome brother.

"I will arrange it with my brother to have my own quarters in your home" he said, without asking Zahra if she agreed to such an arrangement.

He felt very pleased with that idea. Breast milk then began leaking from her breasts, so wee Coinneach cried out loud to be fed immediately and she loved breast feeding him and was glad of the distraction away from her brother-in-law. He passed wee Coinneach Og to her and watched the whole process as the wee bairn suckled strongly on her breasts.

"What has my brother learned from you?" he asked quizzically.

"I don't know brother. Maybe it's in my books, not yet

discovered by Coinneach. We are reading from the books tonight. Would you like to listen in?" Zahra asked.

The prince stayed and listened to the book for a while, as Zahra read out loud to the family about the Seven Glenmoriston Men in 18th century, Scotland. The book was accurate, where it was historical and interesting enough where it was fictional, but he was more interested in how her mind worked, around those historical facts.

"So, brother, have you learned what you thought you would learn from Zahra yet?" he asked, while his quarters were being prepared.

"Aye, I am learning every single day of my married life, brother. It amazes me that Zahra was able to obtain so much information, from so many different sources. She has in fact died for her craft in meeting with those men, across time. They somehow knew that she was talking about them, and they focussed in on her, through the veil. My wife was met, as you know, on Culloden Field by three of them, as spectres, Padruig Dubh Grant, Grigor Mohr MacGregor, and Hugh Chisholm.

Zahra didn't know what she was getting herself involved in, is my opinion" Coinneach remarked.

"Mairi, is it ready yet for my brother?" Coinneach barked.

"My sweet darling. We will read some more tomorrow night, if you like that?" Coinneach asked. Having overheard their conversation, she happily followed her husband to their room awaiting their baths too, when Mairi came and let them know theirs was ready too.

Coinneach and Zahra bathed together like old times, and she enjoyed his teasing or tickling as he bathed her. "Thank you for going to Glengarry, you will love my completed paintings of both you and Wolfie. Now you have me, and I have you, so just you wait for your husband, my sweet one," Coinneach said.

10. Zahra's Art

"Can I try to paint too, if you teach me how?" Zahra asked.

"Oh aye, I would love to teach you, my darling. Do you have any idea of what you might like to paint?" Coinneach asked.

"Aye, but you may think it's odd," she said. "I want a death theme with a corpse, not dissimilar to Malcolm's ex-wife in the stages of decay with tombstones and the like, with ghosts floating about and all that," Zahra replied.

"I see," he said. "That is quite interesting, scientific even with birds pecking out her eyes too I suppose?" Coinneach asked.

"Aye, the birds, the foxes chewing on her intestines, the maggots and the ants crawling all over her, with that bullet hole through her head too," Zahra said.

Coinneach was quite surprised at what his wife had visualised, but he understood that it could be therapeutic from the shock of hearing such dreadful news of a friend's ex-wife's grisly end, and so he thoughtfully agreed. Zahra's art lessons were to begin the next day when breakfast was over after listening to young Hector first giving his plans for his day with his Highland Ponies. His two stallions were busy with his mares and several of them were already impregnated, much to Hector's absolute joy.

Hector MacGregor

Hector mentioned a cave that one of his ponies had found on the property and had automatically run inside of it, so its ceiling was quite high, he said. He wanted to show his Mither, when she had the time, because the pony wasn't inside the cave, despite following her hoofprints there, then weirdly, he heard her neighing outside of the cave. It was a puzzle he wanted his Mither to solve, like maybe the cave had another entrance or exit. "That sounds like an Irish mythological tale. There's a cave in Ireland somewhere dedicated to the Goddess Bridghe who the Catholics re-named to Saint Bridget. The farmer there said a similar thing where a cow would enter the cave and disappear but came out on someone else's land," Zahra said.

His younger fillies and colts were very flighty, so Hector was breaking them in, with Lord Cinaed often looking on with encouragement for his grandson, whom he had a soft spot for. He was grateful to Coinneach for introducing Zahra's family to join with them all, and it was enhancing everyone's lives, despite their rough beginning. Zahra thought they must have been a family of very lonely ghosts, before she arrived with her family. She still didn't know what that pink stone was, that Lord Cinaed gave her, so it just sat beside her bed.

Lord Cinaed loved horses, so Hector taking on the Highland Ponies business was an exciting development for the old gentleman. He would embrace Hector every time he achieved the smallest thing with his ponies, and the two of them talked endlessly about that breed, as well as the other breeds that Lord Cinaed was working with on his own property.

Hector was much taller than Lord Cinaed now and Zahra wondered just how tall Hector would become. He was taller than his brother, Ali too and was now growing stubble on his chin. It never ceased to amaze her how big her sons became so suddenly, when the lassies seemed normal sizes to her. Living on Beinn Coinneach, with the fresh mountain air and lots of beef or venison was the reason for Hector's growth spurt, she thought. His life was now much healthier and happier than it had been before and he could eat as much as he wanted to, so he did.

Zahra's art was exciting and Coinneach thought that she had a degree of natural talent. It was a while before she could achieve the correct dimensions and the human body accurately, like the length of arms, legs, and fingers, however, a dead human body was easier, so it was initially sketched on paper, before it was painted onto a canvas, as she added things to it, like a floating tombstone or the wicked face of a ghost. He smiled at his wife's enthusiasm. She had her own style, that was for sure. His brother rarely ventured into Coinneach's art room, but out of curiosity, he came to see what Zahra was morbidly creating. At first, he drew in a sharp breath, but as he examined it and asked questions as to what each thing resembled, he then grew to like it.

"Do you like it brother?" Zahra asked. She hadn't expected anyone to like it, being married to such a famous and gifted artist like Coinneach.

"I do. I like the morbidity. It is so honest, especially the birds pecking out her eyes, however, are you also going to reflect 'life after death' more comprehensively than just one gruesome dead body, which doesn't quite explain our lives, philosophically?" he asked. Coinneach was surprised that his wife's painting attracted discussion at all, let alone more comprehensive, 'other worldliness'.

"This is your opportunity to reveal the 'Otherworld'. Why not in three stages?" the prince suggested.

"Like three paintings from the moment of death to what happens afterwards. After all, look how long we have all been waiting in this dimension before we will eventually meet with our Creator," the prince said

"If you want to do that darling, there are plenty of canvasses here, but how would the 'Otherworld' be represented?"

Coinneach asked.

"Maybe I should show this corpse, as she was in life in her beautiful form as a young woman looking confused but sitting by a burn. We found someone like that in the Aird, confused and unsure of where he was, wearing odd looking clothing and carrying the wrong currency for life here, but he had just died in a future time and appeared in this time, because he was reading my book about that exact place in the Aird," Zahra said.

"There's a lot we don't know about other people's experiences, after they die," the prince added. "When I died, it was so quick. One moment, I was furiously engaged in fighting a war, then I was in a strange place, and no-one was around. It was completely silent, and I was confused as to where I was. I was utterly lost. But it hadn't yet dawned on me, that I could be dead," the prince said.

"That's a sad story, brother," Zahra remarked.

"I don't want sympathy. I want the art to correctly represent the Worlds. Don't you think Coinneach?" the prince asked.

Coinneach had sat back down on his artist stool, just observing and listening to the conversation between his brother and his wife, and it surprised him. Few people could speak at all with his brother, so easily and fewer people still, would be talking to his wife about art at all.

It was bewildering, but he had to respond to him.

"Yes of course, brother, whatever you are trying to convey in the art, must be understandable and relatively correct, in an artistic sense. I suggest you decide what you want to convey and sketch it out on paper first. Then we will allocate however many canvasses you require. There is no limit as to how many you may need, but aesthetically speaking, three would look pleasing to the eye, as well as fitting into most peoples' abodes. In addition, Zahra is also a poet, and it might assist if the artwork is accompanied by a poem, but that would be up to you Zahra. You are planning to sell them, I hope Zahra?" Coinneach enquired.

"I will buy all three of them. How much do you think but without a poem?" her brother-in-law asked, looking directly at Zahra.

"Brother, I can't ask you to pay for them. It would be just nice just knowing that you wanted them, and they can be all yours, after all, they are not yet finished, and the result might be disappointing," Zahra answered.

"Well just tell me what they will cost, then we will talk later, when they are completed and I will come in with suggestions," he said, then left.

"Alright," Zahra said.

Coinneach was shocked. He had never sold artwork this way and this was his beginner, artist wife. He didn't quite know how to feel about having competition.

"Och, Coinneach, isn't that exciting darling?" Zahra said.

However, he didn't feel that way at all. He wanted to be the only artist in demand in his house. She was the writer or the poet, not an artist, but he knew he was being unreasonable.

"Of course, my love. Let's get to work then," Coinneach added.

The second and third art pieces were of the beautiful woman returning to her youth after death, following a period of confusion demonstrated as Zahra had wanted, by sitting beside a burn and lost without knowing where the female in the painting was, as in the deceased person. The last canvas was of the female then facing her Maker. This painting reflected her journey into hell. Then Prince Griogar came to make comments, not realising just how far the work had progressed and she became embarrassed, at first.

"I love these paintings. Especially her journey into hell. I will pay you. How much?" he asked again.

"Nae brother I can't. You are family, so you can have them, if you like them," Zahra said.

"Well, if you don't give me the price, your husband will, I am sure. Coinneach, how much for your wife's work?" he asked.

"In my opinion, five hundred pounds for each canvas, so in total, fifteen hundred pounds," Coinneach replied.

Both men appeared happy with that reasonable price, as they both continued to look upon them, as they all began to grow on Coinneach. It was becoming a reality now that his wife was officially becoming an artist, like him. They would then need to be framed, so they were sent to one of the MacKenzie workers, who did a wonderful job at that kind of work. Her brother-in-law wanted them hung in his quarters in a few days' time.

"When I receive them, I will give your husband the money," he said. "I just ask you one thing, when you paint gruesome things, please never paint a woman with green eyes. I could not bear to see your eyes in a tragic scene, only a powerful one, like your husband has just painted of you with your magnificent wolf," he added.

Zahra agreed, but thought she would need a rest after all that deep thought. It had made her suddenly feel quite drained and tired, which she mentioned to Coinneach, so she could lie down for a rest.

"Go and sleep then. Coinneach and I need you later, when I need to address some issues with my soldiers and the MacKenzies and you will need to be seated beside your King, as his Queen," Prince Griogar said.

11. That Secret Level

Zahra had no understanding of what her brother-in-law was talking about, so Coinneach took her to their suite to lie down and he explained that some of the prince's men, while intoxicated, had divulged what they had been paid by him, as opposed to what he had paid the MacKenzie men in the recent co-operation with them, that had stood for time immemorial.

Unknown to her, until that moment, it was revealed that beneath their mansion on Beinn Coinneach, was an entirely additional level with rooms beside it. It consisted of enormous court rooms and prisons, used during medieval times for judgements to be passed by the King or the Laird of the land. A tunnel led from the bottom of the mountain through which the soldiers and the MacKenzie Clan could enter, which was heavily locked with a camouflaged, steel door, at the base of the mountain.

From inside her mansion, in the dining room, an innocent looking Persian floor rug was covering a hatch, that concealed a stone, hand carved staircase, that led down into that level. It was currently being cleaned for the occasion. Prince Griogar was the War Chief and therefore he had to make the judgements, while Coinneach and his wife would sit on their ancient thrones of old, which were centuries old, to watch over the event, while he made the decisions as to what would happen to both his soldiers, who were not permitted to disclose such information to the MacKenzie clan and to the MacKenzies, if they had a genuine case needing rectifying.

"Aye but he said that you would be the King, and I would be the Queen. Was he serious?" Zahra asked.

"Aye Zahra, you are my Queen" Coinneach stated as a matter of fact.

She was then too exhausted to take it all in. "I'm too tired to understand this, so I think I need to sleep" Zahra said.

Zahra would need to be dressed as Coinneach's Queen for the occasion, as would her husband, as their King, but their roles were purely ceremonial, so she slept well to prepare for it. Upon being awoken by Mairi, she was told to dress for the event and was re-assured that the old thrones had been taken out of storage, somewhere in the mansion and thoroughly cleaned. Mairi helped her dress in a very ornate gown with huge puffy sleeves, accompanied by jewels from the MacAlpin family of old.

Coinneach came in looking so handsome that she wanted to make love to him, which made him smile but as he held her closely, he said he would make it up to her once this ceremonial event was over and after the princes' decisions were all made clear. He wasn't his usual amorous self, but at least she wasn't expected to watch over punishments, due to her delicacy, she was told.

Zahra hadn't realised that punishments were even involved, until then, which sent shivers down her spine. They both walked down the hidden staircase very slowly, as it was a very narrow, dark and damp staircase, with only intermittent torch lighting, mounted on the walls. The walls were cold stone and damp in many places, but inside the huge Court Room, an enormous fire was raging in its ornate fireplace to keep the large space warm enough and she wondered where that chimney went to. She made a point of counting all the chimneys from the outside, on her mental check list.

Zahra hadn't known of this additional floor to the home and had neglected having that chimney cleaned. The stones around the fireplace looked different to all of the others, as they had a shimmer to them, and she saw engravings in the stone from an unknown source. Spirals she thought. It reminded her of what the water at the base of a waterfall looks like as it crashes down after a heavy downpour, with some force and it creates spirals.

Zahra was asked to be seated to the left of her husband, the King and to keep her hands still and not to utter a single word, to maintain her composure to represent their leader's Queen. She felt as if she was being spoken to like a child and this wasn't the life she thought she had agreed to live with Coinneach MacAlpine and his weird family.

The 'throne' was so uncomfortable, it was hard to sit still. This occasion really had never been anticipated, or even imagined when she married that nice old gentleman, that she had met at the Old Crohn's house. He was truly a King after all, and it was hard to take in. She wanted that nice old gentleman back, not whoever this was seated beside her, giving her condescending instructions.

"Queen who? Is everybody here of the Otherworld?" Zahra asked. It had seemed such a lively place, but they too were just like her and to the outside world, they didn't even exist visibly, unless they chose to.

"Mostly everyone here, now be silent," Coinneach responded, but he was now in a different mood and wanted her silence. Maybe she wasn't welcome in this scenario. Now she knew that her initial judgement of him was way off the mark and more like the first dream that she had of him in the forest where she was disallowed access to him and forced to bow to the King as he rode off on his fancy dressed horse.

"Then Prince Griogar entered from the tunnel below, looking deadly serious, leading his army of Chieftains, who sat to one side, then the ordinary soldiers were in front in order of rank and the MacKenzies, were behind them. On the elevated platform, from where Zahra sat, facing them all, she could see all the way to the back of the enormous, cold hall. On her right was the enormous fireplace and on her left was a line of huge iron bars that closed off an area where prisoners were to be held. There were various iron implements coming out of the walls there too, so she didn't want to imagine what they did in there or hopefully, that was all in the past. Coinneach's eyes weren't good enough to see that far.

The cold stone floor didn't help the atmosphere when the prince commenced his diatribe, complaining of two things. His soldier's disobedience to him, for which he had no tolerance at all and most of the soldiers there looked terrified at what the punishment would be, for breaking their War Chief's orders. The MacKenzies were a mixture between angry men at not receiving the right wages, if that was true, and fearful men in front of the King and Queen, as well as the War Chief.

It was all so barbaric, and she couldn't understand why they would keep up those old traditions in that ghastly, cold, and ancient court room. If it had been a movie set in some old 50's style depiction of medieval life, it may have been tolerable, but they were all serious. Nothing had changed for them, since their 'King' had died, many centuries ago.

One by one, the men involved were brought forward. First each soldier, who were then asked what they had been paid and what they had said and done, whilst intoxicated, to upset the friendly Clan MacKenzie. Then a leader from amongst the MacKenzie Clan, came forward, who was clearly angry and believed that he had lost money in their recent co-operative battle, alongside the MacAlpins. That man spoke disrespect-fully to the War Chief and was immediately put in chains, inside the iron barred prison.

Zahra had never seen a medieval type of court system at work and her brother-in-law was a scary looking individ-ual, when he wanted to be. She was beginning to understand why her husband was keen to co-operate with him. Another more respectful man of the MacKenzies then came forward to replace the first man and spoke for them all, complaining of their alleged, underpaid work and Prince Griogar asked him also how much he and his men were all paid. It was established that both the soldiers and the MacKenzies were all paid the same amount of money, on that temporary basis.

The complaint, therefore, was rejected. All three soldiers who made the claim were to be given six stripes of the whip and all three men would be demoted from sergeant to corporal and their wages reduced. The MacKenzies were required to apologise to the War Chief, the King, and the Queen for wasting their time with their false claim and if other false claims occurred, by the same people, their assistance, would not be sought again. The first MacKenzie who had shown disrespect to the War Chief was to spend one night in chains and was released the following day. No further wages were to be paid.

Before the punishments took place, everyone stood as a sign of respect, for the King and Queen as they were departing.

Coinneach offered his arm to Zahra as she attempted the damp and slippery stairs in her long gown. Going up the winding stairs, the local clans people watched on, unknown to Zahra, as their King and new Queen left them and most of them were in awe of their new Queen and felt a fondness towards her, because she was the brave woman who had faced the recent threat, with her wolf. She was unusually comfortable with wolves, they thought. The older men amongst them, including Prince Griogar thought it most advantageous that she not only loved wolves, but they loved her. A common name for her amongst the MacKenzies was, "*Wolf Woman.*"

Back inside her dining room in the mansion, after the hatch was closed once again, the rug covered over a whole other strange world that lay beneath her feet, to which she was supposed to become accustomed. Zahra needed to speak to her husband about the event.

"Coinneach darling. Your brother takes his job very seriously, doesn't he?" Zahra commented.

"Aye, he does," Coinneach said, with no added remark and with no eye contact. Zahra understood that meant to ask no more questions about just how serious his brother was, in enforcing his regulations, or perhaps her thoughts on the whole matter were to stay unheard.

"I had an idea while I was sitting there and I was dying to speak, but you said not to, so I didn't," Zahra said.

"What idea might that have been?" Coinneach asked seriously.

"You know how it was said that the soldiers were intoxicated when they spread that false information?" Zahra said.

"Aye," Coinneach said.

"Malcolm's farm and others in Glengarry are 'dry farms', as you know, and I wanted to suggest that Beinn Coinneach could also be a 'dry farm' with all those same regulations that Malcolm has in place. I don't mean farms beyond Beinn Coinneach, just our mountain and it wouldn't prevent the growing of barley, but it would prevent making whisky on our mountain or drinking it. Regular searches could be a part of the implementation of that law. Could that work here, do you think?" Zahra asked.

"MacKenzies are all big whisky drinkers, and I occasionally enjoy a dram too. The economy may crash, if that law was implemented due to their reliance on the barley crop, whisky making, selling the product and the occasions where it is enjoyed. We can't be seen as causing any damage to the local economy. They have their own brand of Scotch Whisky. If we made any such suggestion, they would hate us both," Coinneach said angrily.

"Oh, do they? It was lucky then that you advised me to say nothing. As usual, my opinion never counts around here anyway, even though, we are all dead." Zahra said, feeling a little annoyed and walked off, instead of having coffee with her husband.

'When can you have a safe opinion of your own, if not at least when you are dead, she asked herself?'

As she was walking along the long corridor, approaching her room, the prince was back inside the mansion and was red faced from his flogging session, still pumped with adrenalin, unfortunately for Zahra, as she encountered him going in opposite directions in the same passageway.

He saw her and then ordered her into his quarters, which she naturally declined, as entering his private quarters was disallowed by her husband. Despite Prince Griogar knowing this as an in-house rule, he still insisted that she enter his quarters and she knew that it was for violent, sexual activity, all without Coinneach's approval.

Zahra felt afraid in that moment for the first time ever, in Coinneach's home.

She told Mairi to inform her husband immediately. No matter how many times, she rejected her brother-in-law, he grabbed her by the arm to force her against her will, to enter his private quarters. But he was as deaf to her as Coinneach was, it now seemed. That medieval court room had a dreadful effect on both men, Zahra deduced.

"Obey me woman," the prince demanded, and Zahra was forcibly pushed into his bedroom suite and thrown onto his bed, while he began tearing like a mad man, at her many layers of beautiful, expensive clothing and ripping it in the process.

"Coinneach has to be consulted," Zahra pleaded. "Please stop," Zahra pleaded while trying to kick him.

12. The Giant Brown Wolf

Suddenly the door burst open.

At first, the prince just turned to see who was interrupting them, but then in a moment of terrible understanding of centuries of fear, rolled into one second, he knew.

"No Coinneach," he said fearfully getting up and adjusting his kilt again.

All Zahra could see was an open door, but then, she heard what was a very low-level growling sound that she had never heard before, from any wild animal, but if she had to guess, it was like a wolf. Then, it walked in. Its head stood at around five feet high. From shoulder to shoulder it may have measured about two and a half feet across. The longer course, guard hair was a very dark brown, while its soft undercoat was a paler brown.

It was an enormous wolf, looking directly at the prince with predacious intent, as it walked towards him on its enormous paws, making a slight clicking sound with his claws on the stone floor. The wolf was then on top of his brother in a split second in time and it appeared to gesture to her to depart.

She thought for a bizarre moment, that she could hear his thoughts. Was it her husband?

Mairi was at the door ushering Zahra to leave immediately. While she was leaving carrying her torn gown, Mairi mumbled something about all the staff having already departed. Zahra then stopped rushing to her room and went back to hear what was happening, but then the stout, Lord Cinaed also appeared in that corridor and turned her around physically by her shoulders, to escort her back to her room.

"Your brother-in-law has broken the rules, so he is only being punished my dear. Never you mind about these things. You do look so lovely undressed, just like in my painting of you. You can't blame the poor Prince really, with all those nude paintings of you all over the place. All his brothers have one each. Prince Griogar is the only one where you do have clothes on at least. He is always a little stressed after the floggings. He should get himself a good wife like you, not the likes of the one he has. Can't say I ever liked her. He needs a good woman who will avail herself, whenever he needs it, poor fellow," Lord Cinaed sympathised.

"Was that animal I saw, Coinneach, or was it another wolf from around here?" Zahra asked.

"I didn't see any animal, least of all a wolf, my dear. Not since your wolf left us anyway," Lord Cinaed answered slyly.

"Relax now until Coinneach returns back to you," he said and left her room, closing the door firmly behind them both.

She looked at the closed door and wondered at her life, visibly shaking and holding the ridiculous and torn gown. Had she married a werewolf? Did they exist in Scotland? She didn't know her folklore well enough, like her former husband did. He would have known exactly what that was. Could she contact Malcolm the way he and Padruig did, to ask if there were Scottish werewolves, capable of telepathic communication with humans. This animal was on all four legs with nasty, long, and sharp teeth and a growl that seemed to rumble inside your stomach that made her feel nauseous. 'What do I do now?' she asked herself. All three bairns were safe with her, but that didn't answer all of her questions.

Then in walked a calm looking Coinneach, combing his

dishevelled beard.

"My darling love. Are you still annoyed at not having your say around here?" Coinneach jested.

"Nae Coinneach, but I do want to know the truth of what just happened, if you don't mind. I would never disclose it to a living soul. It would also not affect how I would feel about you," she said, still cold, shivering and undressed.

He agreed to tell her on those conditions, so it would never be repeated and neither would her real name ever be repeated. They both had their secrets, each which they both agreed to respect. Zahra always knew he was the giant brown wolf from that day forward, but whether he could shape shift into a wolf, or if he was a werewolf was still unclear. He insisted that none of it was to be revealed to the living or the unalive.

He trusted Zahra with that information and the severely injured Prince never broke those rules again in their home. Everything had to always be under Coinneach's terms. Prince Griogar would never be satisfied with that arrangement, so both men were now back to where they began with their centuries old dispute over a woman.

Breakfast, the following day was the most awkward of times. Glancing at the Prince across the breakfast table, he was sporting shocking injuries that no-one even dared to attend to. Lord Cinaed joined them too for breakfast, in case unnecessary information was leaked, she thought. Hector noticed the injuries, of course but thought better of asking what had happened to his uncle, who may have been in a fight, he thought. Even his uncle's eyes were bloodshot, and bits of flesh seemed to be missing from his ears. The gash down his cheek was so deep that Hector thought that it should be stitched, but he chose to say nothing.

"Grandda Cinaed, are you coming down to see how the ponies are coming along?" Hector asked, hoping to depart the ugly scene.

"I'd love to son. I love anything to do with horses. You might be able to sell one soon," Lord Cinaed said, positively excited.

The two of them walked off very happily together. They were becoming closer than Coinneach was with Hector. Hector had no interest in artistic things, and he wasn't an intellectual either. They lacked common ground. Coinneach also seemed to have a soft spot for Ali who reminded him of himself in some ways. Hector may have been more of a threat, in a masculine way, rather than as a loving son.

Zahra thought of trying that cosmic connection with her friend, Malcolm. This must have been why she had kept thinking of him.

◇

13. What did Malcolm Hear?

"Did Kenneth end up buying that third house Malcolm?" Ailsa asked.

"Aye love, he did. He had enough money with the sales from the nudey paintings. It wasn't as cheap as the first house that we bought for Alex. It cost Kenneth three hundred pounds, but the owners were very keen to move out. It was in a much better condition, thank goodness, but he is employing an architect to design an Art Studio for him and a builder too, so it will all look professional. He still wants to live and work here on the farm, which I am glad about. He wants to then transfer his finished work, or work completed by other artists, like Lord Coinneach, directly to the new Art Gallery, which will have restricted opening times, depending on what there was to sell at the time.

Kenneth is hoping that more artists will want to display their work in the new gallery, so that he isn't only known as the nudey Art Gallery being spread by the church. It will free up our farm too then, especially with the two Clydesdale Teams working out of here soon and Hugh will be much happier," I replied.

"Hugh is taking out two of the new horses each week to train them for my twins, God bless him, so that will take a while, but Hugh is not getting any younger, so he sees he will need to be replaced in time. Presently, we need two working teams, so I hope he doesn't retire for a long time yet. They are also training up two new teamsters, one for Hugh and one for Malcolm Og and Hamish Og. Those young men are also learning Erse from Jean, to take the load off him. They are also paying Jean, so she's thrilled. There were no female applicants for the job if you were wondering. Isobel of Glenmoriston might go down in history, as the only female teamster, ever in these Highlands," I explained to Ailsa.

"Mind you with the Clearances not slowing down, there won't be many people left up here in our part of the world to need many teams, eventually," I added.

My crops were coming along beautifully, despite locals telling me all the time that I would fail with growing oats in Glengarry, but bedrock on my land was much further down than on other properties, except Old John's which was like mine. My coos were calving as well, the goats were all having wee kids and producing milk. Cheese from our farm was now well known and we were selling it at the local bakery by the loch, so they weren't also blocking our farm gate entrance.

My two security guards were both getting along well, and Meredith wasn't bothered at all. In fact, one of the new goat milkers was bothering Colm, he said and asked if he was allowed to respond, given the rules. I asked Colm if he had separated from his wife yet and he had in fact divorced her and his ex-wife was living in his family home temporarily, until all their children had left home or were married. He was then able to respond to young Annie Colquhoun. She was new to Glengarry and lived with her widowed Aunt, who was a MacDonnell, but only Islay knew all their backgrounds from the goat farm, and I thought I would discuss it with her at teatime.

I had some paperwork to complete, as was the usual and locked the office door behind me. I had learned my lesson from leaving it open. Even if Ailsa was at work, I always closed the door now. While deep in concentration, I thought I heard a scratchy sound, like if someone was trying to get my attention at the window. I looked out of my window and there was no-one there, so I went back to work. I thought I heard it again, but this time a more complete, audible sound could be heard. Then I remembered how it was when I was trying to learn how to contact Grandda. I concluded that someone was trying to contact me, who must know me, or I could not hear it at all. It wouldn't have been Cherry. She wouldn't get through and she hated this way of communicating anyway. I listened more closely, as if I was a deaf person and unable to really distinguish sounds.

Then I heard an audible sound that I thought was repeating my name, 'Malcolm'.

I was aware of someone trying to reach me and it was a female voice. I didn't want to believe that Zahra could possibly achieve this cosmic communication right away, lest I be disappointed, but when I heard it again, it became clearer.

"Malcolm, Malcolm, it's me, Zahra. Can you hear me? Malcolm?" the voice repeated.

"Zahra, is it you?" I asked.

"Aye, it's me Malcolm. Can I please talk to you in this way? Sorry I couldn't do it right," Zahra said.

"Zahra, it's amazing you can contact me like this, the same as Grandda. It's not easy. What can I do for you?" I asked.

"Is there a werewolf type of creature in Scotland that can communicate through his mind and have ill intentions only towards an evil doer, not everyone, or is there an ability for some people to shape shift into the body of a huge wolf? It has brownish fur and is about five feet high and more than two feet across?" Zahra asked.

"Aye. The Cu Sidhe. The great fairy dog. It's a malevolent fairy that lives in the Highlands, it may have glowing yellow eyes, its fur may appear greenish. It may let out three howls and if so, you have to get to safety before the third howl, lest it steal your soul. If you are breastfeeding, you may be forced to give the milk to them in the Fairy Realm. If not, they accompany the Sidhe, the ancient spirits. Their paws are bigger than the hand of a man. Is that what you have seen?" I asked.

"Aye, I have I think, but it wasn't green, it was brown," Zahra said.

"On the Isles, there are others, as well as in Ireland and Wales. The Grimm is English which is a black dog. In Irish mythology, shape shifting is found more readily. In Irish mythology men can take the shape of wolves, as well as the Goddess, Morrigan. Also in Ireland, King Nuada, and his entire family were said to all be able to change into the shape of the wolf, in days of auld. It was a transformation of their bodies into wolves while their actual bodies slept," I said.

"In Scotland, Saint Patrick also cursed a tribe of the Picts into being wolves because they howled at him. There's lots of folklore concerning the wolf. If you have just started researching this topic, go to your massive library on Beinn Coinneach and start with Ireland and that curse, then the Cu Sidhe here in Scotland," I advised.

And she was gone.

I heard a knock on my office door and when I opened it, my daughter Islay, just stood there looking at me at first and then with an excuse to enter my office, she proceeded to tell me that her new milker, Annie, was becoming involved with Colm MacKenzie, my new security guard. I was aware already of this, because he had already asked me if he could court Annie.

"He's a MacKenzie, isn't he Da, like my husband, Angus? You could ask him about that 'wolf thing' that you were just talking about," Islay said smiling cheekily.

"Why ask him?" I asked.

"He knows more than you think Da. In the meantime, I can give you my book on the 'Cu Sidhe'," Islay said.

"Were you were listening at the door again, then Islay?" I asked.

"Aye, but you don't exactly speak quietly Da. Besides which, you may as well stop pretending to me that you can talk to the dead, via some method, unknown to most mere mortals," Islay said.

"I was contacted by Zahra. She has never contacted me before. She is concerned about a huge werewolf or shape shifting person and asked me if such a thing existed here in Scotland," I admitted.

"Please do not repeat this to Ailsa," I asked.

"I won't. But speak again with Colm. I heard him call Beinn Coinneach a giant Fairy Dun," Islay said. "You might have been lucky to have been allowed to leave that day," Islay jested.

"I didn't know that you were reading up on the Sidhe too," I added.

"Da, I'm a font of knowledge. I would like to go up there with you next time with our son and both of our daughters unless Padraig is busy," she added smiling.

"What would Angus say about that?" I asked a little surprised.

"He can come too, if he can be spared, however I doubt it. The Teams are very busy right now, what with training up each one of the new Clydesdales, as well as two more men and two more grooms too," Islay replied.

"Nae to the young lassies. But aye to you if you can still remember how to ride a horse," I added sarcastically.

"Don't insult me Da and both of my lassies can ride well too. They are both hard workers on the goat farm and they have never been anywhere, except here. Please Da, Winnifred is almost thirteen now. Your Granma was betrothed at that age, and they are a bit jealous of their cousin April, already being betrothed to that handsome young Ali MacAlpin. They want to meet a young man too and their brother Padraig will be there unless you send him off to another one of your unusual, faraway jobs," Islay added.

"I'll think about it unless Padraig goes to the two places, I need him to go for headstones. Where's Colm? Send him in please Islay," I added.

Colm MacKenzie was doing a good job by all accounts and so far, there had been no complaints about him. The month was nearly up, so I wanted to ask him if he was still keen to stay on in my employ. I also wanted to know why he hadn't told me about Beinn Coinneach, when I had specifically asked him about it, so here was his opportunity to tell me everything he knew, even if it seemed irrelevant. He was looking more confident these days, maybe because they were already handfast, so I asked him.

"Are you handfast yet Colm?"

"Oh aye, the same day I asked you Malcolm," Colm answered quite proudly.

"And if the lass is with child, you will marry her then in the Kirk?" I asked.

"Of course, I will. That'd be bonny, aye," he answered enthusiastically.

"I have other questions relating to Beinn Coinneach. I under-stand there is more that you haven't told me?" I said bluntly.

He sat down and apologised first.

"I am sorry Malcolm, but where I come from, no-one dares to speak of Beinn Coinneach. They have a nasty War Chief, who apparently goes by the name of Prince Griogar, who ensures that no-one steps out of line and that includes my family. My whole family still live near there and I don't want any trouble going their way," Colm replied.

"Now you live here, and it will not be divulged who told me, so what do you know about Beinn Coinneach?" I asked him again.

"When I was wee, all of us lads were terrified of the giant brown wolf that was said to live there, but no-one has ever seen it, so as an adult I thought it must just be a story that was made up to keep us young lads off that mountain, for some reason. My Grandma said, that her Grandma said, that there was a time when you could not see Beinn Coinneach at all, not even on a sunny day. But time went by and by this, I mean centuries of time, it was said that due to some mistake made by one of the MacAlpins, their invisible mountain, became visible once more. There are days when you can barely see it through mist now and rain or cloud descends to cover it, but we are aware that Beinn Coinneach, exists now. It was invisible after the death of King Coinneach of Alba she said to me, and that was where his soul resided and other souls joined him there, as well as his entire family and followers loyal to them, but all dead. It is said that there are still secret levels under the main mansion, where prisoners were kept.

King Coinneach continued his reign in death, she told me, as he was a very powerful King and if it hadn't been for his brother, Prince Griogar, who was also a King of the Picts, in his own right, the mountain may still be invisible. His first wife was stolen it is said from the Sidhe and the Fairy King's fury turned King Coinneach into an enormous wolf. The whole mountain used to be called Fairy Mountain. This part I don't believe. His second wife then died in childbirth leaving him alone, waiting on a woman who was said to be coming to him. A lot of this is pure myth, but my people believe it and are very loyal to the MacAlpins, visible or not.

I am told, that there is a secret tunnel under that mountain to reach the lower levels of the mansion where judgement on wrong doers is passed down. Essentially Malcolm, he is alive in death but functioning still, as a King. The rumour going around before I left, was that he had married, again to that woman, not of our time and they were going to have a royal baby, born into this era. Weird stuff, don't you think? That's why I didn't tell you Malcolm," Colm added.

"You would have thought I was a bit crazy," Colm said.

"Aye, strange indeed but thank you Colm and I don't think you are crazy. Now are you wanting to stay on here. Might as well get that out of the way and sign it off," I added.

"Och aye, I do, thankyou Malcolm. Do you know of a house

Annie, and I can rent together?" Colm asked.

"Ask for her families' permission first, then I can arrange it," I said. "I don't want unhappy parents, turning up with rifles pointed at me," I added.

"Okay, I'll get their permission first. God, that's scary. Can you please write me a reference boss?" Colm asked.

"I can," I said, and he went back to work.

I wasn't sure what to think about my newly acquired information. Somehow the mountain previously having been invisible, eerie as it was, seemed believable. The man I knew as Lord Coinneach being King Coinneach of Alba was less believable. The giant wolf having come up twice now, was becoming scarily believable. I understood from Colm's story of the myth was the mountain became visible after a wrong was committed and that wrong was connected to his brother Griogar and his first wife. This had to have been a wrong of huge proportions. Was she a woman of such piety that her husband's infidelity broke her heart? I didn't believe the Sidhe part.

Scots all used to be so superstitious about the Sidhe, even my Ma still leaves milk out for the Fairies.

I decided, at long last, to read that book on the MacNachten family history, that Matilda's parents gave to me, along with the painting of my grandfather, Nachtain MacNachten. I had never named my bairns after him and I wondered if I should have. My own father was also Nachtain MacNachten, so the name was obviously intended to remain in our family. The first name of the MacNachten woman who married Prince Grigor was unknown to me.

Kenneth and I were due to go to Beinn Coinneach soon and I made sure that I was going to go with him. Islay and her daughters had invited themselves along too. The book that was in my safe, translated by Coinneach, could also contain some answers, but one at a time. That book in the safe felt ominous. Not everything the Druids did was angelic.

14. Back on Beinn Coinneach

While Zahra was feeding her wee bairn, Coinneach Og, her husband approached her lovingly, watching over their bairn, sucking strongly. Coinneach frequently touched his lips as the bairn sucked, as well as her breasts and felt her other breast to feel how much milk she had for him.

"You have so much milk, my darling. Do you always have so much milk?" Coinneach asked.

"Aye, always. It leaks through my clothes sometimes, which is a bit annoying," Zahra said.

"Can you afford to give some of your milk to another?" Coinneach asked.

"Och aye. What wee bairn needs my milk darling?" Zahra asked.

"Well, it's not a bairn. It's my father who needs it, to stay healthy. Can you allow him to nurse from you? I would be there the whole time and it's only for his good health and I will need it too soon. He is here waiting for your reply," Coinneach added abruptly.

Zahra expressed her milk into a cup and gave it to him that way. She was too shocked to comment about breast feeding his father. Coinneach was different these days, somehow and she couldn't quite put her finger on it.

"Coinneach, I need you," she then said and Coinneach took her to their room to make love and his hand massaged her now throbbing, womanhood.

"Does the nursing cause that with Coinneach Og," Coinneach asked.

"Aye it makes me want you," Zahra replied.

"Clever little trick, expressing your milk into a cup. I hope that

I don't have to drink it from a cup too, like my poor father. Do I?" he asked.

"Nae, husband, you can drink it now if you like. There's not much left," Zahra said with a nervous giggle thinking of her husband suckling on her breast. "Do you really like the taste? In the past I have had men feel revolted at my wet shirt, let alone going anywhere near the milk itself," Zahra said.

Suddenly becoming angry, Coinneach stopped nursing from his wife, as if she had become someone else. Someone forbidden.

"What men would that be?" Coinneach asked in a much lower tone.

"It was Padruig, when he tried to kidnap me in Inverness, from Peter Heath's house. They had laid siege to us all and wouldn't leave. In trying to kidnap me, he soon found that my blouse was wet, because my twin bairns were then overdue to be fed. I told you this story. He was revolted by my breast milk, leaking through my clothes, was my point. I was cold because of it and wanted to feed my bairns, who were back inside Peter's house. It was Alex who took me back. They hadn't realised that Grigor and I had bairns, until then. Forgive me Coinneach, please, I didn't intend to hurt you, it was a silly comparison and the MacAlpin family are all different. You love breast milk. I just haven't met a man until now, who enjoyed it. It's too easy for me to make a silly mistake," Zahra said as she stroked her husband across his broad back and shoulders, hoping to placate him.

However, Coinneach remained standing stiff and rigid by their large bedroom window.

"Do you have a particular need for breast milk Coinneach?" Zahra asked. "I don't mind because I can produce a lot of breast milk," she said.

When Coinneach still wouldn't respond to her, she sat back down on the bed, not knowing what to say or do. She couldn't erase her past nor retract what she had said. Did she miss Grigor? She was afraid that moments like this, would make her miss him. She often wondered where he had gone that day, after he had left the mountain. She did feel lonely without all of her family. Maybe it was time to go back to the Aird? It was getting too strange around Beinn Coinneach, even for her and Coinneach was becoming unpredictable, with the 'wolf thing' too. She curled up in bed in the foetal position, hugging her own knees for comfort.

'Oh Grigor, I wish this had never happened', she thought. She was failing in her new marriage too. 'God please don't let me fail again' she prayed. The Aird was the answer she thought.

"I am going home to the Aird tomorrow Coinneach. I want to see my family. I hope you won't mind. Just for a wee while to see Ali and my dear daughters again. I love them all so much. I must see them my love. Are you alright with my taking Coinneach Og with me?" Zahra asked. He was still just rigid and staring out of the window, fidgeting with his long fingernails.

"Coinneach come to bed, you will get cold darling," Zahra said innocently.

He then turned suddenly and growled at her through enormous, sharp, lupine teeth that retracted as quickly as they had appeared, then he hurriedly left the room.

"Oh God," Zahra said to herself, feeling terrified at what she had just seen.

The next morning, she awoke without him by her side. Feeling the sheets where he usually lay, she found them to be very cold. He had never done that since they had been married. Where he had gone, was anyone's guess, but wee Coinneach Og was still there sound asleep, so she fed him and dressed him for a journey to the Aird. When Causantin came in complaining that there was no breakfast, she quickly dressed him too and asked where Dihaoine was and he went to get her, so they could dress her too. She packed a wee bag for them all and dressed in their warmest possible clothing with boots, warm hats, gloves, and her big fur coat.

They all scurried down to breakfast, where there was only Hector who was eating alone at the table.

"Hector, help me feed the bairns, then can you please accompany me on my horse to the Aird with the bairns?" Zahra asked. He put food into a bag too and they ran to the stables with Coinneach Og strapped to her back. Wee Dihaoine and Coinneach Og were both strapped to Zahra and Causantin to Hector, then off they went, down the mountain, not stopping for anything. Mairi hadn't been in the kitchen. There was no staff around at all, and no farmers were on the mountain. It was eerily silent and empty of its people or maybe they had all chosen to be invisible to her.

"Lucky, I sold a few ponies Ma," Hector said. "At least one of us has some coin," Hector added. She had her jewels but no money. It was too quick, and she hadn't prepared to escape quite like this. They galloped a long way before they rested their horses. Even then, Hector was always looking behind himself.

"Are you going to tell me what's going on?" Hector asked.

"Hector, I think Coinneach is a giant wolf," Zahra said.

"And you know this how, exactly?" Hector asked.

Zahra had promised not to disclose her husband's secrets but couldn't help it as she blurted out everything from that terrifying day when she saw that giant animal, entering Prince Griogar's room, with serious intent. The sounds that came from there, made her fear for the life and of her brother-in-law.

"Do you remember the morning when your uncle was covered in injuries at the breakfast table?" Zahra asked.

"Aye, I do. I thought he'd been in a fight, so I said nothing to him," Hector replied.

"That was the morning after it had happened and I asked Coinneach to explain the 'wolf thing,' which he did and it was indeed him, but Hector, please don't repeat it. He made me promise not to tell a living (or dead) soul, so I am breaking my word," she asked. "It rarely happened, he explained, only if he was very angry, or if someone had broken his rules, which Prince Griogar had, then the wolf within him, came out," Zahra said.

"Then what happened last night, to make this all happen and for all of the staff to disappear?" Hector asked.

"The staff disappear when 'the wolf is out,' as far as I have noticed. Last night, I innocently upset him over breast milk, of all things. He wanted his father to breastfeed from me so I expressed my milk into a cup, which must have offended him. Then when he was nursing from me too, as well as wee Coinneach Og, I jested about other men whom I had known before, who hated the sight of breast milk, let alone the taste of it," Zahra explained.

"Then he became incensed. He stood up and went rigid beside the window, just looking out of there. I knew then that I had made a huge mistake, but he would not accept my apology, no matter how often I asked for forgiveness," Zahra said.

"I decided then to return to the Aird, to our family. It was all too weird, even for me, and I can understand a lot of other worldly stuff, but he has changed so much lately Hector, that I was even missing your Da," Zahra admitted.

"That's a coincidence. I dreamed of Da last night. He was in the Aird and I missed him too. He was just like he used to be when we were all happy, albeit an eccentric, family with both Alex and Padruig there too," Hector said.

"So, then what happened last night?" Hector continued.

"He growled at me through huge, lupine teeth, wolf's teeth, which retracted quickly, but he ran then from the room, and I haven't seen him since," Zahra said. "I haven't seen anyone, except my three bairns and you, Hector. I hope your ponies will be alright while we are gone?" Zahra said. "Hopefully Coinneach's not in the Aird," Zahra added.

"Ma, we will have to get going, it's going to snow soon. Can we stop over in Cannich for the night, before we continue and maybe we can be escorted to the Aird by Hamish or someone else from there, to secure Causantin. We have to pick up that harness for the ox too. Causantin is having trouble holding on, even with my belt around him. He is old enough now to ride his own pony Ma," Hector added.

"Aye, he is. Can you teach him then, Hector darling?" Zahra asked.

"Of course. I have been teaching him lots already, so he will be a capable and good horseman one day," Hector said. Causantin was thrilled to hear chatter about him riding his pony.

"Did you hear that, my Causantin? You are going to be a great horseman one day. Hector said so, so it must be true from our hero," Zahra said to the cutest wee lad.

"Now hold on tight to Hector my son," Zahra commanded.

"You will make a wonderful father one day, Hector my son. I should be looking for a wife for you now," she said. Hector liked that idea, smiled and was even a little shy.

"You are so cute, Hector," Zahra said noticing his shyness.

They moved on quickly then, with Causantin holding onto Hector tightly with the belt tied around him. They were all loving brothers, that was noticeable about all of Zahra's lads. Her daughters, Isobel and Fatma were close too, especially since Ali had started working on Craskie Farm and wee Dihaoine was loved by everyone and loved everyone in return, in her sweet little way. Zahra's new lad, Coinneach Og was too young yet to judge, but she hoped that he wouldn't inherit the 'wolf thing' from his father. He did often reach out to his siblings for comfort or to play.

It passed through Zahra's mind that maybe Coinneach's real motive to be rid of her precious pet Wolfie, was in fact wolf rivalry. Her pet, Wolfie would have thought of himself as the Alpha male when the Alpha was already in their midst, unknown to her, who could have warned her and so could have that awful Lord Cinaed.

Why hadn't Wolfie detected Coinneach's scent, or something lupine like that, she wondered also?

15. Grigor Mohr Communes

Arriving in Cannich was a relief to the small family who were yet unaware that Hamish was not there. He was still in Loch Garry. The family were greeted by two grooms, and they discovered that Grigor Og was back in the main house, on Craskie Farm, while Hamish had taken a few days off, with Cora in Loch Garry. Just the same, they were even more welcomed than they had expected. The hungry family could smell food cooking from the kitchen, so Carmel was there too, with Grigor Og.

Zahra asked Grigor Og if they could all stay the night on the way to the Aird and was welcomed to bathe and change her bairns after a cup of hot chocolate, beside the fire. They could stay over for as long as they liked, Grigor Og said. Hector explained that they had a harness to pick up too apparently, that was previously Charlottes, if Grigor agreed.

"Zahra, if you ever want to be permanent, you can have my house, Charlotte House, I love your cooking Zahra and of course you can have that harness," Grigor Og was unfamiliar with Hector but was re-introduced.

"You are half-brothers," Zahra added. They both embraced spontaneously and were thrilled to hear of their family relationship.

"Do you have someone who could accompany us to the Aird tomorrow, Grigor? Causantin may need to be with an adult who is not already carrying a bairn?" Zahra asked.

"I'd love to help you and go to the Aird with you all and help with wee Causantin," Grigor Og volunteered.

They ate first as they were all hungry, while their bath water was heating up over the open fire and Carmel prepared rooms for them all with a bathtub ready for them in both rooms. Zahra offered to make them coffee, but Grigor Og insisted, because having guests was an exciting occasion for him. He was a happy man to have the family stay over and even Carmel was receptive.

"Do you have a problem in the Aird, Zahra, or up on your mountain? I'm sorry, I have forgotten its name," Grigor Og asked.

"Beinn Coinneach," she replied. "Aye, I do Grigor, but I am a failure at marriage, I think. I fall in love too easily, too quickly, trust too readily, speak too freely and in all, I am a better wife now than when I first began here, in this century in Scotland, but not a success. I am an abject failure at keeping a man from either straying or from his own anger," Zahra said, then wept at her own confession of weakness within herself.

As she wept into her hands Hector gave her his handkerchief and disagreed with all of what she had said.

"Ma, having a loving heart is not a failure within you. Trusting people can be worked on, and you must be free to speak openly in a marriage. I would listen to my wife if I was married," Hector said. "You are the best Mither, and the kindest person that I know and trust and I would lay down my life for you," Hector said with sincerity. "Maybe, Beinn Coinneach was only ever intended to heal you with those dreadful facial injuries and love was needed in that context, as was trust. You had to trust Lord Coinneach. Who would ever imagine that he was a giant brown wolf?" Hector said accidentally.

"Oh, sorry Ma, it slipped out," Hector said.

Not to be put off by a slip of the tongue, Grigor Og responded intellectually.

"In our folklore we have many stories of shape shifting, from either human to bear, when we had bears in Scotland, or human to wolf which may have come with the Vikings or more specifically, the berserkers," said Grigor Og. "I have the books on it. Would you like to read up on it, so you are fully informed

Zahra?" Grigor Og asked.

"Is he attacking you or others?" Grigor Og asked.

"Up until last night, it was only one incident against my brother-in-law, however I made him angry over a stupid remark which caused him to bare his lupine teeth, and he growled at me. I was terrified, he then ran from our room and I haven't seen him since. No-one was in the house this morning when we all awoke, so we took the opportunity to leave.

I don't know what I'm dealing with Grigor. Why is Coinneach a wolf?" Zahra asked.

"The MacAlpin family go back a very long way. You must know that much by now. Coinneach, Cinaed or Kenneth MacAlpin was the first King of Alba, but ruthless by all accounts. He had all the Kings and nobles of the Picts killed and that was his idea of negotiating," Grigor Og stated.

"He may be the first King of Alba in his deceased state, but I am deceased as well," Zahra said.

"Aye but he is much older than you and he was half Pictish and most likely a Druid too and they knew magic, unknown to us in these times. Who knows who, or what, he could be, depending on his mood or his needs? It may have been accidental for you to find out, or a necessity arose for the wolf to be revealed, did it?" Grigor Og asked.

"Aye, his brother was breaking his rules with me. If they had fought man to man against one another, Prince Griogar would have won, but pit the wolf against Griogar and Coinneach, as a wolf then the wolf would obviously win. So, that may have been an accidental necessity that I wouldn't normally have seen," Zahra said.

"However, in our bedroom, he bared his lupine teeth to me alone and then growled, when I said something that displeased him, so it isn't only directed at others. The wolf can endanger me and the bairns too," Zahra added.

"I'm frightened Grigor, son." Zahra said.

"Did both instances involve other men? His competition, maybe?" Grigor Og asked. "He is the Alpha wolf in that household, over all you are with. It's very primal, I know, but that is him, I think, no matter how he tries to disguise it with his artistic talent, he is a very primitive man," Grigor said. "The good thing is, that you like wolves and get along well with them, as with Wolfie, so I would not write him off completely yet," Grigor Og said, and it made sense.

"Alright Grigor, I'll go home to the Aird for a while and return with wee Coinneach Og, his son. Do you know if wee Coinneach Og will inherit the wolf shape shifting ability?" Zahra asked.

"I can't say for sure, but it was most likely a curse placed on the King, not dissimilar to the curse that St Patrick placed on a group of Picts who howled at him when he was trying to convert them to Christianity, as well as other alleged 'Saints'. He liked to curse people did that St Patrick, as did many of those early, so-called Christians. It may just be for Coinneach's lifetime, being inclusive of his Otherworld as well, but it should not affect his wee bairn, I hope, but that won't stop 'the MacAlpin' factor and their traditions, entering your wee son's adult life," Grigor Og opined.

"I'll get the book for you while you all bathe and ready yourselves for bed. We need to start out early in the morning and don't fret too much, my friend. Always remember too though, that you have all of us, willing to have you back in our lives. You can live with us in Loch Garry, if you like, or here in Cannich. You too, Hector I have always missed your Mither's stews," Grigor Og said.

The family went about their baths. Hector helped Causantin bathe first and dress for bed, while Zahra bathed and dressed both Dihaoine and wee Coinneach Og. Hector slept with Causantin, while Zahra slept with her two wee bairns.

Before Zahra went to her room, she felt the need to speak with her stepson about his father, whom he clearly loved unselfishly.

"Grigor my son, I am so sorry about your Da. He did come back from the Americas and wanted me back, as his wife. He lay hiding in the heather, up on Beinn Coinneach, then spoke to my grandson, Anndra, when he was overheard by Prince Griogar, whose army readied themselves to destroy your Da. I walked down the mountain then to speak with your Da, and he just looked at me in abject terror and ran away to his horse and I haven't seen him since. Have you seen him? Hector dreamed of him last night, so I thought he must be back here somewhere. Is he?" Zahra asked.

"I only know that he was in the hotel up there in Room 203 with Padruig Dubh, until young Patrick died, then he fled. As far as I know, according to James, there's only two ghosts haunting Room 203 now, Alex and Padruig. Padruig is still waiting for you evidently. You should be aware of that," he cautioned her.

"Padruig might know that you are here already. He has eyes like a hawk," Grigor Og added

"However, he will not disturb you while you are in my house. If you go past the graveyard, then he may trouble you.

Malcolm's ex-wife is buried there in that cemetery too now, did you know? She was shot through the head and wasn't found for a while, so she wasn't a pretty sight apparently, according to Duncan MacDonnell, who stayed here overnight. Malcolm didn't hold a funeral," Grigor Og added.

"Was she predated upon by foxes too?" Zahra asked.

"Aye, she was. Birds pecked out her eyes too," Grigor Og said.

"That's interesting," Zahra added.

"Goodnight, my dearest son," Zahra said.

Grigor Og teared up being called her son and they kissed each other on their cheeks, for the first time ever.

"I was in love with you Zahra when you were my cook. It was most fortunate that Da came for you, when he did, or you would have been my wife, but look how young you look now, compared to me. Now I'm your somewhat, oldish son and I'm happy enough with that," Grigor Og added.

"If I do hear from Da, what message do you have for him?" Grigor Og asked.

"I miss him," Zahra said, and they both went to bed, surprised at Zahra's confession.

Every day she missed him more, which was natural now further removed from what he had done to her and their family, so she had to remind herself of that, to sleep.

Cannich was always a lovely place to sleep, but Zahra had her ex-husband, Grigor Mohr MacGregor creeping into her dreams and interrupting her sleep. She saw him, close by. He was still as handsome as ever and he was alone, without another woman at least, then she saw him walking towards her in a dream and his face was so close to her, that it felt like his warm breath was on her face. Then she awoke suddenly, gasping for air.

Grigor Mohr MacGregor

"Grigor are you there?" she whispered into the cold night air, but no-one replied, and she fell back to sleep. She felt desire coming on and it wasn't desire for Coinneach, her current husband, it was for her ex-husband, Grigor Mohr MacGregor. She was certain she could smell his familiar scent and feel his energy, in that room, as it always had been, and she wanted to enjoy sex with him again. Suddenly her bed indented, as if someone was sitting there on it.

"I am here Zahra. I am always with you. You just don't know it. When you are ready. We will re-unite, but not yet. You will need to return his bairn, then we can start again," the invisible voice whispered and then he was gone. She was sobbing and her bedclothes were wet with her tears. The morning couldn't come soon enough. Her choice would involve losing her new wee bairn and she didn't think that was possible. Her eyes were puffy which Hector noticed at breakfast and even Dihaoine pressed into the puffiness around her eyes.

"Wa wong Ma Ma?" she tried to articulate in her sweet and caring way.

"I am fine my lovely one, I just miss our family," Zahra said.

After feeding wee Coinneach Og, she noticed that he wasn't as happy as usual too. The wee bairn was missing his Da, who would always fuss over him in the mornings and now there were two mornings, where he hadn't seen him.

"I haven't seen him either, my precious lad," she said to Coinneach Og.

"We are going to our farm today to see all kinds of nice farm animals and the rest of your family, like your brothers and sisters," Zahra said, trying to cheer the lad up. Paritch for breakfast was made for everyone by Carmel, who had even milked the goat for fresh milk. "God bless you Carmel" Zahra said. After toasted bread and an egg or two each, the family had coffee to travel with, as well as water, bread, cheese and goat's milk. They all left early, as Grigor Og had stipulated and steadily made good headway to the Aird. Causantin this time was with Grigor Og strapped to him and holding on for dear life.

"We intend to have only one stop," Grigor Og said to Hector, as he led the family at quite a fast pace, compared to the day before. The stop was a 'pish stop,' as Causantin would call it, for them all to pish behind a tree and drink coffee, while the horses drank from a burn and munched on green grass. They then made it to the farm, by mid-afternoon. That was a record from Cannich to the Aird.

The family hadn't yet seen the huge wall constructed in front of the burn, with its enormous iron gates and its new signage that read, "Wolf Ranch." It gave her shudders now with the recent experience of the giant brown wolf on Beinn Coinneach. Now that old and familiar, serene sight of the burn and the huge old growth trees in front of the farm, was all lost, in the name of security.

There was a bell on the gate, like one of those found on the sides of coaches or ships, to ring, if the visitor couldn't get in, which they couldn't. So, they rang the clanging bell that made enough noise, that was loud enough to wake up Hugh Mohr Chisholm, from his watery grave, Zahra thought. Zahra then saw Isobel peering out her front door to see who it was and when she saw her Mither, she ran towards them happily.

"Ma, Ma, Hector. Oh my God, it's really you. How we have missed you all," Isobel said.

Isobel was noticeably heavy with child. It was Lord Cinaed's child, but no-one was mentioning that fact. She was followed by her husband, John Fraser, and their sons, Anndra and Domhnall. They were both calling out "Granma, Granma," and Fatma was close behind them, with her hand fast husband, Simon Fraser, trying to see who it was and upon seeing her, had similar reactions of joy and of course the huge iron gate, was opened. It was odd to have such serious security in such a remote location as that farm in the Aird, miles from anywhere. Zahra felt at home, just the same.

Zahra only ever felt that the Aird was home to her in Scotland. No place had or would replace the farm in the Aird, as yet.

"Where's Ali?" Zahra asked.

"He's up in the fields Ma, but he would have heard that noisy darn bell and he may come down, depending on whether he has finished with the ox or not. He must keep working, if the ox is already harnessed up when he is ploughing the new fields," Isobel explained.

"I'll run and tell him that you're here and we can all have smoko," Fatma said.

Her husband Simon looked quiet.

"You remember your half-brother, Grigor Og?" Zahra said.

"Welcome brother, welcome," they chimed. Grigor Og was in his element because he had been extremely lonely, ever since Helen died and no-one could ever fill that gap, but looking upon his happy face at the welcome, he received, Zahra wondered if his happiness may one day return. That was a nice feeling to bring him some happiness, after what he had been through, and she loved him.

Fishing in Loch Garry had to get boring after a while. Glengarry had its limitations, unless you have created you own big family environment, like Malcolm has done or you were a MacDonnell with all their history, she thought. The Clearances had left a lot of empty wee crofts there in Glengarry and they had moved to New France, now colonised by Britain, and had named a town there also, called Glengarry in Ontario.

The family made their way up to the house on the snow and looking around at all the changes in the Aird, Zahra found it to be quite different. The energy wasn't the same either, with new buildings erected and strange people having been there, had all left their energy behind.

"Have they all gone now, even the fence builders?" Zahra asked.

"Aye, thank goodness. Those men would eat you out of house and home if you let them," Isobel said frankly. She clearly hadn't like them being there and was glad of their final departure.

"Your house Fatma, is it finished?" Zahra asked.

"Och, aye Ma, it's much bigger than it was first intended to be. It's big enough now for Simon and me to have at least four bairns," she said boldly making the lad redder and redder in the face.

"Are you sleeping every night now in your new house then?" Zahra asked.

"Not every night Ma, because it gets too lonely and cold in there, so we try to make it every second night, until Isobel's bairn is born," Fatma replied. "We'd all prefer to be together, so we won't miss each other," Fatma declared.

"Congratulations to all of you, my lovelies. Well, done John. I am sorry we left the mountain in a bit of a hurry, so we don't have anything for your new wee bairn, but next time I see you maybe?" Zahra explained.

As the horses were stabled, the lassies continued to chatter about the bees and how much of it they had sold to the fence builders and the pottery that Simon was now making as neither lass were any good at it, after all. John's Highland Coos and how many calves he had helped birth with young Simon, who was learning the skill, was a big topic of conversation, now that they had plenty of coos, that no-one could possibly steal. The goats were all happy in their new house and Isobel oversaw them all, so she was as bossy as ever when she needed someone to milk or carry a bucket of milk. She had adapted well to life without her Mither. Zahra didn't quite know how to feel about that but would see if they still needed her once she was inside the warm old farmhouse. Her favourite stew was cooking, and it tasted delicious.

"Who cooked this?" Zahra asked.

"Me, Ma," Fatma replied. "I want to try and be as good as you, at cooking" she said.

"Oh, Fatma you are such a good cook now. I am so proud of you," Zahra said. That was when Zahra's son, Ali entered through the back door washing his hands and kicking off his dirty boots.

"Ma," he exclaimed and picked her up and swirled her around. "I love you Ma, I pray for you every night," Ali said. "Is everything alright. Where is your husband?" Ali asked. Zahra already noticed the reference as Coinneach being 'her husband' and not 'their father' anymore. There was already some distance between Ali and Coinneach that she detected for some unknown reason, but he was his father's son and had made the most of Coinneach's financial input into Wolf Ranch.

"Can we have smoko son, and I will tell you all, while we are all together and explain why Coinneach is not here," Zahra replied.

"Hector can add bits too, if you like Hector sweetie," Zahra said.

"Things are uncertain at home, that is true. How would you describe things Hector?" Zahra asked.

"It turns out that our new father is a bloody giant brown wolf, bigger than Wolfie ever was. Sorry Ma, I can't keep this a secret. The man is an ancient, shape shifting man, wolf," Hector said in his very blunt and honest manner. God bless Hector.

"He even growled at Ma through his lupine fangs for refusing to breast feed his dirty, old and disgusting father, Lord Cinaed and to think that I used to like him," Hector added for effect.

"Lord Cinaed? Isobel asked.

"Aye, Lord Cinaed wanted to breastfeed from me. Disgusting don't you think? I compromised and gave it to him in a cup," Zahra said.

"You dodged a bullet there Isobel," said Hector.

"Can he control that condition, Ma? Or is he akin to a were-wolf?" asked Fatma.

Ali was looking worried and listened intently.

"I think and hope that he can," Zahra answered. "I made him angry, as I always do with men and he did that and the mansion was empty when we all woke up, so we all just left," Zahra said.

"Your room is as it was Ma. You can move back in, if you want to or come and go until you both sort it out. It's always your room and remains locked when you're not here," John said.

"How can you sort out a wolf thing like that? He might eat Ma one night when he's hungry, who knows?" Ali objected.

That was when Grigor Og interjected and explained about wolf folklore in Scotland and how he may have been cursed by someone, like St Patrick who did that kind of thing, apparently.

"So, given our Mither gets along well with wolves anyhow, she may be able to work it out. Don't you think?" Grigor Og said. "He did save her life after all. I really liked him when I met him, so even though I don't know him, I think Zahra could give him a chance, after all she has his wee bairn now and if she says no to breast feeding the relatives, then maybe it could still work," Grigor Og added.

"There's also Hector's Highland pony business there, so it would be a shame to lose that. Ma should just rest here a bit and enjoy each other's company, catch up on everything and when your Ma is ready, then be supportive, if she has to leave. But equally if she decides to return to, our father, Grigor Mohr MacGregor, then please be supportive of that too," Grigor Og stated.

"You are only saying that because he was your father, when you were all alive," said Ali. "This is dangerous for Ma if she goes with either man. Why not stay here with us, her family, and have no husband at all? I will promise to look after her, protect her and support her financially until the Day of Judgement," Ali had spoken, and they all knew then to make no objection to his decisions for his Mither, unless she herself decided to leave or go with Grigor.

"Ma if you do go back to our birth father, please do not allow him to live here with us," Ali stated.

"Would you disallow him entry onto the farm then Ali?" Zahra asked.

"That's right," Ali added. Zahra decided to leave it then for the night.

"Alright son. I'll respect your decisions. Both you and John own the farm now." Zahra said.

No-one had seen Ali quite that adamant or emotional about his Mither's plight before and knew that he meant every word. Somehow, Isobel could not see her Mither living under the rules dictated to her by her oldest son, Ali but she just took it all in.

The next day, Zahra wanted to find her beloved pet, Wolfie and so asked if her daughters could care for her bairns, while she went into the forest, on foot to where he had been released. She missed him, and she was confused as to what to do. Opinions and emotions were running high in the farmhouse, and she regretted telling them so much, but it was better than being kept in the dark, as she had been as a child.

She traversed the familiar clearing between the two forests, either side of snow-covered ground, that gradually narrowed into a pathway rather than a clearing, which ultimately led to the old Crohn's house. On one side, there was thick forest which led into a deeper and dense forest, where there were caves and was slightly spooky in appearance for a woman now accustomed to living high up on a mountain, far from the ground. However, it also felt nostalgic from the many times that she had walked this same path. This time was purposeful, however, to find Wolfie.

She hoped she would meet up with Wolfie again. It might mend her heart and add some understanding to her current life, she had thought, until she thought she saw movement flicker, just in the corner of her eye. Then flicker again. There was movement on both sides of her in both forests, thick or thin. It didn't bother her too much at first, after all, she was looking for a wolf. Then they began to appear cautiously one by one, coming out from behind the trees where they were hiding. It was a pack of wolves, not one wolf. Wolfie had found a pack and for a moment, she was happy for him, until there were at least six wolves surrounding her.

Then she stopped. Looked around at her situation and they were not looking friendly. They were the same colour as Wolfie, some lighter but mostly dark grey.

"Wolfie," she called, and her voice seemed to come from a far-away place, too remote to assist her now. She was their meal, if he didn't come. Bursting through the woods came her Wolfie and jumped up upon her and licked her face. "Oh Wolfie," she cried. Then he ran away but the other wolves cowered down and moved no further towards her. He came back nudging his Alpha female to show her.

"Oh, she is beautiful Wolfie darling," Zahra exclaimed sincerely. He then ran away again and came back with a pup in his mouth and dropped her at her feet. Then lowered himself down on his front legs, made a woowoo sound then they all took off very quickly. She could hear him howling as she held the puppy in her arms. He had given her a gift of a female wolf puppy. For a moment Zahra stood there, ensuring that he wasn't going to come back to pick up his puppy. Zahra had to be sure that it was a gift from Wolfie, and it was, as he often dropped things at her feet when he lived at home to give her as gifts, like smelly, dead things. She walked back home to the farmhouse, carrying her puppy to be met by Ali who looked very serious.

"Ma, what's that?" Ali asked.

"It's a wee gift from Wolfie my darling, isn't she lovely?" Zahra said.

"Aye she is. Will you keep her then?" Ali asked.

"Och, aye, I love her," Zahra answered.

16. Coinneach Visits the Aird

"Ma, your husband, Coinneach is here. He appears normal. Like he was before. No wolf signs. What do you want to do?" Ali asked.

"I will meet with him and see what he has to say Ali. Please don't disclose you know anything about the shape shifting, or else it could occur again here," she added. "Ask Fatma to stay in her house with the four bairns, except Coinneach Og please darling," she asked and walked calmly into the old farmhouse. The last time he came to pick her up in the Aird, was an emotional reunion, but this time it was more reserved, waiting each upon the other to reveal themselves. Coinneach Og was deep in sleep. He had finally relaxed.

Coinneach, Zahra's husband, once so dignified and confident, appeared to be lost, upset even. There was no attempt to belittle her reasons for her departure. He completely understood why the family would escape from him. He may have been ashamed as his head was bowed down, not upright, and proud. He wasn't pleased with what he had done in terrifying the whole family, all off the mountain and back to where they had all felt safe. It hadn't been his finest hour, and he feared most of all, that he could lose his wife.

"What's that?" Coinneach asked.

Zahra responded telling him that it was a present from her old friend, Wolfie. He had his own family now and had given her one of his puppies, a wee female puppy. Zahra was obviously elated at receiving this gift of life from Wolfie.

"You have given me a gift of life, our wee bairn, Coinneach Og. A wolf has given you a gift of life, one of his own puppies but what have I given you Zahra? Only terror that sent you running away from me and your new home," Coinneach said morosely.

"You gave me the gift of life, Coinneach. My own life. You saved me Coinneach, you rebuilt my body and what price is there on a human life?" she said sincerely.

"I am sincerely appreciative of all that you have done, both for me and for my family, but I am now in a state of confusion, due to recent events. Not all were due to the 'wolf inside' of you. That can't be helped if you carry a curse." Zahra said. "I am not going to allow your wider family to even think of me as someone that they can acquire breast milk from, unless it is for a wee bairn. Only bairns can enjoy that right?" Zahra said.

"In addition, I want my voice to be heard, and my opinions respected, even if you disagree. I want the right to share my opinions," she added.

"I also wish to wear my old blue jeans, when riding a horse, or whenever I feel like it and most importantly, if you growl at me again, like you did with those lupine teeth, I will be gone from you permanently with all of our children," Zahra said.

"Also, you have said that I have given you a gift of life, being Coinneach Og, but you must recognise too that I am the Mither of that wee bairn and need to be recognised as such and if I must depart from you, I depart with my bairn, wee Coinneach Og," Zahra said. "In addition, I want there to be an amnesty on Grigor Mohr MacGregor, the children's natural father. If there is an occasion to speak with him, I wish to be able to, without your armies' involvement and where no harm would come to either him, or I for speaking together. It is natural for him now to want to know how his family, all are. So, with compassion and understanding of a man who has made awful mistakes, as you too have, can you please accept those terms, if in turn, I agreed to return to Beinn Coinneach?" Zahra asked.

"Aye, I accept those terms if you return home," Coinneach stated, like a man defeated.

"Ali, can you please write that all down and will you please sign it for me Coinneach? Will Ali and John Fraser please witness that written document with your both of your signatures and date the document as well?" Zahra asked.

"I will" Ali said.

"I will," Coinneach agreed, and both John and Ali agreed to be witnesses to the document.

"We also need two copies of it. One to be kept here with Ali and John, and one to be kept on Beinn Coinneach. If needs be, we can see our lawyer, but a lawyer may not understand the wolf part," Zahra added.

"I would also like to address the wolf inside of you. Is it shape shifting, because of a curse, or is it a werewolf condition, where if you scratch or bite someone, they too become a werewolf?" Zahra asked innocently.

"It is shape shifting Zahra. I am not a werewolf, and you cannot also become a wolf unless you request it via the Druid religion. It was because of a curse upon me when I was the King, as you say. I have tried many times to have the curse removed, but it is too powerful," he said sadly after living with this horror for so long.

"Ali in our religion, nothing is impossible from God, is that right?" she asked her son who was listening intently. "Be and it is', is what our Holy Book says. You only need to ask in the right direction, under Ali's supervision, and I believe it will be gone from you," Zahra said, totally confident in what she was saying.

"My dear son, Ali, can you please take your stepfather, Coinneach into your room, to pray for that outcome?" she asked. "Merely ask God to remove it," Zahra said.

Her son Ali too looked confident that any pagan or Catholic curse or Druidic curse, as old as it was, could be undone by belief alone. Zahra left her son together with her husband, while they prayed and she was confident, with the strength of Ali's faith, that this wolf thing would be gone from him. She really hoped so, she feared those teeth that had snarled at her.

That was more than domestic violence, it was domestic terror.

Then her wolf puppy pished on the floor, as puppies do, so as she was cleaning it up, the family were all returning, one by one and asking if they could re-enter. Zahra explained it briefly and it seemed safe enough for everyone to come back in and make lunch.

Anndra and Domhnall were keen to be back in their big warm house.

"Aunty Fatma's house is too cold Granma," they complained. "Can we play with the puppy?" they asked.

"Only inside the house. She might still want to go back to her Mama," Zahra said as she expressed breast milk for her wee puppy into a bowl. At first, the wee pup sniffed it, then looked up at Zahra, then started to lick up the milky contents of the bowl.

"She's having difficulty Ma," said Hector. "Why don't you squirt it into her mouth like you did with Wolfie?" Hector asked.

"Alright son," she replied. Zahra held the cute wee puppy's face with her mouth open and squirted the milk from her full breasts directly into her mouth and she choked a bit but loved it like that. Both were on the floor with Hector, when Coinneach and Ali returned into the kitchen and Coinneach watched fondly upon his wife, squirting the milk into her puppy's mouth. He was proud of her feeding the needy, wee puppy.

"I think the document we all signed forgot to mention wee Wolfie number two, or have you named her something else?" her husband asked, smiling finally. It was as if a heavy load had lifted from him, there was no dark cloud hanging over his head and he was the big hearted, loving man that she knew once again.

"Coinneach, I do love you," she exclaimed hugging her

husband for the first time in many days. He kissed her gently on her neck, then her lips, caressing her head gently, while the family watched on. A sigh of relief filled the room but most especially Ali appeared satisfied. Even John had been surprised how forthright Ali had been throughout the whole family ordeal. Coinneach loved Zahra's long ringlets and ran his fingers through her very long hair, then with both of his hands, caressing her head, he kissed her passionately, which none of them had been witness to before. They did make a beautiful couple, of that there was no doubt.

Lady and Lord Coinneach were together, once again.

Anndra and Domhnall giggled but wanted some affection too and went to them both for a hug and a kiss too. "You are so sweet my lovelies," Zahra said and kissed them too. Causantin was aware he was missing out, so he held onto Coinneach's legs. "DaDa," he said demandingly and Coinneach became a mess of tears, as he kneeled to the wee lad's height.

"My beautiful son Causantin. You are so special, because I once had a big son with the same name as yourself and so you carry his light, like a blazing torch. He was a wonderful human being and grew up to be a very brave man. Will you be brave like he was, do you think?" Coinneach asked Causantin.

"Aye Da Da," Causantin said.

Causantin had all but forgotten Grigor Mohr MacGregor now and there was sadness in forgetting who his real father was. Zahra wondered now if he would even recognise Grigor Mohr if he ever saw him again. Dihaoine would never know him now, so it was only Grigor's older children who would even know who Grigor MacGregor was. Isobel, of course never forgets anyone, so if anyone remembered him, with complete clarity, it would only be Isobel.

It was time to leave the family of Wolf Ranch soon, so they could get back to normal farm work after Zahra bought plenty of honey from Fatma, pottery from Simon, cheese from Isobel and another nanny goat from Isobel too for her robust baby son, when he was to be weaned. Fatma had grown tomatoes, ripened enough to take also, as well as some herbal plants that Zahra didn't yet have on Beinn Coinneach. Her herb garden on Beinn Coinneach was nearly as good now as she had developed in the Aird, but not quite.

Zahra handed them Grigor Og's harness for Ali's ox, which was better than the one he had. Zahra also suggested that Ali change over later to two Clydesdales, if he was going to keep extending the oat fields. She explained the exhaustion effects the oxen more so than the Clydesdales, so long as they are harnessed correctly for deep ploughing.

Coinneach asked her how she knew that.

"It was in one of my books. Can't remember, maybe the first one. You remember Grigor, son? Old Isobel had bought you Charlotte, your lovely ox but the Clydesdales could work for longer periods," Zahra said.

"They can, it's true. I never regretted the changeover, and I still had my Charlotte who followed me around like my pet. They make nice pets too, almost as good as wolves do," Grigor Og jested. He appeared a little sad or disappointed that Zahra hadn't returned to his father or even a move to Cannich. Grigor Og was going to miss the family interaction once more and left Wolf Ranch, feeling lonely once more.

"May I make up for this intrusion into your farm work Ali and give you two Clydesdales. I can have them delivered this week, complete with harnesses, if you will accept my offer?" Coinneach offered.

"Thank you for the kind offer but I would like to achieve it myself bit by bit," Ali replied. "We can't continue taking from you anymore," Ali said.

Coinneach was disappointed at Ali's response and when Ali saw the obvious disappointment, he changed his mind and agreed to accept the offer for the two Clydesdales but nothing more. Coinneach was happier then, but he knew that the charity towards Wolf Ranch was over. He may have succeeded in getting his wife and bairn back but the atmosphere with the family had shifted.

Zahra also arranged for Isobel to deliver her new bairn up on Beinn Coinneach by Malcolm's son, Dr Alex MacNachten, if he was available again, with the same help as before, excluding Coinneach's brothers and including one of the men from the Aird, like John Fraser and Hector from Beinn Coinneach, as well as Coinneach, Dr Heath, the midwife and hopefully, Uncle Malcolm.

Lord Cinaed was obviously going to be discouraged from Isobel's bairn's birth.

It was fortunate that Isobel was blonde like her father Hugh Mohr Chisholm, so if her new bairn was blonde, he or she would take after Isobel. It most definitely wouldn't be a redhead or have dark hair like his or her brothers, Anndra and Domnhall. Her bairn was due in just over two months' time, so it was all arranged, and Isobel would come two weeks before that due date, if they had their dates correct.

17. Enter The Wolf

Having earned so much money delivering the bairn on Beinn Coinneach, both Alex and his wife, Nurse Mairi MacNachten were able to renovate their new home, next door to the Medical Practice, beautifully. It wasn't as dilapidated as Ruth Beaton's house had been. There weren't many homes that bad, unless they were completely dilapidated. When Kenneth bought the third of the houses all in a row, the MacNachten family then owned them all. Homes on individual lots like that were a rarity. Most homes were on Clan land where the tenant had no rights to purchase it from the now, very powerful Lairds who had money on their minds and the whole Clan system of old, was breaking down bit by bit, as the English had moved in with sheep and laws changed.

A way of life that had worked so well for so long was now eroded by the Lairds moving in sheep who earned them more money than a mere crofter, who could only pay them in rent. Many of their homes were burned down to ensure that the crofters left and could not return. New France beckoned to many people and labour was harder to come by as essential trades also left with them, as well as their music, poetry and dance as well as their musical instruments or those who crafted them, which were much missed.

Malcolm's family, while criticised at first for not being MacDonnell's and living on that land, were now appreciated, and looked up to as providing the essential services to that entire community. His oldest son was their Doctor, Alex's wife was their nurse, and Malcolm's wife compounded their medicines, his farm provided the Teams, now two in number, delivering and ploughing farms all over the district with hard working men. The farm itself was becoming one of the very few oat producers in the district and the only goat farm that made cheese, famous for miles around and that was without even mentioning the infamous Art Gallery.

MacNachten was a name whispered now in high regard. People were reminded of how old that name was and how long they had lived in Scotland and worked the land. The MacNachtens just never gave up, being originally Pictish which no-one ever mentioned. Both Malcolm and Kenneth had Pictish ancestors on both sides of their families because their Mither had married Nachtain MacNachten.

Prince Griogar arrived in his old rattling coach one day, unexpected and unannounced from Beinn Coinneach. He pulled into Malcolm's farm, not yet knowing of the new location for art to sell, but Kenneth politely met him on the farm anyway and explained where the new Art Gallery was, for future reference. The prince was alone, surprisingly, and only wanted to part with a set of three paintings that he had purchased from Zahra, some years earlier and all he wanted was his money back, if possible, as there seemed to be some issue, between all of the family members. He also had another one of Zahra, painted by Coinneach to perfection and it was stunningly beautiful. It had to be the nicest painting that Kenneth had ever seen of her.

Zahra really was a beautiful woman that Kenneth could never accustom himself to knowing someone quite as unusual, intelligent, gentle, and beautiful as Zahra was. He had never met anyone like her and never expected that he would again, in his lifetime.

"I just want to offload them all," the prince said. "I'm leaving," he added.

Kenneth sent the groom up to Old John Mac Donnell's sprawling farm, while Prince Griogar was on Malcolm's farm, to ask if he was interested in them. Old John came down in an instant, like he had nothing else to do in his day. He looked at the three paintings, recognising the corpse, as the woman he had shot in 'Donald's Den' and immediately bought them all, in case anyone else saw them. The prince couldn't believe his good fortune, with Kenneth's commission paid, of course. Old John MacDonnell paid two thousand pounds for all three of Zahra's paintings, of the woman whom he had secretly shot through the head and killed and offered five thousand for the other one.

"I think this one might be worth more John," remarked Kenneth. "You don't want to miss out again. This one is truly rare," he said.

Kenneth really meant it and John knew that Kenneth's eye for detail was brilliant, so he offered seven thousand pounds as a final offer and the cash deal was done. The prince drove away in his ornate carriage, without his paintings, but loaded up with cash, which he obviously needed, for a specific purpose. He was much happier then.

He was moving out of Beinn Coinneach permanently. He was a bitter man because he had believed Zahra had loved him more than she had loved Coinneach. The only way to get Zahra then was kidnapping her by force, he had deduced. Coinneach had created this situation, he told himself and he wanted revenge.

A former War Chief and revenge was an ugly combination.

Malcolm and his son Dr Alexander MacNachten received letters on the same day, requesting their presence on Beinn Coinneach for Isobel Fraser to give birth to her third child, said to be John Fraser's, but her confinement was the result of a brief liaison, with Lord Cinaed MacAlpin, Lord Coinneach's father. Malcolm didn't want to go at all to this one, in case the truth was revealed, but Alex talked him into it and they both wrote back agreeing to be present on the day stipulated in Zahra's letter. Kenneth came in then, to let him know of his big win in commission with Zahra in the paintings. He mentioned that there were three other paintings, in passing but thought it may upset Malcolm, considering that was exactly how his ex-wife had died, so he decided to stay quiet about them.

Back at home on Beinn Coinneach, Zahra was much happier with that signed document in place and loving her new wee puppy, except the poor wee thing often pished on the floor, which Mairi wasn't pleased about. Mairi had left for home earlier than usual, so with the prince moving out and Coinneach's father now making himself scarce, it was peaceful on Zahra's side of the big mansion. Hector was over the other side of the mansion, frequented often by Causantin, but even they were both in bed and the wee bairns were all sound asleep.

Contented with writing in bed, Zahra looked up at her bedroom door, as it slowly opened, expecting Coinneach any minute. Who or what walked in was Coinneach, but not in his human form. The prayers had not worked. His lupine eyes looked upon her with desire, as his wet nose sniffed her scent in the air. It was her days of ovulation. Could it be possible between a woman and a wolf? Zahra asked herself.

"So, the prayers didn't work then?" Zahra asked feebly.

Coinneach wanted his wife, although he wished no harm to come to her, being that his size could possibly hurt her, as his lupine member would enlarge, considerably. His heart was pounding rapidly, the desire for her was undeniable. Oddly, she too felt desire for him, even though he was a wolf, and she could feel his love and his familiarity beyond his wolflike appearance.

Her nakedness made her seem so vulnerable and appealing to him. A low amorous growl came from deep within him, desirous of her. He had to have her and as he approached her, she showed no signs of rejecting him, her husband, the wolf after all. She reached out to him and with this one simple gesture, he knew he would have her in his natural state, as a wolf and it was driving him crazy and deeply emotional. She put her arms around his neck as he stood over her as she ran her fingers through the inner and outer layers of his fur, which he could barely feel at first, then suddenly it was like a shock wave, running down each fibre which entered his very being.

She clung to him while ever so gently, he touched her face. Zahra too felt the intensity of sensation through his paws. This was now the moment of the great change that would rock both their inner and outer worlds of existence. She could love him in his most despised and feared state, and in that realisation, her own emotions were too great to ignore, as she wept in acknowledgement of her own love, desire, and acceptance of Coinneach the wolf, as well as Coinneach the man, with a heart big enough to accept her, with all of her faults and failings. Her own low self-esteem would always guarantee that Coinneach could do whatever he liked to his property, as she was to him.

After he had leapt onto the bed, kneeling enormously over her, he didn't wish to put his whole weight onto her, given his obvious size. The slowness of it was maddening to him wanting to respond more readily to the ancient primal, lupine being within himself. Would he enter her from the rear as wolves always did, or would he empale her on his lupine member? He knew it would happen, but he tried to take it slowly. He carefully touched her lips and her face ensuring his claws caused her no injury.

His member was impatiently awaiting her, he lifted her and empaled her upon himself and they were locked in place, and she screamed, holding him tightly, as his body fully encompassed hers. They were one organic form of sensual energy, reaching to the heavens above. As she called out to her God, and he growled vibrating through them both as the orgasmic wave flowed across them in a violent, but unforgettable way. They were attached, stuck, one being, one love and he howled at the climactic moment.

To say that Coinneach filled her completely would understate their experience, but it would define them both forever. For Coinneach, she had been everything the Seer had predicted she would be, requiring all his patience up to this point. She now looked at him when they awoke completely differently and she never challenged him again, he was still her husband, who could do no wrong in her eyes. He needed a wife who stood by his side like that for the rest of their days together and even if Grigor Mohr MacGregor came to see them both, they were stronger now to handle the whole world and whatever it could throw at them.

But everyone can make that erroneous assumption.

Zahra would still have to fulfil her role as Coinneach's Queen, occasionally with Prince Griogar there and that still bothered them both. Even Hector was introduced into the Royal Court, with a new title as Prince Hector, which he laughed at initially, but in time, he too took it all in his stride. He even designed his own new costume for Royal occasions. God bless Hector, Zahra and Coinneach both thought. His Highland Pony business was highly successful with Highland Ponies being sold, even as far away as Glenmoriston and Glengarry.

18. Isobel's wee Bairn

"Sweetheart we must find Hector a wife. I did mention it to him on the way to the Aird and he is keen on the idea. Do you know anyone suitable?" Zahra asked.

"Have you asked Malcolm yet? The available lassies all seem to be in Glengarry or Glenmoriston," Coinneach replied.

"Nae, but I will write to him and ask him, so when he comes on the weekend with his son Alex, he may know if there's a lassie on their farm. Malcolm also has a daughter, Islay, who runs their goat farm, and she has two lovely daughters, Winnifred, and Florence. Do you think we should consider a living soul or not darling? It might be a bit odd for her. Or we could ask around the MacKenzies here or Hamish in Glenmoriston? I should get writing darling," Zahra said.

"The idea that appeals to me is Islay's oldest daughter, Winnifred because they are both a spiritual, as well as an intellectual family. Ask Islay to come with her father to Isobel's delivery and then ask Islay yourself," Coinneach suggested. "She can then meet Hector and decide if she would like him as her son in law and he too should assess whether he likes Islay. He does like Malcolm, doesn't he?" Coinneach asked.

"Aye, he does. He has an awareness of most men's talents in life, as well as their passions and he warned off Malcolm not to harm Wolfie. He has perfect recollection, and he hasn't forgotten that it was Malcolm and the MacDonnell's who dealt with that poor wolf pack in the Aird. I am so glad that they have reformed," Zahra said.

"Have they?" Coinneach asked.

"Aye, there were six at least in the pack, other than Wolfie and his wife and puppies," she replied.

"I didn't realise there were as many as that. That really is wonderful. Wolfie has done a good job. You must be so proud of your wolf," Coinneach stated.

"I am," Zahra said. "I'll write that letter then and invite Islay too, because we are seeking a good match for our son Hector," Zahra said.

"Aye my love, he deserves a lovely lassie who can ride a horse obviously, to be a part of his pony business," Coinneach suggested.

"You do realise that she would live here with us, so you would need to like her too darling? She must respect you, or it wouldn't work," Coinneach said.

"Should Islay bring both of her daughters with her, because Hector might prefer the younger one and so might I and it would give him more choice?" Zahra suggested.

"Aye, I do. So that would be Florence then and they are both MacKenzies, as well. They would fit in well around here, culturally at least, even though they have grown up in Glengarry" he said. The letter was written hastily to ensure that Islay came with both of her daughters.

"Should we send a carriage for all of them Coinneach?" Zahra asked.

Coinneach then decided to send his carriage for Islay and her daughters who were invited too, for Isobel's bairn's birth. Then the lassies could meet up with Hector, although that detail was understated, so that Hector could tell the parents first which lass, if either, that he preferred. They were not yet aware that both lassies were very keen, having missed out already on Ali MacGregor.

Isobel Chisholm Fraser

19. The Carriage Ride

The carriage picked up my son Dr Alex, myself, Islay, Winnifred, and Florence but their brother Padraig had been tasked with other work. We all left Glengarry, then went to the Aird where we stayed one night and picked-up John Fraser and the very delicate, Isobel Chisholm Fraser. After we were finally on our way to Beinn Coinneach, Isobel was clearly uncomfort-

able and began complaining to Alex about feeling unwell. For a while, we continued our journey, but as Isobel began changing colour just as we were approaching Beinn Coinneach, Alex had to ask to stop the carriage, at a humble Croft to ask for their assistance.

Alex had assessed that Isobel was going into early labour, bought on by the movement of the carriage. The MacKenzie occupants of the wee Croft were only too willing to assist and accommodate, despite their crowded and small accommodation, made even more crowded as the occupants of the carriage all went inside the tiny house.

They were unaware of any connection that the family had to Lord and Lady Coinneach at first, until Isobel herself asked for her Ma and in response, Alex asked me if word could be sent to Lord Coinneach, informing him of our location. The man of the house then asked if they were connected somehow to Lord Coinneach and when the response was that Isobel was his step-daughter, they went into a kind of panic and quickly sent their oldest son to let Lord Coinneach know, where they were and in some difficulty. They also sent the youngest two of their bairns to a neighbour, to allow for more space in their home. The lady of the wee Croft, Mrs MacKenzie put a lot of water on to boil as Isobel vomited into a bowl, while Islay assisted, and her daughters watched on with great concern for their Aunty Isobel. Candles were lit as Alex let Isobel know as well as Mrs MacKenzie that he would be performing two things in case she delivered the bairn there and if they could provide some privacy.

An enema is not every woman's delight, prior to the birthing of a new bairn, especially in the presence of strangers. Islay assisted her brother with the enema, followed by small incisions either side of the vaginal entry, due to the obvious size of her large bairn, not unlike the previous MacAlpin delivery. Alex always carried pure alcohol with him, to ensure that no infection could occur, but this was very painful to the delicate open skin. Alex felt it was now an emergency and it needed doing or Isobel would split. He had seen that happen at Medical School and he never wanted to see that again.

This bairn was not wee at all and may have been even bigger than Coinneach Og was upon his birth. That was what concerned him. It could be a twelve-pound bairn by the look of Isobel and her level of discomfort and in addition, she was the only one of Zahra's bairns who was alive, so he felt a moment of panic.

Finally, Lord and Lady Coinneach arrived at the humble croft. They alighted from another elegant carriage, with Coinneach the gentleman, gently assisting Lady Zahra, who were both dressed in warm furs. Hers was a full-length fur with a head piece to protect her head from the freezing cold weather, as well as warm gloves and boots. Coinneach was also in a fur, wrapped around his shoulders, looking taller than I remembered, but together, they were the picture of strength and local royalty from another time.

Zahra looked content, other than having concern for Isobel. Their marriage dilemma had obviously been sorted out, I noted and thanked God for that. I wondered why in Zahra's lifetime, since I had known her, that she had so much difficulty with all of her husbands, but I attributed it to her having an entirely different perspective on relationships, due to where she came from and from her time, but also, I attributed it to her poor choices.

Fleetingly in my mind, I felt that there was still the perfect man for her out there in the world and it wasn't Coinneach or Grigor MacGregor, it was another man, unknown to any of them that may suit her cultural understanding of life. In the meantime, she was doing her best and acting out the role of local royalty. I surprised myself thinking of yet another man in Zahra's life.

"Should we move her to the mansion?" Coinneach asked my son Alex.

"It's too late now my Lord, her waters have broken, and she is in the early stages of labour," replied Alex.

The Croft occupants, were in awe of Lord and Lady Coinneach inside their wee home, and they bowed and curtsied to them, kissed his ring and so much respect had been afforded them both, that even I was surprised at their actual local status. Alex went along with any strangeness, and nothing was going to surprise him now, after his initiation into the MacAlpins, when Coinneach Og was born.

Alex and John decided then to lift Isobel up off the wee bed she was on, to walk her in tiny circles, to hopefully bring on the wee bairn, sooner rather than later. The MacKenzies were keeping the Croft warm, boiling up water and clean bedding at the ready as well as clean baby touls and tea for the non-working observers. Islay's daughters were clearly distressed at Aunty Isobel's suffering, not wishing it upon themselves.

"It's just normal for childbirth lassies," Mrs MacKenzie said to them both kindly, as she gave them cups of tea, as well as I who hadn't yet been asked to assist. It wasn't long though, because John became a weeping mess as Isobel descended into loud screams of agony, only known by those giving birth who just wanted to die.

Alex just worked on steadily, like one of the big Clydesdales ploughing field after field, never stopping, just working on.

Neighbouring Crofts went silent, knowing the King's daughter was the one who was screaming, and her loss, if it occurred, like it did with many of them, could spell disaster for them, they thought. Would they be blamed if she passed away? They decided to all pitch in and help.

The neighbours dropped around food for the King and Queen, as well as for the other occupants, knowing it impossible to afford from that one poor family, who we were all with. Then another family dropped in bread, Bannocks, coffee, cake and cheese. Soon it became a community effort to support Alex, delivering Isobel's bairn, inside the most unlikely of places, a wee Croft. All four horses outside, were taken out of the snow, as it fell heavily and fast and they too were taken into a Croft with a family and the bairns moved to another Croft. It wouldn't be long, and they would need to shovel themselves out of that wee Croft.

More peat was delivered to them from neighbours to keep us all warm enough. They didn't want the King to complain later that they hadn't cared enough for his family. This exercise was costing poor people a lot of what little they owned, in the way of sustenance over the coming winter months. Stews were delivered to feed the hungry amongst them, of which there was becoming quite a number. Coinneach never ate crofters' food however, in case it was poisoned from his old paranoia when he was the living King and people were trying to poison him, but Zahra ate some of the stew and detected a new flavour in it, to which she enquired, amidst the maelstrom and decided she would also get that important ingredient.

Isobel repeatedly called out to her Mither who went to her and took a turn walking her around and told her simply,

"Let it go darling, let the bairn out of her wee prison," and it couldn't be certain if Isobel laughed or coughed, but the bairn crowned, and Alex was there awaiting his or her appearance and then suddenly she slipped out like a fish on one of my fishing trips. It was such a relief, followed by the placenta which didn't go to waste as the Crofters boiled it up to eat. Zahra then decided not to eat any more stew. I picked Isobel up and placed the poor weakened lass onto the bed to allow Alex to perform his unenviable next part of his job, the clots. No woman liked this part of childbirth, and they often swore at my son. Even women who had never sworn in their lives before, were capable of the worse language during childbirth, it seemed.

Zahra relied on Islay to clean up the new chubby, wee lassie, who was predictably blonde, waiting on Alex to check her over while Isobel kissed her daughter affectionately.

"I am so proud of you my darling," Zahra declared, and they both wept together while Coinneach watched over them, placing his possessive hand on his wife's shoulder, always ensuring she was publicly his. The Crofters still looked up to their King, whose head touched their ceiling, so he couldn't stand as erect, as he would normally. His presence could fill an enormous space, so what they felt was a man, who not only filled their tiny spaces but their minds, hearts, and souls as well. It was a bizarre emotion, unlikely to be felt again by another Crofter family. They were relieved that the Princess lived through the ordeal. They congratulated her as 'Princess Isobel', which totally confused her and she asked her Mither about it, who promised to explain it all later.

It wasn't going to be a comfortable ride up to Beinn Coinneach for an exhausted and bleeding Isobel who was delegated to the King's carriage with her Mither, stepfather, John and Alex with the wee bairn. I travelled with the rest of the family in the other carriage after enthusiastically thanking the MacKenzies for their wonderful support and I appeared to have developed a rapport with them all in that short time. I also asked them if they had any needs to replace that had been utilised by us all. They would not answer that but looking around at what had been provided, I took a mental list to give to Coinneach to repay them, no matter what they said, in denial of having done anything other than what was still expected, in these parts anyway, of their Highlands. They were proud people and had such compassion, as did all their neighbours, fearful too once they realised that they were hosting the King's relatives.

'Princess Isobel' was a name that reverberated around the crofts, the bairn was named Princess Zahra Isobel Kenzie MacAlpin Fraser. The name honoured the Crofters. Their deed would be sealed in time, with her lovely name.

Isobel's quarters on Beinn Coinneach had been prepared well ahead of time to share with her husband, John Fraser.

Hector had been anxiously waiting on us all to return, worried sick that his sister may have come to harm, so when he looked upon her alive and well, but exhausted, he embraced her as she alighted from the carriage, then with his great strength now, he carried her to her quarters. John followed him closely behind, still a little shocked and overwhelmed by the experience. The bairn was carried by a lovely looking lass, Hector was thinking.

Her name was Florence MacKenzie, my granddaughter. She followed Hector closely and put the sweet bairn onto Isobel who took her to her breast.

"What's your name again lass?" Isobel asked. She curtsied in response.

"I am Florence MacKenzie, Mistress. My Mither is Islay MacKenzie of Glengarry and my father is Angus MacKenzie and my grandfather is Malcolm MacNachten," she replied. "Can I bring you anything Mistress?" she asked.

"You can ask Mairi to ready my bath please Florence," Isobel replied.

"Aye, Mistress," said Florence and she left to find whoever Mairi was, to ready the bath for Isobel.

"Isn't she pretty Sister?" remarked Hector who was taken with her.

"Aye, brother she is. They both are. Looking for a wife are ye now?" Isobel asked. Hector was too shy to reply, but Isobel knew anyway.

"I'll give you my opinion who is the better of the two of them in time brother," Isobel smiled finally.

"Och Hector, I can't wait to see you with a wife. You think you have the world all sorted out. Marriage changes all of that. You will be her slave. I can see it now. Would you both live here then?" Isobel asked.

Islay MacKenzie

"How many bairns do you both want? Can she ride a Highland

Pony? Does she have a sense of humour? Can she speak Gaelic? How old are they both? Do you prefer older or younger lassies? Do you like their Mither Islay?" Isobel teased.

"Stop it, Isobel. Who is their Mither? Which one is she?" Hector asked.

"She's the bossy, intelligent one who runs the goat farm on Uncle Malcolm's farm. She's Dr Alex's sister, black hair, short-ish but hard working and pretty, married to Angus MacKenzie, Teamster, Hugh Og Chisholm's offsider," Isobel said.

"How do you know all of that?" Hector asked.

"I look, listen and judge," she said, "But I do have a question for you. Why do people curtsy, bow and kiss the ring and all of that for father and Mither, now me as well?" Isobel asked.

"You don't know, after all the discussions we have had? So much for your observation skills Sister. He is the now deceased King of Alba. King Coinneach MacAlpin. That's why they called you Princess Isobel. I get called Prince Hector too, only for royal stuff though," Hector added.

"Is he an actual King, a real King? You are not just joking, are you Hector?" Isobel asked.

"Nae, but he's just a normal fella too. He's kind enough to me. Gives me advice on the lassies too," Hector added. "He doesn't mind if I have a question about my cock like Da used to when he would hit me over the head for even asking anything about my cock," Hector said.

"Och Hector, I miss you. It's so nice to be here with you. Is my bath ready, can you ask please?" Isobel asked.

As Hector was departing Isobel's elaborate quarters, both Florence and Winnifred were there, and Florence bowed to him and called him Master.

"The Mistress's bath is ready Master. Should you tell her or should we?" she asked.

"You both should, so you can assist your Mistress into the tub and back out again," Hector said taking advantage then of his power. He liked them both. It was a dilemma. He would need his sister's opinion about them. They looked a lot alike, only Florence was the younger of the two, by two years and a bit shorter than Winnifred. Winnifred was so quiet. He wondered if he preferred a quiet lass to a bolder lass.

They would both be virgins. What an exciting thought, he was thinking. Trouble was, he was a virgin too. He needed more advice on sex from his stepfather, Lord Coinneach who had offered it. Any advice on his organ was freely given as Lord Coinneach did admire a beautiful male member, which Hector did have. He needed to know what to do, and his stepfather seemed to think that a step-by-step approach a good idea to demystify the needs of women too. His advice had so far been that 'women need to be satisfied son'. Hector didn't even know what 'satisfied' for a woman meant.

Lord Coinneach had gone to a lot of trouble rebuilding his quarters, so that he and his wife could enjoy each other more, he had declared. He had even made it soundproof and had bricked over one of the windows, thereby disallowing visibility and sound from those below. He was serious about pleasing his Mither, at least that's what he claimed. Hector imagined what Ma would do with Lord Coinneach's cock and it excited him. He finally made up his mind, after the excitement over the new bairn had died down a bit.

20. Hector Decides

Over dinner that night, it was to be expected that the conversation described how the group who were travelling in the carriage had to stop and seek aid from the local Crofters. I had already given the list to Lord Coinneach of all that the entire family had consumed, including the horses and for how long that they were there.

Immediate compensation of a flock of twenty goats was given to the poor Crofters, ten goats to each of their door neighbours, as well as the offer of a permanent job inside the house for the primary lady Crofter to help care for Isobel's bairn initially, then work under Mairi, doing whatever duties she enlisted most especially for Zahra's needs. The gentleman Crofter's son was given the job as an assistant to Hector breaking in his horses and grooming them and caring for them, if Hector wasn't on Beinn Coinneach.

 The whole family were then housed in a new larger Croft with more land, on the mountain, within the grounds of the Beinn Coinneach property.

"I prefer Winnifred," Isobel said after everyone had left to go to their respective rooms.

Coinneach, in his very official father role asked permission from Islay for Hector to court one of Islay's daughters. His decision as to which lassie was pending, he explained, until the following day, but Islay had agreed to that and so did I when Islay asked me for permission, as their grandfather, considering Angus, their father, was absent. The lassies were both told about it that night and were both very agreeable but not yet knowing which lassie would be chosen by the handsome Hector.

As a wee bairn, Hector would do terrible things to his Mither that he was embarrassed to mention now, as he wanted to know then, how our bodies all worked and if there really was a hole there to put a male member into. He frequently had made his Mither cry. Hector had been thinking about sex for his whole life, it seemed but growing up on a farm with animals reproducing all the time, made a young lad ask all of those questions.

The windows on the rear side of his Mither's room, were ceiling to floor, covered with heavy purple and green velvet drapes, which were closed at nighttime with a gorgeous view in the daytime and a smaller window on the side, which gave a view all way to the oak grove, where Zahra prayed. The floor wasn't cold underfoot, as it had the thickest of carpets that Hector had ever seen. The lighting was dim, with double candles attached to the walls in elaborate Scottish pure silver holders, as well as an overhead Turkish coloured glass bowl shaped, lighting fixture with candles within it, that Coinneach subsequently lit.

After listening to their advice, Hector knew by the following morning which of the two MacNachten lassies that he liked the most. My quiet granddaughter, Winnifred whom he hoped would do his bidding, whenever he wanted sex, like most of us men enjoy. Winnifred MacKenzie was betrothed that day and hand fast before we all left and both Islay and I were witnesses. My sweet granddaughter then remained behind on the mountain together with Hector on Beinn Coinneach, handfast as his wife. She said her sad farewells to our family as we all left in Coinneach's carriage, without her.

Islay wept the tears of a Mither, as we all left.

Life for both my family and Hector's was forever changed from that day forth. If I had only known the path that Winnifred was on, there may have been a happier path to her story, but she had the strength of my family which surprised us all and God bless her, she later went on to give Hector four beautiful and intelligent bairns, one lassie and three lads.

Unknown to Zahra, on occasion, Coinneach would require Hector to join him in his quarters, where he sodomised Hector hard every time, much to Coinneach's pleasure. The helpful Crofter had a new job now, giving an enema each time to Hector first and preparing him clean and greased for Lord Coinneach, normal for the era that the MacAlpins had all come from. Mr MacKenzie from that wee croft was now his *secret keeper*, which was also normal of those early times. Coinneach found that he wished to control Hector, whom he deemed needed to be controlled, as the rival male of his family on his property, as Coinneach was the Alpha male after all. But what poor Hector had needed was just love, or what he thought was love from a father, not sodomy and he was suffering dreadfully, but he didn't dare tell his Mither, what her husband was doing to him.

What was really happening, was only later revealed. His new wife, Winnifred also never knew of the liaisons with Lord Coinneach sodomising her new husband and neither did Zahra.

Winnifred still enjoyed the sex that she had with Hector, despite being a virgin herself initially, as her man was no longer shy nor ignorant, but his wife had been, so he became very protective of her. She thought the world of him, but naturally she missed her family from Glengarry and milking the goats each day for her Mither, Islay and so she took over that task, every morning of milking the two nanny goats as well as grooming them and feeding them. She then assisted Hector with his ponies, and they enjoyed their partnership with raising them all together. His wife became his right-hand woman with those flighty wee ponies.

As expected, Winnifred was very quiet at the meal table, each time the family ate together, but she had always been a quiet lass. Her Glengarry family made enough noise, without her adding to it she said, especially with the twins, Malcolm Og and Hamish Og, whom she thought of as adorable. Her quiet presence was almost spiritual in quality, so as time passed, the liaisons with Lord Coinneach ceased completely and the quiet but pure soul who sat with them each day, entered Coinneach's consciousness more and more.

"She is almost like a Goddess of Auld," Coinneach declared to Zahra. She could see him at times like this, as the original son of Alpin, with his long-plaited hair, riding on a fine horse, when Scotland was just a new country.

He wanted to give her another name, because he didn't much like Winnifred, as her first name. He suggested Flidas Winnifred Gregor MacAlpin to her and to Hector but to ask her parents, just the same. Flidas was a Goddess of both fertility and cattle. He hoped to lose the name, Winnifred altogether, but maybe that person was a grandmother or some such, so Coinneach kept it as a second name with Flidas as her first name, which suited her, he thought. Coinneach loved to change people's names, so Zahra advised that they just go along with it.

The delightful Winnifred surprisingly, loved her new name, Flidas anyway and even Hector preferred her new name to Winnifred, which was a bit of a mouthful.

21. Enter. Grigor Mohr MacGregor

Isobel had long returned to the Aird with her new chubby wee, blue-eyed bairn, who she had named after her Mither, Zahra Og and not even a visit was had from Lord Cinaed, much to everyone's relief.

Lord Coinneach's brothers had gone around to congratulate both John and Isobel, with a small gift, except the prince and they also let Coinneach know that the prince was temporarily absent and on one of the Outer Hebridean islands. They weren't sure why, but his wife was expecting him to return to her, despite their brief separation.

Life was different, once more on the mountain, but the last person anyone had expected to see was Grigor Mohr MacGregor. Mairi answered the huge front doors one day to an unidentified stranger and when she asked his name, it was Zahra's ex-husband, Grigor Mohr MacGregor. He declared that he was visiting, to see his sons, Hector and Causantin, as well as his daughter, wee Dihaoine so Mairi invited him in.

Seated by the fire, Zahra immediately sent for Coinneach, who was in his art room, once again painting, something special. He came down with some haste.

"Mr MacGregor," Mairi said, and he was offered an armchair, by the warm fire, as it was particularly cold and foggy outside and on top of Beinn Conneach, it was even colder than below. Zahra and her ex-husband then sat awkwardly across from one another, for the first time in many years and since he had harmed her so terribly. Grigor gave her no explanation for his actions at any time, not in a letter or any attempt to communicate with her, other than that one ghostly message.

Grigor had never apologised for sleeping with that other woman, which had led to their marriage eventually falling apart, culminating with horrific domestic violence, and leaving Scotland's shores with Belle MacGregor. All those old memories swam around in Zahra's mind while sitting opposite him. She always thought she would know what to say to him, if they were sitting face to face and speaking once again, but now she was unable to articulate any of it, as her questions continued to swim around and around in her mind, so that it was making her feel dizzy.

"I thought I smelled you not long ago when I was sleeping in Cannich. You were there, I was sure of it. But you are here now only to see our bairns, and not me?" Zahra asked.

"Aye, you are married to Coinneach MacAlpin now," Grigor Mohr replied.

Somehow, she reasoned that if he had come to Beinn Coinneach to see her and to apologise to her, that she would feel better about what had happened, but Grigor had only wanted to see his bairns. Zahra, although oddly disappointed, told him that Hector was married now to a lovely lass, Flidas and had his own business with Highland Ponies. She sent Mairi's husband Callum, for Hector and his wife, so they could meet and asked Mairi to bring both Causantin and Dihaoine to see their father.

When Coinneach entered the room, his face was looking blackened with concealed rage and Zahra hoped that Coinneach could contain it, while he looked upon the face of the man who had caused all those terrible injuries, suffered previously by his wife. She could see Coinneach thinking, 'broken jaw, broken nose, shattered eye sockets, split skull', but somehow restrained himself.

"Mr MacGregor, coffee or tea?" Coinneach asked, trying to remain civilised. "I am Lord Coinneach MacAlpin, your ex-wife's husband," he said, emphasising that Zahra was now Grigor's ex-wife.

Grigor Mohr MacGregor did not stand, bow, curtsy, kiss a ring or show any respect or reverence to the man who had stolen his wife and family, in his eyes. He had long passed the incident of punching Zahra in the face and leaving Scotland's shores on a ship with Belle MacGregor to live in the Americas. Blame, according to Grigor MacGregor was for the crows. Now was now, and Coinneach MacAlpin to him, was the ultimate pig in the greater pigsty of mankind. Zahra hoped he would not antagonise Coinneach too much for what could appear to him, would be more than just a simple pig.

The wolf inside Coinneach was always just beneath the surface and Grigor was playing with fire. "Coffee" was his response, noticeably without a please.

'He hadn't changed that much' Zahra thought. He was still gorgeous. No woman could help but notice how handsome and masculine he was, especially his own wife, with all of those memories of the times they had spent together and the bairns they had shared together, made him appear even more handsome, more masculine than ever before. She couldn't overcome remembering the added tragic sadness  however, attached to their marriage's dreadful and dramatic end, with Grigor's choice to be with another woman, which still shattered her heart, and it surprised her now, just how powerless it made her feel.

As usual, he wore that old plaid, now probably an antique, still wafting its familiar odour across to her sitting by the fire, which often made it smell even stronger. While coffees were coming, the three of them sat awkwardly. Zahra looked at her puppy playing on the floor and picked her up, cuddling her close to herself. It was a comforting gesture. She didn't want to cry looking upon Grigor's face, even though it was bringing out those emotions. She realised that she still loved him.

"I want to see my bairns," Grigor demanded.

"Hector is coming. He won't be long now and Mairi must be changing wee Dihaoine before bringing her to you Grigor," Zahra explained.

Hector and his new wife of only a few months, entered the mansion cheerfully, joking about something the ponies had done, when Hector then saw who was sitting by the fire. It gave him a physical shock reaction. He wasn't sure whether to punch him, hug him or just try to contain all of his emotions also and just sit and be civilised, like his Mither and Coinneach were both doing.

"Hello Da, this is my wife, Flidas," Hector said bravely, through uncertainty, while he sat down, beside his wife Flidas, as well.

"Flidas, this is my father by birth, while Lord Coinneach is now my Mither's husband," Hector declared in front of everyone. Hector hadn't described Coinneach as his stepfather in public, which hadn't gone unnoticed by Zahra, who was a little perplexed by it. Had something happened between them, she wondered?

"I am pleased to meet you Master," Flidas said.

"MacGregor" Grigor stated, "My name is Grigor MacGregor and your husband, lassie, is a MacGregor," Grigor stated firmly referring to Hector.

"Sorry Mr MacGregor. I am pleased to meet you. My name is Flidas MacAlpin. I am the daughter of Angus MacKenzie of Glengarry, granddaughter of Malcolm MacNachten," Flidas said. She looked across at her husband for reassurance, which she received, and he held her hand warmly.

"Why are you here Da?" Hector asked.

"Because you are my son, not his and you were recently

married and this is my gift to you," Grigor added.

He held out a gift in his hand to Hector of an unknown type, until he mentioned that it was from America, made by Indians there. It was an amulet to protect Hector from evil.

"You wear it around your neck son, to protect you from evil," Grigor added.

Hector tied it around his neck, as instructed and thanked his father. Mairi then came in with Causantin who ran to Zahra first, "Ma Ma," Causantin said.

"He has grown so much," Grigor exclaimed. Causantin looked across at the stranger in the room, no longer acknowledging Grigor as someone whom he had ever known.

Grigor knew it was a genuine response from the young bairn and when wee Dihaoine, was placed in his arms, she only struggled to be free and cried to be with her Mither. Grigor drank his coffee quickly, took his leave and left through the big front doors.

If Grigor had stayed, his emotions may have gotten the better of him, as he imagined holding his wife, just one more time, if only he could, but he mounted his horse and left as he had come. Zahra was the picture of good health now and was more beautiful than he had remembered. Her brown hair flowed down to her knees in ringlets and curls. None of the bairns had inherited her hair and he had always thought it was her crowning glory. He thought she looked sad upon knowing that he wasn't there to see her.

He was pleased at how she had received him, and he knew he would be able to get her alone again, one day soon.

◇

Hector's wedding had been formally carried out in the old-fashioned way, led by a Priest and in that secret lower level of the mansion, whereby, Flidas underwent the same horrible intrusive interrogation that Zahra went through, given that she was entering into an ancient, royal family. None of Flidas's family were present on this type of occasion. Zahra tried to help Flidas understand that it was a medieval tradition that was still taken seriously by the MacAlpin family, but it was still voluntary, and she could refuse. Flidas agreed to undergo the interrogation, as Zahra had, just to remain with her chosen man and to assist him in following his families' expectations of him.

Zahra herself was not present while the Priest stood back as King Coinneach and his brothers commenced their questioning of her and all the while, Zahra only felt sadness for the poor wee lass who was so sweet and naïve. She hoped it wouldn't harm her in other ways, psychologically. She hated these ridiculous archaic traditions and hoped one day soon that they would end. Perhaps with the disposal of Lord Cinaed and Coinneach's brothers, it could all go away in time.

When it was finished, this time, it was announced to everyone in the huge room that Flidas was now Princess Flidas of the MacAlpin family to be considered as Lord Coinneach's daughter, Hector's wife and to be respected, as she should be in that position. She had been dressed her in her wedding gown, then kneeled together with Hector in front of the Priest. To the world of the living however, Flidas understood that her title could not apply. Flidas was also now a business partner with her husband, Hector Gregor MacAlpin and both would receive a grant of money, as well as lifelong rights to live on the new wing of Beinn Coinneach's mansion for them and their offspring. They would occupy one third of it for themselves and their future children until the bairns were old enough to be married, or run their own lives. They were also free to decorate it and modernise it at will and all at the family's expense.

Her name change from Winnifred to Flidas was noted and Hector and Flidas were married, followed by an enormous feast put on for the entire community. Only the family from the Aird, were all invited, but not her Glengarry family, due to the medieval and unacceptable aspects of the ceremony. Ali was soon due to marry April which was discussed a lot, and he was disappointed that April wasn't there. The ancient ceremonies and traditions all seemed normal to the MacAlpins, and they thought it was always wise to be cautious when mixing the living with the Otherworld.

Lord Cinaed was always opposed to the involvement of outsiders, even if they were the parents of the bride. They could have another ceremony in Glengarry with them or in Glenmoriston's wee Chapel, arranged by the bride's family, but no mention was ever to be made of 'the previous interrogation. It was an increasingly unpopular ancient tradition, which Zahra could hopefully see ceasing, before April married Ali. Soon he would marry April, and he was becoming excited about it. Thank God neither family would subject her to such an ordeal. They had already stated that they wanted their wedding to be held in the Aird, just to avoid any MacAlpin involvement at all.

Zahra loved her new daughter in law, Flidas, and she wasn't as lonely with Flidas there on the mountain, even though she was so quiet.

"Are you always this quiet?" Zahra asked her one day.

"Aye, Ma it's normal for me. There was so much noise in our house that I didn't want to add to it," she replied. "Then there is Mither, who is so flamboyant by nature which can be a bit embarrassing at times and that made me retreat into myself a bit. My Ma always encouraged me to learn, however as she has done, so I read a lot, like she does, even on the Kings of Scotland," she explained.

"Ma, can I ask you a question?" Flidas asked.

"Aye, my love. Go ahead. I am only feeding wee Coinneach Og, so I am available to answer your questions," Zahra answered.

"I am confused about the whole MacAlpin thing," Flidas said.

"Do you mean the bowing and the reverence to my husband?"

Zahra said.

"Aye, I don't understand it, but I might appear silly if I tell Hector that. Am I meant to know who your husband is?" Flidas asked.

"Nae my love. Only if you are of the Otherworld. You are a living soul, and we are not. Has Hector not told you yet?" Zahra asked.

"Told me what exactly?" Flidas asked.

"We are of the people who have already passed away, like your Great Grandda. You are a living soul, so the people you have met around here are from ancient times who died a very long time ago, while I died relatively recently, after Isobel's birth. We don't usually cross time zones, within this place, where souls wait for the Day of Judgement, but this was an exceptional case where Coinneach and I were prophesied to meet," Zahra explained.

"But you are alive. We are talking together. How can you not be alive if I can talk to you?" Flidas asked.

"Some of us live in and out of the world of the living, by choice, like me. It's a choice but I can make myself disappear, so you wouldn't see me, but then I would not be agreeing to having relationships with the living. Others are never seen and that is what you are accustomed to, or they remain in their graves, asleep. Do you mind living with us as nonliving souls?" Zahra asked.

"I must think about that now. Hector didn't tell me, that he was Unalive," Flidas said.

"Hector may not be Unalive, Flidas. Concerning my bairns, like Hector, there is uncertainty as to their status. Isobel, for instance is of the living souls, because Hugh Chisholm, her father and I were both alive when I conceived, I think or at least I was," I added. "You really must talk to your husband, my child or he might be annoyed with me," Zahra said.

"Coinneach Og however, is of the 'Otherworld', as we prefer to call it, because both parents were Unalive, at the time of conception, however that still doesn't explain how I can conceive at all, in this world. Please do not make it known outside of this family, or we may have to live as invisible souls once again and hide away as 'the hidden ones' do. It can't be known outside of this family that I have conceived, while being Unalive. Do you understand that? It could be dangerous for me especially," Zahra asked.

"There is no scientific, nor religious basis for my ability to have bairns, so even, we don't know what we are dealing with exactly, such as life spans or if my bairns can all reproduce. However, your family is the exception to that rule concerning the knowledge of our circumstances, because of your Grandda Malcolm. I hope that helps," Zahra said.

22. Room 203

Grigor Mohr MacGregor was deep in conversation with Padruig and Alex, in the hotel room once again, as they ate more and more of James's food. Padruig told Alex to order up three meals per day now, if Grigor was staying.

"How? I don't want James to drop dead too, like Patrick did," Alex asked.

"Just leave him a note then and ask for some fruit as well and a jug of highland coo milk. Love that milk," Padruig answered.

James received the message and delightedly added a third meal, fruit, and milk, much to their surprise. James loved being a part of the whole ghost story from Room 203 and he couldn't wait to tell Malcolm, that they had company. He guessed it was Grigor Mohr MacGregor. Those three had been previously inseparable, until Belle MacGregor threw them all into 'new lodgings.'

Grigor was keen to get Zahra back, no matter what, and he let them know that the stinky pig Prince, what's his name, was gone with his army and the MacKenzies were all back to work, as usual and complaining a lot about their wages and so on. The biggest story that he re-told to both Padruig and Alex was that the staff who had worked in the house, were normally disallowed to repeat anything that they saw or heard in the mansion on Beinn Coinneach, but they had indeed repeated a big story.

"A lass, who worked as a cleaner, repeated seeing a giant brown wolf, five feet high at least, two or three feet wide, with paws as big as a man's hand. Mairi, the housekeeper there, told the staff all to leave immediately, but not before the lass had seen the wolf herself," Grigor said.

"She heard Mairi say to her husband, Callum 'the wolf is out' but the MacKenzies didn't believe the lass and told her that

Scottish wolves were grey, not brown, and not as big as that and why didn't they just shoot it after all? And where was the Master when all that was happening, surely, he would have shot it? But the lass and one other lass from another croft repeated the exact same story and they both refused to go back there to work.

She said that the wolf and the Master were one and the same" Grigor said.

Grigor had made himself invisible and sat in on many conversations, listening to the MacKenzies discussing the emergency that had arisen that day. No families could afford to lose the wages from the lassies and were insisting that they were making it all up and they had to return to work. An old woman then from among them, spoke up in their defence.

"When I was wee, there were tales of that giant brown wolf, just as you have described, my dear. My Grandma told me, it was so, in her day too, and her grandma told her, in her day. It's the same wolf and some say that you can't kill it," the old MacKenzie woman said.

"It was said by some, that the King himself, was the giant wolf, but we dared not repeat that. There were never two wolves, nor howling or even a pack of wolves up there on Fairy Mountain, let alone grey wolves, like we all had down 'ere in the Braes and Glens, where the grey wolf would dig up all our graves," the old lady said, slowly smoking her pipe.

"Everyone was too afraid to go near that mountain for a time, because it seemed like a giant Fairy Dun, where you could lose your soul, unless you were a breast feeding Mither, who were frequently kidnapped, but then those women were returned," she added.

"Those were the stories of auld but if you say now lassie, that the brown wolf has returned, then it never did leave, did it?" she said, smoking away casually.

That was what Grigor conveyed to both Padruig and Alex in

Room 203, in Glenmoriston.

"And you expect us to go there, to help you, when there's a bloody giant and unkillable wolf. Are you mad?" Padruig said.

Alex had a lot more to say where Grigor's relationship with Zahra was concerned.

"Why do you want Zahra back anyway?" Alex asked in lowered tones.

"Look what you did to her Grigor. Leave her be, I say. You would just do it, all over again to Zahra. What you did last time was shocking and I never want to see her in that condition again. God forbid. At least, whoever 'wolf man' might be, helped her. Grigor, she couldn't even walk properly after what you did. No, I'm not helping you to take her off that mountain," Alex answered.

"You just might, when I tell you the rest of the gossip that I heard, while I just sat there, minding my own business," Grigor said and that got their attention.

"Okay, what other MacKenzie gossip did you hear, my old friend," asked Padruig patiently.

"You might want to have your coffee on hand, Padruig. This story isn't one you'll ever be likely to hear again, but it is from a credible source. Coinneach's getting one of those MacKenzie men, to give my young son Hector, an enema, and a polish on his ass to prepare him for that monster of a husband of Zahra's. He then fecks him hard up his ass, which causes some considerable pain and screaming is heard from my young Hector, who is barely seventeen years old and only just newly married too.

He is now subservient to the Master.

My son is being fecked up the ass, so if you won't help with Zahra, will you at least help me get my son off that god damn mountain, with his wife Flidas, who is Malcolm's granddaughter, and all of his thirty ponies, so that he can still run his Highland Pony business, down here. There's enough room for all of those ponies here, in Cannich. Three of those wee ponies could fit into one Clydesdale stall in the stables here on Craskie Farm.

In Glengarry, there's the big stables but it hellish busy out there, unlike here. Would Hamish agree to the ponies being here?" Grigor asked, becoming emotional and impatient.

Both men paled at what was happening to poor Hector, who they had all watched grow up from a wee, bairn. A naughty but vibrant lad who you could never imagine being subservient to anyone. Coinneach had learned a method as to how to control that free and wild spirit that Hector always had been before Grigor had abandoned them all and left them for what he thought was a better life in America, with Belle MacGregor.

"Have you seen Hector then?" Padruig asked sombrely, uncertain that Grigor had begun to show an interest again in his family.

"Aye, I knocked on their front door to see my bairns and was allowed in, much to my surprise. There was no army this time, or any objection to my presence. Zahra was there, who seemed disappointed that I wasn't there to see her. She didn't know why I was there, but I had to see my son," Grigor said.

"I gave him a gift for his wedding as an excuse. Something an Indian gave me for protection from evil, he told me, and now Hector is wearing it around his neck. He sure needs it," Grigor said.

"I met his wee wife Winnifred, who they now call Flidas, who is nice enough. She's a bit dim or maybe just too quiet, but there's gossip about her too that Malcolm might need to know," Grigor added.

"You might want to bring Malcolm here to chat about that with Angus, her father too," Grigor said.

"What other horrifying gems do you have to tell us. I'm starting to feel like I'm leading a protected life here, in Room 203,"

Padruig asked.

"There was a wedding up there up on Beinn Coinneach. Did you know?" Grigor asked.

"Aye. Hector is married right?" Padruig asked.

"I'm not talking about handfast. A wedding, with a feast and all that, to which the Aird family were invited, but Malcolm's family, were not invited. There's a whole other secret level underneath that bloody big mansion. Accessible through a secret passage, covered over and sealed. The secret to its opening belongs to the leader of the MacKenzies there," Grigor said.

"Well, the secret keepers over there aren't really reliable, so that could be found out easily enough, I presume," Padruig jested.

"What wedding then, wasn't Malcolm invited to?" Alex asked seriously.

"It was Hector and Flidas's wedding with a Priest and all," Grigor replied.

"Aye. That's normal," Padruig answered.

"Well, no, it wasn't normal, that's why I want you to know what is happening to both the lass, as well as my lad," Grigor added, starting to become emotional.

"They had the lass in front of the Priest, Lord Cinaed, Lord Coinneach, and a couple of Coinneach's sicko brothers, who asked the lass a lot of intrusive questions. She was too stupid and too young to know that she shouldn't have allowed it," Grigor said with difficulty, as he held his head in shame.

"That's why Malcolm wasn't invited then?" asked Padruig.

"Dear God. How can I tell my grandson that?" Padruig asked, then stood up and went over to the window that overlooked the oat fields. Padruig was wiping tears from his face.

"Ponies, here eh, not enough room for thirty, maybe twenty, unless James allows them up here to graze on his golf fields. Hector could live in Grigor Og's house with Flidas." Padruig said as he made up his mind. Count us in, you shit stirrer Grigor, we'll not ignore our young one's plight. Zahra will still not get our help, but they will, is that a deal?" he asked Grigor.

"Deal. I will manage Zahra," Grigor answered.

"But not at the same time. That is our deal. We will need you on task to get your son out of there, with his wife and thirty ponies and all their gear. That's manpower that we will need. So, Malcolm and Angus would be in, as well as that MacKenzie security bloke he has in Glengarry and John MacDonnell. What about Ali? Do you think he'd be of any use?" Padruig asked.

"What we need is someone to convince Hector and Flidas to leave their home with everything there, in the first place and to pack up their stuff, ready the ponies and leave quickly, before that Prince turns up, with his damn army," said Alex.

"Word is, he's in the Outer Hebrides, so now is the time to move. He's up to something." Grigor said.

"Alright then, who is going to convince Ali, to convince them both?" Alex asked.

"Malcolm is the only one with a finger in every bloody pie, the clever wee shite," Padruig answered. "If it must be quick then I'll contact him. Just leave me alone will, you for a while," Padruig said. "In the meantime, Alex, leave a note for James about a few grazing ponies being here and Hamish too, that all of the stable stalls will be needed soon," Padruig said.

"Malcolm, it's me Grandda. Malcolm, I need to talk right away, it's important. Malcolm, I don't care if you have your hand up a coo's privates, I have to talk to you," Grandda said.

"It had better be

important Grandda, I am helping with the calving and my hand is rather busy, so make it quick," I said.

"You are in love with your coos, admit it, Malcolm." Grandda said.

"Okay, I'm in love with my ladies, now can I go, or do you actually have anything of importance to say?" I asked. "Well, you might regret being rude to me, but I'll tell you anyhow. There was a wedding on Beinn Coinneach that you were not invited to, even though she is your granddaughter" said Grandda.

"I know Winnifred was married to Hector. I was there," I said.

"So, you went to the grand feast, held underneath the mansion with a Priest and all that?" Grandda asked.

"Nae, what are you referring to?" I asked.

"I need to know if you want me to tell you about some disturbing stuff, in this manner, or if you want to meet a group of us here in Glenmoriston, intending to remove Hector and Flidas from that mountain?" Grandda asked. "Tell me now Grandda, I am busy," I said.

And he was gone.

Grandda told me the whole gruesome tale of both Flidas, as she was now known, and poor Hector. He asked me if I had others who could help in the way of manpower, because there was a lot of horses to get off that mountain and then driven, all the way back to Cannich in Glenmoriston. I chose my security guard, Colm MacKenzie, my son in law, Angus MacKenzie, Hugh Og Chisholm, and I was yet to talk to both Ali MacAlpin and Old John MacDonnell, with his men to deal with that giant brown wolf, if it became a reality.

As I strolled up the Old Drovers Road to John's place, I felt sick to my stomach, and I vomited by the roadside. 'Oh God help us was my prayer against the sickos in our world'. I was blaming myself for allowing it to happen mixing up dead people from ancient times and the current day, with a living soul like my sweet granddaughter and I owed her the world to rectify it. Before I reached his house, one of his men saw me being sick and came to assist. That was embarrassing, so I brushed him off.

"I really need to talk to John. But please warn him that it is not an ordinary issue," I said.

When I arrived, John was his usual offhand self.

"Malcolm, what do you want? I'm busy," John asked.

"So was I, until a few moments ago, but something important has come up, so I have put down my tools and I have come here to talk to you, because a group of us are meeting in Glenmoriston tomorrow night, to achieve something up on Beinn Coinneach, in MacKenzie lands," I said. "Where you would come in, is to kill a mythical wolf, mythical or real, no-one knows for sure, but it's brown, huge and unkillable for generations, going back beyond anyone's grandparents' memories and it needs to be kept at bay, at least, while I kidnap my granddaughter and her husband off that mountain, with their thirty horses and foals," I said.

"You don't do anything in half measures Malcolm, that's for sure, so do I need to know why you are kidnapping them?" John asked.

"You can be sure to know that it is justified," I said.

"Who has been raped then?" John asked. I told him the bizarre tale, as well as what had happened to Hector, to control that poor lad, and he was so enraged, that he offered up his best sharp shooters.

"John, it may be a shape shifting person, not a real wolf or a Werewolf, it could require those silver musket balls," I added which really raised his curiosity level.

"What have you got yourself involved in, son?" John asked.

"The man who painted all those lovely paintings may not be,

who he seems to be, is all I can say, so if you succeed, it will mean the end of the paintings too," I added.

John had never called me son before, so there was a level of compassion that I had never heard or felt from Old John, before.

He knew we were in trouble. Real trouble.

I was due next to speak with Zahra's oldest son, Ali MacGregor, in the Aird and then somehow convince him of the soundness of the plan, then meet up at the Hart of the Highland Manor, where a very large dinner table was booked already for us all and closed off for privacy, and it was going to be paid for. John, Hugh, Angus, Colm, and Duncan Og would all meet us there, with John's men and stay there overnight before we all left for Beinn Coinneach. I left instructions for Duncan Mohr to manage my property, while I was gone. I needed Duncan Og to come with us, to take care of the many horses.

I sent a letter to Grigor Og, requesting the use of Charlotte House on Craskie Farm, for both Hector and Flidas to live in, as husband and wife and I offered to pay their rent, until they were on their feet, with his Highland Pony business. Meredith insisted on accompanying her husband Hugh Og, to be in Cannich upon our return, to feed us all. My wife, Ailsa packed my few things and food into my saddle bags, and I packed enough ammunition to kill any threatening force, as well as knives, of many shapes and sizes. I clinked as I walked, like Duncan did sometimes.

With my rifle strapped to my back, I was ready and was off to the Aird with one stop in Cannich to see Hamish. We needed him on board too. It was the only time that I wished that all the Chisholm brothers were alive, as mad as they were, they were skilled.

23. Operation Fairy Dun

Thank God for good and loyal friends like Hamish. Not only did he allow the whole pony business to operate from there, indefinitely and to occupy his stables, but he was also going to herd all the horses in, when they arrived, no doubt running all over the farm, with his staff herding them into the stables, unless he also joined in. There would be plenty of feed for them at no cost, initially and we would all sleep at his house, when we arrived back with Meredith's cooking, God bless her. Cora said that she would assist Meredith.

Everyone so far had been helpful.

All that was left, was success with Ali. I don't think I had ever prayed so much in my life before, but I prayed the whole way there to the Aird, only stopping the once for my horse to drink. My horse was a strong old girl but maybe this trip to Beinn Coinneach would be her last. It was time to retire her soon anyway. Uncle Alex had bought her for me to impress Cherry when I first met her and that was a very long time ago. My old mare was so reliable, and it's hard to part with a horse that you know and love, so well. I arrived at the very secure looking Wolf Ranch, which was very unappealing really to look at, but secure. I clanged on the bell to let them all know that they had a visitor, when I saw a confused looking red headed lad, who must have been John's nephew, Simon, so I waved saying my name.

"Malcolm MacNachten to see Ali MacAlpin," I shouted over the wind.

He let me in but still unsure of me and not friendly at all.

"Ali will be down in a while," Simon said.

"Can you take my horse out of the cold weather lad, and rub her down?" I asked.

"I'm not a groom," Simon said.

"Well, who is then lad?" I asked.

"Last groom left. Do it yourself," Simon said.

So, Wolf Ranch wasn't looking too good to start with. I rubbed my poor old girl down, just the same, when Ali came into the stables, looking for me.

"Uncle Malcolm, what are you doing out here in the cold stables?" Ali asked.

"A serious matter lad that you and I need to discuss, in private preferably, away from the, 'I'm not a groom redhead,'" I replied.

"Simon said that. I am sorry Uncle Malcolm. He can be rude at times. I do need to employ another groom. The last one left," Ali said.

"Maybe you weren't all friendly enough to him. Grooms are human too," I said. "Can I have a hot drink before we talk and something to eat, or will someone say they don't cook here either?" I asked sarcastically.

Suitably embarrassed, young Ali took me inside the warm enough home, not as I remembered it, with its homely atmosphere when Zahra once lived there. Had Isobel changed it so much, I wondered? The snippy Isobel served me up some beef stew, reluctantly.

"How's the new wee bairn?" I asked her.

"She never sleeps, John doesn't help, and I'm expected to do all of the cooking since Fatma moved to the other house," Isobel replied, in her snippy way.

"Well, I need a private space to talk to Ali. Can we occupy that new house a while because we need to talk after I've eaten? I need to sleep there too. Ali, do you have a problem with any of that?" I asked.

"Nae, I'll get her to move in here with her husband and you can have that house with me, for the night," Ali replied.

"Good luck with that," snapped Isobel.

He was gone for about ten minutes and finally a grumpy look-ing Fatma and Simon both came into the main house to free up space for us, so we left with our coffee for the night.

Isobel was not a happy new Mither at all.

Relating the story of Hector and his wife Flidas, to Ali was dis-tressing for anyone to hear but Ali's motives for his keenness to join us was partly motivated by his desire to be away from the rest of his family, for a while. We left early the following morning, but he wasn't to embarrass his brother or sister-in-law with the details of the story and so the reason he gave for leaving was a business matter. Which it was.

Thirty ponies. Ali was embarrassed that his farm was no longer the wholesome and friendly place, that it had once been, when his Mither and father were there, running things and John was only good with the coos, not people. Ali was worried about introducing his new wife, April into that environment, because she was so young and there was little doubt that Isobel would eat her alive, Ali thought.

"What's wrong with Isobel then? She wasn't this bad before. Surely, it's not only sleep deprivation?" I enquired.

"My opinion is, that she misses Alex. On top of that, she has never forgiven all the men for destroying, so completely, her biological father, Hugh Chisholm. Even I didn't think he deserved that," Ali said. "She still prays for him over at the waterfall, hoping he will come back, as was told to her," Ali said. "That is truly a tragic sight to see, so I put up with her bad behaviour, for that reason. She was always snippy, no doubt about that, but not like this," Ali said.

"If Ma could see her now, or even how the farm doesn't func-tion properly anymore, she might think of returning home for good. When she does come home, like the last time, as soon as

Coinneach turns up, she leaves and goes straight back to Misty Mountain with him. I have often asked myself whether if she was faced with both of her husbands, Coinneach and Grigor, who she would chose," Ali continued.

"I know Ma cannot cope without a man, because of where she comes from, with her innate fear of being unable to cope without a man, here in the Highlands. It must be easier to live without a man, where she is from originally, so here she is genuinely afraid and so I can't belittle that fear when she is from another entirely different world to us and not Scottish either. At least we can all say that we are Scottish, but what can Ma say? Her country doesn't even exist yet in the form that it existed when she was writing her books. She can't even say, 'Oh I'm Polish or French' or some such, can she?" Ali said reflectively.

He had given his Mither's life a lot of thought and I can't say that I even knew that she was from a country that didn't yet exist. That would be very strange indeed, without anything familiar to draw upon and without the skills needed either, to live in such an environment as harsh as ours is.

"That must be why she suffered from hypothermia then. Her country must have been hot, do you think?" I asked.

"I never asked her that, but that combined with not knowing not to jump into deep snow, like she did that day, would make sense. No wonder she is more comfortable high up there inside that mansion, where no harm can come to her at least," Ali said.

"But what if, as you say, Grigor Mohr presents himself as an option again, would she come back to the Aird?" I asked.

"I don't know. Da did really hurt her, but so has Coinneach, just differently," Ali said. "In Coinneach's defence, no matter what he has done to Hector and Flidas, he did save Ma. Maybe she just should stay there without any of us now," Ali concluded. "I know Fatma doesn't want to go there. She wants to stay at home with the unfriendly redhead. I don't know what she sees in him really," Ali added.

"Why don't you sell your half of the farm then, and take your money and buy a farm, near me in Glengarry. We need people like you. I could give you a job, while you look around and I'll introduce you to John MacDonnell tonight, who has considerable influence in Glengarry, unpleasant though he can be, buying land in MacDonnell country requires his blessings, unless you inherit it, or are English with a thieving heart. Then you and wee April would be close to home, as in her home at least, near her Mither and father and we consider you family. What do you think, would you consider that?" I asked.

"I like the idea," Ali replied. "Hector will be in Glenmoriston and we could see more of each other. I hate him being up there on Beinn Coinneach," Ali said.

"Poor Hector," Ali then added. When we finally arrived, our horses were taken by reliable grooms. Thank goodness for a good groom. My old girl was already tired. Hamish called out to us both and said he was coming with us to the meeting, as well as the meal. He didn't want to be left out and I guessed that he'd want to come to Beinn Coinneach too, so that he was part of the action.

"Who's paying for it?" I asked.

"I don't know, not me is all I know," Hamish said smiling and slapping me on the shoulder. "Are you sleeping at my place, or the haunted hotel?" Hamish asked.

"Your place please," I replied.

I had told Grandda to be present with Alex and Grigor Mohr at the meeting and to pretend that they were my cousins and Grandda just looked a lot like me, was all, if anyone commented on both of our appearances, and I had to call him Padruig, which wasn't pleasing to him at all, but he agreed to that.

At the *'once in a lifetime meeting'* were, Alex MacDonald, Padruig Dubh Grant, me, Grigor Mohr MacGregor, John MacDonald Os'sian, Old John MacDonnell from Glengarry with twelve marksmen, Hugh Og Chisholm, Hamish Chisholm, Ali MacAlpin, Duncan Og MacDonnell, Angus MacKenzie, with a horse and cart and Colm MacKenzie, all with loaded weapons. We numbered twenty-four. Duncan Og was specifically tasked to aid the horses and would assist Hector.

Old John and his twelve marksmen would cover the wolf, or any unexpected return of Prince Griogar from the Outer Hebrides.

Ali was going to go up to the mansion first to convince his brother, Hector and wife Flidas to leave the mansion quickly and pack up their belongings immediately, which in turn would go into the cart, driven by Flidas's, flustered father, Angus MacKenzie. Flidas would travel then beside her father, having been given plenty of food and water for everyone, as well as hay and apples for the ponies and the horses, for the journey back to Glenmoriston.

According to the plan, Hector would ride his own horse to drive his ponies down the mountain, with Duncan Og, me, Padruig, Alex, Grigor Mohr, Hugh Og, Hamish, Ali, and Colm, who always had a gun at the ready, as did I.

The Glengarry shooters would all be at the ready, in hiding initially, after Ali entered the big mansion. Once the group were on their way off the mountain, the Glengarries would hold up the rear, as protection from being attacked from behind, by locals or the wolf.

24. Chaos or Order?

On the way to Beinn Coinneach, Old John MacDonnell was in the lead of the whole party, as he was too suspicious of the true identities of my 'cousins' Padruig Dubh Grant, Alex and Grigor. According to a portrait hung in Tartan Hall, which I had forgotten about, the resemblance was exactly how my Grandda had appeared then and now. Given the 'Otherworldly' aspect of the whole story and John's awareness that the hotel was also haunted by my Grandda and his friends, Old John, therefore took charge and those were his conditions. At least, until we arrived, he said. It didn't help that I accidentally slipped up and called Grandda by his title and not Padruig, on one occasion at the meeting. Two of John's crack shooters didn't trust it at all then, withdrew and went home to Glengarry that same night.

It was familiar to me how Old John ran his team, and it was a fast pace, all the way to Beinn Coinneach, not stopping, not chatting, and certainly never smiling. When Old John got into kill mode, he had only that in mind and he expected everyone else to follow suit. That was difficult for the Glenmoriston Men, who were accustomed to running their own show, but if they needed skilled manpower, they had to swallow their pride. After all, they had killed off three of their own gang. Not too smart a move, it had now turned out to be, as a holistic decision for everyone, especially Isobel Fraser, who was becoming more Clan Chisholm, with every day that passed.

My poor old mare was exhausted upon arrival at the base of that cloud covered, huge mountain and my poor old girl still yet had to climb up there, as soon as we had the signal from them. Ali bravely left our company then nervously, leading, as Old John furtively led his men into hiding, surrounding the mansion. I estimated that by the time my mare had her breath back, Ali would have reached the top and entered the mansion, under the guise of visiting his brother, Hector.

On the way, he would pass the thirty ponies and foals, whom he said later had looked a little skittish and were running around, inside their enclosure. They had already sensed the presence of a large group of men and horses. The smell of horse sweat was in the air and wafting upwards into their flaring nostrils. Not only horses could smell that. It worried me that the wolf could smell, or sense us coming. I had stopped worrying about Zahra, it was the wolf that concerned me the most and the lives of the men from Glengarry and Glenmoriston.

The signal was passed on and we were then to go up the mountain road, as quickly as we could, to herd the ponies back down the mountain. We met Hector there, looking anxious but undoubtedly, clearly desperate to leave, and was following his brother Ali. His wife, Flidas was already in the cart with her father and was going down the mountain track and on her way, hopefully to safety. As Hector opened the ponies' gate, the ponies ran like the devil was at their heels. They were not going to be easy to control, but we just started to herd them carefully on the slippery, wet surface. None of the Highland Ponies slipped on the road downwards, but Hamish's big old horse slipped a bit, and he leapt off, to remain uninjured.

I stopped to assist Hamish, while he helped his horse up onto his feet. Thank goodness his horse wasn't badly injured, and neither was Hamish. That meant that we were however, alone at the rear for a while and vulnerable. I was pretty sure then, that I smelled wolf, but it didn't make an appearance. My rifle was loaded up and ready, while I waited for Hamish to get sorted. I aimed it in the direction of the odour, but maybe the wolf recognised me, was my guess and chose not to launch an attack.

Old John had intended to be behind us, so chaos temporarily reigned.

No-one could wait upon us, due to the incredible pace of the Highland Ponies. The Crofters had all closed their windows and doors, as well as all their shutters. They wanted nothing to do with whatever was happening outside. So much for the MacKenzies all rallying around their King. If I was to guess on where their sympathies lay, it was with Hamish and his horse, trying to get those young folk and their horses off that mountain.

My heart was racing, I admit, not knowing where my enemy might appear from. Thank God, Hamish's horse was well enough to leave that mountain, but Hamish would need to ride in the cart, I thought, for the rest of the journey home, lessening the weight on his poor old horse. A horse's hips were vulnerable to breakage, not unlike humans in a fall, only horses usually have to be put down with a broken hip. I could see the look on Hamish's anguished face over his beloved horse and he agreed to ride in the cart, with his horse following. I had involved so many of my dear friends and neighbours, so it was important to succeed, at this kidnapping at least, with Hector's ponies.

How else would he make a living now that he was a married man?

Seeing my sweet Granddaughter riding in the cart was an emotional moment of both relief and horror. Old John was waiting for me, to my surprise, then he waited for Hamish to sort out his horse and get into the cart, with me watching on, still nervous that the wolf was there.

"Did you smell it?" I asked.

"Aye, I did," Old John said.

We must have both looked awfully serious, but finally the group all moved off, once again at that quick pace, this time led by my grandfather, Padruig Dubh, then Alex MacDonald and Grigor MacGregor. The ponies were behind them and the rest of the group, trying to herd the ponies, behind the three of them. Old John and his shooters held up the rear, enabling me to help the whole droving process. My horse was doing well, in the company of the wee ponies, and I grew to like the funny wee things.

They were strong and flighty and spirited. Some would say wild. I wasn't as young as I once was, and I knew Hamish was feeling that too.

We reached Glenmoriston as an exhausted rabble, except for the ponies who could have kept running, even galloping at one time, which slowed to a canter, thank goodness. I was going to retire my poor old girl after this, I decided. The gates were open at Craskie Farm, as was the plan, even though Hamish was supposed to have stayed home but couldn't stay out of the action.

His grooms and somehow, Grigor Og had appeared to herd the Highland Ponies into the stables and even James Grant was on his border to keep them on Craskie Farm, for the time being. I was sure that I saw a few Collie dogs who herded them too, but I didn't know who had the collies. Then they seemed to disappear, as quickly as they had appeared.

I knew only one man who had kept Collies, Hugh Mohr Chisholm.

All the people who had helped were either staying free of charge in the hotel or with Hamish in the main house. Hector and his wife were given Charlotte House but ate first at Hamish's house with her father, Angus who wept upon arrival, holding his daughter tightly to him apologising to her. Hamish, Hugh Og, Grigor Og, and I stayed in his house with Duncan Og and Colm MacKenzie. Old John was staying up in the hotel and paid the huge bill for the dinner that we'd all enjoyed there, without being asked for it.

He was impressed with young James Grant, he said and was planning to use my cousin's business more often.

<h1>25. The Aftermath</h1>

It was said from the MacKenzies who lived in the Glens beneath Beinn Coinneach, that soon after our departure, known as the **'Day of the Glengarries'**, that another army arrived. It was Prince Griogar with Belgian mercenaries, who had joined him from the Outer Hebridean Islands. He was there to kidnap Zahra and her two small bairns, but not Coinneach Og MacAlpin. They snatched Causantin and Dihaoine but both of those MacGregor bairns were then left in the Aird, with Isobel unharmed and in good health, while their Mither, Zahra wasn't seen again then for a very long time.

The prince took Zahra to the Outer Hebrides, where she was rumoured to have married him. He had threatened to do that, and I may have provided the perfect opportunity for him to succeed.

Grigor Mohr MacGregor then returned with Ali, first to the Aird, to raise his youngest two bairns and to restore balance on Wolf Ranch. Soon after that, Ali left for Glengarry, as I had suggested after selling his share of Wolf Ranch, back to his father. Colm MacKenzie then told us of what had taken place next in Beinn Coinneach, when he went home to visit his own family, in MacKenzie lands.

The local Crofters say that they had seen an enormous grey cloud rolling in, over the top of that huge mountain and they were expecting a terrible storm, so they all closed their shutters and herded their animals under cover.

When no rain, nor lightning, nor thunder came, they opened their doors once again, out of curiosity. There was just dense fog over where the mountain called, Beinn Coinneach, once stood. The giant wolf and all that mythology, if it was indeed a myth, was gone, as was Coinneach MacAlpin himself and his wee bairn, Coinneach Og, born of Zahra. All that remained, was an enormous giant ring of mushrooms, that grew where the base of the mountain once had been. Green grass grew inside that enormous ring of mushrooms, but not even local coos, sheep, goats or hares would go inside that ring of mushrooms, to graze upon the luscious green grass.

Zahra's bairns were then spread to the four winds.

◊

Ali moved to Glengarry, selling his farm share back to his father, then worked for me for a while, until a small farm became available for himself and his wife, April my niece. Hector and Flidas stayed on in Cannich, in Glenmoriston, running his Highland Pony business, living in Charlotte House with Flidas, and paying rent to Grigor Og. Isobel stayed in the Aird with Alex, her second husband and her Stepfather, Grigor Mohr MacGregor and Padruig.

The two Frasers also stayed but were told to pull up their socks or leave.

Fatma moved back into the main house, so that Isobel and all the bairns, with Alex and Zahra's bairns and on occasion John, moved to the new house. More often Padruig as well. Fatma and the moody Simon, stayed in the old house. Zahra's wolf puppy had been delivered with Causantin and wee Dihaoine and the wolf lived with Fatma for a time and eventually left them, to re-join her pack with Wolfie, once more.

Causantin genuinely missed Coinneach, Coinneach Og and Zahra, as did wee Dihaoine and relayed what had happened to them both, to the family frequently and often, describing the event as having been 'stolen' but no-one believed either of them. Grigor never strayed again to another woman and regretted his life decisions but lived in hope that one day, he would be re-united with Zahra, who was fast becoming a myth herself.

James's hotel, was no longer haunted, although it was

advertised as such to still attract new guests of the ghoulish variety, because James had lost his golfing fields to the ponies, but his wife Susan had left him. His Mither Henrietta, never got out of bed anymore, after her husband had died just waiting for death to come, so James hired all new staff, and the food was much better, and the guests returned.

It had cost us all to rescue both young people, but we would do it all over again, if we had to, despite Zahra's unfortunate demise.

I lost my dear old mare soon after, as did Hamish lose his old gelding. Grigor Og paid for Hamish to own a new horse, but I was without a horse for a while longer. I didn't want to replace my old girl. I think it was harder losing my mare, than losing my first wife. Even John offered me one of his horses, but I declined with gratitude. God would choose the right one, at the right time and I had to fall in love with my animals. Call it a weakness, if you like, but I borrowed the lads' ponies for a while. The first horse that Old John tried to give me, was another mare and I had told him that I would feel disloyal to my old lady, so he took her home, unsure of me that day, as I wiped tears away from my eyes. He gave her to Ali, who was more grateful than me, he had said.

I still couldn't replace her. Maybe I was depressed.

I spent nights crying in bed, over my horse. Then finally my dearest and only brother, Kenneth came to me with the most beautiful, but dangerous looking, black stallion. It wanted to bite me at first, but he had a strong character, and he made me smile. I accepted the semi, wild animal because he had fire in his belly. I hoped I still had the skills to handle such an animal, and I admit, he was a challenge, but increasingly as he occupied my thoughts, my old girl was becoming easier to overcome. My wife, Ailsa throughout the whole ordeal of losing my old girl, was nothing less than amazing. She loved me more.

"Oh Malcolm, you are such a sweet and sensitive man, and

I love you so much," Ailsa would say often.

That was a bonus. More sex for me and cuddles and kisses, even cuddles from Islay who rarely cuddled me.

Angus was never quite the same after seeing us all in action that day and knowing what had happened to his daughter Flidas and her husband Hector. He was more respectful towards me and all those men who had all risked their lives and livelihoods that day for his wee lass and Hector. He examined his own values, I suppose, and he had more long conversations about life, with Hugh. My twins were even serious enough to listen in to those conversations. They had matured over that period, and I never wanted them to ever leave my farm, although something told me that they would.

My oldest son was Alex and normally, he would inherit the farm, but he came to me one day and asked if that tradition could change, given what had been spent on him already and he wanted the twins, who were next in line, to inherit the whole farm. I altered my Will to reflect my twins as my heirs for both the farms and their Team but not the goat farm as that was to go to Islay and Angus.

26. Father or Not?

Old John invited me over to his house for a casual chat over coffee and sandwiches, for morning tea one day, which was odd and unlike him to be sociable, but I accepted his invitation, thinking he must have something up his sleeve. He always did. He had the morning tea nicely arranged on porcelain plates and the coffee was Turkish, so it was strong, but I liked it.

He started asking me personal questions like who my father was and more importantly, where he was. Naturally I thought he already knew all that information, with gossip the way it is in these parts. I explained that my father died when I was four years old. He asked then if my Mither had replaced him, to which I said no, until she married Bruce MacDonald in her later years.

"So, you were a Grant though?" John asked.

"On my Ma's side, aye," I explained. "Ma had married Nachtain MacNachten in Loch Insh," I said.

"How did she meet him then? Grants don't usually mix with the MacNachtens," Old John asked.

"I didn't grow up with the Grants, I grew up with the MacNachtens," I added, not knowing where this conversation was going.

"But you are the spitting image of your grandfather. Why weren't you on Craskie Farm like the rest of them?" he asked. I thought John knew all of this, but I explained it all again how Ma was removed as a wee bairn for her safety to a childless couple in Loch Insh, the MacNachtens, which was where Kenneth and I grew up.

"You, poor wee things, separated from your family and for what reason?" John asked.

I didn't want to disclose that the perverted neighbour was a MacDonald, so it stayed as a difficult neighbour relationship that caused Old Isobel, my grandma and her father to remove my Ma, for her own safety.

"They did not anticipate that there was a political matter coming up in 1745, 46 that would end their arrangement with my Mither for a very long time, therefore us as well, when we were born. We were in our teens before we even met Grandma, but Grandda wasn't told of our existence," I added.

"I enjoyed my life in Loch Insh, John. I have no complaints about how I was raised. The MacNachtens were kind people. They were always good to both my brother and I and when my father died, we were raised by my grandfather who was not blood, but he was my Mither's foster father. He was always kind to us and he taught us his craft of stone masonry and how to engrave the tomb stones and headstones in his beautiful artistic designs, some of which resemble Pictish Art," I said.

I started to feel uncomfortable at what would come next and wanted to leave as soon as possible, but his attention then was on my father again. Was I close to him and that kind of questioning? Of course, I was close to my father, and I remember him clearly, fishing together on the loch and the conversation with John was getting to me, as I could see my father's smiling face, as if it was yesterday. I would watch him enter all of the drawings for each stone slab into his book of records with that person's name attached and the date, in a bookkeeping manner, but it was a perfect record of their family art really. He left the book with Grandda MacNachten and he passed it onto me. We were different folk from Loch Insh, which no-one had understood since the move to Glenmoriston, so revisiting these old memories began to break my heart.

"Malcolm, my son," he said suddenly. "I may not have treated you well, since you came to Glengarry, and I regret that. You are a fine young man, and I truly wish you were my son," Old John added, which shocked me.

"You have treated me well enough John. I have no complaints about you. We all have our problems, or our reasons for being who we are," I said. "Now I have to get back to my coos John," I said, feeling keen to leave.

"In a moment my son," Old John said. "You know that I do not have an heir, don't you?" he asked.

"Not really, but maybe?" I replied vaguely.

"I want you to be my son. Not as in, change your life for me, or wipe my bum when I'm too old to do it myself. Just to inherit this land. And so, I can call you, my son. I want to do that because none of these losers around here are worthy of it, but you are. Will you allow me to call you my son, seeing as how you don't have a father, and I don't have a son?" Old John asked plainly.

"I'm not forgetting Bruce, your stepfather, of only a short time, I mean a real father, son relationship," John added.

"I don't know what that is, at this time of my life John. I'm not young either, so what would that look like?" I asked.

"Some warmth between us, as father and son for a start," John declared.

"Warmth?" I repeated.

"A hug and a kiss, that kind of thing and I'll leave you, my land. All of it. If your father was alive, you would hug him, wouldn't you and kiss him? No name change needed or adoption papers. It would be just between us, and it will be known that you are my son. What do you say?" John asked.

Part of me wanted to run out of there, but another very deep part that he had tapped into, was my beloved father and how it would have been today, if he had been alive. That distressed me a bit and I thought I had overcome his passing, but here was someone wanting to stand in for him. If only as a gesture. That felt better than hostility between neighbours and then there was the inheritance. John also spoke to my heart like no-one in the Grant family ever had to either myself or my brother. Except for my cousin, James of course.

"John, don't you have someone to leave your property to?" I asked.

"I don't and you haven't answered my question," he said staring directly at me in the eyes. I had never noticed how blue that John's eyes were before.

"After what happened up on Beinn Coinneach to Hector, I just don't want you to fall prey to such an evil as that, if ever you were in need of a father figure, which I think you are, my son," John added, repeatedly calling me his son. I felt myself becoming emotional, never expecting this tough old nut to ever like me, let alone think of me as a son, whom he wanted warmth from. I thought he would be worse than the Grants ever were, so I was also becoming confused. It didn't help either that my first wife jilted me and had three of my bairns terminated, so trust was big for me and this man trusted me.

"Can you please describe the warmth," I asked.

"Malcolm, son. I am not going to rape you, if that is what your tortured mind has conjured up. Normal warmth between normal people, like with your own family who kiss and cuddle and maybe even eat a meal together occasionally. Do I have to demonstrate it?" John asked.

Suddenly Old John was hugging me, as stiff as I was with my arms both held by my side.

"Not like that you idiot," he jested and smiled a bit. Old John was determined. He kissed me on both cheeks and held me tightly, until I was crying like a baby. It was nice to be held by a trusted man who wasn't going to rape me. I kissed him too, which was weird for me, but he liked it, and he held me by my shoulder and hugged me again.

We then sat together on his big old couch, and I cried for around ten minutes, tears of grief and loss, while he wiped away my tears and it wasn't long, that he was kissing my whole face expressing Gaelic words of love and reassurance, which I had never expected from this old hard nut of a man.

He carefully took my hand with his fingers interlocked with mine.

"You are my son then, Malcolm MacNachten and I love you, as my son," he said kissing me gently and lovingly, as a father would. I felt an unknown stirring from within myself because I had never known this kind of love before, in my adult life.

"My lovely son," John said. "Accept me as your father," John demanded, and I agreed. "We can go out to dinner together one night if you like, at your cousin's hotel and stay there for the night. We can go over the inheritance details and arrange for a visit to the lawyers, so you can believe in it. I'll arrange it all." John said.

"Good son, my good son," he kept saying, wiping away my tears and then he kissed me again. I began to cry again, and he kept kissing me on my face. I was a mess.

"You are my son Malcolm," John said, trying to console me.

He had hit a raw nerve that I hadn't even known was raw, but John had.

It was coming up to lunch time and his house was becoming noisy, as his men were all arriving home to eat lunch.

"Remember Malcolm. You are my son now," he said as I departed. I was going to miss him, already.

 I wasn't sure whether I would tell Ailsa yet, but maybe Hugh? What would he think? What would Kenneth think? Maybe I should keep it to myself, until it was in writing after that dinner in Glenmoriston. I hoped I didn't look a mess going home, so I went to my coos in the brief bit of sunshine, to improve the look of my face, after crying so much. Maybe it was time to visit my birth father's grave in Loch Insh with Ailsa and all the family and our youngest two bairns, Gordon and Eschina.

Hugh came to me, while I was trying to hide in amongst my lady coos, mooching around me like they always did.

"I always know when you're here, Malcolm when the coos all mooch together around, guess who? You. I have never seen coos behave like these ones do with you. They're more your pets. Anyhow. What's up with John then?" Hugh asked.

I was put right on the spot, and I made the decision, to tell a great friend, provided it wasn't repeated.

"He put forth a proposal to me," I said.

"Oh aye? Hugh said curiously. "What proposal?" Hugh asked.

"He wants me to be his son and heir, because he doesn't have a son, that's legitimate anyhow, and I lost my father at a young age, so he felt I was vulnerable to the likes of Coinneach MacAlpin. He didn't want me to experience what Hector has been through. For that to occur, he suggested that we accept each other as father and son and would discuss it further over dinner with inheriting his property upon his passing," I said, in short, leaving out all the emotional stuff.

"Blimey Malcolm, how do you manage to inherit from unrelated folk?" Hugh replied. "Go for it if you ask me. You have nothing to lose," Hugh said sincerely. He noticed my face altering a bit, to a level of sadness and sat down beside me.

"So, you don't want to replace your Da, is that it?" Hugh asked. I hugged my old friend who hugged me back. "How about we visit his grave then, like we did before. You can ask him directly then?" Hugh said.

"You are such a good friend Hugh. Aye. I want to visit his grave again. Can we all go together for lunch by the loch, in Loch Insh?" I asked.

"I would love that. Meredith loved it there and so did our daughter, Ferne," Hugh said.

"This weekend then?" I asked. "Do my lads have any work on the weekend?" I asked.

"Not now," Hugh said firmly. "We'll take my six-horse team and load it all up," Hugh said, patting me on my shoulder and went to arrange it with Meredith. I started feeling excited then about visiting Loch Insh and told Kenneth and Ivy who wanted April and Ali to come too. The group would be me, my son in law, Angus, my precious daughter, Islay, with her son Padraig and daughters Florence and Flidas, with her husband Hector, Hugh Og and Meredith with their daughter, Ferne, my wife Ailsa and our youngest bairns, Gordon and Eschina, my wonderful twins Malcolm Og, Hamish Og, Hugh's brother and our good friend Hamish, with his wife Cora. Ma and Bruce were not to be forgotten this time. It was quite the crowd, so Hugh Og ended up deciding on the eight-horse team, because of the weight.

I loved my big Glengarry family and thanked God for them all.

Alex and Mairi were invited too but Alex was too busy with his patients. Glengarry was keeping him on his toes, but he was earning plenty of money at the same time and he liked his work with his patients, and they all liked and depended on him.

A rider came down from Old John's and then I wasn't sure how to think of him. He was always, Old John MacDonnell, now was he, my father? I really had to visit my father's grave, lest it mess up my mind. The rider gave me a note requiring a response. It was to invite me to dinner at the 'Hart of the Highland Manor' on the following Tuesday evening, leaving Glengarry, early morning in John's coach with him at ten o'clock, then staying over in James's hotel, that night, at no cost to myself.

I accepted in writing and the rider left.

I then had two big events to prepare for. I thought I would wear my kilt to next week's dinner. But the weekend was shorts, underneath my work pants, so I could swim in the freezing, cold water of Loch Insh and maybe do some fishing too and introduce Gordon and Eschina to their grandfather's grave. The twins might remember the grave, I thought, but they had forgotten it but remembered the loch and its ducks, so they were excited. Islay remembered that previous visit clearly, because she saw some kind of ghost behind my father's tomb stone. At the time, she said it was a 'King of Scotland'. Her daughter Florence was looking forward to it and so was Angus. We all needed some family fun, including Hector who found it hard to socialise with people, other than his own immediate family and he missed his Mither, Zahra.

The carriage was filled with bedding for the trip back home with blankets for the bairns and raincoats for the drivers. The women sorted out the food and included stools to sit on. Hugh made sure that there was fishing lines and rods. As usual, upon arrival, I gave my courteous greetings to the family now occupying Granddad's old croft, near the old 'Chapel of the Swans' and they bought down buckets of water for our Clydesdales.

The weather wasn't as warm as it had been on our previous visit, but I dived straight into the cold water of the loch, competing with the ducks whose little legs were competing with the current. It was lovely to feel that familiar feeling of the loch and the warm feeling of home, even though it was a long time ago now. Ailsa was curiously going through the old Chapel and was keen to know where I had grown up.

After I dried myself from my swim in the loch and put some clothes over my wet shorts, my wife then objected. "They're wet darling. You can't wear them. Take them off and I'll stand in front of you while you dress, so no-one can see your glorious manhood," Ailsa said, so I took off my wet shorts.

"Glorious manhood, is it?" I teased.

"Aye it is," she said smiling. "Our sons have inherited it too," Ailsa said.

"Have they? I hadn't noticed lately. Should I look?" I asked.

"Aye, the twins are well put together love and so is Gordon, even as young as he is," Ailsa said.

"Do they have any problems with their foreskins?" I asked.

"Nae, but they wouldn't tell me that. Maybe you could check in with them," she suggested.

After lunch, some rested, some slept, some fished, while I walked up to my father's grave. This visit was different to other visits and given that I was alone, I felt confident to talk to my father. After the usual greetings, I asked him if it would hurt him if another man could stand in for him as my father, now as an older adult, because the man concerned had no heir and was also without a son. Both of us with an emotional need. I didn't know if my father could hear me but sneaking up behind me as usual, was Islay, who had overheard the story.

"Da, I'm so sorry. I overheard you," Islay said appearing saddened by the story.

"There is a ghost there again Da, can you see him?" Islay asked.

"Can you describe him, Islay?" I asked.

"He looks younger than you are now, more like Angus's age. He has black, longish hair, with a black moustache and a wee beard. He is very handsome like you, but with sad eyes. He knows who you are and looks like he wishes he was alive with you. He is your father," Islay said choking back tears.

"Can you ask him if he would mind if John MacDonnell stepped in as my father now?" I asked. She spoke to the ghost, whom she said then looked at her and then me again and nodded in agreement and then vanished. Islay was crying when I looked at her.

"Och, my sweet child, I am sorry. Are you alright?" I asked.

"It's just so sad Da. I am so sorry, I had never thought of you needing a Da too, like I still do," Islay said.

"I don't mind if you feel that Mr MacDonnell can be your

father, even though he is old now. Bruce hasn't done much for you or Uncle Kenneth, but at least, he has been there as a presence, which is better than nothing, I suppose," Islay said.

"Do I have your support then, Islay sweetheart?" I asked.

"Aye Da, you always do. Does Ailsa know yet?" Islay asked.

"Nae, she doesn't. I am meeting up with John to sort it all out on Tuesday evening. I am leaving with him early in the morning, and we are staying in Glenmoriston for the night and back home Wednesday late after we have been to Inverness," I said.

"Sort what out?" Islay asked.

"You mustn't repeat this to Angus or Ailsa yet or any MacDonnells, please promise me that love, but he wants me to inherit from him," I said.

"I promise. So, Mr MacDonnell needs an heir, and you need a father," Islay said in an understanding manner.

"Aye," I said, but others were coming there to visit the graves, so we stopped talking about it.

I was amazed that Islay had the same gift that I had, in talking to the dead without telling me, only she could see them too and I couldn't, unless they chose to.

I felt satisfied then, that day, that my own father had agreed to Old John MacDonnell acting as my father now to me, sad though it must have been for him and Tuesday couldn't come quick enough. I told Ailsa I was going with John to the hotel, if she needed to know where I was, but I would not be home until late on Wednesday.

27. Exit John MacDonnell

Dressed up in my kilt with an additional bag for the following day, my hair washed and tied back, which was a hairdo for me and polished knee-high boots, I was ready on time, as was John. His carriage was almost better than Coinneach's. He was also wearing his kilt, so we did look a fine pair, going out to dinner in Glenmoriston.

"So, you never wear the newly designed Grant tartan, son?" John asked.

"Nae, this is my family tartan, besides which the Glenmoriston Grants had their own tartan that they designed themselves, unlike the other Grants on Spey," I replied.

"What would your grandfather say about that?" he asked.

"I don't know. I'll have to ask him, but from memory, the Glenmoriston Grants' tartan was always different to the rest of the Grant family and Grandda rarely wears his tartans anyway. He keeps it well hidden," I said.

"So, you are one of those who can speak to the dead, are you, my son?" Old John asked.

"Not all the dead, nae. Just Grandda and one time with Zahra, who contacted me, with difficulty," I said.

He put his hand on my knee and told me how happy he was, to be going out with me as my father. He kissed me and said he wanted a warm relationship.

"I do too. I think it will be good for both of us to feel that family connection that we have both been missing," I said.

"I am happy you do too, my son. I love you and I want you to know that. People are afraid to even say that word, love, but I want it to be used with you and I, don't you?" he said.

"Sometimes we Scots think it's too effeminate to use words like 'love' but that's not it at all. Look at Culloden. If the Clans hadn't loved Bonny Prince Charlie, they wouldn't have fought for him. They did love him, rightly or wrongly. Your Grandda was one of those who loved him, wasn't he?" John said.

"Aye he was, but I never speak to him about those times," I answered.

"I admired your Grandda, he was one who was either loved or hated, but always admired by us MacDonnells. He was a very brave man," John said.

"He always calls me a little gobshite, or other rude words, but I am used to it," I said.

"I will never call you that Malcolm, not even in jest," John said seriously. "Have you ever called me names?" John asked.

"Only comments like 'a hard nut,' that sort of thing, nothing derogatory," I said.

"That's unusual, I get called all kinds of things around Glengarry, you've no doubt heard them all?" John asked.

"Can't say I have. I doubt people would speak ill of you around me," I said.

"I thought so. You are indeed my good son. I am just so happy to be with you?" he said. I was enjoying the closeness with this man and excited to be going out with him. It really felt like an occasion. His hand stayed on my knee, and he felt my bony kneecaps.

"You have bony kneecaps. Are you eating enough, my son?" he asked feeling all around my knees. I looked at his knees under his kilt and they were not as bony as mine. "Maybe I should eat more, they are a bit bony. Yours are not as bony as mine," I said. "Let me put me legs on your lap while I lay down a while" he said, and he took a pillow and put it under his head. I helped him adjust it and held his legs across my lap. This was my father now, I told myself. He was wearing hose and in his right-hand side hose, he was carrying a skein dubh.

"I won't disturb your skein dubh. Do you want it on your belt?" I asked.

"Thank you, son," John said. "Will you rub my knees son. I get arthritis in them, no matter what I do for them," John asked.

I massaged his knees for him, which was normal if you have arthritis, I thought, and it looked painful.

"Is your body hair black all over son, with some grey?" John asked.

"Aye, I'm hairy, its true and it's black with some silver now," I said.

"On your legs too?" John asked.

"Aye, black hair. You don't usually see it when I'm wearing pants but with the kilt it's a bit embarrassing, because I'm so hairy like my father was," I said.

"I think a hairy man is a masculine man and that's you, my son, masculine and I love that about you. You are a man's, man Malcolm, masculine, hairy, handsome, intelligent, honourable, honest, and even loving," John said.

"Can you rub my calf muscles too, I'm enjoying this. Just pull the hose down my son," John said. I pulled down his hose and his legs were hairy too, maybe not as much as mine but I liked the comparisons. He wasn't wearing underwear because his kilt occasionally opened when he moved, revealing his man-hood. His cock was larger than I had expected, and he was circumcised, unlike me.

"My legs are feeling much better now. Can you rub my thighs too son if it's not too much trouble?" John asked. I was a bit hesitant about getting too close to his manhood, but I rubbed his thighs for him which seemed to bring him some relief with the groans he made. He lifted his knees to make the underside accessible to me. Trouble was that revealed his manhood com-pletely, as his kilt lifted with his movement. I made him decent once again by covering him over and to my surprise he said I was a good and decent lad.

He asked me if he could massage me too, as it was a long journey.

I agreed as it was a luxurious act to have a massage. I had never been massaged in my life before. His fingers were strong, and he could massage well, deep into my tissues and it was painful. I didn't realise that I even had a need. I kept jumping about in pain, which made him laugh and I had never seen John laugh before, but massaging my legs was hilarious with me jumping and reacting the way I was. Obviously, my kilt lifted occasionally too and he took a peek and commented.

"I want to know how well endowered my son is," John said. I was embarrassed but he said I had a great cock which would be the envy of most men. "Your biological father must have had a big cock," he said. I had to think back to when I was four years old bathing with him and I suppose it was big, but as a bairn, it was just what it was.

I told him that I had visited my father's grave over the weekend in Loch Insh and had spoken to him, but in fact it was Islay who could communicate with him and asked if he approved of me having him as my new father. My deceased father had nodded in agreement. This brought tears to John's eyes, thinking we had gone to all that trouble and the deceased had approved of him. He was emotional then. He stopped massaging me momentarily and just rested his hands there on both of my thighs and was so grateful to me.

"Thank you, Malcolm," he said. "You are really my son now then, if your Da has agreed," he said.

John became deep in thought at how serious I had taken it all and it wasn't a light-hearted gesture at all. We were going to become family.

"You are not circumcised then my son?" John asked.

"Nae. Ma said there were only midwives available to deliver us in Loch Insh and no Doctors to do that operation, so we are what we are. I think the circumcised cocks look more handsome though, don't you think?" I asked feeling a bit embarrassed that I wasn't circumcised when he was.

"Let me take a look son," he said. He felt around the fore-skin and said it was healthy and a fine-looking cock and not to be embarrassed. He showed me his again to see the difference, but he said mine was bigger, so it was better than his, he thought with or without circumcision. Oddly, it felt better to know from an older man that my cock was alright because I had always wondered and was disappointed that Kenneth and I weren't circumcised.

"Well, we really have bonded now my son, over cocks, haven't we?" he said and laughed a bit at us in the carriage with our cocks on show. I wanted to kiss him in that moment, and we kissed briefly. I wanted to be hugged as he had said and fell into his arms for the rest of the journey as he patted my fore-head lovingly. I wished my father had never died in that moment. I had missed out on so much but here was an opportunity to make up for some of the lost love.

"Call me Da, son," he then said.

"I would like that" I said.

From that day on for what life John had left in him, he was Da and we enjoyed regular meals and nights together as his updated Will went through, leaving everything to me. The land, the house, its contents, the weaponry, his art collection, his horses, his furniture and his massive amount of cash in the bank, as well as in his safe.

He must have known that he didn't have much time left, because he only lived for two months beyond the first night that we spent truly bonding as father and son. We slept side by side, holding one another comfortably and I called him Da until his death. He was buried on his own land beside his relatives, who had all gone before him. He left gifts for each of his men and each of the women who had sired one of his bastard army, and that was all. Somehow, I had entered the heart of a hard old nut, as I used to call him, like John MacDonnell who became my father, if only for two months of true happiness for us both.

His funeral was enormous, and I wept so much, I never thought that I could stop. His death knocked me over badly. It had been a tough year and John's life, although marvellous, was an enormous source of the outpouring of grief, for so many people whose lives he had touched, not only mine.

28. MacNachten Enterprises

There was planning to do then over both farms. Even though John had filled me in with everything, like where I could grow oat crops, due to the bedrock, the cattle and all the bills and taxes that were all paid up. I didn't know where to start because I thought we had more time.

He wasn't meant to die, so soon.

I wondered if Islay and Angus should live in my current house with their son Padraig and daughter Florence, or the twins as Alex had suggested? Padraig had been learning my grandfather's craft from me, engraving the tomb stones or their tomb lids and was in high demand. He did a wonderful job of John's tombstone lid, with an almost exact likeness of John, engraved into stone. Kenneth and I had both agreed that Padraig would inherit that part of the family business complete with the books, the history of our art and the many tools.

I couldn't think straight while I was grieving but we did have to move into John's huge mansion and get all the coos together onto his farm and all the goats together onto my old farm, thereby making Islay's business a bigger concern.

I needed Islay to help me and to become an interim manageress possibly a permanent farm manager on MacNachten Farms. Ma no longer needed her wee house on my farm either, so in retirement Ma and Bruce were going to live permanently, beside loch Garry and manage the empty houses, like mine and Hamish's. My house was occasionally loaned out to staff for a wee holiday by the loch, whenever they were looking tired and both Ma and Bruce kept it in a neat and clean condition, including the front and back yards and I gave her coin for that.

Her house on the farm would eventually become Angus and Islay's house, after its many renovations, as it was nearer Islay's goats. I would need to wait until my lads were both married, before they could take over my old farmhouse. Until then, they would have to live with Ailsa and I, Gordon and Eschina, on my new property. I took one of my security men to the new farm and left Colm MacKenzie on MacNachten Farm, which wasn't ideal, but for now that was how it had to be. I asked locals to ask around for a few more security men. I wrote to Hamish too, letting him know what had occurred and my need once again for security men, as well as two young men for crops, one for breeding poultry and two more grooms.

I also placed an advertisement in the newspaper indicating 'no need to apply without references' prefacing the advertisement.

I changed the name of John's farm, as well as mine to be combined as, "MacNachten Enterprises," with signs over each farm entrance. I thought my biological father would be proud of me when that sign went up. That name was recommended by my brother for taxation purposes. My new farm was also blessed with Ali MacGregor and his wife April, living up against one of my long new borders. He had his oats growing along that border, so that was where I planted my crops on my side too where we were safe from the bedrock, according to John.

With the goats gone from my new farm, it freed up space and allowed for more grazing and more chickens, turkeys, ducks and geese, which I bred in large numbers. I built an enormous shed, specifically for breeding them all. I asked Siobhan to set up multiple bee hives for me too and I ordered twelve. One corner of the property was set aside to re-wild around the wee burn and those plants were acquired from my cousin, Alexander Grant. Jean offered to help plant them all and Siobhan assisted.

I also had to employ a second in charge Farm Manager, as well as Islay, for when I had to leave the properties, so I employed a man who had already worked on John's farm before, and he had a glowing reference from John. His name was Ruauri MacAlpin, but no relation to the MacAlpins from

Beinn Coinneach. He had red curly hair and was well liked and known to be a hard worker and tee total. My concern with the new property was introducing it as a dry farm, so a few of my applicants refused the job based on being unable to drink alcohol, on site.

My wife Ailsa was unable to complete the cleaning of the mansion alone, so I bought in a professional cleaning company from Inverness, as well as the help from my son Alex and his wife Mairi, Kenneth and Ivy and on occasion Ma and Bruce. They were a little bemused by how I had inherited the enormous property. It was still not clean enough by Meredith's standards, who was coming with us to work as a cleaner there and the cook on a higher rate of pay while she was teaching her daughter, Ferne, how to cook.

To satisfy Meredith, I bought in the painters to paint all the interior walls and ceilings as well. Hugh and Meredith were occasionally living in Ma's house on my property when it felt too far to walk to the Loch. They would move out only when it was time for Islay to move in there. It had been vacant for a while and needed modernisation.

At last, thanks to John, there was the money for internal plumbing, new rooves, paint jobs all over both farms, as well as the fences. Even the enlarged goat house was painted inside and out, making it the flashiest goat house in the district. Islay gave me her list of needs for her goat farm with the new goats, thereby needing additional stalls and outdoor space for them. She wanted a separate room, set aside for slaughtering the occasional goat and a specialised cleaner employed for cleaning up all that blood, after a slaughter. Her building was looking very exclusive, so it was nearly time to start advertising our existence, with the new name.

I asked my brother to start doing some sketches for me to advertise in the paper, once the chicks were running around from the chickens, turkeys, ducks and the geese. My idea was to include more poultry into everyone's diets with making them more affordable. This part of the farm was extremely successful financially and it wasn't difficult to achieve and the eggs it produced became a sideline business also that Ailsa took care of by holding regular stalls at the roadside and in the Post Office.

The first sketch that Kenneth drew, was of the Clydesdale teams with Hugh's and Angus's team and Malcolm Og and Hamish Og's team with their adult offsider Iain MacKay. My wife and Ivy wrote up an article on both teams dating back to their origins, being from John Grant to Isobel of Glenmoriston, to Hugh Og Chisholm of both Glengarry and Glenmoriston and then to my MacNachten twins of Glengarry, who were the most popular and the most handsome young men in the entire district. It listed all the work that they were able to do and many that they had already completed. Glengarry was proud to own them as much as I did, when they appeared in the newspapers, with local people writing up reviews on both teams.

The second sketch would be the goat farm with a portrait of Islay and her daughter Florence and some of their goats, displaying their many varieties of cheeses, as well as the beautiful new premises.

The third sketch would be of the oat crops, with my crops on my new farm, as well as Ali MacGregor on his property, demonstrating good neighbour relations with the fence in between us showing both a portrait of myself and Ali, looking oddly like one another, although we were not blood relatives.

The fourth sketch would be of the poultry farm with a variety of breeds of chickens, turkeys, and geese with little chicks being a feature. All the sketches challenged our lady writers to accompany each sketch.

I thought we could encourage security men into that role by dressing both my men in their kilts, with their weapons and looking handsome with a description of their jobs. Duncan wanted his hound too in the sketch, so it was the three of them and it proved to be a very popular sketch. Some people even wrote into the newspaper for a copy of the sketch just to put on their bedroom wall.

I wasn't positive of the outcome, but I hoped it would bring more business our way, promoting ourselves and encouraging people into jobs they may have otherwise overlooked. It turned out to be a great success, with the artist naturally advertising himself too with his Art Gallery.

All a part of 'MacNachten Enterprises.'

29. Who Else Read the Paper?

What we didn't think of, was who else would read the newspaper? It wasn't too long before we heard from the family in the Aird. Padruig, Alex and Grigor were all very interested, given that Ali MacGregor was now my immediate neighbour. Hector read it too and was unsure whether he wanted to move to be in Glengarry, rather than Glenmoriston but decided against it, due to the midges.

The most unlikely interest that we had expected to receive, was a letter from the Outer Hebrides, from Prince Griogar MacAlpin, who wanted to see Kenneth MacNachten or whoever it was who now owned the paintings that he had sold through him, to a man named, John MacDonnell. He wanted them back.

I had yet to enter every room of my new mansion, so I collected up the huge bunch of keys and looked for where John would have kept that art spoken of, as I now owned it all, but hadn't yet found it. The accountant advised me where it all was and took me down into the bowels of the mansion, which I thought was for storing corn or something like that. Inside a very large room was John's art collection. Some were ghastly, some pleasant enough, some plain pornographic but I couldn't find one by Zahra, until I came to a pile of canvasses that looked discarded, possibly awaiting destruction and John must have run out of time to complete everything.

I looked at them all and there were three signed by Zahra, representing my ex-wife's death, by a single shot to the head, with her body in its state of decay, exactly as it was. The second canvas was Cherry looking young and beautiful again, then the third was her facing her Maker and being consigned to the hellfire. No wonder John bought these to take them away from my family from ever seeing them, not to mention protecting the identity of the man who shot her.

I destroyed all three of them that day in the bonfire, that was already quite the mountain and all needing to be destroyed. That Prince wasn't getting those paintings back, but what else was there? He had mentioned more than one and the other was one was nude art painted by Coinneach, of Zahra. I went back down to that room and sifted, once more through the art canvasses, until there was a nude painting of Zahra by Coinneach.

I felt like burning that one too, but I gave it to Kenneth to deal with, if that man ever turned up, or Kenneth could write to him and say that this was the only one that was found amongst his possessions upon his death.

As I gave it to Kenneth, he looked at it and said, "Oh yes, I remember this one. It's very well done, and Old John paid seven thousand pounds for it. The other three weren't much to speak of and that prince only wanted his money back on those. He was departing Beinn Coinneach, and he was cleaning out all his belongings, including the art and needed the money.

He was happy with the cash that John gave him.

"So, why is he wanting them back now?" Kenneth asked.

"He hasn't said that exactly, but the other three are unavailable," I said.

"If you want to sell him that one, you can and you can keep the money brother. I don't want it. I was going to burn it anyway, but if you make some money, well and good, keep it, if he ever shows up with that same cash or more," I said.

"The post mark on the letter, is the Outer Hebrides, so they must still be on the Isles and so it won't be any day soon. I never want to see Zahra again after allowing what happened to our young folk," I said.

"In her defence brother, it wouldn't have been her doing, nor her fault," Kenneth said. "Coinneach was too powerful to disagree with, so she must have gone along with everything, whether that was out of fear, or being subjugated herself, we will never know. It's a shame the prince wasn't sucked into the earth like Coinneach was," Kenneth said. "I really liked Coinneach for a time, so he was very convincing. Like a con man really," Kenneth added.

"It wasn't all Zahra's fault, is what I mean brother," Kenneth said quite seriously.

"I have an idea. Grigor Mohr MacGregor wants Zahra back, doesn't he and he's in the Aird now, with his wee ones isn't he?" I asked. "That painting could be left at the farm in the Aird for the prince to collect, without knowing that Grigor Mohr MacGregor is there, with Grandda and Alex," I said. "How about you send it to them in the Aird, saying it is waiting for Prince Griogar to collect and at the same time, write to him in the Outer Hebrides and tell him where it is, what do you think?" I asked.

"I think you've lost your mind in getting involved, that's what I think," Kenneth said.

"Alright, you're probably right. I'll leave it up to you then brother," I replied, and left thinking about those other three paintings and was angry all over again. 'How dare she paint that of my family'. I thought.

As I walked away however, Kenneth reviewed his thoughts, as he remembered the day that the prince came to the farm. It didn't make sense to him that he would now want that painting back. It was also of some risk to his possession of Zahra, now well hidden in the Hebrides. If he returned to Mainland Scotland, he had to understand that he wouldn't be as safe now, as he once was. Beinn Coinneach had its monsters in the minds of simple folk now, and Prince Griogar, as their War Chief, was recognisable.

Unknown to me, Kenneth did decide to send the painting, with a bill too, for the seven thousand pounds, to the Aird, addressed to Prince Griogar. An accompanying letter went to Grigor Mohr MacGregor, informing him that the prince would possibly be there at some unknown time, to pick up the painting of his wife Zahra, as he had requested. At the same time, he sent a letter to Prince Griogar in the Hebrides, letting him know, where the painting was, after the death of John MacDonnell of Glengarry.

Kenneth requested that Prince Griogar pay the bill of seven thousand pounds, in cash and notified him that the other three paintings by Zahra, were unable to be located and were thought to have been destroyed in the clean-up, after Mr MacDonnell's sad passing.

All Kenneth had to do then, was to wait and see what all parties involved did, in response to the painting being in the Aird. Either way, he hoped that it would bring both MacGregor men, face to face, with each other. Hopefully then, none of the MacNachtens would be involved. 'Let the two husbands fight over Zahra, if that was what they thought was still a worthwhile cause. How many men now was Zahra going to send into madness?' Kenneth asked himself.

'To think that I once slept in the same bed with Coinneach and Zahra. They posed no risk to me, like what had occurred with poor Hector. I had felt safe with them both and was warm and comfortable. I never had understood how Coinneach had gone from a person whom I really liked and admired into a monster taking advantage of poor Hector and his wife.

Had he changed that much, or was he always like that? Then Kenneth remembered the bathing room on Beinn Coinneach and that extra-long and passionate kiss on his lips and Coinneach gripping his genitals. He had put it so far to the back of his mind, so that as far as Kenneth was concerned, it had never happened. Now he was gone and so was a valuable source of income with him and we will never know why he went so far as to sodomise the young lad, Hector who was his stepson.' Kenneth thought. He started to feel unwell.

Kenneth had known of Coinneach's tendencies, all along and would die with that memory now that he had recalled it. He then went about sending that nude painting, carefully wrapped, to the Aird.

Kenneth told me later that night what he had done and left it then to those two MacGregor men to sort out their differences, once and for all, and hopefully, he would still get paid, but he was a little doubtful. The advertising for the farms, while at the time seemed like a brilliant idea, led then to the many questions of who else read the newspaper and who may not like MacNachten success and my involvement in kidnapping Hector and Flidas from Beinn Coinneach.

Everyone involved in that exercise now, as time went on, were either dead, injured, had lost horses, lost loved ones, lost jobs, were ill or were generally overwrought.

The mountain disappearing beneath the ground, some say, or just out of sight, was an indication of how much power was unleashed onto the citizens involved and Kenneth worried for himself and his brother. He felt that the mountain would return one day, as it had done in the past, maybe not in his lifetime but it wasn't gone, just invisible and neither was Coinneach MacAlpin or his wee son.

'They would be back too, and not happy either, as Zahra was supposed to have fulfilled some prophecy or another and he wouldn't forget that. That meant three men would still want Zahra back. What was the attraction that led men to do crazy things for that one woman?' Kenneth wondered.

'If only Grigor Mohr MacGregor hadn't strayed, and things would be normal for so many of us,' Kenneth believed.

30. The Painting Arrives

The nude painting of Zahra then arrived, carefully packaged and delivered to Wolf Ranch in the Aird, addressed to Grigor Mohr MacGregor, accompanied by the explanatory letter from Kenneth MacNachten, from the Glengarry Art Gallery.

Grigor hadn't handled one of the nude paintings of his ex-wife, up close before, unlike Grandda who still owned a defaced one, which was well hidden from Grigor. Naturally Grigor exploded with rage and was ready to burn it, as had been my first reaction in wanting to destroy it in the bonfire.

 Had it not been for Alex and Grandda, who were familiar with the nude paintings, it would have been burned instantly. The two men managed to convince Grigor, that it would at least bring the prince to his doorstep, from the Outer Hebrides. He then liked that idea. How else was he going to get that pig of a wife stealer to Wolf Ranch, when he hadn't known of his whereabouts on those damn Islands?

Grigor Mohr MacGregor had overlooked his love affair, now with Belle MacGregor and acted as if he was the wounded party, the innocent husband and somebody whose wife had been stolen from him, who then proceeded to further humiliate him, by doing paintings of her in the nude, just to antagonise him personally. Grandda didn't dare tell Grigor of their defaced painting, with the feigned love making scene, with Grandda's face now painted over Kenneth's.

Grandda and Alex both saved the beautiful painting from incineration, pointing out now how they could all dispose of the prince, when he came to pick it up, supposing he did. In the meantime, they enjoyed looking at it. It was one of the tamer ones they thought, so it was fortunate that it wasn't more revealing, or Grigor would have gone out of his mind.

'What did he think she was doing while he was off with Belle MacGregor? She hadn't wasted her time for sure they thought', both then and now.

They were not sure of the post to the Outer Hebrides and how long that would take to get there and then how long it would take him to reach the Aird if he thought it a wise choice of action. Which it wasn't. Prince Griogar didn't know that her ex-husband, Grigor Mohr MacGregor was back, as half owner of the farm, since Ali had taken his money and left for Glengarry to live next door now to me, Padruig's grandson. If by chance, the prince bought Zahra with him, she wouldn't be able to resist seeing her bairns. They were hopeful that the prince would innocently think that this was merely the location of the art, ready for him to pick up, if he paid the bill, so why wouldn't he have Zahra with him? After all, he was so paranoid, he had never allowed her out of his sight since the kidnapping. His jealousy was such that he could not share her, not even with a wolf puppy, let alone her young bairns.

Prince Griogar was a complete maniac, Padruig had concluded.

Zahra attracted maniacs and he was the only normal man who should have been in her life, permanently all along. He always told himself that they could have had blissful happiness with Turkish coffees served up to him, every smoko and every mealtime and beef stews for mealtimes, like only she could make. Sex would have eventually been achieved happily, he told himself, but that was harder to imagine, after he had raped her and her subsequent reaction. Women eventually give in, was his rationale. She would have given in to his masculine and overwhelming sexual energy. It was a nice thought anyway. He still dreamed of her, having sex with her in all manner of disgusting ways unmentionable to his mates, but he couldn't deny that he still wanted her, despite Grigor fighting to get his wife back.

Padruig just sat back in his usual casual manner to support his friend, occasionally giving words of sympathy, or even a compassionate cup of coffee to convince Grigor, that he was no longer a threat.

Alex would glance across at him occasionally, like 'don't overdo it'.

The howls of the wolf pack were heard that very same night, as the three men talked of Zahra, reminding them of her lupine support. It sent chills down Grigor's spine, recollecting the day that he saw her walking down Beinn Coinneach with a bloody wolf. He knew then that he hadn't married an ordinary woman and yet he had cast her aside for a whorish old woman who stank like hell. Zahra frightened the life out of him that day. Grigor wasn't sure if Zahra had indeed been Sidhe all along. Now he was in awe of a memory.

Like trying to capture mist in your hand, as it disappears with the sun's rising.

◇

A rattle of a carriage was heard a few days later and Isobel's handsome lads, Anndra and Domnhall came running to tell of the coach approaching their big iron gate. The anticipation of who would come for the painting was overwhelming, for all three men, as well as Isobel. She worried there might be another blood bath, like when her father was chopped to bits, but waited to see the outcome, this time. She sent the Frasers away, as it didn't concern them.

Fatma stood beside her big sister. It was times like this that she missed her brothers. Both Ali and Hector were never coming back to Wolf Ranch, and she rarely saw them, especially Ali. They hadn't forgiven their father for the whole Belle MacGregor debacle, or their Mither for yet another husband, they had thought.

They opened the big iron gate, and the carriage rambled on in, as they do. Not graceful like horses, thought Padruig. He'd be on a horse any day, to one of those idiotic carriages, announcing their arrival, for miles around, only to display their wealth with how the carriage was decked out and how many footmen they could afford to employ. He hated carriages and those who owned them.

Prince Griogar alighted, in all of his finery, thinking he was in a royal court to display his superiority. 'No wonder Coinneach hated him' Grandda thought. He was waiting on his partner, so it was a good sign that Zahra was with him. He held out his arm to her while surreptitiously, the big iron gates were being closed behind them, by Isobel's lads, as they had been instructed. Zahra alighted cautiously, wearing fine gold slippers and a beautiful gown with gold lacey edges and big sleeves, never seen before in these parts. It looked like they'd been shopping in Paris or how Paris used to be anyhow.

Zahra didn't look happy, as they had all known her, just co-operative with the prince, after all, Coinneach was gone now, leaving her free to re-marry and to her knowledge, only her son Ali was on the farm and not her ex-husband, Grigor Mohr MacGregor. Zahra suppressed her shock upon seeing Alex and Padruig, but smiled at her daughter Isobel, who stood stationary and unsmiling with both Alex and Padruig and Isobel's two bairns.

It wasn't a welcoming committee, Zahra knew that much.

What was a surprise when they walked inside, to acquire the painting, was Grigor Mohr MacGregor, sitting down at his table, casually drinking coffee.

"Hello Zahra," he said trying to sound like he wasn't bothered or surprised by her presence. Isobel and the bairns were then taken to the house at the rear and only the men remained there.

"Can I see Causantin and Dihaoine?" Zahra asked.

"They are both asleep, so no you can't," Grigor said. It was obvious this upset her, and it may have been the only reason, that Zahra was there.

"My puppy?" Zahra asked.

"Joined her pack in the wild. So, no to that too," Grigor said heartlessly, trying to sound as cruel as possible. Zahra was blinking her tears away, while the prince asked about the painting. Grandda then proudly produced it.

"This one?" Padruig asked.

"Aye, that one. Do you know what happened to the other three?" the prince asked. "Nae, just asked to sell you this for what you paid, which was seven thousand pounds," Padruig said.

"That's correct, here's the money then, if you can give me the painting," the prince said. Grandda carefully counted the money before handing the painting over, while Zahra looked around for any sign of her bairns, of which there was none.

"I let you see our bairns on the Beinn Coinneach, before Grigor, why won't you let me see them, even while they are sleeping. I won't wake them up," Zahra begged.

"Let me help you carry the painting to the carriage," offered Alex, while Grigor conceded and took Zahra to see her bairns as she had requested. Grandda followed closely behind the prince and Alex.

There was another addition to the waterfall that day.

◇

Kenneth was sent his money, and Zahra saw her bairns but then wasn't permitted to leave Wolf Ranch.

The men all hid the carriage behind the stables, which they later sold and kept the horses, as well as the painting. Grigor did get his wife back after all, but for a short while, seriously damaged, though she was, and the wolves howled all night long.

Zahra wasn't going to hold onto this life, as it was, any longer. If only it had been her in the waterfall was her only thought, as Grigor forced himself onto her, that same night in the most revolting of ways she had experienced. He forced her mouth open and told her to swallow his ejaculate, after which she vomited all over the bedding. Grigor was furious and strapped her emaciated body and told her to make the bed up clean, once more.

Sobbing, as she went to the cupboard where the bedding was kept, she knew she had to formulate a plan to escape from Wolf Ranch, hopefully with both Causantin and Dihaoine. She couldn't understand why her daughters both seemed to hate her, when she had missed them all so much, while kept a prisoner on that island, but they did and why was Grigor so cruel to her? As she went through the cupboards, she found her old woollen clothes there and knew what she would wear in the freezing cold night air to give her time to run to her wolf that was still howling. After making up Grigor's bed he fell asleep, and she lay still, until she was certain, that she could escape. Zahra then dressed in her split woollen skirt, woollen boots and layers of woollen jumpers and a coat and gloves. Silently she slipped into the bedroom of her two bairns, when she was made aware of another presence at the door.

It was Alex. "You'll not take the bairns Zahra. I'll lock the front door behind you, is all and say nothing to Grigor," Alex spoke quietly. She kissed the sad Causantin and Dihaoine and left.

By morning, Zahra was gone, into the forest, to the wolves, it was said, and Alex kept his word, as did her two wee ones.

No-one could find Zahra by morning. They searched every woodland, every forest, even caves, asked every neighbour, even scoured the waterfall and the burn, but to no avail. She had simply disappeared during the night, as the wolves howled loud and long. But the wolves then suddenly stopped howling. Not even the old Crohn saw any wolves again, the only thing she did say about them, was that the pack had been recently joined by an enormous brown wolf, known to Zahra, about five feet high and three feet across.

31. Zahra and Coinneach

The Old Crohn had concealed her knowledge of who the brown wolf was and ensured that they were re-united. Zahra mounted upon his broad back and that was the last the Old Crohn saw of them both.

Zahra held on tightly to his big and strong, furry neck. The giant wolf ran like the wind, with his wife, back to Beinn Coinneach. Only one child had survived the whole kidnapping ordeal. Coinneach Og was with Mairi in a Croft off the mountain. Upon first sight, their chubby bairn cried for his Ma instantly and she for him. They all then headed for where the mountain once was, with Mairi, her husband Callum and Zahra and the bairn, who were both still on the wolf's back. They then all walked together, inside the giant mushroom ring and planned to live as they always had done.

The mansion on Beinn Coinneach was invisible to everyone else, but everything was still there, as it always had been. It was not underground as some people said. The farmers who were there at the time of its disappearance were all pleased to see them both back. Coinneach, now bipedal with Zahra beside him.

"I am so sorry my beloved, it was my fault. I left you unguarded and you were taken from me," Coinneach said. Both wept as Mairi prepared their baths.

"Baths, Mistress and Master?" asked Mairi.

"Thank you Mairi. Aye we are both in need of a hot bath," Coinneach said.

Together in the bath, Zahra's months of torture was revealed, and he caressed his beloved, who he had to make it up to somehow and get Causantin back too and Dihaoine one day, when he could catch Grigor unawares. He gently, ever so gently massaged his wife and sponged her face and ran his fingers along her lips.

"My God Zahra, I hope we never have to go through anything like that again. Life has been a living hell, without you and so confusing," Coinneach said.

"It was madness, one army after another. I saw Malcolm with the first army that took Hector and Flidas and I had been about to attack him, until I realised who it was, and I couldn't harm him. I still like Malcolm. I don't understand why there was an enormous effort to kidnap them both and their ponies, when all they had to do was ask, if the two of them wanted to leave. I didn't know they were unhappy. Did you?" Coinneach asked.

"If Hector was unhappy, darling, he didn't tell me. I hope he's happy in Cannich where he is now, I heard," Zahra said.

"So, did Ali sell his share of the farm then back to his father, so he could buy a farm in Glengarry?" Coinneach asked.

"I know less than you do my love. I was stuck all alone in a room, on some very remote island, with no newspapers. Those people were unknown to me, and they didn't know people here, or in Glengarry. It was like a foreign country. Their language was always Gaelic, or Flemish, so I didn't know what they were saying, except some small words that I recognised in Gaelic," Zahra said.

"How long were you like that?" Coinneach asked.

"I don't know for certain. The only measure of time were the sun and moon cycles, if they were visible, behind the clouds. Maybe it was a month?" Zahra said, as she spoke of it with difficulty.

"I can't believe I am back here with you. It was a nightmare that I too did not understand. I didn't know what they were going to do to me, and I didn't expect to survive the horrors of it," Zahra said.

"Did they give you any food and water?" Coinneach asked.

"Nae, not at first, I had to beg to those mercenaries, for water," Zahra said.

"So did my brother rape you?" Coinneach asked.

"Not in that first month or so. When I asked for food, however, they said I could only have food, if I agreed to eat with the prince," Zahra said. " I was starving hungry, so I agreed to eat with him," Zahra said.

"Those are his methods that you have described. I am sorry you've had to experience him as the War Chief. Did you know that Padruig and Alex disposed of him?" Coinneach asked.

"I saw the blood on the snow," Zahra replied. "Then I was suddenly Grigor's prisoner, instead of the prince's prisoner. He was very cruel, and they hated me, except my wee ones. I understood what they had done and a nude painting of me was back in the farmhouse, the carriage was hidden behind the stables and his horses were stabled with theirs, so it was obvious, that I wasn't intended to leave. Grigor raped me that same night," she said and cried again.

"When did my brother rape you then?" Coinneach asked.

"He fed me first, even though I hadn't washed in a month or so. I was then taken by an awful bully of a woman who scrubbed me down with a rough brush and washed my hair, until I was spotless. My skin was sore from her rough scrubbing," Zahra said.

"It was then that his sick, sexual activity began, day in day out. In between, I was scrubbed by that same woman," Zahra said.

"I was at the point of giving up hope, when in the prince's room, I saw the only newspaper for that entire time with Malcolm's lovely twins on the front page, sketched by Kenneth on their big Team with eight horses. Months had passed by, and I was so skinny. My ribs could be easily felt, and my hip bones protruded. He was uncomfortable with my bones, so

I was then fed three times per day to put on some weight. I am still too thin Coinneach." Zahra stated.

"Aye, you are a little, my love. That is what he did in his occupation, so I was desperate, trying to find you, but I was unable to find you anywhere. He must have had that Island pre-planned after he left here," Coinneach said.

"Why do you think that he wanted the paintings back?" Coinneach asked.

"I don't know, but I was crying all the time for my bairns or for you or my puppy, or for food. Maybe I was mentally unwell? I think I was slowly dying, so perhaps, he had gone too far and wanted the things I loved or needed, returned, being to see my bairns, eat more food, have some clothing, get my puppy back and it was his idea to get the paintings back. Initially I was only wearing what I was kidnapped in, and those clothes were filthy. He read in the paper that the man who bought those paintings had died. He then bought me a very fancy outfit to make it seem like I had always been well dressed, all the time, when I wasn't. I was so cold there, so cold," she said, crying incessantly. "I'm sorry Coinneach, I can't stop crying. I never thought I'd ever see you or our home again," Zahra said. "I'm so scared of people like that, who only know cruelty," Zahra said.

"I will get you well again my precious Zahra, as you know. You will be happy once again my dear and we also have wee Coinneach Og to care for. I promise to you that at the right time, I will bring home wee Causantin and wee Dihaoine. They don't belong with that despicable person whom they don't even know. Poor wee things," Coinneach said insincerely.

"I need to get you well first," Coinneach said. As he rubbed down her naked body, he saw the bruises and felt her bones and saw how thin she still was. He asked Mairi to come in to assist. "Mairi, I need some of that special body oil to help my wife's skin. It has all but been scrubbed off," he said.

Mairi was shocked at Zahra's condition and was told to oil and repair her skin over her entire body, every day.

"Oh Mistress, how could they do this to you and why?" Mairi asked and couldn't understand it.

"It was to punish and humiliate me Mairi," Coinneach said sadly. "Now my wife must always have a bodyguard. If not me, your husband Mairi, temporarily. Can you please tell him for me, until we find someone specific for that purpose. My wife will have to like her bodyguard," Coinneach commented.

Zahra heard him also asking how many of the MacKenzie staff had been lost, and it was going to require now asking for staff from amongst the Frasers, who were on the opposite side of the mountain and therefore, unaware of recent events. Her husband was going to send down a Fraser from among them, to look around for the best staff for housework, as well as protecting the Mistress, security and assisting in cooking events, if it was more than just the two of them.

"My darling, forgive me for asking, but why do you still have breast milk, when you didn't have a wee one to feed?" Coinneach asked.

Zahra hung her head in shame and told him that she was ordered to provide the prince with breast milk expressed into a cup, until she agreed to eat with him.

"Then what happened?" Coinneach asked.

"Apart from what I have told you, the prince asked to be breast fed daily, directly from me," Zahra replied. "The first time, his men held me down by my arms and legs, that is why I am so bruised, even on my breasts. He suckled from me, but I didn't want that to occur. The men even held my breasts in place for him to suck from," Zahra said.

"The only good side to that story now, is that you can still feed Coinneach Og," Coinneach said.

"Now my wife, give me your love and everything you must

give to your husband that I have longed for, all of this time," Coinneach said, believing in his expectations of a wife, even after such a formidable experience of torture, rape, starvation, and abuse.

Despite all of that, Zahra did still love him and considered herself his wife. He licked his wife animalistically, all over her genitalia and Zahra tried to unwind and enjoy her body once again, as an object of affection and not of abuse, torture, or blame, but Coinneach had been with wolves for a long time, so sex was very different and unenjoyable.

She knew it was only a matter of time that their relationship would come to an end.

Coinneach hoped that she only needed him, and he was going to feast on her, as his love object, whom he believed was rightly given to him by God in his lupine affected mind and she would never be removed again, nor would her attention on him be diverted, even if she had to sleep beside him every day, while he worked in the art room. He wanted to know where she was, every waking moment now, of every day and every night.

Beneath Coinneach's civilised, outward appearance, was a seething, barbaric, angry man, at what had been done to both him and his wife and their bairns. The brown wolf was just beneath the surface, all the time. Coinneach's wife was deeply depressed, and her body had now become most unappealing to him. Zahra missed her bairns and her wolf puppy, and she was taking a very long time to gain the weight, that she had lost.

However, at no time had Coinneach cursed his brother for what he had done to Zahra, nor did he say that he was pleased to have learned of his disposal, in the Aird.

"Tomorrow night we will start reading again," Coinneach said.

He hoped she might gain interest in her writing once more. Zahra was becoming boring and ugly to him, and she knew that.

32. Fraser Ville

The village beneath the mountain on Fraser land was a small village named, "Fraser Ville," but most people who lived there were of red or ginger hair, ginger eyebrows, and freckled skin. Zahra was asked for a description of a suitable bodyguard, so she would like him. Her description was black hair, handsome, a young man, but not a boy and not an old man, but preferably a muscular person as well. Hairy was preferrable, so long as it wasn't red or ginger hair. Mr MacKenzie found only one younger man answering to that description, who was the blacksmith's son, and he was still working with his father, but not highly revered in social circles, as they were thought of locally as 'silkies', due to their unusual black hair.

Mr MacKenzie had offered him the job of guarding and caring for the Mistress but also working in the Master bed chamber which involved preparing their bed, their clothing, the fire for and attending to the needs of both the Master and the Mistress. His wages were high by comparison to what he was earning from his father, if he accepted the job, but the lad had declined, and the news was passed on to Lord and Lady Coinneach.

"My darling, you may have to have one of the redheaded Frasers, they're good folk. Why don't you want a bodyguard from one of them?" Coinneach asked.

"You are the only man I want in my life with that fair to strawberry coloured hair, with that same-coloured hair on your body too. No-one else in my life can be like you, even if it's similar. I hope you understand. My bodyguard will be close to us both, so he mustn't rival you," Zahra answered.

"Oh, I see," he said and was pleased with her reasoning.

"Can I go to the village, accompanied by Mr MacKenzie and ask him myself? It might be harder to say no to me. I suggest we also pay his father to replace his son by giving him wages to cover training a new employee. What do you think?" Zahra asked.

"I will come too then, and we will both follow you closely from behind and if he wants more money, I can approve it," Coinneach said. "That's only if you like the look and sound of him, my love. You might not like him," he added.

Zahra was bitterly disappointed that her husband was coming, and her heart sank but she knew she had to comply.

"Let's go to the village now and not get too far ahead of ourselves. You really should start writing again Zahra about your recent kidnapping. It would make for a riveting story in the newspapers," Coinneach said.

She had never heard Coinneach express himself in that way and she wondered then what had really happened to her son Hector. Was that why Malcolm's army turned up to save her hero, Hector?

Striding out in front of her two minders, Zahra entered the village of Fraser Ville and was immediately pounced on by the Village Chief, whose job it was to vet outsiders. Dressed in flowing robes, but strong boots in case of village filth and an arisaid to cover her hair, she wasn't recognised, as Lady Coinneach, at first. The old man was duly embarrassed as Zahra removed her arisaid from her head and introduced herself, followed by a scowling Lord Coinneach.

After apologising profusely, the village head then led her to the forge.

 Mr MacKenzie was leading her horse initially and then Zahra took the mare's reins.

"Oh, excuse me my lad," Zahra said, in her sweetest voice.

A handsome, black haired young man was hammering on a horseshoe and looked up at her. He was wearing a tough old leather apron and leather chaps, old shoes of poor quality and an old-style dirty shirt. His hair was shoulder length and tied back, displaying his attractive face in full. His cheek bones were chiselled to perfection and his eyes were a very dark brown, not blue like nearly everyone else in the village.

His father was working at the rear of that small forge, and he was an angry looking, stout, older man who would have had little patience, Zahra deduced.

"My horse was lame just now lad, could you please check her shoes for me?" Zahra asked.

"Certainly Mistress," the lad replied and came over to the mare and checked each shoe. As he leaned over, Zahra noticed that Coinneach was looking closely at the lad's rear end. It was obvious that Coinneach liked this lad and Zahra was reminded, momentarily that he had been living with a pack of wolves and had most likely mated with a few of the she wolves, entering from the rear.

"Lad, what is your name?" Zahra asked.

"My name is Alasdair Fraser, son of Brien O'Neil Fraser, of Fraser Ville, Mistress," the lad replied, surprised at the question.

"My man came here yesterday to offer you a job working for me, Lady Zahra Coinneach, in the mansion on the mountain and I understand that you declined. Is that true?" Zahra asked.

The lad's face changed immediately and went to bow to her when she stopped him.

"May I kiss your hand for this very great honour please Lady Zahra?" Alasdair asked. Alasdair kissed his Mistress's hand, while Coinneach watched on, wanting to take over, but was encouraged to wait, by Mr MacKenzie.

"Your wife has already won him Lord Coinneach. Just wait a moment, please My Lord. You might learn something about your clever wife. She is already doing better than I did yesterday," Mr MacKenzie suggested.

"May I be seated inside your premises to speak with you and maybe you will change your mind?" Zahra asked.

His stout father then came in to see who had entered his premises and frowned.

"Mr O'Neil Fraser, I am pleased to make your acquaintance. My name is Lady Zahra Coinneach MacAlpin and I am here to offer your son a job in our mansion, which I understand means that you would need to replace him?" Zahra asked.

Taking one hundred pounds from her purse, she gave it to him.

"I hope you can train another man to replace your son Sir. If he agrees to work for me and my good husband, Lord Coinneach of Beinn Coinneach. We will pay his wages, if your son comes with us today," Zahra said. "May I speak with your son about the wages and the job and if not, we will not bother you again, but you can keep that money for the inconvenience, that I have caused you," she said.

The stout blacksmith made a grunting sound, pocketed the money and went back to the rear of the forge. Coinneach was beside himself, still listening to the advice of Mr MacKenzie.

"It's nearly over my Lord," Mr MacKenzie said.

"Alasdair, the job is pleasant enough, if you felt us both to be fair employers, with a new uniform provided, as well as food and your own room. I need assistance in my bath and with dressing. Can you do that, do you think?" Zahra asked.

All Alasdair did was nod his head, so Zahra had to ask again. "Is that aye, then lad?" Zahra asked.

"Aye my Lady," Alasdair replied.

"I was kidnapped recently, so I do have some injuries, such as bruising and skin damage. I would need you to oil my skin, can you do that too, as well as primarily act as my bodyguard to prevent another kidnapping?" Zahra asked.

"Aye Mistress it would be an honour to serve you," Alasdair said.

"You would have your own bedroom not too far from our suite, but you would be on call to help me onto the chamber pot and empty them both in the mornings. Can you do that?" Zahra asked.

"You would have to sign a Privacy Agreement. Would you agree to that?" Zahra asked.

"Aye Mistress," Alasdair replied.

"Will you be able to come home with myself and my husband now then? If so, let me introduce my husband, Lord Coinneach, may I introduce Alasdair Fraser son of Brien O'Neil Fraser," Zahra said.

Finally, Coinneach rapidly approached Alasdair Fraser after suffering the previous half hour and held out the huge ring on his hand for the lad to kiss.

"Welcome to my staff, lad," Coinneach said, and Alasdair was overcome and nearly passed out upon meeting Lord Coinneach. When he could finally speak, the lad was a little teary eyed, then he kneeled, bowed then kissed Lord Coinneach's feet, one after the other, which Coinneach had no objection to.

"My Lord, My Lord," Alasdair kept saying, repeatedly.

There was little doubt that he adored Zahra's husband. Alasdair wouldn't stand up, until Lord Coinneach touched his head and raised him up and kissed his lips, as was their custom. It had drawn a few onlookers by then, as Lord Coinneach became recognised amongst the crowd and gossiping villagers started to gather all around the forge.

"We have to go now," Mr Mackenzie advised Lord Coinneach.

The group of four departed on horseback, with Alasdair riding Zahra's horse and the horses climbed up the mountain from the rear side, narrow pathway. Zahra rode together with her proud husband. Alasdair was in awe of his surroundings, as the group approached the huge mansion, then entered the palatial surroundings. Coinneach just couldn't control his utter joy at their success with such a beautiful young man.

Alasdair looked like a boy in love, not a bodyguard for her at all.

Mairi asked if there was a bath required. Then while Alasdair was bathing, Coinneach walked in on him while he was washing his hair and plunged his hand into the bathwater for his penis to feel its length and general size.

"It's perfect lad," Coinneach said.

If Alasdair, was a little embarrassed, he didn't show it.

"I hope you are not a virgin lad, are you?" Coinneach asked.

"Nae Master, I often fecked my schoolteacher and my father has fecked me nearly every day of my life," Alasdair added.

Coinneach led him by his cock, as Alasdair groaned under the pleasure, to his clothes, then kissed him passionately and told him to dress. The young man made a lot of grunts, gasps, and groans, and had no objection to being sodomised. He loved Lord Coinneach leading him by his cock, noticed by Coinneach which was then a frequent, everyday occurrence, just like holding hands would be between teen lovers.

'Alasdair appeared to yearn for the next time that he would have any attention from Coinneach at all, not unlike a puppy really', Zahra thought. This wasn't what she had expected upon her arrival returning home to Beinn Coinneach, after escaping from the Aird, but Zahra had learned from being in captivity, how to survive.

The life that she was now enduring wasn't much better than that horrid island.

The only difference was that there was adequate food, water and warmth on the mountain, but little remained of Zahra's marriage, that she had once known, before the kidnapping.

◇

33. Trouble in Love

Islay came to my new office door as I was setting it up at my new property and told me of a wee problem that I should know about, in case it escalated.

My security guard there on the old farm was Colm MacKenzie, who was courting Annie Colquhoun, but recently, since the arrival of Iain MacKay, as a Teamster, her attentions were now on him. This was upsetting Colm, naturally, as he had sought permission to court her from me. Islay asked me what we should do and preferably, she asked me to talk to all three of them.

Annie walked into my old office, on the old farm while I stood behind my old desk. I asked her to relax and to be seated in one of the three arranged lounge chairs. Iain was next to walk in, after first knocking on the office door.

"Excuse me Mr MacNachten, you needed to see me?" Iain asked, looking afraid that he might be losing his job, so his attention wasn't on Annie. Annie on the other hand was admiring him obviously. Colm then came to the open door, then appeared to take a deep breath, and asked if he could enter.

"Malcolm," Colm said. "Annie, Iain," Colm added.

"Sit down please Colm," I said. "I have heard that there is a small problem with the courtship, Colm and Annie. Is that right?" I asked.

"Not where I am concerned Malcolm," Colm replied, "But I wasn't here last week, as you know. What problem?" Colm asked.

"Iain, do you have any interests in Annie's direction, or is that just gossip?" I asked.

"I do think Annie is bonny aye, I'll not deny it, but I haven't asked to court her, not yet, Mr MacNachten," Iain said.

"Annie, are you still wishing to be betrothed with Colm MacKenzie, as was the first arrangement?" I asked directly to the guilty looking lass.

"I don't like how often Colm is away for work, or visiting his family, I admit," Annie replied.

"Are you now interested in Iain MacKay, more than Colm?" I asked.

"He is handsome, strong, and manly, for sure. Not to say that Colm isn't, I just miss him when he's not here and want the company," Annie said.

"Annie. This is important. You can't agree to court with someone and then show an interest in someone else, unless you bring the first courtship to a close. Look at both men now and tell me which man you prefer," I demanded.

"I love Colm, I want to marry him Mr MacNachten, but he has bairns of various ages to his former wife. Can't he take me to meet them, if I am to be his wife one day, because if not, I might as well go with Iain?" Annie answered.

"Do you love Iain?" I asked.

"Not like Colm," Annie said.

"Have you already committed, in any way with Iain?" I asked.

"No," Iain said vehemently.

Then suddenly, my twins, whom I thought were both working, burst in through the open office door.

"Bullshit. I saw you kissing her, Iain," said Malcolm Og.

"And you told me that you stuck your hand down her dress, and you felt her titties," said Hamish Og.

And that would be the truth, was my opinion. My lads may have been rude, but they were brutally honest.

"Colm, you have a decision to make. Break off the court-ship with Annie now, before it gets worse than this, or forgive her, on condition that it can't happen again. What are your thoughts?" I asked.

"I can't satisfy her anyway with my family, it seems, so sadly I have lost her, and it would be better to break it off now. I have done nothing to her that would embarrass her, if Iain wanted her," Colm said. "I am sorry Malcolm, to have wasted your time. May I leave now?" Colm asked, near tears.

"Can you please wait outside Colm, I still need to talk to you," I asked.

It was sad. Poor Colm. I had wanted to find him a good wee lass, not a two-timing lass like Annie. My daughter, Islay had put forward her daughter, Florence, as she was still upset at missing out on Hector and Ali MacGregor and saw Colm as a much better option to both Hector and Ali, now that Colm was becoming available.

My office was becoming like a marriage guidance office.

"Iain you also must marry this lass now that you have done what you have done. You have compromised her modesty. You can handfast here in my office right away," I said, which they did with Annie weeping and Iain looking pleased with him-self. My lads had run away fast, in case I kicked them up the pants, but I was grateful for their honesty, hoping it wouldn't affect their working relationship with Iain. I then called in Colm again after the others had left and my daughter Islay too, who was waiting in the next room, with her daughter Florence, to enter.

"Colm, I know it's early days and you don't need to answer right away, after what has just transpired. However, I must do what is asked of me, in all honesty.

My granddaughter, Islay's daughter, Florence MacKenzie is nearly sixteen years old now and ready for marriage, she has told us all. She has always thought of you as the most prized man on this property, with good looks and a good job and responsible towards family back home. She has asked me to put her forward to you, as an option to be your wife, to marry whenever you were ready. Would you consider Florence MacKenzie, daughter of Angus MacKenzie, or is it too soon for you to think straight?" I asked.

Florence was looking at him with nervous, adoring eyes and it made me nervous as to what he may say in response. It may hurt my granddaughter, if he outright rejected her, but she did insist and she really wanted him, that was obvious to me, anyway. Islay approved of him and so did Florence's father, Angus and they were both MacKenzies. That might work better anyway, for family relations, so I nervously waited as Colm tried to take it all in. He was shocked at first, then when he looked at her, I detected a longing, so it had potential, I hoped.

"I am honoured that you think of me as good enough Malcolm and Mrs MacKenzie. Florence is indeed the bonniest lass here on the property and in all of Glengarry, I have always thought. I didn't think you would have me after what Meredith told you about me bothering her, when I was seventeen in Kinlochewe. I would indeed like to be her partner in marriage, if it was possible. Is it really?" Colm asked to confirm.

"Aye," Florence said. "I want to marry you Colm," Florence said.

Colm was so shocked at the day's revelations, it may have been a bit too much for him, but Islay assisted the proceedings.

"How about we meet together with Florence's father, Angus over a meal tonight and let Colm take it all in Florence?" Islay said. "Give him some time, maybe, so he can be sure," Islay said speaking calmly.

"I am sure Mrs MacKenzie, I accept your proposal. I mean Florence's proposal, but I agree, we do need to talk to Angus too," Colm said.

"Alright then, tonight come here to eat with us all, if you don't have plans and we can talk to my husband, Angus and please stop calling me Mrs MacKenzie, no-one calls me that. I am just Islay," she added.

"Will they handfast now or later then Islay, what is the plan?" I asked.

"Better wait for Angus, don't you think Da?" Islay said.

"Do you need me here or can I go back home to my wife?" I asked sarcastically.

"Och thankyou Grandda," Florence said hugging me around my waist. It was worth it just to get a hug from Florence, who rarely showed any signs of affection. She was a lot like her Mither.

Back in our new home, Ailsa asked me what it was all about. I asked if I could have one of those nice Turkish coffees with her and a cake maybe, then I would tell her everything. It might even be nice to have a wee cuddle too, I said longingly.

Just as we sat down to enjoy our Turkish coffee together, however and to explain the events of the day, my brother Kenneth burst through my front door, looking pleased with himself.

"Malcolm, brother. I have money for you from the Aird," Kenneth said.

"What for?" I asked.

"The nude painting of Zahra, of course. I sent it to the Aird, like you suggested and here's your share with my commission taken out, amounting to five thousand and two hundred and fifty pounds," Kenneth said, very pleased with himself.

"There is a letter too from Grandda, saying the prince paid for the painting but left Zahra behind who then left, according to the story. Then a happy Grigor Mohr MacGregor was happy no more, because she disappeared overnight to the wolves, the old Crohn has said. So Grandda says here, 'Your weirdo friend prefers wolves to people.' You can keep the letter brother," he said. Then Kenneth asked for coffee and cake too. I hadn't known that my brother was going to do what I had originally suggested.

"Zahra didn't stay in the Aird? I can't believe that. Prince wots' his name, is at the bottom of the waterfall, I'll wager. There must have been some kind of face-off between the two MacGregor men, or three against one," I said.

"Did Zahra not want to stay with her ex-husband then?" asked a confused Ailsa.

"Would you stay with the man after being punched, deserted, humiliated and left disabled?" I asked.

"Nae, I suppose not but I thought he might be a better man now. And she might have forgiven him," Ailsa said.

"Obviously not. You know what I think? That wolf smell on Beinn Coinneach was her husband, Coinneach and he followed us all the way down and stayed with the wolf pack. So, when she turned up in the Aird, he took her back. She's back on Beinn Coinneach. It's just invisible, as it has been before. Don't go there again Kenneth. That man is truly sick," I said.

34. Recovering too Slowly

On Beinn Coinneach, breakfast had always been the happiest time of the day, but with so few of the family now left in the mansion, Zahra wasn't that light-hearted and happy in the mornings, anymore, the way it used to be. She especially missed Hector, Causantin and her lassie, Dihaoine.

Zahra missed the Aird and was questioning why she had left, but she reminded herself what Grigor did to her and felt like being sick all over again.

She needed more time to recover and yet there was so much emphasis on Coinneach's happiness. She felt so lonely as Coinneach was chatting to Alasdair over breakfast and not her anymore. She had thought, when she escaped with him on his big back as a wolf, that she would return to a sense of herself and some happiness, at long last but she had been wrong.

Coinneach was so obsessed with his newfound lover from Fraser Ville, that she now even felt like sleeping in a different room to them both. She was no longer the object of his affection, at least not right now. Maybe she was too thin, maybe it was because being raped repeatedly, had left her ugly and unappealing? She missed her bairns but hadn't even been welcomed by her daughters Isobel and Fatma, when she was in the Aird and she still couldn't understand that.

If only she could see her precious wee Causantin and wee Dihaoine. She adored those wee ones, but she was so far removed from them now. She couldn't understand why Coinneach had even wanted her here on Beinn Coinneach, when there was no longer any affection or love coming from him to her.

Maybe she was a mere possession now, like a pot plant that may need watering occasionally. Reflecting now on her decision to leave the Aird with Coinneach on the giant wolf, she wondered if she had made the right decision. He was now a fully practising homosexual, and she was just a woman who lived with two homosexuals.

Zahra now wondered seriously what he had done to her son Hector, making it necessary for an entire army to rescue him and his ponies. It was a well organised, well-planned rescue of her son and she hadn't even known that he had needed rescuing. How did they know that he was suffering, when Hector lived right under her nose? Would she now ever see him again? Her hero was gone. She just wanted to cry but there was no-one who would listen to her, just like the jailers on that island who didn't care when she cried. Was Coinneach also so heartless now?

There must be a waterfall nearby on this mountain, but if there was one, she didn't know where it was. She asked Mairi and obtained directions and despite the bodyguard plan, no interest was shown in her conversations with Mairi, let alone when she went off to bathe alone, dress alone and walk out of the front door alone and unaccompanied.

Coinneach was still deep in conversation, while fondling the young man, Alasdair. It was as if she no longer existed at all. He had used her to find a lad for himself and not a bodyguard for her at all. Neither Mairi nor her husband appeared bothered by Coinneach's behaviour at the dining table, with the young man.

It was a long walk alone, dressed in appropriate but warm clothing, her long fur coat and knee-high boots. With her rudimentary map in hand, she asked some elderly Crofters, further directions to the deepest gorge in the Highlands, at the base of the waterfall.

It had a long Gaelic name, that she couldn't remember, but it was an adventure, just the same, so it had the effect of improving her mood, surprisingly. It was a cold, damp day but not yet raining and all the grass was wet and slippery. There were wild birds who flew above her head rather closely. Then she saw black crows or ravens, she wasn't sure. They sat on a fence post near her, as she passed by, and one of them let out a loud noise. She thought of talking to them momentarily, because she had hardly heard her own voice in recent days and nights. Crows are nice birds, she thought.

There were no further Crofts or signs of farming as she smelled a large body of water, close by and felt the wisps of moisture in the air.

Zahra was certainly close and was excited at the prospect of ending her misery. It had been a mistake leaving her former spouse, Grigor MacGregor in the Aird, after the disposal of the prince. Her rationale apart from the obvious result of being with Grigor included also being raped, yet again by Padruig. She decided then that her inability to cope with the 18th and early 19th centuries meant that she would no longer even try to achieve the skills needed, the mentality needed, acceptance required of daily violence, accepting rape as a regular part of life, with the role of women so diminished. Zahra could no longer fight uphill, for love or protection needed here in this beautiful, but dreadful place.

After Hugh Chisholm had successfully killed her, leaving her to live permanently in the Otherworld, where souls waited for Judgement Day to come, her life was ticking by, up until this point, where she could bear it no longer. She couldn't pretend to be the subservient, ever pleasing wife anymore, who was married now to a practising homosexual. She had loved Coinneach, but his love was now captured by Alasdair Fraser, and it had been with her assistance. 'Why couldn't I have left it alone with Mr MacKenzie who had failed the previous day?' she asked herself.

There was beauty in this landscape, she could not deny that and understood why the people who were forced to leave Scotland, lamented the loss of their homeland greatly, but she knew how that turned out with Scots in every far corner of the earth spreading their love of the bagpipes, or Gaelic, or tartan or whatever they chose to remember of Scotland when sent to, America, Nova Scotia, Canada, New Zealand or Australia. Very few Scots, in modern times acknowledged how badly women were treated in their societies, if they knew, whether it was the burning of alleged witches or just old-fashioned, domestic violence. Sodomy between lovers in one's own bed, while trying to sleep with your husband, was a new one, she admitted. If she had stayed around to write another book, she thought of including examining the relationships between men and women more closely, especially the sexuality of both husband and wife, not judgementally but openly.

Zahra had never imagined that the manly man, known as Lord Coinneach MacAlpin, would be a practising homosexual, when she first accepted his assistance, after what had happened to her in the Aird. She most certainly would not have married him, but these types of men conceal it so cleverly, so how could you know? All three of her marriages to husbands in this land of primitive Scotland, Zahra assigned to the rubbish bin, as just more of her failures in trying to adjust to a foreign land whose language, she could still not speak. She wanted to depart life completely, permanently and never wake up again.

35. Dr and Nurse Heath

Zahra arrived finally, beside the roaring and raging waterfall with huge wisps of wet air, flowing about her, she hesitated and tried to be careful, not to slip. Every surface was wet, every rock, every blade of grass and all the air was filled with moisture. It was deadly there. No wonder her husband never showed her where it was. Further down, there was an ancient looking bridge, which crossed over the deep gorge that the waterfall had dug deep into the earth. It really was a magnificent sight and if she wasn't so deeply depressed, it would delight her with its beauty.

Why wasn't there a single painting of this amazing feature on the landscape?

From up that high, she could see all the way down to the winding track that led up to Beinn Coinneach, with farmers as small as ants, but recognisable enough because she was sure that she saw someone familiar, Dr Peter Heath. Unable to see the mountain anymore, he knocked on the door to a Croft down there, no doubt he was asking where the mountain had gone. He came out shortly afterwards and to test to see if he could see her, Zahra waved to him first, then took a looking glass from her pocket to capture the sun and reflect the light. 'Maybe he might see it?' she wondered. To her shock and surprise, she saw him stop and look in her direction. She was aghast, still shocked at Peter seeing her mirrored light or her, she wasn't sure.

Zahra had been going to jump down into the deep gorge or the waterfall, but with that one recognition of a person she knew, she decided to hurry back to try once more and hastily depart Beinn Coinneach with Peter, before he left. It was a long way down, so she hoped he would talk longer to the Crofter. She ran past the elderly Crofters, whom she had previously asked directions from, who just watched her running, looking puzzled.

His wife asked him, "Were it 'er agin me luv?"

"Aye, strange lassie that 'un. Runnin' now like the devil's afta her," he replied.

"Maybe he is," his old white-haired wife said, as she lit up her pipe.

As Peter was about to mount his horse, he was satisfied that what he saw was just some kind of reflection playing with his mind, or a trick of the light, until the MacKenzie Crofter asked him a question.

"Is your name Peter?" she asked.

"Aye," Peter replied.

"I was sure I heard a woman's voice, calling out Peter," she said. Then both were astounded when, out of nowhere, Zahra appeared, running for her life and calling out to him.

"Peter, Peter, wait for me please. Can I come with you Peter, please?" Zahra pleaded, breathlessly as he assisted her to ride upon his horse, in front of him.

"Where are we going?" Peter asked.

"To your residence, please Peter. I can work for you as a cook or a cleaner. I don't mind. Please can I stay with you and don't tell Coinneach if he appears out of the blue one day," Zahra pleaded as they both rode hastily into the direction of Inverness.

Zahra had once again escaped, but this time, she had escaped from her need to dispose of herself.

She settled into Peter's medical practice with no trouble, when he told her he had gone to Beinn Coinneach to enquire how her spine was. He had needed the business.

"I was kidnapped from Beinn Coinneach, a while back, did you know?" Zahra asked.

"Nae, I didn't know. I wonder why it wasn't in the newspapers. That's big news if a woman is taken from her home like that. Did Coinneach try to find you?" Peter asked.

"He said he did, but I don't know that for a fact. As far as I know, he never reported me missing. I was kept a prisoner on a remote island in the Outer Hebrides, so no-one could have found me there," Zahra said.

"I am going to make this simple, and you don't have to answer. Why are you leaving this husband, this time?" Peter asked.

"My husband is a homosexual and while I do not have a problem with people being homosexuals, I didn't know that I had married one. There were signs that I don't care to repeat right now. When I escaped from the Aird I thought, we would be happy after my body normalised, but in getting a bodyguard from Fraser Ville, his little friend became his obsession and they are both in love, I think. Today I was going to jump down the waterfall, until I saw you and I changed my mind," Zahra said.

"Alright It sounds like it will take time before you tell me everything. In the meantime, how is your spine?" Peter asked over coffee in his lovely old home in Inverness.

"I am not in the best of health, generally speaking, mostly from the effects of malnutrition and repeated rape, but my skin isn't too good either," Zahra blurted.

"Peter, I can't pay you, but I can work, cook and clean," Zahra said.

"Sounds good. Now take off your clothes, so I can give you a full examination," Peter said.

Peter wasn't expecting to see the bony frame that was now Zahra, with varying colours of her bruises and still with badly damaged skin from the scrubbing with a rough brush. Her ribs still protruded as did both of her hips and after seeing her in those paintings looking picture perfect, it was hard to imagine how much damage now needed reversing.

"Alright. We will take this step by step. First, let's eat. You can be my cook, and I will fix your many issues, my friend," Peter said and hugged Zahra out of empathy for an old friend in need.

She began to cry into his arms, and he wasn't accustomed to a woman crying on him, but he handed her a handkerchief and held her, while sitting in an armchair cradling her on his lap, as she sobbed and sobbed. He couldn't help but kiss her and it felt normal, even though his attraction was to men, up until that moment. Zahra was an exception, Peter felt. She kissed him back in her moment of distress and felt it was only an expression of her deep sadness, but his kiss continued.

"Zahra, can you sleep with me tonight? I am so lonely, that's all. I haven't been with anyone for so long and it would mean a lot to me," Peter said.

"But you are homosexual. Won't it make you sick to be near me?" Zahra asked.

"Do I look sick now? I can perform as well as any man can. I am not completely useless," Peter said answering his own question.

"Alright, but please don't take it as a promise of a future, I have no desire to hurt anyone. Do you mean sex?" Zahra asked.

"If it happens and if not, just cuddles and a nice sleep together. What do you say?" Peter asked.

"I'd like that," Zahra said.

◊

From the mountain, no-one had known where Zahra had gone and the Crofter, who was the last person to see her, did not reveal that she had seen her or the name of who she had departed with. The two old Crofters by the path to the waterfall, however, told everything they knew of the lass who went 'that way' asking for directions to the waterfall, then came running back going 'that way' saying nothing to them, the second time. It hadn't been helpful because she was nowhere near the waterfall, when Coinneach and Alasdair searched. They ruled out that she had destroyed herself, because she had come running back, for some unknown reason.

Mairi did not disclose to anyone that she had given Zahra the rudimentary map, or she would lose her job and so she kept on caring for Coinneach Og. The two homosexuals gave up their search for Zahra, after only a few days of looking and went back to their activities with each other. They also overlooked reporting her missing to the authorities once again and Coinneach's father, Lord Cinaed, carefully protected the family's reputation but fearful this time, that Coinneach had disposed of her, somehow.

Coinneach had found his one and only love, Alasdair, and he had all but forgotten the words of the Seer, from all those many hundreds of years ago. After all, he had what he had needed, which was his heir, Coinneach Og. However, Alasdair had other thoughts, but Coinneach didn't know that. After suffering many years of sexual abuse from his own father, Alasdair knew when to get out and he would do the same eventually, but not before he had obtained what he wanted from the wealthy Coinneach. This had to include money, gifts, clothes, shoes, a new horse with saddlery and ridiculous wages to both him and his father, who was given money also to build a new and enlarged forge on additional land, with their benefits, all from Lord Coinneach MacAlpin.

Alasdair planned to marry a girl one day, when he had acquired premises for a larger forge for himself, was his ultimate plan. Wick sounded like an ideal location, far away from both his father and Lord Coinneach. That old pervert was just a means to an end for Alasdair Fraser and Zahra's loss of a husband had meant nothing to him because his wife had been complicit, in his opinion. With her disappearance, it had only meant more money and gifts, including jewellery for him, to plan his eventual departure. What could be better than that? Alasdair thought.

◇

Zahra and Peter Heath slept side by side on the very first night of being under the one roof. He enjoyed her cooking, and she enjoyed cooking it, after all, she needed to gain the weight anyway, which was Peter's plan for her. When Zahra was in Peter's front garden in the daytime, local people would stop and talk to her and some more patients started attending Peter's Medical Practice, seeing that he had, what they thought, was a sweet wife. For convenience, he called her Mrs Heath, that way too, no one would identify the name, Zahra back to either Coinneach or Grigor Mohr MacGregor, not that it was her real name anyway. Zahra went along with being called Mrs Heath, as it made sense and she grew to like it, as did Peter. The two of them settled into a pleasant routine of working together, eating together, gardening together and sleeping together.

She had gained weight slowly, after a month or more and was looking much healthier and her skin was almost, all healed. Her hair was lustrous, once more and Peter even bought home a new dress for her to wear, as she had nothing of her own, as well as a new Nurse's uniform. She did all the cleaning and never stopped looking after his Medical Practise, paying her own way, never expecting to be found out by any one of those people connected to one of her previous husbands, nor he with any of his. They had settled into married life, without realising it.

They had become Dr and Mrs Heath of Inverness.

Sex was becoming more enjoyable for them both, as they had

few expectations of one another. Being gentle was the primary need for them both, who had deep sensitivities. He began exploring her body, unlike he had ever done in his life, as a homosexual and found it to be pleasant for him, because it was Zahra. As more time went by, more exploration took place, to enjoy more of what they could be for one another, and it was only on the upwards side. Zahra always enjoyed running her fingers through his chest hairs, to feel his manliness and would often rub her face into his chest hair too, as was her habit. He loved her gentle movements of caressing him and he

was never repelled by her exploration of him, as it was all rather new. She had been afraid at first, to touch his manhood, because she worried that it might be too much to expect from a homosexual, until he placed her hand on his member, therefore giving her permission to do what she had wanted to do. That evoked deep feelings that were unexpected, and they then had full enjoyment of each other from that moment on. He brought her to orgasm all the time, as did she to him and they were what you would call, fair to one another in both love and in work. There was only one problem with their relationship, as the months went by, without a hitch.

They were falling in love, inch by inch. Which one of the two of them knew first is uncertain, but it was Zahra who expressed it.

"Peter, would it bother you if I told you, that I loved you?" Zahra asked, carefully expecting it to bother him.

"Do you love me then?" Peter asked.

"Aye, I do. I am sorry about that, but I have no expectations, I just wanted you to know," Zahra said and was going to roll over and go to sleep when he held her gently by the shoulder to roll her back to look him in the eye.

"I love you too Zahra, but I too have no expectations," Peter said. "Can we make love?" he asked.

"Aye," she said and with that Peter Heath entered Zahra knowing they were both expressing themselves in an act of love and they both experienced heightened sensitivity to the act of love making, like she nor he had ever experienced until then. She was almost pulling out his hair, as she came to orgasm and he groaned a deep groan, enjoying the pain of her pulling his hair and kissing him incessantly. He experienced her squeals, at the moment of her orgasm, which gave him the greatest joy too, in knowing that he was the man who gave her that.

The next day they went shopping for food and stopped by for a cup of tea in a tea shop in Inverness. They were both in a world of their own, as they walked down the windy streets of Inverness, holding hands. He would frequently stop and kiss her, a thing he never imagined he would ever do, just six months prior. They arrived back home with their shopping to a waiting room with a few patients, so they both went back to work immediately.

Their front door had a bell that rang each time when someone entered and from behind her nurse's reception desk, Zahra looked up to see, who had walked in. It was Grigor Mohr MacGregor. He had an injury to his hand, requiring the Doctor's immediate attention. He wasn't expecting to see her, any more than she was expecting to see him, but he concealed his shock, as did she.

"Is the Doctor available?" Grigor asked, without saying hello or even acknowledging who she was.

"Aye, he is. Is it serious?" Zahra asked.

"Maybe," Grigor replied, so she ushered him in, ahead of the next patient, whom she knew to be a time waster.

Obviously, he was weakened from blood loss, so Zahra asked Dr Heath to put him ahead of all the other patients. Dr Heath had been training Zahra in his Medical Practice, to assist him and she was wearing the uniform of a nurse. A long-sleeved, full length, white dress with a tartan cape in Clan Gregor tartan and white flat, comfortable shoes, paid for, by the practice. On the counter it read, Dr Peter Heath, Nurse on duty -Nurse Heath. She was paying her way, working, and learning, while not paying rent or for her food or clothing. Zahra worked in his practise and cleaned the house, did all the cooking and they gardened together and shopped together.

Their cosy arrangement was companionable.

Dr Heath saw that it was a serious injury to Grigor's hand and asked Zahra to prepare a sterile tray with all the things that he needed, like needles, stitching equipment, gauze, bandages, pure alcohol to sterilise and all the pain relief that Dr Heath normally used. She was to stand and hold the tray and pass him the items that he asked for, with a pair of tweezers, as he required them. Grigor was beyond objection and was very pale. Their previous relationships with one another, were overlooked in the event of the emergency and all three people, previously all old friends, merely got to work to stabilise Grigor, stop the bleeding and sterilise and close the horrible wound. His heart rate was being monitored and he rested, confident that he was in good hands.

Dr Heath asked him how it had happened, and it seemed that it was while Grigor was working on repairing a broken fence, when the wire re-coiled suddenly, and it ripped open his flesh. It was a nasty wound, and he had ridden his horse, alone all the way from the Aird to Inverness.

It was going to be necessary for him to sleep overnight in the one room only, that Peter had set aside for such emergencies, when people refused to go to the hospital, which Grigor did.

It was a single, sterile room with boiled sheets, a pillow, warm blankets, and a tidy fireplace, to keep the room warm, with a single armchair beside the fire. Zahra was automatically asked to light the fire in that room, not thinking of how awkward that night could be, if Peter and Zahra were sleeping together in their room, with Grigor's knowledge. Just the same, Grigor's health was the priority, and an extra meal was added to dinner that night and luckily it was beef stew, that she knew he loved, and he may not have a big appetite anyway.

After all the remaining patients had gone home, she escorted Grigor to the room that he would enjoy for the night, without any conversation, until he asked her a question.

"So, where's that arty husband of yours gone?" Grigor asked.

"We are no longer married. The marriage has been annulled, Grigor, based on his current relationship. I think he is still up there on the mountain with his male lover," Zahra responded coldly.

"Did you get a payout or something?" Grigor asked nosily.

"I came away holding onto my life, that was enough," Zahra said. "Please make yourself comfortable. There are clean bed-clothes under the pillow. It's beef stew with tomatoes for dinner tonight, in around one hour and Turkish coffee if you feel up to drinking it. Would tea suit you better tonight?" Zahra asked.

"Tea, thank you," Grigor replied and went into his room and sat beside his fire, contemplating life, it seemed.

Zahra busied herself cleaning up the doctor's examination room and changing the sheets on the exam bed for the following day, blew out the candles and smoored the fire in there. Then she habitually washed all the floors, where people had trapsed their dirty shoes, all day long, which then gave off a pleasant sterile, lemon scent. After lighting the lounge fire, she put on the dinner to cook, that she had pre-prepared, so it would not take too long on Peter's wood stove. She was cooking up bathing water for both Peter and Grigor as well as herself when Peter came to assist her to set the table. Peter always liked a white, starched and crisp tablecloth. A throw over from his life in England, she had assumed. He carefully put the knives and forks in their correct places, setting the table for three people.

"Zahra, you take your bath first. The stew might be ready when you are dressed," Peter suggested.

She took his advice. It had been a busy day, and it wasn't over yet, so a bath was a pleasant idea. Washed and clean and dressed and after brushing her very long hair, she finished up the preparation for the meal, as well as making a pot of tea for Grigor and Turkish coffee for Peter and herself. Peter and Grigor both came in looking a little more refreshed and both sat down at the white, starched covered table, while she served them both their meals and their respective hot drinks, surprisingly comfortable with one another.

Grigor seemed to really love the nutritious, hot meal and the Indian tea and some of the colour was returning to his face. He wasn't the happiest soul in the world, but they all had issues, and she hoped compassionately for him, as did Peter, that one night's rest, might do him some good. The two men chatted about the farm and farming in general and how it was all going on Wolf Ranch, as well as how Peter's practise was improving since it had taken that battering in the newspapers, thanks to Matilda Grant writing to London.

Zahra's bairns came up in conversation and Grigor asked if she would like to see Causantin and Dihaoine. It was a question that was so emotive that it caught Zahra off guard. She immediately fell into tears. Trying to stop, Peter helped her with a handkerchief, and she was able to say that she wanted to see them.

"Could we have them stay here, taking it in turns, do you think Grigor, if it suited you?" Peter asked taking over the parental dialogue for her.

That idea really appealed to the tired looking and injured, Grigor Mohr MacGregor. The two men agreed on times and pickup days and Zahra started to clean up when Grigor offered to assist.

"Nae, nae, you must rest your poor hand. I can do this," Zahra said.

She was so happy thinking that she would finally see her wee bairns and dared not ask about Isobel, who seemed to dislike her the last time that they had seen each other. They had all said their good nights, so it was far more civilised than she had expected. Zahra placed all the dirty linen out the back door, ready to wash for the laundry lady and went back inside, only to be faced once again, by her ex-husband, Grigor.

"Are you in a relationship now, with Peter Heath?" Grigor asked.

"Sort of, but we are not married, if that's what you mean. We are very good friends who don't have anyone else. Good night, Grigor," Zahra said and walked to her room.

"What did he ask you Zahra?" Peter asked when she walked into their room.

"Oh Peter, I knew it could be awkward, but he asked if you and I were in a relationship. I told him 'Sort of', but unmarried and very good friends who don't have anyone else. Was I wrong to say that?" Zahra asked.

"I didn't know what else to say, that wouldn't start a late-night argument," Zahra added.

"You did well. It's all true, we are not married but I wonder if we should think about it. Everyone here thinks we are married," Peter said.

"Nae, it's not necessary. Let the patients think that. I like it but it doesn't mean that we have to do the whole thing. It hasn't worked for me so far," Zahra said.

"That's a good point. It really hasn't. But I want to call you, my wife. Do you mind?" Peter asked.

"I'd like it but please don't say it in front of Grigor. The man has feelings, and he isn't well. He still has feelings for me, I am sure of it. What do you think?" Zahra asked.

"He sure does. I felt jealous and my lady, that it the first time in my life, that I have felt jealous over a woman," Peter admitted, and they both laughed.

"So, 'my very good friend', will you allow me to make love to you tonight, even though your ex-husband sleeps just a few doors down from us?" Peter asked not really jesting as he was lovingly looking into Zahra's eyes and began to feel her body. "No wonder you have driven men mad and turned homosexuals into heterosexuals, you are gorgeous. I also have a confession to make from long ago when you were expecting Causantin. I was with Alex briefly, but I was drawn to you then. You and I both have green eyes and then when I helped with Causantin's delivery, I felt an affection for you. I dared not admit it though," Peter said.

"Oh, Peter did you really?" Zahra asked. "That is so nice. You are the sweetest man. I didn't know you at all and to learn so much now about you, I feel I have missed out on such a nice relationship. I do love you Peter, even if we are not married" Zahra said.

"Say it again. I insist," Peter said smiling.

"I do love you Peter, even if we are not married," Zahra said smiling at her sweet friend. He was dying to make love to her upon being re-assured that she still loved him, after seeing her ex-husband. They tried to be quiet, but Zahra wasn't known for being quiet when she had an orgasm and of course he bought her to orgasm just to hear the squeals that she made. He loved it as it excited him. As a precaution, he had locked their bedroom door. They were up early after he kissed her incessantly trying to capture the last of their night together. She was giggling at his games, and she tickled him to equal his games with her.

"I love you Zahra, I do want to marry you one day, so when you are ready just tell me and I'll buy you a nice gold ring," Peter said.

"Peter, you might tire of my feminine company and then what?" Zahra asked.

"I won't. I just know it," Peter said.

It was a friendly breakfast atmosphere as the three old friends, all helped make breakfast together, or set the table and Grigor looked a lot better, as his colour was returning slowly to his face.

"Before you leave Grigor, I have to look at that hand, so I can be sure that you can go on your way safely and I'll give you a tea that has a pain relief in it, that might assist," Peter said.

There were occasional side glances towards Peter, having heard the night's familiar sounds but despite that, Grigor seemed to like Peter but puzzled at what he had known about Dr Heath. After breakfast, Zahra assisted Peter with Grigor's bandage and in assessing the wound. Peter was pleased that it was healing well, so asked Zahra to pass him another of those bandages and he wrapped it up securely once more. Their relationship was very co-operative to say the least, Grigor had assessed. His ex-wife was someone else now and thank God, she wasn't a Fairy, he thought.

"Do you think Grigor might need something to waterproof it going home. It might rain?" Zahra asked Dr Heath.

"Aye, good idea. I have a glove here that will protect it. Is your horse in the stables Grigor?" Peter asked.

"Aye," Grigor said looking on at the pair of them curiously. He wished it was him in Peter's place, but he hadn't given up hope yet on getting her back, despite what he had done. Grigor paid his bill, which was discounted and there was no charge for staying with them overnight, as it had just been a hospitable arrangement, as old friends should be, Peter had said. They all farewelled one another, agreeing to meet up with the bairns in one week's time, in Inverness, where his hand would be checked once again.

That one week felt like a lifetime, both in waiting to see Causantin and Dihaoine with Zahra preparing their rooms in the rambling old house, as well as the adoration that grew between Dr Heath and Nurse Heath. They were often caught kissing, in between patients with his hand on her buttocks, which of course became gossip in their neighbourhood. Neighbours and patients alike, started to say that the whole story of the doctor being a homosexual was entirely made up, to soil his reputation, just due to his being English. His patients grew substantially in number, then and they needed to put their opening hours on the outside of the door, or else they would achieve nothing else. On weekends, patients were transferred to the hospital, to allow family time together and with the new arrangements with Zahra's bairns, naturally everyone believed they were his family, all along.

When Doctor and Nurse Heath walked their two bairns through the leafy park, with the bairns' obvious physical likenesses, there was judgment placed on the 'dreadful rumours' being falsely spread by the newspapers, to such a lovely wee family. Peter Heath was a tall man for an Englishman and was nearly six feet tall who stood erect with perfect posture and walking beside Zahra, who was much shorter than he was, they looked like a perfect pair, both with green eyes and sweet temperaments and wonderful parents. The two of them were frequently stopped while out walking, so their bairns could be admired by an adoring following of patients. Causantin loved the attention that they received and really played up to the local city people, to be especially cute and adorable. Dihaoine was often asked about her name but was too young to know how to answer that question.

"She was born on a Friday," Zahra explained.

Of course, as often happens, even with adopted children, people start imagining likenesses from the father or mither in the bairns, even if they weren't their biological parents.

Finally, Zahra had her wee bairns back after all of the time that they had been forced apart and they adored their Mither and were much relieved to be able to be re-united. They even loved Peter.

"Oh, Dr Heath, your son, wee Causantin looks so much like you," was frequently heard.

Dr Heath enjoyed hearing it so much, that he never corrected his patients' misunderstandings, even when Grigor was right there, listening, whether picking them up, or dropping them off.

Grigor was biding his time, by also not correcting the misunderstandings. The arrangement initially was that Grigor would take them to Inverness and pick them up and that arrangement lasted for around a month, after which Grigor stated that he had become too busy on the farm and asked for the arrangements to be reversed, for a time, or take it in turns. His hand was also much improved and didn't need the frequent checks on it with the bandage changed each visit. The stitches were taken out also and it was looking healed.

Naturally all parents involved were co-operative with the bairns' arrangements, and they decided early on a Saturday morning was convenient, just in case Dr Heath had emergency patients on a Friday night. Zahra was only too keen to co-operate, because she adored her two youngest bairns and didn't want to lose them again.

36. Heaths in The Aird

Hector had given two Highland Ponies to his two younger siblings, Causantin and Dihaoine. Causantin was learning quite well, but Dihaoine was still afraid of the horses and refused to get on one of them, at least for now. Causantin would ride his pony around wildly, like Hector once had and insisted that he could ride all the way to Inverness. It took some convincing to ride on Peter's big horse with him to see just how far it was to Inverness, on horseback. Neither parent wanted the lad to fall off, but Grigor appeared casual about it all.

"Peter can fix the lad if he breaks a bone," Grigor casually stated. Zahra wasn't expecting any hospitality in the Aird, after the last visit and the nude painting of her was hung, very deliberately in the kitchen of the old house, above the mantle. It was the one that had been fought over with Prince Griogar, who lost and was now at the bottom of the waterfall.

"It's a pity you didn't throw that into the waterfall too with him," Zahra commented.

Dr Heath made no remark about the lovely painting, only he was made aware of the men's desire for his future wife, Zahra.

"Hello Isobel, how's your chubby wee bairn," Peter asked upon seeing her, but was met with Isobel's usual frostiness.

"Why are you here, Dr Heath?" Isobel asked.

"Picking up wee Causantin and wee Dihaoine. Are they ready yet?" Peter asked.

"Why are you picking them up?" Isobel persisted in her rude manner.

"You do remember when Grigor took over the role as your father from Hugh Chisholm, I am sure my child? What your

Mither and I are doing, in co-operation with your father, is like what you experienced, only shared arrangements with the bairns, so that neither parent loses contact with them," Dr Heath replied in his most refined English accent, to which she was unaccustomed to hearing. Isobel just frowned in response.

Negotiation was needed with Causantin for him to leave his pony behind. It was decided that he would ride with Dr Heath on his huge horse, much bigger than his wee pony and next time, provided he practiced some more, he could do the long ride to Inverness on his own pony. Dr Heath had a way with bairns, as he had to in every condition, even badly injured ones and so the lad trusted his Mither's new companion, although he still missed Coinneach, and he often asked where Coinneach was, as well as his brother, Coinneach Og.

Zahra saw Padruig's books sitting where they had always sat on the mantel piece in the old farmhouse, once more.

"Your books Padruig, you got them back, I see, but how?" Zahra asked the unsmiling Padruig who barely looked up.

"The post," Padruig answered gruffly.

"What books Zahra?" asked an interested Peter Heath, yet unaware of Zahra as having once been an author, many life-times ago.

"May I Padruig?" she asked politely, expecting a refusal.

"Aye, but I'm watching you," Padruig added, to ensure they never went missing again pointing his finger at Peter. Zahra passed them to Peter.

"Ma wrote those," added Isobel, who then wanted to be noticed.

"What a lovely front cover," Peter commented.

"Aye, my oldest daughter painted that," Zahra said feeling nostalgic momentarily, which immediately upset Isobel.

"I am your oldest daughter," Isobel exclaimed defensively.

"Aye my darling, in the Otherworld, you most certainly are. However, before I died, I had three other daughters and the oldest of them painted that of, 'Isobel of Glenmoriston,'" Zahra explained.

"She didn't look like that," Padruig said, attempting to degrade her work.

"I am sure she didn't, my friend, but I had to use my imagination to obtain a likeness for a lady whom you would have chosen to marry, after all you were an important figure in history," Zahra added, trying to placate him, which worked, while Peter flicked through the pages looking impressed and very curious at the side to Zahra, that he hadn't yet known of.

"Could I please borrow these one day, Padruig?" Peter asked.

"Nae, never again. That last fella never returned them, until a few weeks ago," Padruig said. "You can read them here, while I watch over you," Padruig replied.

It was obvious that coffee was not on offer either, so they both thought it was time to leave with the wee bairns.

"We'll take our leave then Grigor," Peter said politely as they packed up Dihaoine's wee bag and strapped her to Zahra's back, once again, heavy as she was now.

It was wonderful for Zahra to have Dihaoine close to her and with Causantin on the big horse, with her new, most unlikely of men, they headed for Inverness, leaving behind them, all that snippiness that she was pleased to never live with again. Even Isobel was quite unbearable. Fatma didn't even come down from the other house to say hello and neither had John.

What had influenced them to be so unfriendly? Zahra could make no sense of it.

Grigor watched them both leave and closed the iron gate behind them and wandered slowly back up to the house to his companions and Isobel's cooking. After tasting Zahra's cooking again that night in Inverness, he longed for her cooking again.

He had to admit, she had been the best cook that he had ever known, which started from not even knowing what the meat was, when she was given it to cook, back in Glenmoriston. A slab of meat had been put in front of her by John Campbell back then, who just told her to cook it. The bloodied fresh venison sat there wobbling a bit, as bloodied slabs of freshly killed venison does, and she almost vomited. He smiled remembering that day and went inside.

"What's with them then?" Padruig asked.

"What do you mean?" Grigor asked.

"Why is she living with him?" he asked.

"She has work, it's safe and pleasant. Why not? Better than where she was, for sure," Grigor replied.

"But he's homosexual, isn't he?" Padruig asked.

"Better still," Grigor replied.

Grigor knew that wasn't entirely true anymore, but he thought he was safe enough to win her back from Peter, despite the growing love between the pair.

"Take that damn painting down Padruig. I find it offensive for the bairns," Grigor added.

"Me too," added Isobel.

"Put it in your room," Grigor added. Padruig reluctantly took it down and went to his room with his prized possession.

"Da, he is getting more and more sick, if you ask me. He has another one in his bedroom too, that the bairns should never see. I'm not happy that he is living here at all," she added. "Why can't he go back and haunt that hotel?" Isobel asked. "I'm happy with Alex but not with Padruig. Can you ask him to leave please?" Isobel said.

"Not really, but he knows he's not welcome, so he will leave eventually," Grigor replied.

"For you however, if he does leave, so will Alex, most probably and you might want to do more for Alex as his wife, so he knows that you want to keep him, which I think you do," Grigor said. "The alternative you have is now to divorce John and to marry Alex in the Kirk to secure him," Grigor suggested.

"Oh Da. I couldn't do that, could I?" Isobel asked.

"Isobel my child, you are not happy, especially since having your third bairn. You have improved since Alex moved back here, but what is it that your Ma could do to make you happy that I can't do?" he asked sincerely wanting her to be happier.

"I haven't forgiven you all for chopping up my father and completely removing him from my life, without asking me," she said honestly and started to cry.

"You might be happy to know then, that he is back. I first saw his collie dogs, then thought he was back and just hiding somewhere. I started looking around for him and even called out his name a few times. I knew you wanted to see him again and it was a mistake to do what we did, but we acted in accordance with the threat we faced by all three of the brothers that night. Finally, Hugh was confident enough to reveal himself because he isn't quite as handsome as he was, but alive and cheerful like you will remember him. He won't see you unless you ask to see him," Grigor said.

"Oh Da" Isobel cried. "Please tell him I'm sorry that I wasn't nice enough to him and I do want to see him, even if he is ugly. I don't care what he looks like. Does he still have blonde hair like me?" Isobel asked.

"Aye, I will tell him, and he still has blonde hair," Grigor smiled.

"When can I see him then?" Isobel asked.

"Around now," he said, as Hugh Chisholm walked through the back door to visit his daughter.

"Oh Da," Isobel cried, as she ran into the waiting arms of an emotional Hugh Chisholm, who had never expected his daughter to ever love, care or need him. His complete disposal bought out her true feelings for her father, as she had stood praying over the waterfall, every night, since his disposal. Even Ali couldn't tolerate seeing his sister in so much pain and had long left the farm in the Aird, to live now beside Malcolm MacNachten, in Glengarry. It didn't go unnoticed by Hugh, that just the same, Grigor was hurt, and it was going to be harder now for Grigor to share the bairns between different parents. Grigor knew though, that it had all been his fault, having allowed his family to crumble into pieces and could only be supportive of what remained. He had made a start with re-uniting his youngest two bairns, Causantin and Dihaoine with their Mither and now his oldest, Isobel with her birth father, Hugh. Isobel's hug of the big man was prolonged, and she sobbed, saying things that Hugh could barely understand, through her sobs.

Hugh Mohr Chisholm

She cooked a decent meal that night, which proved to Grigor anyway, that Isobel hadn't wanted anyone to enjoy her cooking, but she did now that it mattered for Hugh Chisholm. Grigor felt some of his old resentment towards Hugh returning, but had to reign it in, somehow. He was going to have to show respect to Hugh and that made him feel a little nauseous, but it was all for Isobel, who had made them all suffer with her bad moods, since his disposal, then his own departure and her Mither's plight.

Isobel's third pregnancy and the birth of Zahra Og was bothering him. The actual father of that wee bairn was unaware that he had even sired a wee bairn, or if somehow, he became aware of that fact, they'd all be in a lot of bother from the MacAlpin family. It required discussion between Alex, John, Isobel, Hugh, and himself. His opinion was annulment of her marriage with John Fraser first, as a priority, so she could marry Alex MacDonald, legally, in the Kirk. That would be tricky, as it would need his ex-wife's co-operation by way of a letter agreeing that John was not the biological father of any of Isobel's bairns and John Fraser was considered sterile.

There would need to be an agreement from Alex to marry Isobel, stating that he was the biological father, once that was achieved, thereby losing any control that the MacAlpin family had over Grigor's two grandchildren, Anndra and Domhnall. In his opinion, their bargaining power lay with the third bairn, Zahra Og Fraser, to rid them of the MacAlpin legal adoptions, altogether. It would be hard for a Mither to part with her wee bairn, but somehow Zahra, his ex-wife had overcome parting with Coinneach Og, too easily for her, Grigor thought.

Maybe Zahra too thought that Coinneach Og was 'different' also.

He had to admit too, that the MacAlpin bairns, were a wee bit odd and didn't look like any of their siblings. They were as fat as could be and would no doubt be difficult, as they became older, he predicted. When he became aware that Isobel had given birth to a wee lassie, at first, he had been pleased to know that she would have two lads and one lassie. Naturally, he had thought then that Alex, somehow had fathered the wee bairn, not the ancient old MacAlpin man, who had. Just the same, when he met the wee bairn, he had expected to see a pretty wee thing, but instead saw an obese, unattractive wee bairn, who was strange and had an odd cry, that had a gravelly sound. As she grew older, when he checked in on her, she would just stare at him, with an icy cold stare that had a challenge within her steely, blue eyes.

He concluded that the blood of the ancient race that had long since been watered down by MacGregors, MacNachtens and many others, had been re-introduced in its original form, which included the original Pictish people and was no longer normal, as they understood normal to be, by the standards of the current day. That was what he slept with every night and his discomfort was real. He hoped the wee bairn would be returned to where she would feel normal and so would he, but he also hoped he wasn't being too harsh, at the same time. Zahra Og gave him the shivers, so he hoped Isobel would relent and return her to the weird old man who had sired her.

37. The Heated Discussion

Hugh's introduction into family life was immediate, as he moved into the vacant room in the older farmhouse with Grigor, Isobel, Alex, and Padruig. Fatma had moved back to the newer of the two houses with John and his nephew, Simon. Anndra and Domnhall shared a room with Zahra Og in the old house. When time came for the discussion that Grigor requested, he sent the two lads up to the other house.

"What's this about?" asked Hugh. "Is it about me?" he asked self-consciously.

"Nae, it's not, but I do need your input," Grigor said.

"Do you need me, because I'd rather read," said Padruig.

"You are not required Padruig, so go ahead and read," he stated.

"Shouldn't Zahra be here if it's family business?" Padruig asked.

"I'll ask her afterwards," Grigor said.

"Hmmm," Padruig grunted, disapprovingly.

Opening several delicate topics of conversation wasn't what Grigor was good at, but he gave it a good try, now that he was trying to assert that he was back as head of the family. His first suggestion of annulment of John's marriage with Isobel in order to marry Alex, was met with scoffs, laughs, ridicule and plain no, except from Alex who did want Isobel as his legal wife but hadn't known a way to achieve such a thing. John Fraser was horrified naturally and put his foot down and called Grigor, interfering, and even accused Grigor of breaking their agreement with the farm, as paying for Isobel upon their marriage. Hugh then felt a need to interject and help him out.

"Isobel darling, who do you love the most, Alex or John?" Hugh asked.

"Alex," Isobel replied.

"Who is the father of most of your bairns," Hugh asked.

"Alex," Isobel replied.

"Do you want Alex to be your legal husband in the Kirk?" Hugh asked.

"Aye, I do, Da," Isobel said.

"Alex, do you want to marry Isobel, legally in the Kirk, if she was divorced?" Hugh asked.

"Aye, of course" Alex replied.

"Then there's the answer. Sorry John. Will you give her a divorce, or do Grigor and I have to do the whole annulment thing?" Hugh asked.

"Would I see my bairns again?" John asked.

"Of course, you would. You all still live here on the same property, so nothing much would change except what's on paper," he added.

Grigor was impressed with Hugh's ability to manage the family, after all. Maybe Hugh would be an asset and Grigor needed assistance. The family were all making him feel too tired without having Zahra managing things, the way she used to.

"There's the matter of the MacAlpin adoptions too, which even cover the two grandchildren, Anndra and Domnhall. There is one way we could get them to relinquish control legally, I believe. With lawyers of course," Grigor said. "One of your bairns Isobel, has a different father who I believe wasn't told of the wee bairn's birth. Is that right?" Grigor asked noticing a sudden change of mood in the room.

Suddenly Padruig butted in saying, "The father should have been told about the wee bairn, Isobel. I'm not criticising, but he is the father. You should notify him, or we could all be in trouble here," Padruig stated honestly.

"Shut up Uncle Padruig. Read your book. You're not family. And I'll do what I want with my bairns," Isobel said.

Hugh then asked Alex "How do you feel Alex that Lord Cinaed is the father of the wee lass?"

"Same as Padruig. I think the father should be told about his wee bairn and have the option to see her. Like Hugh was with you Isobel. At least have visiting rights and if he persisted, then I think we should give him custody, because I can give Isobel another bairn. What do you think Isobel? It's trouble, I tell you. That wee bairn is big trouble for us," Alex stated firmly.

Isobel suddenly wept. Maybe Zahra should have been at their meeting after all, were Grigor's thoughts then. Isobel was overwhelmed and outnumbered. If Zahra had been there, it may have brought civility, fairness and calm and a way she had with Isobel to calm her down into making the right decision. This way now, she was lost to the men and what were they were proposing exactly? Isobel suddenly stood up and left the conversation.

"If any of you try to kidnap my wee bairn in the middle of the night, I'll gut you, pure and simple. I've got a sharp skein dubh to do the job," Isobel added and moved Zahra Og into her room with her and locked the door behind her preventing access to Alex as well.

Alex followed his wife to their bedroom door, aware then of their mistake in having overwhelmed Isobel, by numbers alone, without her Mither there.

"Sweetheart, can I please come in?" Alex asked to a locked door.

Padruig was scoffing of course. "You idiots. I told you Zahra should have been here. You can't expect to take a woman's bairn from her, without a mighty fight," Padruig said.

"For once Padruig, you were right. I should have invited her Mither and that Peter Heath," Grigor added. "I can still ask her though, maybe?" Grigor wondered.

Maybe too much damage had already been done, and Isobel was loathe to trust any one of them.

The only man smiling was John Fraser.

"So that was why you didn't want Zahra here, because of a certain Dr Peter Heath? He was Alex's ex-boyfriend, wasn't he?" Padruig said, trying to stir up Grigor and Alex, as well as question Zahra's current circumstances.

"Padruig my friend, there's one thing that you are very adept at and that is stirring up trouble, where there isn't any and where you stand to benefit," said Hugh.

"If I remember rightly, all you ever did when I was married to Zahra, was stir us both up, until eventually you succeeded in breaking us up permanently, even if it was by way of my brothers, joining into your sadistic power games. When poor Sakina was killed, I knew I could never get Zahra back and why would I, when you were supportive of what my brothers had done, except Grigor and Alex. Even in locking out Grigor. I had no hand in that either, but I suspect you do know more about that incident than you have ever revealed.I know I have been blamed as one of 'the Chisholms', but Sakina was my wee bairn that was killed that day, and no-one has ever given me condolences for my lost bairn, just blame for her death, like I was her murderer. You all knew that I had no hand in it, only my brothers, but you didn't clarify that fact, at any time.

So now, don't try to undermine either Grigor's relationship with Zahra, what's left of it, or Peter's if that's who she chooses, going forward in her life now. It's a bad habit you have developed of breaking down the happiness that you see around you Padruig," Hugh said.

"I admit, I did wrong by you in life, for which I have apologised already to you, and I know that it can't be undone. It's not like the late Isobel Grant, your wife, is here by my side now is she, in either of our Otherworld's? She didn't choose either one of us to be with, in the Otherworld. Let it go Padruig, so we can all get on with what we can enjoy from this life here. If it helps, please forgive me for what I did to hurt you in your life as it was, but it wasn't known by anyone other than Grigor Og, who kept it secret for everyone's sakes. You died with dignity and your wife insisted on that. She loved you until the very end and I just wanted to care for Old Isobel, until she passed away. Can you see that now?" asked a very rational Hugh, who'd had plenty of time to go over things in that waterfall, it seemed.

Some of it was news to those listening. Grigor for one, thought that Hugh was also one of the guilty parties.

"Why didn't you help bury Sakina then? Only Alex and Grigor were there?" Padruig asked.

"I was too distraught, but you wouldn't know that feeling Padruig. I had lost another wee bairn," answered Hugh.

"I still want Zahra to know that it wasn't me who was behind it, and to ask her for forgiveness, if she thought I had a hand in it. I need her forgiveness and to take her to Sakina's wee grave, in Glenmoriston, where I visit frequently. I know it nearly killed Zahra and had it not been for Grigor, her life would have ended right then and there. It was bad enough that I was living with the guilt of killing Zahra accidentally and leaving her unable to return to her family, wherever they were. I still don't even know, to this day where she is from, and what time she came from. I only know she is not from here, nor from this time. She came from out of no-where, you remember that?" Hugh said.

"No-one has spoken for a long time of where Zahra came from, as she has been here now for a long time living amongst us, while having bairns, working hard, being someone's wife and it was all lost somehow, after she broke up with me. I was too young at the time and too stupid to appreciate who she was, so if you do get her back Grigor, hold onto her this time, and look after her, is my advice, because she is a rare one amongst us, like a beautiful, but very delicate flower, amidst us thistles," Hugh said.

"You also have a dreadful misunderstanding of why she was with the prince, in the Outer Hebrides. She didn't 'run off' with another man, which seems to be what Isobel and all of you believe. I have investigated it. She and her bairns were kidnapped from her home on Beinn Coinneach, by that Prince Griogar and his mercenaries, who then took only Zahra to the Outer Hebrides after leaving the wee ones here on the farm. Zahra was tortured, starved, and raped repeatedly and when you saw her in that fancy dress, it was the only dress, he had bought her. She only had one dress that she was kidnapped in. He only gave in to coming here to get that painting, because he had nearly succeeded in disposing of her completely and she wanted to see her bairns. I am glad you killed that monster, but you misunderstood Zahra, and you have broken her heart," Hugh said.

"She heard the howl of the wolves that night, calling to her, as well as her own wolf and left here on the back of that giant brown wolf, who was her husband, according to the old Crohn. Trouble was, he didn't remain the man she had known previously, for long. He had lived for too long as a wolf, outside of the human form, in the time that she had been gone, therefore he was thinking like a wild animal. He lives happily now with his boyfriend, Alasdair Fraser. He was the homosexual in her life, not Peter Heath, as it turns out," Hugh said.

"Now I have said enough, so I am off to bed," Hugh said. With that last message, Hugh went to bed, leaving everyone with something to think about.

38. Back in Inverness

After dropping off Causantin and Dihaoine to the farm in the Aird, Peter made the next arrangements with Grigor. Zahra said he was noticeably quieter, pensive and more cooperative. Grigor also asked if he could reintroduce an old friend when he came next time to Inverness, if it was no trouble. So, it was decided to invite both Grigor and the old friend to dinner, with the bairns before they headed back to the Aird. If the weather was bad and late at night, Peter suggested that they could both stay the night in Inverness, getting into the spirit of cooperation and socialising, unless he had an emergency with his patients, which was always possible and had to be said, accompanying any invitation.

For Zahra, it was a bit sad to part with her two wee ones after dropping them off and so for a while, she rode together with Peter on his horse while leading hers, just to overcome the grief of her temporary loss. She just sobbed and sobbed while the ever-patient Peter, not only held her while controlling the two horses but spoke kind words of love and reassurance.

"Do you think we could ever have a wee bairn?" Peter asked.

"I was raped continuously on that island by Prince Griogar and his mercenaries and was never with child. I concluded that my body was worn out. I've had so many bairns now, if you include my first family, as well as the ones here and the ones that I have lost. So, my love, my body might have stopped being able to be with child. You would know better than me, as you are the Doctor, why I never became with child over there. I am grateful for it though, but maybe the malnutrition was a factor. I am sorry that if now you want a bairn and my body can't give you one. That would be sad," Zahra said.

"Oh Zahra, you are so sweet. I do want a bairn from you.

However, I think the reason he failed in giving you a child, could have been that he was unable to. Maybe he was a sterile man. After all, he has been dead for centuries, whereas I am alive at least. Can we try, do you think on your most fertile days?" Peter asked.

"Aye, we can Peter. We might need to marry then, after all, if I am with child. What do you think?" Zahra asked.

"It would mean the world to me Zahra. You are everything to me now. It would make me so happy to have a bairn, but if not, we will share your wee ones. I love them to bits," Peter added. "Do you miss Coinneach Og?" he asked.

"I try not to think about my wee lad. I tell myself that he is better off with his own kind, who are more like him. He was different to my other bairns. None of my other bairns were remotely like him," Zahra replied.

"How was he so different?" Peter asked.

"You might call it, peculiar really. He had an odd way of staring coldly with those steely blue eyes of his, sometimes at the staff, sometimes at Coinneach's family but not his father or me or Causantin and Dihaoine. His voice, or his cry wasn't quite normal either, it had a growly sound. I thought it was related to the shape shifting, because it did have that 'wolf like' quality to it. All in all, it is better that he is with Coinneach's family, even if I miss him terribly sometimes, which I do," Zahra said sadly.

"I miss my sons Causantin and Hector much more, if that assists you in understanding. I hope you don't think me cold, but Coinneach Og, although born of me, needs the other family, more than me. I have a fear too for Isobel's bairn, Zahra Og, from Lord Cinaed," Zahra added.

"All the MacAlpins of that family are not ordinary folk Peter. I really hope I never see any of them, ever again," Zahra said. "Do you want me to ride my horse now darling?" Zahra asked.

"I'd rather you stayed with me. I quite like this ride with my wife, Mrs Peter Heath," he said lovingly and kissed Zahra first on the neck and then on both her cheeks and he told her he loved her, while embracing her lovingly. He was happy, whether they had his bairns or not.

"You have opened up my world Zahra and given me love that I have never experienced before. I am so grateful to you, for that. I never imagined that I would ever be loved like this, let alone even talking about wee bairns in my life," Peter added. "Even my parents would no longer be ashamed of me, if they could see us now, but I know that I will never see them again," Peter added, sadly.

"My poor darling love, you have lost so much and so have I, but we have each other now to hold onto. That's how I feel Peter," Zahra said.

Hugh had left the Aird to follow them from a distance quietly, just to see how Dr and Mrs Heath really got along and once he realised how loving they were towards each other, he decided that he had spied for long enough. They were a genuine couple and his curiosity was satisfied, so he went back to the farm.

"Peter, I wanted to ask you something about our sex life and if I could do a certain thing that I'll whisper to you in case the Angels are listening, to ask permission to go ahead with it," Zahra asked. She whispered into his ear as the horse continued walking along the road to Inverness and Peter almost choked.

"Och, is it that bad?" Zahra asked.

"Nae, I'd like it. I mean, aye. Can we do that tonight then, after our baths?" Peter asked.

They went back to riding on their respective horses, to get home faster and have those hot, soapy baths, gently washing each other. It was fortunate that she had dinner ready to cook, but she now wasn't sure what would come first, the intimacy or their dinner. The hot water was hung over the rekindled fire, while all the while, Peter was caressing his wife and her body in its entirety, now impatient of their next experiment in love making. He was so unaccustomed to the pleasure of a woman, let alone one as gorgeous as Zahra, who so many men lusted after, and appeared in paintings on walls. She was like a dream that he couldn't wake up from. He wasn't jealous that she appeared on walls, it was almost a badge of pride that his wife was beautiful enough to be considered a suitable decoration to grace someone's walls.

She stripped him naked from his meagre attire, after their bath together and sat him on their large armchair in their bedroom, which was large enough for him to spread his legs wide open, as men do at times, but this time, without clothing. Sometimes reticent to do the things she had previously done with her husbands, whom she thought were all heterosexual, she had now asked him permission, in case it was excessive, not certain of what was acceptable in the world of a former homosexual.

Peter waited excitedly as his wife began her enjoyment of his glorious manhood, starting with his testicles. Up until now, she hadn't touched his testicles, in case of offence. She excited him beyond her wildest dreams, with her slow, but deliberate movements with just that area, touching, feeling, holding for some time, while his impatience grew with his erection as hard as it could become, as she deliberately allowed her face and then tongue to rub up against his hardened appendage.

"Oh Zahra, I can't hold on any longer," Peter exclaimed, and he lifted her body and empaled her on his hard and long penis groaning all the while as he ejaculated. "I'm sorry Zahra, I couldn't wait," he said. He wasn't alone with the pleasure of it as she too reached orgasm, sitting hard on Peter's member. Tears were rolling down his cheeks and mingled with hers.

"Why do we both cry?" Peter asked. "Oh Zahra, you make me so happy," Peter said. She lay across his manly hairy chest, warm in the firelight of the room and listening to the beating of their hearts. She loved his hairy chest and fingered it always as a habit as she went through each tiny chest hair giving him an electric shock each time her fingers moved on him. Still with his appendage inside of her, he was reluctant to remove himself nor she herself, connected as they were.

"Mrs Heath, will you please marry me?" Peter asked again.

"Yes, I will, Peter. But first you should learn who I am and where I am from and why I was in Scotland to begin with," Zahra said. "Can we get to know each other more first, then if you still think I'm not too strange, I would love to settle down, grow roses with you and build up the business, have a bairn, if it happens, if not maybe include my other bairns in our lives some more," she said. "I want a fairly simple life actually, that is what I had before I came here and I think you are perfect for me to feel that connection again within myself, without trying to be someone who I am not," Zahra replied. Both Zahra and Peter realising the strength of the commitment became emotional and cried once more.

"We cry a lot, don't we?" Peter asked.

"Nae, it's a normal for tears of joy, of love and of loss also. There is always grief when we have moved onto a new and permanent relationship and we grieve for those who have gone before, be they deceased, moved away, or moved on, in my humble opinion," Zahra said. "I still hold a candle for Hugh in my heart and Grigor, especially Grigor, but not Coinneach, although I do appreciate what he did initially to repair my broken face," Zahra said. "My dear old Aunty and Uncle had a wonderful relationship when I was growing up and I had always hoped that I would find someone like she had and I think now I have found that person in you Peter," she said.

"I don't deny Grigor his feelings, as it is natural, but to be together living with him again would not work. He can't live without his friends hanging on too, like Padruig. And Padruig will destroy anything good in the relationships that he sees around him. Padruig led to the eventual break up of both Hugh and I and he broke me and Grigor up, I know that now. I have loved both Hugh and Grigor, with all my heart, but as you have experienced, there is always someone who wants to crush you and then, love flies out the window, eventually. You and I need a solid base upon which to build and let's face it, both you and I have already experienced the worse things that could happen to any human being, even public humiliation in your case," Zahra added.

"And Coinneach, you didn't mention him?" Peter asked.

"I can't blame Padruig for that," Zahra said.

"I was even willing to accept that Coinneach was a shape shifting, giant brown wolf, despised by all. The test was, could I love him in that form and eventually, like some mad woman, I did," Zahra said. "In all his forms, I was still the centre of his world, but it was eroded by his sole desire for a bairn, of which I was in denial, I admit that now. I didn't want to believe that he had married me only for the royal baby, of which he spoke so often, but it was a factor in marrying me, without a doubt. But when he was completely ignoring me, after I had been through hell on that island with his brother, he had his royal baby and he then only focussed on Alasdair, I knew it was over," Zahra said.

"He didn't even notice me walking out through the front door, to look for that waterfall to jump into. He used me to have Coinneach Og and he wouldn't be too pleased to learn that there is another royal bairn, Isobel's bairn," Zahra added.

"I am concerned about that. I hope Isobel and Alex come to their senses one day and inform Lord Cinaed, so he can at least have visiting rights. It could backfire on them and if he finds out from someone else, God forbid. Isobel thinks it was all her idea to bed that old man, but I believe it was his idea, to compete with Coinneach, so there would always be two royal wee bairns," Zahra said.

Lightening up the atmosphere was required, Peter thought listening to how deep Zahra was getting into the whole MacAlpin issue, which bothered, even him. He recalled his conversation with Lord Coinneach about Zahra's former marriage with

Grigor MacGregor and was told to shut up, basically. He considered mentioning it to Zahra but changed his mind.

"Lie down over there on the bed my sweet lady. I do believe it's your turn to open your legs," Peter said, with manly intent. Lifting his woman onto the bed, he gently spread her legs wide open, and she was giggling before he even started his massage of her. "Open up wide or I'll get those strap things for women in childbirth to hold you open for me," he said in jest. Zahra was sexually excited once more and thought her man was a bit naughty threatening to use his equipment like that.

"You always get me out of my sorrows. I love you for that," Zahra said. He was so naughty, even giving a running commentary on her vagina and its glorious components. His gentle surgeon-like fingers, explored deep inside her and it evoked strong emotion again of both lust and love. Whispering too into her ears to get permission first, she smiled while he proceeded like a man starved of sensual pleasure, while proceeding to enjoy glorious foreplay and observing the change that overcame Mrs Heath.

He massaged her so gently and sensually and while looking into her lovely green eyes, his fingers penetrated her deep first and then he entered her, Zahra gasping in sheer pleasure and delight. The exact moment of her orgasm was when she suddenly grabbed his hair and screamed. It hurt, but he liked it when she hurt him.

"Oh God, God," Zahra screamed. Peter then turned her over as easily as flipping an egg and rubbed over her magnificent buttocks, then put his finger on her anus, to feel if it was an option.

"May I?" Peter asked.

"I am too small there. Don't please Peter," she replied nervously. Rubbing cream onto the area, he asked her to give it a try while feeling her there. He rubbed oil all over her buttocks and told her what a beautiful buttock she had, his big gentle hands caressing both of her cheeks. It was so tempting for him, but it would be injurious to Zahra, he thought, and she was obviously afraid or had suffered from a previous bad experience. He deduced that he was too large anyway to enter Zahra there and kissed her instead, leaving it a question in his mind.

"Thank you for allowing me to try but you are so small for my appendage, I don't want to hurt you," Peter added.

"I am sorry if you feel unfulfilled, Peter, do you?" Zahra asked.

"I would never do you any harm, so how can I feel unfulfilled. A little play there is enough to know that you accept me. Have you ever had anal sex?" Peter asked and when she froze, he had his answer.

"It wasn't voluntary. Does that make me a boring sex partner?" she asked.

"Of course not, never," Peter replied.

"Will you need a man then Peter? I will understand it if you do. I just want you to accept me, as flawed as I am," she said choking back her tears.

Zahra was only reminded of that island and what was done to her there.

"No Zahra my love, my wife. I only want you, now and forever if you want me too. You fill me up completely. I love you so deeply, that it's painful. Do you feel that kind of pain?" Peter asked.

"Oh God aye, I do," Zahra said relieved that they both felt that same pain.

"What are your favourite roses?" Peter asked.

"Och Peter, I love red roses, of course but I also love the big yellow ones too. Do you?" she asked, glad of the change of topic.

"Oh yes. Let's go shopping to the plant nursery tomorrow morning for the rose bushes and get a variety of roses, before we open the surgery for our patients. My parents grew roses in

London, so I think I know enough about them, like those little beasties that live on them," he added smiling.

"Aphids?" Zahra asked.

"Yes, aphids, that's the critters," Peter said.

"We might need horse manure or cow manure too to fertilise them. Do we own a shovel and gardening gloves Peter? We will need gardening gloves," Zahra asked.

"Not yet. But we will," Peter added.

They then went to eat their dinner, finding themselves to be quite hungry.

"Do you think we could have two pencil pines too, with one at each end of the front rock wall? In between them, we could have flower beds too, with two benches to sit on when it's sunny, one on each side of the gate." Zahra added.

"I think it sounds like I need to repair the stone wall too, don't you think and maybe put in a nice black wrought iron gate?" Peter said smiling at all her lovely plans.

"Och, how lovely. With a sign on the rock wall above the letter box. 'Dr Peter Heath, Medical Practitioner," Zahra said. "Do you have a middle name Peter?" Zahra asked.

"I do," Peter said, looking embarrassed.

"Peter Ormond Heath, but please don't tell anyone, I really hate that middle name," Peter said.

"I promise," Zahra said giggling. "I had the same problem with my middle name too but as soon as my Mither passed, I changed it," Zahra said.

"You have the cutest little giggle when you are amused, I love it," Peter said.

"Isn't Heath a Scottish name, yet you are English, so is it Scottish or English?" Zahra asked.

"I am English, but there was a great, great grandparent who

was Scottish from Aberdeenshire, so I do have Scottish ancestry but most of them sailed onto the Americas. I don't know how my family ended up so privileged back in London and with a Peerage, but that was my own lack of interest," Peter said.

"Your ancestor must have been a handsome Scot for you to be so gorgeous, compared to the rest of the English who all seem bald, short and kind of ugly," Zahra said to tease him.

"I always thought I was more handsome than most all of my school friends," Peter said smiling.

"Did you go to one of those posh schools in London?" Zahra asked.

"Yes, Eton College and then I went on to Oxford University to study medicine. I was going to be a surgeon, when things went awry down there, so I only got as far as General Practice," Peter answered very seriously.

"Have your parents written you off, or have they left the door open for you, so to speak," Zahra asked.

"Slammed shut, I'm afraid. My father is a Peer you see, so he got me out of the bother, and I kept my license. He sent me here and paid for this practice, so long as I never saw them, ever again," Peter said.

"That is so sad. You must have suffered immensely when you were just lobbed here like that. It must have been like landing on the moon," Zahra said.

"No more than you did, I wager," Peter commented.

"What if you had his Grandson? Would he visit you then?" Zahra asked.

"I doubt it," Peter said and wanted to change the topic.

"Zahra darling, in that book that you have written, I did note the year of its publication, how is that possible?" Peter asked. "That's just under two hundred years' time futuristically, or is it a printing error?" Peter asked.

"It's easier to tell people that it was a typing, or printing error," Zahra said.

"But it isn't?" Peter asked looking into her eyes.

"It isn't, that's correct," Zahra said.

"I know you are of the deceased folk and somehow living amongst the living and that in itself, is hard enough to comprehend, but how did a book you wrote, get published in 2023?" Peter asked.

"There are two books published now. That second one is 2024 the third was a little later. This was why I wanted us to get to know each other more first, so you won't worry excessively about how strange it all may seem to you. I don't know where to start really, so how about I just start, and you interject whenever you like?" Zahra suggested.

"Alright," Peter said, looking interested, but a bit worried. "I had been wanting to write a book of some kind since I was very young and the only thing, I was obsessive about was horses, when I was ten years old, however it didn't cross my mind to write about that topic or a related topic at that time. In my later years I was an online editor for two different websites then a writer for the website I owned along with two of my daughters," Zahra said.

"Hold on my love," Peter said. "The first problem we have, is in knowing what each other is talking about. What is a website?" Peter asked. Understanding the reply each time was the problem.

So along went the conversation of stopping and starting and explaining, until Peter understood that Zahra's reality in 2023 or 2024 had been quite different to his own in the 1700's and early 1800's, even though he thought his education in Oxford was the best that money could buy, it wasn't the future, which was what Zahra was speaking of. Her name also wasn't Zahra, although now she had become accustomed to it, so she liked it well enough not to change it. Her name was on the front cover of the books that she had written that Padruig was so possessive about. And there were two more to be published.

"How did he get them?" Peter asked.

"I gave them to him," Zahra said. "One of them was here in an old second-hand book shop in Inverness. A traveller to Scotland had died here carrying the second book and so it was given to the bookshop to sell, who thought it was nonsense due to the incorrect printing date, so as a second-hand book, he sold it to me for 6pence," Zahra said. "It was my second published book, so I posted it to Padruig who I knew liked the first one, 'Isobel of Glenmoriston,'" Zahra said.

"What's the second book's name?" Peter asked.

"Secrets of the Braes and Glens, part of the series of 'Isobel of Glenmoriston' books," Zahra replied. "There were facts in the second novel that Padruig needed to learn about and how his daughter Helen had died, as well as how his daughter, Marion went on to live happily. The third and fourth books were given to my daughters when I had Coinneach Og. Do you remember when I was vacant for a while there?" Zahra asked.

"You do mean absolutely, dead with no pulse?" Peter corrected. "Alex and I bought you back to life, remember?" Peter added.

She didn't want to think of it anymore and it had drained her.

"Can we go to bed now darling, I am so tired," Zahra said and promised to continue explaining her life, over the coming days, which she did. Zahra was even more tired than she realised and slept heavily until the morning came, when Peter woke her up. "Wake up sleepy head," Peter said. She reached her hand out for him, and he couldn't resist her loving arms around him and succumbed to the temptation of early morning loving and he kissed her longingly and she kissed him the same, while making love enthusiastically, which was different but very enjoyable with the added strength and vigour of the early morning, behind his movements.

She felt loved and the object of his affection.

"I want to satisfy you Zahra, now let's have breakfast and go to that plant nursery, they might have to deliver everything, and I can also arrange a man to rebuild the stone wall and make the gate as well as my sign. We can buy the two benches while we are there too but that might run me dry of cash for this beautification plan," Peter said smiling.

Peter's old house needed a lot of repairs here and there, as well as a paint job throughout. The plumbing was non-existent, so that would need to come next, she thought, so Zahra started a list of the requested and required works on his house and business, so bit by bit, one day it would be beautiful, she thought. It was such an old, but well-built charming, old home that looked like it was built, well before the Bonny Prince ever came to Scotland. Maybe the roof was next as Peter was no handyman and hadn't done any work on the place, since she first went there, many years ago.

The week passed by quickly, with all their gardening and the rose bushes were all looking healthy. There were four red rose bushes, four yellow, four white and four pink. By Friday, when the bairns and the visitors were due to arrive, the four feet high, front wall was completed, made from Caledonian stone, as well as the lovely black, wrought iron gate and Peter's signs. The garden was complete, but not yet flowering. In the ground and neat and tidy, complete with the two bench seats. The pathway was also finished and made of stone. It wasn't too expensive and there were many local admirers, congratulating them both, for dressing up the old place.

Zahra had been to the markets to buy three wild salmon for all her guests and her bairns, who were due to arrive by four pm. She had a lemon tree growing in their back yard, so she thought to serve up salmon, cured in lemon, lime and brown sugar, served up with the broccoli that she was growing near her herb garden, growing larger by the day. She had to buy potatoes and carrots to accompany her dinner, as she hadn't planted any potatoes or carrots yet and thought she should have done that.

She cooked up two loaves of bread when she arrived home, as well as cooking scones with jam and cream for the wee bairns. The adults were lucky to have a chocolate steam pudding, with a white sauce and if the bairns wanted some too, they could. Their bedroom was ready and warm, as was the extra room with new doonas and pillows in case their guests stayed overnight. She hadn't had time to think who the mystery guest might be, until she went to bathe after washing the floors, as was her routine.

Dr Heath had finished up with his last patient when she had his water boiling for him to bathe also and cleaned his exam room too, in case of an emergency. He was glad of the bath as she was also and all they needed then was for their guests to arrive, so she put on the coffee pot and a pot of tea in case Grigor was still drinking that. She was simply dressed in a woollen tartan pinafore with a warm blouse under it. It was Clan Gregor tartan, and she wore the antique Clan Gregor brooch that Grigor had given her, all those many years ago. Although that was unintentional.

She had bought her bairns a wee present from the markets. A doll for Dihaoine and a plain, unpainted, carved wooden horse for Causantin. What Zahra was unaware of, while in the markets was, she had been recognised by an unfriendly woman, who followed her all around the marketplace and then all the way back to her home, to know where she lived. At no time was Zahra aware of the evil presence that was focussed intensely only on her. At home, Zahra was just nervous with waiting to see her precious bairns.

"Who is it that's coming with Grigor, do you think, Zahra?" Peter asked.

"I honestly don't know," Zahra replied.

39. Dinner with Hugh and Grigor

It was such an exciting moment when Zahra's two sweet bairns arrived. They both ran into the big old house calling 'Ma, Ma and Daddy'. Daddy was Peter and Da was Grigor. Causantin ran the fastest, being the oldest and threw himself into Zahra's arms. Wee Dihaoine tried to keep up, but her sweet little legs couldn't run as fast as her older brother. She was looking cuter than ever and was even dressed in a woollen, long sleeved frock to look pretty with nice wee shoes and long white hose. Grigor had gone to some trouble to dress them both well and they were clearly well fed, even chubby, but so cute.

Peter was excited to see them both too and picked up Dihaoine and swirled her around. "Daddy," she said.

They were both kissing each other as Grigor was walking behind them followed by the most unlikely of dinner guests, Hugh Mohr Chisholm, Zahra's first ex-husband.

Zahra was still holding Causantin in her arms, big as he is, when she saw Hugh. Trying initially to hide any adverse reaction, in front of the children, both Zahra and Peter greeted them both with either the traditional handshake from Peter or the European style kiss on each cheek from Zahra to both Grigor and Hugh. Zahra reminded the bairns that there was a gift for them both on their pillows and the two of them ran into their bedrooms to find the gifts.

"Hugh, it's so nice to see you again after all this time, welcome. This is Dr Peter Heath if you haven't yet met, I don't recall," Zahra said. "Grigor thank you for coming and bringing the bairns. Please come in," she said using only civil language. "Would you like tea or Turkish coffee?" Zahra asked.

"Gentlemen, may I take your coats?" asked Peter trying to be an integral part of the whole social parent gathering. Hugh was taking notice of his surroundings and commented on it being a surgery. Peter added to that and said that they both lived and worked in the same place but hoped that the improvements in the front garden made it look more like a family home now, as well as a family business.

"I like the front garden," Grigor said. "Are they roses?" he asked.

"Yes, we have red, yellow, white and pink rose bushes but they don't yet have roses on them," Peter said.

"And there are flowers and bulbs too, Peter. We have stocks, carnations, and daffodils as well as ranunculi, hyacinths, and others that I can't even remember the names of," Zahra added, who looked proud of their work with the front wall looking beautiful, as well as the gate.

"The sign makes it easier to find at least," Grigor said as they all meandered into the dining room that looked less like a Medical Practise and more like a home now, with Zahra's touch. It was clear to both Hugh and Grigor that Peter's home had been overtaken by 'the Zahra touch.'

"Ma. I like the two benches out the front. Can we sit there in the daytime, when it's not raining," asked Causantin.

"Aye son, you may with me or Daddy. There might be some sunshine if God wills it," Zahra replied. Grigor assumed by the way that she spoke that she still followed that odd religion.

After coffees all round, the group of adults became more accustomed to each other.

"Hugh, can I show you your bedroom, should you both choose to stay. No pressure, just for your safety really. It's awfully dark and cold going back to the Aird. It's up to you both but take a look and I'll light the fire in there too," Zahra said.

Hugh followed Zahra past the myriad rooms, to where their

bedroom was. It had been set up nicely with two large beds with duvets and fluffy pillows. It looked like she had been shopping, just to accommodate them, for this one night. Hugh thought of the comparison to the farm where Zahra wasn't even offered coffee, let alone accommodation when she dropped off the bairns. She lit the fire and put the spark guard in front of it.

"Can you care for the fire Hugh, when you come in later?" Zahra asked simply.

"Zahra, thank you," Hugh said sincerely.

"You're always welcome, my old friend. You were my husband in another life," Zahra said. "I'm happy you are back. You are always welcome here and for medical attention of course. Peter is a wonderful Doctor," Zahra added. Hugh wasn't expecting such a sincere and candid welcome.

When they walked back into the room, Peter and Grigor were both deep in conversation, while the bairns were playing with a jigsaw puzzle that Zahra had prepared on a small table to entertain them both. She had bought the jigsaw puzzle at the markets, and it pictured a highland coo laying down with her calf, while it snowed.

"Would you all like to eat soon then?" Zahra asked.

"Oh aye," was the overwhelming reply.

"I hope you all like salmon?" Zahra said, with a question added to that in case there was someone who didn't want to eat fish. As a precaution, Zahra had an extra meal of beef stew in case there was someone who refused her salmon delicacy. "Salmon please" was the overwhelming reply. Zahra just couldn't present a terrible meal. They all knew that.

Peter had set the table as he routinely did, with his white, starched, and ironed tablecloth. Zahra was glad that there was a laundry lady who had that job of starching for Peter with his English traditions. He had polished the silver cutlery, carefully and placed them in the right order, so that Hugh wasn't sure about what cutlery to use. Zahra quietly showed him the correct one to use.

The salmon was placed in the centre of the table in a beautiful white porcelain bowl, from England as well and Zahra served up each plate with the quantity that everyone wanted, including the bairns, who sat with the adults. The bairns liked it and started eating before the broccoli was served.

"Wait on little ones, there's broccoli, carrots and potatoes too," Zahra said. Everyone loved the meal in its entirety, especially the broccoli.

"Zahra grew this broccoli herself," said a proud Peter.

"Do you need more herbs for your herb garden then?" asked a genuinely interested Grigor.

"Och aye, please Grigor. I need potatoes too. Do you have seeds?" Zahra asked.

"What else do you need," Grigor asked.

"Carrots and other vegetables," Zahra replied.

"Kale?" he asked.

"Och aye. Thankyou Grigor, kale would be wonderful," Zahra said.

"You don't have any chickens for daily fresh eggs. You should have fresh eggs for the wee ones," Grigor stated.

"I've looked, but there aren't any Scots Dumpy chickens for sale, in the markets here," she answered looking a little embarrassed and inadequate.

"I'll bring you some Scots Dumpy's then, with a rooster and a few chickens. Can you build a shelter for them Peter, or do we need to stay and build it for you?" Grigor asked.

"I am embarrassed to say that I don't know how to build one of those where they wouldn't freeze to death, but I would like to learn how. I don't want to impose on you though Grigor," Peter said.

"Hugh, we are staying overnight to build a chicken coup up against the chimney for warmth. Can you pay for the materials Peter?" Grigor asked.

"Does everyone want desert now?" asked Zahra. "There's steamed chocolate pudding with white sauce and there's scones with jam and cream, depending on what you prefer," she said. Most everyone asked for steamed chocolate pudding with white sauce, some with cream. Some wanted both. Pudding was followed by the scones with jam. It was all going beautifully, and all the adults were getting along well, although Grigor did have an issue with Peter being called Daddy. He addressed it head on and asked when they had begun calling him Daddy. The bairns answered him saying,

"Last visit, Da. Ma's new husband is Daddy, and you are Da," Causantin said as a matter of fact.

"Ma isn't yet married son, to Dr Heath. Don't you think you should wait until Ma is married before you call him Daddy?" Grigor asked.

Both Peter and Zahra looked sad, as well as the bairns, which Hugh was aware of, so he interjected.

"Peter is known as Zahra's husband for respectability as the local Doctor. That's important, isn't it Peter?" Hugh said compassionately. "I imagine you both intend getting married?" Hugh asked.

"Aye Hugh, I ask her nearly every day," Peter said smiling and he held Zahra's hand to feel better about the embarrassment created. "She is my wife as far as I am concerned," he said. Zahra was a little saddened and lowered her head.

She had suffered so much from the cruelty of men and her smile from producing the lovely food for the evening had gone, to fearing another awful round of cruelty. It was too clear to

Hugh at least, that there was a lot of suffering, unknown to them, that she had been dealing with, and Peter Heath, former homosexual, was her only support, currently. Grigor conceded to Peter being called Daddy, just so the evening didn't end up disastrously, with him to blame for it. He was sad to see the sudden change in Zahra's demeanour. He didn't think she would be that sensitive. Both adults were too sensitive, he thought.

"Do we have your permission then please, Grigor?" Zahra asked.

"Aye both bairns can call him Daddy but not Da mind?" Grigor added.

So, it was settled. Hugh was happy that he had helped, and Zahra smiled a thankyou across to him, as coffee was served. The bairns, who were uncertain for a while, ran over to both men calling them by their correct titles. Men could be so touchy about this topic, Zahra observed, even if they had abandoned the entire family, at one time. The atmosphere picked up once again and conversation was less controlling and more focussed on daily issues and what was planned to do with the house, in its rambling old state.

"Zahra has an entire list of improvements. But we have to do it bit by bit, so that we can afford it," Peter said.

The two men hadn't known that Peter wasn't the wealthy man they had thought him to be, after all he was a Doctor in Inverness, but that hadn't accounted for the years of struggling to keep it afloat, because of Matilda's letter ending up in the newspapers, which had ruined his business. It had only been since Zahra lived with him that his patients had returned, and numbers were growing by the day, so he was very busy now.

"I am busy now with patients," Peter explained. "So, we will do it all as we go. Plumbing was first, wasn't it darling?" Peter asked, as a matter of fact.

"Aye plumbing, then the roof. Expensive jobs, so it might take us all year to afford that," Zahra said.

"That doesn't mean that we don't have ideas for the bairns schooling though Grigor, which I was going to ask you about," Peter said, but before he could make his plan heard, the front door burst open. At first, Peter thought it was an emergency patient and excused himself and stood up to deal with it, but he was wrong. An overweight, voluptuous, short, unattractive Scottish woman, stormed through his surgery, shoving passed the Doctor and headed straight towards the dining room table.

Zahra automatically held both bairns close to her, protectively.

"Where's that piece of shite?" the woman said.

Grigor turned around in recognition of the woman's voice, whom he recognised only too well.

"You asshole, you lousy piece of shite, you good for nothing liar, you left me behind in the Americas, alone and penniless. I hate you. You, scum bucket," she screamed, then she hit Grigor about his head before he had time to defend himself.

His fists were held tight by his side, wanting to kill her, that was obvious, but he somehow controlled himself from returning the blow. Zahra remembered receiving one of his blows, that he hadn't held back, and it gave her the shivers remembering it in that moment. The woman then directed her attention to both Zahra and Peter.

"I've seen 'er in the markets. Your slut of a wife. She's now living with this 'ere homosexual. You left me for 'er, you fecking fool," she screamed pointing first at Zahra then at Peter.

It was then that Hugh stepped in.

"You'll not behave like this, or speak like this in their home, woman. Now leave," Hugh demanded, as he took her physically by her arm and escorted her to the door, while she kept repeating expletives towards Grigor, Zahra and Peter who didn't speak a word in response. Grigor was grateful to Hugh for removing her and just stood there, in shock.

"Who was that?" asked Peter who was also still in shock.

"Belle MacGregor," Zahra responded.

Zahra descended into tears, covering her eyes and Peter took the bairns from her to bed, to console them and settled them both down. When he came back, he was as upset as Zahra was and Peter held her hand, as much for himself, as for her. They then hugged each other, and Peter held onto her tightly. Hugh watched on in shock but was ensuring that Belle MacGregor couldn't re-enter by another door. He locked the front door, as well as the back door, checked all the windows and put more wood on the fires, at the same time.

Grigor stood stunned for a time, before he knew what to do.

Eventually Hugh asked him if he wanted another coffee or tea. "Tea," was his response and there was a pot already made and still hot, so he poured tea for everyone, who all looked shocked as well as sad, at the words that had been spoken.

"You can't take back those cruel words unfortunately," Hugh said. "I am sorry for you all. Don't take any heed Peter please, I have seen how genuine you are, so carry on, if you can. It's the bairns that I'm worried about, with their questions. Poor wee things," Hugh said.

"Can someone please explain who Belle MacGregor is?" asked Peter.

"It's best if you ask Grigor," Zahra replied.

For the first time since his return from the Americas, after having disabled Zahra, Grigor finally apologised to Zahra for his mistakes in their marriage. It came out halfway in a choke and half in his soul's need to declare his obvious wrongdoings, from which they were all still suffering.

"I am truly sorry Zahra. Not just for interrupting your lovely dinner party, but for what I did to you and our entire family and the farm. I was wrong and I knew it, but not until I was on that ship, on the way to the Americas. I was like a man possessed or cursed by her interest in me, until then. I was blinded by some greater desire, than us and the bairns and the farm," Grigor said, then he wept like a baby.

Grigor never normally cried, or if he did, it was never in front of anyone.

"I have always loved you, even when you were Hugh's wife, I loved you. When you had Isobel, I loved you more, but the wee bairn was Hugh's, so I had to give you both back to him. That was the hardest thing I have ever had to do in my whole life when I watched the two of you leave, to go to Hugh," Grigor said, still crying.

Zahra then stood up, disentangling herself politely from Peter who looked panicky. He was, after all sitting at the same table as two of the Seven Glenmoriston Men. Their strong personalities were felt wherever they went, in any situation, but this was different. A huge declaration of great love, enduring love, going back to the birth of the lassie that Peter only knew as 'the snippy one', never a cute wee bairn.

He was seated with both of Isobel's fathers.

He was in over his head, and he was afraid now that he could lose the one good thing in his life, when Zahra sat next to Grigor.

Grigor continued, "When I saw you, so happy with Dihaoine after her birth, with that awful history of losing Sakina, I felt left out, not unloved, I know that was never the case, but momentarily, there was a void within me and I don't blame you, but Hugh was Sakina's father, so I was a mixed-up mess and along came someone who fussed over me with no history and I felt offloaded from all of that history.

What I did to you with Padruig, I think I did because I needed to have you sleeping with another man to justify what I had done and I thought you liked Padruig more than you did, obviously. When I was jealous, I was always jealous of your attention to Padruig, so when it didn't work to cover my indiscretions, I went nuts. How could I then cover up what I had done with her? I couldn't. The worst thing for me was if you had known that I had slept with her, after lying to you and how much it would hurt you," Grigor said.

Zahra's tears were falling uncontrollably, occasionally wiping them from her cheeks.

"So, on that morning tea day, you did sleep with her then?" Zahra asked.

"Aye, Zahra, I did. I lied to you. Please forgive me. I live only to have your forgiveness and love too, hopefully one day, if possible," Grigor declared.

"But you punched me so hard, I hit my head, and I landed on my face. Nearly dead, but not quite. Hector told me, he had to stop all of you from chopping up my body to throw me into the burn. Is that true?" Zahra asked.

"Aye, Padruig panicked because your body would need to be accounted for, being known amongst the living and he didn't want to be blamed for your death, so his idea was quick disposal. That's when Hector threw himself across your body to protect you from any such thing," Grigor admitted.

"So, to be clear. It was Padruig's idea but you and Alex both agreed?" Zahra asked.

"Aye, we thought you were dead already. You weren't moving," Grigor said.

"A funeral hadn't come to mind at all?" Zahra said.

"Nae, I was too scared," Grigor said.

"I am not going to punch any woman again, not even that woman tonight, even though I wanted to kill her. And after talking to Hugh, disposal is also not something I would ever engage in again, I think," Grigor added, unconvincingly.

"Do you think that you could forgive me one day?"

Grigor asked.

"I already forgave you Grigor. That day that I saw you on Beinn Coinneach, I wanted to talk to you and tell you that, but you looked terrified of me, before I could speak to you. Then you ran away in abject terror. Why did you run away?" Zahra asked.

"I saw a wolf above you, not just the one that you walked with, you were accompanied by another wolf, and I thought you were some kind of Fairy, and I wondered what I had married after all. I had wanted you back desperately, but you were so terrifying," Grigor said.

"What colour was the wolf?" Zahra asked.

"It was grey," Grigor answered.

"Do you still see it?" Zahra asked.

"I have seen it many times with you, above you, beside you, behind you, in front of you, nearly every time I have seen you," Grigor said.

"What about here in this house?" Zahra asked.

"It was waiting for us when we arrived. It's standing there beside you now," Grigor replied.

"Why are you afraid of it, if it can't do anything?" Zahra asked.

"It can by choice, and you don't know it, but you control him by stopping him from attacking, like tonight. It was going to attack that woman and you held the bairns and stopped him, so he stayed with you and the bairns, while that took place," Grigor said.

"Is it Wolfie?" Zahra asked.

"He just turned to you when you said that name, so maybe?" Grigor replied.

"Why can't I see him?" Zahra asked.

"Ask him and maybe, he will appear," Grigor said.

"Zahra, I'm not ready to see a wolf inside the house. Do you think you could do that outside tomorrow?" Peter asked fearfully.

Suddenly Zahra broke out of her intense discussion with Grigor and reluctantly agreed, although disappointed, because she loved Wolfie so much and wanted to know who this wolf was.

"Alright" she agreed, reluctantly.

"Am I forgiven please Zahra?" asked Grigor, once more.

She suddenly embraced him and forgave him crying and he wept once again.

"I am so sorry Zahra," Grigor repeated. Hugh was then unsure of who Zahra would choose. Grigor had always said that he would get Zahra back and maybe he would. It seemed unlikely with Zahra being so happy with Peter, but maybe it would be gradual, as Zahra was accepted once again on the farm.

Hopefully, Peter wouldn't be hurt somehow, but it was likely that someone was going to be hurt.

To lighten up the atmosphere, Hugh said. "I have the solution. Zahra will return to me, the gorgeous blonde," he jested, and Zahra smiled but with three men at the table, all with an interest in her, she would have to make it clear soon who she would choose to remain with, if only for the sakes of the bairns, now calling Peter their Daddy.

The following morning was hectic at breakfast which was lovely and reminiscent of old times. Peter had ensured that his wife and he made love last evening even with the men in the house and he was behaving extra manly, anticipating the comparisons by the bairns.

"What's a homosexual?" asked Causantin, curious about what that woman had said the night before.

"It's when a man falls in love with a man," Zahra answered plainly.

"Eeuhh. Why did that woman call Daddy a 'homosex' then?" asked Dihaoine.

"Because she was a little bit sick in the head, my darling and people with sick minds say things that are untrue. You saw how she hit your poor Da over the head," Zahra said.

"Oh aye Da. Are you alright?" they both asked. Then it was focussed on 'poor Da'.

"She called you that bad word that Isobel calls you too Ma. What does slutty mean?" asked an innocent Causantin.

"Isobel says that. Really? Why? Grigor, why does Isobel say that?" Zahra asked, both shocked and deeply hurt.

"I'm sorry Zahra. There was a misunderstanding about why you were no longer living on Beinn Coinneach, with your former husband and had gone to live with Prince Griogar. It appeared as if by dropping the bairns and your wee puppy to the Aird, that you no longer wanted them or Coinneach Og and went to live with just another man for some unknown reason, so Isobel called you that out of rage," Grigor explained.

"It was Hugh who found out the true story, even though the bairns kept telling us that you were all stolen," said an embarrassed Grigor.

"There was no report in the paper about a missing woman from Beinn Coinneach, so we all thought that you had gone to live with the prince, by choice, wherever he was. Hugh told us, it was in the Outer Hebrides, and you had been tortured, starved, and raped repeatedly, so I have corrected all the bairns now, so they no longer call you that, nor think that. I am sorry but we didn't know what had happened to you," Grigor said.

"I told you Da. But you never listen," Causantin said, becoming upset. "We knew Ma didn't do a bad word, like Isobel was saying. I don't like Isobel anymore," he said.

"Me too," said Dihaoine who was sobbing.

"There's been a misunderstanding, my wee ones. Let me talk to your big sister, then we can sort it all out. She is your big sister who loves you, after all," Zahra said kindly to them both, until they were both calm and loving their Mither. She caressed them both and kissed their chubby cheeks, until they could assure their Ma that they were both alright in their pure hearts and she re-assured them that they would always be believed by her.

"Do you want to go for a wee walk in the park?" Zahra asked.

There was that chicken coup to be built, but the family with Grigor and Hugh, all decided to walk in the park first, while there was rare sunshine where many people gathered around, asking about the fuss they had heard, the previous night, which Zahra managed like a true professional.

"Oh, that poor, mentally ill woman, probably a former old and out of work, prostitute," and so on but no dirt was left on Dr Heath and his family, by the time Zahra had finished with them all.

"She was just some crazy woman disturbing the kindly doctor and his lovely family over dinner with their nice friends," their neighbour concluded.

"No wonder Zahra has bought business back to you Peter. She'd convince these people of anything," Hugh commented.

"Now we can go and build that chicken coup, since the gossip has been dealt with," Zahra said, and they all strolled back home with Dihaoine in the pram.

"This is a nice park," Grigor noticed.

"It is, isn't it?" she replied as she walked alongside her ex-husband. Hugh really enjoyed pushing the pram, which he had never done before and Peter held Causantin's hand, but he wanted to hold his lover's hand.

Peter was jealous, he had to admit it to himself. It was hard having both handsome men with them, who were all obviously in awe of their former spouse. Why that was, was a mystery to him. Was it her beauty, her ability to bounce back after suffering, her compassion, and her humanity? Peter concluded they were right in being in awe of her, as he himself was.

As they approached the house, there was a familiar carriage with two matching horses and Zahra froze on the spot.

"Peter, stop. It's Coinneach. Quick, we must hide. Grigor and Hugh let's go and buy an ice cream or something," Zahra said urgently, and they left again to go in the opposite direction, of the house, towards the ice cream shop. By the time they came back cautiously, the carriage was gone, but a note was left on the surgery door.

"Dear Dr Heath, my wife has disappeared. Could you assist me in finding her? If you know where she is, please let me know too, as I miss her terribly. Lord Coinneach." The note read

"I thought your marriage was annulled, Zahra?" Peter asked tersely, as they entered the house.

"It was. I can show you the paperwork inside," she said.

"Then why does he say, you are his wife?" asked Peter.

"He's a clever man who plays with people's minds, like he did with mine. He has already got you doubting me. Here are the papers if you don't believe me," Zahra said thrusting them into his hands. He read the annulment, and it was clear that the marriage was annulled.

"I am sorry for doubting you Zahra," Peter said. But she wasn't pleased with Peter.

"Let's just build that chicken coup," Zahra said. The two ex-husbands, with Zahra put it together in no time and then the two men had to return to the farm, leaving the bairns with Zahra who would return them back to the Aird, the following night.

"I give them one week," said Grigor on their way home to the Aird. "I'll have her back, I know she's in love with me still and he's not sure of her, that was a bonus," Grigor said.

"What about Padruig? She's not safe with him there on the farm, in my opinion," Hugh said.

"I'll deal with Padruig," Grigor said.

Looking very pleased with how everything went, even the disastrous bombardment of the dinner party had worked in his favour. He was on his way to love, Grigor was certain of it.

"Four husbands in one weekend must be a record, I admit," Hugh added, including himself deliberately in that remark, as one of the husbands, which worried Grigor a little.

'Where did Hugh stand these days with Zahra? She was fond of him. She liked his blonde hair, and he was rather manly in expelling that MacGregor woman', Grigor thought.

"Are you thinking of getting back with her too?" Grigor asked. He felt suddenly worried about his handsome, blonde competition.

"Why not? I'm nice by comparison to the pigs she has had previously," Hugh said.

"Haven't you got someone else?" Grigor asked.

"Nae, they've all got friends, since I was underwater for so long," Hugh said sarcastically.

"She's in love with me Hugh. You saw it," Grigor added, who then kicked his horse and galloped off into the direction of the Aird.

Lying in bed in Inverness, after putting her bairns to bed, Zahra couldn't stop thinking of all her bairns calling her a 'slut,' when all the while she had been in a living hell on that remote and freezing cold island. Had it not been for some peculiar reason that the painting came up as being available in the Aird, she may still have been there, as his prisoner. That was her next question.

How did all of that come about? Her heart was too hurt though to think straight, if her bairns had all hated her, even her hero Hector? Was that why none of them wrote to her and why Isobel didn't even offer her coffee at the farm? She was made unwelcome in her old home. At least now she knew the reason for that, but it didn't feel like she could ever escape from their judgements of her, as their Mither.

They had always loved her. It was so hard to become accustomed to the idea of being an outcast Mither.

Then there was Peter who hadn't trusted her, as soon as he received a note from Coinneach. Peter had been her only strength and support. He was a sort of lifeline, she knew that now, as she was descending into a depression, even though two of her lovely bairns slept just a few doors away. There had been too much information on the weekend that now was threatening to overwhelm her, and it had already overwhelmed Peter. Was she losing him too?

When he finally came into bed, after procrastinating, he hardly looked at her as he entered their room. Was it that bad?

"Do you hate me too?" Zahra asked him.

"Hate?" Peter said surprised. "I wouldn't say hate was your problem. You have three husbands and me who all wanted to marry you, with you not committing to any one of the four. Do you really think of our relationship as a serious relationship, or are you just playing with me Zahra?" Peter asked her seriously.

It was a surprising accusation which made her feel like getting out of bed and walking into the dark night and had her bairns not been there, she may have given in to that immature emotion.

"I have never been playing with you Peter. I think of you as the one who saved me from my suicidal thoughts or actions but if that's not enough, I don't know what is. I do love you dearly, but you are so worried about Grigor, and I know he is handsome and strong and all that, so I do understand your concern, but I thought you knew that I loved you. Then to believe Coinneach, who is the biggest manipulator of all mankind, I don't know what more I can say to you, other than I am sorry for anything that I have said or done that was wrong," Zahra said.

"Have you stopped loving me?" Zahra asked.

"No. I still love you. That is why I am so upset right now. I thought I could handle Grigor, but two ex-husbands, then three ex-husbands, it was just too much for me Zahra," Peter said.

"I imagine if Alex came to dinner too, as your ex, as well as Alex Grant, I might be upset too, but I don't know? You never talk about them, and you don't have bairns with them, so that helps I suppose where a permanent connection to them goes. Even then, I like Alex and Alex Grant, so I can't really see myself hating them or you for having loved them both. I went to Alex's wedding to Siobhan, and I like her too. What do you hate about Hugh, for example. He is Isobel's Da and I haven't seen him for many years now?" Zahra asked.

"I don't hate Hugh, he's a nice man. He helped get that woman out of the house and they both built that chicken coup. I think I just feel inadequate, that's all," Peter said.

"Do you want me to go alone to return the bairns tomorrow then?" Zahra asked.

"Nae, it would be an admission of my weakness. I must be responsible for you and the bairns," Peter said.

"But darling, do you really love me?" Zahra asked as she put her arms around him cuddling him, hoping he would become the Peter she knew. Finally, he rolled over to look her in the eyes.

"You are everything to me that's why its driving me mad. I love you yes, madly, too much, painfully like I said. It's so painful," Peter said with wet eyes.

"Oh Peter, please don't scare me. I am afraid if I think you don't love me for some reason, be it previous husbands, or something that I have said. I can't do all the right things, all the time. I am not a perfect human being and others too, are not perfect. You are unlucky in that the men you had here last night were particularly strong men, who you don't meet every day. That was why I wrote about them in the books. They are still flattered by that, and we are eternally connected by the books. I can't change that now. That's why I asked you to get to know me first, before we got married, so now you have an idea of why I said that.

In addition, I am upset because of my own bairns calling me a slut, so I am not as good a wife to you as I should be tonight. I am very sad imagining Isobel, Hector, Ali and Fatma all saying that I am a slut. None of this was my doing. Grigor went astray, as he said, and it all fell to pieces from there. But if you don't want me, I will leave with my bairns tomorrow afternoon," Zahra said.

"Nae, it's not like that. Please Zahra. Don't leave me. I must marry you. Please don't leave me. I do love you," Peter pleaded sincerely.

"Make love to me then please, my lovely man," she said as the candles went out.

40. Hugh Makes his Moves

The rest of the time spent with the wee bairns for Zahra was like gold, as she showered affection on them and spoiled them with any treat that they asked for.

"You'll spoil them," warned Peter.

"They deserve to be spoiled, my love," she replied They even chased one another through the big old house, like children in a schoolyard. Peter wasn't sure how he felt about all the running through his Medical Practise, but so long as patients weren't there, he allowed it. They still managed to achieve some work in the backyard in readiness for the chickens, around the chicken coup. The grass was long, so they had to borrow a neighbour's lawn cutter that you pushed along, while its blades turning around. It was hard work, but most of the yard was cut low.

"We need a nanny goat now," Zahra said. She would eat all of this, instead of us working so hard.

"She'd eat your vegetables and herbs too though. How do you prevent that?" said a perplexed Peter at the very thought of another animal in his backyard. He was never a chicken or animal person, other than horses, of course. Every well-bred Englishman rode a horse.

Teasing Peter, a bit Zahra said, "I suppose you were one of those English lads who went on fox hunts?"

"Yes, I did," was the unexpected reply.

"Really? I was only joking," Zahra added. "Did you see the poor wee foxes killed then?" Zahra asked.

"Yes, of course. That's the whole idea," Peter added quite coldly. It was a side to him that she hadn't known.

"Were the foxes a terrible pest then?" she asked.

"Yes, they were, but there was the sport of it too, which we all enjoyed," Peter added.

'Somehow the sensitive Peter Heath, who was prone to weeping, didn't quite fit the picture of a fox killer,' Zahra thought.

By the time it came to depart for the Aird, the bairns were reluctant to leave.

"I want to stay with you Ma, I don't want to go back to the farm," said both Causantin and Dihaoine repeatedly. There were tears until Causantin's pony was mentioned but Dihaoine still clung to her Mither hoping to stay. Zahra had no choice in this matter, or else she may never see them again, so gradually they understood that they had to return to the farm, so they could return.

The small family all set out on their way back to the Aird in the early afternoon, to arrive by late afternoon and then hopefully arrive back home in Inverness, before it was too dark and cold. Zahra was not fond of the dark and the freezing cold between the Aird and Inverness. It wasn't creepy like the Great Glen, it was just dark and cold. It now reminded her of that cold room that she had been kept in, as a prisoner on the Outer Hebrides. Cold and dark, with no reprieve from its bitterness. She always felt cold on this journey, even when she wore woollen lined gloves, woollen lined boots, thick underclothing, a woollen tartan skirt and vest with a blouse underneath, with her long thick fur skinned coat that covered her head also, that she had managed to escape from Beinn Coinneach with.

The fur coat was the only thing that she was glad of having escaped with. But she didn't have her lovely horse, who she missed. She was still borrowing one of Peter's horses.

The farmhouse looked homely enough, as they arrived this time, with smoke coming from the chimneys of both houses. Zahra's hurt, however, became stronger as she was now knowledgeable of what her daughter, Isobel had called her, thinking of her Mither as a slut, when she had been kidnapped, so violently from her home, not by her choice, to be in the very cruel and violent company of Prince Griogar in the Outer Hebrides. Isobel had spread this belief to all her bairns. The prince was bitter towards both her and his brother, Coinneach for punishing him for his attempted rape upon her in his quarters on Beinn Coinneach which was met by the shape shifting attack of the giant, brown wolf.

Zahra hadn't known of the existence of the giant brown wolf before that day. So much had happened in that time frame to destroy her relationships now with her older children.

She didn't know what to expect as they entered through the gates of Wolf Ranch, now opened for them by the rude redhead, Simon Fraser. At least he opened it up without grumbling. That was progress. Grooming the horses was a different matter. He refused always to care for anyone's horses. Zahra had originally thought that he was a good choice for her daughter Fatma, but now she had regretted that decision and thinking so highly of the young lad, as he was then. He was Lord Simon Fraser's son and had died in a horse-riding accident. His snobbery was inbuilt, he was lazy, judgemental and of little use to the farm. He had changed since she had first met him. Peter and Zahra rubbed down their own horses themselves, before knocking on the door, but the wee ones had already run inside to keep warm.

Grigor met them warmly and invited them both in, which was friendlier than on previous visits there. Zahra was nervous, just the same, contemplating meeting Isobel, even though Grigor offered coffee himself. 'That was sweet', she thought. He was trying to impress her and was even wearing clean clothing. Peter was keen to leave, but as coffee was served up, it couldn't be refused. Isobel finally came in to acknowledge her Mither. Everyone in the room became aware then of the tension between the two women, as surprisingly, Zahra stood up to her full height, still wearing her fur garment, although not on her head and addressed the issue at hand.

"Isobel, I have a bone to pick with you," Zahra spoke boldly.

"I know Ma. I heard about it. Da told me. I won't say it again," Isobel said, in her snippy way.

That was an inadequate response for Zahra.

"Isobel, I have accepted you marrying two men at the one time, having an affair with Lord Cinaed and stealing his baby from him, but I have never called you a derogatory word or name, describing that behaviour. Why, might you ask, when it is justified to criticise you, when stealing a man's wee bairn from him? But I love you Isobel and you are my daughter. We have been through some of the worse things that life can throw at a person, like losing wee Sakina, your sister, but you on the other hand, have allowed yourself to be disloyal to your Mither, of which you only have one. Not only disloyal but rude, derogatory, and making false accusations when wee Causantin and wee Dihaoine told you the truth, which you ignored. You also hurt them, as well as me.

You didn't only keep this disgusting word to your own filthy mouth, you spread it to all of your brothers and sister, Fatma, which has left me both isolated and disrespected. What have I ever done to you for such a moral judgement, when you entertained yourself, when unmarried to Lord Cinaed? You can't undo the cruelty to me because we were so devoted to one another. Help me understand why you wanted to hurt me so much," Zahra said.

Seeing both Isobel, known as 'the snippy one', facing off with her Mither was a first, for the whole family and friends and the room fell silent. Even Dihaoine hid behind her Mither holding her fur coat, expecting Isobel to explode. Alex was as nervous as any man could be, but didn't interfere, only because he too wanted the third bairn issue dealt with. Peter held his head in his hands, thinking they were never going to get home now to Inverness, before the cold and dark that she hated.

Grigor was interestingly pleased, as he made even more coffee and tea. He had always thought that Isobel had gotten away with too much, but was loathe to chastise her, in case it upset her Mither. Now it was a much belated showdown. Isobel's stance was still stiff, tall and proud. She didn't have her hands in a punching pose, but Hugh, seated at the table beside her, was keeping an eye on any eruption of violence, while agreeing with everything that Zahra had said. He was prepared to step in, if Zahra wasn't satisfied.

"Ma, I have already said sorry. I shouldn't have said that word about you, but it looked that way, so naturally I told all my siblings," Isobel said.

"How do you describe your behaviour then, with Lord Cinaed?" asked Zahra.

"I was lonely without Alex. You know that," Isobel said.

"I asked you. How do you describe it?" Zahra repeated. "Were you slutty?" Zahra asked her daughter.

With that action, Hugh was ready to stop the attack, as Isobel screamed and picked up a sharp knife to throw at her Mither. He took it from her and put his daughter over his knee. He took his leather belt from his waist and strapped his daughter repeatedly in front of the entire family. She wasn't strapped on bare skin, but it would have hurt, and she screamed and wildly kicked her legs, while everyone gave him room to carry it out. Isobel had no defence against the strength of her big, strong father, Hugh Mohr Chisholm.

"Isobel, behave yourself," Hugh chastised. "You ask for your Mither's forgiveness for such a shocking thing from a daughter. Never speak to your Mither with disrespect for as long as I breathe air," Hugh bellowed at her. When he let her go, she then spun around like a wild cat.

"I wish you were still in the waterfall," but she said it with tears that started to roll down her cheeks. Hugh then held his daughter close to him and told her to ask forgiveness properly and respectfully to her Mither and never, ever show disrespect to her again, let alone, throw a knife. Zahra was amazed at what had transpired.

John Fraser was relieved that his wife had finally been pulled into line, at last. Alex was worried if he would suffer in bed that night. Isobel limped across to her Mither, so Dihaoine then hid behind Peter. Causantin was holding his hands over his mouth, not expecting the night to end up like this. His young life was proving most eventful up to this point, compared to most bairns of his age.

Padruig looked on very seriously and sad, saying nothing but had agreed with Hugh. Isobel had been out of control for too long. There was a deep sadness to it. Isobel genuinely hugged and apologised to her Mither, while asking forgiveness and crying all the while.

"I've cooked dinner," said Grigor. "Peter, my friend, Zahra how about a meal before you leave or stay here for the night. There's plenty of room and I have those herbs and vegetables for you too Zahra. I saw you needed a nanny goat too, so I have put one aside for you with the chickens to take back to Inverness," Grigor said feeling very pleased with himself. "Hugh said he'd help you carry it all back," Grigor added.

"My cooking isn't as good as my wife's, but it's edible, every-one," Grigor said.

Peter noted him calling Zahra his wife, as did all the family, especially Padruig. Zahra hadn't even noticed.

"A nanny? Thank you so much Grigor, I was only just saying to Peter that we needed a nanny goat," Zahra said, and the subject was successfully changed.

"I have a beehive for you too Ma," said Fatma trying to make up for her unfriendliness too. "I am sorry too Ma. I believed my sister," Fatma said.

"Heaven is at the feet of the Mither," said an unlikely Padruig. "I slaughtered that asshole Prince with Alex for you too Zahra. He's in the waterfall, for now at least," Padruig said, wanting praise. "Thank you Padruig. He did deserve it. He was the definition of cruelty," Zahra said. "I see you took down the painting too?" Zahra observed. "How did it get here in the first place?" she asked.

Peter was unaccustomed to this type of conversation, and he wasn't sure that he would ever become accustomed to violence in the kitchen and murder approved of by the woman of his dreams. The painting was a challenge, but that was gone. Maybe it would all improve, he thought. He didn't know what, if anything he could add, so he stayed quiet.

Responding to Zahra, it was Padruig who replied.

"Malcolm's brother, Kenneth MacNachten wrote to us saying the painting was Prince Griogar's and he would be here to pick it up," Padruig added.

"So, Malcolm MacNachten was behind the prince and you Grigor, meeting up together in the one place, without him knowing that you were back here in the Aird. Is that right Padruig?" Zahra asked.

"I suppose that little shite was. I never thought about it, but I'll talk to him now and confirm that," Padruig said.

"Can you write to me and let me know of the outcome of your conversation, then please Padruig?" Zahra asked.

"Aye, no problem," Padruig said. Causantin was listening carefully to his Mither, whom he admired so much. She saw his sweet face staring at her.

"Oh, my sweet Causantin, come here to your Ma who loves you," Zahra said and hugged and kissed him to make him wriggle and laugh.

"Me too Ma," asked Dihaoine whom she kissed in the same manner to make them both forget the horrible earlier fight with their big sister.

It was as if it had never happened. John Fraser was accustomed to this and decided to go back to the newer house.

"Will you divorce him?" Zahra asked Isobel once John Fraser was outside of the house.

"The idea was put to me, so I could marry Alex. What do you think?" Isobel asked.

"Good idea love," Zahra said and sort out that adoption thing with the MacAlpins. Get rid of that. I'll write whatever you need but there is still the wee bairn from Cinaed you need to both talk about," she added.

"Ma, how do you feel without Coinneach Og?" Isobel asked.

"Very sad at times, but I deal with most of life's horrors by not thinking about them too much. However, I do think Coinneach Og is better off with his own people. They are very different, and they have their own language. Have you seen her looking at you yet, like staring at you coldly at all?" Zahra asked.

"Aye, I have. Most of the time. Unlike Anndra and Domhnall. She can be so cold, but intelligent too, beyond her years," Isobel said.

"That's true. Anything else?" asked Zahra.

"Aye, it's her voice sometimes, like a growly sound. It gives me the creeps," Isobel said.

"Do you and Alex both think she might be happier with Lord Cinaed?" Zahra asked in a low and calm voice.

"I can't part with her Ma, but Alex wants her to go to Lord Cinaed," Isobel said.

"That's understandable. A Mither can't be forced to part with a wee bairn, but one day, it might just happen, in the meantime, you should both write, once you are married mind and let him know it is his wee bairn, if he wishes to visit her. After all, he might not want a bairn at his age, but do not go to Beinn Coinneach, for any reason and if he meets you here, don't be alone. Remember too, that Lord Coinneach can shape shift into a dangerous, giant brown wolf, who will not like a rival, royal bairn. The good thing is, your bairn is female and the younger one in their traditions, so Coinneach Og is still the superior of the two wee bairns," Zahra added.

"Grigor, do you know how to make those musket balls made of silver? The wolf is unkillable with an ordinary musket ball?" Zahra asked.

"We all know how to do anything, and a wolf is a piece of cake," Grigor replied.

"It's five feet high at least, thick brown fur, huge head, paws as big as a man's hand and nearly three feet across his shoulders," Zahra said. "It's Coinneach. That's how I departed from here, after you disposed of the prince that night. I heard his howl and left, and I rode upon his back," she said.

Peter was becoming afraid at the talk of wolves and asked her why she would ride off on a wolf.

"It's just like riding a small horse really and easy too by just holding onto his fur," Zahra answered honestly.

"I don't mean that. Why didn't you stay inside the safety of the house?" Peter asked.

Both Grigor and she knew why, but they both didn't disclose that they'd had an issue where he was mean to her that night, then he raped her, as skinny and damaged, as she was and still married to Coinneach. Grigor was relieved that she didn't tell him, but how would she explain why she hadn't stayed then?

"I was still Coinneach's wife, and it was him that was howling," Zahra replied.

"Bedtime for me," said Alex and both he and Isobel left, and Fatma had already gone, so the core group was small, as Causantin and Dihaoine had already put themselves to bed.

"You can borrow one of my books Peter, but one week only, then the other one," Padruig said as he gave one to him.

"Thank you Padruig," said a grateful and surprised Peter.

"At least you have more material for your next book Zahra,"

said Padruig, "Like that shape shifting, bloody giant wolf."

"You can both sleep in our bed," Grigor said referring to his and Zahra's marriage bed as 'ours'.

"Zahra, I have patients early tomorrow, we will have to leave around four o'clock in the morning to get there on time," said Peter.

"I'm coming too, don't forget," said Hugh "To help you out with your house and carrying a goat. Food and lodgings for free, while I do the work, so long as Peter pays for the materials. Okay Zahra?" Hugh asked as she made her way to the bedroom.

"Och Hugh, that is so generous of you. Isn't that wonderful Peter?" Zahra commented.

"Come out the back" ushered Hugh and Padruig, to show Peter where all the things were to be taken with them into Inverness, in the morning. They took their time showing him how to strap the chicken cage onto his horse, while Hugh would have the goat and Zahra would have the beehive, along with the vegetables. That left Grigor inside the house, alone while Zahra who was attempting to go to sleep in her old bed. Grigor climbed into her bed beside her and before she knew it, he had entered her, made passionate love, and ejaculated.

"Oh Grigor," she said quietly. "I'm in one of my fertile days" she said.

"Then you'll have to marry me again. I don't have a life without you. Come back to me," Grigor pleaded.

"Oh Grigor, I've never stopped loving you, but please don't hurt Peter," she implored, and he left the room after doing what he had planned to do all night long. Now he was satisfied.

The last of the adults left in the kitchen chatting, were Padruig and Grigor, discussing how to kill that 'bloody shape shifting wolf', as Padruig called it and it became a quiet murmur as Zahra lulled herself into a restful sleep curled up into the warm arms of her lover, Dr Peter Heath.

Grigor wasn't all together trusting of Hugh departing with them both as well, in the morning and being alone in Zahra's home with her, albeit in a back room, even if the 'dull Peter' was present. Grigor deduced that he might have to go to Inverness midweek, just to keep himself front and centre in Zahra's mind.

No doubt Peter was going to read those books of Zahra's from cover to cover. Grigor wasn't even sure if he entirely trusted Peter, but he was still sure of himself. She had never stopped loving him, she had said so, herself. She hadn't tried to fight him off in their bed either and that was a good enough sign. He was far more handsome than any of the other men, even the blonde one, although he may have to make concessions for him.

A new plaid was all he needed, not a philibeg, she laughed at him for wearing one of those things once. Maybe a visit to the barber shop too? Aye, he could feel it in his loins. Love was coming soon.

41. Malcolm Receives a Letter

It was unlike my Grandda to communicate with me by mail, but I thought it must be important enough, so I decided that I would respond also, in writing.

Wolf Ranch,

The Aird, Scotland, 1830

To my Dearest Grandson, Malcolm,

I hope yourself and your good wife, Ailsa are both well and life is everything that you hoped it would be in Glengarry, in your new premises.

I am writing to enquire with you as to how it all came to be, that we received, the nude painting of Zahra from your good brother, Kenneth.

To be clear, none of us here nor Zahra herself have a complaint about its presence here at all. I personally love the painting which now adorns my bedroom wall.

It had resulted in Prince Griogar, as was arranged, to pick it up and was subsequently paid for, so Kenneth was paid as you already know and please give my thanks to my Grandson Kenneth. Alex MacDonald and I were departed of the soul of Prince Griogar as you have also been informed. Zahra MacAlpin was, as was predicted to be, accompanying that Prince, on that day in his carriage, coming from the Hebridean Islands, where she had been living for several months.

However, that having been said, there has been an enormous and most dreadful of misunderstandings, as to why Zahra was with him, which I hope to clarify first in this letter.

You and I and many other loyal friends were all involved in the kidnapping of Hector MacGregor from Beinn Coinneach and his wife Flidas MacKenzie, which was successfully carried out, although the giant brown wolf was thought to have followed us all down to the Aird.

However, that isn't the reason why I am writing.

The absence of Hector and the alleged 'brown wolf' meant that Zahra MacAlpin and her three bairns were alone in her mansion, without protection on Beinn Coinneach, except for the maid Mairi, who took care of wee Coinneach Og.

The brown wolf has now been identified as Zahra's shape shifting, now ex-husband, Coinneach MacAlpin, as their marriage has since been annulled.

Unfortunately, because Hector wasn't there to protect his Mither and neither was Coinneach MacAlpin, an army of unknown kidnappers, from the Outer Hebrides, struck the mansion, kidnapping Zahra, her two bairns and her wolf puppy, leaving behind only wee Coinneach Og with staff.

The mercenaries dropped off the two bairns, Causantin and Dihaoine MacGregor and the puppy to the farm in the Aird, but Zahra was taken to an unknown destination. Her then husband, did not make it known that his now ex-wife, had been kidnapped, because he either didn't know, or he didn't want his family to attract controversy or worse still, he could have been complicit.

I cannot describe the severity strongly enough in this mere letter, as to how badly Zahra was tortured, starved, raped, and beaten but somehow, Zahra has survived it, up until the letter from Kenneth arrived.

Her family, in the meantime, all thought that she had run off with yet another man and had lost all respect for her, given that she was still married to Coinneach MacAlpin at that time.

Could you please tell Ali that his Mither is not what Isobel Fraser has accused her of and Zahra was in fact a victim of a most heinous crime, unreported by her own now, ex-husband. If it hadn't been for the meeting of the two MacGregor men in the Aird, Zahra would still be in the Outer Hebrides but no longer of this world.

Thank you from the bottom of my heart for at least getting 'the worm out of his hole' for long enough to destroy that evil. However, most disappointingly, her own family, in not believing in her intentions, forced her to feel that escape that night on the giant wolf, to return to Beinn Coinneach was her only option made necessary, which subsequently vanished out of sight, along with Zahra.

Coinneach now, however is a practising homosexual with Alasdair Fraser of Fraser Ville and Zahra wanted desperately to leave Beinn Coinneach and fortunately a certain Doctor Peter Heath wanted to visit Zahra, as her practising physician, which enabled her to miraculously depart by attracting his attention with a looking glass.

She is now living and working in Inverness studying nursing, should Ali wish to see her, but if further information could be furnished about the painting, from Kenneth, it would be most appreciated. Zahra is now living with Dr Peter Heath. They are lovers it seems and unmarried and her marriage to Coinneach was annulled but oddly, Coinneach is now looking to locate her.

Please do not reveal to Coinneach MacAlpin where she is, if he should contact you, as I cannot emphasize strongly enough, just how dangerous an outcome that could be for both Zahra and whomever she may be with, at the time.

Affectionately yours, signed Grandda

I asked Ailsa to read the bizarre letter which was a shock to me. I too thought Zahra was with that man by choice, abandoning her baby Coinneach Og, as well as her two bairns, both born with Grigor Mohr MacGregor, and not by kidnapping.

"My God Malcolm. That poor woman. You said yourself that you no longer cared about her. Oh Malcolm, look how wrong we can be," Ailsa said.

I didn't have time to take in all the new facts, before seeing Kenneth, but what struck me as most odd was the kidnappers knew to only target the MacGregor bairns, not the MacAlpin wee bairn, the MacGregor ex-wife and pup. It felt ominously like the days of proscription when it would

Outer Hebrides

have been legal to commit such an act of violence against MacGregors. I wondered why Grigor hadn't thought of that and had also followed Isobel in her belief of her Mither abandoning another marriage. It was clear, however that he still didn't see his ex-wife as a MacGregor and maybe never had and never would. That made me feel even worse, as if I had been complicit in a crime against Zahra's wee family.

I told my wife that I'd take the letter first to Kenneth, then to Ali and she agreed, as we had enough time to deal with it. Most of the work on both farms was complete. Kenneth told me on the day that I had taken the painting to him, not to be involved, but he had changed his mind about not getting involved and sent it, as well as letters and so on, to make it all happen. He didn't quite expect a disposal of the bloody kind, no doubt. Kenneth was pleased he followed his intuition and sent the painting to the Aird, 'after all it was your idea initially', he commented to me. But after receiving his money, Kenneth thought nothing more of it and knew nothing more. Neither did I, other than the three paintings by Zahra that I had burned and that might be what Grandda wants to learn about.

I hoped not, because they had been destroyed.

I would never curse my benefactor and new father of only two months, beyond his death, but John MacDonnell's obsession with all things 'Zahra' and art, was continuing, well after his death and I wasn't comfortable with dealing with any of it at all. The money was paid and that should have been the end of it, but now there was a serious line of enquiry, but why? Just because her bairns were calling Zahra bad names, surely not, I thought. So, I went to Ali's farm on my new big, black horse, which meant I needed to go around the entirety of my new estate, to get to his front door, which I had not yet done, and I suppose that wasn't very neighbourly.

Ali and his wife, April were eating lunch, which I disturbed, and I offered to return later, but they insisted that I join them for lunch, which I did. It was nice tomato sandwiches, and I was hungry and thirsty, so it went down well, considering the conversation was going to be awkward with my neighbour.

It felt like I was intruding on his private family business.

"Ali, there is a matter I need to talk to you about, it's not concerning farming, it's concerning your Mither, because I received a letter today requesting of me to pass on some information to you," I said, trying to sound confident as he looked intensely at me, at the mere mention of his Mither.

It was a touchy subject, after all.

"I have been informed that your sister, Isobel misinformed you all about something to which she has since apologised. It was about your Mither, Zahra MacAlpin. I hope you will hear me out, as I do have it here in a letter, if you would prefer to read that?" I asked.

Ali said to continue reading awkwardly and was embarrassed in front of his young and impressionable wife.

"You were all misinformed that your Mither had ran off, willingly with another man, Prince Griogar MacAlpin, to an unknown location. In fact, after we had all left Beinn Coinneach with Hector, that very same day, another army of unknown men, went to the mansion on Beinn Coinneach, where Zahra, your Mither, was left unprotected without either Hector or Coinneach, who had subsequently followed us as far as the Aird," I said.

"That army, in fact, kidnapped Zahra and the two wee bairns and the wolf puppy, but not wee Coinneach Og," I added.

Before I could go on, his wife became upset.

"Kidnapped. Och Ali," April exclaimed.

"Who were they?" Ali asked.

"Mercenaries from Belgium, paid for by the prince, from the Outer Hebrides and that was where Zahra was taken and kept prisoner for some time," I said.

"Ali the rest might upset your wife, so if you can read the content from this section here in the letter, it would be better, to which I indicated," I said.

Realising his Mither had been an innocent party and so badly mistreated, it bought him to tears. He was remorseful for having believed his sister, Isobel.

"Is this Ma's new address now, in Inverness?" Ali asked.

"Aye it is, and I do know that Doctor who was also present at Coinneach Og's birth. He does have a history in England, concerning male patients of his and was known here as a homosexual and it was in the papers when Matilda, Uncle Alex's wife, let it be known to them. She wrote to London first to obtain the information, and he isn't permitted to practise medicine in England, only Scotland. So, he lost most of his patients as a result, and he was a struggling doctor, when I met him, with low self-confidence, but a nice temperament and a sound medical background.

He had befriended your Mither, a while ago, when she had her leg broken and that's how they met, I think, and he helped deliver Causantin too in the Aird. I personally haven't seen him since Coinneach Og's birth, but Zahra clearly needed him to escape from Lord Coinneach's grasp, which I will explain later. Her marriage has since been annulled, so you can probably apply to no longer be adopted by him, I'm not sure, but in my opinion, you should get rid of that, if you can and return to using your birth name of Ali MacGregor," I advised.

"Hugh Og and I are going to Inverness for items that I need, and we can take you, if you wish to visit Zahra this Wednesday, and we are staying overnight. Are you interested or not?" I asked.

"It would be a very early start, around four in the morning, not arriving there before lunch, so if you were to eat lunch with us first, then we can drop you off at your Mither's place of work, then you could have the afternoon with your Ma and meet us back at my cousin, Aonghus and Annabel's home, unless Zahra invites you to stay with them. Let me know before Tuesday night, okay?" I said, and I took my leave.

I took back my letter, before I left, and I replied to Grandda the same night, informing him that the message to Ali had been delivered.

◊

Ali was at my door with his overnight bag in hand Tuesday night, asking to stay over in my house, so he could be ready, early in the morning with both Hugh Og and me. I also let him know that my cousin, Aonghus MacGregor was a lawyer, so if he needed him, I advised him to take advantage of that, while he was there in Inverness.

When we all arrived on the Team in Inverness, we ate lunch and then headed for the Medical Practice to drop off Ali. It was the lunch break there for the Medical Practice, so there were no patients for a while. Only Zahra could be seen from the road, sweeping their front path, from her front door and all the way to the road, and she even swept the footpath, before re-entering through their lovely new iron gates, closing it behind her.

Ali had observed his Mither sadly with me, Hugh Og and Angus, then Ali left us before Zahra went back inside. All of us felt sad watching Zahra, with the new information that we had learned from Grandda. Ali then approached his Mither, who was wearing the traditional nurses' long white uniform and cap with her woollen, Clan Gregor traditional nurse's cape, to keep warm.

Ali was naturally nervous having to face Zahra, after having treated his Mither, so badly by not even inviting her to his wedding with my niece, April MacNachten, while he did invite his father, Grigor Mohr MacGregor, who was far more guilty of domestic crimes, than Zahra could in several hundred lifetimes.

Ali alighted the carriage and we said our farewells, but I watched on, while Hugh Og managed the Team with Angus.

Before Zahra went inside, Ali called out, 'Ma' to her. She swung around in recognition to the sound of the voice of her beloved son, Ali from Glengarry, now. The shock of seeing him, caused her to faint but luckily, she fell into his arms, and he carried her carefully to sit on the bench seat, near the front wall of their practice. He placed her head between her legs for a while, before she sat up and looked at him in utter disbelief. Then I lost sight of them.

Zahra must have been distraught, at not having seen her son Ali for all the time that had passed, to have reacted that way and all due to the false information that had been believed by all of her bairns, except the youngest two, who themselves had been kidnapped and their sad story had also been disbelieved.

"Oh, my Ali," she cried, and she couldn't stop weeping, when her companion came out to see why she was taking so long to sweep the front path.

"Zahra are you alright?" Peter asked a very pale looking, Nurse Heath, as her name badge now read.

Ali stood up saying "Hello Dr Heath, I am Ali Gregor MacAlpin, Ma's oldest son. I came to visit, but Ma fainted, when she saw me. Can we take her inside out of the cold please?" Ali politely asked, respectfully standing as he spoke to the Doctor.

It wasn't obvious that Peter was a strong man, but he lifted Zahra up with ease and took her inside and lay her on their bed.

"I'll get you some water my love," Peter said tenderly. Ali sat with her to talk, while the fussing Doctor wiped her forehead with a cool cloth and gave her water to sip.

"Did you get a shock seeing your son my love?" Peter asked kindly.

"Aye, Peter, I did. I am so happy to see him. I'll be alright in a minute darling. My head is swimming a bit, is all," Zahra replied.

"Lie still then, you can have the afternoon off from work to catch up with Ali, unless something urgent comes up," Peter said to her. "Welcome to our home son," Peter said to Ali and shook his hand.

"I'll make you some tea or is it coffee?" Peter asked.

"Coffee please," Ali answered.

"Ma, I am sorry that I haven't visited you, nor written, either. Will you please forgive me?" Ali asked. "I am married now Ma. Do you remember April, my father-in-law, Kenneth and Ivy MacNachten's daughter? She is my wife now and she is with child," Ali said.

As Peter walked in, he caught the end of the conversation.

"Married are you son? Congratulations. Don't stand up each time I walk in either. Here's your coffee and Uncle Hugh Mohr Chisholm is in the back yard, if you wanted to catch up with him too. Now, I must get back to a new patient. Your Mither has made me a busy Doctor, God bless her. If you like, you can take a walk in the park, or eat something. Please help yourself. I hope you're staying over for dinner and the night lad. Glengarry is a long way from Inverness," he said and hurriedly left to go back to work.

"He's nice Ma," Ali said.

"Aye son, he is a very sweet man. Congratulations to you both too and I hope your April has an easy time of it, giving birth. You have your Uncle Alex in Glengarry, so he will be wonderful for delivering your wee bairn," Zahra said.

"I like it in Glengarry Ma. I'm next door to Uncle Malcolm and he has been very helpful with farming advice. He has inherited a huge property now that was formerly, the estate of Old John MacDonnell," Ali said.

"Did Mr MacDonnell pass away?" Zahra asked. "That's so sad, I really liked him."

"Uncle Malcolm loved him too. The funeral was enormous Ma. I hope you will come and stay with us some day. My wife has asked that you accept our invitation," Ali asked.

"Did she now?" Zahra said. "That's nice of her, I'd like to come and stay over, with Peter too though. We can ask him," Zahra said.

"Did you decide against visiting me or writing to me because of what Isobel had falsely claimed to you all, about my character?" Zahra asked.

"Aye Ma, I am sorry. Uncle Malcolm read me a letter that he received from Wolf Ranch in the Aird, with the factual story, concerning the kidnapping from the mountain. He offered to bring me here to see you, because he was coming to Inverness and staying with his cousin, Uncle Aonghus MacGregor," Ali said.

"Is that so? I'm feeling much better now son, let's go and say hello to Uncle Hugh, who you may or may not have met. He is Isobel's Da, my first husband. He's staying here to do some work for us in the garden and the house," Zahra said avoiding how the truth was revealed finally and her fight with Isobel, Ali's older sister, over this very emotive matter.

After introducing both Ali and Hugh, it was realised that they had met on one occasion in the Aird, before Hugh's demise with both of his brothers. Ali seemed pleased to meet the older, yet handsome man, but also pleased that Zahra had support from her first husband. While in the backyard when Hugh was controlling the goat from entering the vegetable garden, Dr Heath unexpectedly called for Nurse Heath's assistance, after all.

"I have an emergency, Nurse Heath. I need your assistance, now please," Dr Heath demanded.

Hugh's palings needed to be nailed onto the fence, so Ali offered his assistance to Hugh. Dr Heath on the other hand had an unexpected enema to conduct, followed by an exam on a very stout gentleman's rectum, for some reason. The result was a lot of faeces in a bucket from the examination room, which Nurse Heath had to quickly empty outside into the privy, at the back of the yard. She ran past Hugh Mohr and Ali holding her nose and deposited the contents of the pail into the privy, then went to the well to wash the pail clean. It was clear that Zahra was feeling ill from the smell of the faeces, but it was her job to wash the pail clean of any remnants of faeces.

As Zahra was returning to the surgery, she stopped near the rear door, went even paler than when she fainted, and vomited into her herb garden. Hugh watched upon the woman, to whom he was married once and recognised the familiar signs of Zahra being with child. 'Oh God, whose bairn was this?' 'Did Grigor achieve it after all. Hugh wondered asked himself.'

"Let me help you and take the pail love," Hugh said kindly.

Hugh then returned the bucket to Peter, whom he informed that Zahra was sick. The old and stout man had an enormous belly that rolled out and over his tiny wee penis, that was barely visible, as it was the smallest penis that Hugh had ever seen on a man, and he was embarrassed when Hugh walked in, naturally. Peter wasn't aware of the man's shame, sitting there completely naked, waiting upon the Nurse to continue.

"Can you get her please Hugh, just this one job, then she can go with Ali," Peter said. As he was departing the examination room, Peter could be heard asking the patient to 'bend over, bottom up please'.

"Nurse Heath," Peter called again. Zahra recovered after taking her last breath of fresh air and ran inside to answer Peter's request. With Peter's hand examining the man's rectum, Zahra was really feeling ill and luckily there was nothing much left in her stomach. It was some kind of exam for the prostate gland, Peter explained. The patient's enormous, white and flabby backside, pointing upwards, was really a sight to behold and not one, easily forgotten.

"Nurse, pass me more lubricant please," Peter said. Peter was then better able to examine him internally. Still not satisfied, he asked the patient to push up his bottom further with Peter's finger endeavouring to examine inside the patient's rectum. The patient was involuntarily grunting like a pig, as it must have been very uncomfortable.

"Nurse Heath, to learn how to complete this exam, you will need to examine his testicles," Peter said. Instructing the patient to then stand up and turn around, he asked Nurse Heath to hold the man's tiny penis aside then gently grasp each testicle in her small hands. The technique being forefinger and middle finger on the underneath and her thumbs on the top. She was directed to gently turn each testicle between her thumbs and fingers feeling for any lumps or abnormalities as this was a part of her nurses training. There was no chance that his tiny penis would ever become erect, Zahra thought and hoped, while feeling around the poor man.

"Now tell me what you feel," Peter asked.

"The right testicle is swollen with a hard lump and the left testicle is soft and appears healthy, Doctor Heath," Zahra replied.

"The patient has to be admitted now to the Cancer Ward at the hospital. Do you agree Nurse Heath?" Peter asked.

"Aye Doctor," Zahra replied. Peter smacked him quite hard on his enormous, flabby, white, English bottom, then told him to get dressed and get himself off to the hospital, while opening the windows up for ventilation, then Peter and Zahra both thoroughly scrubbed their hands, up to their elbows, once more.

"My bill has to be paid first, Mr Jones," Peter demanded.

 It hadn't mattered to Peter that the man could be dying from cancer, only the payment of his bill was imperative.

"Well done Nurse Heath," Peter said. "How are you now?" Peter asked.

"Much better," Zahra replied. "Am I free to go now with my son, Peter?" she asked.

 Mother and son both departed, finally. Ali apologised for interfering with her workday. He hadn't realised how hard she worked in the Medical Practise, or that she was training to be a nurse.

"Don't be late Zahra, so dinner is cooking for us all and you will have to sterilise this room top to bottom, more than usual," Peter called out as she was departing.

"Yes Doctor," Zahra added.

"I'm quite glad you chose today to come son. I'm not feeling that well. It'll pass, no doubt," Zahra said.

The two of them strolled arm in arm through their lovely park with the leaves of the trees rustling in the wind. It was comfortable it if was just breezy in Inverness, but if the wind came up, it was bitterly cold and it could blow right through you, she felt.

"You bought a farm in Glengarry, I hear, that's an achievement, Ali? Did you become tired of the Aird, or were the crops failing?" Zahra asked.

"I love my farm in Glengarry. It was Uncle Malcolm's idea, as I wasn't happy any more in the Aird. Isobel was snippy, all the time and she was going to be too hard on my wife, so I had to leave for April's sake, really. The crops were doing very well. I worked hard there," Ali replied.

"Tonight, it might be better if you stay with Malcolm and his cousin because Peter is in a discontented mood being as busy as he is. Can you drop in tomorrow before you leave?" Zahra asked.

"Aye of course," Ali said.

"Ma, I am sorry for not inviting you to our wedding. I feel so guilty now that I have been told the full story," Ali said.

"You should have all given me 'the benefit of the doubt', my Mither would always have said. Why were you all so certain that I was guilty of a wrongdoing and deserving of that dreadful word that you have all been calling me, especially in knowing that I no longer had your brother there to help protect me and the wee ones?" Zahra asked.

"I don't know. We all followed Isobel blindly," Ali said.

"I hesitate to ask you this, but did Hector also believe the 'slut' story too?" Zahra asked.

"Aye, all of us did, except the two wee ones," Ali admitted in shame. "It's different with Hector though Ma, he misses you so much all the time, so maybe he had his doubts, because he knew what Lord Coinneach was capable of. Please ask him yourself to clarify that," Ali said.

"I am a writer, as you know, son. One day, I will write it all down, so you will all know what truly happened to me there on those islands," Zahra said, but it felt like an idle threat directed at them all.

"Do you still feel isolated Ma, from us, I mean because we all let you down?" Ali asked.

"Aye, of course I do. I never imagined that my bairns would ever betray me," Zahra said.

"Betrayal?" Ali asked.

"Aye, that's what it is son, betrayal. Does the word offend you, or do you deny it?" Zahra asked.

"I don't deny it," Ali said, finally accepting it as a reality.

"Ali, concerning your wedding with young April, I do have to speak my mind about that. Even the worst of parents, are still invited to their bairns' weddings, just because they are the parents. Did you hate me that much, or were you all so embarrassed to even want to acknowledge my existence?" Zahra asked.

"It was shame, not hate. I never hated you Ma. I could never hate you. I do love you, please forgive me," Ali asked.

"I forgive you son," Zahra said. "But how do we all get past a wedding that can never be re-celebrated?" Zahra asked. "After all, you had two parents who were both alive and both living in mainland Scotland. I still don't understand it. Your father and I should have both been there," Zahra added.

"My wife invited you to stay on the farm with us. That's a start, isn't it? Can we start with that?" Ali said.

"Is that so that no-one else sees who your Mither is? Maybe son, but you were the son who led the prayers. What has happened to your faith? Has that gone too?" Zahra asked. "Only your father was invited to your wedding, wasn't he?"

Zahra asked.

"Aye, he was," Ali said.

"And did you feel shame towards him for doing what he did to me and with Belle MacGregor and the farm?" Zahra asked.

"Nae, I was over that by then," Ali said.

"Did he take a partner, another woman, I mean?" Zahra asked.

"Nae, he was alone. He looked lonely too. He was a sad sight to see. Ma, he misses you terribly. Can you please consider getting back with him?" Ali asked.

"It sounds like all my bairns will judge me, no matter what I do, and I have never stopped loving your father. And it's none of your business if we re-unite or stay apart. We are the parents. Remember that, Ali," Zahra said.

"When did you all start judging me? Was it when I married Coinneach?" Zahra asked.

"Nae it was when we found out that Hector was being sodomised, right under your nose," Ali said accusingly.

"So that was my fault too now, was it?" Zahra asked sarcastically.

"You don't know what it was like living with Coinneach. He had absolute power. Do I have a cock to sodomise someone with? Nae, I think not. At risk to myself, I asked the man with the cock, being Coinneach, never to hurt my son. You do understand that he was a shape shifting bloody wolf, don't you, or are you completely stupid, Ali?" Zahra said getting grumpy at the assigned blame.

"You had choice Ma. You could have left him for Da," Ali said.

"I re-call being on Wolf Ranch after finding out that Coinneach was a shape shifting wolf and you expressly told me, to dis-allow Grigor MacGregor onto the property. So you seem to have conveniently re-written history to suit yourself," she said

"Your father raped me upon my return, in my poorly condition as it was, coming off that damn island, while unmarried to him and him believing also in the false story that I was nothing more than a slut, while I was still married to Coinneach MacAlpin. I was someone else's wife, who had been violently removed from her home and taken with a hood covering my head, to a freezing cold isolated island, with no food, or water. Can't you even begin to comprehend the crimes committed against myself and your little brother and sister?" Zahra asked angrily.

"Who would you have chosen upon your escape Ali, if you had been in my position? Your wife, or your ex-wife, if it had been you then?" Zahra asked. "I was still married, call me old fashioned if you like. Your father divorced me remember?" Zahra said angrily.

Finding herself enraged with the attitude still, of her immature bairns, Zahra stormed off back home to put on the dinner for both Peter and Hugh. She departed from Ali.

"Give my regards to Malcolm, Hugh Og, Angus, Uncle Aonghus and his wife, Auntie Annabel. Enjoy your night in Inverness Ali," Zahra said, and Ali just watched as his Mither strode off, independently of him and them all. She was now a stronger woman than she used to be and was deeply hurt by the actions of her own bairns, except wee Causantin and Dihaoine.

He wondered if their relationship was now lost, forever? He felt utterly ridiculous for just offering her a visit to his tiny farm to compensate for their wedding, as he just stood there, all alone in the park. He had never felt so alone. How could they have all done this to her and it wasn't yet the end? She was a writer, and it was going to feature in some newspaper or magazine somewhere and her bairns will look as guilty as the kidnappers were. He knew he had forgone his only opportunity at any reconciliation with his Mither, who had always adored him, prayed with him, taught him everything he knew, until he went to live with Hamish and that was all her idea too. His wife

April was her idea and yet he didn't invite her to his own wedding, with full knowledge that she was already off that island.

He knew in that moment that he was going to regret that decision for the rest of his life. He owed her too much and he was so idiotic then to try to assign blame to her, about his brother Hector, when she wasn't responsible for what had happened to Hector.

The truth was, that she was too good, too perfect as a Mither, almost flawless.

Why had he said that?

42. Just a Stomach Bug

Cooking dinner that night was just for three people when Hugh came in and asked where Ali was.

"At his Aunty Annabel's house with Malcolm and the other Glengarry mob," Zahra answered with attitude. Hugh knew that the visit hadn't gone too well but he was still more concerned whether she was with child or not.

Running to the outhouse, several times that evening and eating very little, answered that question. She just had a stomach bug, not what he feared she had.

"What happened with Ali then?" was the repeated question from Peter.

"He was condescending in trying to make up for not inviting me to his bloody wedding with April by asking me to stay over at his farm, like some senile old Granny, unable to think for myself, let alone judge their judgments. I introduced April to him and set them both up since they were both young, but Grigor was invited to their wedding, despite everything he did to all of us, and yet I wasn't. I was the one who was raped by Padruig and yet ended up with a busted-up face and forced to leave my home in the Aird. I was the one bloody kidnapped and kept in a freezing cold room on an island, starved then raped some more. What is it about 18th century Scotland, raping women and thinking it's alright?" Zahra said tersely.

"Well, it couldn't have been worse than Mr Jones shitting all over the exam room," said Peter.

That made her giggle a bit at the poor man with the tiniest penis in the world.

"I didn't know that men could have penises that tiny, let alone his tiny balls," Zahra said, and they both fell into raucous laughter which Hugh thought was very entertaining and very different conversation to normal table talk.

"You won't repeat it will you Hugh? We shouldn't repeat it, should we love?" Zahra said to an amused Peter, still remembering his miniscule balls.

"I'm sorry I made you squeeze his balls love, but we did find that abnormality. The man might have cancer after all," Peter said. "He pissed all over me, before you came in, did you know?" he added. "I had to go and change my clothes, before I called you in, that's why I needed you," Peter explained. "At first, when I was examining his rectum, he up and pissed on me," Peter said.

"You two sure are a funny pair to listen to," Hugh said, "And what with Ali visiting, Zahra vomiting, fainting then shitting all night, it's been quite an eventful day," Hugh added smiling, but he was pleased to see Zahra was getting over the visit from her son.

"It was just a stomach bug and not what you were thinking Hugh. I saw it on your face," she said.

"I admit, I thought for a moment there that you had one in the oven, but thank God it was just a stomach bug," Hugh added. "Ali is a bit of a temperamental wee shite these days, isn't he then?" Hugh judged.

"Yes, too temperamental, judgmental, disrespectful and he even told me to get back with his father. The cheek of it," Zahra said.

"Did he?" asked Peter. "So, he didn't like me then?" Peter asked, looking disappointed.

"He said he did like you in one breath, then in another breath, he told me to go back to Grigor," she said incredulously. "It's not the business of bairns to say such things," Zahra said.

"I agree with that," Hugh said.

"Is he coming back?" Peter asked.

"Maybe tomorrow to say goodbye, but I'm not sure. I'll be busy working anyway," Zahra said. "I've got water on cooking for both of you, for your baths, after we wash the dishes, if that's alright?" Zahra added.

"Peter, if you were pissed on, you had better go first," Zahra said and giggled again.

"We can wash up, can't we Hugh?" Zahra asked smiling.

"We can Zahra," Hugh said trying to join in the humour of it. Living with constant unpleasantness like cancer, especially involving the possible death of a patient, leads to a dark sense of humour he surmised. However, Hugh re-called all the prisoners who kept naked on prison ships after Culloden, whose genitalia appeared shrunken due to the obvious freezing cold conditions, and he never re-called anyone laughing about it.

At last, their day came to a pleasant close, as they all went to bed and after baths, Peter was reading Zahra's first published novel.

She kissed Hugh goodnight, which he enjoyed, and she put out the candles and the lamp in the kitchen. Hugh felt it in his loins and planned a moment alone with her to talk her into glorious sex with him, not a rape situation like both Padruig and Grigor seemed to think was the way to go, he wanted her to remember them, when they were married and how they were before poor Sakina's demise and to visit her grave that he frequently visited alone, in Glenmoriston.

It was the one place where he could cry over their loss, not only of their unborn bairn, but of their marriage too. He had never appreciated Zahra enough and couldn't understand why. Was it his obsession with Isobel Grant or had he found Zahra just too unusual, without any Clan credentials by calling her an 'out of towner'?

Hugh just knew that now, because he had matured, that he needed Zahra to be his wife once again.

The friendship and acceptance of each other, provided him with a new window into a different side to Zahra and her new life and her developing character. She was now disallowing the put downs, that she had always tolerated. Were they all always so unkind to this stranger in their midst? He was thoughtful as he was nodding off, but he couldn't help remembering the days when the two of them were as one and sexually compatible, before he allowed Padruig to interfere. He couldn't blame her for the breakdown of their marriage, any more than her children could blame her for the family breakdown, but it looked like her bairns were not sincerely forgiving, despite their words of sincerity.

His daughter, Isobel had deserved that strapping that he gave her, but Ali wasn't his son, and he didn't have parental rights over him, because if he was, he would have put him over his knee and strapped him too, if only for not inviting Zahra to his wedding.

He felt a sadness and empathy for Zahra. No parent can be perfect, he thought, most especially him, but Ali's visit had been a complete failure, despite Zahra being the model Mither to Ali, throughout the lad's entire life. Hugh planned to speak with him when he came to say farewell to her, despite Ali's masculine company from Glengarry, being Hugh Og, and Malcolm MacNachten.

They would both support Ali, that was obvious, Hugh thought.

Those Glengarry people all stuck together he had observed in the past. They even dared to criticise the Glenmoriston folk as 'clicky, introverted and inward thinking'. He preferred Glenmoriston any day to Glengarry, with all those midges. Hugh finally fell asleep convincing himself that Glengarry was a shitehole after living there for a while with Ruth Beaton, one of his wives. It made him feel better to call Glengarry a shitehole, even if it wasn't.

To the people who farmed the land there, it was home.

◇

Peter was due to go out for his medical supplies, to stock up on everything from bandages to medicine and was going to a specialty shop for those items and would be gone for at least two hours, he told Zahra who had some time then to clean up the surgery. The sign on the door gave him two hours off, to prepare for the next unexpected enema in the exam room. He hadn't been prepared for that exam on the previous day and that man had to have been constipated. It was rather disgusting when he remembered it. Peter cheerfully waved both Zahra and Hugh farewell, before he left, first thing in the morning. If Ali was coming around, it would be after lunch as he was going to visit a lawyer named Aounghus MacGregor, Malcolm's cousin, Ali had told his Mither the previous day.

Hugh was set to finish the additional privy, the stable and the small goat enclosure, then the neat backyard would be complete, before starting on the plumbing, inside of the big old house. He was enjoying his work in Inverness, especially the food, so he asked Zahra what was for lunch. She had prepared a beef stew, which was his favourite, with tomatoes that were ripening, in her own garden.

"Where do you get your beef?" Hugh asked.

"It's a specialty shop in Inverness, that only sells meat," Zahra said. "I know it's not as good as the freshly killed Highland Coo beef on your farm, Hugh. I am sorry about that," Zahra said, as she turned towards him, and found that he was standing very close to her.

"I'll bring you a coo then, next time I go back to the farm and kill it here, then you'll know for sure that, it's really fresh," Hugh said with that cheeky smile of his.

Then surprisingly, as she was about to walk away, he took her hand gently.

"Zahra, I do want you, I make no secret of that fact, but not to harm you, or force you to do anything that you don't want to do," Hugh declared.

Zahra was a bit taken aback, at first and was unsure of what to say.

"You and I were husband and wife, and we had a bairn together and we lost a bairn too, but now that time has passed, and you know that I am not the guilty party in that matter. I have been guilty of many other things. I had a wife in Chisholm country, and I was having an affair with Isobel Grant. I am sorry for all of that and for lying to you and for hurting you," Hugh said.

"Och, Hugh that was a long time ago now, and it is all forgiven, really. Isobel Grant obviously didn't choose to spend her time in the Otherworld with you and neither did your wife, Mrs Chisholm, or Ruth Beaton," Zahra added. "I do have many lovely memories of us. I hold onto those memories and think of us as a nice couple and not of what we became, so don't worry about that now. After Dihaoine was born, I finally recovered from the loss of our Sakina. It took a long time, and Grigor was patient and quite wonderful, up until then," Zahra said and as she was about to get back to work, Hugh took her hand again.

"Do you remember how we felt?" Hugh asked.

"Aye Hugh, of course I do, but I don't torture myself like that," Zahra replied.

"So, Zahra, how much did you love me, please tell me now. I won't harm you in any way," Hugh said as his hand slowly moved up her bare arm.

"Why Hugh? Why do you need to know that now?" Zahra asked.

"Because I need you, sexually and while I have no desire to hurt either you or Peter, I want you the way it was, in secret. No marriage, just sex as it was," Hugh answered.

"That is not an appealing proposition Hugh, after I've just been called a slut. Wouldn't that just be confirming the bairns' accusations?" Zahra asked.

"We are adults Zahra, not bairns and no-one needs to know.

Not Peter, not Grigor, no-one. Just like it was between me and Padruig's wife, Isobel, we had sex for years and years. We were great lovers. I was her greatest love, and I was Ruth's greatest love too," he said. "It frustrates me that the most beautiful of all of my women, being you, can never be my greatest love, unless you concede," Hugh said. "I never had a living child with any of my women, except you," Hugh added.

"What about your wife. There were lots of bairns and grandchildren too?" Zahra asked.

"They were not from me, they all had black hair, as you saw and they were all of my neighbour, not me," Hugh said looking sad. "I had spent too much time apart from her due to the Rising and then being a Jacobite in hiding, so I can't blame her entirely."

"I am sorry Hugh, that's just awful," Zahra said.

His hand then touched her face which gave her a jolt. Then he ran his fingers along her lips and told her to take his manhood and feel it.

"Nae, I have work to do Hugh," Zahra said as she was attempting to break away.

He took her hand gently and placed it over his manhood.

"I'll only ask you. Do you remember this inside of you?" Hugh asked Zahra who felt his hard member as firm and large as it always was and waiting to enter her. Touching his member and being asked that question, took her back so many years in time. It was like another lifetime, not even of her anymore, but she felt the very same emotion as she had felt then but reminded of the tragedy of her lost wee bairn.

"Oh, Hugh, we lost her," Zahra said and melted into his arms for the first time ever, acknowledging that each other both had lost a wee bairn on that shocking day, not only her, but Hugh as well. She cried and so did he finally, crying the tears of grief, for a lost wee bairn who was murdered, so gruesomely. She allowed him to hold onto her tightly while they both sobbed, for what was lost. The child was lost, but so was their marriage, because of the false accusations made against him. He had played no hand in harming his own wee bairn and she knew that now.

"I'm so sorry Hugh, I believed Padruig and Grigor that it was all three of you brothers who conspired to do it. I have never understood it. Please forgive me," Zahra asked.

"It wasn't your fault, you suffered so much too, and I don't blame Grigor either for taking you away from all of us, just to allow you to recover. I thought you would come back to me, but you didn't," Hugh said, and he wept even harder.

"Oh Hugh, please don't cry, it makes me so sad. I will make it up to you somehow, I promise," Zahra said.

"Will you be my lover then?" Hugh asked. "Or my wife, which-ever you prefer, we could hand fast, and no one need know, if you like? I'll even accept you and Peter together for now. He is a homosexual, so he will go back one day, to be with a man, so you need to protect yourself from that hurt. This is one way to do that," Hugh offered. "I could live with you both, take my time with the house. Accept me please Zahra?" Hugh asked again and held her private area and rubbed it, which she enjoyed and then he held her up against the wall and was inside her before she could decline. He was thrusting hard while holding her up by her legs. She remembered his way of having sex, it was frequently like this with Hugh or outside, or on a table, or on the beach, in the most unlikely of places. He didn't care where it was. His strength meant he could do it standing up.

The world was his sexual expression, and it provided the spaces for that.

It was glorious sex that she had forgotten even existed. Hugh was a perfect sex machine, there was no doubt.

"We can hand fast until we marry properly, but no-one needs

to know, please Hugh, for now," Zahra conceded.

Hugh and Zahra handfast that day before Peter came home and Hugh went back to work on the privy and the stables, while she was cooking and sterilising Peter's exam room. Once Peter was home again, they all ate lunch together. It had been a great day, and they all had smiles on their faces, until Ali arrived to say his farewells at their front door.

"I'll take this," Hugh said to Peter, guessing it was Ali.

"Hello Ali. Off to Glengarry then?" Hugh asked.

"Yes, Uncle Hugh, I do have some news for Ma, if I may enter and speak with her?" Ali asked.

"It depends on if you'll upset her again. Because if you do. You'll have me to answer to," Hugh threatened. This shocked Ali who always thought he was in the right and could never be criticised.

"I hope it doesn't upset her Uncle Hugh. Could you be present then?" Ali asked.

After sitting to drink his coffee, Ali explained that he had been to his lawyer, Aounghus MacGregor, who had sorted out the adoption matter and Ali was no longer adopted by Lord Coinneach MacAlpin and had returned his name back to Ali Gregor MacGregor, and had written out his Will, leaving the Glengarry farm to his Mither, in the event that he predeceased her. He also re-iterated that we were all welcome to stay on the farm at any time.

"What do you think Peter? Should we visit the farm one day?" Zahra asked.

"Count me out. I've had enough of farms for a while. You and Hugh can go," Peter said.

"Do you have a spare horse, Ali. I'm still borrowing Peter's?" Zahra asked.

Before Ali could answer, Hugh jumped in, saying he had a

horse for her, so Ali need not worry about that, but he made it known to Ali how displeased he was, that none of them, most especially Zahra, had been invited to his wedding and he may have to put on another feast, in order to feel included in his exclusive wee family and if he didn't, then he would simply be cut off from them all. Peter, Hugh, and Zahra all sat together waiting on his response and were met with, 'there would be another feast with all three of you invited.'

Then Ali joined us on the Team. Peter, Hugh Mohr, and Zahra all waved to Hugh Og, me and Angus, as we all departed Inverness.

It was going to rain, so it would be a wet ride back to Glengarry for us all, but somehow, I thought that Zahra didn't really care, if we were all soaked through to the skin.

43. Midweek and Grigor

It was midweek and Grigor had been to a tartan mill to buy a new plaid. He then went onto a barber shop to have his hair washed, trimmed it a little and shaved around his small beard and moustache, now trimmed to look very neat and sculptured. The barber plucked his nose and ear hairs, which hurt like hell, and his face was splashed with a pleasant smelling, but stinging liquid. He had already been to the public bath, so he was as clean as he could ever remember being. The barber also offered nail clipping for both his fingernails, as well as his tough toenails.

Grigor then bought himself new, knee-high leather boots, to go with his new highland shirt and his new plaid, he was set to win the heart of his ex-wife, Zahra MacAlpin. He would certainly impress. All that was left was a gift and he was unsure of what to buy. He entered a jewellery store where a lovely gold bangle was engraved for him, and he left with it boxed and wrapped up nicely with a ribbon tied around it. There was also a flower shop from where he bought red roses, which he knew that Zahra loved.

Grigor MacGregor then rode his horse onto the *"Heath Medical Practice"*, in Pebble Lane, Inverness, Scotland. It had a nice ring to it, and it matched his fancy attire.

He had only just missed the departure of his eldest son Ali, with all his Glengarry friends, on the Team of six horses that had blocked the entire lane. The neighbours were all starting to gossip amongst themselves, that their quiet Pebble Lane, was no longer the quiet wee lane that it once was.

With a little healthy nervous tension, Grigor told himself how handsome he was, as he walked into the Medical Practice, where he looked directly ahead to the desk where Zahra sat to take the patients' money and to make appointments. Nurse Heath had her head down, taking some notes, as he walked past Dr Heath's examination room. There were two women patients seated to his right, waiting to be seen by the doctor, but they looked up at the handsome man, carrying flowers and began gossiping immediately. Zahra must have thought that he was just another patient, so he was at her desk, before she had even glanced up.

"Och Grigor, it's you. I thought you must have been another patient. Have you bought the bairns here?" Zahra asked.

"Nae Zahra, I've bought you flowers, long deserved," Grigor said, and her ex-husband passed them to her. The patients were murmuring to each other, which then sounded very gossipy, with Nurse Heath receiving flowers from a patient and a handsome one at that. Zahra stood up and kissed him on each cheek in the European way and received the beautiful roses.

"Thank you so much Grigor, they are so lovely," Zahra said as she smelled them.

"Nurse Heath," called out Dr Heath.

"Oh, excuse me, Grigor. Please go through to the kitchen Grigor. There's coffee on and Hugh's out the back," Zahra said as she went to see what Peter needed.

Peter wanted her to hold a tray with all his bandages and instruments and antiseptic and suturing equipment to sew up an injury, she thought. She stood there with his tray with all his needs and passed them to him, as he requested them. It wasn't a terribly serious bite from a wee dog, so it didn't take long. She thought that it shouldn't be closed over, in her opinion but she dared not contradict the Doctor. When he finished, she let him know that 'Mr MacGregor' was here to visit. He wasn't too pleased because it wasn't a day for the bairns, not to mention, being a bit jealous.

Grigor spoke to Hugh first and they were both in the kitchen pouring coffee when Zahra came out and took that patient's fee and sent in the next patient with the patient's medical notes.

"Coffee for me too please before I have to work again," Zahra asked jovially.

"Look Hugh, lovely roses," she said admiringly and put them in a vase and displayed them right in the middle of the table.

"Thank you, Grigor, I love them," Zahra said. "Is that a new plaid too, can I feel it?" she asked. "It's gorgeous. Great bold colours, are these colours still Clan Gregor? Mine's different to yours. Is this a new colour?" Zahra asked. "Is that a new brooch too?" Zahra asked. "I still wear the old one you gave me from the field, every day," she said. "Why are you here?" Zahra asked.

"I have something to give you," Grigor said. Hugh was watching on intently, but he was rolling his eyes. Grigor was wearing a brand-new woollen plaid, he smelled sweet, was carrying a bunch of roses, now what else?" Hugh wondered.

He knew what Grigor was up to and he had to get ahead of him.

"What is it?" Zahra asked. Grigor pulled out a gift-wrapped, small box and gave it to Zahra.

"Can I open it?" Zahra asked excitedly.

"Aye, it's a gift," Grigor replied proudly. Peter walked in, just as she was opening the gift and surveyed the scene of her two handsome, ex-husbands, once again.

"The bill, Nurse Heath," Peter said, impatiently.

"Oh, sorry Peter," Zahra said and had to put the gift down temporarily, while the patient paid, and the next patient was ushered in. She then locked the front door for their lunch break with a sign on the door.

"One moment, Grigor," Zahra said, then excitedly opened it up. It was a lovely gold bangle. She read the engraving on the inside but put it on quickly. It fitted her narrow wrist, and the gold suited her skin colour.

"It's lovely. I've never had a gold bracelet, ever. This is amazingly beautiful," Zahra said, admiring her gift.

"Nurse Heath," Peter yelled again. "The bill please," Peter said, now becoming impatient with her. She wrote out the receipt, while Peter was watching on, as she was writing.

"Where did that new bangle come from?" Peter asked.

"Thank you, Mrs McKinnon," Zahra said to the patient.

"Peter, it's a gift from Grigor," Zahra said quietly, as she escorted the patient to the door and locked it once again.

"A gift? Can I see it?" Peter asked. She disallowed him to take it from her wrist, in case he read the engraving.

"It's quite nice indeed. I was looking at a similar thing, just the other day, so at least I know now what not to buy my sweetheart and kissed her, very deliberately in front of both men.

"Who would like to eat lunch now?" Zahra asked. Naturally they were all hungry and she asked Peter if she could go to the shops later to get some minced lamb meat as well as something to go with it, like Turkish pide, which she could make. They all might like something different, or she could just cook lamb with rice if she could procure rice somewhere. It was quite hard to get specialty foods in Scotland, that she was accustomed to cooking back home.

"Can you please tell me of a specialty store that sells things from other countries like rice and noodles and the like Peter?" Zahra asked.

"There's that Turkish shop. They might sell rice," Peter said.

"I suppose it's too cold to grow rice here in Scotland, isn't it?" Zahra said thinking out loud.

"I was reading your book last night Zahra and I quite like your style. It's different to anything I've read. Your facts are all correct. I've checked them all to ensure your accuracy," Peter said. "I like the way you weave the fiction in and out of the non-fiction or the other way round really," Peter said.

"Have you read the books Hugh?" Peter asked.

"Aye she was working on it when we first met her and so we were well aware of what was going into that first book, until she featured me of course then it got hot and sexy as I am, of course," Hugh said, smiling.

"Yes, well it does get a bit too much for bairns to read for sure, I am surprised they allowed it to be published where you come from. The Presbyterians would have banned it here," Peter said with some knowledge.

"Peter, will you go over some pages that I have written for the newspaper about my kidnapping to ensure there's nothing in it that would prevent it from publication?" Zahra asked.

"You want me to go over it without anyone else seeing it yet?" Peter asked.

"Aye, you seem to know what might be prevented from publication. What if the Editor is a Presbyterian?" Zahra asked.

"A criminal offence is in a different category my love, but I will do as you ask and not tell a living soul of course," Peter said suddenly feeling that he had worth, all over again and lunchtime became enjoyable. How did Zahra swing men around like that?

"I can even go with you to the newspapers when you have completed writing it, so they will feel more pressure to publish it, if you like," Peter added.

"Nae, bad idea Peter. I want it to be my story and not anyone else's. But you can take me there and wait outside if you like," Zahra added. "Grigor asked if there was any money in writing articles for the paper. That would be good, wouldn't it?" she said. "It would be like making money for nothing. I'd like to write a gossip column like who has just had a baby, who's married or betrothed, who died, that kind of thing," Zahra said.

"Very boring Zahra," said Hugh and Peter agreed but Grigor

thought it was a good idea. "Marriages, engagements, deaths, births, new jobs, latest news on any topic that interested people, even for the farmers like when its harvesting time or planting, so to involve the city folk more with the country folk, like the dates of the Highland Games in each town and any cei-lidh along the way, great idea," Grigor said.

"Most of us are born here in the one place and stay here, until we die. Zahra here is all over the place, the country, the city, the farms, working woman and having bairns. You are unusual for here, where we don't usually leave, like as you say in that first book about Isobel of Glenmoriston who was born on that farm, and she wanted to die on that farm, and she did. I respected that about her," Grigor said.

"I am not so unusual anyway. You keep saying that, but I just don't have parents or any family here, like Matilda had, so I can't inherit a place from parents," Zahra said. "And what about the Clearances then? They've all gone?" she said.

"You make me sound like a nomad, Grigor, "and she got up to wash the dishes.

"You shouldn't have said Zahra is unusual, Grigor, she is an ordinary, soft, kind-hearted and intelligent woman, who got stuck here because of me," Hugh said in her defence. "I'm sorry for that Zahra and for your bairns back at your home," Hugh added.

Wiping away tears from her cheeks, thinking of her three other daughters, who would never have betrayed her, she missed them terribly.

"They would never have betrayed me like my Scottish bairns have, except our two wee ones, Grigor. Never. Ali has betrayed me," she said, still clearly hurt by Ali.

"You always put too much emphasis on the bairns. That was your mistake, Zahra. The main emphasis in our marriage should have always been on me," Grigor argued, and he really meant it.

Their argument was interrupted by a loud knock on the door. Patients were disallowed treatment over lunchtime and were to attend the hospital instead. Zahra stood up to deal with the annoying patient, she thought, as she wiped away her tears from her eyes.

44. It Wasn't a Patient

"Zahra, my dear child, it's you finally," Coinneach said as he stepped boldly inside their old house. "Where have you been my dear?" he asked. From an onlooker, Zahra was like a stunned wee animal, just before you kill it. She was unable to speak or move, it seemed. Seeing Coinneach was a shock, but it was more than that, Hugh observed. Suddenly, Hugh was the married man again, handfast to Zahra, who needed to save her from whatever the control was that Lord Coinneach had over her. Was she hypnotised or just stunned, he wondered? He just knew he had to get her away, with some excuse.

"Zahra, I'll help you pack your things," Hugh said as he lied to Coinneach and led her to his bedroom, not hers, where he attempted to wake her from Coinneach's influence.

"Zahra, Zahra, it's me. Wake up," Hugh said.

Suddenly, her eyes were not glazed over anymore.

"Hugh, it's you. Why are we in here?" she asked looking confused. Hugh had to explain to her what had happened and the danger that she was now facing from Coinneach. Hugh wanted to take her away from the house, escaping through his bedroom window.

"Where's your long fur coat, gloves and boots?" Hugh asked.

"It's all on the back veranda for when I go outside," Zahra replied.

They climbed out of his bedroom window after Hugh put on his own coat, beret, boots and gloves. He held her hand and led her to the back veranda to see if they could get those essential items for her, as he knew that she suffered from the cold. Grigor saw them sneaking about and stood in the way of anyone's vision of them both. Realising that they were escaping, he knew that they would need money and his was all spent. The only money was in the tin that Zahra kept the Doctor's payments in, which he stealthily took. As Hugh was reaching for Zahra's big fur coat, Grigor passed him the cash, boots, and gloves.

It wasn't the time to regret his last few words that he had spoken to his ex-wife.

Ensuring that no-one could see them, Grigor saw that the two of them took two horses and they left from the stables and out into the lane, behind the house. Peter too was trying to assist the escape by keeping Coinneach busy but lived to endure long-term suffering from Coinneach's wrath.

Peter was raped that day by a very strong and angry Lord Coinneach, who wanted to punish the Doctor for hiding his wife, as he saw it. Grigor had to choose who to assist, his ex-wife or Peter and he chose Zahra and heard the horrible screams of the suffering Doctor.

When Coinneach came out of Peter's room, it was as if Grigor wasn't even there. Coinneach ran from room to room searching for Zahra, then he angrily realised, that Hugh had spirited her away. Screaming like a wild animal, he was pulling at his hair and his eyes were rolling backwards. He briefly then saw Grigor, growled at him, as the wolf, through huge, sharp, lupine teeth, then ran out of the front door, from where he could use his carriage to chase them both down.

"My God. Zahra. What on earth were you living with?" Grigor said out loud.

Left alone then in the house, with the flowers still in their vase, it was all a bit surreal. What a contradiction, first red roses accompanied with joy, then in less than an hour, a rapid escape from inevitable harm, but to where? Where would Hugh take her that Coinneach didn't know of already? Grigor himself would need to get to his own farm soon too, in case they too could suffer from the wrath of the giant brown wolf.

"Peter are you alright," Grigor asked a sobbing and naked

Peter, sitting in a corner of his bedroom. He quickly covered him over and helped him put his clothes on. Grigor tried to make him feel better, but he knew Peter had been raped and as a former homosexual, the poor man was devastated. Peter could barely look up at him, but Grigor held him just the same and made him coffee and sat him gently, back down to the remnants of his meal.

"Peter, I have to leave. Coinneach might harm my bairns on the farm, if I don't return. I am sorry but I don't know where Hugh has taken Zahra. Can you guess?" Grigor asked.

"Ali's farm maybe? It's the only farm Coinneach doesn't yet know about," Peter suggested. "Please don't let him get her. Oh my God, what a monster. Zahra was hypnotised, did you see that? That explains why she was under his spell and didn't know what was really happening to her son Hector. Tell Hector what he did to me. No-one else, just Hector and tell him to protect himself. I'm sorry I was jealous of the bangle Grigor. Will I ever see any of you again?" Peter asked.

"Of course, you will. You are still the family Doctor. Take care, I must leave now. By the way I had to give your takings to Hugh. He didn't have any money and neither did I," Grigor said and left hastily to check on his family, in the Aird.

Hugh and Zahra were galloping like the wind, to put as much distance between Inverness and Hugh's planned destination. Hugh knew they couldn't get to Glengarry that night, maybe the next day, so he drew on old memories when he had taken his former lover, Old Isobel Grant, Padruig's late wife, to make passionate love to her on one of Padruig's frequent and long absences. Hugh was looking for an old boarding house, and he just hoped that it was still there. He was relieved upon seeing light in the distance where he thought it was, in his memory with the chimneys all billowing smoke. There was good stabling for the horses, with a groom to feed them. The older lady who ran the boarding house, looked suspiciously at the two of them, even a little accusingly at their marital status. She thought they were immoral and unmarried.

"We are married, woman, a double room please," Hugh demanded.

Their room was nicer than was expected and there was a large bed, which made Zahra feel suddenly shy, but Hugh was rather pleased.

"Anything else?" the woman asked dryly, as she raised one eyebrow.

"Aye Ma'am, can we please have two meals and tea to the room?" Zahra asked.

"Anything else?" she said again with a tone attached.

"Aye, do you happen to have any lost property that hasn't been claimed. I need more clothes," Zahra said.

"Do ye now?" the suspicious lady said. "There was a port left here well over a year ago now by a lass, who never came back for it. You can look see, if it might fit ye," she said looking at her up and down as if she was fat. "Well come on then lass," the lady said, and Zahra followed her to where the woman kept the lost property. The port was a nice yellowish, soft leather one with 'MacLean' printed on the outside.

"MacLean?" Zahra said questioningly.

"Aye. Know her do you lass? Thought she was a 'lady of the night', that one. Cherry was her name," she added.

"I know her ex-husband. Do you want me to return the port to him?" Zahra asked.

"Aye take it. I am sick of it, takin' up room," she added. Zahra walked upstairs, carrying the port. Inside the port was a lovely woollen split skirt, that didn't appear to have ever been worn. There was also a pleasant blouse that she could wear, but most of it was sexy looking underwear, or tops which she showed Hugh and they both laughed at it for a while. Their meals were delivered while she was showing off the underwear which the lady ignored, with raised eyebrows, said nothing and left. "Zahra, we do have to leave early in the morning. That man has that lupine ability. He will be able to pick up on your scent, wherever you are. You have a wolf too, according to Grigor. Can you bring it into being now, to see if it can help us?" Hugh asked.

Zahra hadn't known how to communicate with her wolf, but she tried. Much to her surprise, the large wolf immediately appeared in their room.

"What is your name?" she asked him as he sat in front of her.

"Ulvy Stoirm," the wolf communicated through his mind.

"Can I call you Ulvy," Zahra asked.

"Aye, ye have a brown wolf on your tail, did ye know?" he asked.

"Aye, we do. How much time do we have?" Zahra asked.

"Sleep the night. Then we leave immediately," Ulvy said. "I will become invisible again, but you can now call on me at any time and I will try to kill it, but it is known as one of the nasty ones from ancient times," Ulvy said and disappeared once again.

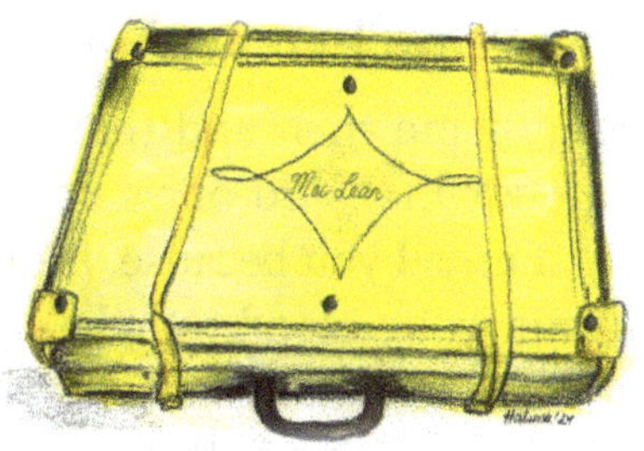

"But why do I have a wolf, Hugh? I never used to have one," she asked Hugh.

"With me, you had no wolf, with Grigor, you had no wolf but since you were with Mr Wolf Man, you have a wolf. Take one guess," Hugh said. Zahra had never disclosed to a living soul that Coinneach, in his wolf form had made love to her and had ejaculated. Had there been some chromosomal mix up since then, she wondered?

"Zahra, did he make love to you, as a wolf?" Hugh asked.

"Will you leave me alone to fend for myself if I tell you the truth?" she asked nervously.

"Lie down my lovely wife," Hugh said. "I do not judge. Just tell me, so I know. That is all," Hugh asked.

"Aye, then he did. He wasn't cruel to me at all. He was so careful not to hurt me. He entered me and it was stuck like that for a while. It was like nothing you can imagine. I was on another planet, not in pain but I screamed, I think which lasted for over fifteen minutes from memory," Zahra said, feeling ashamed of herself.

Sex with an animal, was indeed different for any of them and Hugh looked on and smiled at her and said that she was the sexiest woman alive. That wasn't what she had expected to hear.

"I wouldn't tell Isobel, or God only knows what she'd start saying," Hugh said with a lovely smile.

"I haven't told anyone. Not even Peter," Zahra said.

"So just me then and that's how my 'wolf woman' will stay. Your sex life is no-one's business, except mine now, my sexy one. I asked you because, it may have become mixed up somehow in your blood. Maybe that's why you can't have bairns anymore too. God you are so sexy," Hugh said. He rolled over in bed massaging both her breasts now she was alone with him. His big hands explored all over her lovely body as he remembered all of her. "You have lost some weight, but you are still incredibly beautiful," he said. "Zahra, I want you to stay with me now always. I do want you passionately. Can that wolf see us when we are like this, do you think?" Hugh asked.

"Ulvy please don't watch," Zahra asked.

Zahra felt at ease also with Hugh as she sat up to run her hands through his beautiful blonde chest hair that she remembered so well.

"I always loved your chest hair that grows all over you, I've missed it, Hugh. I did miss you, despite everything," Zahra admitted. "I never imagined us apart, but there we were apart, and I couldn't forgive you. Do you forgive me?" she asked. Hugh's eyes teared up again, but he said he had been a ratbag who had never deserved her. Grigor did, he had thought until just before Hugh had been waterfalled, when he felt that Zahra needed to be removed. He had learned of Belle MacGregor and Grigor going astray with her which had broken Hugh's agreement with Grigor, of many years previous.

"Just the same, I am a friend of Grigor's now and I hope he will still be a friend when he knows that we are married. He will find out Zahra. Are you ready for that?" Hugh asked. "Can you face him and tell him, or don't you feel committed to me?" Hugh asked.

"I can't tell him Hugh. I couldn't hurt him, knowing he wants me back," Zahra said.

"Are you committed to me? No pressure. I'll not force you if you can't feel it," Hugh asked.

"Can you give me time Hugh please? I have just escaped Inverness, leaving poor Peter behind, God bless him. We were such good friends. Let me come to you in my time and we'll be handfast in all that time," Zahra replied.

"Do you love Grigor, Peter or me the most, do you know that much?" Hugh persisted.

"Hugh, I'm tired of the competition between the men. Let me come to you, as I initially did when I first asked you to spend eternity with me. Do you remember that I asked you that, but you were with other women. I was foolish then, and I don't want to be foolish again. I did choose you however, but since then, my family has been with Grigor, other than Isobel, and she hates me now.

It's not easy now, it's complicated. Part of me loves Grigor, a big part loves you, another part loves poor Peter, but I hadn't a plan to marry him. I do love you. Is that enough for now?"

she asked. "We may all need to live together, so we can all see the bairns. Some other arrangement maybe? I must see wee Causantin and Dihaoine and they are Grigor's bairn's too," Zahra said. The events of the day were just too much then, and she wept for so much, as she tried to come to terms with not waking up in Peter's safe environment, and for Peter. She crawled up into the big arms of her man, Hugh Chisholm, who wasn't pleased without an absolute reply, as Peter too, wasn't but that was all she had left in her.

Coinneach and his family had drained her almost dry, and she was only just recovering when Coinneach resurfaced and why had he resurfaced, when he had a lover, a boyfriend?

45. Call Me Husband

They knew they had to leave early, but it hadn't stopped the passionate love making that only Hugh was capable of anywhere, anytime.

"I do love you Hugh," Zahra said. She held his face in her small hands looking at tiny changes in his face.

"I'm not too ugly, am I?" Hugh asked.

"Hugh you were always like the Celtic God Lugh to me, so handsome, like Lugh himself, but now you are a better version of Lugh because you are more human and so loveable," Zahra said.

"That'll do. I'm happy with that," Hugh said. "Hold me Zahra," he asked. Feeling her small hands around his member was ecstatic for Hugh who had waited for so long, imagining this moment.

"Och Zahra, I love you so much and you will be mine. At least introduce me to Ali as Isobel's father, your ex-husband who you've remarried by handfasting for respectability," he said then kissed her laying on top of her with one arm on either side. His love making over and over was rhythmic and torturously pleasurable until her orgasm was reached as she screamed too loud for a boarding house.

Paying the bill was one of those times when you do feel like saying a rude word to those taking your money and giving you side glances, like that woman hadn't indulged in sexual activity herself at some time.

"Never heard a married couple before, lady?" Zahra asked

which amused Hugh no end.

"Breakfast is included, Mr and Mrs Chisholm, through there to the dining room," she said, extending her arm in the direction of the dining room, not taking any offence.

She may have even liked the couple.

Mounting their horses, this time carrying the yellow port, Zahra was glad of both the thick woollen split skirt, as well as her long fur coat, boots, and gloves. It had snowed overnight, just lightly but enough to make it bitterly cold, as it turned to ice. She felt for the poor horses, as they trudged through the difficult terrain, until they came to more familiar territory. They were eventually getting closer to farmland and not too far from Glengarry. She didn't think that Glengarry could be this cold, but it was. They had removed too many trees she thought as well as the wildlife and lots of birds. The sky consisted of many shades of grey, but it didn't look like it should be this cold. She was hoping that hypothermia wouldn't get her. It was like a thief in the night for her that could sneak up on her and stay too long, like an unwelcome guest.

When Loch Garry finally came into sight, it was easier to follow and then all the way to her son's farm. Inverness then, seemed like a very long way away. The sorrow of the parting now was replaced with a kind of excitement, wanting to see her son's house, no matter how humble. She saw Marion's wee houses come into sight beside the loch, where Zahra had once stayed. There were local people there, milling around gossiping and she was nervous. Should they avoid Malcolm's Mither, if they could?

"Hugh darling, that's where Malcolm's Mither lives. Do we go around it, or straight past?" she asked.

"Hugh darling now, am I?" Hugh teased.

"I can call you what you want me to call you," Zahra said blushing. Darling was a word that came so automatically to them back together again, after all those years had passed.

"Husband," Hugh said. "Call me husband," Hugh Chisholm said to Zahra MacAlpin.

46. Ali's Place

Both Hugh and Zahra, with their weary horses, trudged through, snow, ice, sleet, mud and water, to finally get to that row of wee houses where Malcolm's Mither, Marion lived, beside Loch Garry and Zahra asked Hugh to wear his most unfriendly face, with a sternness about him, so they wouldn't get caught up in a 'MacDonald information seeking mission', from Bruce, Marion's husband. Zahra would hand over the port, thereby losing that responsibility, while asking Marion to wait until the evening or the following day, before giving it to Malcolm. That would allow them time to settle in at her son, Ali MacGregor's farm, without an unwanted visit from Malcolm. As much as she loved her good friend, it wasn't the right time.

Ali's farm was certain not to be known by Coinneach for many reasons, one of which was its location, another was due to it being so difficult to find. Once they eventually came to be on the right property after being barked at by many dogs, honked at by many geese, after asking suspicious locals, along the way, they cautiously approached the front door, as Ali wasn't expecting them and neither was his young wife, April, Kenneth's only daughter. Looking around, it didn't have that busy farm feeling to it, but it was a small place, just big enough for Ali to manage alone, Zahra thought. The homestead too was small, but sturdy looking, built from Caledonian granite and it looked like his wife had been planting flowers all around the house. Zahra would have planted something edible first and later, she would have planted something pretty.

She felt a sudden pang of sorrow for those rose bushes and flowers at the Doctor's surgery in Inverness that she and Peter had planted together and for Peter himself. She would never see those rose bushes blossom, she felt and there was sadness in that. In that instant, she wondered why she always did that to homes that she had lived in. Ever since she had lived in Scotland, each place she had lived benefited from her herb gardens, at least. She told herself she did it out of necessity because shops were too far away, or closed, or the herb was unavailable, so one had to grow it if you wanted it, but she had never planted roses, until she was settled in Inverness.

"Are we going in?" Hugh asked cautiously having already dismounted.

Zahra was still looking around reflectively at how her son and his wife had set up their lives together. It was cosy, safe, and humble, but nice enough. He was never going to be rich on this amount of land with so few cattle, chickens, and a few goats with just two small oat fields. Glengarry didn't grow many oats, so that wasn't too surprising. There must be vegetables behind the house, she hoped, or they would starve, with just one bad winter. Not even any corn crops, kale, or potatoes could be seen growing.

"Can you see any corn or kale, neeps or potatoes growing Hugh?" Zahra asked.

"Nae, tis a wee farm is all love," he said, and he helped her dismount. He snuck in a kiss, which was so nice, that he kissed her some more. "Husband, remember?" Hugh reminded her.

"I can hardly forget, husband," Zahra said smiling.

She then saw a wee face staring at them from behind the front door. Was it April? She couldn't remember what she looked like, but she did have red hair and freckles, so it probably was her. Hugh took the reins of her horse, while she went to the front door and asked if either Ali or April lived here or if they were at the wrong farm?

"Aye Mistress," the lass said. "I am April MacGregor. My husband is Ali MacGregor. He is down at the oat fields working. He'll be back soon, or you can go there yourself," April said, barely opening the door wide enough to be seen.

Zahra chose to take directions and go together with Hugh, to the oat fields. There was no groom for the horses, so Hugh continued to lead both horses. Ali struck a lone figure working hard, as he always did, and it did give her a pang of sorrow to see him like that, after parting, like they had in Inverness. Maybe she had been too hard on him? It must be so lonely out here, without any family at all, she thought after growing up closely with a twin sister and a house that was always full of people, coming and going. Perhaps this visit with Hugh would be good for him. At least he would have real masculine company and some guidance, and so would April. It looked like they both needed it.

"Ali, my son," Zahra called. "It's just me and Hugh, Isobel's Da," she added.

Ali looked up in shock to hear the voice of another person, let alone his Mither, of all people, all the way out in Glengarry. He dropped whatever implement he was using and ran over to her and hugged her immediately.

"Ma, what are you doing out here? Uncle Hugh," he said, and he shook his hand.

"This is my husband now Ali, can we please take you up on your offer and stay over a while with you and April?" Zahra asked. Hugh was thrilled at the introduction and was hoping young Ali would accept him, given that he was Grigor's oldest son.

"Of course, Ma. Congratulations both of you. That is good news. Have you seen my wife, April yet?" Ali asked.

"We saw a wee lass who directed us here lad, but I wasn't sure if it was April. She is a pretty wee thing," Zahra said.

"Would you like to come down to the house to have smoko then? I can have smoko a bit earlier than usual, and I can show you both to your room," Ali said.

Ali was thrilled at the company and the visit from both his

Mither, as well as Hugh Chisholm and it pleased him that Hugh was now his stepfather. Maybe there had been anxiety over Peter after all, having formerly been a homosexual, hadn't given her family a lot of confidence. Only his patients had fallen for the whole, 'married man' appearance. Then Zahra remembered all his patients, while they were stabling their horses. She just couldn't immediately forget her responsibilities in that Medical Practice, and she was certain that something awful had occurred there to Peter. Zahra decided to write to Peter, after they had settled in to tell him where they were and to ask him how he was and to let him know how much they owed him, because the money was nearly all spent.

Peter had been much busier though, than they had both expected.

He had finished the last of the editing on the lengthy article, written by Zahra MacAlpin and had already taken it to the newspaper in Inverness, where the owner had to be consulted due to the seriousness of its content, who in turn had contacted the police.

It was due to be printed on the front page in the papers, on the following day after Hugh and Zahra's arrival in Glengarry, but due to the article's length, however, it was going to be printed in three parts, it had been decided, between the owner and the Editor. This also gave the police more time to arrest both the mercenaries from the Outer Hebrides, known already by them, for their many crimes, as well as Coinneach MacAlpin, for the rape on the Doctor himself, as well as multiple crimes against his former wife, Zahra MacAlpin and Hector MacGregor, formerly known as Hector MacAlpin.

Zahra had all but forgotten the article that she had agonised over, so the evening with Ali was relatively uneventful, while Hugh and Zahra asked to bathe, then due to being weary from travelling, asked to go to bed early. They had been given a double bed in a lovely room that overlooked the vegetable patch after all, which much relieved Zahra.

47. The Newspaper

I hadn't read the early papers yet on the following morning, but my wife, Ailsa was at the Post Office buying one as usual, when my Mither, accompanied by her husband Bruce, came knocking on my door early and was carrying a yellowish coloured port.

"Morning Ma, Bruce. Care to eat some breakfast? Are you moving in?" I asked.

In the Aird, similarly Grigor was waiting upon his newspaper from young Simon, who always went to buy one for him. The only thing he was good for, Grigor would often say. Peter anxiously waited at his local Inverness newsagency for the first newspaper and bought several copies. It was there on the front page with a sketch also of Peter and Nurse Heath, drawn by one of his patients in her Nurse Heath uniform. Ali never bought the papers. Lord Coinneach had servants who always bought his newspaper for him and was waiting upon his copy for a little light reading, he thought.

"What's in the port Ma?" I asked.

"Zahra dropped it off just yesterday, son and asked us to give it to you, because it belonged to your late wife, Cherry MacLean and it had been left at a boarding house, just waiting for Cherry, all this time.

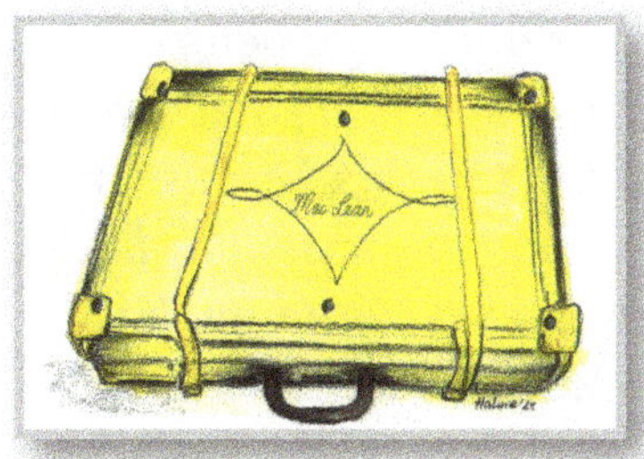

Zahra offered to bring it here for you and the boarding house lady was glad to be rid of it, apparently. Zahra informed me that she borrowed a split, woollen skirt and a blouse, which she said she could pay you for, when she had the money. They're currently staying with her son Ali," Ma said.

"Zahra is in Glengarry? Is Peter with her then?" I asked.

"Nae, an unfriendly looking man, with the name of Hugh Mohr Chisholm, Isobel's father and Zahra's husband," Ma said.

"Don't you mean her ex-husband Ma?" I asked.

"Nae. She was clear to say that he was her husband," Ma said.

"Ma, I'm not sure of your facts, but I need to see Ali anyway about corn crops, kale, and potatoes, today. You say they are there on Ali's farm? Both Hugh and Zahra?" I checked.

"Aye son, I'm not senile," Ma replied.

Ailsa arrived back from the post office and gave me the newspaper and started to go through the port. I'm not sure who was more shocked, Ailsa, at the contents of the port, or me with the front page of the newspaper, featuring Peter Heath with an article written by his former nurse, named, Zahra MacAlpin, to be published in three parts.

Kenneth then walked in with his copy of the newspaper asking, "Have you read this?"

The whole family read the article word for word, needing to know every detail of her life from when she had unfortunately had to leave the farm in the Aird and her bairns, except the youngest two, due to an incident with her husband, leaving her disabled.

The newspaper article started very simply, *"My name is Zahra MacAlpin. It used to be Zahra Chisholm, then it was Zahra MacGregor, but I was forced from my home in the Aird with a near total stranger whom I had met only once before but who appeared to be a healer, and I desperately needed a healer. I had no choice but to put my trust in him because my jaw was broken in several places, as was my nose and both of my eye sockets and there was a three-inch cut on my head, behind my right ear, that bled a lot. My neck and spine were out of alignment, but I couldn't remember all that had happened. The healer's home was on the top of a misty mountain, named Beinn Coinneach in MacKenzie lands, bordering also on Fraser land."* ....

Just seeing the name of someone you know in the newspaper is shock enough, but to also just learn from my Mither that she was one property away, staying inside the house of her son, Ali my neighbour, was jarring and serious. She wanted us all to know what had really happened to her and so did Peter. Equally something had happened to Peter, committed by Zahra's ex-husband Coinneach MacAlpin, on the same day we had all departed from Inverness. It made my skin crawl, thinking that we all could have been there, at the same time.

The separate report on Dr Peter Heath stated that he had been raped by Coinneach MacAlpin and Hugh was there, that same day. I needed more information.

"Son, I know you are going to just ask a lot of questions, but this is a little more serious than the usual everyday problem. You need to be more delicate than you are normally. Hugh is obviously looking after her, so watch your step," Ma advised.

"Should I come?" Ma asked.

"Nae Ma, you're a MacDonald," I said.

"See what I mean?" Ma said.

I was worried about going around to Ali's farm then, as I didn't think that I was that blunt as Ma implied, but maybe I confused truth and bluntness at times. I took the seed potatoes as well as corn and kale with me, to help with my reason for being there.

"Hello Uncle Malcolm, nice to see you. We have visitors. Ma came to visit after all, with her husband, Uncle Hugh," Ali said, looking happy at the reunion and I detected that Ali may have even been proud to call Hugh Mohr Chisholm, his stepfather.

"It's nice of you to help out lad," I said, forgetting to ask if he had read the papers. "Coffee or tea?" Ali asked. Hugh was seated at the small dining table with Zahra as I walked in, and it was uncomfortable. I was one of those who had betrayed her, as her bairns had. I found it hard to look her in the eye, so I found myself looking across at Hugh, most of the time.

"This story was in today's papers Zahra. We all thought you both might like to know. I see that you have written it, but Peter has had it published for you in Inverness," I said.

Zahra's face had been one of friendship at least but she immediately turned away and looked out of the window to the birds flying past, or just to see something or anything, more pleasant than what I had just said.

"Is it the complete story?" asked Hugh.

"Nae. It will be in three parts, due to its length," I said then realising that Hugh was taking care of her after all. "I'm sorry to tell you both also that your good friend Peter, was raped the same day that you both escaped from Inverness, by Coinneach MacAlpin and the police are now involved. They have said that they do need to talk to you both, when you feel ready, or if you like, I can ask them to come here as I know the men from Fort William, due to Cherry's death," I said.

"That would be better," answered Hugh. "I am her husband," Hugh said bluntly.

I left the corn, and the seed potatoes with Ali and as I departed, I heard Zahra begin to wail.

"Oh Hugh, poor Peter," she cried, with the saddest wail that I had ever heard from Zahra, and it made me want to cry too.

It must have taken some time for Ali and April to take in the news and understanding why Zahra and Hugh were both in Glengarry, married once again. Now because Fort William knew me, they were relieved that they had a local to go through, who could be trusted, so I let them know where they both were and to go through her husband Hugh, due to Zahra's distress and I could take them to Ali's farm, the following day. I thought it wise to take Duncan with me as an additional witness and the officers of the law were able to confirm all of the details. They were wanting to arrest Grigor also, but Zahra did not press charges against him, due to him being the bairns' father and was reformed. Their threats against him, however always weighed heavily on him and his face wore the look of a guilty man.

◇

Both Hugh and Zahra discussed the many ways by which to kill the giant brown beast, as the police didn't know what they were dealing with and if you told them that it was an ancient, shape-shifting being that could morph between wolf and man, they might lock both Hugh and Zahra up, for madness alone. Zahra had already thought of the silver bullets but acquiring enough silver wasn't going to be easy.

"Hugh, I have an idea. In the wee chapel in Cannich, there are pure silver, double candle holders on the inside walls, do you remember?" Zahra asked.

"I do, but we can't steal from a wee Chapel. That would be sacrilege," was Hugh's opinion.

She had forgotten that Hugh was one of those closet Catholics and when it came out, it was a surprise, because he covered up his religion for the best part of the time, due to the fanatic Presbyterians.

"Frasers sell the same type of candle holders in brass. We could ask Grigor Og, while we are here, if we can take them all down off the walls and replace them with the brass ones, then melt down the silver, to make those musket balls for the firearms. What do you think?" Zahra asked.

"It sounds too good to be true, but it could be done," Hugh said thoughtfully.

"As you say, we are in Glengarry, where Grigor Og lives in retirement and we could ask him and get his permission, also get some shooters organised, go to Cannich, see Hamish and

Hector, talk to your wolf Ulvy Stiorm and once we have a gang of men prepared to lay down their lives to kill it, we will," Hugh said.

"Okay, write down who we need in the shooters because we don't have Old John anymore, just Malcolm, Hugh Og and his gang, Grigor, Padruig, Alex, Hector, me, you, and Isobel. She's a good shot now," Hugh added.

"I don't own a rifle or a horse. This horse belongs to Peter, and I need a rifle. Do you think Ali has a rifle that he can loan me?" Zahra asked.

"I don't know, but we need to write this all down then take it step by step, because we need money to buy the brass candle holders. That must come from somewhere. So, money must go on the list of needs, as well as a rifle for you and a new horse. That old one of Peter's won't last long anyway," Hugh said.

"Malcolm looks like he has inherited from Old John, so he might be able to fund it all?" Zahra suggested.

"Why don't we rest up a while then and when we get up for lunch, we can get to organising it. Sound like a plan?" Hugh asked.

"Oh, aye please, I am already tired after crying too much Hugh," Zahra said.

"Just think of your darling husband then, so it will put a smile back on your beautiful face," Hugh said.

"By the way my sweet husband, no one here is surprised that we are married, are they? It's like they expected it," Zahra said.

Laying on their bed in Ali's house, they both made themselves comfortable for that rest, but Hugh always had a hand that roamed around, and around, which Zahra was really allowing herself to enjoy.

"I love feeling that it's your hand Hugh and not some monster from the Outer Hebrides," Zahra said.

"That isn't romantic Zahra, but I'll take it as a compliment, seeing as it's all in the papers now. Can we marry properly in the Kirk while we are in there stealing the candles?" he said cheekily.

"There's no Priest there," Zahra said.

"There will be on Sunday. How about you wear your best woollen skirt from that port, and we get married in front of a Priest?" Hugh asked.

"I'm not a Catholic Hugh. We would need a Muslim Imam or at least a Muslim person too," Zahra added.

"No, we don't, if you just become like me," Hugh said

"You never give up, do you?" Zahra said patiently. "Ali is a Muslim, he will do," Zahra said thinking where she could look up the right words to say for a wedding.

"Alright. Ali and a Priest," Hugh conceded.

Poor wee April wasn't much of a cook, so teatime mostly consisted of showing her how to do it, what to add and how much, what not to add, what cuts of beef were suitable for different things, how to cut it up, or mince it, how much salt was too much salt and that was without even trying to explain the role of both herbs and spices. Poor wee thing hadn't been taught much at home by her Mither, maybe because Ivy is an academic really and not much of a cook. By the time Sunday came, April was baking bread beautifully, her beef stews had improved, her herb garden was now exploding into wider varieties of now known plants with little labels, her vegetable patch was now large enough, Ali had planted the corn given to him by Malcolm, as well as the potatoes and Hugh built them a potato storage unit, so they wouldn't starve. The kale and the turnips were planted in a greenhouse, so if it snowed, they would not be affected.

Zahra told him to get in two students to help him, who could live in their house with them, after we had left, and more oats were needed planting where there was no bedrock. She also suggested that they plant fruit trees all along their borders, like green and red apples, pears, plums, nectarines and apricots.

They then took that list that she and Hugh had compiled to Grigor Og, before Sunday came around, for that permission, who was totally excited about it all, and he gave Zahra his spare rifle and ammunition to keep and a letter to Hamish to give her a horse from Cannich to keep, that he knew wasn't being ridden. Marion had also learned of them getting married from Ali repeating it here and there in his excitement, as he was reciting his part of the ceremony, as well as Hugh.

Marion came out of her front door one day, carrying a magnificent crimson coloured, Persian, taffeta, wedding gown.

"I just made this for you my dear," Marion said, like it was as easy as mopping a floor.

She was an amazing seamstress, as it turned out. It even allowed for the cold weather, with its many layers of warm petticoats and warm undergarments. It had a sexy looking, bust line that she was a bit uncomfortable with, but Hugh was thrilled to see her in a sexy looking wedding gown, in its crimson colour. Hugh had asked her once, a lifetime ago, if she had a choice of gowns, what colour would it be, to marry him in, and she had said crimson and he had remembered that, and Hugh then had told Marion. The measurements were perfect because Hugh was behind it.

◇

The big surprise for both Hugh and Zahra was that James Grant, from the Manor House, had prepared a magnificent feast in the hotel for them both and whoever arrived, to celebrate their marriage. An enormous suite, just for the two of them after the wedding, was provided also to stay in, for as long as they had wanted it, only with free publicity as his reward, so the press was invited too. Of course, Grigor, Padruig and Alex and all the family from the Aird were all invited, as were all friends and family from Glengarry, as well as Doctor Peter Heath, who was to be accommodated as well in the hotel, free of charge.

As Zahra's story came out in the newspaper each day of Zahra's horrific ordeal, it was a harrowing read and even Zahra herself, couldn't read it. And only she knew just how much they'd had to edit to make it suitable for ordinary folk to absorb. The gross and unspeakable parts had all been left out but not unknown by the editor and the police.

She just hoped that both Grigor and Peter could eventually be happy for both Hugh and her. The last thing that either of them wanted, was to hurt people, but it was inevitable, most especially Grigor and Peter.

Malcolm had his shooters all prepared, and the candlesticks were all changed over to brass inside the wee chapel, and the silver was melted down to make the silver musket balls, as Zahra had suggested. Isobel was one of the shooters, with her pistol that she always carried in her apron.

Zahra was yet to meet up with her big son, Hector, face to face, before their wedding. In preparation to see him, Zahra had acquired a mating pair of charcoal-coloured, Irish wolf hounds from Duncan Mohr MacDonnell, for Hector as a gift, before the wedding, which he adored. Hector was dressed up nicely in his Clan Gregor kilt with his wife Flidas, standing by his side, also in a long Clan Gregor tartan pinafore.

He looked very shy and emotional at the sight of his Mither, but he loved the hounds that she gave him, who took to him too, immediately. Zahra was overjoyed at the sight of her hero, Hector, after all of their time apart and she threw her arms around him spontaneously, which he then returned, holding onto her tightly. Both dogs were invited to the wedding too.

Oss'ian

"Ma oh Ma, I have missed you too much, too much," Hector kept repeating, starting to cry. "Can we both live wherever you and Hugh live? I am too lonely without my Ma," Hector said weeping. He had taken no part in Isobel's gossip and hadn't believed any of it.

"Aye my hero Hector," Zahra said. He was the Best Man for Hugh to hand over the rings, which had materialised from out of nowhere. It was never disclosed to her, how they were paid for, but both Hugh and Zahra were to receive a gold wedding band each, to make it known to all, that they were a married couple. Zahra thought that Padruig had something to do with it.

Niamh

The Priests arrived at Craskie farm, Glenmoriston and Ali was nervous but prepared with his lines for both Priests. Both religions had agreed to work together, given the two religions, represented. A lot more people had arrived to attend the wedding than was expected of the two most unlikely of people, who were to remarry.

Zahra's name was read out as Zahra Shushannah Grigor Chisholm, honouring both of her husbands, the exception being Coinneach MacAlpin. Ulvy was ready and he had forewarned them both, that Coinneach hadn't been put off by the newspaper articles.

On the contrary, he was enraged, in his lupine form and was out to rip Zahra and her new husband apart, hoping to enjoy every minute of it.

Ulvy committed himself to fight the giant, brown wolf to the death and had warned Hugh that in the event of his death, that it may leave Zahra feeling an emptiness within herself, for some time, but that was his role in life.

48. Clash of the Wolves

No one had ever seen, nor heard the like of it before, let alone inside such a wee Chapel, known only for its peace and tranquillity. All the pews were full, and people lined the walls to watch Hugh Mohr Chisholm, re-marry his beloved Zahra. Grigor Mohr MacGregor, although upset at the loss of the woman he had hoped would remarry him, had reluctantly accepted Zahra's choice and had taken their bairns in their best clothes, to attend their Mither's wedding to Hugh and sat in the front pews. No one yet mentioned what Hugh would be called by Zahra's bairns, but Hugh naturally wanted to be called Da. It could be possible to have two Das, at least for the wee ones, but the older ones, like Ali and Hector could most likely call him Dadaidh, which is Scots Gaelic.

As the Priests and Ali all stood at the front to read their parts of the wedding ceremony, Zahra and Hugh then kneeled in front of them, until it came time for the rings to be exchanged. Hector proudly walked across and passed the rings to the older of the two Priests. Hugh placed Zahra's ring on her beautiful long finger, a moment in time which he thought would never arrive and his emotions were rising, within him. He hoped he wouldn't cry in front of his friends. Then she placed his ring on his finger, which then sealed their marriage and their commitment to one another. They then kissed and both of their faces were wet with tears and the Priests gave them both a handkerchief. Not even the Priests had expected this level of interest, love and emotion, felt between these two, mature adults.

Just as the young Priest was about to ask them to sign the formal marriage document, the unthinkable happened. The tranquillity was shattered, when the Chapel door suddenly burst open and an enormous, giant brown wolf, familiar to Zahra, walked in, striding like as in slow motion, but powerfully towards the two of them. Before anyone had an opportunity to take out their weapons, the brown wolf had launched itself into the air, to attack both Hugh Chisholm and Zahra Chisholm, but its attack was met suddenly, mid-air, by Ulvy Stiorm, Zahra's tough spirit wolf that no-one was prepared to see, least of all, the unprepared, giant brown wolf.

The sounds of the vicious fight between two Alpha males in the small Chapel were horrendously, terrifying as all of the women in the Chapel quickly rounded up their bairns of all ages, to remove them all to the hotel and to safety, followed by the older folk and those men, who were unarmed. That left Padruig Grant, Alex MacDonald, Malcolm MacNachten, Hector MacGregor and Isobel Fraser avoiding the crush of people who were all departing hastily, and trying to load their weapons, at the same time, along with Hugh who was also attempting to take Zahra to safety.

Zahra's wolf was committed, as he had told Hugh, that he would kill it and fight to the death, and despite Hugh's attempts to remove his wife, Zahra couldn't leave Ulvy alone to fight the wild beast, determined to kill his rival. There was fur flying in the air and blood was spurting in all directions from wounds, inflicted. It was obvious that the brown wolf had not prepared himself for a rival Alpha male wolf and the first round saw him badly injured and on the stone floor, bleeding. He was still alive and lifted his head to attack once again, which gave both Padruig and Malcolm just enough time to load their weapons with their silver musket balls.

Their next round saw Zahra's wolf Ulvy, falling into a pool of blood, fur, and teeth.

His opponent, the giant brown wolf, stood back for just a split second, to take another breath, before he was to launch into his last killing attack onto Ulvy's throat. A shot then rang out through the air, making a deafening sound in the small Chapel. As Zahra went quickly to her wolf, who lay dying, she wailed as only the banshee can wail. Her wolf died in her arms, as she held him and rocked him backwards and forwards, holding his beautiful, but bleeding, lupine body. Hugh went slowly to his new wife to comfort her. The Priests and Ali were hiding behind the pulpit, but that didn't help the ringing in their ears.

Where had the shot come from? The brown wolf lay down on the floor, bleeding and was then slowly returning into the naked, human form, of Lord Coinneach MacAlpine.

Isobel Fraser was standing there, holding her pistol, where she'd had a clear shot of the beast. Malcolm was in disbelief that it was Isobel Fraser, who had destroyed the beast that had plagued the Highlands for centuries. As the monstrous wolf was becoming Coinneach MacAlpin, Hugh then aimed the final fatal shot into the beast's head to protect his daughter, Isobel from any threat from the law.

The person who was both Lord Coinneach MacAlpin and the giant brown wolf, was now dead and the newspaper reporter had witnessed it all.

Holding his wife gently once again, Hugh then spoke to her quietly and gently.

"Zahra, my love, I am so sorry. Please forgive me. I have been shot too. The silver musket ball must have ricocheted off something, and it has hit me too. My life is now leaving me, my beloved, please forgive me. I am sorry. Please don't marry another man. I am your first here and let me die knowing that I will be your last," said Hugh Chisholm.

He slumped backwards as everyone present, then realised that there was a third death, Zahra's new husband, who had not yet signed the wedding papers.

Malcolm, who was quick thinking, called the Priests over with some urgency.

"The Wedding Papers, quickly!" Malcolm yelled.

Putting the quill into his limp and dying hand, Malcolm assisted him to sign that Hugh Mohr Chisholm was indeed the husband of Zahra Shushannah Grigor Chisholm, and four others there present and witnessed that they too had seen them marry, as well as the shaking, crying, wailing mess, that was the true and tragic form of Zahra Chisholm. The Priests attested to their marriage as legitimate, as well as then reading Hugh Chisholm his Last Rights, as a Catholic.

Ali too then descended into the same grief that had beset his Mither and kneeled beside her in prayer and was joined by both Hector and Isobel.

Grigor Og sent word to James Grant to inform him that it was now a funeral for Hugh Chisholm and not a wedding and Hugh could have Henrietta's grave, inside the Chapel, which James gave up to him gratefully, as did Grigor Og. Malcolm agreed to make the new tomb lid, engraved for him.

All the while, Zahra was inconsolable, "No, God, no. Why did you leave me in this God forsaken place, only to be left repeatedly. Why did you take Hugh from me again. Why?" Then she started to tear at her garments, as she wailed and struck herself repeatedly, on her chest. What had once been her beautiful wedding gown, was now hanging in shreds when James went to their room to collect clothes for her from her port, adequate to keep her warm, as well as her long fur coat. It was a truly tragic sight, like no other. James Grant had never had a wedding turn into a funeral at his hotel before and he had to try and do his best, for a friend and because that would end up in the newspapers too.

People who had hidden in the hotel, drifted slowly back to see what had happened, only to find Zahra striking her chest repeatedly and tearing apart what was left of the once beautiful, crimson wedding gown. Dr Peter Heath was one of those who came back to see what had happened to his dear friend, Zahra. He helped James put some warm clothes back on her, while talking to her compassionately, like only Peter could.

"You'll be alright my lovely friend, you'll be alright. I am still your friend. You can live with me, if you want to, there is always a place for you in my home and I will help you get through this. Trust me please Zahra," Peter said. Hugh was laid to rest inside the Chapel in Cannich. Ulvy Stiorm was given his own grave, in the same cemetery with a headstone that Malcolm also engraved that read;

"A great and loyal friend of Zahra and Hugh Chisholm. Died in defence of them".

The newspaper reporter who saw it all, decided not to write it up, unless he was forced to, because it had been all too strange. It appeared as if a wolf had jumped out from inside of the bride. The police arrived to question him, and he wept saying it was too crazy to repeat and so it was decided that a stray wolf had crept into the Chapel overnight to keep warm and was met by a wedding taking place by morning.

When the reporter did tell them, they all agreed that it was an attempted murder, resulting in death, by a misfiring weapon, that the crazy naked man who was lying dead, was carrying on him, intending to kill both the bride and the groom, but succeeding in killing only himself and the groom.

No mention of Isobel Fraser, shooting anything or anyone,

made it into the police report, in case she was blamed for the death of her own father, Hugh Mohr Chisholm, nor was there any mention of another wolf. As far as the public knew, there was only one wolf that day, as Coinneach's naked body was retrieved by a greatly humiliated, Lord Cinaed.

Alex MacDonald

Only Alex MacDonald remarked about the appearance of who was once, Lord Coinneach.

"I thought his body might turn to dust, considering that he's been dead for so bloody long," Alex said, but Coinneach's naked form was still healthy in appearance.

"I don't think I'll ever understand the complexities of the Otherworld," he said.

He was told to be quiet by Padruig, because they were both amongst the living and needed to get back to their haunted, Room 203 before their names were included as having been present at the wedding.

Lord Cinaed had been urgently asked to collect his son's remains that day, which he did, as soon as he could, but due to the distance from the MacKenzie lands, he had missed the funeral, of Hugh Mohr Chisholm. He did take the opportunity to speak with the now quiet and spell bound woman, that was once his beautiful daughter in law. He had known of the shameful reason for her departure from Beinn Coinneach, while his son was making love to a young man, Alasdair Fraser, who had since left him to live in Wik and run off with a woman, whom he had married. He also knew of Prince Griogar and what he had been done to the beautiful lady, who was once Lady Coinneach.

Lord Cinaed told her that Beinn Coinneach and the mansion was hers now as her inheritance and to call it her own home, as compensation and he would pay her for her suffering, an amount of five hundred thousand pounds. Zahra didn't have a home of her own in Scotland and it did make sense, despite her brain not functioning well enough, to take in what he was saying.

He sincerely apologised for the suffering that the MacAlpins had all caused her and wanted to help in any way possible, while he was busy raising Coinneach Og. He asked if she wanted to see him too, which she obviously did, but the bairn was truly one of them and he might find her to be a stranger. She was offered paid staff in the old mansion and ownership of everything that his son had once owned. Zahra asked for a lawyer to put it all in writing and then she would like to see Lord Cinaed again, when she was thinking straight, as well as Mairi and wee Coinneach Og, but not Lord Cinaed's other sons, to confirm it, take possession and negotiate terms, if Hector too, was compensated.

Zahra stayed in James Grant's hotel for a while, visiting both graves, unable to leave Hugh, still in disbelief that he had been taken from her. She talked long and often to James Grant, to get it all off her chest. She then rode her horse, accompanied by Grigor Og, to briefly see her wolf friend, Wolfie in the Aird, and told him all about it. Wolfie allowed her to hold him for a while sensing her sorrow and he then returned to his pack. Being accepted by a wolf at least, gave her some hope. Her family tree hadn't mattered to him. She walked alone back to the farmhouse. Zahra was too afraid of rape, yet again on that farm now that two men were guilty of that crime there, if she stayed too long and so she stayed only long enough to visit both Fatma and Isobel and her two grandchildren Anndra and Domnhall, accompanied by Hector and Grigor Og.

Hector swore never to leave his Mither ever again.

Her two youngest bairns, Causantin and Dihaoine still wanted to live with their Mither, so Grigor said they could stay permanently with her, if they chose to, which they did and he relinquished custody of them in law, acknowledging his guilt and their devotion to her.

49. A New Reality

The four of them rode off together to Beinn Coinneach, to decide what to do with that big mansion on that cloud covered mountain, and all their lives together, leaving Flidas to look after the ponies in Cannich, briefly.

There was a Queen on the British throne now, Alexandrina Victoria. Zahra reasoned that life in Scotland, might improve for them all with a new Monarch and not continue to worsen, but she couldn't remember reading the early history of Victoria's long reign, other than further changes to the kilt. Grigor wouldn't like the new Queen's ideas but what did he like, after all?

Not too much would ever please Grigor, she concluded.

Zahra had given up making any further personal changes to adapt to life in Scotland, because no matter what she did, or had sacrificed, it hadn't worked out. Nothing worked for her in the harsh environment of the Highlands, and she couldn't smile any more with having lost Hugh and she didn't care anymore what people thought of her and her small family. She was tired of the continuous questions of her Clan origins, her family, her father's name and her genealogy, which didn't exist, because she wasn't from Scotland and her parents were not even born yet, in their separate countries of origin.

She had always been looked down upon in Scotland, even from the poorest of the Crofters.

She wondered about Lord Cinaed, waiting upon their arrival. How would he receive her and her family, as it was? He always had thought that she was an 'oddball', which he had verbalised. He had accepted her daughter, Isobel more readily than he had accepted her, as a member of their very peculiar and medieval family and yet he had made promises to her. She was yet to see if it was to materialise in law, as she had requested. She had never trusted Lord Cinaed from the very first day that she had met him, and her opinion hadn't changed.

As the four of them made their way up that treacherous, slippery track on the mountain, she halted temporarily to take Dihaoine onto her horse, while leading her wee Highland pony.

Hector monitored Causantin, who insisted that he could manage the slippery track.

The portly, Lord Cinaed was holding Coinneach Og in his arms effortlessly, while awaiting upon their arrival. The bairn was a big lad now. 'Almost too heavy to carry', Zahra thought. He was always going to be a big lad, but upon seeing him for the first time in a long while, she was surprised at how much he had grown. Zahra was certain, that he wouldn't remember her, but to her delight, as she approached the two of them, he reached out to her saying, "Ma".

She was pleased to see the wee lad again and hugged him too, as heavy as he was. She was surprised that the lad loved her at all, but she did love him, despite his rotten father and she had missed him so much. Zahra held her son and kissed his chubby cheeks.

"Oh, my sweet son, how I have missed you too much," Zahra said. It was times like that when her belief in a greater power was always going to be there to pick up her broken pieces and help her once again to put herself back together with her lovely small family who loved her and love was everything to Zahra, after all.

Coinneach Og MacAlpin

Lord Cinaed had arranged staff for their arrival, so the usual grooms were back and took their horses and ponies upon arrival. Mairi was slow to come out to greet her, at first, but when she did, she was sorrowful and curtsied to Zahra.

"Mistress," Mairi said. "I am so sorry Mistress."

The two women hugged, and Zahra told her, no curtsies, no bows, and she was just Zahra. Lord Cinaed did not agree, so it was, Mistress Zahra. Hector had always liked Lord Cinaed and the two men shook hands. Lord Cinaed also gave him his condolences for the loss of his stepfather, Hugh Mohr Chisholm. It always seemed like Hugh could return to them, so Hector hadn't yet accepted that Hugh was permanently gone from him. He was obviously taken aback by the condolences, as the family all moved indoors and out of the cold.

Coinneach Og could walk by himself, but Lord Cinaed picked him up again, much to the bairn's frustration, because he wanted to walk or run with his brother Causantin and his sister Dihaoine.

Beside the big and familiar fireside, there was a rather serious looking lawyer, which had been Zahra's request, after all. She was introduced to him as being Mr John Alexander Hamilton, from Inverness. Zahra had dreaded even being inside that mansion, which smelled different, but she tried to overcome her dread, as did Hector, who was also obviously uncomfortable. Sitting down by the warm fire, was at least a chance to warm their hands and her wee ones stood close by the fire, to warm their buttocks.

"They did well on their ponies Zahra," said Lord Cinaed. Small talk was awkward.

"Thankyou. Hector has been teaching them, as well as their father, so they should be competent enough, but I did bring Dihaoine on my horse on that last slippery bit," Zahra added.

"You used to tell me that you had a greeting from your time Zahra, but you didn't greet me like you showed me, that time,"

Lord Cinaed said.

The memory of that day bought immediate tears to her eyes, when she remembered happier times with her former husband, Coinneach. She had stopped crying for over a week after her husband's death and so it was a surprise to her that she had tears left to cry over anything, let alone remembering trying to get along with Lord Cinaed.

"You liked me more than I liked you at first, but that all changed when I grew accustomed to you and your funny little ways and I confess, I have missed you, Zahra," Lord Cinaed said. "Will you greet me like you did that day in the dining room?" Lord Cinaed asked.

"Nae, I will not, Lord Cinaed. I don't touch men anymore. It's nothing personal but please can we get on with the business?" Zahra said.

Lord Cinaed was trying to achieve power over her. She recognised it all now, but she had been so naïve then. No matter how simple and pleasant a hug might be, it meant more to the rendy old man, without a wife, than it meant to her, no longer seeking companionship. Hugh had asked her upon his death, for him to be her last husband and that was going to be how it was, for the rest of what remained of her miserable existence in Scotland.

The lawyer spoke up then, verifying her new name now as Zahra Shushannah Grigor Chisholm.

"That's correct" Zahra said.

"May I witness the wedding certificate to verify the name change," Mr Hamilton asked.

He saw what was obviously, a blood-stained Marriage Certificate, that was signed, as her husband had lay dying and he handed it back to her thanking her, with his eyes now cast down and ashamed, as much as a lawyer can be, she thought. Lord Cinaed didn't know the whole story in truth, only the one that was printed in the newspapers. He only knew that his son was going to Glenmoriston that day, dressed up nicely for her wedding. He hadn't known of his evil plan to kill either her or Hugh, so he claimed. He had never known of her spirit wolf, Ulvy Stiorm. To know that, meant you would need to know that Zahra had, at one time had sexual relations with Coinneach, in his dreaded brown wolf form and only Hugh had known that, and the secret died with him.

Zahra did have her questions as to how or why Coinneach had become the brown wolf in the first place. Maybe that conversation would be in private, away from the lawyer and her bairns one day.

The lawyer was a typical representative of the law, in many ways, but one. There was a humanity about him, which was unusual with these types of men. It appeared in all the paperwork that Zahra would receive the entire property in her own name, of Beinn Coinneach, which was enormous, including the land, the mansion, its Crofters and their rents, the home's contents, staff, stables, and all other outbuildings, except for Hector's horse stables and yards, so that he could re-commence his business there, in his name now known as Hector Cinaed MacGregor.

Hector was asked if he still wanted to keep Cinaed, as his middle name, which he did, so he was happy with his arrangements. He would be able to write to his wife, Flidas to help drive the ponies back up to that mountain soon, if it was all agreed that the family move back in.

"Would I still have two paid farm managers?" Zahra asked. The answer was yes, it was as before with Mairi and her husband, Callum and George and Rose MacKenzie who dealt with outside issues, such as fencing and livestock.

"Are my bees still alive?" Zahra asked.

"Aye they are, I come here every day to tend to your garden and I use it too. Lovely herbs and vegetables Zahra, lovely.

The Nannies are both at my house for Coinneach Og, but I can return one, because he needs one at my home," Lord Cinaed explained.

"Can I please look around the mansion, before I sign?" Zahra asked.

She wanted to see her former bedroom suite with her ex-husband and get the feel of what needed to be destroyed, to eliminate any remnants of Coinneach's energy, let alone that of his former lover.

It was even worse than she had expected, with no memory of her ever having lived there. It was now a homosexual boudoir that was all to be removed and burned. She asked if Lord Cinaed had any objection to any of that room's contents being destroyed.

"Go ahead, burn it all," Lord Cinaed said.

The art room was not a room that the younger two bairns could enter. It was all enormous paintings of male genitalia. Coinneach had become obsessed by that young man and his genitals, it seemed. She asked also if she could destroy all of those, to which Lord Cinaed agreed. She could no longer find one of herself in there. There were only three of her in the main sitting room, high up on the wall, near the Fraser sword. The one of her and Wolfie was there too, which confused her because it hadn't been there, when she left.

"I don't know who put that up there," Lord Cinaed said.

"It's a nice painting at least", she added. "Lord Cinaed, do you know why he wanted me back when he was still in love with that young man?" Zahra asked.

"He did still love you my dear, despite his obsession with that young man and when Alasdair tricked him, he went a bit crazy. He then realised his loss, where you were concerned, reading the papers especially, about his brother's treatment of you made public. He then seemed to deny any wrongdoing and had just expected to fetch you back and it would be as easy as that," Lord Cinaed said.

"Coinneach hadn't factored in your new life, surviving without him and he hadn't tried to find you at the time that you went missing. He didn't even report you missing. He just wanted to get back to his lover at that time, until there was no lover," Lord Cinaed said. "He was certain that you would crawl back to him, no matter what he had done in your absence. When he found you in Inverness, he wouldn't stop the pursuit to find where you had gone with Hugh Chisholm.

I know he raped your good friend the doctor, Peter Heath. I am so sorry Zahra for that. The police were here on Beinn Coinneach, searching for him, so he reverted into the wolf form, in order not to be found. That way he followed your scent and found out somehow about your wedding, but I don't know how he found that out, let alone where you were getting married. It's an horrific end to your story, I am so sorry, eternally," Lord Cinaed said.

"He wasn't himself anymore and he had lost his grip on reality," Lord Cinaed said sadly.

Zahra pointed out, "The marriage had already come to an end on the day of the two kidnappings. Hector was saved by the Glengarry army from being sodomised by him and then he was taken to safety, however myself and my youngest bairns were violently attacked by your son's mercenaries, and I was taken to the Outer Hebrides. As the brown wolf, Coinneach followed the first army that had kidnapped Hector, leaving me vulnerable. I had neither Hector nor Himself for protection then. He was humiliated by his brother who then took advantage of the first kidnapping in order to take me and my bairns, except Coinneach Og, then we were victims, too easily.

That's why it was never reported in the newspapers. None of you reported me and my bairns missing either, did you?" Zahra pointed out.

"I am guilty too of not reporting you missing, that is why I hope the amount I have offered you is enough," Lord Cinaed said, riddled with guilt.

"And my son, Hector, for the sodomy? What about his compensation? He is not a homosexual man," Zahra added.

"I will gladly add another clause for Hector then for a sum of two hundred thousand pounds sterling, if that sounds agreeable to you both?" Lord Cinaed asked.

Hector then began to negotiate. He would only agree, so long as his Highland Pony horse business was exclusively his only and not a part of any of the MacAlpin businesses and asked for a further 50,000 pounds, therefore amounting to 250,000 pounds sterling, to which Lord Cinaed agreed. Hector further insisted, that the land upon which his stables and yards stood, be on its own separate title, separate to the rest of Beinn Coinneach, in his name only, being Hector MacGregor. Lord Cinaed was a bit taken aback at the forthrightness of Zahra's, son but agreed to his terms.

"In addition, I want clean water plumbed to this old house for the kitchen, a laundry room and every single one of its many bathrooms," Zahra added.

Zahra explained that the small bedroom on the ground floor, at the rear of the house behind the kitchen area, was to be converted into a large laundry room, complete with the latest in laundry technology of the current day, with the water plumbed into there, as well as a small wood stove suitable for pressing and cabinetry for the household sheets. Additionally, a four-line clothesline was to be erected outside of that laundry room, which would have its own secure, separate door leading to the outside. Plumbing and all the renovations were agreed upon and to be paid for by Lord Cinaed, including the wages indefinitely for the laundress, who would live on site and the rest of the staff.

Zahra insisted on regular, week about, access to her son,

Coinneach Og MacAlpin and agreed to care for him whenever Lord Cinaed was busy or tired and she would provide him with his own bedroom. Then, if anything happened to Lord Cinaed, her son was to automatically become her full responsibility and the child was not to go to any of his other sons, while also expecting that Lord Cinaed set up an education fund for him, to enable him to be university educated with Zahra as the trustee on the account. He wasn't as pleased with all of the custody chatter, but he surprisingly agreed to it, and it was also signed off with the lawyer.

"Can I please see the library first?" Zahra asked before signing anything, knowing of the value of those rare books. One look at the library, and it was obvious that many books were missing.

"Will you be returning my books, Lord Cinaed?" Zahra asked.

"Aye, they were just on loan, my dear," Lord Cinaed said.

"My name is Zahra, not 'my dear' and please send your man for the books now and I will sign, along with the money too for Hector and I, if you have it," Zahra said.

His accountant came back with the money looking flushed, for both Hector and Zahra and his servants carried around one hundred rare books, back to her library and carefully put them back onto their collapsing old shelves.

"Please feel free to borrow a book when you wish, Lord Cinaed. Have you taken anything else?" Zahra asked.

His lawyer was looking increasingly disappointed in his client.

"Aye, there may have been twenty nude paintings of you Zahra," Lord Cinaed added.

"You may keep those on loan, if you like them, but I want them all back, undamaged, in the event of your eventual passing, Lord Cinaed with a complete list of all of them and their value," Zahra said and then she signed.

"You drive a hard bargain Zahra, but thank you," Lord Cinaed said.

Cleaners were arranged, as were removalists for things that she wanted destroyed or paid for by Lord Cinaed.

Zahra and her small family watched on as Lord Cinaed left in his carriage with his lawyer and her wee son, who she had arranged to see again on the weekend. Hector seemed happy with his arrangements, but his facial expression was sour, just the same as a disappointed grandson would be, who had loved the old man, at one time.

Zahra's small family watched from the back balcony that night, as the bonfire lit up the night sky, burning even the velvet drapes and the thick carpets from her former bedroom suite, that she had previously occupied with Coinneach MacAlpin. Zahra basically gutted that suite and even had the walls all re-plastered, as well as the ceiling and the ceiling roses.

The light fitting, with its many crystals was taken down to be cleaned and renovated by a family living on her property. She burned sage, incense and Udd for days to rid the suite of any evil, she thought.

Where the bedhead once leaned up against the stone wall, it revealed stones that had been built into the thick wall of the mansion, not yet plastered over, of an unusual variety that sparkled and had similar drawings or symbols on them, etched into the stone, which perplexed her. She had seen something similar in that awful lower level of the mansion, around the huge fireplace and wondered where they had all come from. She didn't plaster over those stones, only the ones around them because they looked so ancient, but in a good way.

Eventually, that one room felt clear of her ex-husband, but it was an enormous mansion, and he had dwelled there for an eternity. The most troubling part of the complex was the area beneath it all. She asked the MacKenzie staff to gut it all and be rid of anything reminiscent of medieval times to make it into something worthwhile, but to keep all of the iron that could be useful later. There was enough room in there to drive an entire herd of cattle on a cold winter's night, up through the MacKenzie entrance and she thought that was a good idea, as she wanted to breed Highland cattle. She sold the two ancient old thrones, so she could buy her coos.

While Hector attended to his ponies return to Beinn Coinneach, with his wife Flidas, Zahra went from room to room, noting down with Mairi what had to be removed, destroyed, sold, given away or just tidied up. Hector spent some of his money on improving and extending both his stables and yards, which received a coat of thick white paint and looked professional.

Zahra asked a Professor from the Edinburgh University to come and assess her books and value them too for insurance. He would prove to be quite an asset to her in explaining the myths of old, surrounding that family. The books were so rare that they were worth a fortune, so a locked door had to be put in place for the library. He advised her to donate some to a museum, so she pondered on that idea for a while. There were ancient medical books too, from the Beaton family that she decided to give to Peter Heath, as a gift to him because of his suffering and loss.

The poetry section was huge also and included the rare books that she thought no longer were in existence of Captain Alexander MacDonald of Glenaladale of Skye. Padruig would love to read those poetry books, but Zahra couldn't read Erse, even though mysteriously, she always could recognise the work of that genius. She decided to give one book of poetry to Padruig and sell all the rest to an historian that she was familiar with, to help with her expenses.

Zahra was due to visit Inverness to choose fabric for those drapes that she had burned, as well as thick woollen carpet, along with a new large four poster bed and the bedding for herself, and other matching bedroom furniture needed, that would then require a Teamster to deliver it all. She wrote to Hugh Og Chisholm to ask if he was busy, or the twins, Malcolm Og and

Hamish Og, in moving some shopping from Inverness to Beinn Coinneach and awaited their response. Hugh Og wrote back and said he was very pleased to hear from her and informed her that it was only the twins who were available.

Therefore, the best idea was, if the lads picked her up from the mountain and took her to Inverness and then delivered it all back there, so long as they could stay on Beinn Coinneach overnight, in both directions and to be fed and accommodated also.

This timing coincided with Hector moving his ponies back to the mountain, with his wife Flidas and a few friends, who were helping him to drive them. That one narrow road was covered with Highland Ponies, as well as their drovers and then the Teamsters, Malcolm Og and Hamish Og, both hoping for a girlfriend along the way. There were a lot of raucous exchanges between the young men, all in the prime of their lives, except the overweight Iain, who was also with Malcolm and Hamish MacNachten.

Zahra had written to Peter Heath from Inverness, also, to ask if he would like the Beaton Medical books and if she could visit with him, and maybe stay overnight, accompanied by her Teamsters, Malcolm Og and Hamish Og MacNachten and Iain, because of her shopping. He was so excited to hear from her that he wanted to return with her to Beinn Coinneach to help her to re-decorate the massive old place. She thought that was a wonderful idea, because it was an enormous job and his input, as well as physical help, with an old friend, was just what she needed.

Keeping herself busy was helping to take her mind off losing Hugh, but at nighttime when she went to lie down to sleep, his face would always be there and the tears then, were inevitable, sleeping alone now, in that enormous house. She could never put Hugh completely from her mind. Her love for Hugh had never left her but when he too revealed his desires and love for her, it was a dream too good to be true and it turned out to be just that. Too good to be true. She spent only a few days alone with him and now if she had known that was all that she would have, she may have done it all differently. She continued to wear both the ring that Grigor gave her after giving birth to Dihaoine and the gold ring that Hugh gave her on her wedding day as well as the gold bangle from Grigor.

 Her heart still ached, so much for the man she fell in love with, while writing a book.

"Oh God Hugh, I miss you so much," she would often say as her last words before she could sleep.

50. Twins MacNachten

Zahra was ready with her extensive list of shopping needs, as well as a wee bag to stay overnight in Inverness with Peter. She hadn't seen him since the day of her wedding, which was also the day of Hugh's death, and she couldn't remember the things that Peter was trying to say to her in her state of grief. A lot of it was a blur, once she had realised that her husband had been a victim of the violence too. She still had not comprehended how that musket ball had entered Hugh's body and who it was that had fired the weapon responsible, but then she would tell herself that it was better that she didn't know yet, at least while her heart felt so delicate.

Her Teamsters were the lovely twins MacNachten, Malcolm's precious sons. He had done a wonderful job of setting up his lads in the tricky business of Teamstering, with Hugh Og's training. The last time she had anything to do with the lads was when they were a lot younger and climbing over the back of the carriage and balancing like mountain goats, as only they could. They were a unique sight to see, as they were both identical twins, gorgeous looking lads, now about seventeen, with long jet-black hair, just like their father, but she had lost track of Malcolm's bairns. They bragged about their prowess over womenfolk, was all she knew and competed as to how many ladies they had had sex with. It sounded a lot like Malcolm, their father and Kenneth when they were both growing up in Loch Insh. Those two brothers must have been a handful for a Mither, whose husband had passed away when they were both young.

The twins were staying overnight on Beinn Coinneach, as instructed by Hugh Og Chisholm and she personally cooked the food, to ensure that it was to their liking. They also had liked chocolate pudding, so she was preparing that too, when she heard the Team coming up the narrow mountain track. The grooms had all been prepared to care for the Clydesdales and room was made for all six of them. She wasn't sure how many horses that they would bring, but she hoped they were all prepared well enough. The staff all knew that these were no ordinary Teamsters and were to be given special treatment.

The raucous lads jumped down from their high seat on the carriage, while their other number, Iain had to climb down, with some difficulty, with his weight being an added problem.

"He's fat Aunty Zahra," they said and laughed at Iain.

They all assisted in stabling their own precious Clydesdales, whom they spoke gently to in Erse. The horses were so well cared for, as all six of them were each rubbed down, with their hooves and shoes and feathers all checked. They were given a lot of feed, as they needed it, they explained. They asked for oats in the morning for the additional energy that they would need, going back down that mountain. At least the carriage was empty going down again, posing less of a danger but just the same, the overweight Iain's job, was to hang off the back to stabilise the carriage and prevent it from slipping forward. They prepared branches of small trees and hay in preparation for the slippery road.

"What's first for you, a bath or food?" Zahra asked all of the men. "Food," they chanted in unison. She was glad that it was ready, and they all finally went inside her old mansion. She indicated where they could wash their hands and sat them all down to the big and wide, dining table. Hector was with his ponies and had returned after finally stabling them all, as well. They did some masculine punching each other pretence games and accused each other of hogging the drover's road in general hilarity.

Flidas came in looking tired and washed her hands ready to eat too, followed by their two friends, David Mathieson, and Cameron MacDonald. Flidas was glad to see Zahra, once more and the two women hugged and Flidas called her 'Ma', which she liked. Causantin was watching on in wonderment at the two young Teamsters, whom he thought were like Gods, to be able to drive a six-horse team like that.

Dihaoine was shy around Malcolm Og, in particular, who she could tell apart from Hamish Og which Zahra wasn't able to do at first, then she wanted to sit right next to Malcolm Og at the dinner table and said boldly, "I'm Dihaoine."

"Really, Miss Dihaoine, I am Malcolm Og, because my father is Malcolm Mohr, who you may have met before. I'm pleased to meet you," he said, and he shook her tiny wee hand. She may have fallen in love with Malcolm's oldest twin, and he was as smooth as butter. Poor wee lass. 'A broken heart would plague her for a lifetime, if she followed the twins MacNachten,' Zahra thought. But she didn't interfere in the lassies first ever interest shown in the opposite sex at the age of just four, nearly five. Ali had arranged his betrothal when April was very young, so it did happen in this country. Zahra wondered if Malcolm Og could mend his adventurous ways, so she asked him directly.

"So, Malcolm have you met any lassies along the way this time?" Zahra asked. Unexpectedly, he was reluctant to reply.

"Och, Malcolm," was Hamish's response, "I saw you going into Mrs MacNab's wee Croft, and you weren't there for her cupcakes, while her husband was in the oat fields," he said, revealing his brother's antics.

"I was in there for business as well as her cupcakes, I'll have you know Hamish," he answered, and both Iain and Hamish both laughed, as well as Hector.

"Bullshit, cupcakes, my arse," said Hamish Og.

Malcolm Og then appeared a little annoyed.

"Shut up brother. And you weren't screwing Mrs Henderson either I suppose? You were just eating cupcakes with her too, is it?" Malcolm Og asked.

"Nae, I was screwing her 'tis true. Her husband is never there, and she likes me, she does," Hamish Og said.

"Who's for dessert, our handsome Teamster lads?" Zahra asked.

Cleverly she had found out that young Malcolm Og did like her wee daughter and didn't want her to think poorly of him. Knowing wee Dihaoine, she would never think poorly of him anyway and covering it up, made no difference to her. He had captured her heart already.

"Dihaoine, why are you staring at Malcolm Og?" Causantin asked Dihaoine.

"None of your business Causantin," Dihaoine said.

After serving them all dessert and a hot beverage of their choice, like hot chocolate, she asked Mairi to start preparing baths in two separate rooms, one for the lassies and one for the lads. Mairi's husband was there to help her, so they both prepared the hot water to be ready on time for the guests, who were very amusing. Mairi's husband, Callum, was enjoying the banter so much that his wife had to kick him into action. Baths were completed in a flash, and they were shown to their rooms, but the lads asked for musical instruments, when everyone else thought it was bedtime.

But all those young men wanted to continue well into the night.

Zahra asked Mairi to put the young ones to bed while Hector, David, Malcolm Og, Hamish Og and Cameron were directed to the large cupboard, where all the musical instruments were kept. Zahra advised them not to play Coinneach's ancient pipes, in case they were diseased, so she confiscated them and decided to take them to Inverness to have them restored.

"Use my uilleann pipes lads. They're new and I can't play them yet anyhow," Zahra said. All the other young men took out a fiddle, a flute, two bodhrans and the newer highland pipes.

Flidas went off to bed, too tired for more socialising, but she had hoped that Hector would follow her.

Zahra had started to drift off to sleep, while the young men entertained themselves. Singing was even heard in the most lilting of sounds. The twins really had hidden talent. When Flidas was tired of waiting for Hector, she went into Zahra's temporary bedroom and asked to sleep with Zahra. Her room was warmer, and Flidas' room was so dark, she said. She was a bit afraid of the dark, so she climbed in beside Zahra to sleep. While in Inverness, Flidas was going to stay behind and help care for both Causantin and Dihaoine, as well as the ponies. The ladies both chatted a bit about how the bairns liked their eggs cooked in the mornings and then Zahra fell asleep easily, for the first time since moving back to the mountain.

The twins MacNachten could even sing. Who would have thought?

Bundling up the old pipes for restoration to take to Inverness, the twins asked Zahra if they could bring the good instruments with them too and return them when they all arrived back home. Zahra hoped Peter wouldn't mind if they were noisy at his place in Inverness. Overall, the twins MacNachten liked Zahra and were pleased with how they all got along so well. They liked how easy she was to get along with, despite knowing of her recent loss. They especially loved the huge mansion on the mountain and how much noise they could make, without disturbing neighbours. They loved the spaciousness of it. Zahra was pleased that their energy filled every corner of the mansion, further removing any bad energy that remained of Coinneach MacAlpin.

Breakfast was quieter the next day and Mairi was glad of that. Zahra wondered what it was like for Ailsa every day, living with Malcolm's big boys, who never seemed to tire and were forever loud. However, Malcolm Og had revealed another side to himself in liking Zahra's daughter, who once again, sat beside him at the breakfast table. He was old enough to be married already, so wee Dihaoine was indeed hopeful, if she expected him to wait until she turned twelve years old.

Dihaoine MacGregor

"Did you like staying here with us, Malcolm?" asked Dihaoine. "I'll see you again when you come back, do you want to see me? I like you Malcolm," she said boldly.

The sweet bairn was very brave to speak up.

"Aye, Miss Dihaoine. I love staying here with your family. Of course, I want to see you too," he said and stopped at that without pledging how much he liked her.

However, he did approach her Mither, Zahra and declared his interest in a betrothal with Dihaoine with a view to marriage, when she became of age, like her son, Ali had done with April, if Dihaoine still felt the same way.

He asked Zahra if he was acceptable to her family, but it would mean upon marriage, that Dihaoine would probably need to live in Glengarry.

"What if I build Clydesdale stables for you both, then you wouldn't need to live in Glengarry?" Zahra asked.

Zahra was happy to hear his offer of a betrothal, but he would need to ask his parents as well and then, even though she agreed, they would all have to agree as one family, as April's family had. Then, it would be drawn up in a contract that wasn't too serious if either party needed to withdraw, for a genuine reason. Zahra also declared her dowry amount of ten thousand pounds for Dihaoine's spouse, paid at the time of an actual marriage. She only had one stipulation and that was the wedding wasn't to be held in Cannich.

Hector was staying on the mountain, while everyone else was in Inverness, because he had to feed his two Irish Wolfhounds and Hugh's three Collies, that had come with them. In total, there were five beautiful dogs. Hector worried about breeding, because the male Collie wanted to mate his female wolf hound, which was causing some tension between the dogs. His dogs were wonderful guard dogs, while the Collies were better at rounding up sheep. Zahra hoped the collies could round up cattle, as old as they were now, after she acquired them, because she wanted at least sixty highland coos, but she would need Grigor's help at the saleyard, in Inverness. That was another job after the house was completed.

While Zahra was in Inverness, the plasterers and the painters continued their huge job of renewal on the old place, which included the ceilings and the ceiling roses. She was glad to be away from the smell of it, for a while. She planned to buy Turkish light fixtures to replace most of them, that were still candle lit. Her kitchen also was to be completely gutted, and a new kitchen built with a lot more cabinets, almost up to the ceil-ing and including an enormous walk-in pantry and she hoped the new kitchen would be completed by the time that she came home, with its huge, new wood stove. The Frasers from Fraser Ville were doing all her cabinetry and had planned the new plumbing into the kitchen.

There was food to cook for hungry Teamsters when they came back, but more modern appliances had become available, since Mairi had her old fire in place. Zahra had bought a woodstove, considered modern, but twice the size as the normal household one, as there were often many people to cook for. Mairi was told that if the kitchen wasn't ready, she was to cook in her own home, then bring it up, when they returned. Zahra had also given the husband-and-wife team, their own quarters in the mansion for when they worked late, in the new wing, away from family and on the top floor. She allocated rooms to other servants, like two cleaner lassies who became permanent, a window cleaner man for inside and out who was also the chimney sweep for all the many old fireplaces. He then could co-ordinate when he was cleaning the filthy chimneys that were dangerously dirty, followed afterwards by the windows.

Zahra also employed the laundress who had to take down all of the many household drapes and laundered and pressed them all, as well as all the clothes, sheets, and general bed linen. It

was an enormous job, and it required an additional laundress who lived in too, in the same room. The main laundress in charge, was Anastacia Fraser, a strong, middle-aged widow, who went home to her cat on the weekends and attended Kirk. Her off-sider was her niece, Francine Fraser. Mairi managed all of the servants' quarters and ensured that it remained decent, moral, and clean, with no visitors or alcohol permitted. Coinneach had disallowed servants to sleep under his roof at all. Zahra thought that to be impractical, so long as they kept to themselves when they were not working, and her own life remained private.

They all had to sign a privacy document, agreeing to maintaining the confidentiality and dignity of her family and her home.

When the Team arrived in Inverness, Zahra was dropped outside her first shop on her list, while the lads took the Team to stable them and to check their shoes. They would meet up again once all the shopping was complete, then they would take it all to Peter Heath's Medical Practise, where they were to spend the night. When they finally arrived, after an exhausting day's shopping, Zahra ensured her belongings could not be stolen and was re-assured that it was all watertight, given she had bought one dozen mattresses and duvets, two dozen sets of very expensive sheets, two dozen duck down pillows, as well as a huge four poster bed which was rather wide and long and would require the lads to carry upstairs for her, when they arrived home. She had also bought all the matching furniture to go with the beds. Some of it had lovely carved oak on the doors of each draw or each cupboard door. It had a Celtic feel about it.

She had gone to the Turkish shop in Inverness too, to replace several of the shabby light fittings, that were candle lit. The ones she had purchased were pretty but required careful handling, so they wouldn't break. One Turkish chandelier was to be in the entrance of the man-sion with its matching one further inside the huge room with a long drop from the high ceiling. She also bought two dozen new Turkish and Persian floor rugs of varying sizes to match the new décor, as the old floor rugs were almost thread-bare. She hadn't noticed how poor the home's condition really was in when she was living there. Had it become worse since she had left maybe?

The other Turkish light fitting, which had more colour, went over the dining room table, and had wall lamps to match and two free-standing lamps as well. The house would then be much better lit, as well as in better condition, clean and Zahra's idea of beautiful.

Zahra bought an entire range of matching, hand painted Turkish porcelain plates, bowls, cups, saucers and serving plat-ters for those busy times with many guests.

She decided to keep the heavy old wooden dining table but had all the chairs re-upholstered to be cushioned and covered in velvet, to be more comfortable to sit on. She had also bought four big beautiful new armchairs to be arranged by the fire-side, as well as a long couch which would sit on top of one of the newly purchased, Turkish floor rugs. New drapes were in place there to match the colour scheme. It was coming together at last, she felt.

Before arriving back home on Beinn Coinneach, the chimney at that popular fireplace would have been thoroughly cleaned, as well as all the windows, before the team of plasterers and painters had started in that room, as well as the ceiling. But she prayed that they would all be finished as well, by the time she was back home again.

She had a plan to halve the enormous sitting room by way of a partition to keep it all warmer too when the front door was opened.

51. My Friend Peter

Then there was her friend, the kindly Peter Heath. As they approached his house in Inverness, Zahra was uneasy remembering, all of what had occurred there.

Zahra had his rare books to give to him as a gift of thank you, but she suddenly felt nervous, with her nurse's uniform to return to Peter. It would be the first time going back there, since she and Hugh had to escape through Hugh's bedroom window and out the back lane on Peter's horses. She only recalled then that she had been hypnotised by Coinneach MacAlpine, upon his unwelcome arrival, and the end of her life as Nurse Heath.

The lads had known of a stabling facility nearby for the Clydesdales, which meant leaving all that precious shopping there, inside the carriage.

The lads delegated Iain to stand guard over it all, as well as the horses, and to sleep with it all. They would bring down his dinner to him they said, but he knew his place and the twins were in charge. Iain would miss out on the music night this time, if they chose to have one, now they were down to Iain, David, and Cameron. It would be a much quieter music night and Zahra hoped it would include some of their lovely singing voices which had been a well-kept secret, until this visit to her. Mairi had also given Zahra an enormous list of ingredients that she needed to cook with, to add to the huge pantry, so all that food shopping came with them also, into Peter's house, in case they had mice.

On approaching Peter's house, still uneasy, she saw their lovely roses in full bloom and suddenly she felt emotional, at the sight of them. How could she ever forget how happy they both were in planting their new garden in front of the Medical Practice, when she was Nurse Heath? But she had forgotten those roses until then. Her brain had gone into survival mode on that terrible day, as she felt under threat. She couldn't physiologically think of anything, that she may once have enjoyed, until she felt safe enough, once again. Maybe that was what this visit to Peter was all about, not décor. It was her brain releasing herself from fear and from the next threat.

Peter Heath and Zahra had enjoyed a simple, but happy life together and she was learning nursing, as she went, so there was a sense of satisfaction too, in having learned new things about medicine. They had been happy.

But now it was different, as she began to get a real sense of Peter's loss and Peter's pain too, not only of having been raped, but in losing her and taking it so graciously, as he did. Would he want her to share his bed with him, was her next question that concerned her and so it would have to be addressed early on, unless he had found another of course? Could they, as friends, just sleep alongside each other for comfort, warmth, and friendship, with no sexual element? 'Would Hugh have minded'? she asked herself.

The aroma from the roses was uplifting as she walked in through the lovely wrought iron gate, and it put the first smile on her face she'd had since Hugh's death. Zahra wondered if she always appeared miserable to others, or at best, serious or thoughtful. Why hadn't she thought to buy rose bushes too, for her new home? What a difference that would make to the whole feeling of that ordinary looking mansion, as well as the beautiful aromas from each coloured rose as she smelled each one?

The MacNachten twins were impatient to enter through Peter's front door and were confused as to why there was a delay, caused by the roses. Zahra appeared to be in a world of her own, temporarily. Eventually she just opened the front door and walked right in, to find a few patients seated on the right, as they always had. It was like walking back in time for her. For the lads they just followed her, feeling a little confused.

"Nurse Heath, you're back," one patient exclaimed. At that remark, the Doctor's exam door opened quickly, and Peter rushed out to greet her.

"Zahra," Peter exclaimed. He was so thrilled and excited to see her that he was overcome with emotion and held her close to himself. She hadn't allowed anyone to touch her, let alone wrap themselves around her so completely, not looking like letting her go. The twins were just watching on with a lot of interest and offered to go into the kitchen and make the coffee together. The two lady patients said they'd been looking after the Doctor for her by bringing him meals and cakes or scones, every day. They said they'd leave them to their privacy and come back the next day. The door was locked after them.

Peter took her to the kitchen and cradled her on his knee, still delighted to see his friend. While holding her around her mid waist, Peter noticed something that felt different in her body shape. He then felt her lower abdomen and asked her if she was with child.

"With child?" Zahra repeated. "Nae, I can't have bairns anymore. I told you that," Zahra said.

"What do you think lads?" Peter asked both Malcolm Og and Hamish Og.

"Show them Zahra," Peter said unashamedly.

Zahra revealed her stomach to the young lads who both agreed.

"With child. That's what Ailsa looked like, when she was with child," Hamish Og said.

"Where's the looking glass?" Zahra asked. She then looked into Peter's long looking glass.

"I just ate too much last night Peter," Zahra said dismissively.

"When did you last have your courses?" Peter asked.

"I don't know. I haven't paid much attention to myself, to be honest my friend, but now you have me worried," Zahra said.

"Who did you make love with last?" Peter asked, hoping it had been him.

"Hugh," Zahra replied, looking sad.

"When?" Peter asked.

"The night before our wedding. His death," Zahra replied.

"Oh, please Peter, surely not? How can I raise a wee bairn without him?" Zahra asked and then began to cry.

"Please, be wrong Peter. How can you prove it?" she asked, choking back her tears.

"Can I please have a sample of your urine?" Peter asked.

"Yuk, that's disgusting," said Hamish Og.

"What can the urine reveal?" asked Malcolm Og who was more interested in the science of the question.

"It's an old test young Malcolm. Piss Prophets were who they were called, by identifying the colour of the lady's urine, which had a cloud upon the surface if there was a bairn coming," Peter said.

"Are you a 'Piss Prophet' then?" Zahra asked.

"Not really, although I have done it once before, in Medical School in London," Peter said. "But I was right. She was with child," Peter said.

"Alright. I'll pee into the chamber pot for you, and you can look for that cloud," Zahra said.

"This is going to put me off my dinner," said Hamish Og.

"Shut up, Hamish. It's science," Malcolm Og said.

Taking a very good look at Zahra's urine, Peter was convinced that he saw that cloud and that she would soon be experiencing morning sickness. He was certain that she was with Hugh's bairn. Dinner was much quieter then, than the night before, contemplating having a bairn, without Hugh. It was both a gift from Hugh and a burden. How could she raise the child alone on Beinn Coinneach? She imagined what he or she would look like with his lovely curly blonde hair and the wee bairn would be beautiful, that's true, but she had never even tried to raise a wee bairn alone, as a widow. She had yet to come to terms that she was now a widow, and that Hugh was never coming back, let alone having no-one to share her wee bairn with.

"Zahra, I can help you. Don't worry," Peter said.

Zahra then gave him the rare books, which he absolutely loved and finally they sat down for dinner.

"Oh shite. We forgot Iain," Hamish Og said. All the talk of being with child and pissing in a pot made everyone forget poor Iain, alone with the Clydesdales and the shopping, as well as thirsty and hungry.

They quickly then ran some food and a flask of coffee up to him with apologies and came back. The two lads got the uille-ann pipes and the flute out and sang a sad Gaelic song which made it even worse for Zahra, thinking of what was growing within her which was not going away and she had to deal with it, eventually. It was fortunate she had already completed the heavy work in the mansion on top of Beinn Coinneach.

◊

Peter had arranged a locum to replace him while he went to Beinn Coinneach with Zahra. He thought it would only be for a week or two, but he had the distinct impression that it could be for much longer. If only the wee bairn had been his, he thought. He had so wanted a wee bairn with his beloved Zahra, but only Hugh had managed to miraculously achieve it.

Peter didn't even know how they had grown close once again, while Hugh was living and working there in his house, but Hugh had been her first husband and her last, she said. She might change her mind when people started to gossip about her being heavy with child, without a husband, in the

Highlands of Scotland. But there was no disgrace in being a widow, only extreme difficulty, especially if it was a lad.

How would Grigor react now, Peter wondered?

Peter and Zahra did not sleep in the same bed together that night. Maybe it was because of Malcolm's twins, maybe it was her knowledge of being with child, maybe Hugh's presence was felt by them all, or perhaps it was that sad Gaelic song? Either way, the Team was ready to go very early the next morning and Peter rode his horse all the way to her huge mountain, after buying all of those rose bushes that Peter promised to add to the whole load, with gardening gloves and shovels.

It was a strange and eerie part of the world, Peter had always thought, as they approached her mountain, more like the land of the Sidhe, but he was looking forward to seeing what Zahra had bought, now that her enthusiasm was lost, thanks to him. Iain was grumpy the whole way there too, having been forgotten the previous night. The huge mountains, one after the other, were always an imposing sight, but her mountain was always up in the clouds, with fast flowing waterways coming from them all from many directions into various, burns, rivers and Lochs.

The twins were always energetic, only more thoughtful this time, as Zahra sat in between the two of them, with a thick blanket over their legs. She was growing close to them both and was going to miss them when they left. It was only one more night with the twins and she may not see them again for some time, at least until Malcolm Og's parents were told of Dihaoine and Malcolm Og's plan to be betrothed with her daughter. She would have to write to them and invite them over one day for that discussion. She hadn't seen Malcolm Mohr since her catastrophic wedding day when she lost Hugh.

It's funny how close friends can become so distant once again, after a tragedy, but they too had to process that shocking event, she pondered. She hoped that she wasn't going to always be a reminder of that traumatic event.

Unloading the shopping on that mountain, with the help of a few additional staff was hard work, especially the enormous, four-poster beds and its very heavy mattresses. When it was all in place, it looked lovely, Peter thought. The plastering and paint work had all been completed by the hard-working teams of Frasers, complete with nice clean fireplaces and the fires were all lit to ensure that the paint and the plasterwork was all completely dry in preparedness for Zahra's return. The Turkish chandeliers and light fixtures all looked spectacular, she thought. Peter had never been a fan of Turkish décor before, but he was going to need to become accustomed to it. The Fraser plasterers told her that it was essential that the job was completed on the ceilings especially, because they all had had a very peculiar odour, which they attributed to the age of the mansion, which thankfully was now gone. They had decorated the ceiling roses in beautiful intricate designs, which made her ceilings around each light fitting, now look spectacular.

Zahra's new kitchen was also completed with that enormous wood stove and oven which she thanked God for. Zahra went immediately to the village and paid the cabinet makers and asked them to come back to re-make the shelves in the library as well, which looked like they were all but collapsing in parts and discuss that partition.

She felt grateful that finally, in this century that all the bathrooms could now be plumbed, and they all badly needed to be renovated, as well, and the workers started work on those. Fresh water was now coming up from the wee burn that ran behind the mansion and was one of the many water ways that led into her small loch, above that deadly waterfall. She was now wishing she had flushing toilets but that was a way off. She had needed new bathtubs, which she bought also in Inverness, with a copper for each bathroom with a nice fireplace, ready to use each time, complete with the wood.

The bathroom walls had already been plastered and painted

but Zahra wanted the floors and walls all to be tiled as well, to avoid mould, with the Turkish tiles that she had bought that had a pretty pattern. Some were blue and white only, others were blue, red and white with birds in many patterns. There was a lot more work to do on the bathrooms, while she investigated toilets, because she was sure she had been to an old castle that had an indoor toilet where the waste went down several floors, to be collected by the unlucky gardener whose job it was to clear out the poop. Anyway, what she achieved was both the floors and walls covered over with tiles, after the plaster had dried, eventually.

The bathroom windows were all changed to open inwards and there were shutters in place, on the outside walls to protect all of the windows, from storm events. Many window frames were found to have wood rot, which all needed replacing in the bathing rooms, as well as the door frames and most of the doors too, which she had replaced but at least the old doors made good firewood. With her concerns about storms approaching, she asked Mr MacKenzie to scout the entire exterior of the property, to ensure that every window had strong shutters. Some windows did and some didn't, as it turned out, and some were just hanging from their hinges. That became another big and urgent job, along with a lightning rod on the rooftop. The farm manager's job had just become a little more difficult.

Her mountain was prone to severe storms, and she had that feeling that they were in for a big storm soon. She was in disbelief at how unprepared for a major storm event that Coinneach had been. Zahra instructed Mairi to stock up the kitchen too and the gardeners bought in all the ripened vegetables and as many of the herbs, as could be spared, some of which went into drying cabinets. Mairi was happy with the kitchen.

There weren't many Highland Coos on her property at all, maybe only fifteen if she counted them, but Zahra also had a coo slaughtered and butchered, when Hector wasn't busy to carry out that task. Hector had been busy breaking in ponies and had even sold a few ponies already. He also told her, that his father, Grigor Mohr MacGregor had been there to visit, while she was away in Inverness and said he would come back on the following weekend.

"What was Grigor here for?" Zahra asked.

"He wanted to talk to you about something," Hector said.

"Did you invite him in for coffee?" Zahra asked.

"Aye, of course I was hospitable enough and invited him to stay the night, so he did, much to my surprise. He even ate dinner with me and watched on, as all the renovations were taking place. I think he expected that you'd be back by Sunday, but when you still weren't back, he left because there was work to do on his farm," Hector said.

"Did he comment on the new work being completed on our mansion, or not?" Zahra asked.

"He didn't say anything Ma. You know what he's like? He doesn't give much away. He might have loved it, or he could have hated it. I really don't know with him anymore," Hector said.

"He would have made a good gambler with a face like that then," Zahra said. "Is there any other news while I was away son?" Zahra asked.

"Aye it all happens, the minute you leave. Lord Cinaed wanted to leave Coinneach Og with you and I informed him too, that you weren't here, because you were shopping in Inverness to replace the bedding and lots of other stuff, that I wasn't sure of Ma," Hector said.

"That's a shame. I would have liked to have looked after Coinneach Og, if I'd been here. Is he bringing my son back anytime soon?" Zahra asked.

"Aye, and he was more interested in how your renovations were going and asked if you needed any help but didn't say what day he'd be back. Soon I think," Hector said.

"Well done with your pony's son," Zahra said. "Son, there's something I need to talk to you about, when you have time. Is it your smoko soon?" she asked.

"Looks like it is. I'm curious. Let's have coffee Ma. I missed you and so did Flidas," Hector added.

"Would you mind son, if there was news of my being with child again, from Hugh?" Zahra asked.

"Och Ma," he said embracing his Mither. "That would be wonderful news. Are you with child again then?" Hector asked.

"Peter thinks I am. Do I look fatter than I was, do you think?" Zahra asked, as she showed her son her stomach.

"A little bit aye, but that's a good thing after you were so thin. I wouldn't have thought you were with child though," Hector added.

"Me too, but Peter did a test on my piss, and he says that test means that I am with child," Zahra said.

"Ma, you were always sick or nauseous at least, when you were with child with Da. Was it different with Hugh?" Hector asked.

"Aye it was. I didn't know that I was even with child, until the birth. Sickness wasn't bad, like it was with your Da," Zahra added.

"So, you might be then, if you slept with Hugh before your wedding day, which you did, because you were handfast," Hector added smirking.

"Aye, we were son. It would be like a gift from Hugh, but without his help to raise the wee bairn," Zahra added.

"He wasn't much good at that anyway, so accept it as a gift from him Ma. Congratulations. I'll have another sibling. Will you tell Da?" Hector asked, smiled then finished off his coffee. He embraced his Mither warmly, welcomed her home, and hoped it would go well with the wee bairn.

"Good luck with Da," Hector said very naughtily, with that

cheeky expression of his.

After the MacNachten twins had finished their work, they ate dinner and stayed over one more night, were paid handsomely in cash, then left early the following morning before the weather turned and it was fortunate that that they did leave the mountain, when they did. Zahra had decided to give Malcolm Og that letter for his father, Malcolm Mohr MacNachten, concerning her daughter Dihaoine, so they could discuss the betrothal, when they all arrived home in Glengarry. She kissed both lads and hugged them both and noticed that she was already becoming more accepting of hugging men again, but especially fond of the twins.

Each hour that passed, looked like the weather was building up and she was just pleased that the twins would already be home, safe in Glengarry before it broke, and she advised Hector to bring all the ponies back in, under shelter. There was always the option of underneath the house, but the stables were now large enough.

52. *Storm on the Mountain*

Most everyone felt Zahra was exaggerating the dangers of a major storm on top of Beinn Coinneach. Peter just kept chatting about where he was going to plant all the roses. It was a subject of interest, but she kept pacing up and down, checking each floor to ensure each level had no way of a storm breaking a window, or water entering somehow. She hadn't thought of the roof, up until then.

"Oh God, the roof," Zahra exclaimed out loud.

"What Zahra?" asked Peter.

"I hadn't thought to replace the roof, Peter. What if water comes in through the roof?" she asked genuinely. She hadn't owned a home in Scotland before and she was particularly afraid of storms up that high on what she was now calling her 'Misty Mountain'.

"Can you ask Lord Cinaed when it was last replaced, or is there an office here with books revealing all of that stuff?" Peter asked.

"An office?" Zahra said. "I haven't gone through any books yet. I don't know where it is," Zahra said.

"Near the library perhaps?" Peter suggested. The cabinet makers were in there working on replacing some of the shelves when both Peter and Zahra walked in and spoke to them.

"Mistress. I'm glad you came in, because there's something very odd about this entire section of shelving, if we can show you, please?" Mr Fraser asked.

"There's an odd handle behind these damaged shelves that you wanted us to replace and when we opened the handle, it revealed another large room behind it," he said. "We didn't touch anything in there. It's too dark in there anyway, but what do you want us to do?" Mr Fraser asked.

"Can I have your torch please Mr Fraser?" Zahra asked.

Tentatively entering the very dimly lit room, she discovered an office, of some sorts. It was not a well organised office with papers of varying ages, lying all around the place, as well as quills from centuries ago and ancient cabinets and desks, where no doubt some poor soul had worked in near dark conditions, to do the book work.

It had previously been known as MacAlpin Industries, it appeared. That worried her because it might well still be that, and that name wasn't on her paperwork. Another visit to the lawyers maybe? She looked for the most recent date on anything at all, to see if anything was relevant and it had only been a short while ago. To be exact, it was when neither her nor Coinneach were there in the house and that was when the books from those shelves were taken down, maybe looking initially for the way into his office.

 What else had Lord Cinaed stolen, was her immediate question?

It did look like someone had been rummaging through the papers, but had they found it? It may still be a treasure trove, or it may once have been, only now its secrets were probably gone. Either way, she couldn't find a current ledger revealing if a new roof had been installed or not. It was more than disturbing not to even have the most recent of taxation bills and payments. She may owe taxation without knowing it.

She instructed Mr Fraser to continue replacing the shelves as someone had been too violent in trying to access that room and the damage was too great.

"Please don't enter this room Mr Fraser but do you know an honest lady or man who are accountants or bookkeepers with some historical knowledge? I need help to sort this mess out. Most importantly, I need to ascertain what my current account status might be, concerning taxation," Zahra asked.

"I certainly can. I know an old man who once worked here Mistress. He never told us his secrets about the MacAlpins, but this might be where he worked. He would never say. He was a bookkeeper, name of Martin Fraser, from Fraser Ville", he said.

"Can you get him for me please Mr Fraser? I need to know when the roof was last replaced," Zahra said.

"I can tell you that", Mr Fraser said. "The newer wing didn't need replacing, but the older one, where your room is situated, needed a lot of work. We had a big team up there replacing it all, with good slate and were paid well by the former Master," Mr Fraser added.

"Thankyou. That's good to know with a big storm brewing, Mr Fraser. Can you still ask the old gentleman if he will see me, please?" Zahra asked. "I want him to go through that room and see if there's anything missing and only, he would know that. Tell him I will pay him," Zahra asked.

"Do you think that you might have a thief?" he asked.

"Might have, Mr Fraser. It was Lord Cinaed who stole those books," Zahra added.

"Opportunistic then, when neither of you were here. That family would slit each other's throats if the money was right," he added.

"I read about what that Prince Griogar did to you in the papers and I am so sorry Mistress, so sorry. We, of the village, are not like that," Mr Fraser added.

"Thank you, Mr Fraser. Just call me Zahra. This is my friend from Inverness, Dr Peter Heath," Zahra added.

"Dr Heath. I am sorry to you also. I read about what happened to you too. I didn't know the former Master was like that," he said, shaking Peter's hand.

"Thank you," Peter said, not wishing to discuss it any further.

"I'm glad the two of you can comfort each other," Mr Fraser added.

"I am with child too Mr Fraser, to my late husband, Hugh Chisholm, who was killed on my wedding day. So, when folks start gossiping, please clarify that, in the village. You know what gossip can do to a person's life and I don't want my wee bairn to suffer?" Zahra added.

"Aye Mistress, I will. My wife would love to help you with your wee bairn, alone as you will be. Keep her in mind if you need a hand," young Mr Fraser offered. "Your life really didn't improve much in losing your new husband like that, right on your wedding day. What a terrible thing to happen. My sincerest condolences Mistress," he added.

As the two friends walked away, they heard the carpenters gossiping, in shock that they had met the two people from the newspapers and were going over the gruesome details, as well as the death in the Chapel in Cannich, Glenmoriston and the dreaded wolf.

However, at least Zahra was pleased to know that the roof wasn't going to leak.

"Peter, I owe you a horse and the saddlery too," Zahra then remembered. "I forgot to repay you, and I don't even know where the horse is," Zahra said, suddenly feeling foolish.

"It's alright, my dearest Zahra. James sorted it all out with me and I picked him up and he had been well cared for there too," Peter said.

"Did you? I am so sorry Peter. I couldn't think straight. Please forgive me?" Zahra asked.

Holding his dear friend Zahra, he remembered that day, only too clearly.

"It was an honour to do anything, even as small as that was," Peter said tearfully.

Peter and Zahra did sleep alongside one another that night, as the enormous dark clouds came billowing across the ranges, but couldn't quite get above their mountain, and the wind blew furiously, making a whistling sound. There was thunder and lightning, like she had never experienced before. Then there was the continuous heavy rainfall, she thought was never going to stop. Zahra briefly left her bed and prayed that it would all stop, when Peter picked her up and put her back into the enormous bed, ever so gently and they spooned with one another, to feel comforted as well as warm.

Zahra was crying and so was Peter, until both Hector and Flidas came in and asked to jump in bed with them too. They all comforted one another, as the Gods expressed their anger. Then both Causantin and wee sweet Dihaoine came in too, clutching each other while they cried out to their Mither and crawled over everyone, clamouring to be near their Mither, in between bodies, just to feel the safety, warmth and comfort of the Mither who they had been parted from.

All of Zahra's bairns, who had experienced that separation from her, made the most of the comfort, that only she could give them. In all, six of them slept together, clutching onto one another, throughout the wild, wet, and stormy night, not even judging that Peter was there too. It was expected that he was like them and needed her as much as they all did.

Zahra was afraid of what she would find when she went outside the next day.

It was a frightful mess with a few trees down, branches lay everywhere already being chopped up for firewood by the Crofters. Peter was pleased he hadn't yet planted the roses, or they too would have been victims of the storm, or firewood. Hector ran down to his ponies, madly doing a head count. He was pleased they were only a little scared but none missing nor injured. One mare had given birth early to her foal and other than that, the poor wee things just needed some re-assurance. Flidas' soft touch with them always calmed them down.

"Ma, next time I will take you up on the offer of the downstairs level," Hector said.

All the other farm animals were also alive but badly affected. Zahra walked all around the mansion and there were only two shutters hanging on by a few screws. She asked the whole family to search every room to ensure that there were no leaks or any other damage.

Peter's biggest suggestion was major improvements on the access road to her Beinn Coinneach mansion, which was now very badly eroded and covered in all manner of rocks and stones of varying sizes and fast flowing water. There were minor burns running across the entirety of the property, including across that road, causing erosion deep into its already eroded surface. And more rain was expected.

Peter came up with the ingenious idea of making the surface of their entry road, solid first by digging down about three feet, or one metre, then adding a lot of small stones for drainage, then laying hard wooden sleepers that were used on railway tracks, atop the drainage stones, then ultimately topped off, completely covered over in thousands of smooth cobble stones, cemented in, like in Edinburgh, so that they couldn't move a single centimetre and held on at the sides, by a cemented ridge with a deep drain on both sides of the road to take water away and down the mountain rather than across it. The drain also would need to be deep enough for these storms and cemented.

It sounded good in theory, but it was a better idea than any that Zahra had. She asked him to draw it all up, so she could see it in a picture format. Zahra suggested an additional two asphalt mounds in two places to slow down the traffic for Hector's ponies, who needed to cross the road, without damaging it, as well as widening it, so cattle, horses and carriages could use it, at the same time. Of course, it also needed its own sign. "*Misty Mountain Road.*"

"Peter, maybe you missed your vocation. You could have been

a road engineer," Zahra said. "I think we will give it a try, you are such a clever man", she added and kissed him.

Mairi remained calm during the clean-up, as did her husband Callum, but he was busy ordering other people around to clean it all up, including Rauri who swept the front and rear patios, which became his permanent job.

Shortly after breakfast, Mr Fraser, the carpenter came up from Fraser Ville with an older gentleman who was wearing glasses on the end of his nose. The bairns were all excited after the eventful night and sleeping with both Peter and Zahra. It had been a crowded bed, but even by Zahra's standards, she was as happy as she could be, knowing her bairns were all safe and happy, as were her son's ponies.

The elderly gentleman introduced himself as Mr Martin Fraser, a former bookkeeper from Fraser Ville, no flowery credentials and no handshake.

"Mistress, how do I address you please?" Mr Fraser politely asked.

"Zahra. My name is Zahra Chisholm, formerly Zahra MacAlpin, but my husband passed away on the day of our wedding. My marriage with Lord Coinneach had already been annulled," Zahra explained.

"So, you are no longer Lady Coinneach then?" Mr Martin Fraser asked.

"I'm not sure, Mr Fraser. Is that relevant?" Zahra asked.

"It may have a bearing on taxes, Mistress. Do you now own Beinn Coinneach?" Mr Fraser asked.

"I do, aye. As compensation for the things that happened to both me and to my bairns. I'll get you that paperwork to show you, before we enter that room Mr Fraser, that your carpenter showed us yesterday," Zahra added.

"Do you also have proof of both of your marriages Mistress? I'd like to see that first, before I disclose anything of importance about the MacAlpins," Martin Fraser declared.

The unassuming small man, sounded more like a wary lawyer than an accountant, who was afraid of the MacAlpins or maybe just afraid that the room had been found at all. Zahra showed him what he needed to see, before he believed who she was. "I also appear up there in those three paintings, that Lord Coinneach painted in his better days," Zahra added. That was what made all the difference to the suspicious little man, because she was clearly identifiable from the paintings alone, and he knew the man's style of painting and Zahra's hair is unforgettable.

"He is a loss to the world of art, that is for certain," Mr Fraser added.

"Hmmm", Zahra just made a noise, and they went into the library to open the bookcase to enter the old and dark secret room, both carrying a candle.

"Did you work in here?" Zahra asked him plainly.

"Aye, I did for thirty years, until my eyes could not tolerate the dark any longer. The Master disallowed too much light in here, else the room be found out," he added.

"I need to know if this was how it was when you left it and if you see anything that may be missing?" Zahra asked.

"This is not how I left it. I was always meticulously neat and tidy. Not a paper out of place, Zahra. And there's a lot missing from this room. Along that side wall was a pile of gold, high enough to sit on like a chair with your legs dangling down. A massive quantity of gold, both Spanish and French. I don't see any now, so that has all gone," he said as he walked around examining the room, holding the candle.

"There was another cabinet there that had the oldest scrolls in it, from ancient times in another language. Pictish I think. They were Title Deeds to this land. But he didn't give you the deeds, is that right?" he asked.

"That's right," Zahra said.

She couldn't conceal her shock, and neither could the other Mr Fraser, imagining all that gold, right there and someone had stolen it, only very recently.

"I also saw a name, MacAlpin Industries. What is that?" Zahra asked.

"He didn't tell you much, when you were married then, I take it?" Old Mr Fraser asked.

"What is MacAlpin Industries please, Mr Fraser?" Zahra asked again.

"It's where all the MacAlpin brothers, along with their father, Lord Cinaed MacAlpin, invested their money, all over the world and in many companies and in real estate. Money earned from that, goes to the group of them, which used to be six people. Now it is only four people, consisting of Lord Cinaed, Padraig, Cinaed Og, and Anndra. If I was to guess who was behind the heist, it would be Anndra. He would have done it with his brothers, but with their father's full knowledge." he said.

"If you can prove that you were married to Lord Coinneach, which you can, even though it was annulled, you can take it to Court, as 'missing inheritance' and as one of the groups in MacAlpin Industries. I would advise you to see a lawyer in Inverness, as soon as possible, because that gold will disappear into thin air. You will need Lord Coinneach's Will and I can give you the name of the lawyer, who wrote his last Will. His name was Aonghus MacGregor from Malcolm MacGregor Law Rooms. You have access to his child, Coinneach Og, so apply also for custody, because the child inherits from his father and without this, there is no inheritance for the lad," he said. "As for the missing documents, ascertain with the lawyer, that this land is indeed in your name and not MacAlpin Industries. A lot of their properties are under the business name and not their own names," he added. "Do you want me to come with you Zahra? I am concerned for your welfare, as have many people been around here, since you married him." Old Mr Fraser asked.

"Yes, please Mr Fraser and I will pay you for your services. My friend Dr Heath is returning to Inverness the day after tomorrow, so can you come with us? Then you and I could see Mr MacGregor?" she asked. "I am familiar with him, because he is the cousin of a friend of mine, so that helps. Do we need to stay overnight?" Zahra asked.

"Aye, I can and aye, we need to stay overnight," Old Mr Fraser replied.

"We can stay with my friend, Dr Heath then, if that is to your liking?" Zahra asked.

"So long as it costs me nothing, Zahra and you said you would pay me today?" he asked.

"Aye, I did. How much," Zahra asked.

"One pound, Zahra," Old Mr Fraser said, and he left with his pound. The young Mr Fraser left with him to clean up from the storm.

53. Glengarry Home

My lads were overdue from their Teamster work taking them to Beinn Coinneach and Inverness and I was anxious the entire time, just knowing that they were with Zahra. I now thought of Zahra, like she was bad luck. I didn't want my innocent lads to fall into any strangeness. Ailsa thought I was being unkind to a poor, grieving widow and so did Hugh Og, so I was outnumbered, and I resorted to prayer. I really couldn't stand it if anything happened to my twins. I loved those lads so much, that even Alex accepted my boundless love for them, without envy.

Alex believed that I had a mental illness, where the twins were both concerned, because my ex-wife was going to kill them, before they were even born. My love for them was boundless, knowing they nearly hadn't been born, because of my evil first wife. I paced Alex's office floor in his medical centre telling him that they weren't back yet, repeatedly. He was now the only person who would listen to me, without judgement, concerning my lads. I guess he learned that skill in Medical School. Either way, I stopped bothering Ailsa and Hugh Og, while the twins were with Zahra.

I just thanked God that she didn't live in Glengarry.

Of course, the moment the Team was back, I was down there at the stables, like a shot. I wanted to see them with my own eyes and hold them again to overcome my parental anxiety. Hugh was regretting giving them the job he had thought was the easiest of the two that he had on his books. Hugh and the lads were now using my old office in the old house while I used my new big one in Old John's place, that I had inherited.

The sign read "Teamster Office," with another sign outside pointing to the old house for enquiries concerning both Teams.

I was proud to see my sons' names on the sign, which I had suggested. Team I was Hugh Chisholm and Angus MacKenzie. Team 2 was Malcolm Og and Hamish Og MacNachten. They left off Iain from the sign.

Malcolm Og and Hamish Og were both in good spirits but their offsider, Iain looked grumpy. I held them so tightly, even they were surprised at my anxiety upon their return.

"I am so pleased you are home, lads. Ailsa has cooked a special meal for you both," I said.

"Da, I've missed you too," said Hamish Og hugging me back.

"Da, I have to talk to you over dinner, after I give this money to Hugh. Can you come with us to the office first?" Malcolm Og asked.

"Hugh," Malcolm Og said, "This is the job's payment in full, in cash with some extra," he said.

"You two keep the extra lads. It's a tip from Zahra," Hugh said smiling at their innocence and their honesty.

"I'll take the rest, and we'll sort out the business on Friday. Okay?" Hugh Og said. "How are the horses?" he asked. "Weather's coming up, so when you finish with them, close up all of the stables." Hugh demanded.

"They're really good, but need a farrier to check their shoes tomorrow," Hamish Og added.

"Have you written up the job?" Hugh asked.

"Aye, and where we stayed all of the nights, as well," Malcolm Og replied.

"Where did you stay in Inverness?" Hugh Og asked.

"Dr Heath's house, free of charge. Nice beds, warm and comfortable. We had a good dinner, but Iain was grumpy because we forgot him for a while. Zahra's nice, so is Peter," Malcolm answered.

"Did you know that Zahra was with child, to poor old Hugh Mohr Chisholm?" Hamish Og stated.

"Didn't know that, but not enough time now to catch up before this weather breaks. Can you deal with the horses now and the stables, then get yourselves inside," Hugh said seriously.

I helped them with all their gear, as well as rubbing down two of their six horses. I put out too much feed for them which my lads laughed at but allowed it. I gave each horse a carrot and thanked them for bringing my lads home safely. I kissed the horses on their muzzles and patted their necks.

"Oh Da, anyone would think we weren't coming home. It was only Zahra's shopping for that old house on the hill. It will look nice when she has finished but now, she's with child, she's not too pleased without having Hugh Mohr with her," Hamish Og said.

"We met up with Hector too and his wife and his drover friends on the night we arrived, and we had a music night and made a lot of noise. It was great fun with all her musical instruments," Malcolm Og said.

"Wee Dihaoine fell in love with Malcolm, Da," Hamish Og said.

"The four-year-old lass?" I asked.

"Aye, Malcolm's taking them out of the cradle now Da," Hamish Og said.

This started a bit of a fight as the two lads then swung punches at each other and returned them, falling over then swung again, disturbing the horse's tranquillity.

"Come on lads let's just do what Hugh asked and finish up here before the storm breaks. Ailsa's waiting for us," I said.

Of course, I hadn't taken it seriously and had no idea that this was what Malcolm Og wanted to discuss. We all strolled up the road as we saw the enormous clouds rolling in and the atmosphere changed.

"It's not going to hit us head on. Maybe further north. It's lucky you are home lads, it might hit directly where you just were," I said. Just the same, we hurried inside to where Ailsa had the house nice and warm, with hot baths ready for my lads and dinner with desert. I kissed her on her cheek and thanked her.

"Their clothes are very dusty looking," she observed. "I've put out clean clothes for you lads," she said chasing after them. Hamish was cheeky and swung around and kissed her and spanked her bottom.

"Oh Hamish," she said. Ailsa was still embarrassed by that way of theirs and left them to it in case Malcolm spanked her too. However, Hamish Og called out to her.

"Oh Ailsa, you can come into the bathing room if you like. My hair needs washing," he said.

"I'll do it Ailsa," I said.

"Your hair is it Hamish? Let me help," I said, as I poured warm water over his head. He was much cleaner and less cheeky then.

"Need help too Malcolm," I asked.

"Nae Da. I'm good," he replied.

I was so happy to have them home, it was heavenly, and my heart was finally at peace again. Over dinner, they talked about Hector's ponies that sounded as flighty as ever, being moved back to Beinn Coinneach. I didn't envy those drovers. They are not easy horses to drive. I was given full details about the interior of Zahra's home that was being pulled out and replaced with new things that Zahra had purchased or was to purchase. They even told of the enormous bonfire she told them off to rid the house of all things she hated. Of course, I didn't tell them her ex had become a homosexual and understood why she would burn the contents of her bedroom.

The funniest tale was of the Piss Prophets who could decide if a woman was with child or not and Peter had decided she was after Zahra pissed into a pot, transferred into a glass implement to determine the colour of the pish. "It was gross Da," said Hamish Og. "Aunty Zahra pissed right there into a chamber pot. They're sure not shy those two," he said.

"I am so pleased for Zahra that she has something of Hugh to hold onto. That is so nice," Ailsa said.

"Not if it's a lad like Hugh. Imagine trying to raise a big lad like that, with the way he used to be, when he was young anyway," I said.

"If it's a lassie, it'll be like Isobel, pretty but snippy, bossy and disloyal to her husband," added Malcolm Og.

"Are you thinking of what type of woman you would like to settle down with then, are you Malcolm?" asked Ailsa. Not realising that she was opening the flood gates.

"Aye, Da, Ma, I am. I have a plan, and I am going to stop sleeping around now with all my married ladies. Hamish can take over my ladies, if they all agree. I'll give them flowers and say goodbye," Malcolm Og said.

"Da, I have this letter to give to you. It is about a betrothal to wee Dihaoine, until she turns twelve years old," he said.

I was astounded and so was Ailsa. Neither one of us could respond at first. Maybe I was in shock.

"She's just a wee bairn Malcolm. She will change a lot. Grow up and meet others. How can you know from one or two meetings and such a young one? I would hate to see you miss out on someone who you could marry now. You can't marry her for years. You will have needs son. You will want your own wee bairns by then. Its thirteen years difference in age," I said. "Show me the letter."

Truth was, I didn't want my family to be forever related to Zahra Chisholm.

"I told you Da. Pinching them from the cradle, he is now. That's sick Malcolm in my opinion. At least the other women were all over thirty, some forty even. I thought you liked the old ladies, then one little lass says, 'I like you Malcolm' and you're all gooey and stupid and want to marry her on the never, never plan," Hamish Og said.

"Don't be so harsh Hamish love. Your brother has different ideas to you. He needs your support now especially, not enmity," Ailsa said wisely.

"Do you need me then brother?" Hamish Og asked. He was then worried that he had let Malcolm Og down.

"Aye, I do. You're my twin. My other half. We have always decided things together. I don't want to make a mistake. I want you to like her and the plan," Malcolm Og said through teary eyes. The twins at last embraced and overcame their differences of opinion.

I said I would think about it and discuss it with Uncle Kenneth who had done a similar thing with wee April, who married Ali MacGregor, my neighbour. She was a shy wee thing who barely spoke to anyone, except her parents and her husband. She knew Ali was the one too as soon as she met him when she was wee and they had a betrothal for years but she wasn't quite as young as Dihaoine. Then there was Islay, my own daughter who chose Angus, when she was barely six years old.

"What's Dihaoine's name now. Is it Chisholm, MacAlpin or MacGregor?" I asked.

"Zahra said Dihaoine's name had been changed by Lord Coinneach when he adopted her, but it was changed back to MacGregor and Zahra said she and Hugh were not changing any of the bairns' names. Hugh was firm that they had the Father's Clan name. Her name in full is Dihaoine Freya Dorothea MacGregor. It had been MacAlpin for a while only. Hugh was sensitive about hurting Grigor because of Isobel, so wouldn't insist on adoption, unless they had all wanted it or it became a necessity, like if Uncle Grigor, ran off again," Malcolm Og answered.

"That means a discussion needs to take place with both Zahra Chisholm and her ex-husband, Grigor MacGregor," I said. I tried not to make fun of the plan or get angry or both. My emotions were all over the place, so I closed my eyes and asked myself what Old John would have done. I was asking him to myself, *'John why did you die? I need you now. You would know what to say to these lads. Should he get betrothed?'*

I felt impotent. Trying to be the father they always knew, I promised to support them both and would write letters to both Zahra Chisholm and Grigor MacGregor and arrange a discussion in the bairns' place of residence, being Beinn Coinneach, soon to be named 'Misty Mountain Ranch' after Zahra had arranged it with a lawyer.

I then decided to see Aonghus MacGregor in Inverness to get legal advice and even have the betrothal with Dihaoine MacGregor written up legally, to be armed with knowledge and paperwork.

"Did Zahra mention a dowery at all, son?" I asked.

"Aye, she said if we both decided to marry when she was twelve years old, or beyond depending on what she was doing at the time, she would pay you a dowery of ten thousand pounds," he replied. "If that wasn't enough, it would form part of the discussion," Malcolm Og answered.

In bed with Ailsa that night, she was unusually amorous and for once, I wasn't, but I had to respond to her needs with little enthusiasm, I performed but I was only fulfilling my husbandly duty. I was not myself. I dreamed a lot that night. It was Old John MacDonnell. It was like he had come when I had called on him and just seeing him made me weep in my sleep. He spoke to me seriously.

"Malcolm, my son, there's a lot more to this. Listen to your son. The wee lass needs you. They both need you. Gold, son, a heap of gold is never where she would guess it to be. Look for me at their waterfall, but bring your weapons," he said.

"I miss you Da. I really need you this time, I was saying,"

And he disappeared into what looked like an opening in that mountain side by the waterfall on Beinn Coinneach.

"Darling, are you alright my darling? Wake up," my wife Ailsa was saying, and I stopped weeping then.

The storm was raging outside. It felt like God was telling me something. It had stopped raining by early morning, but everything was soaking wet and large water droplets fell from the roof, as I stepped onto the veranda. Ailsa came and put her arms around me as I stood still, just remembering John in the dream and gold and the waterfall. It made no sense. What gold?

"You had a bad night last night darling. Why does this disturb you so much? We can deal with it like everything else, can't we?" Ailsa said.

"Nae Ailsa, we are heading into the eye of the storm," I said.

I left to talk to Kenneth, my brother about betrothal with the young ones. Then onto Inverness to see the lawyer.

"Ailsa, I'm staying overnight in Inverness," I said.

She just co-operated these days and didn't complain.

I rode my big black stallion that Kenneth bought me, with my saddle bags full of snacks and a flask of coffee in readiness for Inverness. Kenneth was helpful and the process seamed simple enough and he expressed his uncertainty too, at the time, as April was not only young but also their only wee lassie. He still missed having her home but was grateful at least that Ali lived in Glengarry with her, so they saw her as often as possible. He advised that my son's lassie live with us in Glengarry, for the Team and the family.

He then asked if he could come with me to the lawyers and stay over with our cousin, Aonghus. At least he didn't charge for us to sleep overnight, and Annabelle could cook quite well, admittedly not as well as Zahra or Meredith but I liked her cooking. I hoped he wasn't busy with appointments because I hadn't made one. Hopefully a lot of people were still cleaning up after the storm. Some folk said it was only the first of many storms this season, like Grigor MacGregor would say. I never could understand how some people seemed to know that about the weather and folk like me just had to look up at the clouds.

We left then in a hurry to make it to Inverness to see my cousin. Kenneth's horse, as well as my new one, named Jet, made it in good time before it was too late in the day and Aonghus was pleased to see us both. He was a little surprised too at the age of the wee lass, wishing to be betrothed, as did my brother, until she was old enough to marry. He made a comment that lassies were becoming more forward these days, and some were even proposing marriage before the man had even asked. What a scary thought. If one didn't have the home to give her and a job with enough to support you both, it would be embarrassing to say no to a lass you liked but could not yet afford.

"Odd co-incidence with you coming in today," Cousin Aonghus said.

"Och, aye why is that?" I asked.

"Well, I might as well say, at the risk of it sounding unprofessional, that Zahra MacGregor Chisholm is due here any minute now to see me, with some very interesting issues indeed. She's coming in with the old bookkeeper, formerly employed by the late, Lord Coinneach MacAlpin.

Incidentally, you were there in the Chapel that day when Hugh Chisholm died, weren't you?" Cousin Aonghus asked.

"Aye we both were," I said.

"What's this I hear about two wolves, not one, or is that just gossip?" Aonghus asked quite plainly.

"Cousin, we are staying overnight with you and Annabelle, so we can tell you there, where the walls can't hear, so to speak. It's not a story many would believe anyway, but it would have to be strictly confidential, for Zahra's family's sake," I said.

"Okay, free accommodation and free food, for free information cousin," he said very cheekily, spoken like a true Grant.

"You are sounding more like Grandda, every day, cousin," I said.

"Have you already written to the father, by the way, as well as the Mither of this wee bairn?" he asked.

"I have and I have asked to meet them both up at Beinn Coinneach," I replied.

"When will you meet?" Aonghus asked. "Zahra might ask me this question today," he asked.

It was then that his secretary came in with a message that Mrs Chisholm had arrived for her appointment, but so had Grigor MacGregor, unexpectedly.

"Do you all want to talk together now on this topic? *You* are all here?" Cousin Aonghus asked.

The secretary came back saying, "Mrs Zahra Chisholm wants a private meeting today, accompanied by her bookkeeper, Mr Martin Fraser only, but she asks to meet both Mr Grigor Mohr MacGregor and Mr Malcolm Mohr MacNachten, up at her home tomorrow midday, concerning betrothal between Dihaoine Freya Dorothea MacGregor and Malcolm Og MacNachten, with overnight accommodation and meals provided," she said.

"You can tell us what she said anyway, can't you cousin?" I asked.

"Nae, that's why I suggested that you chat here, but never mind, it will cost you all another fee, when you draw it all up, if you all go ahead with it," Aonghus said. "She must be pretty for all of this fuss," he added.

"Family discount?" I asked.

"Aye," he said reluctantly.

"I'll just have to eat dessert tonight then, too," I added.

"Chapel gossip costs too," Kenneth added smiling.

"Were there two wolves or one?" my cousin asked again.

"Tonight cousin," I reminded him.

Walking through Aonghus's waiting room was awkward, but I gave my greetings to Mrs Chisholm, as she was now known, formerly. She was standing beside a short, thin, very old, and small framed, short sighted, looking man, wearing thick lensed, pince nez glasses, perched on the end of his nose. I had never seen him before, but I suppose he did look like an old Fraser who should have already died but that was unkind of me to think. He looked as if he had been stuck inside a sunless office, for many a year.

 Grigor Mohr MacGregor was trying to avoid us all and wished he hadn't arrived there, at that precise moment in time, as both myself and Zahra. There was no avoiding it, so at least Zahra gave her regards to us both and her eyes lit up upon seeing that Kenneth was with me. She embraced him spontaneously, which surprised all onlookers, especially Grigor Mohr who was clearly still in love with her.

The poor man had suffered for a long time now for his indiscretion with Belle MacGregor and his face wore the suffering and the loss. I shook his hand and hoped to see him on the morrow. He nodded a kind of confirmation without speech, but I think that meant, he would be there. He hadn't changed much really and was still wearing his old plaid.

Dinner at Aonghus and Annabel's house was animated conversation that we all enjoyed, covering years of catch up, including funny tales from his work, as well as my farm and Kenneth's Art Gallery.

"So, you were the popular one today, Kenneth, getting a loving embrace from the lovely Zahra. How did you get to be her favourite then?" Aonghus asked.

"I slept alongside them both on one cold night and it was a lovely warm and friendly atmosphere. Better than sleeping alone in one of those cold old rooms in that huge drafty place," Kenneth replied.

"You slept with them both?" Annabel asked incredulously.

"Aye it seems odd to say now, but they were in love then, and they were making love most of the night. I just fell asleep and found myself cuddling up to one or either of them and awoke to find Coinneach helping Zahra with her toileting," Kenneth answered honestly.

"Now the wolves. You promised Malcolm," my cousin said. He was holding back the dessert if I refused.

"There were two wolves. One brown one, one grey one," I said. I didn't know then what to say, so I asked if there was anything I needed to know before going to Beinn Coinneach.

"You say I am like Grandda, you are more like him than me. Alright then, I have an idea. How about this? I give you one bit of information, then you give me some information in response?" Aonghus said.

"That sounds good, don't you think Kenneth?" I said. "My turn," I said, "Who was the Fraser bloke with her and why?" I asked.

"His name is Martin Fraser, former bookkeeper for thirty years for the late Lord Coinneach, until he was too blind to continue, because he was working in a secret room in that mansion, for

MacAlpin Industries," he said. "Your turn," he then added.

"Is Zahra with child and if so, whose is it?" Aonghus asked.

"Aye she is and Dr Peter Heath thinks so and if she is, it's Hugh Chisholm's wee bairn," I replied.

The night went on like that backwards and forwards trading information with my cousin and it reminded me a little of the game that Ali and Hector played with their Gaelic obscenities back and forth, back and forth.

We lost Annabel to her desire for sleep, then Kenneth, long before Aonghus even looked tired. "Who are MacAlpin Industries?" I asked. This was one of my questions that required a lengthy explanation. And what happens if Zahra's home is in the business name and not in her own name?" I asked.

"It would belong to them. I will investigate that, however. I also have some neat little documents here that I thought you might like," Aonghus said, like he was a detective, of sorts.

"Lord Coinneach MacAlpin has had many legal Wills, which have all been overridden by the next Will. The oldest one is so old that I thought it was a mistake, but it wasn't. His first Will, where his wife died in childbirth, left everything to his son, Causantin who died in a battle and was killed by Vikings, or something like that. I know it's all unbelievable, but these people weren't even alive," he said.

"His next Will was also overridden at a much later date when he married Zahra. He renewed his Will with me, and I do remember him coming in, to do that. He left everything to Zahra MacAlpin, including his share of the business, known as 'MacAlpin Industries' and the house, contents and so on, as well as custody of any bairns they might have.

'MacAlpin Industries' involved his father and all four of his brothers, so it was Coinneach's share of that business. Of course, now that number has been reduced by two people at least. It leaves Lord Cinaed, Padruig, Anndra and Cinaed Og, with Lord Cinaed as the Chairman. It's a crooked organisation, with the little I know of these types of businesses with old money," Aonghus opined.

"Then he came in once again to change it. Everything then was to go to a young man, 'Alasdair Fraser'. His bairn, Coinneach Og MacAlpin, was to live with his father, Lord Cinaed, not Zahra MacAlpin. Coinneach Og was to inherit his share of the business, kept in trust by his father," he said.

"Then, only one day before that tragic event at the Chapel in Cannich, he changed his Will, yet again," he said.

"Once more, he left everything to Zahra Shushannah MacGregor MacAlpin, despite their marriage having been annulled. Alasdair was to get nothing at all. He was certain that Zahra would return to him, even though she was living in Inverness, at the time, with Dr Peter Heath. I lodged it and it is the only legal Will of Coinneach MacAlpin. Zahra was to have custody of his son, Coinneach Og MacAlpin and to manage his inheritance of the business, not Lord Cinaed. Nothing was to go to his father, Lord Cinaed MacAlpin, he was adamant about that. Lord Coinneach may not have known that Zahra was marrying Hugh Mohr Chisholm, being the most likely reason for his attack on them both, upon discovering that," he added.

"This most current and legal Will, however, is what you need to give to Zahra tomorrow, because there is missing inheritance. You'd be familiar with that problem cousin. The old bookkeeper, Mr Martin Fraser, told me that there was a lot of gold missing from that secret room. She will need to get investigators in, so the wood from those bookshelves that she is replacing, should be kept as evidence, that there was a break into that room," he added. "I have also asked Martin Fraser already to write up a statement and bring in all relevant information from when he worked there, declaring what is missing," Aonghus said.

"Once we get it all together, we can act on it. He is our main witness. Let's hope he doesn't die before we can act," he added.

"I did have a dream about gold up there and it made no sense, until now. However, in the dream, Old John MacDonnell told me to go to the waterfall and look for him there. He said there was much more to this, than we knew and young Dihaoine, as well as Zahra needed my help. It's a big deal then and the gold does exist?" I asked.

"I can't say about your dream, but the gold certainly does exist. Old John might be telling you where it is, do you think?" Aonghus asked. "Is there a waterfall up there?" he asked.

"Apparently, there is. Zahra has mentioned it once before," I replied.

"There might be access behind it where the gold is hidden?" Aonghus said.

"I'm done in now Aonghus. I've got to sleep," I said.

"Thank you for all these documents. I hope Grigor is there. I might be in over my head. I wish Old John was still alive. He'd know what to do," I said feeling very limited with this type of thing. Chasing up inheritance wasn't new to me though, so I wasn't looking forward to any of it. I thought my son's plan of betrothal was bad enough, now it was way bigger than that.

Sleeping was a welcome state after the exhausting night with the mentally active, Aonghus MacGregor. Kenneth was snoring in his deep sleep which didn't help, so I blocked his nose briefly, so he would stop but it started up again. Morning came too soon with breakfast and the chatty Annabel.

Saying our farewells to our cousins, Kenneth and I headed up to Beinn Coinneach, but we took it slowly, as we were both feeling a bit tired. I filled Kenneth in about the gold, as a fact in missing inheritance and then I told him of my dream, which he took more seriously than what Aonghus said.

"He exhausts me," Kenneth said. I smiled at the Grant family genetics being stronger in our cousin than us. We must have more Clan MacNachten in us than Clan Grant we both concluded.

"Ma isn't a true Grant, anyway, is she?" Kenneth asked.

"I don't know any Clan Grant women, other than Ma, and she wasn't raised a Grant. Maybe, it's who raises you, is stronger than the genetics," I concluded.

"Either way, we are MacNachtens for sure. Aonghus is just exhausting," Kenneth said. I had to agree. It was indeed wise to have sent him to university and enter law. It was old Isobel's idea, I had been told. I wondered if my youngest two bairns were being educated well enough. He is as sharp as a tack. 'Maybe Grandda was like that when he was young', I thought? To have survived those times he had to have been sharp.

Once we arrived in the region of Beinn Coinneach, I wasn't looking forward to the meeting and prayed that Grigor would be there too. I didn't feel comfortable alone anymore with Zahra. I wish I felt differently, but after seeing that wolf jump right out of her that day of her wedding, I wasn't sure what to expect next. No-one spoke of it, but we had all seen it. Was she Sidhe, of some variety, yet unknown to us all?

As we started the upwards climb, we observed that serious work had commenced on improving the road that led up to her mansion, at long last.

Thank goodness, that road had really needed it and had been the source of many discussions concerning safety, as to how to reach the top, alive. It looked like they had dug down deep into the wet earth, then they were laying small greyish stones, suitable for drainage, then on top of that layer were very heavy hard wood sleepers, to be a solid foundation for the road. Then it appeared that the next step was covering over the wooden sleepers with a layer of cobble stones, all cemented well together.

Along both sides of the road, they were allowing for water to run off, by having a cemented edge with a type of wide gutter, allowing for water drainage, about three feet deep and three feet wide. The road itself was also a lot wider than it had been formerly, to allow for both the coos, as well as carriages to pass one another, at the same time. They had only finished the lower half of the road, so there was a long way to go. So long as it was solid, it would survive the next storm, but they would need to work faster, the weather was already looking like another storm was brewing.

We rode the rest of the way on the much-eroded, old track. Stones were still strewn all over the old section. They must have borne the brunt of the wild storm, I concluded for it to have moved even the bigger stones like that and decided that the volume of water must have been far greater than usual. I glanced across at the grazing fields and noticed a new yew tree had been planted, beside an ancient old rock and wondered why they would plant a yew tree there. I didn't know if cattle ate from the yew tree, but I hoped not, as they were very poisonous, however it had the appearance of someone's seat on the rock under the yew tree, or it was an unmarked grave as some were after Culloden, Grandda had said, so no-one would dig them up again. Druids also used to preach under yew trees, as well as oak trees, my Ma told me to receive some sort of hallucination, but the tree was too young yet to give off any sort of hallucination, I was thinking, as I was going up slowly on the newish road.

Upon reaching the mansion, was an even bigger surprise, as there was now a newly built, and very large, two-tiered rose garden in front of the wide stone paved frontage, which was very pleasant, not to mention clean, after a storm. It had Peter Heath's touch with different coloured roses on either side of the road and on two levels. It was lovely and not dissimilar to the way the two of them had begun preparing their garden in Inverness, when they were Doctor and Nurse Heath. On the exterior of the big old stone mansion, now were torches attached to light up the building at night.

There were also quaint looking pole lights at the top of the road, and on both sides of the paved frontage area, as well as at the bottom of the road where we had entered, so the whole area would be better lit up. I liked the new look for Misty Mountain Ranch, and it was obvious that Peter had been a great help to his old friend and for that I was pleased for them both, as it would have been a therapeutic exercise for them, as well as a lot of hard work.

They both had issues that no-one spoke of anymore, except my cousin.

There was a new sign too, in two places with Zahra's new name for her property, "Misty Mountain Ranch." One on the new big wrought iron gate and one sign above the two enormous, newly carved oak, wooden doors. I couldn't make out what the carvings were in the oak at first, then looking closer, it was an attempt to copy ancient Pictish symbols, but in wood. Carved into the wooden door were horses with their riders under the many swirly patterns, geometric patterns, and a carving of two people seated upon what looked like thrones. Around the edges were hares, salmon, deer, heron, swans, wolves, bears, lynx and weaponry of old, like spears and swords, tools of trade and targes. It was an original work of art, and I wondered who had completed such a beautiful piece of art.

There was also an enormous, big lock. Maybe it had been Grigor?

New enormous stables were also being built on the left-hand side of the mansion, of huge proportions, more like a stable for Clydesdales, than for the Highland Ponies, who already had their stables further down the road, which we had already passed. Signage was also on that building in Calligraphic lettering, reading "Misty Mountain Ranch Stables" and the year. The mansion also had Zahra's name above her door and the year. Zahra must have lodged the new business name with Aonghus.

Inside Zahra's newly renovated home, it also had two planks of wood to ensure you could close off those huge, heavy front doors. Either side of the front doors on the outside, Zahra had also placed huge planter pots with big blueish, pink flowers that had big green leaves. Zahra said they were called hydrangeas. It was all looking very different. It even smelled different to how it had smelled before. I liked it, in an unusual kind of way. I was glad there wasn't an awful statue of an Indian colourful elephant or some such, beside the front doors, which would have been too much.

Zahra welcomed us both, happy and smiling at having company, especially upon seeing that Kenneth was accompanying me. She kissed him of course, but not me. She had a soft spot for my brother, and I hoped, that was all it was, but they did share a family connection now too, with April and Ali marrying. I often wondered why Kenneth hadn't insisted on Zahra being at the wedding for April and Ali, but it was a sore spot, so I thought better of raising that issue too. Zahra could easily dissolve into tears still, I imagined. She was deserving enough to have been given the '*old place on the mountain*', as my twins called it. Compensation, Zahra said and even Hector was given his own compensation, so I was pleased for him too, after suffering as much as he did and so silently, without ever complaining to his Mither.

Zahra had never known of her son's torture.

When Kenneth saw all the interior changes to Zahra's family mansion, he raved about it to her, especially the pretty interior Turkish lights. I liked the big comfortable couch chairs, by the fire and being waited on by the, ever-loyal Mairi. We were served up Turkish coffee with sweets. Then, before any conversation had begun, Grigor arrived and the lovely young Dihaoine ran to him and jumped up into his arms. She had finally grown to love him again, after their time apart when Grigor had chosen to be with Belle MacGregor. He still carried the shame on his face that all men do, who have deceived their wives, to that degree, then beaten them up in the process.

He was a calm looking man now and I couldn't imagine he was that same man who had punched Zahra in the face, causing those horrific injuries.

54. Betrothal & the Waterfall

Grigor was friendlier to me on this occasion, than he was the day before, but lawyer's offices had that effect on people. I probably looked stressed there. I still felt stressed. A lass like Dihaoine? I felt like it was almost immoral to even mention a connection with my son, but I had to. She was so young.

Zahra got the conversation started but Grigor was more direct.

"What is it you want of our Dihaoine?" Grigor asked. He wasn't a man to mess with words and I think I was already stepping on his father toes.

"My son Malcolm Og, one of identical twins, wishes to be betrothed with Dihaoine, with the view to marriage when she turns twelve, unless she is otherwise occupied or has changed her mind," I said. It was blunt and out there with no frills. It was as it was.

"How old is your son, Malcolm Og?" Grigor asked.

"He is seventeen, he has his own Teamster business, in partnership with his twin brother Hamish Og and he lives with me and my wife, Ailsa in Glengarry," I said. When he marries, he will move to the other house on MacNachten Farms.

"He's a Teamster then?" Grigor asked.

"Aye, he is" I said.

"Speak Erse, does he?" Grigor asked.

"Aye, he does," I said.

"How many Clydesdales do they both have?" Grigor asked.

"Eight Clydesdales," I replied.

"Did they recently assist Zahra then with her shopping in Inverness?" Grigor asked.

"Aye, they did," I said. Then he turned to Zahra and asked for her opinion about the lads, and particularly Malcolm Og.

"They're efficient Grigor, very hardworking and funny. They enjoy themselves, as they work and never overlook any detail. They were polite to me the whole time, as well as to Peter in Inverness, when we stayed there for the night. They are beautiful singers in the Gaelic language too," Zahra said.

"Are they?" I responded, a little surprised.

"You didn't know?" Zahra asked.

"Nae, they never sing at home," I added.

"They play a lot of musical instruments. I just opened up the cupboard over there and the whole group of them, with Hector and his friend's, played music for hours and I went to bed," Zahra said.

"What gave Malcolm Og the idea to be betrothed? Why not wait until he's old enough and meet the right person?" Grigor asked.

"My son Malcolm Og had the idea from Kenneth's daughter, April marrying Ali, your son, when Ali was betrothed to April as a young lass and then waited until she was twelve years old to marry. Then you know the rest, the wedding that you were invited to Grigor, but not Zahra. I suggested to Ali that he moved to Glengarry, if he sold his share of your farm back to you, because of his concerns for his young wife suffering with trying to live with Isobel, being so snippy," I explained.

Both parents hung their heads in shame for different reasons. Grigor's shame was that Zahra hadn't been invited to their son's wedding, believing that Zahra had run off with another man. The truth was revealed in the newspaper articles, explaining how she had been kidnapped and forcibly removed from everyone, suffering all manner of atrocities. Her shame was her daughter Isobel was being so difficult to get along with now, that Ali had to move to Glengarry, to protect his vulnerable young wife. Both parents appeared sad and had little more to say.

"What do you think Zahra? Come here, I want to speak privately with you," Grigor said. As Zahra willingly approached her ex-husband, he took her by the waist. "Sit here with me" he said. His strong arm held her tightly, so that she had to sit beside him. She was confused at what he was doing and wanted to wriggle free politely, if possible, without embarrassing him, but he wasn't letting go of her. "Sit down," he demanded. Zahra appeared to concede defeat and just sat there.

"Now, Mither of our Dihaoine, what are your thoughts?" Grigor asked seated very closely together to Zahra and was attempting an awkward kind of intimacy. I was afraid that it was going to be forced on her any minute, and I couldn't quite understand his intentions and his timing. Kenneth stood up and decided to leave our company and go to the kitchen to assist Mairi in making cups of hot chocolate, he said.

"Will you agree, if I do?" Grigor asked.

"Aye, she does really love him," Zahra replied.

He then turned and kissed his ex-wife passionately groping her as well and it was time I helped with the hot chocolate and let them sort out their relationship, for once and for all. He was that type of man who was going to get what he wanted, and in that moment, he wanted Zahra, and he was tired of the waiting. He had been excluded when she chose to marry Hugh Chisholm, despite all of his efforts then. No-one would blame him now, for still wanting his former wife back. I didn't want to judge him, and she wasn't in any danger. Eventually I glanced across from the kitchen and they were both equally involved in their amorous attentions towards each other. Zahra's next husband, I wondered.

"Mairi, can you please handfast the two of them, for decency, don't you think?" I suggested. She agreed and went across to them both, with a ribbon in her hand and they both held out their arms for the procedure.

Zahra was married once again and I felt oddly pleased for them both.

Then it was safe to bring up the subject of the missing inheritance and the legal Will from her former husband, Lord Coinneach MacAlpin. Aoungus had sent the investigators around and the bookshelf wood had been kept, as was instructed, which they took with them when they finally left after the lengthy discussion with Mr Martin Fraser who arrived shortly after the marriage of Zahra and Grigor. They also had his testimony concerning the missing gold.

All the while, Grigor kept looking at Zahra, in awe of her. He finally had her.

"You will have to live here," Zahra had ordered. Their arguments had already begun, but eventually it was decided that Grigor would live there on Beinn Coinneach and leave the farm with John Fraser, Isobel Fraser MacDonald, Fatma Fraser and Simon Fraser with Anndra and Domhnall, as well as wee Zahra Og with Padruig, if he wanted to still live there too.

"It was getting too crowded there anyway," Grigor Mohr said.

After giving the documents to Zahra, as Aonghus had instructed, I still didn't have permission for my son to be betrothed, so we stayed the night on the mountain in the hope of achieving that, the following morning. Considering I had it in writing already, I rose early the next morning to ensure that I could get their signatures. Kenneth was keen to get home to Glengarry, as was I, so as soon as it was signed, but we first went to the waterfall to see if the spectre of Old John could be seen, as I had seen in my dream.

It was a beautiful part of that property, that I had never seen before and it was quite awe inspiring, with a view all the way to the bottom of the entry road that was being re-built. There were beautiful enormous, native trees, still standing with hundreds of birds and native animals, scampering here and there. Even wee red squirrels ran around, plentiful in number and then we saw a beautiful hare who just sat in front of us and stared without fear of us or the horses. The hare seemed to open my vision somehow of the 'Otherworld'.

Then, I saw who I thought was Old John MacDonnell.

He looked happy to see me and healthier than he had ever been, when he was alive. It made me miss him more, but he beckoned me to an opening in the face of the natural rock wall, beside the waterfall. He vanished, then returned. I didn't understand how he had found an opening of some description, so we both searched, until we found a small hole that only one man could climb through. Kenneth is thinner than I, so he went in first and it opened into an enormous cavern, and it was all there. Loads of gold, both French and Spanish. Kenneth started to haul it out from under the waterfall.

I rode my horse, Jet back to Grigor and Hector to tell them both what their job was that day, hauling up all that gold with Hector's pony and cart. We had to get home to our wives and businesses. The road was almost finished, and I was glad to get off that mountain, before the next storm was due to hit, so with the required signatures on the betrothal agreement, we both departed.

I had told Ailsa that I would be gone for only one night and it had been three nights, and we were unlikely to arrive before midnight, even if we had kept on riding. We always used to stop off in a wee bothy, or shieling on the way home, so I ran it past Kenneth, who was very tired. I thought it better that we did stop, in case he fell off his bloody horse. It was a cold old bothy, but it did have supplies of peat to keep warm enough. Sleeping on straw beds, was a far cry from the plush new duck down mattresses, that Zahra had purchased, with her compensation payout. I felt grateful to my new father for his assistance, because I wouldn't have had the confidence to be one of the signatories to my son's betrothal and no doubt both

Zahra and Grigor felt it was a nice wedding present in getting Zahra's gold back.

The next morning, it was dreich, but luckily, we had our waterproof coats. My wife coated everything in bees wax, she claimed it was the best way to keep me dry. We were then home by midday instead of midnight, but I wasn't expecting a great reception at either farm, as I dropped off Kenneth, I wished him luck with Ivy and went on to Ailsa. I was nervous I admit. If she had done this to me, I'd be irate. Instead, she ran towards me, when she saw that it was me on my horse, Jet and she began to cry.

"Och Malcolm, my darling husband. I thought you were dead, don't do that to me again please," Ailsa cried.

I had a lot to make up for now that I had upset her so much. I promised her a night out in Glenmoriston, eating in James' restaurant and staying overnight in his hotel there, if she liked that idea. She calmed down thinking of what to wear at that restaurant and then asked all about what had happened.

"Where do I start?" I asked. "Zahra's married again to Grigor Mohr MacGregor."

Book 3

"Misty Mountain Ranch"

1. Cattle on The Mountain

"Grigor, now that you're here to stay, I am so pleased because I can ask you all about buying cattle. We need lots of them, with a good bull, preferably yellowy, orange ones," Zahra asked. It was the first morning after they had spent the night together and he hadn't quite expected her to get straight down to business, so quickly. He had hauled all that gold up the day before and his back was a bit sore, as was Hector's.

"Ma, what do we do with that gold now?" Hector asked. "Do we put it into a bank where it's safer than here?" he asked.

"Nae son, it's too old. It's Spanish gold mostly, as well as French, so we will have to melt it down and spend it bit by bit in small bars," Grigor said.

"But Da, whoever hid it in the waterfall, could come back. Can we find a better place to hide it in the meantime?" Hector asked.

"We could brick it into a wall," suggested Zahra.

"But we will need some of the money to buy the cattle, so we will need to work out how much to melt down for sixty coos, then bricking into a wall is a good idea," Grigor replied.

'We could bury it," Hector also suggested.

"Do you know of any caves here Hector that are not near the waterfall," Zahra asked.

"Oh, aye there are lots," Hector said. "They're dotted all over this mountain and it could be hidden in separate caves in small quantities, so it can't all be lost, all in one go," Hector suggested.

Grigor seemed to know how much would be needed for cattle, including a good bull to start the new industry. Hector and

Grigor were busy melting down gold bars into little ones without a Spanish or French identity while keeping the value.

"Do you know a trustworthy bank manager?" Grigor asked. "We need someone who can keep quiet about this who has a vault, we might be able to put some of it, as it is, into their vault," Grigor said logically.

"I don't know any bank managers Grigor," Zahra said. "How about we get Mr Fraser back. He would know a bank manager. We'd just have to pay him," Zahra added.

"Why don't we just employ him and be done with it," Grigor said. "He has a son too who can help him, doesn't he?" Grigor added.

Mr MacKenzie was asked to visit Mr Martin Fraser in Fraser Ville to visit the mansion once again. He was happy to do so, if he was paid and he was accompanied by his accountant son, so we then employed them both, as accountants and they were given an office on the top floor of the new wing at the rear, with plenty of light and a desk each.

He was astonished to learn of the gold being back where it had once been. All his suggestions were followed. "Those iron bars that you have downstairs, can be built across behind the bookcase, so if they break in again, the bars will stop them from going any further," Mr Fraser said. "That will be easier than finding a cave," he said.

So, the men who worked on the bookcase came back again to forge the iron to the correct size to cover over the secret room's entrance, for the entire length of the room's size. Mr Fraser was happy with the result, but Grigor still wanted a bank involved as well, that had a vault. He also wanted to learn how to melt down the bars into smaller bars in the best way to pay for the cattle, else it attracted attention and resulted in all of us being followed home and robbed.

Mr Fraser introduced Zahra and Grigor to his brother-in-law, who lived in Fraser Ville also, but worked in Inverness with a group of people who all travelled to work together each day, on a horse and cart. He was a trustworthy Bank Manager from a small bank who agreed to keeping part of the gold in his small vault in Inverness, then Grigor was happy. It was a good start with the Spanish gold, especially for that rainy day when Grigor and Zahra might be in debt, unexpectedly.

Most of Zahra's cash from Lord Cinaed was nearly all spent, with having repaired the long entry road, with the cost of the small drainage stones, the heavy hard wooden sleepers, labour, cement, and thousands of cobble stones but it had been worth it. The drain, either side of the road, worked an absolute marvel, with every downpour. The result looked amazing and so much safer, especially with the lighting as well and the garden alongside both sides of the new road that Peter had suggested. He wanted pine trees and roses all the way along both sides of it. Peter seemed to think that the money would never run out, but with the new road, the Clydesdale stables, improvements to Hector's yards and stables, plus everything else inside, the bathroom tiles and road renovations, money was fast running out.

It was fortunate that the gold had been found, thanks to Malcolm's dream.

Grigor had decided where the cattle would roam, and the family finally had the small gold bars, and they all went together with Hector to buy the Highland cattle and a beautiful big docile bull. They asked Flidas to stay behind in charge, as well as minding the two young bairns. They were wondering about the merits of a front gate, in order to stop unexpected visitors from even arriving at their front door or stealing the coos. The bull was going to be hard to handle with droving all the cattle home. He was a strong, big bull that Grigor swore was the best bull in the market. Getting him home was another matter, especially with a whole fold of lady coos.

"Won't he want to mount them on the way home, Grigor?" Zahra asked.

"He might, but that won't take long," Grigor said.

Zahra hoped he was right because she was afraid of bulls, even docile ones and she was going to manage the ladies, unless he disturbed them.

"I would prefer it if you kept him separate, Grigor until we get to Misty Mountain. Hector and I can manage the ladies, if they're not chased around by the bull. Please Grigor can you manage the bull, separately somehow?" Zahra pleaded.

Grigor then had to employ staff from the market to get the bull home first, then Hector and Zahra would leave with the ladies after the bull, who was accompanied by Grigor. They had spent so much money, that the market gave them two more men to drive the ladies home. It wasn't that hard, but luckily Hector was very experienced now at droving, while Zahra had only ever mustered sheep on horseback as a youngster. Even with their three collies and the two Irish wolf hounds, it was difficult. Arriving at the base of 'Misty Mountain Ranch', the road upwards became a race for some coos and a slow old meander for others. One thing Zahra did decide on was closing that big, wide gate. They'd be too easy to steal, once it was known that they were now in the cattle industry so up went that sign. Zahra did love her signs.

Grigor wanted to use the Clydesdale stables for the bull, but it was only temporary. Zahra showed him under the house where there had once been that medieval court, which still gave her the creeps. In a storm, she hoped it would be suitable to protect the coos in there, if they built a separate section for the bull. The tunnel from the base of the mountain was certainly wide enough, allowing for their horns, if the coos walked in single file, but the lights were too low. She would have to move them all up the wall, so their horns wouldn't catch on to them and thereby start a fire. Grigor was shocked at the complexity of the house that Zahra now owned.

Zahra asked Mr MacKenzie to change the height of all the lights and organise a strong enclosure in there also, for the bull, as well as a separate section for the feed which was where the old thrones used to be located with old unused antiques. All that iron that was previously used for monstrous things in there, would finally have a decent use. It was a huge area and was big enough for all of the cattle, or all of the ponies but not both together, so the ponies could have the Clydesdale stables in a storm, she offered.

"Zahra, why have you built Clydesdale stables when we don't have Clydesdales?" Grigor asked.

"Because Dihaoine's fiancé has Clydesdales. It's for them when they come," she replied.

"This is for Malcolm Og?" Grigor asked incredulously.

"Aye and whoever needs it, like your bull or Hector's Ponies," Zahra said.

Dihaoine looked pleased at her Mither's planning for Malcolm Og's next visit to see her.

Dinner that night saw an exhausted family after droving the cattle all the way from Inverness. It was near dark when Zahra arrived home, but luckily Grigor had prepared the feed for them and where they would be penned off from escaping again down that road. The wrought iron gate would stop them from escaping, and it may discourage people from entering too or stealing the new coos. Just the same, they put a bell there like the Aird farm did, so if it was a genuine visitor, then the gate could be opened for them. Grigor disagreed with that idea.

"It's too much fuss," Grigor said. He was right and eventually the gate was only closed at night.

Life with Grigor was always a discussion, most of which resulted in Grigor winning with his point of view, but at least Zahra and Grigor no longer fought. Hector watched on nervously at first, mostly in disbelief that his father was back with his Mither. He didn't dare ask his Mither about Hugh's last dying wish, but he knew how to live with them both, so long as his father didn't hurt his Mither again, was all he cared about. Zahra saw his concern for her across his face one day and, as tall as Hector was now, she held him around his thickening waist and thanked him for being so understanding.

"I love you so much Hector, can you please tolerate your Ma and your Da?" Zahra asked.

"For you Ma, I will," Hector answered.

"He is trying hard, my love," Zahra said.

Hector just nodded in response.

2. Pigeons Fly

"Grigor love, I need to talk to you about Lord Cinaed and my wee bairn Coinneach Og," Zahra asked.

"I want my bairn, wee Coinneach Og back with us, permanently. Should we tell Lord Cinaed that he has a wee lassie?" she asked.

"Alex would love that, and the father should know anyway, so aye, tell him. You and Isobel are not getting along anyway," Grigor said. "Where are those homing pigeons, you said sent messages to him?" he asked.

Zahra led Grigor out the back of the mansion to where the pigeons were all happily housed in their dovecote, and she explained the two varieties of pigeons to Grigor. One for eating in the winter months and the homing pigeons, but each bird went to a particular member of the family. She didn't know which one was which, so they guessed. The main bird at the front of all the other birds, had to be for Lord Cinaed, was Grigor's reasoning. Looking at how it was done, there was another problem.

"Grigor, they wrote in their own language, and we don't know that language," Zahra said.

"Then write a wee message in English. He knows your handwriting," Grigor said. "If the wrong person gets

it, he ends up in the waterfall," Grigor said, as a matter of fact. One by one, that family all had to be disposed of, was Grigor's plan anyway, then they would own MacAlpin Industries.

"Short cut," Grigor said. Zahra had forgotten how blood thirsty her ex-husband could be but, in this instance, she thought it was a good idea. As they released the bird into the air, she wondered who was going to turn up, but decided coffee was in order. Food too maybe? As they sat in the kitchen, drinking coffee and eating sandwiches, Grigor became amorous. Did killing someone turn him on? Maybe it did.

"Where's your axe love?" Grigor asked.

"Just by the back door," she replied. Grigor walked back in with both the tomahawk, as well as the axe.

"Please don't mess up my new Turkish rugs," Zahra said. Grigor rolled up the Turkish rugs and leaned them up against the wall.

"Anything, else?" Grigor asked.

"Aye, if there is blood splatter on my newly painted walls, you are paying the painter next time," Zahra said.

"Sounds like I should do him outside to save me some hassle?" Grigor said smiling.

"How can you smile, contemplating murder, Grigor?" Zahra asked.

"It's not murder. They're already dead and they're crooked assholes, that's why," Grigor said, then kissed Zahra passionately and rubbed her private parts which was, admittedly, very enjoyable, but as she began to want more, there was a loud bang on her big front door.

"It might be Lord Cinaed," Zahra said.

Lord Cinaed was indeed standing at their ornate front door, waiting to be invited in. He was holding onto Coinneach Og. The wee bairn held out his arms again saying 'Ma'. She took him into her arms and a reluctant Cinaed parted with him.

"Och, my sweet wee Coinneach, aren't you so handsome. Your hair is getting curly like mine," Zahra said.

The sweet lad played with her hair to feel it and laughed. He was the first bairn to have anything of Zahra. Hugh's bairn was nothing like her in looks or personality, Grigor's bairns all looked like him, just a better version of him. Hector had a bit of Grant about him for some unknown reason but was clearly a MacGregor, maybe a bit taller. Zahra was busy with Coinneach Og playing with him, reading to him and as time went by, she did wonder where the other two were, when she noticed the two axes were missing.

"I've prepared your new room. Do you want to see it?" Zahra asked wee Coinneach. She had it all arranged beautifully for him with a rocking horse and his own special bed. He had a nice outlook to the front garden, and he could see Hector on one of his ponies. "Heto, Heto," he said.

"You are so smart, aye that's Hector on his pony," Zahra said. Then she saw her husband carrying bags of heavy things and was headed in the direction of the waterfall.

'Oh God. He's done in the old man,' she said to herself. Another one down, let's hope he can't put himself back together again, like Hugh did, she thought.

Mairi offered to take the lad, for something to eat with Causantin and Dihaoine, when Hector came in to speak with her.

"Ma. Has Da done in Lord Cinaed?" Hector asked.

"Aye, maybe, he has," Zahra said. "Coinneach is living here now," she replied.

Grigor came in wiping his hands on a rag and looking puffed. It reminded her of when Coinneach wiped his hands on a rag, when he was painting.

Mr Martin Fraser let them know a few days later that Lord

Cinaed had been missing for a few days and no-one knew where he was. Zahra declared that he had dropped off Coinneach Og on that fateful day but knew nothing more and acted surprised that she would now have full custody of wee Coinneach Og.

Neither party were expecting a visit from Anndra MacAlpin, the worse brother after Prince Griogar. He was enquiring about his father. Zahra answered him in the same way as they both had to Mr Fraser. Their father had dropped off Coinneach Og for her to care for, while he was going somewhere, but did not disclose where he was going and they hadn't been interested to ask. Anndra wasn't in a hurry to leave and perused his surroundings. She offered him tea or coffee, which he accepted and sat beside the fire.

"New couches, I see." Anndra said.

"Aye, from my compensation money, Anndra," Zahra responded.

"New Turkish lights and floor rugs too?" he added.

"Aye," she responded.

"The walls have all been painted, have they?" Anndra asked.

"Plastered and painted. Ceilings too," Zahra replied. "It's an old place that needed a lot of work," she added.

"Were they Highland coos that I saw mooching around?" Anndra asked.

"Aye, that's our new business," Zahra said.

"It's not a part of our industries and you didn't get my permission," Anndra said boldly.

 Zahra could not believe his attitude of power and control, that he was now assuming.

"I don't need your permission Anndra and you need to start paying me for my share in MacAlpin Industries," Zahra said.

He then stood, half smiling, half smirking at her.

"This is ours you fool, so now the cattle are ours too," Anndra said.

But just as he said that his eyes rolled back, as he received a fatal knife wound to his kidneys from Grigor.

"I know. The Turkish rugs," Grigor said to Zahra and Grigor quickly pulled Anndra's lifeless body out through the front door with Hector holding the big doors open.

"Mairi quick. There's blood on the new couch chair," Zahra said.

"Then wash off that trail of blood and keep it to yourself," Zahra said worried only about the new furnishings. Hector helped his father to be rid of Anndra into the waterfall. They were also both carrying the axes that Grigor had just sharpened.

Only two MacAlpin brothers to go. Cinaed Og and Padraig.

"I need Padruig Grant and Alex to help. This is getting too close to the bone," Grigor told her later that night.

"So long as Isobel doesn't come here too and Padruig doesn't stay," Zahra said.

The new groom was tasked with riding to the Aird with a letter from both Grigor and Zahra.

The letter read: *Padruig, Alex, Need two hands with that waterfall here. Grigor and Zahra MacGregor.*

Grigor had all kinds of weapons ready for the last two brothers, unsure if the MacAlpins would bring in mercenaries, once again. There weren't many left of the Glenmoriston Men, so John Campbell aka Ossian, was also called on by Padruig.

The cattle were a lot of work for Grigor, let alone everything else, Causantin was helping Hector with the ponies these days, along with Flidas too, although they all helped Grigor when needed. Dihaoine stayed in the house a lot and helped Mairi learning how to cook. She had overheard her Mither's criticisms of April's cooking and being unprepared for marriage, so she was determined to be prepared. Coinneach Og helped Zahra with her herb garden. He liked gardening and getting his small hands dirty.

The three Glenmoriston Men arrived, before there was any sign of the two MacAlpin Brothers, or any mercenaries and the farmwork was under control. Zahra had planned bedrooms for all three of the men in the new wing, a long way from herself and Grigor. They hadn't remembered not having even told them that they were married. Grigor just hadn't come home one day from after seeing her, but no confirmation had been made of any formal marriage.

"We are hand fast," said Zahra.

"I'm arranging a proper wedding with my wife, and you'll all be invited," Grigor said cuddling Zahra and kissing her, to ensure that they all believed it.

"Are you? That's nice. We should leave off Ali and April from the guest list, jesting of course. In fact, everyone who left me off their bloody guest lists shouldn't be invited," Zahra added. In a more serious tone.

"I agree Ma," said Hector. "See how they feel about not being invited, especially Isobel," Hector added. Grigor still looked guilty for having gone to their wedding, without Zahra there.

"I am sorry Zahra. I felt lousy the whole night, if that makes you feel any better," Grigor added.

"It does a bit Grigor," she replied.

"I brought the books over for you to read to me Zahra," Padruig said.

"I have a bone to pick with you Padruig Grant. If you had revealed more details to Rev Robert Forbes at the time, my book would have been much more detailed about what happened here in the Highlands. It was only known that you were back from France, due to the Inverness Rev John Stewart that you had passed through Leith and avoided talking to him. Why did you do that Padruig? What was that all about? If you had time to see Rev Stewart?" Zahra asked. And I quote from the book the "Lyon in Mourning":

Quoting *Rev. John Stewart, Inverness, March 24, 1763. I had two visits this winter and spring from your old friend, Patrick Grant, whose picture, I am told, hangs in Tartan Hall. He made a notable figure in North America, one campaign only, against the French owing to a particular friend who would not dispense with his attendance, and he has returned safe and sound, and has Chelsea pension. He was a night in the neighbourhood of Leith but had not countenance enough to visit a certain friend, being afraid of being bantered for something.* ®

The whole room was agape at how Zahra had memorized, what was contained in that part of The Lyon in Mourning, owning up to Padruig's avoidance of the Reverend upon his return from France. Zahra had needed more information about Culloden and the atrocities afterwards. It hadn't mattered that he had fought in France, she had just needed the information. He only thought of Zahra as a smarter than usual, oddball but sexy as hell, who had appeared out of nowhere and should have been grateful to them for looking after her, especially Grigor, when things went pear shaped. How did she memorize all of that? She was still angry at her unfinished work and dying while on the job.

Grigor knew his wife was smart but now understood the underlying issues with Padruig. She may never forgive him. Under the current Monarch in that time, all was peaches and cream with the empty Scotland now that the rebels were all dead and or cleared.

"I am sorry Zahra. I couldn't speak to him at that time," Padruig said.

"You were in Leith," Zahra said. "I feel that I have failed, that's all. That book was meant to achieve more than what it did," she retorted

Hector put his arm around his Mither. "You're smart Ma. I could never memorize a book like that, but you could do better with your understanding about snow," Hector jested.

"Very funny my beautiful son. Any way you can memorize all those Gaelic sayings that you and Ali play with. You have an amazing memory, and you can repeat all of the names of your wee ponies. Your father is lucky to remember his own children's names, isn't that right, Grigor?" Zahra teased. "I might have to put signs on all of the bedroom doors too, now that we have Coinneach Og here, as well," Grigor said.

Mairi had cooked stew for them all, expecting an animated conversation over dinner, but it had gone quiet now with each man delving into the past and things that they would rather have forgotten, but they never could. At least her husband, Grigor seemed to appreciate his wife's depth of emotion for a people far removed in time from her. Maybe the recent events had been too much, reminding her of how brutal they had all had to be, to survive but he knew that if anyone understood that, Zahra did. She had married two of the Glenmoriston men twice now, and the oddball was Coinneach MacAlpin, not her.

"Just one thing Zahra, if you don't mind me saying too Grigor," Padruig said. He was careful now not to upset Grigor this night.

"I never thought of you as an oddball, I just couldn't make sense of where you came from, that was all. I heard you and your family talking about us during Samhain before you came to us and I told Alex that you weren't a threat, but we weren't sure what to make of you and when you had affection for Hugh, I was worried at first. We knew he was married and had a reputation with the ladies, so you were going to be hurt, we knew that much, that's all. We couldn't judge people, when we were hacking people up and you were just trying to figure out how to cook a stew.

I liked you actually and that's all I think I should say," Padruig said.

"I was both in awe of an historical personage, as well as a bit afraid of you at first," Zahra said. "Raping me, however, will not help, so please do not entertain that idea again, or do I need to sleep with my skein dubh?" Zahra said.

Hector and Flidas both thought it was now time for bed and kissed their Ma goodnight and took all the wee ones with them.

Mairi was with her husband, Callum in the kitchen and when Zahra went in to assist her, Mairi hugged her Mistress and told her she didn't need any help. Her husband had adopted a sad looking demeanour now, understanding who she really was and how sad it was that her marriage had ended with Grigor in the first place.

"I have a question Zahra, about the wolf in the Chapel. Where did he come from?' Alex enquired.

"Aye?" she said warily "His name was Ulvy Stiorm and he was a 'spirit wolf' who hadn't been with me for long and I wasn't even aware of his presence, until Grigor told me, when he was visiting me in Inverness with Hugh. Peter didn't want a wolf to materialise in the house, so it wasn't until I was with Hugh, that we asked him to appear, because we needed his help. We knew that the brown wolf was on our tail and could follow our scent. Ulvy Stiorm then told us who he was, and that he would fight to the death, if the need arose, which he did as you saw. It was unlucky that Isobel's musket ball ricocheted and hit Hugh in the Chapel in that process," Zahra said sadly.

"I thought you were here to assist my husband with the MacAlpin brothers, Alex?" Zahra said, not wishing to disclose any more personal information to Alex.

All the men were morose over the incident in the Chapel. They had all wished they had been more supportive of them both, before their wedding.

"But how does a 'spirit wolf' occur if you didn't always have one?" Alex probed.

"Are you going to assist my husband and I with the MacAlpin brothers or not?" Zahra asked again.

"I will," Padruig said.

"I will too," John Campbell said.

"And you Alex? Or are you here, only to satisfy your own curiosity?" Zahra asked. "Because I am not answering any more personal questions that you have. I have never asked you a personal question, have I? Do I ask you. 'Why do you walk around naked?' No, I don't bother to know the answer. Do I ask you. 'Why you were in love with Peter Heath then suddenly in love with my daughter?' No, I was hoping you could recover, that was all. Have I even chastised you for leaving my entire family when I was removed after Grigor knocked me out? No, I am glad that you are back now with my grandchildren, who love you," she said emotively.

"There's a time and a place to enquire and in addition, I am your mother-in-Law, and there is supposed to be a level of respect from you to me, which I am not hearing," Zahra said critically. "Just because my daughter is disrespectful to me, gives you no reason to be the same. I have never been disrespectful to you," Zahra added.

Alex and the entire group were surprised at her new directness and if anything, agreed with Zahra. He was bordering on disrespect to his mother-in-Law. No-one could remember her being unkind to Alex, only kindness was ever shown to him.

"You have only ever shown me kindness Zahra. I thought it would change, however when you became acquainted with Peter Heath, that's all," Alex said looking down. "Has it changed towards me?" he asked nervously. "Peter's rose gardening is all around here, even all the way up the misty mountain road, to the house," Alex said.

"Peter's rose gardening now, is it?" Zahra asked in a sarcastic tone. "Peter and I both bought the roses together for his Medical Practice. We both loved roses. It was a pleasant activity that we did together. It wasn't just Peter. He has continued that on to include this property, because I don't have the time to do everything. He offered to assist and that's what he did, because he knew that I would like the roses, and I love them. The aroma of the roses has a way of altering your mindset, for the better," Zahra explained.

"Just because Peter and I no longer live together, doesn't mean the end of our ongoing friendship. It had nothing to do with you. He is a lonely man, and we like each other. He is always welcome here," Zahra added. "On top of all that consideration, is that he was raped by the man who was searching for me. It was therefore, my fault that he was raped," Zahra added sadly.

"Can't you also befriend Peter again?" Zahra asked. "Alex Grant no longer sees him either" she said. "Why can't you even have a cup of tea together? It would mean so much to him," Zahra asked.

Alex was looking ashamed and embarrassed then, remembering that he was once in love with Peter Heath, and refused to show his softer side, not even a cup of tea with Peter Heath.

"Did you think that Peter had spoken ill of you to me?" Zahra asked.

"Aye," Alex admitted.

"Peter doesn't speak ill of people, who were once in his heart. Give him a break Alex," Zahra said. "Give me a break too. I'm wondering now if the reason for Isobel hating me so much, may have been because of you. Was it?" Zahra asked plainly.

"I didn't help, I admit but it was all your daughter, when you disappeared from here and I am sorry that we all got that story, so horribly wrong," Alex said.

"Have you finished now with all of your questions Alex because I am going to bed? I'll leave Grigor to explain the rest to you all. Goodnight," Zahra said and left their company, disappointed.

Zahra kissed her husband, spoke quietly in his ear and left the room.

"Thanks Alex. We needed Zahra for the inside information," Grigor said.

"You might as well all go to bed and if you are unwilling to help, then leave early in the morning, will you?" asked Grigor.

He followed his wife blowing out the candles as he left, indicating they had better go to their rooms, or it would be too dark to find their rooms again in that big house. Padruig smoored the big loungeroom fire too and they headed up the opposite stairs, carrying a single candle each. The night had not gone as well as Grigor had hoped. Zahra was different and who wouldn't be, after all that she had been through, even after losing Hugh?

'Her life was a book in itself', Grigor thought.

3. The Next Day

Mairi was up early preparing breakfast for the Glenmoriston Men, but the whole time they were present, Mairi's husband stayed with her. The staff were all busy in their tasks, not noticing what the men were occupied with, but the men's beds were stripped and made up clean once again and their windows opened briefly while there was sunshine and closed again, soon after. Their floors were all washed, and all of the surfaces were dusted then wiped clean. The men had never seen such clean rooms in a residential house.

The long and wide, dining table was beautifully set, with fresh roses in vases and two big fires were lit, once again. The nanny goat had been milked and there was fresh goat's milk, and on this occasion, there was even a jug of fresh Highland coo milk, for Padruig. The floors had already been washed and cleaned and the Turkish rugs beaten outside, then brought back inside again. The kitchen was busy with both Mairi and her husband and as soon as the three men sat down, their parritch was served, then Grigor and Zahra came in. Zahra went straight into the kitchen to greet Mairi and carried a plate of toasted bread with jam across to the table. She could barely look at the men but was clearly close to Grigor, who took every opportunity to hold her hand or kiss her lovingly.

Grigor shook the hand of Mairi's husband, and they all seemed to have a close association, especially Mairi with Zahra. Padruig saw that Mairi knew a lot more than she would ever disclose and deduced that she must have seen Zahra, at her very worst, when she had been first taken there, as a victim of violence. Grigor's violence. Padruig wondered if they knew it had been him and if so, how they felt about him.

Zahra stayed in the kitchen with Mairi, discussing staff

uniforms that she wished to change. Currently they were all wearing a black and white, midcalf dress which Zahra didn't like. She was suggesting to Mairi something warmer, longer and more colourful. Zahra had always felt the dresses were too short, especially for the cleaners but the former Master wanted it that way, she said and black was his choice and there was no discussion. Mr MacKenzie hated his wife wearing both black and short dresses, so he was involved in their discussion, which was more interesting than theirs.

"Why don't you all have breakfast with us and tell us about your uniform and we can all give you our opinions too. Will you eat with us Mairi and Callum?" Padruig asked.

 Zahra asked the wary pair if they wanted to, who then agreed, only if she wanted them too.

"Aye I want you to," Zahra said.

Coinneach must have been so cruel to them too, that even a small thing like eating together was a frightening prospect.

"What I suggest Mairi is a long dress in all your own respective tartans. With a matching blouse underneath," Zahra said.

"My tartan has red in it. Would a red blouse be appropriate Mistress Zahra?" Mairi asked.

"That would be nicer than black and white, don't you think? How many blouses do you need for one week?" Zahra asked.

"Aye and I'd need five Mistress," Mairi said.

While they ate breakfast, it was decided how many different tartans were needed as well as capes and measuring would start that day.

"I'll put the order in, if you all agree on the design, between two," Zahra said.

One was a simple long skirt with a waist coat and blouse to match the tartan. The other choice was a long sleeveless dress or pinafore, with long sleeved blouse underneath and both with an apron and a cape. Both uniforms had a cap, to cover their hair. Grigor said he liked the pinafore dress and matching blouse to keep the ladies decent. Mairi's tartan was an old MacKenzie tartan, which was nice, and it would help Zahra in recognising who everyone was, when the staff changed over to the Clan Fraser. Padruig was very interested in the dresses and agreed to the long pinafore dress, because his wife had worn one like that.

Alex said nothing at breakfast. Maybe he had said too much the previous night.

"Mr MacKenzie, what about you?" Zahra asked. He had been quiet too, while eating his breakfast. Hector was watching on and listening. He wasn't going to leave the room, until his Mither had.

"The long one too Mistress, not the short skirt," Callum said. He looked pleased his wife would cover up her legs at long last.

"Oh, that's wonderful," Zahra said. "Mairi, can you help me with measuring the permanent female staff?" Zahra asked.

"Mr MacKenzie, would you object to wearing those tartan long pants, not the pillibeg kilt, with a highland shirt and matching waist coat in MacKenzie tartan?" Zahra asked.

"Me, Mistress. Nae I don't need anything new?" Callum replied.

"But if you did, would you wear them?" Zahra asked.

"Aye. If it were all wool and were warm enough," Mr MacKenzie said reluctantly.

"Would you prefer plain tweed woollen trouse?" she asked. Mairi was smiling at this conversation, then giggled.

"Tweed then, in plain grey with matching waist coat or clan tartan?" Zahra asked. He was pleased with the tweed.

"I think you had better come with me to the Mill to choose the fabric, Mr MacKenzie. You might be harder to please than the ladies. Mairi, can he stay over for one night in Inverness with us?" Zahra asked.

"Grigor darling, do you mind if I stay over one night with Peter?" Zahra asked.

"So long as you take Coinneach Og with you," Grigor said. "He's a demanding lad that one," he said.

"Aye, I can take all three little ones if you like?" Zahra said.

"Can we take the carriage then Mistress, for the little ones. It's certain to be a wet day?" Mr MacKenzie asked.

Sidling up beside her husband, Zahra asked him if he would like a new plaid.

"Aye, I would," Grigor said and kissed his wife too passionately for company, but he was beyond caring.

John Campbell asked a question, relative to their visit.

"Could you describe what the two MacAlpin brothers look like, before you get busy, please Mistress Zahra?" John asked politely.

"Cinaed Og isn't too tall, not short either, average height I suppose. Pale blue eyes, blondish, reddish thick, curly hair, small goatee, blonde eyebrows and speaks too quietly. He is quite nice. He helped me with delivering Coinneach Og, doing Alex's old job. He's lean and fit, doesn't like his wife, I think. Cinaed seems a bit effeminate to me and he wears old fashioned clothing. The other brothers all seemed to dominate him but there's a humanity about him, that's not present in any of the other brothers. Padraig is more masculine than Cinaed, but untrustworthy. Similar height to Cinaed Og, he's a snappy dresser, likes the ladies, dark blonde hair, short back and sides, no goatee or moustache. Confident stride when he walks. Stands as straight, as an arrow, like a military man. Bit sharp, possibly ruthless, but not as sharp as Anndra was. They look a lot alike really and if it wasn't for the goatee, I doubt I could tell them apart," Zahra said.

"I don't know much more about him because he has stayed

in the background, but his name isn't pronounced like your name Padruig. It has the Irish pronunciation, so it sounds like they're saying porritch," she added finally smiling. "My preference is for Cinaed because he is also intelligent and maybe spiritual too."

"Let's go Mairi," she said, and the two women walked off, leaving the breakfast dishes to the men.

Measuring wasn't an easy task with women of all shapes and sizes, demanding tartans of all unknown varieties. So, it came down to one tartan only for all the MacKenzies and one for all the Frasers. The trip was planned for the following day, so Hector also wanted to come, to protect his Mither and his siblings. She thought she had better bring farm produce also for Peter, as it was a surprise visit and would cost a lot for him to feed, now that there was going to be two men and one woman, with three bairns, who all ate a lot, as well as Peter. She included a shoulder of beef, goat's milk, vegetables of many varieties, cheese, and a sack of flour for bread, salt, ground coffee and their own honey.

She had Peter's front door key just in case he was out, so she could let herself in, at any time.

"Gentlemen I think it would be a bad idea to kill both brothers. We need Cinaed Og to assist us with the lawyers when we change everything into just the two companies. His and ours. So, this will be Misty Mountain Ranch Industries, with whatever else we inherit from all the others, split into two and Cinaed Og, can take on another name. The old name of MacAlpin Industries will be dissolved. Everything will be split down the middle between Cinaed Og and I. Then whatever I leave in my Will to my son, Coinneach Og would be no different to what I leave to Causantin, for example or any other of my sons or daughters.

Can we please agree on that, or we will have too many investigators here looking for them? I want to be the Chairperson of the company that Cinaed Og and us will run, Grigor, while it all goes through. There's no need to be greedy is there? You three men will be paid for coming here and carrying out the one deed well, ensuring that one brother cannot come back to life again, like Hugh did from the Aird waterfall.

The only question I have is when Prince Griogar's estate goes through, is whether I am entitled to more from his estate, minus his house, or at least a greater part of it, than Cinaed Og is, due to the multiple crimes against myself and my youngest two bairns, Dihaoine and Causantin. I want separate trust accounts in my young two bairns' names, to be kept in trust for them when they come of age, paid directly from his estate, if I can achieve that. Hector has his compensation which he has had to spend on his stables and my compensation has all been spent on renovating this house. I would like to see my youngest two, who were kidnapped also, set up for life, if possible. However, as I've said, at this stage it's only a question, so bear with me on that one. His wife gets his house but all his assets and as well as income, after the initial split it could be a 70/30 split between me and Cinaed Og instead of 50/50. Cinaed would obviously have to agree," Zahra said.

All the men had lost understanding Zahra back at the prince's name, so none of them could follow her train of thought on that matter.

"What about payment for doing him in?" Padruig asked.

"Good question. That too can be paid to you but not from his estate, until it's in my name and if you can tell me what you would like to be paid for that job, I assume you'll pay me for those two paintings you have too, Padruig?" Zahra asked.

"Never mind," he said.

4. Salmon on Misty Mountain

"I also need someone who knows about salmon fishing, Grigor.

Can you find someone in the village while I am gone, so we can also start up salmon fishing here? I think it might work. Salmon can jump up waterfalls, can't they? Then there's the wee loch that they could swim around in, so we can sell them. What do you think, Grigor?" Zahra asked.

"Wouldn't Hamish and Hugh be better to advise you on salmon?" Padruig asked. "They know everything there is to know about fish. Hamish is also getting tired of working so hard in Cannich. An easier, laid-back job here with just him and Cora would be better than Cannich, now that he's getting older," Padruig added.

"His bairns are all married and with their own bairns all living elsewhere. Hamish is also a bit lonely without his bairns and his friends. He'd love it here. If you had a wee house nearby the waterfall, that would be perfect, or he could live in the big house. You could sort that out. That wee house by Loch Garry is always empty. He might as well sell it to Malcolm who has plenty of money, for one of his bairns, like Alex. Hamish would love working with fish all the time," Padruig added.

"Thank you Padruig. That's a great idea. Hamish is such a nice man, and he has helped me out many times. I owe it to him really. What do you think Grigor?" Zahra asked.

"Aye, if you're serious Zahra, about salmon, then write to him tonight, before you leave, then post it in Inverness. I like him too. Not sure about building him a house though?" Grigor said.

"We need to know first if it's possible to breed them here and if they can jump up that high," Zahra said.

"I don't know anything about them, but I did see lots of fish, at least two types, in the loch the other day, so it might be possible and if it was possible to breed salmon here darling and they were making us a pretty penny, we could afford a wee house for Hamish and Cora, couldn't we?" Zahra asked. "I'll buy a book tomorrow in Inverness on salmon farming. Do you want one too on Highland coos, in Gaelic or English?" Zahra asked.

Zahra was now a businesswoman.

5. Inverness and Peter

It had been an ordinary day for Peter in his Medical Practice. There had been some disgusting things to deal with, but that was all in a day's work. The last thing he was expecting was a visit, late in the day from his dearest friend, Zahra, along with Mr MacKenzie, her Farm Manager, her sons Hector, Causantin, and wee Coinneach Og and her daughter wee Dihaoine.

Poor Peter had a minor panic attack when he saw them all arriving, because he hadn't been shopping yet and his cupboards were all empty. Zahra had been to the post office and the book shop during the day but was fully prepared to cook at Peter's house, but he didn't yet know that. 'What could he feed everyone for dinner was his first panicking thought?' Fortunately, Zahra pulled out all the farm produce that she had with her, to start cooking for him, then he was overwhelmed with not only relief from his loneliness, but all that food too. He cried onto her shoulder.

"Oh, Zahra, I have missed you so much and I am so disorganised, without you here," Peter said as he wept with both sadness and joy. Each of the bairns were cuddled and kissed in much the same way.

He had been so lonely since being up on the mountain with them all and then being back in Inverness alone was making him feel low, he had to admit. He couldn't believe it when the stew was cooking and the house was active once again, with the sweet little bairns, even Coinneach Og this time.

"Coinneach Og has grown a lot since I saw him last," Peter said. He picked him up joyously.

"You are such a big and braw lad," Peter said to Coinneach Og. "Zahra darling is he growing hair like yours now?" he asked. "It's not as blonde as it was and he's growing your ringlets. Isn't he gorgeous?" Peter added.

Coinneach was loving all the attention that he received from the caring and parental figure of Peter Heath.

Mr MacKenzie had the horses stabled nearby, like Malcolm's lads had, but they bought all their shopping inside this time. Zahra showed him the few new uniforms that she was able to get on the day, while all the rest were on order, due to the sheer size of the order. He loved the colourful tartan uniforms, with the matching blouses, even the aprons and caps.

"I love all of these plaids. Who are they for?" Peter asked.

"One is for my husband Grigor, in the MacGregor modern red tartan, but the others are for Padruig Grant in the Grant Glenmoriston colours and Alex MacDonald of Aonach in their tartan and his friend John Campbell MacDonald with his confused identity. They are up at our house now if you wanted to see Alex again. Do you?" Zahra asked.

"Why is Alex MacDonald there at your home? That sounds positively sinister," Peter said.

"Reason enough to give them each a gift then, don't you think? Do you want to see Alex? Isobel's not there and we have the carriage. We can tie your horse to the back," Zahra added.

"I'm not really busy this week and I suppose I could hire the Locum again," Peter said thoughtfully.

"You might be able to put Alex in a better mood than what he was with me," Zahra said.

They were all ravenously hungry and ate the entire stew together, using some of the vegetables from the garden that Hugh and Zahra had planted. Mr MacKenzie was very surprised to watch Zahra in action, in the kitchen with her culinary skills.

"It is a wonderful garden, Zahra. I use it every day. It reminds me of both you and Hugh, all the time," Peter said a little sadly.

"He only left good behind him Peter. I hope we can all do that in our lives for whoever we leave behind, to enjoy. You deserved this," Zahra added. "It makes me miss him when I look at it all and remember him working here," she confessed. "His daughter, Isobel has a lot to live with now, being responsible for his death. She never talks to me now," Zahra said. "I can't say that I have forgiven her though, so I'd rather not see her, for now anyhow. Grigor and I are happy but if she was with us, she would create antagonism. Alex wasn't exactly kind to me either. Your name also came up in conversation. He thought that you may have spoken ill of him to me, but don't worry, I defended you. He has a lot of misunderstandings, I think," Zahra said.

"Were you his first male lover?" she whispered, out of earshot of the rest of the family.

"Aye, I was, but he became embarrassed about that and changed his mind about being with me. That's why I sought out other company. It wasn't the best decision that I have made, with Matilda hating me like she did," Peter said. "There wasn't anyone after the two of them, until I met up with you here and I fell in love with you. So, I am not really a true homosexual, am I?" he said reflectively and out of ear shot.

"I think you love humanity Peter, like a true healer must and I loved you too. I am sorry I let you down," Zahra added.

The two of them hugged and held one another and it was like they had never been apart.

"Will you sleep with me?" Peter asked.

"I can't have the bairns tell Grigor. He will be upset, so it would need to be after they were all asleep and I would need to get up early before any of them," she said.

"So, you will?" Peter said.

"I will, my friend. Just get me out of bed very early," Zahra said.

They kissed outside under the stars that were barely visible behind the clouds.

"Do we have another storm coming?" Zahra asked.

"It's on its way. Not yet, but soon," Peter answered.

"Do you like the tweed uniform for Mr MacKenzie?" Zahra asked.

"I do. Nice and warm, yet smart and practical too," he said.

"Do you like the little sewn on badge?" she asked.

"Zahra, you are preparing for something big, I can see that. 'Ranch Manager, Misty Mountain Ranch,'" Are the ladies also all getting that sewn on?" Peter asked.

"Just Misty Mountain Ranch?" she answered. "Taxation reasons. Mr Fraser advised it and I'm keeping every receipt," Zahra said.

"I wish I lived nearer to you," Peter said.

"What if you fell in love with Alex again?" Zahra asked smiling. "I think it could happen. You can soften him up," Zahra added.

Sleeping alongside Peter was warm, comforting, and familiar. It felt as if like they had never been apart. He made love to her surprisingly quickly.

"Don't forget, I'm with child my darling," Zahra said.

"I'm gentle remember?" Peter said.

She was up early and bathing when no-one was aware, and it was a cold morning to be bathing when Hector walked in.

"Hector, Peter's coming with us to see Alex today," Zahra said as she climbed out of the bath.

"Ma, what could possibly go wrong?" Hector said sarcastically. "Ma, you are so beautiful. Your body is lovely," Hector said, as he looked at his naked Mither.

"Hector, my son, I'm your Ma. Mither's aren't lovely,"

Zahra said.

"Mine is," Hector said, with that cheeky sound in his voice.

The family then all departed for 'Misty Mountain Ranch' after picking up the re-furbished highland pipes, musical instrument. They even looked nicer in a brand-new bag. While she was in the music shop, Zahra picked up some music sheets as well as wooden music stands, another flute, a small organ and a few more instruments to make a more complete band for when the lads came again.

She also registered the name of their business in the land office for when her meeting was to take place with Cinaed Og, if they hadn't already disposed of him. She hoped they hadn't, because there was too much information that she was yet to discover, that only Cinaed Og had access to.

6. Tartans and Tweeds

All four men were seated on the wooden benches outside in front of her home on the mountain, drinking coffee and looking very comfortable and pleased with themselves. Someone at least had been disposed of successfully. Hopefully not Cinaed Og, Zahra thought. Immediately Grigor answered the question that must have appeared on her face. He confirmed that it wasn't Cinaed Og. It was the other one.

"Done, good and proper. Fish food now," Grigor added. She then wondered if her salmon would eat human flesh and that was off putting.

"Then you all deserve a gift each," Zahra said cheerfully. Firstly, she gave her husband his new plaid with a loving kiss, which he liked. It had that nice new smell. She then gave Padruig his Grant Glenmoriston plaid and hoped it was the correct one.

"Is it the right one Padruig?" she asked.

"Aye, its perfect Zahra," he said and before she could stop him, he came in for a big wet kiss. It was kind of revolting, but she was more wary then, with each gift she gave.

Then Peter alighted from the carriage, unexpectedly for them who were yet unaware of his presence. The expressions on all of their faces were of shock or disbelief, she wasn't sure, but the most stunned of them all, was Alex, who hadn't stood up yet to receive his gift. He remained seated and silent. She gave his plaid to Peter to give to him and she gave John's to him. They were all well received but Alex couldn't look Peter in the eye. Peter was hoping for physical contact, but it wasn't forthcoming.

John thanked Zahra for his plaid, and he said he liked it.

Eventually, sometime later that night, Alex thanked Zahra

too, but much later. Grigor was shown the uniform for Mr MacKenzie before it was given to Mr MacKenzie. Grigor approved of the smart outfit with its sewn-on label, and he handed it to him personally, so that was far better, from man to man.

"Where is Mairi, Grigor?" Zahra asked.

"Inside cooking," Grigor said.

"Would you like to see her uniform first, which he did?" Zahra asked.

"That's much better," Grigor confessed.

"I've ordered the rest. I could only bring home one for Mairi and one for the Fraser cleaning lady lass, because there's a wait of two weeks," she added. He looked at the other one and approved that one also. He was enjoying his new 'Master of the House' role, and it suited him.

"Mr MacKenzie, would you like to give these to your wife. One for her and one for the Fraser lass?" Zahra said.

"Grigor, these are the refurbished bagpipes too," she added. "Try them out Padruig, if you like," Zahra said, which he did and the tune that Padruig chose was, 'A Lament for the Children'. A very sad lament, that echoed across all the mountain tops and could be heard all the way to Fraser Ville, as well as to the Crofts down below. Zahra sat down for a moment to listen, as Coinneach Og and Dihaoine sat on her knee and listened too. Padruig was quite the talent on the bagpipes with his hidden gifts in poetry as well. He was a walking contradiction. She wondered if the MacNachten twins had inherited their musical talents from him.

"That's a sad tune Ma," Dihaoine said.

"Yes, it is," Zahra said.

She was then pleased to see that both Alex and Peter had moved away and were now talking pleasantly to one another. Maybe they would re-unite? Maybe not? It was hard to know with these men.

"I've registered our business name too Grigor, in readiness for my meeting with Cinaed Og, if he turns up one day soon. And here is your book on Highland Coos in both Gaelic and English. Hector, my son, here is your book on Highland Ponies, breeding and blood lines and so on. And this is the Salmon one for me to read. I posted the letter to Hamish to ask him to come here and advise us on whether we can breed salmon here or not.

"Why did you bring back Peter here?" Grigor asked critically.

"Because Alex was here and I thought it might be good for them both to sort out their issues," Zahra said.

"What if Alex then leaves Isobel?" Grigor asked.

"Is that really our problem? We can still mind Anndra and Domnhall, or they can go between houses. Isobel's not nice to anyone anymore. Not even Alex," Zahra added.

"Aren't you interfering?" Grigor asked.

"Yes, but so are you with killing off Padraig MacAlpin. My methods are a little less violent. We are both interfering types of people Grigor, don't you think?" Zahra added smiling.

"I suppose you're right," Grigor said.

"Aren't you going to kiss me darling? Or maybe you didn't miss me?" Zahra asked. He turned and looked at her very sensuously and told her it was lucky there were people around or she'd she stripped naked for him, right this minute which made her giggle.

"I love your giggle," Grigor said.

"I love how sexy you are, Grigor MacGregor. Let's go inside love, it's getting cold out here. There's another storm coming apparently," Zahra said.

"Hector put the ponies away. Storm coming, we think," she added. When she went inside, Mairi was wearing her new uniform and looked lovely and so was Mr MacKenzie.

"Do you need to put the coos under the house Grigor?" Zahra asked.

"I'll wait to see first if it's going to be a real storm, after all it's only raining and then we'll move them," Grigor said.

"The pen is ready down there for your bull with the feed and his fresh water is already there," Zahra added. "If you want to check it all, just lift the rug here and open the hatch and go down there this way, revealing the dark stairway. It's dark, so take a torch with you," Zahra added.

"Mairi the house is a bit too cold. Can you please stoke up the fires and Mr MacKenzie can you bring in some more wood please?" Zahra asked.

"Padruig please light the fires in your bedrooms now, so your rooms won't be too cold later on," Zahra added. Padruig wasn't accustomed to taking orders from Zahra, but he followed her instructions with some withheld judgements.

Alex and Peter were still talking out the front of her mansion and were becoming cold.

"Come in now you two. Sit by the fire. It's getting cold now, so we'll just eat, then go to bed tonight. Mairi it's too cold for baths for the bairns. They can just eat as soon as it's ready," Zahra said.

'More orders' thought Padruig. 'Good luck to Grigor this time', he thought.

Grigor went downstairs to the lower level, prepared now by his wife for the cattle. He thought Zahra was a little excessive these days, always coming up with the next money-making scheme, but bringing Peter to the Ranch, with Alex there, was too much. He didn't approve of Alex being amorous with Peter, and he hoped that nothing would develop between them again. Zahra was too liberal sometimes he thought.

He was surprised to see that the pen for his huge bull was perfectly arranged, with feed and water already prepared. The lights had all been moved up higher, as he had asked her to do. He decided to move the bull first, then see how the weather was. He lit up the lights, then yelled out to Zahra to hold his dinner, while he got the bull. He noticed that there were additional torch lights there now too, so it wasn't as dark and gloomy and a bit scary down there, as it usually was, when he first looked at that ominous level. It gave him the creeps.

"Padruig, can you please assist Grigor with that big bull. I don't want him to get injured," Zahra said.

The two of them moved the docile big bull, without any drama, as lightning was just starting up and a few rumbles of thunder, could be heard. The two of them drove the co-operative big bull, up through the tunnel, without any drama and into his pen where he started to munch on his hay. The collie dogs were trying to look helpful, but they weren't, and Hector must have kept his two dogs with him all the time these days, so the collies just floated about, looking a bit lonely. They missed their old Master, Hugh.

"What would scare me, is if that big fecker just said, 'blow this', and turned 'round and charged in our direction, knocking us both over," Grigor said.

"Thanks for the confidence, Grigor. No wonder your wife sent me down here to help you," Padruig said.

"Help me? I didn't need your help Padruig, I thought you just wanted to come. Did Zahra tell you to help me?" Grigor asked.

Realising then that he might have made an error, Padruig tried to cover it up.

"Umm. She might have. Call it love, Grigor," he said in jest. "How did you two get back together anyhow?" Padruig asked.

"I was here on some family business, and I wasn't going to let her slip through my fingers again," Grigor responded.

"The Alex and Peter thing? Is Peter sleeping here the night with Alex, or on his own?" Padruig asked.

"Wait and see my friend. We have to get the coos now as well, so can you ask Hector for his help?" Grigor asked.

All the men wandered over the entire property, droving all the sixty cattle calmly, on foot, slowly into the tunnel, so there wasn't a rush into the narrow space, which was successful in taking twenty coos at a time, instead of sixty, all at once. By then it was already bucketing down with rain, the thunderclaps were right over head and then the lightning came, and one lightning bolt struck a tree nearby and split it right down the middle, but it didn't catch on fire. Good firewood now Grigor thought.

Grigor was already wishing that he had acted on his wife's earlier predictions.

She knew that mountain better than him and so did Hector, who took it all in his stride. When he glanced across at his tall son, on occasion it appeared as if the lad had been born there and into that mountain lifestyle. The mist, the clouds, the rain, and the storms overhead, were all in a day in the life, on Misty Mountain.

Like snow in the Aird, the mountain had its own climate, that Grigor was only just growing accustomed to, but following his wife was new and he found it hard to agree with her, even if he knew when she was right.

At least she did not ridicule him, when he was wrong, or even crow when she was right.

He was missing having sex with her and couldn't wait, until they were in bed once more, that night and together once again. He had had enough male conversation and their friend, Alex had gone off on another tangent with Peter, once more and the two of them were leaving the following day for Inverness, not Glenmoriston. Alex and Peter bathed together, after the coos were all settled beneath the house, so Grigor didn't want to know any more details than that. The bairns didn't seem as frightened of the storm that blew overhead on this occasion, making it hard to even hear each other. Maybe it felt like safety was in their numbers.

Padruig was leaving with John on the following morning, so he wanted Zahra to read to him, one last time before he left, riding in the opposite direction to both Alex and Peter. Hector and Flidas listened intently too, but gradually, the wee ones all fell asleep, one by one to the calming sound of Zahra's voice. Even Grigor felt tired and calm, as her voice helped them all drift into slumber. Hector then carried Coinneach Og and Causantin to bed and Flidas carried Dihaoine.

Once again together and happy, the eccentric family drifted off into their respective directions, bidding goodnight to all. Zahra gave Grigor cash for the men who had assisted in what-ever it was they had all accomplished together and she didn't want details, so long as they had felt appreciated. Mairi and her husband had long gone to bed and the big sitting room was emptying out and it left only the three of them.

Zahra closed the book until the next time that they would all see each other again.

Waving farewell to everyone was harder than both Grigor and Zahra had expected. The following day was wet and cold, as they all went happily on their respective ways and Grigor let his coos back out, then his bull was last, who was a very active animal, determined to mount any female coo, he came across.

Grigor knew how to choose his bulls, that was for certain.

"You chose well my darling," Zahra said.

7. Cinaed and Zahra Go it Alone

Of course, no day would be an ordinary day, unless something challenging came along for the two of them, which it did. First came Cinaed Og looking for his brother Padraig who Zahra denied having seen, because she was in Inverness, which was all true, even all the bairns hadn't seen him, including Hector and the Farm Manager. Poor Cinaed Og was despairing with all of his family disappearing or dying and asked Zahra for advice.

"What will we do sister, there is just the two of us now?" Cinaed Og asked. It was perfect and exactly what Zahra had wanted.

"It leaves just you and me in charge of MacAlpin Industries brother, and we have already changed our half of the name, so why don't you change your half as well and we just split it all down the middle? And then MacAlpin Industries won't exist anymore," Zahra suggested.

"I'd like to be the Chairperson then you and I can meet once every month, as we divide it all up. Can you go and get all of the paperwork now, so we can make a start on that?" she said simply to him, like it was as easy as that.

"I'd love that," Cinaed Og said. "I've always wanted to be independent, but what about the wives?" he asked.

"We give them outright ownership of their homes, as you and I also will do," Zahra said.

"And Coinneach Og?" Cinaed Og asked.

"He is my son. No different to my other sons and will remain with me in my custody with my husband, Grigor Mohr MacGregor," Zahra said. And so, it was in law with no objection to Zahra's custody of Coinneach Og. Who was left to object, after all? Cinaed Og went and collected all of the paperwork, and they were assisted by Mr Martin Fraser and his son,

Charles Fraser to ensure that it was all legal. The two industries were separated finally, and the old one was abolished, and they used her lawyer for that. Zahra needed to be sure that she owned her property outright, with its lovely home.

Lord Cinaed had been missing for long enough for his Will to be read and considered. The same applied to Prince Griogar and Lord Coinneach's which had already been dealt with. Zahra then retrieved her paintings from Lord Cinaed's home.

There were at least twenty of them. Kenneth might like to sell a few, but she decided to keep most of them. It was her history, after all.

There were some duelling pistols that she retrieved for her husband, that she thought he might like. There were swords, targes, and rifles of so many kinds, that she and Cinaed Og went halves in, as well as other weaponry that they also shared. Cinaed Og gave her all the antique China. It was truly lovely as well as the cabinetry, that it was all housed in, found its way to Zahra's house. She took multiple pure silver candle holders, candelabras and leather goods like satchels, belts, saddles, bridles and outdoor dining seats and potted plants. But when they entered a room full of rocks, Zahra exclaimed.

"What are these?" she asked. "Lord Cinaed gave me one of those pink ones," Zahra said.

"They're pink diamonds, but uncut from Africa or somewhere obscure. Collecting rocks was a hobby of Da's," he said.

"What are these big rocks?" Zahra asked.

"Break one open and you'll see," Cinaed said. Reluctantly,

Zahra broke one open, and it was purple crystals on the inside. It was purple amethyst crystals.

"Oh, this is gorgeous," she said. "But where could I keep them?" Zahra asked.

"There's that prison room underneath your house that would be big enough, near the court off to the side of the tunnel," Cinaed said.

"Is there? How do I get into that room?" Zahra asked.

"One of the lights acts as a doorknob. Just turn it," Cinaed said.

"But I just had the lights moved," Zahra said.

"Then where it was, just attach an actual doorknob, but flattish. It's a big room, but a miserable place and I never go in there," Cinaed said. It was obvious that he had trauma attached to the memory of that room, just mentioning it. "There's an additional storeroom beyond that room for cold storage in the winter months". He added

 Zahra agreed to take all of Lord Cinaed's gemstone collection, so long as they could get Malcolm's Team back to move them and open that secret doorway.

"You can have all of his clothes Cinaed, we have no need for any of those, except two warm coats for Grigor and Hector," she said. Cinaed liked his Da's weird clothing, even his shoes, so he took all of that. There were two pairs of boots she saw that Grigor and Hector might like, which she asked for and looked like they'd fit.

When it came to the horses, Cinaed Og was most adverse, as he said they were costing the business money, despite their pedigree. There were at least twenty pure bred horses including the sire, his mares and their offspring and not one of them had ever won a race but Zahra wasn't interested in racing, just the beautiful animals. To her joy, Zahra inherited all the lovely horses, with their bloodlines. She thought each of her sons might like one, even Ali, reluctant though she was to give him one. Causantin will be big enough one day too. Then she owed Peter a horse. Grigor would love one and she loved one in particular.

Overall, she was happy with what she obtained from the late Lord Cinaed's house, including some of his late wife's old jewellery and furs. Prince Griogar's family home was put into his wife's name for her to upkeep and his name was removed from the family companies, as it was dissolved. She then wrote to Hugh Og Chisholm and asked if Malcolm Og and Hamish Og could come and move the rock collection for her. Hector and Grigor could move the horses, as soon as possible, or else they would starve and as it was, they were looking thin. Padraig's estate too, was soon to wind up, as was Anndra MacAlpin's, so those two were the last.

Zahra succeeded also in obtaining additional finance from the prince's estate, as she had wanted, to go to her two young bairns who had been kidnapped also and had not yet been compensated. Cinaed Og was apologetic for not thinking of that, as well as her own suffering from his brother directly and paid her an additional huge sum of money for her bairns to be held in trust in her name. She was delighted upon receiving the unexpected amounted from Cinaed, which she banked immediately.

Lord Cinaed had known about the birth of Zahra Og, his daughter after all, and had left a minimal amount to her, for when she turned twelve. That was achievable enough by selling up his property in its entirety, leaving the amount stipulated to Zahra Og with Isobel Fraser as the trustee for her daughter. Isobel would not be pleased however, that it wasn't her own to keep. The rest of his property and income was to be split up between Cinaed Og and Zahra MacGregor. Cinaed Og and Zahra dealt with all of that, upon seeing Aonghus MacGregor, their lawyer, in Inverness and it was placed in Zahra Og Fraser's bank account, kept in trust for her twelfth birthday. Her inheritance included a diamond necklace that had belonged to his late wife that was to go to Zahra Og on the day that she married. There was a sadness to it learning that he had known all along about Zahra Og, and they could have known one another.

It took several visits to Inverness together to sort out the legalities, including dealing with the investigators, seeking out what had happened to the MacAlpin family. They questioned Zahra again, about her abduction by the prince and when she had seen him last, so it was intense and tiring. The princes' income and his entire wealth was then split in two, between Zahra and Cinaed Og, with his wife being given the house, but she had no access to anything else, including money or other real estate that had previously been a part of MacAlpin Industries. Those all went to Zahra and Cinaed.

The investigators enquired from Fraser Ville to the local MacKenzie Crofters, to Inverness and there was no one who had any information on either Anndra or Padraig MacAlpin. Zahra wasn't under suspicion, nor were any members of her family, who were also investigated, as well as others that the company had dealt with. The MacAlpin family had been such a tight knit group that it was only a few people, like their wives, who might have known where they were going, at any given time. No one ever knew of Lord Cinaed's movements, because trust was a big part of their function and that was their final undoing.

In waiting to see if Anndra and Padraig materialised, the law allowed the wives to take possession of their homes, as well as the finalisation of the company but had a clause whereby if their husbands returned within a twelve-month period, their position on the new company could be reestablished, being their portion of what Zahra was earning and their portion of what Cinaed Og was earning. Should they never reappear, then half would go to Zahra and half to Cinaed. The finalisation would occur then in twelve months' time.

Zahra was very grateful for the legal services of Malcolm's

cousin, Aonghus MacGregor. Cinaed didn't need to visit anymore with dividing the company up into two, unless his brothers did reappear, therefore would see less of him. Cinaed wished both Zahra and Grigor the best and as he left, he thanked her for all her assistance in dealing with such an enormous problem. Zahra had only just started to take in what her income was going to be, so she asked Old Mr Martin Fraser to ensure first that taxes were up to date, which he worked on for some time.

There was a substantial amount to pay in outstanding taxes, which she told him to deal with. Both his son, Charles Fraser and himself were given a dedicated office on the top floor in the new wing of the mansion, where there was plenty of light, for Old Mr Fraser with his failing eyesight. Their office was at the rear of the building. Other members of staff also lived now on that same level. The chimney sweep, two laundresses, two cleaning ladies and the farm manager and his wife. The gold remained closed off behind the bookcase.

The gems were to be kept hidden in the secret room, near the old courthouse, with the newly installed handle to open it. That room was accessed from the tunnel leading to the old courthouse, through opening one of the lights. That then revealed a large room as its door slid to one side. It made an awful noise when opening it with stone-on-stone grinding and at first it was pitch black in there, until it was lit up by a torch to see within. When Zahra looked to see where the gems would go, she was expecting some old rubbish in there, but it was completely empty, however it didn't feel empty, and she couldn't make herself enter the room. There was another door in there that led to the additional cold storage room, but she put off entering it until it was necessary. It must have been for corn she assumed.

The Team had arrived with Malcolm Og, Hamish Og and Iain to move Zahra's rocks, which they did, with some difficulty. Thanks to Iain, who was quite strong, all those rocks ended up in that secret, but horrible room. Zahra still refused to go in there. She decided she'd just leave the gems to do their work. Dihaoine and Malcolm enjoyed their time together, getting to know each other.

Before the brothers left, she gave Malcolm Og and Hamish Og a horse each from Lord Cinead's property and she asked the lads if they wouldn't mind dropping off a third horse to Ali, who lived next door to them in Glengarry. She'd already gifted Grigor his and Hector their horses, as well as Causantin for when he grew taller. Zahra had the most beautiful Chestnut mare, with a white blaze and white socks, and she understood why she would never have won a running race. What was Lord Cinead thinking?

These horses were just droving horses at the most. Perhaps they may be able to jump a few things. So, that only left Isobel, Fatma and John, so she wrote to them and told them that they could come and get them, if they wanted them.

She decided to keep them temporarily in the big stables, especially the Sire, unless the Clydesdales were there, but the property wouldn't be able to manage the grazing of that many horses, as well as cattle but she intended to keep the gorgeous Sire and two brood mares.

8. Hamish Ascends the Mountain

Hamish Chisholm and his wife, Cora arrived on horseback, leaving Cannich for a while.

Grigor and Zahra were both happy to see old friends and they were invited in with cakes, tea and coffee on offer. Hamish was a bit shy to see Zahra married again, with child and in her new surroundings, but pleased to see Grigor and Zahra back together again. Cora was more forthright and asked if they were married yet.

"Aye, of course we are," Grigor answered a little offended.

"Sorry Grigor. Was there a wedding we weren't invited to?" Hamish asked.

"Nae, we are hand fast for now, until we get all the businesses sorted out around here. I am planning a wedding for us both, but you are all invited, and no one is excluded, even though my wife wants to exclude Ali and April for having excluded her," Grigor said jesting.

"I wasn't invited to that one either Zahra, when I was sure that he would invite me," Hamish said looking a little hurt about that.

"Really, you too?" Zahra said.

"Well, Hamish my friend we do have something in common, but I suppose, I shouldn't hold a grudge. I don't usually, but this hurts, if you know what I mean. He's my oldest son. It's hard to get my mind around it still, that he believed some gossip that was spread by Isobel," Zahra said a little too emotively.

"You'll get over it love," Grigor said. "He does still love you, even though he has become somewhat of a loner, out there in

Glengarry," he added.

"Aye, Hamish dear, imag-
ine if it was one of ours
who didn't invite one of us
to their weddings. We'd
be devastated. That's what
Zahra is dealing with, isn't
it Zahra?" Cora asked, surprisingly understanding.

"Aye, I didn't even know that they were married, until I was
back out of captivity, then they had moved to Glengarry. Hugh
and I went there just the once, as we were escaping from
Coinneach, when he was chasing us. It's such a small farm
next to Malcolm. We helped them with a few things and Hugh
built them a potato storage unit. The poor lass can't cook. I had
to teach her every step of the way, how to cook a basic stew,"
Zahra said. "They were unprepared for marriage. Even worse
than me, when I was lobbed in Scotland, not knowing beef
from venison," Zahra added.

"That badly off, were they?" Grigor asked humorously.

"They were love, but Hugh and I improved things a bit for
them like planting corn and kale, else they would have starved,
as well as potatoes that Malcolm bought around. I built up the
vegetable garden but what they need Grigor, is more land for
more cattle," she added.

"Is there land for sale around there that we could buy them to
enlarge the farm then?" he asked.

"I'd have to ask Malcolm darling and if you want to do that, we
can," Zahra said.

"I would if there was the land," Grigor replied.

"I'll write to him then darling. With Glengarry there's that
problem with the bedrock, so crops can only grow in a few
select areas. However, I'm forgiving and if we can achieve it,

I am happy to, but we would need local knowledge. He would be wiser, to invest in cattle," she said smiling.

"Now my friend Hamish. The reason that you are here is, I have a question concerning salmon farming and if it could be possible here on Beinn Coinneach. I don't know how high that salmon can leap, but we have a waterfall that's rather tall and a wee loch, so I was wondering if we could farm them here and then sell them from the loch, if that's how it all works. We will pay you to tell us naturally, and please stay here for as long as it takes. I'll show Cora your room first and then Grigor and I will take you both to the waterfall," Zahra said.

"Zahra is quite the businesswoman now Grigor. You must be proud of her. It's a good idea. I'll tell you if it's feasible," Hamish said to Grigor.

"It's quite the walk. Do you have boots with you Hamish?" Grigor asked.

The four of them were all enjoying the walk to the waterfall, accompanied by her younger bairns, Causantin, Dihaoine and Coinneach Og who, in this instance, was riding on Grigor's shoulders, due to the distance and the danger of the waterfall. Cora noticed that Zahra was with child again and remarked on it.

"Och Zahra, you are with child again. I stopped being able to conceive, a long while ago. How do you continue to have bairns?" Cora asked.

"I was unable to also, but Hugh left both Grigor and I a gift from him, a wee bairn, so we are both thrilled about it," Zahra said, feeling like Cora had trodden on her grief.

Grigor was happy with her reply because it made it still sound like it was his wee bairn.

The outlook up at the waterfall for both Hamish and Cora for their first visit was breathtaking.

"This is such a beautiful place, Grigor, I love it here. Such a change from Cannich," Hamish remarked. "I admit, it is getting tiresome there nowadays," Hamish said. "James comes down occasionally to say hello, but I hardly ever see anyone from the old crew, except when we go fishing with Malcolm and he is always a good friend with a lot of news," he said.

"Please don't arrange a wedding in Cannich for us Grigor. I couldn't bear that again. I'd be worried sick, that you'd leave me too," Zahra said out of the blue. She almost looked as if she would cry at the thought of a wedding in that Chapel, or even in Glenmoriston at all.

"Can we get married here, then I know you won't leave me too and no weapons either, especially Isobel," Zahra said. That was a raw topic. "Get Priests and Imams to come here, rather than us go there please and Mairi can arrange the food with the MacKenzies," Zahra almost begged.

"Zahra, I am arranging it but don't worry darling, it won't be in Cannich," Grigor said, and he held his wife closely to re-assure her and kissed her gently. He was pleased at the display of love in front of Hamish and Cora.

Upon a thorough inspection of all the waterways, as well as the waterfall and the loch. Hamish was excited.

"Yes, it's possible to breed salmon here," Hamish said, glowing at the idea.

That night over their dinner with the whole family, Hamish put forward his plan for 'salmon on the mountain' and how it could be achieved successfully and then the fish could either be sold, eaten, or fished and thrown back in, to catch another day. Grigor admitted that he was surprised and offered Hamish the job with Cora to set it all up, and if it was successful, he could stay on permanently.

Even if unsuccessful, he offered him any job, he wanted to work on Misty Mountain. If the salmon made enough money, Grigor offered to build them a house near the waterfall, but not too near as to spoil the pristine outlook.

In the meantime, they could have quarters in the new wing on the level beneath the staff quarters, where most of the guest rooms were.

He said to take their time to think about it and do whatever was needed to commence the industry. Grigor and Hamish retired beside the fireside to discuss wages and Cora was offered either to assist her husband, or an indoor job cleaning.

She chose to work with her husband. Grigor jokingly warned them that Zahra would most likely make them wear a uniform with a stitched little badge saying, 'Misty Mountain Salmon.'

The industries now on the mountain were developing with, Misty Mountain Cattle, Hectors Misty Mountain Highland Ponies, Misty Mountain Salmon, and Misty Mountain Thorough Bred Horses. Zahra had a sign made up listing all their businesses at the bottom of the mountain.

9. Hector's Role

Discussion over her expectant bairn had made Zahra feel emotional and she feared for the future if someone tried to dispose of Grigor. She worried for the future of her wee one, as all expectant Mither's do, but Grigor had known his wife in this condition, many times before, even when she was in tears, weeping insecurely. He told his son Hector, that he was now her oldest son, as Ali had let his Mither down. Therefore, there were responsibilities that Hector needed to know and assume, in the event of his father's demise, just to make Zahra feel secure.

He explained how his Mither was when she was in her extreme emotional, expectant states and how to hold her firmly, until she stopped crying. This always worked before and it should work again, Grigor said. Hector took his role very seriously and understood that if Grigor was to be disposed of by someone, then he had to care for his Mither and not by another husband. Flidas wanted to assist too with it and wanted to help where she could.

Zahra was always emotional when the wee bairn was mentioned, especially this one.

The room next to Zahra's suite and Grigor's was prepared for two purposes, a small lounge room, doubling as a reading room, as well as a nursery. The window had previously been bricked up by Coinneach, which was all taken down and the bricks were all removed, flooding the room with lovely, bright light. The smallish room had already been plastered and painted white, so Zahra had it painted again in a soft peach colour which was more conducive for a bairn, she thought. The builders took all the brick's downstairs, then the bricks were left out the back of the house, to deal with later.

Zahra furnished the room with five new velvet couch chairs, not purple this time, but a lovely shade of peach, the same as the walls, with a nice low oak table in between them all. A smaller bookcase was made by the Frasers, so the family could read just the books that they were reading, or interested in, at the time, rather than the entire enormous library. The open fireplace was large, and it warmed up the entire room and water was heated over it for anyone still wanting tea or coffee, rather than going to the kitchen. In addition, there were two large candelabras from Lord Cinaed's house to give off sufficient light, as well as several smaller candles and lights attached to the walls, called sconces and an overhead Turkish light. The window curtaining was half covered in a peach-coloured silk at the top half and a darker peach velvet, on the bottom half of the long, ceiling to floor, windowpane. The old carpet had been discarded and a new very thick woollen carpet was fitted, so that it was all clean, fresh, soft, warm, and plush in soft blues, peach and orange.

In front of the fireplace was a traditional hearth containing an iron implement, then the hearth was covered with Turkish tiles in case a bath was needed in there, for either the new bairn, or an adult.

The new wee bairn's bassinet was in one corner with of all his or her baby things and Zahra was ready. Hector was nervous at his role because now he would be walking his Mither around when she was about to give birth and maybe even delivering the wee bairn, as his father had done before, with Isobel. Flidas had to keep re-assuring him.

Most nights then after dinner was over and Marie was cleaning up, the family would retire to that lovely room where Hector would read his pony book, Grigor would read his book on highland coos and Zahra would read her book on salmon, while Flidas would read the book that Zahra bought for her on bees, so she could take over making honey and putting boxes all over the huge property, under different trees, for different flavoured honey. Causantin and Dihaoine read their children's books for a while, until they fell asleep, as did Coinneach Og, before the younger ones were all put to bed, eventually leaving just the four adults.

Zahra had decorated the walls with the nude paintings, which were numerous. In addition to this she hung her favourite of herself and Wolfie on the mountain slope. She thought of moving that one back to the dining room area.

When Hector went to deal with the bricks, as he had been asked to, he noticed some of the lime had been dislodged, revealing a yellowish colour beneath. It looked a lot like those gold bars kept in the secret room. Surely, the bricks hadn't been gold bars all along, he asked himself, so he investigated further and kicked off more of the lime. He concluded that it was more gold but didn't want to make that decision himself without asking his Mither.

"Ma, can you come and look at those bricks that we took off the window please? It won't take long," Hector asked.

Walking hand in hand with Coinneach Og, they strolled outside together, where it was a bit windy and what her son had found was yet another shock of concealed wealth from her former husband, Coinneach MacAlpin. He had covered over the gold bars in a lime or cement type of substance, making them appear as bricks.

At the time that he was covering up the window, she wondered why he didn't get a tradesman to do that work, but he did it himself and she had always hated that bricked-up window. It had been a lovely source of sunshine and light and it had been a beautiful outlook from that window. The pile of gold bars was quite high now that she understood that it was gold.

"Hector, can you quickly cart these into the secret room in the library and put them with the others?" Zahra asked. "You can clean them off later when no-one is around to see what they all are," Zahra added nervously. "I'll go and tell your father." she added. Hector did as she asked to get them out of sight quickly.

Grigor was amusing himself with their new coos, walking

around with them, as John Fraser used to do, intending to walk them further down the mountain, where there was more green grass. Zahra interrupted him temporarily to tell him the news.

Most people would be pleased at the ownership of a pile of gold, but it only caused Zahra more anxiety.

"Has anyone else seen that they were gold bars too?" Grigor asked.

"I don't know. I really hope not," Zahra replied.

"Never mind love, we'll deal with it later and Hector and I will melt them all down into those small bars," Grigor decided. The two of them were busy half the night both cleaning the gold bricks and melting them down, until they were both exhausted.

"Da, can I buy more Highland ponies with some of this gold?" Hector asked. "I'd like to expand my business".

"On one condition. We drove these other horses of your Ma's to Isobel, John and Fatma at the Aird. Ask your Ma if Domnhall and Anndra can have one horse each too, as well. There'll be too many horses on the mountain, if you buy more horses as well. That'd be five less horses, but Ma might not agree. She only said no horse for Simon Fraser. Maybe she just forgot the grandchildren?" Grigor added.

"We can drive them down tomorrow and come back, the same night, or else your Ma will get upset. Hamish and Cora are due next week with their things, so she'd be alone. I'll talk to Mr MacKenzie and Mr Fraser to watch over her," he said.

"Ma has employed a groundsman, too Da, so he can keep a watch out as well," Hector added. "His name is Rabbie Fraser, younger son of Mr Charles Fraser. His job is to sweep our entry road from the bottom of the mountain, all the way up to the house, removing any manure and putting that on the rose bushes, as he goes. Then he has to sweep all of that paving in front of the house, as well as the back. He has to tidy up the benches and the pot plants too, if they've been moved.

Weeding the rose garden is also his job and he has to fertilise the entire rose garden and prune the roses, when its pruning times, so that garden will be meticulous. He also cleans all the outdoor privies and empties their buckets of shite and buries it somewhere, off site," Hector explained.

"He's not permitted inside the house either, because he's too dirty, nor can he just sit around looking like he lives here. The only place he can enter is underneath where the coos are kept in a storm, to clean up their mess and prepare it for them, if there's another storm coming. He gets paid weekly by Mairi when he leaves the property, after he finishes sweeping the entrance road, back down again one more time," Hector explained. "So twice per day. That road of ours will be the cleanest entrance road in all this district Da," he said smiling at his Ma's plans. "He can watch out for anyone too while we're gone and maybe we can lock up the gate too Da?" Hector added.

"Son, it sounds like you have it all in hand, so long as you tell your Ma," Grigor added.

"Why can't you tell her Da? I don't want to upset her," Hector said. "Ma likes those horses" he added.

"What you're wanting to say is, Isobel doesn't deserve one, is that it?" Grigor said smiling. "Aye. I don't want to get between the two of them, that's for sure. "I'll tell her then, but it might be later on because I have to walk my lady coos back once they've had a munch down there and it'll be a while then, before she knows," Grigor said.

"Alright, I'll tell her that we are both taking five horses to the Aird, very early tomorrow morning back by night sometime, depending on the weather and how the horses behave," Hector added.

He was looking forward to adding another twelve Highland ponies, at least to his herd of horses and Flidas and he were very proud of them. He was selling more than he could keep up with. He needed to breed more.

10. Lonely Day

Zahra knew it was going to be lonely without her big son, Hector, whom she had become dependent upon and her husband Grigor, who she had grown more and more in love with and needy. With them both away, driving the five big horses to the Aird for their family, she was desperately lonely and a little afraid. It reminded her of when she was alone, just before she had been kidnapped and she began to shake, with nerves and anxiety. She didn't trust that Padruig wouldn't talk Grigor into staying overnight in the Aird. She knew it would be wise if the weather came up to stay there, but it was relatively calm, and she wanted them both back for her own selfish reasons. She couldn't bear to be alone when she was with child. Flidas had decided to join both men too to help them drive the difficult big horses. She was alone, with only her staff, Mairi and Mr MacKenzie and her three young bairns, Causantin, Dihaoine and Coinneach Og.

Mr MacKenzie and Mairi both went to bed immediately after cleaning up after dinner and Zahra was left alone with her young ones and they all wandered off up the stairs together, holding hands, to her bedroom. All the bairns sensed that their Mither was upset and they all wanted to sleep in her bed with her, to comfort themselves, as well as their Mither. Coinneach Og started to cry, wanting more love and attention, but Dihaoine also wanted attention too, leaving Causantin who was trying hard not to cry, but he ended up really upset.

Crying, he then asked "Where's Da Da? Has he gone? Has he left us?" which made Zahra cry even more. If only he was here. They'd be happy, if only Grigor had never left us, we would not all feel so insecure. She joined in with them crying too, as the whole wee family wept themselves into a deep sorrow, she sang them a sad lament which made it even worse and they didn't even hear the door opening, as Grigor walked into his wee family, all weeping for him.

When they finally heard him and saw him standing there in disbelief, gazing upon his sad wee family, they all threw their arms around him, one after the other, as well as Zahra whose face was wet with tears. He was shocked at first, hoping nobody had been injured or died.

"I didn't think you'd come home husband, thank God you're here. We all love you so much Grigor," Zahra sobbed.

"I love you Da, Da," came in its many forms climbing all over him as he climbed onto the bed to allow them access to him. Even he hadn't expected his own bairns to miss him so much, in such a short time.

"My family, I love you all. I came home as quickly as I could, but it looks like you've looked after your Ma, very well," Grigor said. "I tried Da Da but I cried coz I missed you," Causantin said. This meant the world to Grigor who had shared these bairns with Coinneach, Hugh and Peter. His own eyes were wet with tears.

"Don't cry Da Da," said Coinneach Og who ran his fingers through Grigor's hair for the first time ever. They had all made their choices of who their real Da was and would be. Coinneach Og was the most touching of all who wouldn't stop playing with Grigor's hair.

"Da Da's hair not like my, Ma's like my," he tried to say, then played with Zahra's ringlets in her long brown hair, to compare with Grigor's hair.

"Whose hair do you like the best my son?" Grigor asked the wee lad.

"Da Da's," he said and played again with Grigor's hair.

"I like Ma's the best," said Causantin. "Ma is so pwetty," he said.

Hector called out to the family and asked if he could come in.

"Aye son," said Zahra. She then leapt from the bed to hug her big, tall, and handsome son.

"The horses are all good and delivered Ma," Hector said.

"I missed you both. I was scared without you," Zahra said.

"Come with me then when I buy the ponies Ma, so you won't be scared," Hector said caressing his Mither. "Is that okay Da?" he added. "Can the bairns come too?"

"Why don't we all go, and we can have a nice ice cream in Inverness?" Grigor decided. All the children were thrilled about that.

"I can ride my own pony," said Causantin.

"Me too," said Dihaoine. The mood was already improving when Flidas came to say goodnight and took two of them to bed while Grigor carried Coinneach Og, for the first time and tucked him in his wee bed and kissed him goodnight.

"G'night DaDa," he said putting his arms around his neck.

"Goodnight my son," Grigor said to his son, Coinneach Og who loved him. There's nothing quite like the love from your family to make your heart feel complete and fulfilled and this was the moment that Coinneach Og had bonded with Grigor as his father.

"Thank you, my darling Zahra, for giving us both this wonderful family. I am sorry you were worried. I'll always be more aware of your feelings. You're all so sensitive in the right way and I understand why. Coinneach Og is braw, isn't he?" Grigor said.

"Aye, he was a poor wee lad. He didn't like Lord Cinaed, so he's so much happier now with you, my love," she said wrapping her arms around his neck.

He leaned down over his wife supported by his arms, one arm on each side of her body, staring into her big green eyes. His legs were opening her legs.

"I think, I am a very lucky man that you still love me after what I did," he said.

"I never stopped loving you, Grigor. I love you even more than ever now and I need you more than ever. I am sorry that I am so needy," Zahra said.

"You can pretend all you like that you are the strongest businesswoman in all of the Highlands, but I am the one who witnessed you all crying for me, my dearest," he jested with his sweet smile. "Do you want me now then?" Grigor asked opening her legs further.

"Aye, I do," she said smiling. He then sat back on his haunches looking at his wife and began to excite her and looking at her opened legs rubbing both of her inner thighs. He kissed her first gently on her clitoris then began to lick vigorously and then sucking her. He remembered the effect it used to have on him. How had he forgotten that? It was driving him mad instantly.

"Open up further," he asked as he pushed her thighs gently exposing his wife's private area. His hand fell across her bush running his fingers through all of her until she was calling his name. He wouldn't give himself to her until he was satisfied that she really wanted him. When he entered her, it was an explosion of fulfillment that he hadn't felt until then, even compared with the other times that they had made love.

This was different. "Hold me Zahra," he asked.

This always meant to hold his cock and bring him back to life yet again. Her fingers gently roamed across his cock feeling his every centimetre and his testes feeling her way around them until there was a response and she sat up and kissed his cock on the tip licking it all around while his hand sat on the top of her head rubbing her hair then lifted her under her armpits and impaled her on his hardened manhood. Both reaching orgasm and letting out all the built-up emotion of the night of missing him. She squealed in pleasure and Grigor always enjoyed his wife reaching orgasm, as well as himself. Seeing her face like that, was a joy like no other. They had reached a part of their life's journey that had matured to that point of no return. She was his wife, whether they had married in a Kirk or not.

"My Zahra, I know there's a lot of your life when I wasn't with you, that you have not told me about, and I do respect your privacy. I do see however, little things about you that were never there when I knew you before I left you, which I know was my fault. Please tell me what you can about what happened when you were kidnapped. I have read the newspapers version of it, but I see your face sadden every time that it's mentioned, especially because of Ali's wedding. I know there's more to that story than what I know. Is that right?" Grigor asked.

"Please Grigor, don't ask me to tell you. What if you hate me when you know some of those things?" Zahra replied and started to weep.

"You are having our bairn, Hugh's bairn, you need to be healthier, mentally too Zahra, to deliver him or her safely," Grigor added.

"I know Grigor. Peter has the whole story, with all its gruesome details which he advised me to write down. He said it had to be edited for publication, so there's a lot that they left out, but the editor read it, as well as the police. You don't need to know what they did to me on that island Grigor," Zahra added.

"I do because you are my wife. My wife in life kept secrets of her ravaging from me and it literally killed me. I died once I found out. I don't want to find out from Peter and end up in the waterfall by choice. It might finish me," Grigor said. "Show me this paper that you wrote please, with all of the details," Grigor asked. Very reluctantly, Zahra went to her sideboard where she kept a leather satchel, containing her important documents, and it was in there. Pages and pages of it.

"Grigor, what if you feel differently about me, when you read this? What will I do then?" Zahra asked.

"I wouldn't ask for this information, unless I knew in my heart that you would still be my wife and loved as always," Grigor said. Zahra wanted to leave the room, but he insisted on her being there.

"This is what we share Zahra. Stay with me," Grigor insisted.

Zahra was sodomised repeatedly on the island as well as other unmentionable horrors to demean her and to break down her spirit. He had known of the rape but not sodomy. She felt ashamed of herself, and she couldn't look at him.

"Look at me, darling wife. There is nothing in here that makes me love you less. Hate them more yes, but if anything, I love you more. You survived this when others couldn't have. This is why you are so hurt when Isobel said those things about you, and you lost attending your oldest son's wedding. Is that right?" Grigor asked, and Zahra couldn't stop crying into her husband's loving arms, as he held her close to him.

"I understand that much now, but the wolf is one you need to tell me about, don't you?" Grigor asked.

Nodding in agreement she told him of how the grey wolf came about, when Coinneach, in his giant brown wolf form, had copulated with her, his human wife. That resulted in Ulvy Stiorm becoming a part of her, without her understanding that would happen.

"I had guessed as much, I just needed you to be honest with me, so our relationship is honest, going into our future. You can tell me everything, as we go. It doesn't have to be all at once, or you will exhaust yourself, but it might be better for your mental health having this wee bairn, I think," he said gently caressing her stomach.

"It's a boy again, I think" Grigor said. "Did Hugh know about the wolf?" he asked.

"Aye he did," she said sadly. "It was going to remain a secret.

I see him occasionally you know. Just occasionally. He likes that you are here. Can we have him bought here to the mountain to bury? I hate that Chapel now so I can't visit him, and I think he would like the nice outlook here. He must be so lonely there in Cannich," Zahra added.

"Aye, we can of course and get the grave top too that Malcolm made," Grigor said.

"Then we can show him the bairn, when he is born," Zahra added. "He'll have blonde hair like him, do you mind?" Zahra asked.

"It's an honour to be Hugh's bairn's father. Tell him that when you see him," Grigor said smiling.

"He's just over there, listening to us. You can tell him yourself," Zahra said as she pointed across the room to the corner where Hugh stood.

11. Hamish, Hugh Og & the Waterfall

Hugh Og was assisting his brother, Hamish Mohr Chisholm with everything they needed to set up the salmon farm for Zahra and he offered to assist in building the infrastructure too. Hugh Og was almost as excited as his brother Hamish was and Cora loved the plan to live on Misty Mountain. She had been long tired of Cannich, since Helen killed herself, to be exact, and was disappointed that her husband had taken on the job as the Manager there. Grigor Og was back there now and looking for a replacement, while I had been asked to purchase Hamish's house by Loch Garry.

Word spread around Glenmoriston and Glengarry, that Hamish was selling his share in the fishing boat too and was leaving Cannich to live in MacKenzie country to start salmon fishing for Zahra MacGregor and her husband Grigor Mohr MacGregor.

I heard that I had missed out, once again on employing Hamish, to of all people, Zahra MacGregor.

Malcolm Og had taken Ali's new thoroughbred horse around to him, after their last visit to Misty Mountain Ranch, as a gift from Zahra to him, which came to Ali as a bit of a shock. She was such a lovely mare, and he had needed one, complete with saddlery too. His Mither knew how to make him feel guilty for not having invited her to their wedding. His wife, April had warned him against taking that action and so had Uncle Kenneth and Aunty Ivy too, who were now Ma and Da.

Now Ali had to live with his mistake that wasn't even fixable before Hugh's tragic end.

Malcolm Og and Hamish Og also told him that his sister, Isobel was getting one of those horses too, as well as his twin sister, Fatma, John Fraser and Zahra's two grandchildren, Domnhall and Anndra. He didn't know where the horses had come from, other than from his Mither, but they were all pure-bred beautiful horses with their bloodline papers. In addition, there was a gift of a strange pink rock for his wife, April.

Malcolm Og took the opportunity to ask Ali whose idea it had been not to invite Aunty Zahra to his wedding, which they had all attended. Ali was loathe to respond at first but admitted that it had been his decision, because of his sister.

"Isobel had threatened not to attend the wedding if her Mither was there, with all of the false accusations that we were all made aware of," Ali said.

"Do you regret having made that decision now, brother with both of your parents now back together again and the truth now printed in the newspapers?" Malcolm Og asked, his future brother-in-law.

"Every day of my life," Ali said, gloomily.

I had been around too, to ask him if he wanted additional land in the area, if it came up, as his Mither and father wanted to buy it for him, if he agreed. While I was there, I filled him in on the latest news that Hamish and Cora were moving to Misty Mountain Ranch, as it was now called, to start up a salmon farm. He was shocked and it seemed like everyone else's lives had moved on, leaving him behind.

Hugh Og and Hamish were too busy and too excited about the new venture to be bogged down with other people's woes and had the plans drawn up for the salmon farm and had purchased everything that they needed, paid for by Zahra. Hugh Og was taking time off from Teamster work, leaving Malcolm Og and Hamish Og running that business while he was gone, assisting his brother. Hugh Og was being well paid too and was staying on the Mountain, in luxury and had even taken his wife, Meredith with him, by invitation. Meredith was totally excited to be returning to her home country.

When Hugh's Team trundled up the newly renovated road to the Misty Mountain mansion, they were both impressed by the new road and the groom and Hector directed them into the beautifully built stables for the Clydesdales, that Zahra had built, especially for the Teams. Angus wasn't with Hugh this time because he had stayed at home with his wife, Islay. It was the season for considering the wives, it seemed. There was also a long discussion between us brothers, Kenneth, and I at home, about the share of the boat that was now available for sale and who might be suitable to buy it. The two choices left remaining, from the short list were Alex, my son and Angus, my son in law. Ali's name had been put forward but rejected and so had many others. We hadn't realised that our little time share, fishing boat idea, had caught on. Kenneth's preference was Angus, because he was younger and stronger than some, like Bruce now, who was too old to help lift the boat.

"I wish Bruce would sell his share too," Kenneth said, "Then both Alex and Angus could buy a share," he added.

"Are you sure about Ali?" I asked. "He's not too sociable, it might help him loosen up a bit," I added.

"I'm sure," Kenneth added.

"I think we have to rule out, my son Alex too, in case of medical emergencies. How can he be contacted if he's in the middle of Loch Ness?" I pointed out.

"That leaves Angus MacKenzie, my son in law. He'd better not think he's getting a discount, on family grounds," I said.

"So have we decided then brother?" Kenneth asked.

"Aye, it's Angus, if you agree brother," I said.

"I do, so long as he does his share of lifting the damn boat," Kenneth said.

"By the way brother, I received a polite letter from Mrs Zahra MacGregor who wants me to sell a few nude paintings, on commission. She has too many up there that she has inherited from the old Lord Cinaed. I didn't know that he could die, again. Hugh said he could bring anything back, that she wanted to sell. What do you think?" Kenneth asked.

"Well, considering you have fewer people now interested in buying them, like Old John, don't get more than two, then if they sell, get more. They may not be as popular now. Has anyone asked lately?" I asked. "They stopped asking, when I kept saying that, the artist had died," Kenneth said.

12. Is Coinneach Og Fat or Braw?

When Hugh Og and Meredith entered the newly renovated home on Misty Mountain, Meredith gasped. Accompanied by the ever-smiling Hamish, with his wife Cora, they were all set to build a salmon farm.

The brothers had decided to build it together.

"This is so beautiful," Meredith said. Hugging Zahra, both Meredith and Cora were pleased to see her again.

"You are so big now with child, Zahra. He's not a wee bairn that you are carrying, for certain. Another fat one, like Coinneach Og, do you think?" Cora asked.

Unfortunately, Coinneach Og heard her calling him 'fat', then immediately began to cry. Grigor told her not to speak like that in front of the lad, as he was a very sensitive, braw lad.

"Poor wee lad. You're braw is all. Da Da's going to give you a pony riding lesson. Will that make you happy lad?" Grigor asked.

The two of them went off and left everyone, even Hamish and Hugh, while the horse-riding lesson took priority. Grigor found his love for Coinneach was a joyful one.

To keep her guests occupied, while Grigor was then unexpectedly busy, Zahra decided to read from a book concerning the 11th Lord Lovat's salmon fishing, in the days before he was beheaded [(4)]. She was sure both Hamish and Hugh Og would be interested in these facts. She was now fascinated about anything connected with salmon.

"The soldiers were puzzled by the seasonal running-in and then disappearance of the salmon. The Fraser Highlanders explained that the fish bred in the River Ness and the Beauly then went to sea for several years and for some reason

returned to the place they were spawned, in order to lay their eggs. Analysing their commodity 'by way of experiment, they clipped their tails into a forked figure like that of a swallow and found them with that mark when fully grown and taken out of the cruives'. The Frasers understood the life cycle of this precious asset as well as how to kill it and market it," [(4, p220)].

"However, as you all know, Lord Lovat came to grief after the 1745/46 Rising." Zahra glanced up only to see that both Hamish and Hugh appeared irritable and were hoping that the reading lesson would come to a quick end.

Fortunately, Grigor then came in as the shocked audience couldn't have taken much more of Zahra's history lesson and Grigor passed Coinneach Og into Hector's capable hands, who was giving Coinneach Og his weekly lessons now.

"We have learned a lot about poor old Lord Lovat. He was a wonderful salmon fisherman. I didn't know that. Thankyou Zahra. I hope we do as well as Lord Lovat and don't disappoint you. He has raised the bar somewhat. I wonder why they've never farmed salmon here before?" Hamish commented.

Meredith was chatting to Mairi in the kitchen about meals and what the men all liked to eat and when, and offered to be her assistant, which was her way of saying, that she was taking over the kitchen. Zahra didn't mind, because everyone loved Meredith's food and she was a MacKenzie, after all and this country was hers and you could see it in the way she carried herself, compared with when Meredith was in MacDonnell country, in Glengarry. It was an unusual cultural observation that Zahra had made and wondered if they'd all be like that in their own countries. She didn't even know where Grigor's country was. She thought it might have been Argyle once. At least before proscription.

Cora was looking a little less confident, after being chided by Grigor, but at least she now knew the boundaries. No fat shaming was allowed for wee Coinneach Og. Grigor was now the lad's very protective father, since the braw lad, cried for him, played with his DaDa's hair, and kissed him goodnight.

Grigor was such a softie, underneath all that bravado, Zahra was thinking. All three big men then left together, leaving Zahra behind, when it was supposed to be her project.

"Wait on me please," said the very pregnant lady, who wanted to be included in her own project. She had trouble keeping up with all three big men, so her husband decided to carry her on his back. That was a bit embarrassing, but at least they all arrived at the waterfall, at the same time. Hugh Og was admiring the view so much, that he briefly hadn't seen where Hamish had gone. He was busy telling Grigor what was going to be built and where, and what it was all called in 'salmon fishing language'. "Would there be lads from the local village who would know how to make the boxes too? We need to make enquiries about employing two more lads to make up the cruives?" Hamish asked.

"Aye, most likely, whatever gets it underway," Grigor replied, now having taken over.

"Maybe you and I can go to Fraser Ville to find those lads?" Zahra asked Hugh Og. He asked Grigor first of course and then they slowly walked to the village to find two unemployed salmon fishing workers. The Village Head always knew who everyone was and who was out of work and what their occupations, all were. He was a very nosey person, but he did point them in the direction of who they needed, even though they turned out to be unemployed herring fishermen. They in turn, recommended two older men who'd had that job, in Inverness, many years ago.

"It wasn't on the river Ness, was it?" asked Zahra.

"Aye, it was. Rebuilt some of the old Lord Lovat cruives, but it was then banned in public waterways and permission had to be sort and all of that. However, on your own property, that's not a problem. We're not young men now, so are we who you need?" Mr Fraser asked.

"Nice of you to ask Mr Fraser. Please come with us and we can ask Hamish Chisholm, who is in charge, and he can talk to you," Zahra said.

"What happened to the Master then?" Mr Fraser asked.

"My husband, Grigor MacGregor is now the Master, but if you mean Lord Coinneach, he died," she said.

"But you are still the Lady Zahra?" Mr Fraser enquired.

"I don't think so," Zahra said.

"Just because he died, doesn't mean that your title dies too," Mr Fraser said. "Nae, you'd still be Lady Zahra. You'd best investigate that. Methinks you're still Lady Zahra and the fishing rights on your waterways are yours, but investigate it, just the same," Mr Fraser advised.

"But my husband isn't Lord Grigor, so that wouldn't be fair, would it?" she asked.

"A Peerage is still a Peerage which means influence, like if there are issues with the salmon fishing rights. People can be touchy about Scottish salmon," Mr Fraser warned.

He was right of course, and he knew what he was taking about.

When Zahra finally received her letter back, confirming her Peeress, she went ahead and applied for the exclusive salmon fishing rights over the waters on Beinn Coinneach. That took about two weeks, including her Peeress, informing Aonghus MacGregor at the same time. It went through with a battle over her continued use of the Peeress title, even though Lord Coinneach was deceased, and Zahra having married twice since his passing. Zahra kept it all quiet, so that Grigor wouldn't be upset, until it all went through, then she told him. She just produced the 'salmon fishing rights' and framed the letter, thus ensuring that it could not be questioned. Mr Fraser knew what she was doing, and he was proud of her.

"Well done Lady Zahra," he said very quietly but he never said it again.

"Look Grigor darling, we have exclusive salmon fishing rights, and it can all go ahead," Zahra said.

Grigor hadn't known of there being any doubt over the project, let alone how she did it and only Mr Cinaed Fraser, knew how it was achieved, thanks to him. She gave him a gift of one of those pink stones, and he knew what that was too.

"Thank you, Mistress," he said and smiled. Watching on, Grigor was frowning and wondering what wee secret there was that the two of them had.

"Okay Zahra, out with it. What don't I know now?" Grigor asked.

"Apparently, we needed that 'fishing rights' thing which Mr Fraser told me about and considering that you, Hamish and Hugh Og were all busy, I did the paperwork, that's all," Zahra said.

"Paperwork?" Grigor asked. "You will need to tell me, eventually Zahra. If there is a secret, I will not be pleased," Grigor added, unsmiling.

Zahra was standing beside the waterfall, very heavy with child and Mr Fraser overheard her husband and had known and seen how Lady Zahra Coinneach had arrived on Beinn Coinneach and knew then which husband must have been responsible for her broken nose, broken jaw, split head, and her disability over time. It was well known in the village but never spoken of. He decided upon risky action and went to Grigor, calling him Master.

"It was because of me, Master, I just told Lady Zahra of the need for that paperwork, or else you might lose your money. I am so sorry, Master, if I spoke out of line," Cinaed Fraser said.

The very suggestion of losing money was enough and it wasn't mentioned seriously again, but Grigor did know that there was more to it, especially when Lawyer Aonghus MacGregor sent his bill to Zahra. Then after the salmon farm was set up, he asked Zahra why there was a bill from a lawyer.

"I needed representation to achieve it my darling. I might be clever, but not clever enough, to achieve it without Aonghus. I'll pay for it," Zahra said.

He opened the letter where it referred to her as a Peeress, Lady Zahra Coinneach.

"The mountains name is still Beinn Coinneach, while the business name is Misty Mountain Salmon," Zahra said.

"Have you used the old Peerage to achieve it?" Grigor asked.

"Aye, it wasn't going to be as easy as we thought. It was recommended that I use it, which was challenged, because Coinneach is dead and I had remarried twice since his death," Zahra said. "I won the case Grigor. One of us had to help Hamish and one of us needed to push it through the Courts, somehow," Zahra said. "I knew you'd hate it. I am sorry if it has upset you," Zahra said.

Surprisingly Grigor turned to her and said, "You clever little bunny rabbit."

"You're not angry then?" Zahra asked.

"Are you joking? I am proud of my wife. I'm telling Hamish." Grigor said.

Off Grigor went and excitedly told Hamish, Hugh and whoever else would listen that his wife had taken it to Court as a Lady. Raucous laughter then was heard all over the loch and then she wasn't sure how she felt about that. Both Mr Fraser and Zahra shook their heads but were pleased at the outcome, just the same. She smiled a thank you to Mr Fraser who was now more aware of her background, than she knew.

13. Arsenic and Green Toys

Zahra went back inside her beautiful home. It was becoming too wild and windy for her, and she was missing the bairns.

Cora and Meredith had found things to do. Meredith was in the kitchen swapping recipes and talking herbal improvements and a meal was cooking, with cakes, scones, and all kinds of food was being prepared for the bairns and the men, for when they came in to eat. Coinneach Og was seated by the fire, occupied with something, so she went over to hug him. He was holding onto a wooden carved toy. The toy wasn't one of hers. It was painted green, and she was instantly horrified because she knew that meant, arsenic. He went to put it into his mouth, as small children always do, and she ran to him and took it from him.

"No, don't Coinneach," she said urgently to the shocked wee bairn.

"I gave it to him Zahra. It's a new toy to make up for upsetting him," said Cora looking very pleased with herself. "Don't you know that this has arsenic in it? That green colour in the paint is arsenic. You could have killed my son. When did you give it to him?" Zahra said panicking.

"Just now," Cora said, looking disturbed.

"Arsenic?" asked Meredith. Zahra picked up her son to check on his health.

"Are you feeling alright son?" Zahra asked. "Mairi please don't allow any new toys, without my approval," Zahra ordered.

"I'm sorry Mistress," Mairi said. Zahra washed Coinneach's mouth out and he seemed alright when Grigor and the men walked in to eat their lunch.

"Ma, is Coinneach alright?" Hector asked.

"I hope so son. He was given a toy with arsenic in the paint. Children are poisoned by that. I found him putting it in his mouth," Zahra said, and Grigor overheard the conversation as he was walking in.

"Who gave my son a poisonous toy?" Grigor exploded.

"It was me, Grigor. I didn't know that it was poisonous. I am sorry," Cora said.

"Family, there are some things you need to know about in this period. Please sit down for your lunch and I'll talk as you eat. This era is known an era of progression, whereby experimentation on the public will occur. Some of these experiments will improve and eventually stop killing people, but Britain stays lagging behind the rest of the modern world, legislatively. As you can see, I still have a wood stove in my kitchen, not the new gas ones, now available or gas lights. They are not yet stable or safe enough, so my choice is still whale oil outside for lighting, not gas and candles for the inside, even if you all laugh at me for my lack of modernity.

"This house has just been painted but in trying to buy more paint, the changeover has already occurred whereby lead has been introduced into the paint also and it could be a long time before we can paint the house again. Lead in the paint, is also toxic. People will start using wallpaper in colours, especially green. The green is achieved, like in that toy, with arsenic, please destroy that toy far away from the house Grigor or bury it deeply underground. Grigor stood up and took it outside to bury far from the house. People will die from their own wallpaper, wee bairns especially. I do not allow toys for my bairns, unless I approve of them first, even dolls. We make our own dolls. Don't give my bairns anything, without my approval first. It is a serious matter," Zahra said to a shocked audience.

"Heating the home is also going to be gas and then later, electricity. As I said, right now, the gas, especially gas in combination with electricity, results in explosions in some peoples' kitchens. Grigor, I hope you like staying old fashioned, because we will be called that but it's important to wait, until it's proven to be safe. Wallpaper is out, so washing our walls is all we can do right now, unless we can buy paint overseas when lead is banned in paint?" Zahra asked.

"Cora, please stop causing issues with wee Coinneach Og. That was too terrifying to think that my wee lad could have been poisoned," Grigor asked. "You might be pleased to know that Hamish and I have talked, and we can build you a wee house of your own, then you might be happier," Grigor added. Which they did.

"Zahra, how do you know what happens with the ''Victorian era?" asked Cora with a sarcastic tone in her voice.

"My wife knows what she knows," Grigor said, shutting her down.

"Cora, shut up," Hamish added.

Watching over Coinneach closely for any changes in his health, Zahra hadn't eaten.

"I'll take him love. You eat some lunch," Grigor said. "Och my braw lad," Grigor said as he kissed him on both cheeks, much to everyone's surprise as to how much Grigor loved the wee lad while the lad chuckled at the attention from his father.

Hamish's Croft

Grigor had been the stepfather to several bairns and he was good at it, fortunately because Zahra was giving him another wee bairn to be father to, from Hugh Mohr Chisholm. Zahra wondered how Cora had been allowed to teach children for all those years then gladly ate some lunch and she was becoming tired and was needing to rest after eating and thought a lie down with wee Coinneach was a good idea. Grigor and Hamish retired by the fire with Hugh Og, to design the new house for the two of them, with everything they needed in it, built from solid Caledonian granite.

The Frasers from the village were experts at building that kind of thing, being up so high on a mountain which needed an expert, so Grigor was going to get quotes first to see if they could build it while they continued the salmon farm project, or whether the three of them had to build it. He had to also think of his coos that Hector was looking after in the interim period, and he was looking forward to getting back to his normal routine with his coos.

The women made up before she lay down to take a nap and a quick hug was had with Cora.

14. Bedtime Questions

It had been an exhausting day for everyone, so an early night after teatime was in order, however Grigor always seemed to wait until bedtime before he began asking Zahra things he had been thinking over, even after great sex. He was like that.

"Zahra darling, you normally talk about wee bairns' names by now, this far into your confinement. You haven't mentioned it once. Why is that?" Grigor asked.

"It was a bit amusing wasn't it with Dihaoine? Poor wee lass. One minute she was Freya then Dorothea then finally Dihaoine," Zahra answered hoping to change the subject.

"Good try," Grigor said. "I'll ask again patiently Zahra. Why haven't you mentioned wee bairns' names, for either a lad or a lass?" Grigor asked again becoming impatient. "Look at me my wife. You try not to look at me when you don't want me to know something. So, look at me and tell me the truth Zahra?" Grigor persisted.

"Oh Grigor, please don't," Zahra asked, as she began to tear up.

"You want to cry now because I am mean to you, or because the wee bairn will have a name?" Grigor asked, as she sobbed.

"You're not mean," Zahra said as she sobbed.

"Okay, so there's a problem with his name, if it's a lad, is that right?" Grigor asked patiently. And Zahra nodded crying as he held her in his arms.

"I know you want to call him Hugh, my love, so please just say it," Grigor said.

"But he should be Grigor, I know that, but Hugh wants him to be named Hugh and the second name Gregor," she said.

"So, you're talking to Hugh now?" he asked incredulously.

"He communicates. It's not the same as talking," Zahra said.

"So, Hugh wants the lad named Hugh, named after him and the second name, Gregor named after me, so Hugh Gregor MacGregor?" Grigor asked.

"Almost," she answered intrepidly.

"He can't be Chisholm," Grigor said. Zahra then cried into his chest like she always did, and he asked her if that was what he wanted.

"Aye," she said hoping the sound was somehow muffled in his chest hair.

"Did he want Hugh Gregor Chisholm MacGregor?" he asked.

"Please don't be angry Grigor," Zahra asked.

"He can be Hugh Gregor Chisholm MacGregor and that's, that Hugh," Grigor said speaking to the ghost of Hugh Mohr Chisholm.

"Lassies names?" Grigor asked.

"Freya MacGregor, after your Mither," Zahra answered sincerely.

"Well, that is nice. Good choice my sexy woman," he said, satisfied at last.

"By the way Zahra. Too many men look at you when you're at the waterfall. I don't like it Zahra," Grigor added.

"Maybe they hadn't expected me to be with child again. I really didn't think that I would be either, so just let them stare. They will tire of staring, if you tell them that they will lose their jobs, if they upset me by staring," Zahra said.

"Darling Zahra, I just have one other question," Grigor asked cautiously.

"Bedtime is more like question time these nights. Would you prefer to have these conversations in the sitting room?" Zahra asked.

"I'll ask when it comes to me and not a planned question time, as you suggest. So, will you answer me or not?" Grigor asked.

"Of course, darling go ahead and ask," Zahra said, as she began to caress him sensuously. She wasn't expecting what was to come and it was a shock to her. She no longer felt sexually stimulated, at all, upon hearing what he asked.

"How was your nose and jaw fixed? I am sorry Zahra. I know it is a sensitive question, but you were a bloodied and broken mess, and I never imagined with those facial injuries that it would ever be repaired, but somehow you are even more beautiful than you ever were?" Grigor asked sincerely. "I didn't want to ever ask you, but my curiosity is overwhelming, and I am asked by others as well, like when Alex and Padruig were both here. They saw you at the time and couldn't understand how that flattened mess could be repaired," Grigor asked.

"It is indeed most fortunate that I both love you and understand your way of communicating, in the way that you do, because your question is in poor taste, to say the least," Zahra said.

"I know it is Zahra. I don't know how else to speak delicately. English is my second language, so it doesn't come out too delicately, does it?" Grigor said.

"Oh sweetheart. I do love you and I wish I knew how to give you all the answers to your questions. In the Aird, there is little that I remember, so 'the mess that my face was in', as you describe it, is not what I know about. No-one has called me that, until just now, nor described it in that indelicate way. I too did not want to see the damage. However, because I found it hard to stay conscious then, there's little that I do remember. I re-call snippets here and there but not of the actual look of it," Zahra said a little thoughtfully.

"I can tell you that my husband, as he became, Lord Coinneach, was a healer and a Druid and capable of magic or so he said, but rarely used it. It would have been too weird to think of him as a normal person, so he concealed his identity, especially the wolf. All I can tell you of my face was that he ran his thumb and fingers gently down by nose, barely touching it. Then there was no bleeding from my nose, which was pleasing to me because Dihaoine wanted to be breast fed. I couldn't open my blouse, so I had to ask him to open it for her to feed. He then repeated a similar thing, ever so gently with his fingers, along my jaw line and both of my eye sockets, under both eyes. I hadn't known that my jaw was broken at all, but Mairi then looked happier because I was unable to speak properly, up until then then.

The bleeding then stopped from both my nose and my mouth. Mairi was out of the room at the time that it occurred, as she had been tasked to give Causantin a bath.

Coinneach was fanatical about everyone bathing frequently. Mairi's husband helped her with me, I think, but I don't remember him on that day, other than a nice, helpful presence. I felt there was someone else, but I have asked and there was no-one else.

I do remember my head being stitched, because that did hurt and it was Mairi who had to do it, due to Coinneach's poor eyesight. Coinneach took off my arisaid, when I gave him permission to do so, in case there were more injuries and then I had to be bathed too. As I said, I was in and out of consciousness, but he kept me awake, in case I drifted away permanently which was a real possibility, he said. I might also have remembered things in the wrong order, so maybe Mr MacKenzie, Mairi you and I could speak privately about it, if there's more you need to know? Coinneach carried me. I remember that. I couldn't walk properly, so Mairi had the bath ready, and she undressed and washed me. I think then, I remembered some of what had happened on the farm," Zahra said and began to weep.

"I told him that I had upset you and Padruig had raped me, but that was all I could truly remember. I'm not trying to be evasive," Zahra added.

"I was more concerned, over the following days, that I couldn't walk, nor write properly. I walked like a duck. It was called my 'wobble,' until it was fixed slowly. My handwriting was all over the place, which upset me, so Coinneach was teaching me calligraphy. He called on Peter Heath then to see what he could do about the wobble, because I was with child by then and it was a threat to the success of the birth of Coinneach Og if I stayed liked that. I had written to Isobel to be here to assist me, and at that time she was happy to come and live here with her two bairns. It's hard to imagine her hating me now, when she was so upset on the day that Peter had to manipulate my spine and put my head back to where it was supposed to be," Zahra said.

"What do you mean?" Grigor asked.

"As a result of the strong blow to my head, it was knocked off the top of my spinal column and Peter said it was lucky that I was still walking at all, but he was going to try to fix it," Zahra said. "Peter stayed for several days and repeated the work on my neck and spine, so I could deliver the wee bairn, or it would have been too agonising, causing death of either or both of us," Zahra said. "But here we are again, and I need to write to Peter to get him back soon. I need him here for wee Hugh Gregor," Zahra added.

"I am sorry Zahra that I've put you through telling me this, but so that our relationship has no barriers, we need to both know that we can last the test of time," Grigor explained.

"I understand love," she said. "If you want to talk to Mr MacKenzie, please can it be the four of us together, but not with Hamish and Hugh or the bairns, because I don't think they should know those details," Zahra said. "Please don't tell everyone that Coinneach was a Druid also, as well as a wolf obviously, especially Cora, she's so inappropriate," Zahra asked. "Can we move them into their own home as soon as possible please?" Zahra asked.

"I am happy with everything you've said, Zahra and I don't

need to talk to Mr MacKenzie. I just hope that the folk around here don't think that I am a monster. I've just caught a few glances is all and I hoped that they hadn't judged me poorly. And I agree. We need to move Cora and Hamish into their own nice home, so long as they are happy with that," Grigor said.

"The locals don't think that you are a monster, darling. On the contrary, everybody here really likes you. Especially after having put up with Coinneach for all those years. You are a breath of fresh air, because you are so normal. Are you having some difficulty in coming to terms in knowing what you did to me Grigor?" Zahra asked.

"Aye, I am, there's something still that I don't understand about the whole matter, but it will be revealed in time I am sure," Grigor said.

"Thank you for getting Cora's house built soon, darling. Let's get their house built before Cora kills our sweet Coinneach Og," Zahra added seriously. "So, you know too, Coinneach Og has an entire blanket box, full of safe toys in his bedroom, that he loves," Zahra added.

"About us Grigor my love. It's not to say that our story isn't impacting and terribly sad, because it is, which might account for some of those glances, but we are obviously back together again and that speaks volumes for now, doesn't it?" Zahra said.

Zahra and Grigor both spooned in bed together that night. He threw his leg right over her to possess her completely and his arm right around her big belly and they both fell asleep, with Grigor satisfied that his wife had forgiven him somehow, despite those horrific injuries, that he had caused. Her ability to forgive, was her greatest strength but there was something niggling at him over how a broken nose and jaw and eye sockets could be fixed like that by the magic man, when her neck wasn't.

That sounded more like Fairy Magic, he thought to himself, not Druid and he knew there was a missing piece of information but not from Zahra's side, it was from his side.

15. Zahra's Peace on Misty Mountain

The letter to Dr Peter Heath was posted the next day, requesting his assistance in the lead up to the birth, expecting that her wee bairn may come early. There were two dates where Zahra could have been with child, with a difference of one week, in between those dates. Zahra asked her dear old friend, to deliver the wee bairn this time, with assistance from both Grigor and Hector, but not Isobel. Mairi offered to clean the wee bairn after his birth, this time. She told him, she had named him Hugh because he was Hugh's wee bairn and didn't want that kept a secret, with his Clan name also included in his birth name.

Hugh Gregor Chisholm MacGregor was his full name, if he was a wee lad and Freya Zahra Chisholm MacGregor, if she was a wee lassie. She also told Peter that Hugh's body was also currently being moved from Cannich, to be buried near Zahra and her bairn on Misty Mountain, thanks to Malcolm Og and Hamish Og, so the new bairn would know who his or her, father was, if she and the bairn survived the birth, this time. Then Hugh, Zahra and the new wee bairn could all be buried together, if they didn't survive it.

Grigor and Zahra made the decision as to where Hugh would be buried, up on the mountain, with the tomb lid that I had already made for him, leaving a hole once again in the Cannich Chapel. Zahra asked me to engrave a headstone for her as well, given that Hugh would now be buried in the ground in a coffin. I helped my grandson, Padraig and my twins achieve it with Grigor Og's knowledge, which was a sad and unpleasant job to complete, but the hole was already dug near her mansion on Misty Mountain Ranch, so she could visit his grave every day.

If Zahra was to die in childbirth, she asked to be buried beside him, with her bairn if the bairn died too and Grigor would join her, one day. She asked me to make her a tomb lid too to match, but on hers she wanted a black swan and a likeness of her wolf and a headstone, so Grigor wouldn't have to pay for it. It read; *"Zahra Shushannah Chisholm MacGregor, wife to Grigor MacGregor, beloved Mother to Hector, Causantin, Coinneach, Dihaoine and five siblings and three grand-children. Dearest friend to Peter Heath, Ulvy Stiorm and her pet wolf.*

Misty Mountain Ranch, Beinn Coinneach had the beginnings of its first wee cemetery complete with aromatic shrubs and bulbs that flowered every year, including daffodils, hyacinths, tulips, and gladioli, surrounded by yew trees. Mr MacKenzie placed a nice bench near Hugh's grave for Zahra to sit and talk to the wee bairn, about his father, once he or she was born, within a short walk from her mansion. Zahra would be able to visit Hugh, instead of Hugh being in the Chapel in Glenmoriston. Callum was very kind to her once Hugh was buried there and the tomb was in place, as he then understood, who the wee bairn's father was. Grigor was hoping to pretend that the bairn was his, but it was not to be, and Grigor went along with the truth, finally as a true gentleman.

She was often asked why there was a black swan on her tomb lid, when Scotland only had white swans.

"We had black ones," was all Zahra would say, which just added to her continued mystery.

Either way, she was preparing for her own end with her Will in order and the businesses all in order too. Grigor asked her why she was so well prepared for her own end, when it was unlikely to occur. She told him of the day she had met Lord Coinneach when all the troubles first began and he told her that she would have one more bairn, before her time was over. That bairn was Coinneach Og. She wasn't expecting to survive childbirth this time, neither did she expect the wee bairn to survive either, but she just hoped they both would. Like all Scottish women in those days, they still made their own shrouds, which she adorned with wildflowers that Grigor had never seen before, which she told him the many names of.

"This Victorian era sees my family first entering the west coast of a vast continent, part of which was called, 'The Swan River Colony'. There were black swans there," she explained. "That was where I was born of multiple ancestries, including Scottish, German, and Irish and my hometown had an Aboriginal name," she said.

"The farmers there grew wheat and sheep, and I had my own horses when I was growing up and I often mustered sheep for a local farmer, needing help to move them to the sale yards," she explained to Grigor for the first time, feeling safe enough to say it.

While never having spoken of her hometown or how she had grown up, Zahra did so on this occasion, never thinking of it as terribly important to anyone, which it wasn't, truth be known. Grigor felt it was like getting to know his wife for the first time, without all the suspicion or wariness about the Sidhe.

Mr MacKenzie empathised with her and took Zahra by her arm to visit the new grave. As Hugh's body was placed carefully into his new resting place, there was a peace that descended upon the whole mountain. The storm clouds simply went away and there was no storm, as her tears flowed uncontrollably. Birds sang and butterflies came fluttering about, as if to welcome the newcomer. Zahra sat on that bench with Coinneach Og sitting on her lap.

"Who is that Ma?" Coinneach Og asked.

"That's Hugh Daddy, the father of this wee bairn in Mummy's tummy," Zahra replied. "Hugh loved you. Do you remember him?" Zahra asked.

"Hugh Da hab hair like my, but more yella?' Coinneach asked.

"Aye that was Hugh and this wee bairn might have yellow hair too, do you think, or do you think it'll be like my hair with my brown ringlets?" Zahra asked.

"Bairn with yella hair some curls like yours Ma," he said. Coinneach loved hair.

She remembered that day like it had just happened when Hugh was shot by Isobel's musket ball after it had gone through the body of the brown wolf then hit a metal frame of the pew in the Chapel and into his big and beautiful body. It just missed her and there were many times that she had wished that it had been her and not him. She could still feel his warmth and his familiar love and wished so much that he hadn't died from a deadly bullet, made from silver. Both Ulvy Stiorm and Hugh died that day, along with her ex-husband, Coinneach who caused it, by entering the Chapel, intending to kill them both.

"Mr MacKenzie, where did Lord Cinaed send Lord Coinneach's body when he picked it up? It wasn't at his home. I mean there wasn't a grave there when Cinaed and I went there. Do you know where the body was sent?" Zahra asked.

"Aye, he was sent to Wick, Mistress, to Alasdair Fraser and he is buried on his wee farm there," he replied. "Lord Cinaed was too ashamed to have his son openly known as a homosexual and buried on his farm, even though that is what he was, or became, so he sent him far enough away to his homosexual lover. He would be the only one to accept him, he thought," Mr MacKenzie said. "I spoke to the cart driver afterwards and that lad didn't want the body there either and had to be paid to have him buried there. Alasdair Fraser was married to a lassie by then, and his wife hadn't known of his previous love affair with the Master," Callum said.

"I am truly sorry Mistress what happened to you here. I was relieved to hear that you escaped from the mountain on that horse, with Dr Heath that day. He was a good man," Mr MacKenzie added.

"I was going to dispose of myself that day, when I asked Mairi for that rudimentary map to go to the waterfall, Mr MacKenzie. I felt unloved and ignored. I really couldn't take any more, after the horrors of the island. But just when I was going to do it, I saw Peter Heath down below, looking for the mountain, because it had been made invisible, as you remember. Peter was talking to a lady Crofter, so I tried to wave at first, but he couldn't see me, then I took out a looking glass, that I carry which reflects light, to get his attention. Then he saw it and looked up at me and I ran like the wind, trying to get to him before he left. I only just made it on time, before he left and then climbed onto the back of his horse and that was how I got away," Zahra said.

"Thank you for telling me, Mistress," Callum said very sadly. "Is that grave there for you then Mistress?" Mr MacKenzie asked.

"Aye it is in case I don't survive the childbirth. I didn't want to cost Grigor anything and this was where I wanted to be buried, near Hugh and if the wee bairn dies too, then we can all be together," Zahra said.

"I think you will make it Mistress. Dr Heath is coming today, and he will make sure that you make it," Callum said.

"Today? Is he? That's wonderful news," Zahra said.

"Mr MacKenzie do you see Hugh standing over there near his new grave, or is it only me who can see him?" Zahra asked.

"I see him too Mistress. At first, he was confused where he was, then when he saw you and heard your voice, he was calm and now he likes where you have put him and your grave next to his. He doesn't want the two of you to die in childbirth. He would like the wee bairn to have a good life, even a university education, so try hard Mistress, for him and the wee one," Callum said kindly.

"How can we better communicate with each other do you know?" Zahra asked.

"Just talk Mistress. Start talking directly to him, as if he was still alive," Callum said.

This made her cry. She wasn't over Hugh's death yet, no matter how much time had passed, or how busy she kept herself or how much she loved Grigor. She was still raw and feeling those same emotions of seeing Hugh die right in front of her, on her wedding day from her daughter's musket ball.

"It was his own daughter's musket ball that killed him," Zahra said.

"When I was first with child with Isobel, I was a living soul and despite him accidentally killing me, she was still alive in my womb and she was born alive, so she is the only one of my bairns where there's no doubt as to her condition," Zahra said. "In my religion, if you kill your father, even for a righteous reason, there's no sin on you, but it does reduce your life span. Isobel is already looking older than I am and she envies me for that, but what she may not know is her time has been shortened too and she is ruining her life, what is left of it," Zahra said.

Just then the two of them heard a horse coming up her road.

"Is that Peter?" Zahra asked. "Can you help me up, I am so heavy with child, Mr MacKenzie?" Zahra asked.

"Aye, it is the Doctor Mistress. Take my arm," Callum said, and he walked her slowly to where his horse would meet the groom. However, it was two horses. Peter Heath was accompanied by Alex MacDonald and Zahra's heart sank. She anticipated another evening of unpleasant conversation with Alex. Zahra didn't think she could tolerate him once again. She smiled at Peter but had to force a smile for Alex. She heard Grigor coming up from the waterfall with Hamish and Hugh Og too, so it was going to be another testosterone filled evening. She decided to go to her reading room after dinner, to avoid them all. The groom then took both horses, and Peter hugged his old friend Zahra carefully.

"Peter, I have so missed you," Zahra said.

"I always miss you Zahra," Peter said. He noticed the graves and then asked who had died.

"This is Hugh. I had him moved here to be with me and his wee bairn. The other grave is mine in case I don't make it," Zahra said seriously. Alex was shocked at what she said but went over to Hugh's grave to pay his respects. Simultaneously, Grigor came up and jovially called out his greetings to both Alex and Peter.

Unexpectedly then, another horse came up the road and it was Cinaed Og. She went across to her former brother-in-law and kissed him on each cheek in the European way.

"Would you please join us for coffee my brother, Cinaed?" Zahra asked.

"Sister, are you about to have the wee bairn?" Cinaed asked, looking worried.

"Aye brother, it is soon. That's why the Doctor has just arrived. Have you met Peter Heath?" Zahra asked.

"Not formally, I saw him helping you with Dr MacNachten with wee Coinneach Og," he said. Zahra introduced Cinaed to Peter and they appeared to like each other.

"These are also our other friends Hamish and Hugh Og Chisholm who are building the salmon farm, and you know Alex," Zahra said.

Grigor looked unhappy that Cinaed was visiting but Zahra felt it was a pleasant distraction.

"Over coffee sister, I need to talk to you about Coinneach Og. Don't worry, its good news. Can we sit by the fire? You should go in out of the cold anyway sister," Cinaed advised.

She took his arm and the two of them led everyone back inside. Mairi quickly served up coffee or tea and scones, jam and cream. Enjoying his coffee and scones, Cinaed asked Zahra about her health.

"I am alright. Not brilliant but the bairn's due soon and I confess that I am worried this time," Zahra said.

"I will assist you again, then you will be fine. I am the only one of us left," Cinaed offered.

Cinaed obviously still thought of Zahra as a MacAlpin, which annoyed Grigor.

"Thank you Cinaed brother. I'd appreciate that. Can you be one of my walkers then?" Zahra asked.

"Peter, when is my sister due?" Cinaed asked.

"I haven't examined Zahra, yet Cinaed as I have just arrived, but possibly a few days or any moment really, if Zahra's waters break," Peter said.

"Then I had better stay overnight and for dinner. Mairi, do you have enough to feed an orphan like me too?" Cinaed asked, humorously inviting himself over to stay.

"You can sleep in Prince Griogar's old quarters, if you like brother," Zahra said.

"I am here to deliver you this paperwork sister, which arrived just this morning. Coinneach Og has now received his Peerage as did I. He is Lord Coinneach McAlpin now. Isn't that wonderful?" Cinaed commented.

Coinneach didn't understand the fuss, but he asked just the same.

"Is that like Ma? Ma is Lady Zahra," Coinneach Og said a little proudly.

"Aye, just like Ma," Cinaed said.

"He can attend university like all of us. I would be honoured to pay for his studies. A surgeon would suit him, I think or politics," Cinaed said.

"Aye, I agree. While he is sensitive, he is very intelligent and capable of Medical School in Edinburgh, but I don't want him to go to England. I would really appreciate knowing his uncle will do that for him Cinaed, you're a good man," Zahra said.

Mairi and Meredith then invited everyone to eat at the large dining table as they had gone to quite a lot of trouble to make very tasty meals of several varieties, including stews, but salmon as well and fried chicken. Over lunch, Peter hadn't wanted any tension to build up and it was obvious that Zahra was uncomfortable with Alex. He knew it wasn't because of his sexual preference, so it was just Alex's unkindness towards her most recently, he thought.

Alex surprised her by then asking if Anndra, Domnhall and Zahra Og could all live there on Misty Mountain Ranch and go to the village school in Fraser Ville. Isobel and John Fraser weren't getting along, and the bairns were suffering, Alex claimed.

"Why can't they live with you in Inverness? Peter is a wonderful father," Zahra said. Peter was shocked at that suggestion but was happy to be a parent again, just the same, so long as Alex looked after Zahra Og, being that she was so young. The lads were ready for high school, but wee Zahra Og was a long way behind them.

"You could be a stay-at-home father and help Peter with his business, like I used to, can't you Alex? If you can't, then of course we will, but I am not sure about this wee bairn, so if I don't make it, then Grigor couldn't care for all those bairns, as well as run the businesses. Can't you have them in Inverness?" Zahra asked again. "John wouldn't mind, would he? You could also take it in turns, so neither one of you is overworked. However, I think Isobel may not like parting with Zahra Og," she commented.

"For this household, Anndra and Domhnall could work out, but wee Zahra Og and her needs, with me like I am now, may not work. What do you think Grigor?" Zahra asked.

"They're our grandchildren, so we can't turn our backs on them, can we?" Grigor said, suddenly being the righteous grandparent.

"Peter, can you mind them in Inverness or not?" Zahra asked.

"I'd love to, but Alex hasn't asked me. He has asked you," Peter said, feeling a little hurt.

"Why can't you and Peter raise the lads at least? You are their father, Alex?" Zahra asked.

"People would gossip about us, wouldn't they?" Alex said.

"It's your life choice, so shouldn't you get used to that Alex?" Zahra advised.

"Can I help?" asked Cinaed. "I do believe that wee Zahra Og was my father's wee bairn and I can look after all three of them. My wife and I don't have any bairns, you see, and Zahra Og is my sister after all," Cinaed added enthusiastically.

"That's a nice idea Cinaed and then I won't be run off my feet, we can see each other often as well, then when you want to pick them up to visit you, I suppose you'd arrange that?" she said.

"Are you two gentlemen in a homosexual relationship? Is that why you don't want the bairns there?" Cinaed asked. Peter looked stunned at the candid question, but both Alex and Peter just looked at each other silently and Hector answered for them.

"Yes, they are," Hector said.

"But didn't you live with Peter too Zahra?" Cinaed asked.

"Peter loves humanity, not just men or women. And he is a wonderful father and so is Alex. It's a shame, you are too embarrassed to be parenting together Alex, when you know the bairns need help. People don't need to know what your private life is about, you could be cousins, or Alex might be an employee, there are many reasons why two men would be raising bairns together," she added.

"Have you asked Isobel if you can raise them?" Zahra asked.

"I have asked her, and she refused," Alex said.

"Have you spoken to a lawyer then for a legal opinion?" Zahra asked.

"I have and their opinion is the bairns should stay with Isobel, unless her Mither could take them," Alex said.

"Have you not seen my condition, Alex? Grigor can't look after them," Zahra said.

"Why can't I look after them?" Grigor asked.

"They can't swim and you're still working on the waterfall. They could drown up there. It's too dangerous Grigor, unless you're watching them all the time. I can make a compromise and take the two lads, provided they stay away from the waterfall and Cinaed can take Zahra Og," Zahra said. "But I think you should be allowed to have them all," she said.

"Zahra Og is welcome with me. Is that an agreement then?" Cinaed asked.

"Can you take the lads on some days too Cinaed but only if Isobel agrees to this mind. I'll write to her to confirm it," Zahra said.

Peter looked ashamed of putting more burden onto Zahra when he was there as a doctor. Both Mairi and her husband looked unimpressed too.

"Cinaed brother, do you want to come with me and Peter now for my examination to see how long I have before this bairn is born?" Zahra asked. "Peter, are you still actually available, or do you want me to consult with Alex MacNachten?" Zahra asked.

"I want to Zahra, but Alex is very jealous of my friendship with you," Peter said.

"That's a problem, isn't it, so he doesn't want you to deliver my wee bairn?" Zahra asked.

"Not really, but I have insisted," Peter said.

"I'll write to Alex MacNachten tonight then. It's short notice and he may not be able to come on time," Zahra said.

"Let's hope you have the wee bairn tonight then, while Peter is still here," Cinaed said flippantly.

"So, Peter, can't we have the same friendship that we had, because of Alex's objection to me?" Zahra asked.

"Nae, we can't. He gets too upset. Really upset and hard to manage. Let me look at you now Zahra. You haven't had morning sickness or all the usual symptoms, so it's probable that we won't even know when you're going into labour. Is that what happened with Isobel?" Peter asked.

"I didn't know that I was with child with Isobel, and she just came out and Grigor delivered her," Zahra said. "Hugh's bairns are different to both Grigor and Coinneach," Zahra explained.

"Who else is assisting?" Peter asked, suddenly sounding serious.

"Cinaed, Grigor and Mairi said that she would wipe down the wee bairn once he or she was born," Zahra said.

Then the atmosphere suddenly changed after Peter examined Zahra.

"Cinaed can you urgently please get Mairi with the things for the bairn and tell her to boil water and get Grigor and Mr MacKenzie? You're in labour my love. Can you take off some of these clothes? I'll prep you now and we are having a bairn tonight, Zahra," Peter said.

Peter gave Zahra an unwelcome enema and then shaved all her private area to make it as clean as possible. Grigor came in horrified at the emergency oncoming birth.

"Are you in labour now Zahra?" Grigor asked as he came rushing in.

"Aye darling. I am sorry to spoil your dinner Grigor,"

Zahra said.

"When I've finished here Grigor, you and Cinaed and maybe Hector too can assist," Peter instructed. "Can you go and tell them to wash themselves thoroughly with soap and they will have to help too, as well as Mr MacKenzie who will also have to wash up."

"Do you have clean aprons here?" Peter asked. Mairi was sent for the clean aprons and additional sheets and bought in the water and towels and prepared a table for the bairn.

"Alright Zahra my love you can have him when you are ready, so we can stand you up. Hector, one side, Cinaed the other. Mairi, mattress and doonas on the floor please. Now do your wee walk, while I see how advanced you are," Peter said as he sat on the mattress on the floor watching the cervix opening quite quickly.

Suddenly Zahra let out an almighty scream.

"He's coming Zahra. Good girl let him come," Peter said. No-one had been prepared for the sudden arrival of the new bairn but he slithered out and Zahra screamed, "Hugh" and it trailed off into an 'oo' sound. Poor Grigor felt the sadness of a husband, whose bairn wasn't his but assisted just the same. Zahra was oblivious to having called out Hugh's name and then asked for Grigor.

"Grigor, is he alright? Is he alive?" Zahra asked. Her new wee bairn was a blonde curly haired lad, just as Coinneach Og had predicted and the lad came running to see him.

"Can I see him," Coinneach Og asked. "His hair Ma, its yella but curly like yours," he said totally excited by his new brother. "Can I hold him please?" Coinneach Og asked.

"Aye he can hold him, as long as he sits on the floor with Hector then he won't drop him," Peter said. Coinneach Og loved the wee bairn so much he kept on kissing his face and telling him he loved him.

"Coinneach you always have to wash your face and hands before you touch him, okay?" Zahra said. "Have you washed your hands?" she asked.

"Aye Ma, Mairi told me," Coinneach Og said.

"Can I hold him Zahra, I'm clean," asked Grigor.

"Of course, you're his Da," Zahra said.

Gently taking the wee bairn from Coinneach Og, Grigor held the wee lad in his arms ever so lovingly.

"He does look like you and Hugh, both handsome and sweet looking," Grigor said tearing up. Then everyone wanted to hold him, when Peter stepped in.

"Enough of the holding. Only immediate family in case of germs. He's a new bairn," Peter said.

Alex looked in but didn't come in.

"Mistress, do you want me to bathe him properly now and we can take him to his proper wee bed where its quiet?' Marie asked.

"Aye and Mr MacKenzie can you light those fires up there please in both rooms and you can go with Mairi," Zahra said. "Thank you, Peter. Are you finished?" Zahra asked hopefully.

"Not yet. Nearly darling. Hold on," he said as he pressed on Zahra's lower abdomen for any clots after the placenta came out. "I wish all child births were like that one," Peter said. "You were amazing. So much for dying in childbirth and having the grave ready," he jested. Zahra then was overcome with extreme tiredness.

"Are you alright love?" asked Grigor.

"I am so tired Grigor, can I go to bed once wee Hugh has fed," she asked. "Please thank Hector for me. Where is he? Where's Cinaed?" she asked.

She thanked them both and kissed them both affectionately.

"I love you both. Cinaed please stay the night. Its cold tonight," Grigor was a little surprised at how her relationship had grown with Cinaed and they both seemed to love each other as a real brother and sister.

"I'll help with Coinneach Og too, if you like," Cinaed said.

"I'm managing just fine with Coinneach Og. I'm his father," said a very possessive Grigor over Coinneach Og. "You can mind Zahra Og, if she ever lives here," Grigor added.

"Grigor, I don't want any of them near the waterfall or the loch," Zahra insisted.

It was decided that Cinaed would look after both wee ones, while Grigor and Hamish were still salmon fishing. Then bit by bit, Grigor handed it all over to Hamish, so Grigor could get back to his cattle. Cora and Hamish had settled down nicely into their stone home, near the Loch, above the waterfall. Cora was happier there in her own home without Zahra dictating terms as to how they should all have to live. Cora still doubted the truth of the green paint being poisonous.

Cinaed's wife didn't seem to mind where he was. It was only Isobel's reply that Zahra was waiting for.

◊

Meredith didn't want to return to Glengarry now that the wee bairn was born and Mairi was needed to assist Zahra. She asked her husband, Hugh Og, if she could stay on just for two more weeks until Malcolm Og and Hamish Og were both due next, then she could return home to Glengarry with them. Hugh Og sadly agreed to departing without his wife, all the way back to Glengarry, alone. Meredith was going to do all of the cooking on Misty Mountain Ranch, morning, noon, and night, for the entire two weeks and she was paid well for her work.

She liked the idea of the extra cash in her pocket, as well as being in MacKenzie country, but she did miss her handsome husband, once he had left. She enjoyed her moments with the wee bairn too and was sad that his father had died, despite Grigor being a devoted father now, she just hoped it would stay that way. Meredith didn't like the look of Alex and Peter's relationship while they were there and wondered if Peter wasn't being subjugated by Alex. John Fraser had always fallen under his stronger influence and so she expected Peter Heath would too. She was glad to see Alex leave.

It was a dreadful shame for both Zahra and Peter, once it had appeared that they had lost the strong friendship that they both once had with each another, because of Alex.

When Hugh Og reported back to me in Glengarry, without Meredith, who was staying on to help, he explained the situation and asked if the twins could bring Meredith back in two weeks time.

"That's not a problem Hugh. New bairns are a lot of work. That's nice of Meredith. Ailsa might have to get used to cooking for me. I like it, especially breakfast," I said. "What did Zahra have this time?" I asked.

"A cute wee lad with yellow hair. God, he looked so much like Hugh Mohr but Zahra too. It was uncanny. She called out for Hugh when she was giving birth. I felt for poor Grigor, raising another man's wee bairn. He has done it before and he's doing it again for Hugh. She even named him Hugh. I'm not complaining mind. Hugh is a great name, but she's naming him after Hugh Mohr Chisholm. That's not all. His full name is Hugh Gregor Chisholm MacGregor, so he has his Father's Clan name in there too," Hugh said. He was unsure of what I would think.

"That's a great idea. Should be more of it, more honesty and honour to the actual Father. Good on her and Grigor for accepting it," I said.

"That's not all. She had Hugh's remains moved from the Chapel with that tomb you made. He's buried there, right near the house," Hugh Og added.

"I knew that, Hugh. I had to make one for her too. In case she died," I explained.

"She wanted a black swan on it. I had to write back and check because I told her our swans were white. She said that where she comes from, swans are black. Can you imagine a black swan?" I asked.

"How are the horses?" I asked.

"Really strong and healthy, Malcolm. Zahra has built new stables, especially for Clydesdales, for your sons, I think, and the two grooms were good, fussing over them all the time. Then I could help Hamish and do whatever was needed. I even went to that odd little village behind that mountain with Zahra, called Fraser Ville, looking for two more employees to work on the salmon farm," Hugh Og said.

"How was Zahra?" I asked.

"Tired most of the time, big with child Malcolm. She didn't much like Cora and neither did Grigor," Hugh added.

"Oh aye, why?" I asked.

"Cora called her wee son Coinneach, 'fat', which he is, but the lad is sensitive and cried when Cora called him fat and Grigor was mighty angry with Cora, so he took the lad for a riding lesson. The next day Cora thought to make it up to him for making him cry, so she gave him a wooden toy, green in colour, and Zahra walked in, just as the lad was about to put it in his mouth. Zahra then hit the bloody roof," Hugh said.

"Did you know that the green colour had arsenic in it?" Hugh Og asked.

"Aye but only recently. Ailsa warned me about it. She gets that information because of her job. Dangerous stuff. Down in London many folks have died from it as well as the green wallpaper, so Ailsa told me not to buy wallpaper and even the paint now has lead in it, which is poisonous too. Luckily, we just did all the painting, before they put the lead in it," I said.

Hugh was shocked that everything that Zahra had said was true.

"Zahra said not to get those gas lights yet too. They're unstable. Can I sleep here Malcolm? I'll be lonely without my Meredith," Hugh Og asked.

"Aye big fella, your old room is still as it was," I said.

16. Isobel Fraser Visits Misty Mountain

Baby Hugh was adorable, and he did have his father's softness of character, in such a wee bairn, which drew Coinneach Og to him frequently. Seated on the carpet by the warm fire in the sitting room, the two wee bairns were together when a loud knock came on the door. Mairi answered it and it was Isobel, carrying Zahra Og. Zahra was trying to think what Zahra Og's relationship was then to Coinneach Og and she thought that she must be his Aunty, even though she was younger.

Thank God Cinaed was still here, was her second thought, so she called out to him, even though he was occupied in the kitchen with Meredith.

She was still very tired and couldn't think quickly enough to deal with Isobel. Zahra put wee Hugh Gregor on her breast to suckle a while, as Mairi indicated to Isobel where her Mither was. After Mairi offered tea or coffee to both women and Master Cinaed, as she still called him, she looked worried at what might eventuate, and went to fetch her husband Callum, while Meredith made the refreshments.

"Hello Isobel and Zahra Og sweetie pie, nice to see you both. Do you remember Uncle Cinaed?" Zahra said. "Are both of the lads with you?" Zahra asked.

"Ma. Aye, they're outside," Isobel said, not being very friendly.

"Bring them in out of the cold, for a hot chocolate," Zahra said.

The door was opened once again and the cold wind blew into the warm mansion, then the lads ran in, saying "Granma" and they kissed their Granma and wanted to see the new wee bairn.

"You have to wash your hands first, lads," said their Great

Uncle Cinaed. Mairi had the wash basin with soap and a towel ready for them and took the opportunity to wash their faces thoroughly too. If it had been up to Mairi, they'd be put in the bath before touching anybody, but Isobel was already glaring at Cinaed for insisting on the hand washing.

"Lads, you can call me Uncle Cinaed because it's too much to say Great Uncle," Cinaed said. "You can sit on my knee Domnhall," Cinaed said. "We can both look at the new wee bairn from my knee. Look he has fallen asleep," Cinaed said.

"Mairi, can you get me Hugh's cradle please," Zahra asked. Zahra put her wee bairn down to sleep while both lads looked at him. "Get comfortable Isobel with your coffee," Zahra said. Zahra Og reached out to Cinaed, which was sweet.

"Do you want me to take her Isobel?" asked Cinaed.

"Not really, I don't know you," Isobel said.

"I'm her half-brother" Cinaed said. "Zahra Og is a MacAlpin." Cinaed added proudly and Isobel just ignored him.

"Your letter Ma?" Isobel said, looking at her Mither questioningly as she took the letter from her apron.

"Aye, I was asking if you had given permission to Alex for those plans of his," Zahra said. "Have you?" Zahra asked.

"Nae, I have not and why are you involved?" Isobel asked.

"Alex was here and claimed that you and John were not getting along anymore and claimed that all your bairns were suffering. Is there any truth in that?" Zahra asked.

"John and I are not happy together anymore, that's true because Alex left me. What do you expect, he left me, so he could go and live with a man?" Isobel said, disgusted with Alex's life choice.

"What is John unhappy about and how is it affecting the bairns?" Zahra asked. "Surely you can still care for the bairns, even if Alex has gone. You have done it all before?"

Zahra asked.

Zahra Og was wriggling to get out of Isobel's arms and reached out then to Granma.

"Can I take her now?" Zahra asked. The poor wee lass was finally handed over to her Granma.

"You got new bairn Granma?" Zahra Og asked.

"Yes, sweetheart. His name is Hugh, just like his father," Zahra said.

"Is he my full brother then?" asked Isobel.

"Aye he is your brother," Zahra said. Isobel reluctantly then looked at the new bairn.

"He does look like Da, a bit," Isobel said reluctantly.

"Aye, he's a lot like Hugh," Zahra said sadly.

"What's your decision Isobel please, I need to lie down soon," Zahra said.

Zahra couldn't take much more, and it was fortunate that Grigor came in for lunch. Grigor wasn't impressed to see his wife clearly overtired from giving birth, then being hounded by Isobel. Cinaed had tried to assist, but Isobel wouldn't listen to him. Mr MacKenzie and Mairi both came to help Zahra and wee Hugh.

"Master, can we take the wee bairn Hugh and the Mistress to bed for their rest now?" Mr MacKenzie asked.

"Me too?" asked Coinneach Og. They all went to Zahra's bedroom with Coinneach Og in bed with her and wee Hugh beside her, in his own wee bed. Zahra was so exhausted, that she fell asleep right away, with Coinneach Og holding onto his Mither. Mairi covered them both over warmly with a woollen blanket and left the room with her husband Callum, after stoking the fire and closing the big drapes.

Mairi said to her husband Callum, that she was worried about her Mistress because she wasn't herself and was not recovering at the speed that she had done previously.

"It's grief Mairi, pure and simple. The Mistress is grieving for Hugh the father of the wee bairn. She's not recovering because she can't talk to her husband, the Master about the man she still loves and misses. Grief can kill, I've seen it kill. Her daughter isn't helping because she used to have a nice relationship with her, but the lass shot her own father. Not intentionally but it happened in Cannich, and in their religion, it shortens their lives when that happens. That's what the Mistress told me," Mr MacKenzie said. "Master Grigor is a jealous man, but he can't see what she needs. She just needs him to sit and talk with her, go for a walk together, holding hands. She's a romantic type of person, poor lass," Callum added.

"Now not even her friend, Peter Heath is allowed here, to visit," Mairi said.

"Who is the common denominator Mairi?" Callum asked.

"Alex MacDonald," Mairi said.

"Aye, Alex the troublemaker," Callum added.

"How can we help then?" Mairi asked.

"I had one idea only," Mr MacKenzie said. "When I saw Master Hugh standing by his grave, I could see that silver musket ball was lodged in his right hip. We could tell Master Grigor where it is lodged and get Dr Heath out here to operate on him in secret, to remove it," Callum suggested.

"Oh my God, Callum. Operate on him in his grave. Is that a sin?" Mairi asked.

"Nae Mairi, just that Master Grigor might not want him back alive, because Master Hugh will be her legal husband again, unless she keeps Master Grigor in a bigamous marriage?" Callum said.

When the two of them went downstairs some developments had occurred, because Grigor had threatened Isobel with the strap for upsetting his wife. Grigor had decided that Zahra Og was now going to be one week with Cinaed Og on Misty Mountain, in their own quarters and one week with Isobel on Wolf Ranch with Isobel and John. Both lads were going to live full time with Grigor and Zahra, with Alex and Isobel both having visiting rights on Misty Mountain Ranch.

The lads would attend the Fraser Ville School, and they wouldn't be allowed near the waterfall, but Hamish would teach them how to swim in the loch in summertime.

That seemed like a good start and then Mr MacKenzie asked if he could speak to the Master for a while with Mairi. Both expressed concerns over the Mistress's condition. Mr MacKenzie identified her poor condition as unexpressed grief, out of concern for Grigor's feelings, to which he agreed. He then added his suggestion of bringing in Dr Heath to operate on Master Hugh's body, to remove the silver musket ball, which was the reason for his death, for those who are already deceased.

"How do you know where the musket ball is lodged, Mr MacKenzie?" Grigor asked.

"I see him too Master like the Mistress does, standing by his grave or thereabouts. He's happy now that he is here near his wife," Callum said. "I think if the musket ball was removed, then with prayer over his grave, he may be able to return to us, but only if the Master thought it was a good idea," Callum added.

"Right hip you say?" Grigor asked. "I can write to Peter and ask him to operate on it, on the quiet so Alex won't know, and I'll pay him well. He had better not tell Alex where he's coming, or it might not work. I confess that I am worried about my wife too, but it means she would have two husbands then and she won't like that too much," Grigor said.

"Master Hugh would still be her legal husband, so she would have to make a decision," Callum said. "How would you feel

Master, if the Mistress asked you to remain here, but not as her husband?" Callum asked, looking worried.

"Surely she will have us both?" Grigor said. "I am not giving her up now," Grigor added.

"I understand. Do you think, it may help if the Master could take her for a few wee walks, when it's sunny, holding hands, so you keep her love, have wee chats by his graveside, holding the wee bairn, riding a horse together to see the tenants, that kind of thing," Callum said.

"Mr MacKenzie you have been around women for a long time to have kept Mairi happy all this time, so I'll do as you suggest. Wee walks you say, holding hands, chats by the grave, holding the wee bairn, riding her horse might be too soon, but I'll start with that letter and get all romantic after that," Grigor said.

"The Mistress likes her hair being brushed too," Mairi added.

"That's a lot of hair Mairi. Can't that be your job?" Grigor said.

"Yes Master of course it's always a pleasure," said Mairi, as she curtsied to Grigor. He liked being the Master and he even liked the wee curtsy. It made him feel respected. 'Men need that respect', Grigor thought.

"Are you staying Isobel?" Grigor asked.

"Nae Da," Isobel replied.

"Then best get home before it gets dark, and we'll take care of your bairns. Write it on your calendar. You never know love, you and John might enjoy each other's company, now you're not thinking of trying to make more bairns," Grigor said.

Isobel left Misty Mountain feeling unhappy with the arrangements but pleased at least that they were not with Alex and understood that her parents had been dragged into her miserable life.

The loneliness of riding off alone, without her bairns was heart breaking, just the same.

17. Cinaed Moves In

"Cinaed, brother you'll have your own quarters with wee Zahra Og and the lads can sleep in the room near Causantin and Dihaoine," Grigor commanded, feeling in charge and in control. He sat down at his desk and wrote that letter to Peter Heath, without giving him an option other than to operate on Hugh, but without telling Alex where he was going. Zahra wasn't too well, unless Hugh could spring back to life, by some miracle of God.

He had to get accustomed to the idea of being romantic. Sexy he was good at, and he was going to do his best in that department. Romantic, not so good.

Mr Callum MacKenzie had been more and more occupied with domestic issues in recent days and so he had allocated many more of the Farm Manager tasks to the second farm manager, George MacKenzie, who was doing a wonderful job and was also in complete sympathy with the happenings in the 'big house,' as he called it.

Meredith planned to cook up a delicious meal for when Peter arrived the following day, because after such a difficult job, food was all she could think of. Mairi posted the letter and when the family all disturbed from their rests, they had a normal dinner with delicious fresh vegetables from Zahra's, incomplete garden, after a very long day. Cinaed was now a semi-permanent addition to the table, but Meredith found him easy to please and he made suggestions for better health for the Mistress, such as kale, spinach, and celery.

Hamish now went to his own croft with Cora, which was a relief without Cora causing more issues. Cora was aging faster than Hamish and her arthritis bothered her, so that added to her moods. She felt unattractive and she was becoming difficult to socialise with. It was hard to imagine that she had once sang like a nightingale at the wool waulking or in the Chapel. Being near the waterfall might be aggravating her arthritis, too but Meredith didn't have that problem, so she wasn't sure.

Coinneach Og and wee Hugh both woke up from their rest for wee Hugh to feed while Coinneach was also wanting milk from Zahra, when Cinaed knocked on her door. He asked her if she needed help with the bairns' nappies.

"Actually Cinaed, they all missed out on their baths this morning. Can you see if Mairi has the hot water ready for their baths yet and you can bathe Zahra Og first if you like?" she said. He saw that she was breast feeding and asked her if Zahra Og could have a drink too while he talks to Mairi and prepares the baths. Zahra Og and Coinneach Og had a drink as well as wee Hugh Gregor.

"Thank you, my sweet sister," he said, kissed her forehead then patted wee Hugh on his bottom. "I'll talk to Mairi and get those baths and clothes ready," he said.

"They need wee furry boots on their feet too Cinaed, and bonnets," Zahra said. He stood watching on as Zahra breast fed the two bairns, momentarily not having had a wife who'd delivered a child, let alone seeing breast feeding in motion, it was a moving sight for him.

"I've never been up close to breast feeding. It's so amazing," Cinaed said.

"I'm just like a dairy cow, that's all," Zahra said.

"Why didn't Coinneach paint you in the act of breast feeding?" Cinaed asked. She didn't like the mention of his brother, so just she ignored the remark.

"Are you a Druid too Cinaed? If you are, can you teach me what you know?" Zahra asked.

"I am, aye, but you can only learn if you are of the royal blood line. Do you know if you could be?" Cinaed asked.

"I don't know. Do you have a series of tests to identify me, if I am, because Coinneach did identify me as a MacGregor, that is from the MacAlpins, but I don't know what is truthful now," Zahra said. "Can you do those tests again?" Zahra asked.

"Did you copulate with the wolf," Cinaed asked very quietly, eyes down.

"Do you need to know that?" Zahra asked, feeling momentarily shocked at the direct question.

"It's one of the tests," Cinaed said. "If one of our wolves attaches itself to you after copulation, then you are automatically identified as being of the blood line," Cinaed said.

"But Ulvy Stiorm is dead now," Zahra said and began to cry. She held onto her former brother-in-law and sobbed in grief for both Ulv and Hugh. "They're both gone from me now. I feel so alone," Zahra said sobbing. He held her and explained that it can be rectified.

"You can have as many wolves in a lifetime, as is needed. They will fight to the death for you, like yours did. However, it requires copulation with another, like Coinneach was," Cinaed said rather vaguely.

"What do you mean Cinaed? Coinneach is dead now?" Zahra asked.

"One day, when your husband and all of the bairns are out, or asleep, with doors locked, I can perform that duty for you," Cinaed said. "It's not a quick process, as you may remember, so it would have to be carefully timed. Its' not a sexual need that I have. I want to make that clear. It would be a means to an end in order to achieve it. It's not always successful, but if both parties co-operate and my wolf is gentle with you, then we could achieve it," Cinaed said.

"You have a wolf too?" Zahra asked.

"Aye, we MacAlpins all did, but Coinneach's was by far the oldest and the most vicious and it hadn't been of his choosing to endure a life with that cursed brown wolf of unnatural proportions, because Coinneach had been cursed," Cinaed said.

"No Seer nor Druid nor Priest, could break that curse" Cinaed said seriously, "So it then became a MacAlpin tradition to each have a spirit wolf, within the boundaries of the Druid faith, to protect ourselves," Cinaed explained.

"Would you agree to copulate with me, as a wolf?" Cinaed asked, still looking down.

"I'm asking this of you because there is something that you are unaware of, currently taking place and the family are all busy by your husband's graveside, with Dr Heath. He is operating on Hugh to remove the silver musket ball that is lodged in his right hip. If we do it now, they will all be unaware," Cinaed said.

From that act, a most beautiful grey She Wolf appeared in Zahra's bedroom. Down below, beside Hugh's grave watching on intently, Hamish thought that he had heard a wolf's howl coming from inside the mansion.

"Did anyone else hear the sound of a wolf's howl coming from inside the house?" Hamish asked.

"Nae, Master Hamish, 'tis not in the house, but 'tis true that the sounds of the mountain echo, so if there was a wolf over beyond the waterfall, then it would echo and make it sound like it was from here. I have lived here my whole life, so I know. Isn't that right Mairi?" Callum said to his wife, looking to her for support.

"Aye husband," Mairi agreed. Mr MacKenzie had become aware that the only person missing from the group, apart from the Mistress, beside Hugh's grave was Master Cinaed, which meant only one thing. Another wolf would join them soon.

He deduced that Cinaed was introducing her to his world of the Druids.

Coinneach had known all along that Zahra was of the royal

blood line, as did Cinaed, but Coinneach didn't want Zahra to know that about herself, least she become like a Priestess of Auld, or even more powerful than that, if she was introduced to the Sidhe. A Goddess.

All the bairns, even wee Hugh held in Grigor's arms, were present by Hugh Mohr's grave, while Peter Heath cut into the side of Hugh Mohr Chisholm, in order to remove that silver musket ball, responsible for his death.

Mr MacKenzie and Mairi insisted that it would distress the Mistress too much to see him cut open, keeping her asleep had been their overall decision. Then Hamish, who had very good hearing, had heard the Mistress scream.

"I'll go," said Mairi followed by her husband, Callum. Then they would bring her back and tell her what had taken place in Hugh's grave.

The activity was all over in the bedroom and Cinaed was dressed once again and no longer smelling like his wolf, when Mairi knocked on Zahra's bedroom suite door. Thankfully, Zahra too was dressed, tidy and wanting to see what was happening to Hugh's body.

"Mairi, I'm glad you came. The Mistress was having a bad dream, but she is alright now. I told her that Peter Heath was here, operating on Hugh, hoping to remove that musket ball," Cinaed said. "The Mistresses bedsheets and pillowcases all need replacing. Can you do that and tidy up in here with air freshener too please?" Cinaed asked.

"I'll take the Mistress to the grave, Master Cinaed?" Mr MacKenzie said.

"Aye, please do and I'll soon follow you down," Cinaed said still feeling a little shocked himself at his accomplishment, as well as the absolute joy it gave to him.

Taking Mr MacKenzie by the arm to go down the stairs, Zahra was wanting to see Hugh's grave immediately. Meredith was preparing for an influx of the family all wanting refreshments and was busy in the kitchen. She was a little suspicious of Cinaed. He was still handsome after all. He was tall, intelligent, elegant, quietly spoken and yet strong somehow. Meredith's life had been boring compared to Zahra's, but she didn't envy her at all and missed her own smelly, horsey, Hugh Og back at home in Glengarry. She had heard the wolf howling too but was similarly convinced that it was just an echo. It still meant that there was a wolf on the property, somewhere.

The scream Meredith had heard, however, wasn't a bad dream, of that, Meredith was certain.

As Zahra approached the grave surrounded by the entire family, Grigor offered Zahra his arm.

"I hope you don't mind darling. I took the initiative to help Hugh get that silver musket ball out of his troubled body. Then if you pray over his grave, asking for him to return, he will as he has done before, we hope. That is the theory anyway," Grigor said. Peter was washing up as he had finished ensuring the site that he had operated on was totally sterile. "Is it thoroughly sterile Peter?" Zahra asked.

"Aye it is Nurse Heath," Peter said in jest.

"Is he going to be warm enough now when he starts to wake up?" Zahra asked. Suddenly people were offering their socks and coats and blankets to keep Hugh as warm as possible.

"Zahra my dear, here is the deadly culprit," Peter said, producing the silver musket ball. "What a truly ingenious idea that was Grigor, my friend. I truly hope this works," Peter added.

Grigor released his wife's arm and walked over to the other side of the grave, sensing another presence in their midst. He had always been able to see or feel the 'Otherworld' since he was a wee bairn. He knew there was something else that had joined them. Then as Grigor looked across the grave to his wife, who stood beside Cinaed, there it was, not only one, but two spirit wolves. One of a very docile nature with Cinaed's hand on his head and Zahra's new wolf, that had somehow appeared to replace her old one, Ulvy Stiorm.

Zahra's new wolf was not as docile in appearance, but still a grey wolf, with a lovely white mane. He wasn't a young wolf either and appeared to be a very strong male. Zahra was clearly unaware of his presence, as she had been previously, but she did look happier. She was no longer depressed, as she had been since the birth of the wee bairn. There was only concern on her face for both Hugh in his grave and baby Hugh. If he was to examine closely who she was closest to, it would be both Cinaed and him, other than baby Hugh and Hugh Mohr in his grave.

Cinaed stood beside Zahra and they both exchanged glances of both gratitude and warmth. Wee Zahra Og ran over to him extending her arms up to him to be picked up and called him Daddy.

"I'm not your Da. I'm your big brother, but you can always rely on me my sweet wee sister," Cinaed said, as he lovingly picked up Zahra Og.

"Brudda?" Zahra Og asked.

"Aye brother" Cinaed replied. Coinneach and Causantin both wanted attention too with all the wee ones getting most of it lately and Causantin went to his Ma and climbed onto her with Coinneach Og wanting to be lifted too, so Hector lifted his young brother.

"I'm your big brother," Hector said.

Dihaoine moved along the side of the grave to get a good look at her Daddy Hugh, inside his grave, who was supposed to be dead, and it seemed like everyone was waiting for him to leap up out of his grave.

She put her hand down into the grave and asked him, "Are you alive Da?"

Then turning around in her crouched position, the person

closest to her, was her Uncle Cinaed and she looked up to his kilted self.

"Uncle Cinaed, you got a 'stiffy' like Hector gets. Is your cock cold? That's what Hector gets. He says his cock gets a 'stiffy' when it's cold. You should put on panties like me," she said.

Cinaed was very embarrassed, as he pressed down on his obvious erection and everyone's eyes were glued on Cinaed's erection beneath his kilt, so he thought it better to go indoors to keep his obvious desire for Grigor's wife, well hidden. Zahra's reaction was one of amusement, as she covered her mouth trying not to laugh at her bairn's honesty, not realising Cinaed's erection had been because of standing beside her.

Grigor was at least pleased to see that Zahra wasn't guilt ridden, or some other emotion that might have revealed any desire for him also, but there clearly wasn't any. Meredith had come out to let everyone know about the refreshments and had heard it all and had also the need to cover her mouth, so she wouldn't laugh out loud. Mr MacKenzie and Mairi however, did both look very awkward and went inside. Hamish was catching onto the odd ways of Misty Mountain that were quite entertaining, but Cora was still more concerned about her arthritis and needed to sit down.

Dihaoine was the sweetest little bairn and Hector wasn't the least bit embarrassed about having regular 'stiffies' obviously. He might have even been pleased that his erections were now known about by the entire family.

18. Grigor's Nightmare

"May your cattle wander off at night,

May your chickens cease to lay,

May the wolves eat your sheep,

And your wife's face turn to mush...

by your violent hand....

Lost be your horses, your bairns and your life.

Never again will love return to your marriage bed.

Only a wolf like stranger can ....

Her face restore.

But love for you will be....

Never more.   – A Druidic Curse.

Grigor woke up in a sweat. Shaking all over and bathed in sweat, he gasped at the horror of what had been a curse placed upon him. He had been cursed all along.

Had it been Coinneach McAlpin who had cursed him the day his wife went to the Old Crohn's place where she had met him? Grigor then understood why everything had happened the way it had, even his poor wife's face. He rolled over to hold onto her and feel her face once again, to ensure it was as it should be. Zahra responded to his loving touch, "Grigor darling," she said in response to his gentle touch. He was so relieved to hear those words. The curse must have been broken or else, they couldn't both be back together in their marriage bed. She became amorous then and they made love, like it had always been. His heart sank thinking he had lost her due to a curse and she had suffered so much and as a result his eyes welled up in tears.

He never cried after making love, but Zahra felt how wet his face was.

"Darling. What's wrong?" Zahra asked. She ran her hands across his hairy chest and as she spoke in her loving way, he had to tell her about the nightmare before the words of it were lost to him.

"Druidic Curse you say?" Zahra asked. "It must have been Coinneach then describing what occurred before my face was damaged. I didn't know what a Druid even was before I met him. There is something you need to know Grigor," Zahra said.

"That entire family were Druids. Cinaed just told me that yesterday, including himself, so he is the last of his line. I asked him to teach me what that is exactly," Zahra said.

"There is also something you need to know too my love," Grigor said.

"Oh aye, what?" Zahra asked.

"You have another wolf. Cinaed has one too, so now it makes sense if he's a Druid and it's a Druid thing," Grigor said.

"I do? It's not essentially a Druid thing, it evolved from the MacAlpins or the Picts, I'm not sure," Zahra said. "Do you mind if he teaches me?" she asked.

"So long as he doesn't get any 'stiffies' or makes a move on my wife," Grigor said smiling.

"That was funny. Poor Cinaed. I thought it was the other way round with your cock and the cold weather. I thought it shrunk, not go into a 'stiffie," Zahra said.

"It does shrink. Don't start taking lessons from Dihaoine and Hector," Grigor said.

"So why did he go stiff then?" Zahra asked.

"He was standing too close to you. So, when you have these lessons with him, don't sit too close. Maybe it's that perfume you always wear. It is rather nice," Grigor said.

Zahra giggled at the memory of it and they both laughed and made love once more.

"Poor sweet Dihaoine," Zahra said.

"That curse got it a bit wrong anyway love. We didn't have any sheep, we only had goats," she said. Kissing as they both fell back to sleep.

Zahra had forgotten to tell Grigor that the night before, she too had a bad dream where she thought she saw the ghost of Coinneach MacAlpin standing in their lounge room looking unhappy, dishevelled, unclean and wearing very little. If she remembered, she'd tell him the next day.

Operating on Hugh was causing a degree of disharmony in whatever world it was that Coinneach now lived. She had prayed again that night for Hugh to return to a healthy life, with few side effects from the hip injury.

19. Meredith's Departure

Dihaoine was spoken of, quite a lot after the incident at the graveside looking up Cinaed's kilt and inadvertently seeing his erection, just before her betrothed, Malcolm Og, was due to visit her again.

"Should we be worried Zahra about how advanced in maturity, Dihaoine seems, with her betrothed coming on the weekend?" Grigor asked.

The weekend also meant Meredith would depart when both twins did, which inevitably meant buckets of tears from poor sweet Dihaoine. Meredith would leave behind a most welcomed addition to Zahra's family's ability to manage their life over this difficult period, experienced by all, on different levels and in many ways.

"I hope we don't have to worry with Meredith leaving too. Life will be a bit more challenging," Zahra added feeling concerned.

"Has anyone checked Hugh's grave yet?" asked Peter. He had already eaten his breakfast and was due to return to Inverness soon, but he wasn't in any hurry to get back to his demanding and jealous lover.

"Nae, that's your job but I'll come with you, my friend," Zahra said as they both then hurried outside to move the tomb top from Hugh's grave. As they both moved it, they saw that Hugh was bleeding from the injury site.

"Oh my God, Zahra, his heart must be beating but he could become hypothermic. We must get him beside the fire now," Peter said urgently. Peter can't have even been expecting success, or he would have been better prepared.

Zahra rushed inside to call on both Grigor and Hector to help carry Hugh to be laid by the fireside.

"Mairi place a single bed with lots of blankets and furs by the fire," Zahra asked.

"Mr MacKenzie, stoke the fire and put a big log on to burn and bring in more wood please," she asked.

"Mairi boil water too please over the fire too," Zahra added.

Hamish was the only one who was thinking of who was going to be Zahra's husband if Hugh was truly returning miraculously back to life. Maybe Grigor didn't believe it possible, because they hadn't had that wedding with Zahra that he had spoken of, so often. As far as everyone knew, the two of them were still handfast, not married in a Kirk. By comparison, Hugh's wedding with Zahra was an unforgettable one, with blood stained and signed wedding documents, without a known death certificate, to Hamish's knowledge. Would she have to choose between Hugh and Grigor, or could they come to an amicable arrangement, in much the same way as Isobel had with her two previous husbands?

Zahra had always been a one-man woman. Grigor was aware then that they had a problem, as Hugh's lifeless body began to show signs of life. He was regaining his colour very slowly and there was joy at the man who was regaining life, however painful, it appeared to be. Hamish was even worried about the stability then of his job, if the Master of the mountain, was then in question.

Cinaed thoughtfully walked across to Peter, who was carefully monitoring Hugh's vital signs, as his heart picked up pace very slowly. Hamish saw Cinaed whisper quietly into Peter's ear, to which Peter agreed. Cinaed then compassionately took Peter's place on a stool beside Hugh, then appeared to just run his hand across his face and Hugh then opened his eyes. Cinaed then ran his hand gently down his arms reciting words in another language, and Hugh was then able to move his fingers and then his arms.

"Hugh, can you hear me?" Cinaed asked. Hugh closed his eyes

and opened them again as if to say he could hear him.

"I am Cinaed, Zahra's brother, can I touch your legs to assist you to move?" he asked. Hugh closed and opened his eyes again, so Cinaed ran his hands down each leg and both of his feet.

"Move your toes please Hugh," Cinaed asked.

Cinaed ran his hand in a sweeping motion across his chest and stomach and lower abdomen area, then stopped at one point near his right hip. He pressed into his hip with some pressure increasing it bit by bit. Then Hugh tried to speak.

"Hurts," Hugh tried to say in a raspy voice. Cinaed then went around to the back of where Peter had operated and the hole seemed to vanish completely, applying pressure there with a rounded fist.

"Is that better?" Cinaed asked. The look on Hugh's face showed a significant improvement in his pain level.

"Hugh, I am going to wrap my fingers around your throat, with Zahra's permission." Cinaed asked.

"Zahra may we both wrap our fingers around Hugh's throat together please to release Hugh's voice box? This is your first lesson. Just do as I say," Cinaed said.

Hugh closed his eyes and opened them again to indicate yes and looked happier in his eyes. Zahra came into his view and Cinaed held his hand over Zahra's hand linking her fingers with his and they gently touched Hugh's throat. Hugh's eyes were the voice of his soul upon seeing Zahra. He began to tear up which was a good thing, cleaning out his eyes of any foreign particles. Cinaed wiped his eyes so gently, then continued teaching Zahra as he went on telling her what to touch and what to visualise whilst holding his throat.

"Zahra," Hugh said. It was much clearer.

"Hugh, come back to me," Zahra said. "We have a wee bairn."

Mairi passed wee Hugh to Zahra, and she showed him wee Hugh.

"This is wee Hugh Gregor Chisholm MacGregor," Zahra said.

"Grigor and I are hand fast. He bought Peter here to bring you back to life. Are you happy to be back or not?" she asked. He lifted his right arm with difficulty reaching up to his bairn and Zahra's hand and she met him halfway. As they held one another's hands the two of them were both crying and with difficulty Hugh sat up to hold his wife, who was crying out his name repeatedly 'Hugh'. Zahra was all that Hugh could say, it seemed. The two of them embraced and the question then was on everyone's lips of who would Zahra's husband be now? Now that she was married to them both.

Zahra whispered something into Cinaed's ear and he in turn, then asked for everyone to turn around for Hugh's privacy. She and Cinaed were going to ensure that Hugh's male member was working too as they both held it to bring blood back into the area and within seconds it was erect. Zahra was so thrilled that Cinaed quickly took off his helpful hand, giving Zahra all the credit for that and Mairi asked for a screen for privacy and everyone, except Zahra remained with him as she sat on his erect penis. It was a lifegiving force like no other, but everyone felt for Grigor.

The bairns then started asking questions.

"Will we have two Da's now?" Causantin asked.

"That would be the best outcome," Hector replied. "A Master for the Farm and a Master for the Family, what do you think Mr MacKenzie?" Hector asked.

"What a bonny idea Master Hector, but it will the Mistress's decision to make and a hard one at that. She loves them both and couldn't part with either man nor could she part with wee Hugh. I pray to God that it can be a happy arrangement that both men can accept. The staff will respect whoever is chosen, as Master or master's both. Mairi and I will prepare quarters next to the reading room upstairs now, so the Mistress can be close to them both. There's no hurry, is there?

Master Grigor is doing a wonderful job on the farm and Master Hugh will have a hip issue that might slow him down. He may well be suited to dealing with the complicated problems with Alex having access visits to Zahra Og, as well as his daughter Isobel when she visits all three bairns. He will be an active Grandfather, then to all three of those bairns.

Keeping an eye on Dihaoine and her betrothed is a big job, and he does know Malcolm Og's father already, so that's helpful. You could help me Master Hector in arranging the suites for all the family on that floor. Would you like to assist Mairi and I, because we all want them all to be as happy and as comfortable as possible," Mr MacKenzie said.

"Aye of course Mr MacKenzie," Hector said.

Zahra's beautiful bedroom suite on the top floor had an outlook across the mountains, and the braes and the glens at the rear of the mansion and on the righthand side of it, if you were to be looking at the mansion from the front. This location not only captured the prettiest view from all angles of the mansion, but it was also the quietest and therefore, the most peaceful location. The room next to Zahra's was the family's reading room and nursery.

Formerly it had been a bedroom but now, with its lovely sunny side outlook, for reading as well as warmth, it was perfect for reading at night and day, with its fireplace hard up against the fireplace on the other side of it, being Zahra's bedroom. This made both rooms especially warm, which was necessary on such a cold mountain.

But where was the perfect spot on that same level for Hugh and should the husbands each have their own room and visit each other when it was their turn? Hector felt Zahra had so many belongings like her new clothes now, that she couldn't be moving around from room to room, whereas a man with just a few plaids or trous wasn't as important and Zahra wasn't giving up either man which she made clear to both men. It would require a lot of grown-up, adult behaviour from both men to share their wife now, because Grigor had forgotten the wedding, that he had promised Zahra.

It had now diminished his claim over her, of which he was made aware. He didn't want to fight it, else he lose not only her, but his bairns as well as the businesses that they had built up together. Just the same, he thought it wise to bring out Padruig's lawyer Grandson, Aonghus MacGregor. He knew it couldn't be argued in a Court, but at least they might get good advice. Grigor waited until Hugh's health had improved.

Zahra bathed Hugh daily and she'd oil his poor dry skin and massaged his aching muscles. She also needed Cinaed to limber him up, as he was too stiff to ride a horse. Cinaed simply ran his finger and thumb down each stiff muscle which appeared to make them well again. Each time he did this, Cinaed showed Zahra his healing methods and she learned from him as she went, learning chants or poems too that were to raise his ability to become stronger.

She was learning the secret arts of the Druids.

Sacrificial Pond

All the while, Mr MacKenzie and Hector worked on the ideal rooms for each adult. It was decided that Zahra would keep the room that she was in currently with no change, other than her man would change. The suite beside the reading room was a beautiful large room and it was given to Hugh with the bathing room next door to that, making it easier to bathe him while he was a little stiff.

The view from there enabled

him to see all the way to the very edge of the Misty Mountain Ranch property, where there was a native forest and an oak tree grove with a well and running water. It was an ancient place where Druids once met to be taught or to teach their auld ways. No building, no written word, just an oak grove with its sacrificial pond. A burn ran through the area giving it an air of simple and natural beauty. The rock faces beside the rock engraved stairs going to the burn, had many Celtic or Druidic symbols.

There was something beautiful and magical about that and Zahra thought that Hugh would admire that view.

The bathing room was large with Turkish tiles because of Zahra's renovations, with a copper that cooked up the hot water and an enormous porcelain bath. The room became very steamy, so opening it up in the daytime was essential, so that mould wouldn't start to grow. Then the last suite on that level was to be given to Grigor, but she feared he would need a reason to like it, apart from the view to the front, as well as the side view giving him a more complete overview of what or who was coming onto the property.

Zahra had always wanted a turret built in between the two halves of the mansion but had not decided where the internal staircase would lead and so it was never built. Now, however, it could be built leading into that room with Grigor having control over the turret and its weaponry. She thought with both men's approval, it could work and so did Hector and Mr MacKenzie. Before Aonghus MacGregor was due to arrive to talk serious business, she had that turret built by the Frasers and the MacKenzies, all giving their opinions where it should all face. Zahra was more concerned that the stone matched the rest of the mansion, and the stairs led to Grigor's room, without enabling water to enter the house during a storm, or a criminal on the roof top.

It had a pointy roof that must have a name, but she described it to the builders, and they knew what she had meant. It was therefore extremely well secured from both criminals and water from any storm event. On top of that, Grigor was given a beautiful suite with lovely fixtures and his own bathing room as well as an enormous bed which had a plush goose down mattress, doona and pillows.

Zahra was satisfied that Hugh was mentally agile enough by the time Aonghus MacGregor had arrived to discuss their relationships and arrangements between the three adults and their bairns and the grandchildren, as well as the businesses, currently owned by Zahra on Misty Mountain Ranch. Zahra's Will, as well as both men's Wills, were going to be updated, to be in line with all their decisions made on that day. Hugh had had many conversations with Grigor and Zahra, before Aonghus arrived.

His loving moments with Zahra were cherished as the two men shared her time and affection. Alternate nights with Hugh and Grigor. It was agonising for the men, and they didn't hide that fact and would have preferred a clean-cut decision, but until the meeting with Aonghus, that wouldn't happen, in the name of fairness.

It was the worse time for Meredith to have left, but she had to go home to her husband, as she had promised and to her employer, Malcolm MacNachten. She was glad to leave, although she had valued all the experiences she had had there.

She certainly had never seen someone come back to life after having died, twice and wasn't going to tell anyone in Glengarry what she had experienced there, except her husband Hugh Og.

Both Malcolm Og and Hamish Og had spent two days on Misty Mountain with their beautiful Clydesdale horses and were told of all the news with Hugh 'recovering' and were due to leave with Meredith, just as Aonghus arrived with his pony and cart. Mairi was back full time in the kitchen, but in the time that Meredith had been there, she had learned new recipes and methods of cooking, as well as how to use the new herbs that she had never used before. Her first meal cooking without Meredith was for Aonghus, the family, the staff and the two husbands, as well as Zahra, all eating lunch together.

Aonghus was invited to stay for as long as was needed, because it was late, and the weather was expected to be poor. He needed to be familiarised with everyone again anyway and was happy to occupy one of the many lovely guest rooms. Aonghus felt the weight heavily upon his shoulders and thought that perhaps his grandfather was using him to delay any possibility of being removed from Misty Mountain once Hugh took over once again as Zahra's husband. Aonghus knew this wasn't any ordinary situation, but he had become accustomed to his deceased relatives and being in communication with them.

Lunch was a success and even Cinaed liked it and he wasn't always easy to please. There was a low level of tension with Aonghus's presence and with the tradesman all having finally left, Hector's first honest question was, "Ma, why did you build that war like thing up on the roof?"

"It's called a turret, and I thought your father might like it, Hector. It has stairs that lead into your Da's newly re-furbished bedroom," Zahra said.

"I'll show you after lunch Grigor, now that the tradesmen have all left, if you'd like to see it. Would you like to see it?" Zahra asked, feeling a little unsure of herself.

"What's it for?" Grigor asked.

"It's for an invasion of some type, or an attack, or English trying to steal our land, something like that. There are a lot of weapons too," she added trying to add to its appeal somehow.

"Is this so that I'll be happy with losing you, while I entertain myself shooting at imaginary targets?" Grigor asked.

"I was thinking more of the responsibility of the Mansion. But you can keep it locked if you don't like it," Zahra said.

"I'd like to take a shot at any unwelcome person Da. Can I have the key to get up there?" Hector asked.

"Take a shot at Alex for all I care," said Domnhall.

"Aye. Shoot Alex." said Anndra.

"Nae, nae, it's not to shoot the family, lads. It was meant for an attacker, like kidnappers or the English. Aren't you calling your father, Da anymore?" Zahra asked.

"He left us. Why should we call him Da?" they both said.

"I'm sorry lads. Do you miss the Aird then?" Zahra asked.

"Aye we miss home, and we miss Ma. We love you Granma and none of this is your fault, but why should we have to live here all the time, when our home is in the Aird with Ma?" Anndra said.

"Ma is snippy we know that, but we still love her, and we want to go home. We understand why Zahra Og would stay with Uncle Cinaed and you, but we are not related to him like wee Zahra is. Ma must be lonely, and she needs us to look after her now," Domnhall said.

"Aye lads, you are right of course. If my husbands both agree, then you can go home to your Ma. I'll not stop you," Zahra said.

"Can we go home please, Grandda and Grandda?" both lads asked both men.

It was in action in front of everyone that the family had already accepted the two men as equal Grandda's. The lesser problem had become who Zahra was married to and of greater concern was Isobel's custody of her two sons, so that was dealt with, thanks to Aonghus being there. Both lads were old enough to know their own minds and Alex had fallen out of favour for having left their Mither. She had loved him, but he had lost his love for her. Wee Zahra Og also had papers drawn up between only two parties, Isobel Fraser and Cinaed MacAlpin, who were Zahra Og's only real family. Cinaed had custody and Isobel had visitation rights. It meant a visit to the Aird to sign off on it, but that part was dealt with.

Then the conversation, with Cinaed listening in, came back to Hugh and Grigor's rights.

"I am not happy with the current situation. She is my legal wife and as such, I demand rights over her all day long, every day and every night, all night and to sleep in the same bed, every night. I appreciate that I have a room of my own to take a nap in the day or to read or write a letter but when it comes to sleeping at night, my wife is my wife," Hugh said.

"I am also unhappy with being unable to make love to her whenever I choose to and being stuck in a room that's not even close to her," Grigor said.

"I am unhappy too my husbands, but my solution may not be appealing to you both and that is why I have given you your own spaces. I am sorry you don't like the front room Grigor, I really am. I feel foolish for building that turret. I didn't know what to give you. I love you both and I don't want either of you to leave me. I am shy to say it but what I wanted was all three of us to sleep together. It's so warm and cosy, but I thought you would disagree, so I didn't suggest it," Zahra said.

"What a great idea," said Cinaed. "I wish someone wanted me in their bed. My wife doesn't ever want me in the bed anymore, so even if I was sharing, I'd be happy," Cinaed added.

"It's so warm when there's two people in the bed with you.

Kenneth MacNachten slept with Coinneach and I and it was so nice. Nothing sexual occurred between us and Kenneth, but it was such a nice loving experience. It could be like that for you Grigor and Hugh either side of me. At least we would be warm and then whoever wanted to make love to me, could do that," Zahra said simply.

"I love your idea Zahra," Cinaed said. "What do you think Mr Lawyer?" he asked.

"That would be a personal decision they would make at the time spontaneously. I do agree about the rights of the husband, however. It can be achieved two ways. Zahra divorces one of you and the other has those rights. The other way is that this remains a private matter between three adults, and you choose to be together or not. You have the rooms to go to if you choose to be apart, but where sex comes in, either husband currently must have the right to make love to his wife, even if there is someone else in the bed. So, in agreement with Zahra actually, it would be better that you all sleep together for as long as you all wish to, making love and doing what wives and husbands do. If you are comfortable sleeping together, it would be the perfect solution," Aonghus said.

"Great Uncle, what are your thoughts?" Aonghus asked.

"It would be better than sleeping alone in the front room, while I still want that room, as my room as a private space and a place to keep my belongings," Grigor said.

"Uncle Hugh what are your thoughts?" Aonghus asked.

"If I can make love to Zahra, whenever I wish to, then I am happy. It won't matter if Grigor is in the bed, I grew up sleeping with all my brothers, in the same bed, so it wouldn't be much different to that," Hugh said.

"I suggest that you trial that idea and see how it works then, because there is too much to lose for all of the other options," he added. "I heard one of the staff suggest Master of the Farm and Master of the Family. Would that work?" he asked. "Great

Uncle Grigor as Master of the Farm and Uncle Hugh as Master of the Family?" he asked.

"I would like that," Zahra said. "I want to keep both of my husbands, keeping them both happy and ensuring the businesses still run well," she said. "I do have an opinion concerning Master of this and that, however. While it is best to have those titles for staff to show respect to both men, which they do need, but in practical application, the two husbands, and Hamish, the two farm managers and myself would need to meet once a week to discuss farm matters. It could be that Hugh wants to plant a crop, which we need, but he may want it in the wrong place because we might know the weather is better and the soil better than Hugh does at this stage. However, it doesn't exclude Hugh from growing crops, which he is good at," Zahra said.

"The crop that I need is a crop of hardwood trees for a sustainable supply of our own wood and I can show you where they are to be planted Hugh and I can help you plant the wee trees. The other matter that could come up is chopping down the oak grove for the oak. You can see it from your bedroom window. This can't happen. It's a religious site and can't be chopped down for the wood. If they fall in a storm, would be the only occasion where we could use that oak. Is that understood by everyone?" Zahra asked.

"Cinaed and I will be using the oak grove for my lessons, when the weather is fine," Zahra said.

"What lessons?" asked Hugh.

"I am learning about Druidism," Zahra said.

"I might have already broken one of your rules then Zahra. When the twins were here with the Team, I thought it was easier if they ploughed a section of land for cropping, up behind the stables where the manure pile was, so that was ploughed in as well. It's for corn, potatoes and kale. Hope you don't mind. It gets enough sun from what I could see, and the soil was pretty good. I'll keep adding manure to it," Hugh said.

"That's brilliant Hugh, I am happy with that. Are you Grigor?" she asked.

"So long as he looks after it and builds a storage bin for the potatoes," Grigor said.

"I've already started on that, and the corn can be stored under the house where the cattle feed is stored," Hugh said.

"I need to know something about your new wolf Zahra," asked Hugh.

"We both knew how Ulvy Stiorm was made, so how was this new one made?" Hugh asked.

"She doesn't have to tell you anything about Druidism, Hugh, it's a secret religion," Grigor interjected.

"Am I going to meet this new wolf then? Are we both safe from him?" Hugh asked.

"I would like you to meet him too. Can we meet him Cinaed?" Zahra asked.

"Aye, we can if the bairns are not going to enter the room. Just ask him to make himself known to you now Zahra," Cinaed said.

Everyone gasped, except Grigor who had seen him at the graveside, and he was aware of his size and his mean appearance. He stood beside Zahra looking at her and he smiled at her lovingly and she patted his head.

"Can you tell me your name?" Zahra asked him.

"I'm simply called the Winter Wolf," he conveyed.

"Are you able to protect me if am under attack?" Zahra asked.

"Aye, just as your last wolf did and died for you. I will fight to the death for you also. And I will not attack either husband, unless they are threatening to kill you," Winter Wolf conveyed.

"Do you know that both Hugh and Grigor are both my

husbands?" Zahra asked.

"I do," he conveyed, without judgement.

"Thankyou. Can I call you just Winter please and can you tell me if Lord Coinneach can return, or if he has already returned?" Zahra asked.

"Aye, you may call me Winter. That man to whom you refer, is out of his grave," he conveyed. "He has no wolf presently, unless your brother, Cinaed offers him one. Currently he is not dangerous, but you will need to talk to your brother, to ensure there can be no wolf from him," he conveyed.

Then Winter returned to the Invisible World.

"Cinaed, please can you assure us here that you won't give another wolf to your brother, now that he is out of his grave," Zahra asked.

"Nae Zahra, I can't do that. He is a Druid too. If my brother asks for my help, then I must give it," Cinaed replied.

"What options are there to change that?" Zahra asked.

"I can offer a compromise, but your husbands won't like it," Cinaed said.

"I'm listening," Grigor said.

"Regular lupine copulation with your wife's wolf," Cinaed asked.

Hugh punched him so hard that he fell to the floor and appeared to be dead for a while.

"Have you killed him?" Aonghus asked looking worried.

"He's already dead and no. Filthy foul-mouthed creepy rake. There I was thinking he was a good man, and he says a thing like that," Hugh exclaimed. Cinaed eventually got up off the floor and took himself to bed.

He had fallen foul of one of the Glenmoriston men, which wasn't a good idea.

Grigor was pleased to see Hugh respond in that way and so was Zahra. Only Aonghus was disturbed by the violence. Hugh had all the businesses explained to him and their Wills were updated, so that it all remained in the group of three. Grigor was happy too, realising then that he had help driving coos in a storm, to the protection under the house.

"One thing not to ignore Hugh. If Zahra says, 'Oh dear it looks a bit stormy, I wonder if the coos should be under the house', then move the bloody things with me as quickly as possible. She has a way of communicating that's easy to ignore, but if anyone knows the weather up here, it's Zahra. She and Hector have learned the mountain's own peculiar climate. It's unlike the Aird, Glenmoriston or Glengarry because it's up so high. You can wake up one morning in the middle of a cloud. It bothered me at first, but both Zahra and Hector looked as calm as anything, so now I just follow her as soon as she says it," Grigor said.

Hugh wasn't surprised about that because she had always been a bit of a weather beacon, just not snow aware. He looked a bit proud of his wife and he was gaining confidence from their discussion. He wasn't looking forward to returning the lads to Isobel and asking for her signature for the future of wee Zahra Og.

Domhnall and Anndra wanted to go home the next day, so that was his first job.

"I can come too Hugh. I'd like the ride, and I can give you one of my new horses," Zahra said. "The two lads will ride ponies because they left their horses at home in the Aird and I'll have to carry wee Hugh on my back, if you want me to come. Isobel would love to see you again," Zahra asked.

"That'll depend on the weather," said Grigor. "Be back before nightfall, if you both can. Do you need Hector, too?" Grigor asked.

"I think you'll need Hector sweetheart, so I'd prefer he was here to help you. Anything could happen, especially if Alex turns up. You'll need to keep him here," Zahra added. "I am only expecting one delivery of all of the uniforms, which are all paid for, except for the delivery man, so I'll leave you coin for him. We will endeavour to be back by nightfall, unless a storm brews and we have to stay there," Zahra said.

"I'd love you to come with me Zahra," Hugh said smiling.

The paperwork was completed, and it only then required Isobel's agreement to wee Zahra Og and the two men's comfort level with sleeping arrangements.

"By morning, if the sleeping arrangements have definitely changed, please tell me before I leave," Aonghus, their lawyer asked.

"I'll send you all your copies of the Wills," he said.

20. Bed With Grigor and Hugh

As all three adults entered Zahra's room, there was a degree of tension. Two very large men, both with their usual masculine needs and desires, complicated now with sharing one woman, between the two men or face losing everything and everyone.

Zahra was there waiting upon them with hopes that it could all work out. She undoubtedly loved both men, but she had chosen Hugh first when she first came to Scotland, so Grigor's fear was if he upset her, she would return to her first choice, despite how many bairns she had with him.

There had to be tension, even from Zahra herself.

As the two men made their entrances, Zahra was sitting on the blanket box beside the window, dressed casually with the room heated up already and the bed folded back in readiness.

"I hope you are both comfortable. Did you want to chat before we go to bed or not?" Zahra asked.

"Yes," Hugh said. "I told you not to marry again, but here we are, so now we have to decide who makes love to you first. It's unnatural for me," Hugh said.

"I'm sorry Hugh. Yes, you did and at first that was my plan, to never re-marry," Zahra said.

"It was a truly tragic time for her Hugh. It was my fault, and I felt that she needed me. That's why I imposed myself on her," Grigor said.

"I don't regret it Hugh, Grigor has been a wonderful husband to me, and I just hope that the three of us can work this out maturely. Can we all at least try?" Zahra asked.

Zahra climbed onto her comfortable huge, four poster bed peeling back her nightdress and waited then for her husbands to decide which side of the bed that they preferred. Hugh was decisive and climbed in and wrapped himself around his wife, with one leg over her possessively. Grigor was wondering if he could bear this for a moment, then gained his manhood back as Hugh had already begun to make love to Zahra. The sounds of the love making were maddening to him, as he lay beside her only occasionally being able to catch a whiff of her beautiful scent. He couldn't stand to watch the big lusty man, thrusting hard into his petite wife, after only being in the grave so recently. Why had he helped him come back to life? It was all his fault, so he couldn't complain really.

He heard his wife's familiar sounds of reaching orgasm and felt jealous of another man being able to give her that same joy, as he could. Before Hugh could start up again, Grigor rolled over to embrace his wife kissing her lovingly and she responded, as she would normally. It wasn't going to be as good, being the second man with Hugh's sperm inside Zahra already, but Grigor had his needs and was quick to make love, without any foreplay. He satisfied himself but there was little time to be as responsive as usual, although she enjoyed her love making with her sweet Grigor too.

During the night, she became tired and each time that she was about to sleep, one of the men wanted her attention. At one time when she had fallen asleep caressing Grigor from behind, Hugh wanted her to turn to him and caress him, which she did. It was a demanding night. No arguments, just exhaustive loving with either one, or the other. It was harder than she had expected, physically. She would need to take a sleep with wee Hugh during the day, but she had promised to go to the Aird with Hugh.

She prayed for forgiveness for having two husbands at the one time and finally got some sleep, but it was nice and warm, at least. By morning, Zahra was sound asleep and was awoken to more early morning love making but hadn't yet opened her eyes to even know which man it was. Luckily, she heard her needy bairn, wee Hugh, wanting to be fed and then changed. Naked, Zahra climbed out of the bed to change her wee bairn, when she was pleased of the assistance from Hugh who finished dressing him and stoked the fire while she fed him. She caressed Hugh's big and beautiful body from behind and thanked him, while wee Hugh fell back to sleep. He was a good wee bairn.

Hugh said he was going to go and get ready for the trip to the Aird, so he asked her to get ready too, soon. He kissed her lips and left the room. Grigor, however, was still needy and so they made love one more time and the affection was more meaningful, when they were finally alone.

"We can't talk when there's three of us. I can't tell you I love you," Grigor said.

"Please give us more time darling. I can't lose you again Grigor," Zahra said. "I have to get ready now to go, my darling," Zahra said and kissed him passionately. He knew that she loved him, and nothing had changed between them, and she knew also that she loved Hugh, as well as Grigor.

"The farm couldn't manage without you now Grigor. Please can we try again, or alternate nights if you must," Zahra said.

21. Isobel and Cinaed

Zahra bathed after such a busy night and then dressed in her warmest clothes. She even wore her long fur coat after she had fed wee Hugh again and strapped him securely to her back and was met with an impatient Hugh.

"Which horse is mine?" Hugh asked. They had to round up the horses and she indicated which one was his.

"I like him," Hugh said. The two lads were impatiently waiting and had already saddled up their ponies.

"Should we bring Zahra Og to visit Isobel?" Zahra asked.

"We are out of time now. Let's go." Hugh said.

It was a pleasant enough journey, although cold and frosty, but Zahra always enjoyed the trip between the mountains and could wave occasionally now to people whom she knew, which was heart-warming. She hadn't planned what to say to Isobel, because Isobel didn't know that they were coming. John Fraser may not be pleased to see them either.

They were on their way now, so there was no going back.

Isobel was standing on her veranda when they arrived in the Aird, seeing them coming and just meandered down slowly and looked unenthused, to open the gate. The only pleasant surprise was her father was alive, once again. But in true Isobel fashion, she wasn't even overjoyed to see him.

"Why are you here?" Isobel asked. The lads answered by saying that they were home and ran to their Mither. She hugged them both, which was a relief at least she still loved her lads.

"For good?" Isobel asked.

"Aye for good Ma, Grandma has the papers." Domnhall said.

"So where is my daughter then?" Isobel asked.

"Back on the mountain love. However, I do have an idea that

I would like to talk to you about darling, regarding wee Zahra Og," Zahra said.

"Can we go inside out of the cold please?" Zahra asked.

The horses were all led by Hugh and the two growing lads, to the stables, while Zahra and Isobel went inside with wee Hugh. Zahra was concerned that he would get too cold out there, in the Aird, being so small.

Zahra then began her explanation to Isobel and her plan, that she believed would work for them all.

"Cinaed currently has custody of your daughter, Zahra Og and you only have visitation rights, according to these papers. You do have full custody, however now of both of your sons, Anndra and Domnhall MacDonald Fraser. They have both asked to come home to you and wanted to kill their father, whom they now call Alex, did you know that?" Zahra asked.

"Aye, they hate him now for leaving us," Isobel said.

Hugh came inside as she said that.

"Where's the coffee love?" Hugh asked.

Isobel prepared them both coffees and then asked her Mither what her idea was.

Isobel was noticeably more co-operative, since her father gave her the strap and his presence was going to ensure that she behaved.

Cinead Og MacAlpin

"You were very attracted to the old Lord Cinaed when you went with him. Do you remember that?" Zahra asked.

"He was a rendy old beggar is all Ma, and I was lonely,"

Isobel admitted.

"There is another one of those rendy, but young and handsome beggars, who just happens to have custody of your daughter and whose wife hates him. He has a nice big home on lots of land on a nearby mountain to us. You could move in with him and marry him, for his money. He's not Catholic. I'd prefer it if he wasn't living at my house all the time now that he has upset your Da, then you could always see wee Zahra Og," she said.

"Do you want to make a play for him?" Zahra asked.

"Cinaed Og, do you mean? He's a bit dull, isn't he?" Isobel commented.

"Nae, not dull, just so long as he can still give me my lessons, then I would approve. Would you approve Hugh? He won't bother me for sex then," Zahra said.

"I approve," Hugh said. "How will you arrange it?" Hugh then asked.

"I think Isobel shouldn't sign these papers just for visitation rights only for Zahra Og, which gives the wee lass over to him completely and I will say to Cinaed that Isobel wants to see him in person, with the wee bairn, to talk it over here together, in the Aird. Cinaed comes here and we leave it all up to Isobel," Zahra said.

"Then, you will all live on his lovely property with him and his wife, which isn't far from us, and the lads can still go to the local school in Fraser Ville, God willing," Zahra said.

"Sounds good love. Now we had better go, the weather is changing," Hugh said feeling concerned.

"Sign these papers for your two lads and Alex can't worry you over them again," Zahra said, and they left once more, to trek back home, only now it was much windier, and Zahra had wee Hugh inside the front of her fur coat this time, protecting him from the wind, for rain was sure to come soon, and it did. Luckily, they weren't far from home, as the light was becoming dim, and the rain was in their eyes. Hugh was having more trouble going up the mountain than Zahra was, so he followed her, now that she knew it blind, as Coinneach once could.

Grigor was pacing up and down, impatiently waiting for them both to come home and had already secured all of the animals, as had Hector. The weather looked menacing on top of Misty Mountain. Both Hugh and Zahra trotted their horses up their road to the top, where they were met gratefully by the grooms and they hastily went inside, waited upon by both Mairi and an anxious Grigor.

"Zahra I was worried about you both," Grigor said, as he took wee Hugh from inside of her fur coat.

"The poor wee laddie," Grigor said. "Is he cold?" he asked as he took him beside the fire.

Hugh had a smile across his face, admiring that Grigor cared for his son so much. Mairi took a blanket and wrapped it around wee Hugh. Grigor sat by the fire rocking the wee bairn back and forth like an old grandfather would and he was the picture of domesticity.

"What took you so long?" Grigor asked. Zahra then explained her idea, ensuring first that Cinaed wasn't in the room.

"That's a good idea. I hope it works. Mairi's cooked us a nice stew and has made bread. Did you see Padruig?" Grigor asked.

"Nae. Did you Hugh?" Zahra replied.

"Aye outside, he was. Said he was thinking of leaving the Aird because Alex was no longer there. Can he move in here? I said I'd ask you both, or he'll go back to haunt that hotel of his," Hugh said. "If Isobel moves into Cinaed's place with him, then he could have Cinaed's room, couldn't he?" asked Hugh.

The last person on this earth, apart from Alex, would be Padruig that Zahra would want to move in with them. She would prefer all the MacAlpins resurrected than Padruig, not yet having forgiven him for imposing himself on her. Grigor saw the look on her face and knew that was a terrible idea.

"He is welcome to visit occasionally, of course as an old friend, but he cannot move in on a permanent basis. Why doesn't he find himself a woman?" Grigor asked.

"What about you Zahra?" Hugh asked. "Nae, he can't move in. As Grigor says he can visit on a short stay basis but not permanent. Never. I cannot trust Padruig, and he has never apologised for raping me and he would do it again. He is a rapist, can't you understand that, Hugh?" Zahra said.

Cinaed then came in with wee Zahra Og and Coinneach Og who had been playing together. "Welcome home you two. Am I interrupting anything?" Cinaed asked.

"Nae, I do have news though for you my brother Cinaed, which might please you. My pretty daughter Isobel, while not signing the custody papers, has said that she wishes to speak with you alone, personally, as she finds you very appealing," Zahra said, feigning a smile.

Hugh remembered the word 'dull' being mentioned but overlooked his wife's tactics.

"Are you at all interested in finding another woman Cinaed, who is pretty and blonde, like yourself and able to have bairns. Your father thought Isobel was a charmer?" Zahra said.

"You did say that your wife didn't want you in the marriage bed anymore. All three of us here, as Isobel's parents, would approve of a union between Isobel and yourself if her divorce comes through with John Fraser. Can you divorce your wife?" Zahra asked plainly.

"I don't mean kicking her out of her home at all. It would still mean your wife could live in her home, as well as the five of you," Zahra said.

"Five?" Cinaed asked.

"Aye, Isobel has three bairns, wee Zahra Og, Domnhall and Anndra," Zahra said.

"Are those the handsome lads who wanted to shoot their father, Alex the homosexual?" Cinaed asked.

"Aye, that's them," Zahra replied.

"I liked them. They're smart and handsome lads, for sure," Cinaed said. "I'd like to talk to the pretty Isobel and see how I feel about her. How does that sound?" Cinaed asked.

"Sounds reasonable Cinaed. Thank you for considering it," Zahra said.

"Can we eat now?" Grigor asked.

22. The Storm that Killed

The storm was a bad one and it worried Zahra, which was unusual. It wasn't usually this windy, this wild and wet. The noise that was made by the wind was something she had never experienced. There was a whining noise made by the wind, whistling around every corner of the big old mansion.

Zahra asked Hector if all the ponies were away safely. He'd had the foresight to put the last of the horses, including her horses into the big stables built for the Clydesdales, so that all of the horses were safe. They all hoped that the salmon farm would survive the night and thanked God for the protection of the lower level of the house for all the cattle. Grigor had even put away anything that could fly around in the strong wind.

In bed that night, all three of them, just lay there listening to the horrible sounds, unleashed onto the mountain. The bairns all climbed into bed with them, one by one, to be comforted, crying, or just needing re-assurance.

Coinneach Og clung to Grigor's neck and wouldn't let go of him. The wee lad kept saying "Da Da. Da Da" There hadn't been so much as a chicken left out in the wild weather, but it was a mess by morning and it was still raining.

It almost felt like they were all lucky to have survived the night.

"Grigor, I am worried about Hamish and Cora, as well as the salmon farm. I hadn't thought to tell them to come here in bad weather. Can Mr MacKenzie go with you to check on the salmon farm, as well as the two of them?" Zahra asked.

Hugh was aware that she hadn't asked him but offered to go too and the three of them all covered up after breakfast to find what they hoped wasn't a disaster.

Both Cora and Hamish had died during the night as their wee house had been obliterated, like a hurricane had targeted their home in the strong wind and their bodies were retrieved far from their home. It was a totally unexpected tragedy. Even the Caledonian stones that the home was solidly built from, were found far from where the home had once stood.

The salmon farm too was all broken apart, needing complete reconstruction, if at all.

Zahra's project had failed.

The volume of water that came down from that waterfall destroyed everything in its path. That was possibly why it had never been farmed before, she concluded. But how could she now tell Hamish's friends in Glenmoriston and Glengarry that Hamish had died, twisted around a tree in a frozen wet and wild night on Misty Mountain? Mr George Fraser had acted like the parent she didn't have, during this tragic time. He revealed to her he was also of the deceased ones, like she was, and for as long as he had lived near the mountain, there had never been a storm like that. Zahra had her tradesmen checking all the chimneys and the roofing slate, while Grigor and Hugh were dealing with the two bodies and the authorities, while also making two large coffins. They employed the MacKenzies to assist in the clean-up, while Hector attended to all of the livestock's needs, but didn't allow them yet to wander freely, until all of the debris was removed. A few rose bushes were lost and a few of Zahra's pot plants were smashed, but losses were minimal, except for the tragic death of Hamish and Cora, and Zahra's beloved salmon farm.

Grigor put his arm around Zahra at one stage saying, "I'm sorry about your farm love".

Not one of the oak trees had fallen in that wild wind.

They weren't prepared for the Constabulary visiting about three skeletons that were found on MacKenzie land in the path of their waterways, behind the Crofts, after the storm. Grigor was angered by their presence and stated it wasn't on their land, so it wasn't their problem who the skeletons belonged to.

They left accepting his explanation because after all, they were found on someone else's land, not Misty Mountain.

◇

Hamish and Cora Chisholm were buried in the dreaded cemetery on Craskie Farm, in Glenmoriston and the funeral was huge for a humble man from humble beginnings. Hamish had loyally worked there in Cannich for most of his life, until asked to work for Misty Mountain Ranch, where he and his wife both died in that freak storm. Although Zahra attended the funeral, along with the Unalive, as well as the living, she felt that it was her fault, no matter how many times Grigor insisted that it wasn't. Freak storms were the decision of the Almighty, was the Priest's opinion, not that they could have protected both Cora and Hamish, as well as the cattle and the horses.

Somehow Hamish had always seemed invincible. Their croft was supposed to have been strong enough, but not strong enough to sustain those winds. The story even made it into the newspapers. What surprised those of the Unalive attending the funeral, was the presence not only of Hugh Mohr Chisholm but both of his brothers, Alexander, and Donald, invisible to the public as they were, but back to cause havoc, no doubt.

Malcolm MacNachten, with his Grandson Padraig's help, was called upon once again, to make their tomb stones and head stones as well as to engrave their names inside the wee Chapel, built by Isobel Grant of Glenmoriston, paid for by Zahra MacGregor. Padraig MacKenzie would be taking the tombstone business over soon. No-one called Padruig Grant's former wife Isobel, Chisholm, anymore. She was either Isobel of Glenmoriston or Isobel Grant, so Padruig had achieved that much at least. He had also moved back into his hotel to haunt it for a while. Zahra was just pleased he wasn't moving in with them.

"Why was I named Isobel, Ma?" her daughter Isobel asked, on the day of Hamish's funeral.

"Your father was having an affair with Padruig's wife, whose name was Isobel, and he named you after her but it was after your birth so I didn't know anything about that affair, until much later," Zahra said.

"He must have loved her then?" Isobel asked.

"Aye, your father is a loving man," Zahra said.

Cinaed had accompanied Isobel and the family in the carriage to the massive funeral and he overheard that she had been named after Hugh's Mistress, whom he did later marry, if only briefly, until she died. He felt sorry for the beautiful young woman who had been named after someone who wasn't even a member of her family. Even worse was learning that she had another half-sister who had died too, whose name was Fleur.

"You have a lovely name Isobel, no matter where it came from. I like it," Cinaed said. "If you marry me, I wish to name you Christaline Zahra Chisholm MacAlpin," Cinaed announced.

Isobel just rolled her eyes.

"Och, Ma, how have you put up with all of these men and their ways?" Isobel asked.

"I have loved them darling. That is all. Now, let's go home," Zahra said, after putting a rose on Ulvy Stiorm's grave.

There was no indication that Isobel had accepted that name, but Cinaed was certainly interested in Isobel now. Cinaed loved wee Zahra Og, his half-sister, and the idea of a bairn of his own was appealing too. He had spoken to his wife about having a woman move in with them both and the only provision she gave was that he had to provide a cook who could do that work and not her, as well as a paid laundress for all their laundry and a cleaner.

He was surprised at his wife's immediate agreement to him sharing his bed with another woman. There was a sadness to it, as he thought of the many lost years of happiness that he could have had. His father had chosen his wife for him, and he'd had no say in that marriage, when he was a young man. Now his father was gone, and her family were no longer even living in Scotland. Cinaed wanted Isobel.

He wasn't concerned about those skeletons that were found after the storm, even though he too had been informed by the Constabulary and he asked them not to bother Zahra's family, who were already upset by the tragic loss of both Hamish and Cora and the destruction of their salmon farm.

Cinaed was beginning to enjoy the freedom from his MacAlpin family and the prospect of a new wife, the pretty blonde, Isobel.

23. Mr Fraser of the Trout

When Zahra and the family arrived back home after the exhausting funeral, she passed wee Hugh to Grigor, after the bairn had been fed, and told him she was going for a walk by herself, beside the waterfall just to clear her head. She sat there and cried at the loss of such a good friend as Hamish and all the work and all of those poor fish. However, as she sat there, a shadow fell across her and it was the familial, Mr George Fraser.

"May I sit beside you Mistress?" he asked.

"Of course, Mr Fraser," she said.

"Let's breed fish in the wee loch, instead of beneath the waterfall?" he said out of the blue. "Trout maybe?" She smiled for the first time in days, and she wiped away her tears. "I can do it for you with my friend Mr Fraser. It won't be huge, but a farm just the same," he said "And you never know with salmon. The ones who were born here will come back one day maybe, as they do, so keep an eye out for the ones whose tails we clipped," he said.

"Mr Fraser. Where is your wife?" Zahra asked.

"She passed during childbirth, as many women did in my day, but I haven't seen her in this life, so she can't have chosen to be with me," he said. "We men were all expected to punish our wives if they did wrong and it wasn't easy, but our wives were all young and needed to be taught life's lessons," Mr Fraser said. "I know what you have experienced, so it can't be nice to hear that I have punished my deceased wife, and you come from a different cultural understanding, but here, the men are in charge and must be obeyed, as you may have learned by now," Mr Fraser said.

"I learned that, very early on and I have complied," Zahra said.

"I want to draw you up the plans for the new fish farm. Can you come down to my house now and I can show you," George

Fraser asked.

Not having told either husband, Zahra hesitated but he assured her that it wouldn't take long.

"Alright, if it doesn't take long, or my husbands will worry where I am," Zahra said.

He took her hand and gently assisted her to stand, then offered his arm for the trip down the hill to his croft on the outskirts of Fraser Ville. His shared croft was isolated from any neighbours and was very quiet, surrounded by big, tall trees that were all unaffected by the storm.

"Tea or coffee," he said smiling. They drank their tea, and she awaited the plan to come to fruition, when he stood up suddenly and expected her to show an interest in more than a trout farm. He expected a sexual liaison and took her hand and forcibly placed it on himself saying he wouldn't tell her husbands, if she did what she was asked of her.

Zahra was so shocked and was in disbelief and then realised that the door behind her was locked. She was trapped and she had walked right into the trap.

"Mr Fraser, I want to leave now and don't touch me?" Zahra insisted. Mr Fraser stood close to her while she pulled away as he grabbed her by the arm.

"Nae, nae let me go," Zahra yelled.

"Not until you give me what I want," George Fraser demanded. He pushed her hard up against the wall, "Open your legs or I will do you harm," the cunning old man said as he removed his leather belt and threatened her with it.

"Grigor, help me," Zahra screamed.

"Hugh, help me," she yelled as she dodged the creepy man around the room and tried to open his door. "Grigor, Hector, Hugh please help me," she screamed as loud as she could.

Lucky for Zahra, Hector had gone looking for his Mither and

thought that he heard her screaming and ran like the wind, in the direction of her screaming.

"Hector, Hector, Grigor," she kept screaming while kicking and punching at Mr Fraser, when he tried to grab her again.

Grigor was alerted to his son, running in the direction of Fraserville, unnaturally fast and that was sufficiently unnerving, so he followed him son, hastily. As Hector came to Mr Fraser's door, Hector kicked down the door and found his terrified Mither, trying to escape the assaults of Mr Fraser.

"Hector, help me please," she yelled. Hector thumped Mr Fraser so hard that he hit the floor unconscious. Hector then swept up his precious Mither and they both went to escape, as his father, Grigor appeared at the door.

"What happened here?" Grigor demanded to know.

"That man was attacking Ma, so I hit him Da," Hector said.

Grigor went berserk and then began beating up the man.

"That'll do Da. Let's go and report him to the police," Hector said.

Grigor couldn't stop himself until that man was mutilated.

"Where's Hugh when you bloody well need him?" Grigor said out loud.

"I'm here," Hugh said. "Leave it to me and get our wife back home. Waterfall in bits?" he confirmed.

"Aye," Grigor said, and they took a very shaken Zahra back home.

Home was another story. Zahra then had to explain herself and how she came to be in that man's house to begin with and why, when she hadn't told any of them where she was going, other than to the waterfall. It was one of those events that had previously led to a strapping, so she calmly handed him her own leather belt with tears in her eyes, asking forgiveness for making a mistake like that. She had believed Mr Fraser's story of another fish farm and so, she awaited the strapping, as Grigor stood there feeling helpless, holding the belt in his hand but, unable to do it anymore.

"I can't do this anymore Zahra. You must comply with our agreements, or it just won't work. I'm not going to hit you anymore, you know that. Promise me to obey or we quit this marriage now," Grigor said. Hugh walked in at that very moment, having disposed of Mr Fraser, and took in the sight and heard what Grigor had said.

"It wasn't her fault Grigor, she was conned, and she wasn't in her right mind, following the funeral," Hugh said. "People make mistakes. Some more than others, admittedly but she loves you and both of us need you for this all to work," Hugh said. "I'll move to the other room if it helps, but emotions are running high right now. Give her a chance mate. She can't always get it right," Hugh said.

"Do you want to leave me, Grigor?" Zahra asked sobbing.

"Nae, I don't. I want you to comply is all I want," Grigor said. "If you decide to go to Fraser Ville, then tell one of us, or take us with you. You can't trust those people and people are often taken advantage of, after funerals," Grigor said.

She then ran to her husband and hugged him in both relief and love.

"Grigor don't leave me please," Zahra begged. "I promise that I won't do that again. I don't know why I trusted him, but I really did. I don't know who I can trust."

"Us three, is all who you can trust. Hugh, me, and Hector, no-one else," Grigor stated.

"What about Mairi and Mr MacKenzie?" Zahra asked.

"They are like secondary trustees," Grigor added.

"Cinaed?" she asked.

"Only for lessons, unless Isobel marries him," Grigor

stipulated.

Isobel had been there with them all after the funeral with her two handsome lads, back on Misty Mountain, once more and she pitied her Mither, whom she knew adored both men and if anyone understood that predicament, it was Isobel.

Isobel's divorce had come through and she hadn't yet told Cinaed, else the pressure would begin, but she had intended discussing it over dinner. Although now, she was wondering if the time was right.

"Hugh, Grigor, and Hector, I have something for you all, that I forgot to give you from my father's house that day Zahra and I were there sorting it all out," Cinaed said.

He then went to a large port, that he had left behind from the funeral. Inside it were two dark brown, bear skin coats, complete with their heads, still attached and one complete coat of wolf furs, all stitched together, large enough to be full length. "My father hunted and shot all of them and was very proud of his kills which made me sick as a wee bairn, but I have seen how warm Zahra's coat keeps her and after that shocking storm, I wanted to give them to you all. One bear skin fur for each of Zahra's husbands and the wolf skin coat to our new hero once again, young Hector if you like them," Cinaed said.

"I hope to marry the lovely Isobel, one day, if she will have me, then you might trust me too," Cinaed said.

"Are you even divorced yet, Cinaed?" Hugh asked.

"It's before the Courts currently and I think it will go through. We are not Catholic and my nearly ex-wife has agreed to another woman living in my house with me, so long as I pay for a cook, a cleaning lady and a laundry lady for all of us, so it's all good I think," Cinaed replied.

The bearskin coats did take Grigor's mind off their issues, as he admired the bear skin, not having ever seen a real one, up close before, since bears had all been eradicated from Scotland.

"Thank you for the coats, they're bonny. I admit to never having been up close to a bear, before they were all gone. This might need airing," Grigor said, smelling the musty smell.

"Aye, mine is a lot of wolves, Ma. Why didn't your wolf help you today?" Hector asked thoughtfully.

"I'll have to ask him about that coat in case they are relatives of his before you use it, and I will ask him that question. I think I was supposed to call on him," Zahra said.

She called on 'Winter Wolf' to sniff the new coat given to her son, which he did with sadness as he made a sorrowful sound and lay upon it, as if he was in mourning.

"Oh Ma, they must be his family. How sad is that?" Hector said.

Winter Wolf conveyed that they were all his pack and of him when he was the Alpha male, at that time. Hector offered the skins back to him, but Hector was given permission to use it, so long as it was never sold and kept only in his family. Concerning Mr Fraser's advances, he answered that his role wasn't to stop sexual activity, which was intended to be, unless he was asked to, because that would put her husbands at risk, so it was left as it was, unless she called on him.

Isobel spent that night with Cinaed to decide once and for all, if she thought he was dull, or sexy enough for her. The morning saw smiling faces on them both, so it was presumed that he was sexy enough, like his father had been and he had a big cock too, she told her Ma. But her Ma knew that already.

"Did you like him then darling?" Zahra asked.

"Oh aye, I do. He just looks dull, but he knows how to make a woman really enjoy sex," Isobel commented.

"Let me know what your plans are then," Zahra said.

Zahra was reflecting on her own night of loving both of her men, one after the other and it was becoming more manageable, and the men were more comfortable being in the same bed as one another and being heard, making the sounds we all make when making love, that we would prefer no-one else heard. It was an intimate sharing for the three of them, to eventually accept those sounds and even the occasional smells that one lets off during the night, inadvertently.

The closeness that Zahra saw grow between the two men, was something she thought she would never see, being men of such different characters and especially with Grigor's belief in his rights over everyone, as well as his royalty. Zahra had reminded him who the royalty really was, and the Glenmoriston men had thought so little of them, that they had disposed of them all, except Cinaed.

Cinaed was lucky to have survived and now with Isobel liking him, it further protected him from another 'waterfall incident'.

During the night, Hugh had sweetly fondled Zahra's face and kissed her lips gently and asked her how she was, after what had happened to her. She ran her fingers through those lovely chest hairs of his and told him out loud that she loved him, so it was becoming easier to express themselves when in the one bed together, as the nights went on and there wasn't jealousy at all and if anything, there was just deep concern for each other and all the bairns that they shared.

The bairns loved the new arrangements with both men in the bed with Zahra and climbed all over both fathers, while she breastfed wee Hugh. Causantin wanted attention from Hugh because he had missed him so much when he was in the grave and sometimes, he found it hard to believe that Hugh was back permanently. He frequently asked Hugh if he was really staying alive or going back into his grave.

24. Maybe a Trout Farm?

A knock on the big door one morning was Mr Fraser's friend, another Mr Fraser holding a large paper with drawings on it. He apologised for interrupting anything, but he couldn't find his friend or else they would be together to explain a plan that he had had. His idea had been that instead of salmon fishing at the bottom end, beyond the waterfall where heavy water could once again destroy the farm, a better idea might be a smaller farm of trout fish instead, in the wee loch up the top. He was sorry he couldn't find his friend, but he was certain he and his nephews could build it, if the family were still interested. The family was interested but it was too soon after the deaths of their two friends and it felt disrespectful, until more time had passed.

Hugh's patch for crops that he had the twins plough, had also been turned to a slushy, muddy, mess after that stormy night, so he had to re-evaluate if that was indeed the right place after all. Zahra thought that storms like that didn't occur frequently, and corn, potatoes and kale were all needed desperately, so once the soil settled, he became busy planting the seeds with Zahra's insistence and Hugh put palings all around the crops too, to keep out other interested creatures like the curious deer, when they came to forage.

The uniforms had all arrived-on time, which included Hamish's new uniform, so Hugh said he could wear most of it. The sign beside the gate at the front of the property was altered once again and 'Salmon Farm' was removed until the family decided what to do. It was hard to imagine 'Trout Farm' but Zahra thought that eventually, she may do that, if Grigor and Hugh both agreed. Everyone else looked smart in their uniforms like the cleaners, the laundry ladies, the chimney sweep and the grooms, Hector and Flidas with his business name, Grigor with his cattle which left her with the dilemma of what to have on Hugh's shirt. For now, he wore Hamish's uniform, until she had a suitable one made for him.

She decided that Master for both Hugh and Grigor would be acceptable, and they liked that.

Zahra had ordered all those small trees that she had wanted planted for a small sustainable forest and they arrived eventually. There was around one hundred small trees which didn't look much when small, but when large they would, so she was pleased about that. It meant that Hugh would have to build a nice fence with railings, so they wouldn't be easily stolen. It ran from the iron front gate to where the trees ended. Grigor was surprisingly impressed at the look of it, as well as the concept finally, as he then understood that they were providing their own wood for the future. He loved that Zahra had disallowed the oak trees to be cut down, so out of curiosity, he went down there himself to see if there was anything special about that outdoor space, where his wife and Cinaed held their lessons.

It was a special place, and the old growth trees did give off an energy, unlike other trees with the sounds of wind rustling through the leaves in a musical way. Some of the older trees were over five hundred years old. The water pond there was interesting but needing to be cleaned and there was a small-ish stone circle there too, that looked Pictish to him, being familiar with that stone and its many carvings. Carved deep in the ancient stones, there was the Pictish beast, the spirals, the wolf, an unknown King and Queen seated upon thrones, many ponies with men riding upon them, salmon, snake and others that he had seen before, none of which had the Christian cross, so they were all of the pre-Christian era. It was an ancient meeting place, there was no doubt which he felt stirred by, so he acceded then to whatever it was about the oak grove, he wasn't going to cut down these trees. They made his wife happy.

On one of those days taking her lessons from Cinaed, he just wanted to gossip about Isobel which wasted some of her time because her questions on that day concerned her Winter

Wolf, who was a protector for her only. She had known that her former husband, Coinneach and obviously Cinaed, could also shape shift into the wolf form itself and this was what she also wanted, so she could do all of the things that a wolf could do. She also wanted to know, when in that form, if the shape shifting wolf, could procreate and have puppies of their own, if a male and female shape shifter were involved. He was surprised at the level of interest that Zahra had on this topic, and while he did have the answers at first, Cinaed seemed reluctant to answer.

"Aye, currently you have a lower level of wolf, if you like, who is only there to protect you and not for you to become one, which is a much higher level. Did Coinneach not explain this to you?" Cinaed asked.

"Nae, he explained nothing to me, in fact he never told me that in having had sex with him, as the wolf would result in my having a spirit wolf at all," Zahra answered.

"He wasn't supposed to do that, without your consent, but moving on, you have reached the stage where your inner voice has told you that you want it and that's a good thing, if it's not from another source, not even from a book," Cinaed replied. "Are you sure that you want to be able to become a wolf? You will be able to run as fast as a wolf, you will have the strength of a wolf, the needs of a wolf, in terms of food and procreation. Basically, if you stay in that body for too long, you will think like a wolf, even when you return to your human form. Currently, you have an Alpha male wolf protecting you, so it is possible to procreate with either him or me if you are the Alpha female. It's not sexual, as you now understand between you and, I but if your husbands knew, would they understand if it was me? Either way, you as a shape shifting female wolf could procreate with Winter Wolf during the mating seasons, of which there are four in one year, if my memory serves me correctly. I have never mated with a wolf to procreate, so it would be an experiment," Cinaed said.

"Are you also able to disappear?" he asked.

"Aye, very well," Zahra answered.

"What I suggest then is this. We copulate as we did before, to upgrade your status to a 'shape shifter', which means two wolves will be with you, once that's completed. You may feel a bit different afterwards. It's important not to allow the wolves to overtake your personality. When I can see that you do have her, then we can copulate again, in the right season, once again which is now anyhow, but still invisible for the sake of safety from your husbands and Isobel too, who must not know. In the old days, the Celtic Druids made love to their Mithers, but not now, and there aren't many of us anymore. How does all that sound? Is that still something you want?" Cinaed asked.

"I do want it badly but how do I feed the pups?" Zahra asked.

"Your own milk. You don't have to shape shift into the wolf to feed them always, but you can if you want to, however it might not be possible with the family around," Cinaed said.

"My husbands might understand if I have to feed them at night with the door closed. I am sure Hugh would at least," she said.

"Wolf litters could be up to six pups. Can you feed that many?" Cinaed asked.

"So long as wee Hugh has been fed and there's enough milk for them all. What do you think?" she asked.

"I think I should get Isobel with child, so there's additional milk to feed the pups, if you run short," Cinaed said. "Then what do you plan to do with the pups?" Cinaed asked.

"I want to breed them and have them live with us all on our mountain, like dogs can," Zahra said. "I can shape shift, if they misbehave, can't I?" Zahra asked.

"Aye we both could tell them off, when they're naughty," he said smiling, starting to like the idea.

"I have another question too. How do you turn a man, like Hugh into a shape shifter wolf?" she asked.

"Once you become one, you can do it and I will explain to you the actions and words to say to bring it about, but he also must want it. You can't just make him one, without his knowledge. That is against our practices, despite what Coinneach did to you. A moral code if you like. I have never indulged in going against the rules," Cinaed said.

He wrote it all down for her and she put it away in her apron and looked at his fob watch and the sky to see how much time they had left whether they could achieve both today or just one.

"I think we can achieve only one today, Ma, then you can get accustomed to him being a part of you and not make mistakes, like accidentally becoming that wolf and scaring the staff. I did that when I was just starting out and the maid ran away and never came back. I had big sharp teeth, and she thought I was going to attack her, poor thing. I still feel guilty about scaring her," Cinaed said.

"How do I shape shift. Do I just think it in my head like, now I'm the wolf?" Zahra asked.

"Aye nearly. It's all in your mind. A request, but you can be partial too like just the teeth to scare someone, or your entire body. So, you need to make it clear when you request it," Cinaed said.

"We have time now if you like, but invisible, in case someone comes, or someone is spying on us." Cinaed said. "We will need to make the puppies another day, then I can get Isobel with child, so that would be better. My divorce came through, so I wanted to ask permission to marry her. Can I please do that?" Cinaed asked.

"Aye, you can of course, then later we can ask both husbands," Zahra said.

The two of them were happily copulating in the oak grove, to ensure that she had the ability to shape shift into a wolf and it was that lucky that no-one could see them, because Causantin came looking for Granma, then left again.

"Thankyou Cinaed, it becomes more enjoyable each time. The first time with Coinneach was overwhelming, like my head was going to explode," Zahra said.

"I enjoy it naturally as a wolf, but I don't want Isobel to be a wolf, so it will only be with you if we have a need. The wolves' needs are too intense. I'm glad that I am human, but occasionally the wolf takes over. Can we help each other out on those occasions? I don't want to get hit by Hugh again, so it would have to be kept secret," Cinaed asked.

"Aye, but one day, they will understand because Grigor can see both of our wolves. Yours and mine. He will see that I have two, as soon as we get back," Zahra said.

Domnal and Anndra MacDonald

"Can he really? Is he a Druid?" Cinaed asked.

"Nae, but his family of auld were Pictish," Zahra said.

"You probably should know more about this mountain too, in that case in our next lesson," Cinaed added.

Zahra took Cinaed purposefully to Isobel's other two parents, Hugh and Grigor, where they were both working at the time, to ask them if Cinaed had their permission to marry Isobel. Isobel was standing on the front porch watching over all four adults and anxiously, awaiting the reply from them all. Grigor asked him where they would all live and with whom else. He was told about Cinaed's former wife and was shown the divorce papers, as was Hugh, all with serious demeanours.

Cinaed told both of her fathers that Isobel would have a cook in his lovely mansion, a laundress and a cleaner and she wouldn't have to pay for anything, nor would her bairns, whom he would take full responsibility for. He was going to pay the university costs for both Domhnall and Anndra, as well as for Zahra Og, if she wished it. Isobel had requested for the wedding to be held on Misty Mountain Ranch.

Cinaed stood there waiting for a while, looking nervous, while the two men asked him to wait while the two of them spoke. Isobel wandered down and held her Mither's hand watching the two men quietly speaking in Erse to one another, having a secret discussion, just to make Cinaed feel nervous. Cinaed then turned to Zahra.

"Ma is there anything else I could offer just so that I can secure Isobel's hand. I'd do anything for her?" Cinaed asked.

"Aye, there is one thing Cinaed. You could offer to pay a dowery, even though you are not required to, but given that she has your father's wee bairn, it might help if you offer at least twenty thousand pounds for her and her family, if you can afford that," Zahra answered.

Cinaed was thrilled to make that offer and immediately went back to the intimidating pair of men.

"Excuse me fathers, I forgot to mention that I'd like to offer a dowery for your beautiful daughter and grandchildren and because Isobel is the Mither of my father's bairn. Would it be acceptable to offer twenty thousand pounds?" Cinaed enquired.

Grigor knew the man had more money than that, so he made an ummm sound and so did Hugh and looked like he was going to walk away from the discussion with Cinaed, but they liked the clever idea of getting dowery once again, for Isobel.

"Twenty-five thousand pounds is a much better price. Would that be sufficient fathers?" Cinaed asked once more.

"Hmm" said Hugh this time. "Maybe and you'll pay for her wedding gown of her choice and you'll buy her a nice wedding ring?" Hugh asked.

"Aye of course, I'll take her shopping to the best bridal shop and the best jeweller in Inverness tomorrow, if she accepts," he added.

"There's one more thing. You'll never strike her," Hugh said dead seriously.

"Nae father, I'll not ever hit a woman, not ever, least of all, the beautiful, Isobel," Cinaed said with love in his puppy dog eyes. Grigor thought that he didn't know Isobel very well yet and he'd feel like hitting her in the first week of their marriage, if not before, so it was a good clause to have added for how snippy Isobel could get. Hugh and Grigor both settled on twenty-five thousand pounds. Twenty thousand of which would go into Isobel's own bank account and five thousand to be shared between the two fathers.

Cinead Mac Alpin

Isobel Mac Alpin

25. The Wedding Plan

A MacAlpin wedding was to be planned on Misty Mountain, with everyone invited, including Ali and April, Kenneth and Ivy, Grigor Og MacGregor and Carmel, Bruce MacDonald and Marion and Hugh Og Chisholm and Meredith. The twins were coming too of course with Islay and Angus MacKenzie but Iain was left at home in Glengarry with the security guard. It was sad that Hamish hadn't made it to the wedding and his loss was going to be felt. Padruig, Alex and Peter were included. Zahra thought James and Susan would be nice and then everyone could stay over in their home on the mountain as well as, Dr Alex MacNachten and his wife, Mairi.

Hugh and Grigor wanted to build an internal balcony, overlooking the large sitting rooms and dining room below, because Cinaed did lose many of his big oak trees in the big storm and offered the wood to both men for that purpose, especially Grigor. The balcony would give a complete view of who or what was happening on the lower levels, accessible from each level's staircases. It was high enough so that none of the bairns could climb over it and the wooden railings were built close enough together so that their wee necks couldn't get caught between each railing. It really was a Celtic masterpiece once it was polished up with inlaid carvings of Highland life and animals and people.

Their wedding was catered for by local MacKenzie and Fraser people and waited on also by local people. It was a lovely wedding, and they were married by a Catholic Priest again which Zahra thought unwise, but they went ahead anyway. Isobel and her sons had been living at Cinaed's home for some time, before they married, and he offered to send them to university, because they had completed their high school certificate ahead of time. They were both very smart lads and Alex now rarely saw them, after they had moved to Cinaed's house. He and Peter had settled down to life in Inverness and slowly, the family saw less and less of them both, unless there was a medical reason to see Peter who had grown accustomed to Alex's overbearing ways.

Padruig came over occasionally to see everyone, mostly when he was lonely, but he never overstayed his welcome anymore and went back to his hotel where James wanted him to be. Both James Grant and Padruig stayed over on the mountain, after the wedding and had grown close to one another, as the years had passed by. Bruce MacDonald had passed away in his sleep before Isobel's wedding, leaving Marion a grieving widow in Loch Garry, but she had enjoyed her life with him and then was able to see more of the grandchildren and her sons Malcolm and Kenneth. Kenneth wasn't well, on and off, on occasion and went fishing less and less. Marion, Malcolm, Ailsa, Kenneth, Ivy, Hugh, Meredith, Islay, Angus, Alex MacNachten and his wife Mairi, with their two sons, Malcolm Og and Hamish Og, all came to Isobel and Cinaed MacAlpin's wedding.

The mansion was once again filled with old friends, as well

as new ones, wedding gifts and all the wee bairns, wee Hugh, Zahra Og, Coinneach Og, Causantin Dihaoine and Fatma, without Simon this year, because they didn't re-new their hand fasting, and they had never formerly married and decided not to again. It also didn't help those relations on Wolf Ranch that never quite recovered after Isobel had left John, divorcing him, then moving in with Cinaed with John's bairns.

The sounds of the bagpipes were heard on the day of the wedding, as well, as Padruig played the uillean pipes beautifully. Malcolm Og and Hamish Og sang songs, so beautifully, it was enchanting. The fiddle and the flute were played, and Meredith played her harp too with her wee daughter, Ferne.

Alex played the bodhran and he even seemed a little sad at losing, Isobel, his former wife of many years and his two sons, to a nice and wealthy man named, Cinaed MacAlpin. That odd man who walked around naked most of the time, even on a cold day, was gone from their lives, but never quite forgotten.

Sleep came easily as an exhausted family finally fell silent, until there was an echo of a different kind, heard early in the morning. Fatma came quietly into her Mither's room to awaken her.

"Ma, Ali's calling the prayers," Fatma whispered.

Zahra kissed both of her husbands, who were reluctant to let her leave, but she said she'd be back soon and kissed them again. Zahra attended to her ablutions and put on a prayer robe over her warm underclothes, stoked the fire and put on a log, then left her tired husbands, confused to what that echo was. As she walked down the stairs, Zahra saw that she was the last one of the ladies of the family to join in and Ali had finished calling the prayer. It was Hector now who was leading the prayer. She had never seen Hector lead prayer before, so she just stood in line with her daughters Fatma, Isobel and Dihaoine and her daughters in law, Flidas and April. In front of her were the younger lads, Coinneach and Causantin, joined by Ali.

In front of the family group was Hector, leading prayer for the first time. His voice was now deep and loud and resonated throughout the whole mansion, as had Ali's during the call for the prayer.

Both Malcolm Og and Hamish Og came onto their balcony with their Grandmother Marion, to watch the family do whatever that was, out of curiosity. Opposite them on the opposite balcony were two tired looking fathers, both needing to know what was going on. Mairi scurried quietly into the kitchen and Mr MacKenzie was stoking the lounge fire and adding another log to warm up the mansion, as was his morning task. The prayers were a curiosity, for most of the onlookers as, one by one, people came out to watch and listen to whatever language that was, including Padruig, James, then Peter and Alex who were caressing one another. Cinaed stood stunned that his new wife was one of those in a line, with the other women praying and following Hector in a language that he recognised, as Arabic.

Domnhall and Anndra arrived a bit late, but quickly stood in front of the ladies with the lads, their hair all messed up from sleep. They all seemed to know what to do, which made Hugh feel oddly proud, but he didn't know why that was. He nudged Grigor in the side.

"Wonderful isn't it. They're all our bairns?" Hugh said.

Grigor was still confused how watching Zahra in the Aird get out of bed to pray, all those years ago, had led to this and now they were all doing it and she wasn't even leading them. They were leading her. And he still could not understand a word of it. But he conceded that it sounded nice. Then at the end, it seemed like it went back to Ali, who did another prayer on beads which they all suddenly produced and followed along. Cinaed walked down the stairs, rather than just stare at them all and when he waited for the end of the prayer, they all either kissed each other or shook each other's hands, then Cinaed wrapped himself around his new wife, of one night and told her how much he loved her. It was a wonderful sight and then Mairi offered coffee or tea if anyone wished it, and many did, and some went back to bed.

Grigor was happy that Zahra kept her word and went back to her husbands, and they snuggled back to sleep a while longer before their busy day started again.

"Did you know that Hector and Flidas were already following your religion?" Grigor asked. "Nae, I don't pry. Religion is up to the individual and you can't make someone believe a thing, can you?" she said.

"Us Catholics were forced, so I like that attitude, but I am still Catholic mind," Hugh said.

"We weren't forced so much, but if you didn't, everyone thought there was something wrong with you," Grigor said. Zahra made her cute giggle sound that he loved, and he kissed her passionately and made love to his beautiful wife.

"Hugh felt proud of you all didn't you Hugh?" he said.

"Aye, I am so proud of my family. You all looked and sounded so heavenly. It gave me goosebumps," Hugh said, and she reached out to him with her hair falling across her arms. Hugh lifted her hair and told her how proud he was of her and kissed her again and then made love slowly each time and it was perfection for Zahra. It had worked for her and her two husbands.

"Do you know who I noticed was watching Fatma a little too much and maybe even a little shyly?" Grigor asked.

"I thought you were too tired to notice stuff like that, but tell us who?" Zahra said.

"Hamish Og was watching Fatma like a hawk, he was. You'll see. The next marriage after Malcolm Og with Dihaoine, which is soon, will be Hamish Og," Grigor predicted.

"Fatma has already asked if she can move in here darlings, because she doesn't want to live with Simon anymore. She just wants to collect all her bees and her goats, seeing as how we lost nearly all of ours in the storm," she said.

"Well, Simon Fraser has to pay me out then. I own half of that farm," Grigor said.

"It'd be worth a bit now with those renovations that you never paid for Grigor," Hugh said sarcastically.

They both realised then that they'd already lost Zahra's attention, as she had already fallen asleep.

26. Miracle on the Mountain

Zahra was waiting on Cinaed for her lesson and decided to look over the waterfall because she used to enjoy that, before the tragic deaths of both Hamish and Cora had occurred, when of all things, a miracle was there before her eyes. Zahra's salmon were back and jumping up the waterfall. There were lots of them and they had come back home to where they had been born, God bless them. She was so excited that she ran to tell both Grigor and Hugh, calling out their names, as she ran. "Grigor, Hugh" she was yelling. Hugh had been planting and Grigor was tending his precious coos, when they both panicked hearing her voice calling out to them.

"What, what?" Grigor asked as she ran to him.

"Grigor, it's the salmon," Zahra said. Hugh came then. "It's the salmon they're back home. Come and look," she said. She ran and they followed her and Coinneach Og was with Grigor, so she asked him to carry him, in case he fell into the waterfall.

"See, them over there and up there. They came home Grigor. They came home Hugh," she said, and she cried as her fish were jumping up the waterfall.

"Mummy's crying DaDa," Coinneach Og said.

"That's happy crying wee Coinneach," Grigor said.

Salmon Fish

"Poor Hamish. He never saw his babies come home," she said.

Salmon Fish

27. The Fairy King

Zahra was still keen to farm her fish on Misty Mountain and was now aware that her salmon would leave when they wanted to, as salmon do, so contacted Mr Fraser, accompanied this time by Hugh, to show her the plans once again and to tell him that the salmon were back on the mountain, at least for a while. Hugh and Zahra strolled hand in hand, back home after arranging plans with Mr Fraser to make the trout farm made from wicker at the top end of the wee loch, which was less volatile, waterfall wise. It would take some time, so they weren't in any hurry.

It was her lesson day with Cinaed and no doubt he'd be gossipy about his wife Isobel, instead of the lessons, but she was patient. Zahra had some specific questions about the Sidhe that day. She had dreamed of a tall and thin, male fairy, perhaps the King, who was standing there, just looking at her. He was atop a mountain which looked like her mountain, but without the mansion, so she wanted some background information too on what her mansion was built on. She wasn't in the mood for making puppies either, so she hoped he wasn't. Hugh then asked her some questions as they strolled along, and she was expecting it to be related to the trout, but it wasn't.

"How did you get the second wolf Zahra?" Hugh asked. "Was it Cinaed?" he asked quite bluntly.

"Aye it was, Hugh. Cinaed Og is the only Druid of Auld, left to make these things happen and it wasn't sexual, as you know, because he is to married Isobel," Zahra said.

"Does Grigor know?" Hugh asked.

"Nae, only you know. Please don't tell him Hugh, I can't lose Grigor," Zahra pleaded.

"He knows you have two wolves, so he will figure it out. I am not comfortable with keeping secrets from him. I want him to know how you achieved it," Hugh said.

"Even if he leaves us?" Zahra asked.

"He won't leave us. Not now if you tell him what you are doing with Cinaed," Hugh said sternly.

"It was just once Hugh, to make the shape shifting possible, it's not all the time," she said.

"Are you doing it again?" Hugh asked.

"In order to make the puppies, we need to do it again, but after that, both myself as a wolf and Winter Wolf, create the puppies," Zahra said. "I don't feel anything for him as a man, nor he for me, it's just the process, but if you insist, it could risk ruining our relationship with Grigor," Zahra said.

"Don't you feel disloyal to either one of us?" Hugh asked.

He then looked sad and upset.

"Nae, I don't because it's not sexual and it's with a wolf, not a man. I only love you and Grigor, and I would never be disloyal to either one of you. Grigor might think I am disloyal, so I haven't told either one of you, but I will tell him if you insist," Zahra said.

Instead of walking to the oak grove, the two of them walked across to the cattle who were mooching around Grigor, both looking concerned about what the outcome might be.

"Grigor darling, Hugh wants me to explain something to you about my two wolves," Zahra said.

Grigor had already seen her second wolf and was already aware of what had taken place.

"Let me guess. Cinaed, as a wolf and you copulated to make it happen?" Grigor asked.

"Aye, Hugh wanted me to tell you, so you knew how it all worked," she said.

"I know how it works. I saw the second wolf the same day that you had obviously done it, like the first time and I know it's not sexual from your part, but I am unsure about him, even though he has married Isobel," Grigor said.

"There's one more process to make the puppies. Do I have both your permissions?" Zahra asked.

"I knew when I first married you, that you were an unusual lady, not quite this unusual, but it took me some time to make up my mind, if we would marry, even with your unusualness, being not of our time. Once I had made up my mind then, it was for eternity, and except for that curse, being a wee glitch along the way, nothing changes. However I appreciate you telling me, but I knew anyway," Grigor said.

"Hugh, do I have your permission?" Zahra asked.

"Aye, so long as this is the last time and never again. I don't like it, even if I understand it. You belong to us alone," Hugh said.

She felt sorry for her husband, Hugh because he was clearly upset by it.

"Nothing will happen today darling. I want to ask Cinaed about the Sidhe today, I think you call them fairies. I saw a male Sidhe in a dream last night. He looked like he was a King, and I didn't know that there were male fairies, let alone Fairy Kings, but he was here on this mountain, so I need to know what was here, before this mansion was built. I can ask Cinaed if you can sit in on this lesson because it's only about the Sidhe, then you might feel better, do you think?" Zahra asked.

"Aye, I'd like to hear what he has to say about that," Hugh said.

"So do I. That sounds ominous," Grigor commented.

Cinaed arrived a little late, but he gave his horse to the groom, who was wearing his new uniform, which Cinaed admired and took the time to admire the groom's new uniform. Then he looked around for his student and Zahra was waving to him from the coo paddock and went to greet him.

He waved to everyone once he saw where they all were and

Grigor asked if the two husbands could sit in on one of Zahra's lessons that day, as it was only about his wife's dream, and they would leave once it concerned the Druid religion. Cinaed was thoughtful at first, but agreed.

"Are you alright Zahra?" Cinaed asked probably addressing the frown on her face, after Hugh's objection to the wolf copulation.

"Aye, I am," she said and the four of them walked together to the oak grove.

"I do feel as if I am intruding on something private, so I am sorry Cinaed," Hugh said.

They each sat on one of the many ancient old rocks found in that grove, for that purpose and Zahra told Cinaed of the enormous cloud covered mountain, that she had seen in her dream, which she thought was her mountain but without the mansion yet built on it. But atop that mountain was a circle of many stones around a huge mound with some kind of entrance tunnel leading into it. Standing in front of it, was a man or a being that was much taller than the average man, as well as very lean, with long, fine, silver hair, who she knew in the dream to be a fairy or one of the Sidhe who was maybe the King of them all, and wanted to ask if there was such a thing as a male fairy, a King of fairies or the Sidhe and also what was underneath the mansion before it was built, many centuries ago, and was their anything there now?

Cinaed's usual expression was happy enough, sometimes dull like Isobel had said, but this question altered his facial expression completely. He became very serious, almost sombre. He dropped his head a bit, as if to decide what to tell Zahra and he then lifted his head once again and looked directly into Zahra's eyes.

"No chit chat today then?" Cinaed said, trying to lighten up the atmosphere.

"Aye Ma, there are male fairies, as well as female fairies and there are Fairy Kings and Fairy Queens. Sadly, on top of this mountain there was a large mound shaped tomb of some kind, circular in shape with an entrance, as you have described. It was said to have belonged to the Fairy King by all the locals, a long time ago. My brother, Coinneach, being a King himself, didn't want competition and believed there could be no other King but himself. He, therefore ordered its destruction," Cinaed said.

"This mountain was formerly known as Fairy Mountain or Mountain of the Sidhe, before it was re-named Beinn Coinneach, by my brother," Cinaed said. "There are still some ancient maps with that name on it because it's the largest mountain in the entire district and fires were lit up here to mark the change of all the seasons, like Samhain. He was an important Fairy King by all accounts.

Zahra gasped at the very idea of destroying a mound of such ancient significance.

"Oh no, he didn't," Zahra said.

"I was the youngest in my family at that time and I had no say as to what could happen at anytime. When Coinneach built the prison, where your gemstones currently are, he imprisoned them all in there, without food, water, or air, in the dark, hoping they would all die, like any ordinary mortal, would. They suffered and their cries could be heard all over the mountain. He expected that one day he would just walk into that prison, and they'd all be lying dead. What he found instead, was an empty room, like as if nothing, nor anyone had ever been in there. Even the dust on the floor wasn't disturbed," Cinaed explained.

"I was cautious of what my brother was capable of from a very early age, but I never demonstrated it, because he always had my father's full support," he said.

"Not even Prince Griogar had done anything like that, until he locked you up on that island, recently to starve, Zahra," Cinaed said. The mood of all four of them was sad and thoughtful of the Fairies' suffering and where the family stood now being on top of their old home.

"Was, that mound a home or a grave?" asked Hugh.

"It was their home, as well as a grave and a portal to the 'Otherworld' and this mountain then was in the Pictish language called Fairy Mountain, not Beinn Coinneach," Cinaed said. "It was a portal of some kind into the Otherworld with many carved inscriptions on the inside which only they understood. My brother used some of those stones to help build your mansion, so those stones are all over your mansion, in the walls, everywhere," he added.

As soft and as silent as anyone could move, the very tall and lean Fairy King entered the group of four. Zahra looked up immediately and knew that he was the Fairy King from her dream with his bluish glow and silver hair. Cinaed looked up and knew him from the many centuries ago, when he had been imprisoned, along with all his people. Grigor turned to see him for the first time, but Hugh was unaware at first.

He spoke like a quiet musical lament to Cinaed.

"I know you lad from when you were wee and weeping, as they locked us all in that dark room," the Fairy King said. "I know you Grigor as one of the men who have taken our revenge for us, for which we are grateful. I know you Hugh, as the one who was under the ground for a time, and we assisted you, to keep you alive. I know you Zahra from the day you first came here, broken and bleeding. I repaired your face when he wasn't in the room. He was going to leave you like that, bleeding. Do you recognise my touch?" the Fairy King asked.

The Fairy King touched her face as soft as a butterfly's wings.

"Yes, I do. It was you, not Coinneach," Zahra replied.

"You have no need to fear from us, who dwell beside you. Occasionally leave us some milk by your front door, that would be nice. Go in peace my friends," the Fairy King said.

And then he slowly faded away.

None of the men asked about the revenge that the Fairy King mentioned and to what it referred, after all, it could refer to anything? Grigor was hoping Cinaed wouldn't piece it together with the three skeletons found after the storm, to add to the story. They all went back to work and Cinaed and Zahra set up a date to make the wolf puppies before the next wedding, which was for Dihaoine and her betrothed, Malcolm Og.

28. Horses, More Horses

Malcolm Og and his twin brother, Hamish Og were driving their team of eight Clydesdale horses up the Misty Mountain Road, and as they did, they raucously yelled out to Hector, who galloped alongside them, until they had reached the top. It must be a heavenly life for a young man', Zahra thought now that the worst of life's tribulations in Scotland were over, even though people were still leaving, either by choice or cleared to make way for sheep. Zahra often compared her own life to Isobel Grant and was glad that she hadn't led the life that she'd had to live. Her lovely tall son, Hector was showing off his beautiful pure bred Highland Mountain ponies and his were the best in all the Highlands. Even Beth Fraser was going out of business, because of Hector, so she had taken to teaching horse riding in her older years, instead of breeding. She had even offered her own remaining stock of Highland ponies to Hector at a reduced price, but he rejected it, as they were not of the same quality as his and where the family lived on that treacherous mountain, they needed good mountain ponies, where you could trust that they knew where they could put their feet, without falling over, or slipping.

Beth's letter had reminded Grigor, however that her late son, Simon Og Fraser, owed him, his half of the farm in the Aird, so Zahra helped Grigor pen a letter to the aging Lord Simon Fraser, in such a way that it appeared that Grigor had purchased it for the young couple, in readiness for marriage, which did not eventuate. He then asked Lord Simon to re-pay him and invited him to go there to check on its current valuation.

It wasn't long before Grigor received his half share of the farm, straight into his personal bank account, with many thanks for taking such good care of his son. Grigor didn't mention that the rude little shite, still lived there in his spectre form and would forever be a nuisance to the world of the living and the dead. Grigor was just thrilled to feel like a rich man with the value of the property having gone up considerably with the additional house and all the other renovations, paid for by Coinneach MacAlpin.

Of course, he spent some of it on the coos but surprised Zahra with a nice wedding ring in eighteen carat gold with three small diamonds. It was beautiful and she was delighted.

Their daughter Fatma was especially pleased to see Hamish Og arrive with his twin brother, both gorgeous looking, even more handsome than their father. The twins still had their long black hair tied back in a ponytail, while they worked. They were a lot like Malcolm and their skin colour was slightly olive, which must have been inherited from their deceased Mither, from the islands. Dihaoine was excited waiting upon her betrothed, as nothing had changed over the years and if anything, they had grown closer and closer, with knowing each other so well. It had been a risk to take at first, they had thought, but it had all worked out and now the discussions were underway for their wedding. As her older sister, Isobel announced being with child again, Zahra Og was in school, and Isobel's two sons were at university, one studying medicine and one studying law.

Zahra's family and the farm was finally as she had wanted it.

The trout were breeding, and the family ate salmon when the fish came home, and Zahra sold what they couldn't eat. Hugh's crops were growing frantically, and his corn was stored downstairs, as were the potatoes, all in preparation for a famine.

These were men who had farmed through famines and were prepared and couldn't understand why even Zahra, was so productive. Fatma was proud to show Hamish all over the property to where she had placed her bees, having taken over from Flidas and he helped her to prepare the day's honey, as well as milking the goats with her. They were looking very domesticated together. Grigor had been right. They were to be the next wedding after Dihaoine.

Dinner was the usual time for serious conversations to take place and on their first night on Misty Mountain, the twins put an unexpected proposal to Hugh, Grigor, and Zahra, with family all listening in. Malcolm Og began a little nervously and reminding those listening that he was marrying Dihaoine on the following weekend, he asked if it would be in the family's best interests if the Team could move onto the mountain and not Glengarry. They would then run their teamster business from Misty Mountain Ranch. Malcolm Og would then be with his wife, and she wouldn't need to leave her home. Zahra first waited on her husbands' responses, and they both turned to her for her opinion.

"What do you think Zahra?" Hugh asked.

"I think that if you have already discussed it with your parents, as well as both Hugh Og and Angus MacKenzie and they have all agreed, then I would agree to it," Zahra said. "Have you

discussed it with Hugh Og, especially with the work that both teams have?" Zahra asked.

"Aye Mistress we have both discussed it with our parents and with Hugh Og and Angus. At first Hugh Og didn't agree, but he does now that Hamish Og wants to ask Master Grigor something important," Malcolm Og said.

"Ask me what then, lad?" said a stern looking Grigor.

"Master Grigor, may I have the hand of your daughter, Fatma in marriage, if yourself and your wife both agree?" Hamish asked, starting to stammer.

Fatma was smiling from ear to ear, and everyone was happy for them both.

"What do you think Zahra, Hugh?" Grigor asked.

"You first Grigor," said Hugh.

"If my wife agrees and Fatma herself agrees, then I am happy with that, if you explain to me again where you are running the Teamster business from," Grigor said.

"From here if that's alright with you and your family. There's a lot of work, out this way and between here and Inverness, so we are keen to move here and use your stables, if that's to your liking," Hamish Og said.

"We get wild weather up here sometimes lads and it can get mighty cold and wet, not to mention, cloudy and misty. If you can care properly for your horses, ensuring they are indoors, the minute there are signs of bad weather, then it would work, but you would need to know that about the climate on this mountain. We lost Hamish and Cora, as you know, as well as the whole salmon farm we had built, so that was a freak storm, but you must care for your animals on these occasions. I keep the coos under the house here, so they are all safe. Hector has all his horses well stabled as soon as there's a breath of wind.

Can you promise that you would care for those wonderful horses, knowing that about the climate up here?" Grigor asked.

"Aye, and we would also pay for another groom. Can we bring our own groom with us too?" Hamish asked.

"Well Zahra, my wife, it looks like you built those stables for these lads, after all. Do you agree with the plan?" Grigor asked.

"Yes darling, if both you and Hugh agree to the Team operating from here and to having all three lads living here in the house, not outside in the stables, marrying not only Dihaoine but Fatma too, then it would be a lovely family environment, so long as they know what we are. I don't want them to wonder why Ailsa is aging and I am not, so please, tell them my love," Zahra requested.

"My Da, has already explained it Aunty Zahra. We know that the three of you are already of the Otherworld, but it's uncertain about your bairns, except Isobel. Is that right?" Malcolm Og asked.

"The staff here also are also of the Otherworld, as you say, as well as Master Cinaed, when he visits, but we don't talk about the bairns, because we just have to wait and see. Coinneach Og looks healthy, and he is growing up big and strong now, so we just don't know about life spans, or whether Fatma can reproduce either," Zahra said. "As you know, a few of us, like Hector and Flidas are Muslim and in that religion, it is permitted to have more than one wife, especially if she cannot reproduce, so if Fatma cannot give you bairns, it is permitted, if you are Muslim, to have two wives," Zahra added.

"You don't have to call me Mistress Zahra either. When you marry my daughters, then I am 'Ma', unless you don't like that. Hugh and Grigor also would both be 'Da' and you know they are both my husbands, I assume?" Zahra asked.

"Aye Ma," said both Malcolm Og and Hamish Og.

"Mairi will take you to your rooms and you can choose which ones you prefer. The top floor is all staff on that side, so you would be beneath them until you are married. The rooms are cleaned by my staff and sheets washed by my staff, so that is of no expense to yourselves, but when you are married the married quarters are on this side of the mansion with plumbed bathing rooms unless the ladies insist on renovating that side with marriage suites. Mairi will also insist that you wash your hands every time you come inside and please leave your boots by the door but there are indoor shoes or slippers to wear in the house," Zahra said.

"You can use the library whenever you wish but please return the books. Also, I keep my horse in the same stables as the Clydesdales, as well as her stallion, so that my three horses are close to the house, if that suits you both," Zahra added.

"Oh Ma. I almost forgot. Our Da gave us these books for you to read. They were translated from Pictish into English by Lord Coinneach when they were still talking. The books belonged to my Foster Great Grandfather, Gilcrest MacNachten and were found in the ceiling of his croft in Loch Insh. Da thought you should read them. He mentioned something about a curse," Malcolm Og said.

"Please thank your Da for me. A little bit of light reading then?" Zahra jested.

Then the night was just going over who was invited to the Malcolm Og's wedding, where to be seated and what food they all wanted. Neither lad mentioned dowery, but Grigor let it go and thought he'd ask the father, Malcolm MacNachten when he saw him.

Like Isobel's wedding, there was a crowd, only this time there were more young people, as well as many nice wedding gifts for the two of them, being so young. They chose a person to hold the ceremony, who was neither Catholic nor Protestant, so he said, but had a licence to marry folk, so long as it was legal, was the family's main concern as this was a new concept to people of the nineteenth century. For Zahra, it was nice to see Malcolm Mohr again, still wearing his hair long, but it was greying now, and he had a lot more lines on his face, as did

Ailsa. He seemed pleased to see his sons settling down finally, with such a lovely lass, as he said. He commented that he never thought he would see the day when both lads would want to be settled down and discussed dowery with Grigor who looked pleased. Doweries had been put aside for both daughter's weddings, but some people could expect too much, however Malcolm was a reasonable man. Malcolm was accompanied by his Mither, Marion also, who was looking tired of life, after losing her husband, Bruce.

Zahra didn't want to disclose to Marion, that death wasn't the end of all that exertion, just a new beginning. So, she gave her condolences instead.

It might have been then that Zahra decided to take up writing again and publish in Scotland. After all, she could never go back to her old home and everyone she knew now would all be gone. She had been reading those books from Malcolm which were in part, informative but the most interesting thing she found was a section on curses both simple and more complex to achieve. It seemed they were right, and they had all been cursed but luckily it was of the simpler variety of curses that could be broken. Coinneach clearly wasn't much of a Druid at all, and she wondered if he attained the curse elsewhere, like the Old Crohn who had introduced them, in the Aird. She had a lot to gain, after all and it would explain why she didn't know that they didn't have sheep, when nearly everyone else did, by then.

Alex and Peter were not invited to this wedding, but Padruig was invited with James Grant, so he could take him home the next day. Apparently Padruig and his ghostly presence was good for business and James needed him there at his hotel, so long as he didn't scare anyone to death again, like his son Patrick. It suited Padruig who had his room cleaned every day and meals provided with his spectre friends dropping in from time to time, except the family from Misty Mountain. As Zahra was talking to everyone, she decided what to call her first novel. It might be a good, bad, and evil kind of romance novel but her two wonderful husbands of the current day would feature prominently as the heroes of her life in Scotland. Sex was too controversial to put into print, she thought but it could be played around with a little because she did have the best sex life anyone could ever imagine. Just thinking of her sex life, drew first Hugh, then Grigor to her side, both putting their arms around her. They were both her men, her gorgeous handsome big men. She felt so lucky, despite all of her hardships.

"What were you just thinking of my sweet wife?" asked Grigor.

"Sex, and how lucky I am," Zahra whispered.

"I know when you're thinking of sex. You give it away on your pretty face. Shall we three escape the mob for a while and enjoy ourselves?" Grigor asked.

"I'm in," said Hugh.

"Aye my Misty Mountain Men. I was thinking of writing another book. What do you two think?" she asked.

"Aye, so long as I am the most handsome one," Grigor said.

"Nae, me. I'm the most handsome man with my blonde hair," Hugh said smiling. Zahra chuckled and the big man Hugh picked her up and they went to their bedroom all together. The young people all started up their musical instruments, as Zahra closed her door. As Zahra lay beneath Grigor, he was hungry for oral sex that he had missed in a while, and it drove her crazy as she reached orgasm and he enjoyed what her body gave him. Then as he was on his haunches, now unphased by the presence of her other husband, he began to thrust slowly at first speaking to her in romantic Gaelic tones as he used to in the Aird. The romance of it and the depth of feeling always bought tears to her eyes, as he spoke then thrusted slowly gaining momentum. His orgasm was always a deep heart felt groan that made her love him so much more every time. When he lay gently across her chest, she said to him.

"Grigor, I learned some Gaelic to say to you. Can I try?" she asked.

"Aye," he said. However, it all came out incorrectly and Grigor couldn't help himself but to laugh out loud at her efforts at poetic Gaelic and getting it all wrong. Hugh was trying hard not to laugh also but thought better of it.

"Did I get it wrong then?" Zahra asked. "I tried to memorise it from Cinaed's lesson, but I won't try again," she said. She was embarrassed at her poor Gaelic, but Grigor was still smiling at her and said he was pleased that she tried and then told her what she had said in English.

"The words are easy to mix up. Don't give up. It's a difficult language," Grigor said.

He held her while speaking genuine words of love as she nestled her face into his hairy chest, that she loved. Hugh was suddenly shocked saying, "Jesus, Mary and Joseph," Her Winter Wolf leapt out growling and baring his teeth.

Zahra then became aware of the Fairy King in their presence.

"Mistress Zahra I am here to tell you, that it is time," The Fairy King said.

"Time for what?" Zahra asked.

"Your wolf pups are due and Cinaed is busy at the wedding. My wife has made you a wicker basket for them and Winter Wolf to lay together," the Fairy King said.

"Can you shape shift into the she-wolf now, to give birth to your wee pups. Master Hugh, you have experience with delivering pups. Can you assist me please, with your wife?" the Fairy King asked.

"Lay on your side Mistress Zahra please," The Fairy King asked. As Zahra shape shifted into her, she-wolf for only the second time. She became aware, then that she was uncomfortable with labour and tried to lick herself from where the pups were going to arrive and was whelping at the same time. This was a female wolf having her first litter of puppies and she was frightened at what was happening to her lupine body, as her eyes looked longingly into Hugh's. Hugh could still see Zahra in there, asking him for help. She kept making a whelping sound, then standing up and turning in circles wondering at what was happening to her body. The Winter Wolf was disturbed that she was so upset and stood full height with his front paws on the bed where she lay. These were his puppies due to arrive, after all and his Alpha female was afraid.

She was a beautiful wolf, despite being a wolf and laying in their marriage bed, having made love just moments before, Grigor was shocked at what was happening. Maybe Hugh was handling it better than him, knowing his old Collie dogs like he did, as well as Zahra. Grigor had to pull himself together and try to be helpful and patted her on her head lovingly, hoping that might help.

"Say your Gaelic stuff Grigor, it might calm her down. She's panicking" Hugh said.

Grigor began to say the same words to a wolf as he was saying to Zahra which impressed the Fairy King and his wife, who appeared in the room somehow too, with the wicker basket. Luckily the noise of the music downstairs drowned out the sounds that were emanating from their room. Baby Hugh, however, was disturbed and was awoken and began to cry for his Mither. Grigor had to nurse the youngster because there was no breast milk forthcoming for quite some time. The new pups had to be fed, once they were born, before wee Hugh could be fed again. Wolf pups were now a challenge that the Fairy King had to help them with, because Cinaed hadn't done his job properly.

As each wolf pup was born, she whimpered and the Fairy King gave it to the Winter Wolf to lick off its protective sack, as Zahra was unable to do that. In nature, it's the female wolf who licks it all off, but reluctantly the Alpha male was doing that job, then carrying each one to the wicker basket, indicated by the Fairy Queen, until all of them were born.

There were five pups born alive, each with their own placenta which the Winter Wolf ate reluctantly. Then as Zahra's milk was ready for the puppies, the Winter Wolf bought each puppy back to suckle on the mother wolf, who had finally settled down but unhappy, because she could hear wee Hugh crying. As soon as they were fed, Winter Wolf carried them by the skin on the backs of their tiny necks, back to the basket now, with a warm blanket.

Zahra then shape shifted back, needing to feed her wee bairn, Hugh.

Grigor only wished for her sweet chuckle to be heard once again, just to be reassured that she was still Zahra, once again.

"The Goddess's of Auld were accompanied by wolves. Your wife is like a Goddess," said the Fairy Queen in her musical voice and the two of them, then departed having completed their task.

Her husband Hugh hadn't had the opportunity to make love to her that night, before this had all happened, and he was feeling the need to make love to her, as soon as she had finished nursing the wee bairn, to make himself feel normal again. Wee Hugh was settling down, once again and was warm in his bassinet, near their bed. Hugh took his wife into his embrace, re-assuring her and as soon as she started to fiddle with his chest hairs, he made love to his wife. She began to weep both out of love and out of relief, that the scary ordeal was over.

"I was so frightened Hugh," Zahra said.

"No more litters of pups," Grigor demanded firmly.

Grigor was wondering how to tell the family where the puppies had all come from, and a lie was going to have to cover it up, temporarily. They had live people living there now, not just the unalive. The alive would want to shoot the wolves, which made it risky for Zahra if she ever shape shifted outside in the site of someone's, long rifle.

"Grigor, we may have to tell the new family members the truth, so I am not shot. Grigor, where is my wedding ring that you bought me?" she said suddenly panicking.

"It's okay my love, do you think I would risk that ring after Causantin and I went to so much trouble just finding that old jeweller and his shop, let alone have it designed and made especially for my clever wife. Do you realise how many times per day that you will have to feed these little deaf and blind, dependent wee creatures?" Grigor asked. As she put her ring back on, she replied.

"Nae, Cinaed didn't tell me much, it seems," Zahra replied.

"You will need to feed the pups five times, per day for around five minutes, each time. They can't open their eyes yet, but when they do, they will be blue, but as they mature, they change to yellow. They will have a funny little waddle in about two weeks time. After that two-week period, there will be attempts to stand and walk, growl, whimper, and squeak and their first attempts at howling. They will also get their first puppy teeth in two weeks, and they can then eat regurgitated meat. Good luck with that Zahra and don't ask me to vomit up meat for them," Grigor said.

"How did you learn all of that Grigor?" Zahra asked.

"When I was wee and all the wolves were being shot, I hid one injured Mither and her five puppies, until they were strong enough to all leave safely, from under our house. My grandmother would have shot them all or drowned them, if she had known," Grigor said.

"I'll vomit up the meat for them. I can help with them. I love them. They are so cute." Hugh said.

"Trust the 'Celtic God' to swoop in for points," jested Grigor.

"I mean it Grigor. I miss my Collies. This is perfect for me. A wife and a dog, all in one, with pups," Hugh said gleefully.

Zahra and her Puppies

"You're sick Hugh," Grigor said.

The two men were proud of their achievement, despite their joviality.

"Hugh, before I forget to mention it and I know it's off topic, but can you please do two things for me before the next thing happens. One is growing carrots in two separate places. One location is between the rose bushes, out the front of the mansion, for domestic use only, and a larger commercial crop of carrots, out the back, beneath my window here, so I can see you when you're working, while I am nursing the pups, or wee Hugh. You can wave to me from there," Zahra said.

"And the second thing?" Hugh asked.

"The price of kelp will increase dramatically from now onwards, until the end of this century, then it will crash again, leaving many people hungry, nearer the coast than here. Therefore, we need to ask the twins to go now to the coast to get one large load of kelp, before the change in price commences and depending on the price, we can ask them to go one more time to prepare for your carrots. We also need to plant oats too, following Ali's advice," Zahra replied.

"Okay, I'm curious. Why?" asked Grigor.

"The kelp becomes needed, as a component for the glass manufacturing industry, so poor farmers will no longer be able to obtain free or cheap kelp, and the price becomes unaffordable, before it crashes. I don't usually tell you these things, in case it changes history somehow, but this is the survival of our family. The fence around our property will have to continue to be built also, as people become hungry and you may need that turret after all, my darling Grigor," she said smiling cutely.

"The carrots, please explain Zahra?" Grigor asked.

"The only cash that can be earned by the coast, will come from the sale of carrots for the horses. It's a small cash earning industry for a short while," Zahra replied. "Don't repeat that to any of the other growers, who will then grow carrots too and I also think we need turnips," Zahra said.

"Okay, enough of the business now it's my turn to enjoy my wife," said Hugh as he tickled her and finally, Zahra was giggling once again.

"Grigor, my love, did you say that Causantin went with you to the jewellers?" Zahra asked.

"Aye, he did. He has a flare for it and that old man asked me if the lad wanted to become a jeweller like him, but I forgot to tell you. Sorry, I forgot". Grigor said.

"Darling, we have the diamonds and the gold. All we need is someone who knows what to do with it. Causantin is old enough now to do an apprenticeship. Can you please take me there to meet him, when the two weeks of intense puppy feeding is over, and we can see if Causantin would like that as a career? What do you both think?" Zahra asked.

"I agree," said Grigor. "Me too," said Hugh.

"By the way, I need Coinneach Og to collect the manure for me. Will he do that, if we give him a pony and cart?" asked Hugh.

"Grigor and I will tell him to do it and give him a pony of his own, from Hector. As for Malcolm Og and Hamish Og, I think you should tell them both about the shape shifting and the wolf pups, please Grigor," Zahra asked.

"Nae not yet" he answered. "Feed the pups by the window and watch the Celtic God plant carrots, until Hamish marries Fatma first," Grigor said.

"Enough business chat. It's time for me now," said Zahra's Celtic God, with his blonde hair, flowing down to his elbows. "Love me my clever woman," Hugh said, and Zahra chuckled as he took her into his big, strong, blonde hairy arms. He kissed her passionately and sat her on his manhood and she squealed her joyful sound. She was surprised that he was already erect and had been waiting for her but was delighted.

"By the way you two, Padruig's coming to Hamish Og's wedding. He demanded it tonight. He's up to something," Grigor said.

Zahra was tired after the night's events, but still had time to run her finger down Hugh's beautiful aquiline nose and his perfect features and perfect skin. She ran her fingers through his long blonde hair that now came down below his elbows. She didn't really take in what Grigor had said seriously. She was thinking of what they would all wear to the next wedding.

"Is my hair dirty?" Hugh asked.

"Nae, my sweetheart, but on the night of Fatma's wedding I want to show off my two glorious men with their handsome faces and to be dressed better than anyone else. Can I buy you both new jackets, with matching vests, so you are both my handsome men with your hair clean and hanging out freely? Maybe Cinaed can do a painting of you both with me, in the middle, so we can have a lovely big portrait hung high up on the wall?" Zahra asked.

"Cinaed is a better portrait artist than Coinneach ever was and who cares what Padruig is up to Grigor?" Zahra added.

"My turn before those pups wake up then," Grigor demanded.

Coinnech Og's Cart Pony

Grigor took his wife firmly in his grip and when he lay her down beneath him, he spoke to her again in Gaelic before he made love to her romantically. With each thrust, he looked deeply into her big green eyes. He had a level of concentration and self-control, she always amazed at, which drove her to her maximum pleasure while he watched her reach it, before he then allowed himself to come to orgasm himself. He knew her eyes so exactly as he had mapped them both out. Grigor thought that Zahra had the prettiest eyes in the whole world. He also knew that somehow a part of herself understood what he was saying. Zahra felt safe between her two big, loving men knowing there was enough room in their big hearts for her.

Her needs and her demands, along with her lack of skills living in nineteenth century Scotland, made her aware of her dependency upon them both and only men with big hearts, like they had, could put up with her. At least that is how she thought, and it frightened her to be without them both now. She had learned a lot and had come a long way but was still aware of how much room she occupied in their big hearts.

29. Carrots, Jewels and Another Wedding

Hugh planted his crop of carrots, as Zahra had requested of him. The domestic supply was planted in between the rows of roses, as Zahra had asked him to do also, then with Coinneach Og busily picking up manure for the commercial crop, Hugh was right underneath her bedroom window. Her lonely life in her bedroom, allowed her to wave to both him and Coinneach Og. The sweet lad was so young, yet very big for his age and he could drive his pony cart picking up every coo paddy, or horse manure from all over their mountain, which he dropped back to Hugh. It wouldn't be enough fertiliser, so Zahra had to have that conversation again about what the future held. The cost of kelp was going to rise to an unaffordable price very soon.

◇

My twins left the next day for that first load of kelp, hopefully getting in before the price rose. While the twins were out, Zahra and her wolf family all went for a run, all over her mountain, through snow and the pups were awkward and not yet able to discern what was what, in nature. She would need to run around her mountain with them, more often. Even if it was to familiarise them later as adult wolves free from domestic life and roaming across the mountains.

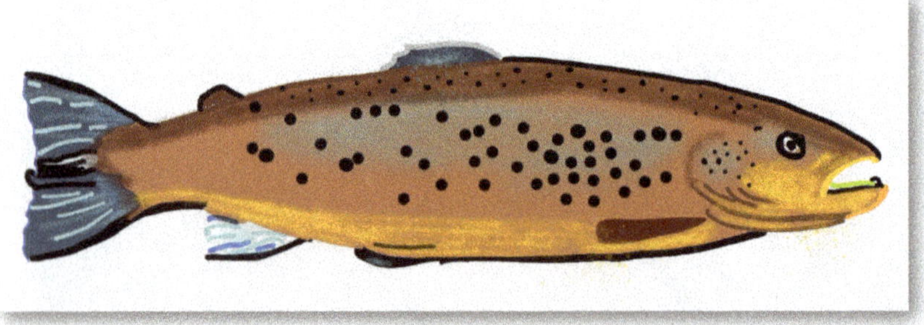

Scottish Brown Trout

There was lots of news in the papers, but Zahra no longer read the papers and only waited on Grigor to tell her if there was something to worry about, like the weather. She knew what was coming anyhow. The trout farm had been built well by Cinaed Fraser and his two nephews, so when the salmon came and went each year, they still had trout. They never tried again to farm the salmon, but they didn't need to with the same families of fish returning each year. Zahra's sign had been altered once again to read Misty Mountain Trout Farm and in addition, it now had MacNachten Teamsters, Misty Mountain. My twins also painted that on the side of their big carriage. Isobel gave birth to another wee lass, and they were happy with wee Annie Chisholm MacAlpin and Dihaoine took a little more time.

Causantin went off to his apprenticeship to learn the craft of jewellery making and becoming qualified in that trade, while living on site. Master Urquhart had been vetted and was excited to see a few of the stones that were delivered to him, which they could transform into fine diamond rings, bracelets, necklaces, tiaras and brooches, even large brooches for Highlander men to hold their fly plaids in place.

They were very expensive and only the wealthy could afford them, but Zahra's beautiful son, Causantin had a system with old Master Domhnall Urquhart. They charged the Campbells, twice the price and the English tourists paid, three times the usual retail price. That enabled the shop to be kind to the young couples wishing to marry, who had little money, so their price could even be free on some occasions, or at least cheaper, as in Hamish's case when he bought a magnificent ring for my daughter in law, Fatma.

Bit by bit, the gold or the pink diamond rocks and the amethysts found their way into Master Urquhart's shop, so that Causantin didn't have to pay for his board or food while still earning a good wage and qualifying to become a jeweller in a wonderful new craft. It was a well-kept secret that there were diamond rocks, as well as amethysts and gold going into that jeweller's shop from Misty Mountain.

Fatma finally married my son, Hamish Og and as Padruig promised, he was there, without James this time, along with a huge crowd of the living and the Unalive. After the formalities were over, the portrait of the three parents was hung, Padruig came over to Zahra, Grigor and Hugh and he wasn't happy.

What happened next was unexpected.

"You are doing the wrong thing Zahra. Choose one man, not two. You can't be married to two men at the same time," Padruig ranted angrily to Zahra, not to either Grigor or Hugh.

She knew that she was out of her depth with him, being in such an ugly mood and as he was, so close to her in proximity so she placed both of her small hands on his big, broad chest.

Causantin MacGregor

"Padruig, I respect you as one of the Seven Glenmoriston Men and if you think you are the leader of such heroic men, then I implore you please, for your permission to be married to both of my men, Grigor Mohr MacGregor and Hugh Mohr Chisholm," Zahra asked sincerely.

Padruig was silenced by being touched like that and stood back, still staring at her. Grigor was worried about Zahra.

"I am the head of this family Padruig. If you have something to say, say it to me," Grigor said firmly.

Hugh began to sob, fearing the worse outcome, that he could lose Zahra, which broke both their hearts.

"I have a signed wedding certificate for my marriage to Hugh Chisholm," Zahra said. "And Grigor and I are both handfast," Zahra added.

Zahra concluded that Padruig must have had been drinking, even though there was no alcohol in their house, so he may have taken it with him.

"Why did you not consider marrying me then?" Padruig asked which shocked them all.

"Because, my old friend, I am aware that I take up a lot of room in both Hugh's and Grigor's hearts. There isn't enough room in your heart for the likes of a strange one like me," Zahra said.

Grigor was almost about to hit Padruig, when the Fairy King quietly waltzed on through the wedding crowd, who were now all listening in and worried. He was well dressed, as if he was a well-known guest. He went straight up to Zahra, putting his calming arm on both Hugh and Grigor, then announced that he was qualified to marry both Grigor and Zahra and did so, so that both men would be her husbands, equally. He spoke some unknown language, that nobody understood and pronounced them both man and wife.

He then touched Padruig on his forearm, saying, "This is their Unalive Time, my friend, not their Judgement Time, so it is permissible, Mr Padruig," the Fairy King said. "Besides which, Master Grigor here answers for all three of them, not the sweet Mistress Zahra. What do you say Master MacGregor, are all three of you married equally?" the Fairy

Fatma MacNachten

King asked.

"Aye we are," Grigor said and smiled at both Zahra and Hugh and that was the end of that. Padruig never questioned the validity of their marriages ever again and neither did anyone else, to their knowledge. It left hurt feelings behind, which was unavoidable with Zahra's and Hugh's sensitivities, but they had a wedding to finish.

The last business of Fatma's and Hamish Og's wedding day was, all of the jewellery that Causantin had been busy making with old Master Urquhart, but Zahra was aware, that she was running out of time and needed to feed her wolf pups soon, so would only be able to complete some of it.

Zahra began by saying, "My dear husbands, my dear friends, both old and new and my wonderful family and the Fairy King and his wonderful family. Thank you all for coming to this auspicious occasion of our daughters' wedding to Hamish MacNachten, son of Malcolm MacNachten."

"My son, Causantin, is an apprentice jeweller with Master Domnhall Urqhuart and has completed some special gifts for this occasion. First, we wish to present for the two recent weddings of Malcolm Og with our daughter Dihaoine and Hamish today with our daughter Fatma and they are asked to come forward to receive these gifts from myself, Grigor, and Hugh. For both Dihaoine and Fatma we are gifting pendants of pink diamonds with a setting of amethysts, with gold latches. For both of their husbands Malcolm Og and Hamish, who we are so pleased to have as part of our family, we are gifting solid gold necklaces with their names on them, so we all know them apart. We thought rings might get in the way of their work with their horses. We hope the four of you all like the gifts and enjoy your lives together, as much as we do and may God bless you all, as well as Master Urqhart and our son, Causantin," Zahra said.

"For my husbands, are solid gold plaid brooches with a

solitaire pink diamond stone in the centre, but engraved on the backs of each one is their identifying Clan motto. Like my gown today represents Clan Gregor as well as Clan Chisholm, may I pin them on, as they might be handy to hold on to the fly plaids?" Zahra said. "My husbands will complete the rest," she said. There were many other smaller gifts, but she had to ask Grigor and Hugh to finish them off for her, as she took her leave.

Hector was confused why his Mither tried to look unnoticed and then ran quickly up the stairs to her bedroom on the top floor, without completing her task of giving out all the jewels. Hector asked himself what could be there, that was more important than the wedding. So, he decided to slink off, unnoticed and he followed her up the stairs. When he reached the reading room, next door to her bedroom, he was sure he heard whimpering sounds and then a wee wolf's howl, albeit a quiet one. He knocked on the door, then entered.

"Ma?" Hector said.

What Hector saw was a beautiful Alpha female grey wolf, with her five wee pups, now with their eyes open and suckling on the mother wolf. Winter Wolf leapt out to protect them, when the she -wolf made a guttural noise to make him obey her and not to attack her son, Hector. It was obvious that Zahra, in human form, was not in the room, but her Winter Wolf was.

Hector's mind didn't want to conclude that the female wolf before him, could possibly be his Mither, but her dress, worn to the wedding, was laid out on her bed, along with her wedding ring and he didn't know then what to do with his discovery.

"Ma, is it you? Are you feeding these wee wolf puppies?" Hector asked.

He looked into her eyes and saw tears rolling down her cheeks and he knew that it was his Mither.

"Ma, how did you become a real wolf and have baby wolves?" Hector asked. He sat down beside her, and her pups and she licked his hand and nudged him to pat her, which he did lovingly.

"Och Ma, I always knew that you were some kind of miracle from God, but I wish you had told me. I could have helped with these little fellas," Hector said. "Aren't they cute?" "And you Ma, even as a wolf, you are so pretty. How are we going to keep you all alive with Malcolm and Hamish here now? They will want to shoot you all?" Hector asked.

The door then burst open with two worried looking husbands both coming in.

"Hector you can't tell Hamish and Malcolm Og yet. Please it's a secret," Hugh asked pleadingly.

"Son, we were going to tell you at the right time. This is your Ma. Not permanently, you understand, it's only to feed the wee pups," Grigor said. Zahra nudged his hand again for acceptance and he patted her on her head as Winter Wolf watched on, protectively.

"Don't worry Ma, I'll keep it a secret, but you will have to reveal it, as soon as these people have all gone home, for your own safety," Hector advised.

"This was your gift son, but you had left the room, so we came looking for you. Your Ma had Causantin make it for you," Grigor said.

Hector received a gold kilt pin shaped liked a pony with 'My Hero Hector' engraved on it.

"Och Ma, it's so lovely. Thank you," Hector said, and he kissed the wolf. "You even smell like Ma does. How do you get back to being yourself?" Hector asked. Hector had so many questions which the husbands both answered and truthfully and it all shocked him that Cinaed was also involved.

"Who was that man who married you both Da?" Hector asked.

"He is the Fairy King, son. This house was built on top of their home by the previous owner, who tried to kill all the Sidhe. He is the one who cured your Ma's injuries on her face, not Coinneach," Grigor said.

"I liked him," Hector said.

"Well, that's fortunate, because he can pop up at any time. He helped deliver the pups," Hugh said. With feeding time over and the pups cleaned up, Zahra was able to return to herself, naked as always, covered over quickly by her husbands, who helped her adjust again and held onto her tightly.

"You three must really love each other. Ma, I'm sorry for barging in on you," Hector said. She embraced her son, and he was relieved to be holding his real Mither again. He kissed her face again and again and re-assured her it was a secret, but they should tell the family as soon as the guests were all gone.

"I'm sorry son. They needed feeding and I did want you to know," Zahra said.

◇

"Da I think we need a security team here too to protect Ma, like Uncle Malcolm has on his farm. One of his men is Colm MacKenzie. He might want to come back here, or he might know other people here. Think about it please for Ma's sake," Hector asked. He then left the room with one last kiss and a soulful look.

It was a good idea, so both Hugh and Grigor quickly returned to the party, seeking me out before I went to bed to ask about Colm MacKenzie.

"You are welcome to employ Colm MacKenzie. He is good at his job, but Meredith still hates him. I'll ask him for you and if he is interested, he can come to see you both," I said. They said their goodnights with tiredness as their excuse, but the young ones had already taken out the musical instruments and it was about to get very loud with the pipes and all the other musical instruments, as well as the lovely singing voices of their new sons in law and my sons.

Hugh was keen to get back to his wife and Grigor ran up the stairs after him.

30. The Day of the Wolf

The night had come to reveal the wolf pups' existence and Zahra's ability to shape shift into a wolf whose name was Crystal, as well as her protector, Winter Wolf, to both Hamish and Malcolm Og. Grigor and Zahra had asked the Fairy King to be present also, not being wholly confident of their success, as well as myself, the twins' father, and Ailsa, Cinaed and Isobel, along with the whole family, including the now aging, Grigor Og. Hector was supportive, they knew that, as was his wife and my granddaughter, Flidas. Causantin would be there too, as it was his weekend at home. Ali and his wife April as well as Kenneth and Ivy had to be there too, so no-one was left out of the loop. I had chosen that night to bring along my security guard Colm MacKenzie, to see whether he would like to work on the mountain, as I had found a replacement for him, and Colm was keen to move back to the MacKenzie lands to be closer to his growing family.

They all arrived independently of one another except Ali, April, Kenneth, and Ivy, who arrived all together in one carriage. My oldest son, Alex with his wife Mairi, also came accompanied by Angus and my daughter Islay MacKenzie. They were all curious as to what the big announcement was.

Both families were now very intermingled.

A feast had been arranged by Zahra's, MacKenzie staff, consisting of salmon, trout, beef stew, vegetables of every kind from Hugh's Garden and homemade bread and bannocks enough to feed an army. Dessert was an enormous chocolate roulade with home grown strawberries and cream from the goat's milk. Fresh fruit juices from carrots, celery, apples, plums, and cherries were plentiful, so hopefully no-one would feel the need the bring any alcohol. Padruig wasn't invited this time, but Zahra's, three trout farmers were present and all were Clan Fraser. All the staff were invited too, including cleaners, cooks and chimney sweeps, the Fraser accountants and even Aonghus

MacGregor, my cousin and lawyer with his wife Annabel, with everyone's bairns. It was even more exciting than a wedding, but the atmosphere was more controlled and mature, with respect for both Masters of the house, as well as the lady of the house Zahra, herself.

Upon entering the mansion, the first thing you see is the enormous portrait, painted by Cinaed, of the three lovely parents of this huge happy family, growing by the day.

It was Grigor Mohr MacGregor, who spoke to everyone after dinner had been served and everyone had said all their greetings and had caught up with one another.

"My dear wife Zahra and fellow husband, Hugh Chisholm, my family and respected in laws and my dear friends, may God grant his blessings on this gathering here on this auspicious night. Amen. Our wife, Zahra has a particular talent, yet unknown to you all, except to our son, Hector and our dear friend, The Fairy King of the Sidhe, for those who are yet to meet his esteemed self and his wife. Zahra has learned from Cinaed a very rare skill indeed and one not to be repeated. She has learned how to shape shift into another form, which was practised in the days of Auld by the Druids and our last genuine Druid sitting here is Cinaed," Grigor spoke in a grandiose manner.

Then the daughters of the Sidhe had all been tasked with carrying a wolf puppy each, into the room.

"Some of you may be surprised to see that we have wolf pups in our mansion, but they are part of our family now too and we will train them as they grow up. These pups are only now four weeks old. Their Mither, is our wife, Zahra and the father to these pups is Zahra's protector wolf known as, Winter Wolf," Grigor said.

The Winter Wolf was then instructed to appear. Then Zahra went over to her husband's Grigor and Hugh and stood between them.

"Zahra can shape shift into a lovely, harmless grey wolf whom we ask you all, not to shoot, even if you feel inclined to do so, as she is our wife," Grigor said.

Zahra then demonstrated the shape shifting into the wolf and played around the lounge room with her pups, while everyone watched on in shock and some in sheer amazement. Others were stunned, some joyful and others speechless or the shock, made them feel like reaching for a rifle.

"I have seen Ma feeding her pups and then change back to her human self, so I can personally verify this as a fact and this is not a magician's act," Hector said, adding to the validity of what his father was saying.

"We intend to keep them all on this mountain, enclosed by fencing that is underway now and their training will be rigorous. As you know, my wife is very knowledgeable about wolves and they are inclined to her, for an unknown reason, so now we offer you all here to ask any questions you might have," Grigor added. "Hugh is a very good dog trainer from his Collie dog breeding days and his knowledge has been invaluable as has been the Fairy King and Cinaed to whom we show our gratitude for this opportunity to return wolves to Scotland who will do you no harm," Grigor added.

Grigor then waited on a response from the gasping group, especially when Zahra then returned into human form covered, over once again by her husbands, then she dressed.

My son, Hamish was bristling at the sight of a wolf and felt the need to reach for a weapon but didn't have one, due to it being a family dinner. He had been practising with me, to be accurate in his kills, so as not to just injure a poor beast, but to kill it outright. Hamish was faced then with a dilemma. His Mother-in-Law could be in his line of site one day, and he could accidentally kill his wife's Mither.

Dihaoine was so excited by the sight of the puppies and automatically ran to play with them, horrifying, both her new husband Malcolm Og and me. I was well known to be a wolf killer, and this all flew in the face of my son's understanding of the environment, in which they lived, and I probably said all the wrong things.

"How can my sons feel safe living here now with their wives, if you have a wolf pack roaming all over this mountain?" I asked. "If they are not permitted to kill them, excluding Zahra if she chooses not to shape shift into a wolf, my sons' families will have to return home to Glengarry, where it is safe," I said.

"I can learn to live with it Da, if both my new Da's and my Ma take care of us all," Malcolm Og said. "I don't want to return to Glengarry now. I love it here on the mountain and my new family are so honest. They didn't have to tell us all tonight, but they have, in the hope that we will accept Ma as a wolf Mummy for a time and it must feel awful if we can't accept her as a wolf Mummy," my son added.

"My wife Dihaoine loves the wolf puppies, and she would be upset if she was forced to leave her home. I can't do that," Malcolm Og added. "I am married now Da, with all due respect to both you and Ma, I have to mind my wife and her family, and we are all settled here, even if Hamish has reservations, I don't," Malcolm Og said. "Both our Da's are big strong men who have weapons, which they would use if they had to, if we were ever in danger. Is that right Da and Da?" Malcolm Og asked.

"That's correct son," Gregor said.

"I love it Ma and both Fathers. Congratulations. Can I please do this too Cinaed?" Isobel asked.

Cinaed looked thoughtful momentarily.

"I can help you achieve having a wolf protector, my darling, but you don't need just a wolf, that was your Ma's choice. You could have a bear for instance to protect you, which would be terrifying when you think about it, but it wouldn't be able to propagate anyway. There must be two bears, two wolves and so on, one male one female. If you did want the wolf, like your Ma, the danger could be an eventual larger pack of wolves that would become known about, and this must be kept a secret. That would bring the hunters here, especially the English. I would prefer it if you helped Ma with these puppies that we already have my darling," Cinaed said patiently.

"Can I help with them too Ma?" Isobel asked.

"Aye darling, you can," Zahra said.

Coinneach Og was already playing with them, as was Causantin while the adults all watched on.

"Mistress Zahra, may I speak," asked Mr Fraser from Zahra's trout farm.

"Aye, Mr Fraser please speak," Zahra said.

"There have been stories of wolves here on the mountain for many centuries and I am also of the Unalive and have watched and heard them come and go but never have we in Fraser Ville ever experienced any attacks on people or livestock from wolves from this mountain and I trust Mistress Zahra and Master Grigor and Master Hugh with our lives, enough to keep working here, without any concerns. Thank you for telling us and we will keep your secrets Masters and Mistress and will take our leave now, while you decide what to do. I wish you all well," he said, and the three Frasers left and went home.

Aonghus MacGregor asked if he could give a possible legal perspective which was agreed to. "If it becomes known that you are breeding wolves, with no intention to kill them and an unfortunate matter, beyond your control occurs, whereby one or more of your wolves' attacks or kills either local people or livestock, then you may be taken to Court over it. We don't have the laws yet to blame an individual for such a thing, but it could still be argued in Court. Of course, shape shifting could not be a part of the legal argument, so where or how you came by the wolves would be asked of you. Therefore, my advice to you is to ensure you make the fencing secure, so they can't leave this property, have them wear collars perhaps to make them appear like pet dogs, include other breeds of dogs here also with collars to confuse people what dogs you have, other than wolves, such as Collies and Irish wolf hounds," he suggested.

"They can all still form packs, no matter the breed of dog or wolf and attack the local livestock. I do agree with the collars though, but mixing those breeds isn't wise," Hugh advised.

"Just so long as you know that people will fear them, as Hamish Og here tonight has demonstrated," Aonghus said.

"Nae Uncle, I'm not fearful. I just needed to protect my wife," Hamish Og said.

"Do you wish to come home to Glengarry lad then with Fatma?" I asked.

"Nae Da, thank you for asking. Misty Mountain is our home now. It was a shock at first, that was all. I'll get used to the idea slowly and I promise that I'll never shoot you Ma," Hamish Og said.

"Don't shoot any wolf son on our mountain, as one of them will be our family," Grigor said. "What you do with your Da, elsewhere, is none of our business but these wolves are our business. Can you all keep them a secret and all keep them safe?" Grigor asked.

Looking at the sweet little faces of the pups, it was hard to imagine them ever as a threat, but Scottish people had been conditioned into believing that any wildlife, like bears, lynx and wolves, were to be destroyed. The Fairy King had words of wisdom from the days of Auld when people and nature were once at peace with one another.

"Once the seasons became established and the snow melted, the lochs grew in size and were filled with numerous varieties of fish, plants and trees grew and herbs of many kinds. There was peace amongst us, the Sidhe and the Gods and Goddesses of Auld, as well as all the earth's beasts that walked upon her. It all started to change when the newcomers came and started to take over and then peace was no more. Magnificent forests were burned down to kill the wolves and the bears and the Sidhe. The majestic forests then were all gone and so was the peace. Now to achieve peace, we must all work harder at it. This is what our friends here on Misty Mountain are trying to achieve," The Fairy King said.

"In addition, the Druids kept their teachings from being written down, as did the Pictish people to protect the knowledge from invaders such as the Romans, the Nordish folk and the Normans. But who taught the Druids? We the Sidhe taught them shape shifting, so if Master Cinaed is uncomfortable with you revealing this secret of auld of yours Mistress Zahra, I will teach you, with your husbands' permission," he added.

"If authorities start making witchcraft accusations of ye, we will help you vanish the mountain once again and they will never find any of you, including the wolves," and the Sidhe all departed with their family. "Go in peace my friends." He said.

Kenneth MacNachten, Art Gallery owner, artist, and close friend, as well as my brother was then asked for his opinion.

"I am always sad when I come here to Beinn Coinneach. I enjoyed it here one time when I was once friends with Lord Coinneach, now Zahra's ex-husband. I thought we all shared a closeness. You were still disabled then Zahra and I had to help you put your boots on, after he dressed you. There was a time when he wasn't all bad, although I know what he did to you later and who he became, but I still have difficulty when I am here to think clearly. All I can say is I don't care if sweet little innocent lives, like those puppies can enjoy life in preference to meeting a gruesome death, because of the fears of some people, then so be it. Let them live.

I also need to tell you all my family and my friends, that my doctor and nephew, Alex, seated with us all tonight, has told me that I have little time left in this living world, because of the damage done to my body, when I was an alcoholic. I hope to meet you Zahra and family again, after I pass away. Anyway, leave the wee puppies alone Malcolm my dearest, sweetest brother. If anyone deserves some happiness, it's the gentle Zahra. She has suffered too much, but never complains and the puppies make her happy and her good husbands can see that. Now it is time for me to sleep. Goodnight my friends and family," Kenneth said.

Ivy and Kenneth then departed for bed as the tired and sickly friend, struggled up the stairs.

Kenneth's announcement was too much. April, his daughter hadn't been told of her father's illness, neither had I, nor my wife Ailsa. First it was April who burst into tears over her father's illness and Ali, her husband had to comfort her, but I was the one that no-one had seen cry in a long while, since Old John MacDonnell's funeral. I held my head in my hands as tears flowed freely, while my wife, Ailsa consoled me. Ali took April to bed but passing past me, he patted me on my shoulder and offered any assistance I needed.

"I will leave your wolves alone Grigor and family. All the best in training them," I said, before going to bed as well.

It was an unexpected and sad ending to the night, with Kenneth's news that then overshadowed everything. He was the gentle and loving soul, who had helped Zahra on more than one occasion, but the most memorable occasion was the time he mentioned, when he slept in the same bed as she and Coinneach, when they were happily married. It was always a raw topic when raised with Grigor, still carrying the guilt of her being in the mansion, due to the curse on him inflicting terrible injuries to Zahra.

He hadn't yet forgiven himself, even if she had.

"Zahra have you forgiven me for why you were here at all, with being disabled?" Grigor asked tearfully.

Zahra was already upset at the news of Kenneth's illness, but to then see her husband taking on blame was too much for her, as she threw her arms around her precious husband. "Of course, I have. You and Hugh are everything to me. It wasn't your fault, you know that. It wasn't your fault, my darling, sweet Grigor" she said wiping away his tears. She sat down with him holding him and Hugh held his shoulder.

"We support each other my brother" Hugh said. "The good news is the wolf pups won't be shot." Hugh said.

Both Malcolm Og and Hamish Og came over to the three of them seated now together looking miserable.

"Did you tell everyone about the pups because of us, Ma and Da's?" the twins asked.

"Aye lads, we had to make sure that you didn't shoot Zahra, if she ran outside one day to chase her puppies, on impulse. She's like that. Impulsive," Grigor said.

"Would you prefer that we left, Da's and Ma?" they both asked.

"Nae. God forbid, nae. This is your home now my precious lads. We all love you both and our daughters love you and it's done now," Hugh said. "You might even like the wolves one day, perhaps?" Hugh said.

Dihaoine led Malcolm Og to them, and Zahra asked if Isobel could take them all together back to Zahra's room into their bigger wicker basket, accompanied by Malcolm Og and Hamish Og too, if he wanted. Isobel held one lovingly, so the others followed and went up.

31. The Coast Story

Coinneach Og looked upset, so Grigor picked him up, as heavy as he was.

"What's the matter my son?" Grigor asked.

"I wanted to tell you all the story of what happened when we went to the coast with Da's carrots and how I helped sell them too," Coinneach Og said, sobbing.

"How about you tell everyone at breakfast time, then my son. I am so proud of you selling carrots too," Grigor said.

"Are you Da. Are you proud of me too?" Coinneach Og asked.

"Aye, my sweet lad. You clean up all the manure for the carrots and you went on that big team with the big lads and Da and you sold carrots. Of course, I am proud of you, and I love you too," Grigor said giving him a big kiss on both of his cheeks.

"I love you too Da. I'll try to tell my story at breakfast then," Coinneach Og said.

"One mean lady tried to trick me Da into giving her free carrots in her basket," Coinneach Og said.

"Did she now?" Grigor asked. "Now off to bed with you my son, or you'll be too tired to tell the story at breakfast time," Grigor said.

"Hugh, what's this about young Coinneach nearly being cheated, down by the coast with the carrots?" Grigor asked seriously.

"I was going to tell you both, but this took precedence. He did good though. He knew that she was up to no good. He's a clever wee lad," Hugh said proudly.

That conversation then overtook wolves and Kenneth's poor health, all the way up the stairs with Zahra passing the others, as they went down. They didn't interrupt, as it was obviously a family matter that the parents were all discussing and were still going on about when wee Hugh needed a feed, so Zahra began to feed him listening in on all that happened at the coast.

Hugh began to tell the story.

"The first commercial crop of carrots had all been loaded up onto the Team to take to the coast a few days ago, where they would undercut the price of the other man, also selling carrots, which made us very busy and women came running from all directions from every wee Croft to get the cheaper carrots, for their families to eat, not just for the horses. Obviously, those people were already hungry, and the famine must be in its early stages. The lads kept moving the horses forward, as they emptied it more and more and to steady the horses too, who were getting upset by the sudden appearance of such a large crowd.

Coinneach Og had to get down out of the back at one stage to give one lady her basket of carrots and she had already paid, when another woman at the end of the line asked him to fill her basket for her, so she could jump the queue, as well as not pay. When Coinneach Og filled her basket with the carrots, he realised that she hadn't paid and brought them to me, while I was busy with all the other ladies," Hugh said.

Pointing to her in the line Coinneach said, "Da this is for that lady, but she hasn't paid yet."

Hugh then described the wild scene.

The woman then yelled out at wee Coinneach, "You wee shite, you could av given em to a hungry family".

He might look four years old, but he is not yet three and it really upset him to be yelled at. I then yelled back at the old Crohn and said, "you won't get any you old Crohn if you speak to my son like that and you'll pay twice what the rest pay, so apologise or you'll nae get your basket back," I said.

"So that's what happened. She said sorry, then stood in line, real quiet like and when it got to her, we charged her the same and gave her, her carrots," Hugh said. "But Coinneach pished on her carrots before we gave em to her. Real proud of Coinneach," Hugh said smiling and laughing at the memory of it.

"He didn't pish on her carrots, surely not. Och Hugh, that's disgusting," Zahra said.

"Och, she can wash 'em darling," Hugh said. "It's nae half what he does in the carrot garden. He shites in there too, as well as pish. "Good manure Da" Coinneach says, and then he laughs," Hugh said.

"Does he shite in the rose bush carrot's garden too?" Zahra asked.

"Nae not there, he's quite the character. I had no idea he was so cheeky while being sensitive too, but I don't stop him, and he enjoyed himself with the big lads sitting in between them both. He wanted to steer the horses. He might make a Teamster one day. He loves it up there and they really have taken to him. They said he's a lot like they were when they were young," Hugh added.

"Och nae. I hope not," Grigor said. He was aware of the twins' exploits with married woman in the past.

"Do you mean the music and the singing then my darlings?" Zahra asked innocently.

"Aye, musical lad one day, maybe," he said, hiding their exploits.

"Grigor, you are not telling me something aren't you?" Zahra said.

"It's nae Grigor's fault," Hugh said.

"What isn't?" she asked.

"You tell her Hugh, not me," Grigor said.

"The lads used to have a reputation with the married ladies on the Teamster runs. According to Hugh Og, they had a competition as to how many married women they could service, while their husbands were out or away, until Malcolm Og met Dihaoine and gave up all his women to Hamish Og, who got bored with so many and with no competition, so he wanted to settle down too, like his brother and luckily, he fell in love with Fatma," Hugh said looking guilty.

"And you both didn't tell me this?" Zahra asked.

"Sorry love, they were just rendy lads," Hugh said.

"It's healthy, and it kept all those women happy and no doubt a few bairns too. Malcolm has raised them well, like real men," Grigor said.

"Yes, like men," both Hugh and Grigor agreed, so it could not be argued.

"Well, if my sons in law are real men, I don't mind," Zahra said. That then worried them.

"Not as manly as us, mind," Grigor added.

"Prove it then, my manly men," Zahra said, and the pleasure began.

"By the way Hugh, if Coinneach is going to learn how to be a Teamster, he has to start learning Erse now," Zahra said. Hugh tickled her and she was unable to speak any more with Hugh on one side and Grigor on the other, both keen to prove themselves.

One thing that they all enjoyed was a healthy sex life, as well as the love and devotion to one another. Padruig Dubh, however was never far away in the background doing what he was best at doing, which was breaking up couples in love, whether it was Alex and Peter, or Zahra, Hugh, and Grigor. It was not surprising that Zahra's nightmare then in the early hours of the following morning, was Padruig Dubh Grant doing just that and trying to entice both of her husbands into one of the many battles of the Victorian era with British colonial expansion. Zahra awoke crying as Grigor and Hugh both were asking her what was wrong.

"Oh, Grigor and Hugh please don't leave me. Promise you won't leave me, or baby Hugh and wee Coinneach," Zahra pleaded and kept crying.

"Tell me your bad dream Zahra," Grigor patiently asked.

"Padruig goes to all seven of you, to re-unite to become 'warriors again' were his words. He entices Alex to leave Peter, whose Medical Practise has suffered because of the homosexual rumours, once more circulating. Peter becomes a shattered man both emotionally and in his business. But then Padruig starts on you both as well. He makes you both feel immoral at first, for being in the type of marriage, that we are in, then he makes you feel like you are not real men and encourages you both to fight in one of the many of Queen Victoria's battles. There are endless wars and battles under her reign, and it gets worse into the next century with the first and second world wars. We have to protect our sons from all of this, as well as Hector's horses, because they will come after them," Zahra warned.

"We are not leaving you Zahra or wee Coinneach, or wee Hugh. I want to see my son grow to be a man, like me and to protect you and all of the family, not fight for that fat German sympathiser. He can't even speak English and yet they force it upon us," Hugh said.

Grigor was thoughtful, however. "Padruig has already done as you have described Zahra, and your friend Peter is most likely in need right now. Padruig has not yet spoken to Hugh, only me and he tried to make me feel weak, but I will never do to you what has been done to you, ever again. Please trust me and be warned Hugh, that you are next. He is relentless in trying to break us all up. It isn't because he loves Zahra, it's because no-one can love him, not even a ghost, not even his wife in life, Isobel. Women don't like him. When he speaks of love, it has only been for men, never of women. He never wants to satisfy a woman, but he is jealous of what we all have, just the same," Grigor said.

"When did he do that?" asked Hugh.

"After Fatma's wedding, the same day he attacked Zahra," Grigor said. "I can't respect a man who speaks to my woman like that. If he comes here again, don't invite him in Zahra, but if Peter comes, invite him in and help him. Now let's go and hear wee Coinneach Og's story, that he wants us all to hear over breakfast," Grigor said.

Coinneach Og was a classic performer and waited until the whole family, including his parents were there at the breakfast table and began his long story of the day that he went with my twin sons and his Da, Hugh to sell the carrots. The mood was not expected to be light after hearing the awful news that my faithful and loving brother Kenneth was ill and would soon pass away. I, especially, was a man weighed down by grief. The loss of my first wife felt like it had re-emerged as an additional loss, as well as the loss of old John MacDonnell, whom I saw as my second father figure. It didn't help that Bruce had recently died too, as well as my best friend, Hamish on Zahra's Mountain.

I watched on and listened, unenthused at first, as Coinneach Og stood on a chair to be seen by everyone to tell his story with great exaggeration, with Hugh or my twins chiming in to add to it. After a while, I stopped listening, but I was thoughtful. I saw the happiness on the wee lad's face, talking of his first experience in the wider world and concluded that he was needing more experience than just that one trip to the coast. Coinneach Og had rarely left the mountain before that day, that he could remember. Only once when he was a wee bairn but since then, life was between the late Lord Cinaed's house and Misty Mountain.

"Why don't you go more often with my lads, son to see more of the world and learn more about human nature? It can shock you, like that dishonest woman calling you that bad name. I married a prostitute, without my knowledge, but everyone else in Glengarry knew, just as I was trying to establish myself as a farmer, in a new area. The men were all laughing at me, behind my back, at what an idiot I was for being deceived by her, but you were cleverer than I was, so no-one will ever laugh at you, behind your back, be sure of that, young Coinneach," I said and then prepared to leave.

"Not everyone laughed at you Malcolm, I never knew about that, so how could I or Ma or Bruce? You only found out because of the wolf hunt. Sorry Zahra but that was how Malcolm found out, in your house in the Aird," Kenneth said.

"I am so sorry Malcolm about what happened to you and with her and her grizzly end," Zahra said.

"Was it you who painted my ex-wife's corpse then, in that forest?" I asked candidly.

"Aye it was, I wanted to know if you had a killer there in Glengarry and the paintings did sell but they were never dis-played, so it never helped find out who killed her," Zahra said.

"Och, aye it did. The killer bought them and hid them beneath other unwanted items and had prepared to burn them, before he passed away," I added.

"So, who was her killer then?" Zahra asked out of curiosity.

"A man who was justified in doing what he did and who car-ried out justice for me and my unborn wee bairns, that she had killed, as well as his. You don't need his name," I said. "She was going to kill my twins too, but for Hugh here when he was living with Ruth Beaton. I have never thanked you Hugh, but thank God you were there, or my lads would never have taken their first breaths of air," I said emotionally.

"I'm sorry for the paintings then Malcolm and I'm glad they were never seen by your lads, our lads too now," Zahra said.

"At least you know now, why I always want them to be safe," I added.

"I know my friend," Zahra said, sadly.

Both Ailsa and I mounted our horses to leave but just before leaving, I stopped and turned to Zahra and Grigor.

"It is stunningly beautiful up here. I do understand why you would live out your 'Otherworlds' here. I hope it all works out with Colm MacKenzie," I said, and left. Grigor was already walking off to his coos waving as he walked, and Hugh kissed her and told her he was seeding more carrots.

"You won't need as many now, I think," Zahra called out as Hugh walked off too, not imagining that we would be attending Kenneth's funeral in just one more week.

The world would be a much smaller place without him in it.

◇

Zahra had hoped that she wasn't going to be left with the job of explaining the security job to Colm, but she was, and so the first half of the day was either introducing staff, explaining the job, taking him to his room or riding the entire property with him with wee Hugh strapped to her back. The trout fishermen were all pleased to meet him and to learn that Colm's role was security, and they told him what their concerns were in terms of fish theft, poisoning and other possibilities.

Colm asked where Hamish's house had been and was shocked that it had been a safe home, built from solid stone, in a safe location and not in a wind alley, either.

"I'll get your new shirts made Colm if you can give me your measurements. It'll just have Misty Mountain Security embroidered on it. Do you think five shirts and two vests will be enough?" Zahra asked.

"Och, aye Mistress" Colm said.

"Just call me Zahra" she added.

"There is just one other matter. I am hand fast with Florence MacNachten, Flidas' sister, but she didn't come today, awaiting the outcome. I like the look of the job, but I am married, so the room might need to be larger. Do you have a suite suitable for a married couple?" Colm asked politely.

"Och, Jesus, Mary and Joseph, I didn't know you were married. The married quarters aren't where I showed you, they are on the other side of the mansion. Come with me then," Zahra said.

Zahra allocated him Prince Griogar's old quarters, so everything was complete in there, even though she hated that room, but it had a bathing room adjoining it, suitable for newlyweds. His quarters then were underneath Grigor's room, that he rarely used, with an outlook to the front of the property. Zahra showed him the turret also, opening the locked door with her big bunch of keys.

"I built this for Grigor, but he didn't like it at all. The stairs are from his room that he rarely uses, but in case he's in the room, please knock first or ask his permission to use the turret," Zahra added. "Talk with both my husband's tonight too so they can both tell you of their concerns. My concern is Padruig Grant talking down to me when he comes here, so if you can stop that, I'd appreciate that and if you want a proper wedding with Florence, I can arrange it here on our mountain, but not if you were to want it in Glenmoriston," Zahra added.

"That'd be bonny, aye Mistress, the mountain would be fine. It's only for a small wedding anyway. My parents are too old now to come up here," Colm said.

"That means we will have two of Malcolm's sons, and two of his granddaughters. He can't be that worried about the wolves then, if he bought you here and he knew Florence, his granddaughter would follow?" Zahra said.

"We have no fear of wolves. Malcolm is a sharpshooter is all. He shot two wolves in the wolf hunt. It was in all the papers," Colm said.

"So, you know not to shoot any of my wolves, don't you Colm?" Zahra impressed upon him.

"Aye Mistress," Colm added.

Zahra wasn't convinced and was going to keep a close eye on Colm MacKenzie and her pups, who were now hungry, so she left him with Mairi to eat his lunch. She heard her husband's come in later giving him strict instructions to care for their wife, as well as general guard duty of the entire premises. He seemed to think that he had to wear his kilt, but both husbands told him to wear tough long pants, preferably waterproof, because of the weather, and they laughed at Zahra's plans to put him in a Misty Mountain shirt, with security written on it.

"Don't worry Colm, our wife does it to everyone, even Mairi here. It has something to do with tax," Grigor added.

"I love my work shirt Master Grigor and so does my husband Callum. It gives us a sense of belonging and knowing the Mistress cares about us too," Mairi said. "Colm are you going to mention your wee wife, Florence MacKenzie who is moving in as well and we will have yet another wedding?" Mairi prompted her clansman.

"Another one of Malcolm's bairns, is it?" Grigor asked.

"Nae, Master Grigor, Malcolm's daughter Islay and her husband Angus had one son, Padraig and two daughters, one of whom wanted to marry me, even though I am a divorced man with children. Islay's second daughter, Flidas married your son, Hector and mine is the oldest of the two lassies, Florence, so she is Malcolm's granddaughter. We are handfast, so your wife suggested we marry proper like, here on the mountain, if the two of you and her parents all agreed," Colm said.

"I wonder why Malcolm didn't mention that" Hugh pondered. "How many of his offspring will be here then, in total?" Hugh said.

"Can't you count Hugh? That's four. Malcolm Og, Hamish, Flidas and Florence," Grigor said.

"We'll become the House of MacGregor, MacNachten and MacAlpin. Can't forget wee Coinneach and Isobel's new bairn," Hugh said.

"You forgot yourself, ijit, the House of Chisholm," Grigor chipped.

It was amusing to listen to them, and Zahra's heart swelled just knowing her men were downstairs including wee Coinneach in their conversation. She worried about wee Coinneach's feelings about his biological father and dreaded the day that she would have to tell him who he was, but both of her husbands loved him, that was evident.

"Another wedding. Hope your lot aren't as noisy as the others. MacKenzies then, are they?" Grigor asked.

"Aye Master Grigor, my parents are old now and won't come up here, but Malcolm and Ailsa, Islay and Angus will, I imagine, if you all agree to it," Colm said.

"Can you just call us Grigor and Hugh too. It's too formal," Grigor asked.

"Och aye. Every week, can we meet in an office to discuss any concerns I might have, if that's okay?" Colm asked.

"It'll have to be the library for now, until we sort out a special office for that. The accountants have all of our office space," Grigor said.

Hugh and Grigor then went back to work mumbling about Colm. Grigor said to Hugh as they walked off. "He's a bit formal, isn't he?"

"Aye, special office, and all that. Suppose we do have spare rooms on the other side. We could use one of them, but they always seem to have guests in them, just when you think the house is empty," Hugh said.

"He clinks when he walks, have you noticed that. No chance of sneaking up on the enemy, the way we used to," Grigor remarked.

"Aye and a wedding at our expense too. Malcolm knew when to pass him on," Hugh added.

"Revenge for not being able to kill the wolves I reckon," Grigor added. They both grunted the way men do and worked hard all afternoon.

Zahra put pen to paper after feeding her pups to ask permission for Colm MacKenzie to marry Malcolm's granddaughter and Islay and Angus MacKenzie's daughter in their home on Misty Mountain Ranch. In the same letter she asked when Florence was due to arrive and maybe, instead of two trips, they could make it just one for the wedding which would be a small affair, according to Colm as his parents were too old or too superstitious to come and also felt it unwise to invite his teenage children because the fear and legends of Misty Mountain were too real for some folk, who believed they would never return if they went onto the mountain. A Priest could come who was known to them, but if they objected and had other plans, please let them all know, by return mail.

After Mairi posted the letter, she just waited on Malcolm's decision.

While she had her pen out, she also wrote to her son, Ali for his advice on growing two oat crops for both bread and parridge on the mountain and given there may be another wedding, he could attend that as well, because Malcolm's granddaughter was handfast to the new security man, Colm MacKenzie. Of course, she gave him intricate details of where she wanted the oats to grow and how much trouble they had gone to, to acquire the kelp. She sent her regards to his wife, April and hoped to see him within a few weeks.

Malcolm was glad of not having to organise a wedding and just sent a small list of guests with a contribution enclosed for costs. He thanked her for arranging it and said two weeks' time suited them as it did the Priest who was an old man now, since she last met with him, but he came up to Misty Mountain Ranch to arrange it with Colm and Zahra. The MacKenzies were once again tasked to cook, and serve the guests, as well as clean up afterwards.

"This must be the smallest wedding that we have ever had Mistress," remarked Mairi.

"Aye. None of his family are coming," Zahra said. It was a relief when it was all over and done with and the two of them, Colm and Florence could live as a married couple normally and the two sisters were thrilled to be re-united. It had the effect of helping Flidas to finally be with child. She had been waiting for her sister all along. Both young women were with child together, so Peter was needed and once again Zahra penned another letter to Peter asking for his services, hoping he was still at the Inverness address and hoping that he was still practicing medicine.

32. Peter's Broken Heart

Colm saw a horse and rider limping up the long road to the mansion on Misty Mountain Ranch whom Zahra identified as the old horse that had belonged to Peter Heath. To onlookers, Peter appeared to be slumped forward in the saddle, so Zahra urgently sent out both grooms to bring him in with Colm, who was strong enough to lift Peter from his horse. Cinaed, who was still there fortunately, helped him to the mansion, together with Colm and were ushered into the small room, now always used for medical or first aid reasons, on the right-hand side of the entry way, as one walked in through the enormous oak, front doors.

Zahra tapped on the floor near her dining table, attempting to attract the attention of the Fairy King not knowing how else to summons him. Peter's problem was not a minor one and he looked close to death.

"I am here my dear Zahra, you don't have to tap on the floor. Just think of me and I am here for you," The Fairy King said as he embraced her. "Tell me your need." After explaining Peter's peculiar condition and who Peter was, the Fairy King then asked.

"Was he a close friend of Alexander MacDonald?" The Fairy King asked.

"Aye, he was, and Grigor said that Padruig had broken up their relationship just recently," Zahra added.

"May Cinaed and I examine him alone, while Mairi runs two separate clean hot baths. One with saline added?" the Fairy King asked.

"I will need the window open, and you need to light scented candles all throughout your mansion. Tell Grigor and Hugh that I need them too, after Cinaed and I have treated him," he said very seriously.

The Fairy King and Cinaed closed the door, and no-one could see what their treatments entailed, but they succeeded in extracting an object lodged well up inside his anal passage, thereby blocking Peter's ability to pass excrement and it was extremely painful. His buttocks had been whipped by someone using a horse whip, as well as his back about twelve times and his skin was broken in places. During this time Zahra was able to make a few clear decisions while lighting the aromatic candles that Dihaoine had made and opening windows.

"Grigor, Hugh can he live here with us for now?" Zahra asked. "Can I send the lads with his keys to collect all of his chemical supplies and medical instruments as well as all of his clothes and those valuable books that I gave him," Zahra asked. The two men agreed while waiting on the work Cinaed and the Fairy King were both completing. Hector went with the lads to help, which was fortunate, because there was another horse left there, who had been left to starve and was in desperate need of care.

"Mairi, can you prepare two hot baths and his room underneath the accountants office," Zahra asked. "Grigor, please prepare yourselves for the smell. Hugh cover, your nose, when you go in there, to ensure that poor Peter passes all that he has inside of him," Zahra said.

In case they vomited, she also gave them a wooden pale to vomit into, which was needed and several chamber pots.

Looking at the extended pantry that she had built for the house, she asked Mairi to free up space for Peter's medicines up high at the end furthest away from the cooking ingredients, and provided no-one went near them, it would work. Mairi put a sign on those shelves, so only Peter could access those medicines, with one of those warnings about poisons signs. Finally, the door opened, and the foul smell wafted out of the door, as Grigor and Hugh both went in then, to assist him to pass what was left inside of him, into several pails. His bowel had been blocked by the object that was intended to kill him.

The family needed a Doctor on the Mountain, and the village needed one too, so Peter didn't need to go back to Inverness anymore. His reputation had been destroyed, once again and his lover and friend stood accused of torturing Peter.

The life of a homosexual, in that era was unthinkably shocking.

"Zahra, I need Zahra," Peter kept saying.

"You will see her my friend after we give you a good wash?" Grigor said as he took the sickly man to his first bath. Blood and excrement continued to make its way out of Peter, so the men called on the Fairy King again.

"My friend. You will heal. Do not despair, you are safe now with friends to stay with, for as long as you want or need," Grigor said.

Grigor's eyes were wet with tears and was reminded once again of what humankind was still doing to one other and his prime suspect for that evil, may have been known to both Hugh and him, but they didn't yet have the proof for that.

"Hugh can you please lift him from the bath with Grigor and take him to the other clean bath, with the clean salted water?" the Fairy King asked. Colm MacKenzie also helped carry Peter to the salinated bath water. The Fairy King spoke some words over the water first, as they put him in and there was no more blood or excrement leaving his body.

"Zahra, you may now come in my dear," the Fairy King said.

"Zahra, oh Zahra my friend. I'm sorry. I am ruined," Peter said.

"Nae my dear friend, you are not ruined. You can stay here for as long as you like or need, and all your medicines and clothes are being collected as we speak and you will have a room of your own here in our home. We will care for you as you have cared for us," Zahra said.

"They jammed an object inside of me that was impossible to remove. It was agony, then they horsewhipped me," Peter said.

"Who did that to you, Peter?" Zahra asked.

"First, Alex broke up with me and left with his possessions and I was simply heartbroken. I didn't understand why he was leaving me," Peter said. "Then I received your letter, so I was preparing to come here. But then he came back in a disguise with a tall friend, also in a disguise, who was wearing black pantaloons and a black shirt and smelled like Turkish coffee," Peter said.

"It was terrifying, just like when Lord Coinneach raped me," Peter added.

"It won't happen to you here Peter and my husbands and I will care for you with our Fairy King and Cinaed, my son in law," Zahra said.

"I don't know how he got it out Zahra but thank God he did, I could have died," Peter added.

"Death's not so bad, so long as you are in the best company, after all I am dead," Zahra said smiling.

"Och Zahra, I have missed you so much. You were always so kind to me and all of the patients. My business is ruined now," Peter said.

"You can practice medicine here Peter. If you like that idea. The village needs a doctor, and we need a doctor. Just think about it while you are getting better," Zahra said.

Peter was dried off with a toul, by Zahra's husbands and they dressed Peter in their own clothes waiting on his to arrive. Mairi had cooked broth, soup, and fish, allowing for Peter's condition.

"Do you want soup now?" Mairi enquired.

"Aye, I could eat. I'm thirsty." Peter said. Everyone sat down then to eat the soup prepared especially for Peter and the bairns all looked on in sympathy at their sickly guest.

"Dr Peter, will you get better?" asked the sweet enquiring,

Coinneach Og.

"Och, aye lad. Thank you, because of your magical family. You are a lucky lad to be a part of this family," Peter said.

"I sold carrots at the coast with my Da and a lady called me a little shite, because I wanted her to pay for her carrots," Coinneach said.

"Really? That's awful. I'm sorry wee Lord Coinneach, you are not that lad. You are a lovely braw lad," Peter said. "Now I think I have to lie down and sleep. Would you all please excuse me?" Peter said still with his English manners and was aided by Zahra's husband upstairs.

"Master Peter, before you sleep, just so you know, my husband, Callum and I are just down the hall from you and up one floor if you need anything in the night. We can also assist you going down the stairs for breakfast early in the morning," Mairi said and gave him a bell to ring, in case she was needed.

There were a lot of questions from the family as to what had happened to Uncle Peter, so Zahra and her husbands decided to tell them that he had been horsewhipped by intruders and Fatma offered her honey to apply to the wounds in the morning because it had antiseptic qualities in it.

After the lads had returned from Inverness, the news of the sick horse didn't go down well as Hector and his father had to put the poor animal down. Zahra's thoroughbred horse that she had given Peter had been stolen also by the thieving intruders. Zahra's brood mare was in foal, so it would be a long wait for another well-bred horse for him to train up, unless Hector loaned him one of his. It was fortunate he wouldn't be keen to ride for some time and would need daily salt baths to prevent infection and manage the obvious pain and to reduce the swelling. Regular walks amongst his roses would be therapeutic, so she planned to ask him to prune them for her in his spare time, given his love of roses. And maybe get rid of the wee beasties on them too.

"Ma, we should stay and help you with Peter so you can still feed the puppies and wee baby Hugh and take them for walks now, as they are ready for that if you have wee collars for them," Cinaed said.

"Thank you Cinaed, male company would be good for him too as well as me. We can all help him as a family I think in our own small ways," she said.

"When he can ride Ma, he can borrow one of my ponies until he gets one of his own," Hector said.

"Thank you, son. It might be a while before he can ride, but please tell him and he will appreciate your kind offer," Zahra said.

Bedtime wasn't the usual happy time that they all experienced together and the three of them lay there on their backs staring up at the ceiling for a while, taking in the day's dreadful events.

"Thank you both for today. You were marvellous," Zahra said. Grigor seemed to need to be held and to hold Zahra more than to make love and he rolled over to hold his wife and began to cry.

"Zahra, was it my fault? Could I have stopped Padruig and Alex? I didn't imagine they were ever capable of what we saw today. Forgive me if I didn't do enough for your friend," Grigor said sobbing.

"My sweet Grigor. I do love you so much. It wasn't anything to do with you. You couldn't have stopped it, despite knowing that Padruig had broken them up, you couldn't have known they would do what they did, if it was them and we must give them the benefit of the doubt. They were in disguise. It may not have been them. I really pray it wasn't them, or maybe you have just accepted that reality and I haven't yet," Zahra said and sobbed too.

Hugh rubbed her back and rolled over to hold them both. "The Fairy King has offered to have him live with them if he is willing to procreate. They have a need to add to their population and Peter needs care and protection. I'll miss him if he goes with them," Zahra said.

It was lucky they had some sleep because during the night Coinneach came into their room crying,

"Mummy, my legs hurt. Da's my legs hurt. Can I sleep with you?" Coinneach asked.

"Aye son come in between Da and I to keep warm. What's wrong with your legs my darling?" Zahra asked.

"I don't know Mummy, they just hurt from my knees down," Coinneach answered.

"My niece had a condition in her legs when she was about ten years old or more, I can't remember exactly, but it was what they called a growth spurt," Zahra said quietly trying not to wake Hugh.

"What's a growth spurt?" Coinneach asked, still crying.

"It's when your body grows suddenly, instead of slowly growing, so it hurts because you can't keep up with how fast you are growing. Do you think you are growing fast?" Zahra asked.

"Aye Ma, I'm going to be the biggest bairn aren't I? Why am I bigger than everyone else in the family Ma?" Coinneach asked.

"Your natural father was Lord Coinneach, you know that son, and he was a very big man, even bigger than your two big Da's here," Zahra said.

"Bigger than Da and Da?" Coinneach asked. He couldn't imagine a man bigger than both of his Da's.

"Aye bigger than these two huge, big Highlander, handsome men with long legs, so maybe he had this problem too when he was a wee bairn. We'll have to ask Uncle Cinaed, or you can ask your uncle if Lord Coinneach had sore legs when he was growing up too," Zahra said.

"What happened to your niece then? How did they treat the soreness?" Grigor asked.

"She had to wear braces on her legs, one leg at a time but we also need to ensure that Coinneach is also getting enough sunshine for his bones to be healthy and maybe drink more milk. Can you drink more milk son?" Zahra asked.

"Can I drink yours please Ma?" Coinneach asked. "Please Ma I won't take too much from wee Hugh," he begged, and she gave in, and he settled down and then slept like a log. After that night, she allowed him to feed from one breast and wee Hugh from the other one as her body adjusted to the nutritional needs of each bairn. Wee Hugh had thicker, more nutritional milk from the left breast and Coinneach had a thinner milk for his nutritional needs from the right breast and sometimes they fed at the same time and Coinneach would pat Hugh or Hugh would pat Coinneach when they reached out to each other, until they both slept peacefully. It helped the pain considerably.

Coinneach didn't need braces but in asking Cinaed about the condition, it appeared that it was a deficiency that the MacAlpins all suffered from and in having a bairn with Zahra, Lord Coinneach was hoping it would go away. The illness is like a type of arthritis that stays with them, through to old age and that was why the old Lord Cinaed had wanted Zahra's breast milk when she was breast feeding, according to Cinaed who was drinking Isobel's breast milk for his pain.

She was shocked to learn that Cinaed suffered from it as well.

In asking Cinaed why they all suffered from this illness, he reluctantly told her that long ago, one of his many times great grandparents had lain with an unwilling woman of the Sidhe, who subsequently was with child and kept prisoner with him, until she had his bairn. He then had her taken away and one presumed that meant that she was killed somehow. The wee bairn developed the illness then from around three or four years of age, and they have all had the same illness, ever since then. Breast milk was all that helped to ease the pain.

"So, was it a curse then?" Zahra asked Cinaed.

"Yes, we thought so," Cinaed said sadly. "It was wrong what he did, and we have all suffered because of it," he said.

"Have you spoken about this to the Fairy King?" Zahra asked.

"Coinneach destroyed their home, why would he help us?" Cinaed said.

"Because he is so kind," Zahra said.

"The Sidhe are not always kind Ma," Cinaed said, and he went about his business. It had an ominous ring to it with centuries of knowledge about each other.

"Be careful how much he does for you. There is always a price to pay," Cinaed said walking away.

33. Coinneach's Grave

"Ma, where is my real father's grave?" Coinneach Og asked.

"Don't you feel like my two husbands are your real fathers, Coinneach darling?" Zahra asked.

"Aye, I do but I still want to know, who he was and where his grave is, Ma," Coinneach said very adamantly.

"Do you remember when Lord Cinaed went missing, presumed to be dead?" Zahra asked.

"Aye," Coinneach answered. "I expected your father's grave to be there on his land when Uncle Cinaed and I had to go there to sort out everything, because it was Lord Cinaed who picked up his body from Cannich, not us. So, I asked Uncle Cinaed where it was, if it wasn't there, and he told me it was in a town named Wick, further north from here. A long way away and on privately owned land where your father's friend, Alasdair Fraser is a tenant. I haven't been there because he could send us away after going all that way," Zahra explained.

"Can we try Ma and go there one day, so I can visit his grave?" Coinneach asked.

"I will try son, but I can't promise anything. I will talk to both your Das and see what they say," Zahra said, and she hoped that the lad would forget it, but he didn't. Asking both Grigor and Hugh about this topic was bound to arouse all manner of discontent, even jealousy, given Zahra had married the lad's father. Zahra didn't know how to go about it, where it would create the least anger or guilt. She certainly couldn't imagine Grigor going with them, to a remote place like Wick. She scoured her brain to remember anything she had ever learned of Wick. It had formerly been Vik, she thought like a Viking name, because originally the old town was a Viking settlement, as well as a fishing port. God only knows who lived there now, with the Clearances in Ross and Caithness.

In 1854, there was a massacre of Ross/Strathcarron [5] mostly of women of Clan Ross in Greenyards. The Landlord was a Munro. Sixty women were violently assaulted by the police who were wearing hobnail boots and carrying truncheons, resulting in deaths and horrific injuries, especially to their breasts and skulls, was all she could remember. Their houses were all burned to the ground and some women were kept in prison in Tain and others in a church in Strathcarron, before many, if not all were transported to British colonies. Alasdair himself may have been cleared, so she asked Colm to accompany her to Fraser Ville to visit Alasdair's father for the address of the farm and wasn't expecting to see the dreaded Alasdair himself. He was sitting inside the forge, nursing a black eye and a head injury, fussed over by a young lady, whom Zahra deduced must have been his wife.

"Hello Alasdair, do you remember me?" Zahra asked.

It turned her stomach when he looked into her eyes, as she clearly remembered her former husband cavorting with this young man. It was enough to lead her to wish to dispose finally of herself had it not been for Peter Heath visiting her on that fateful day.

"Aye, Lady Zahra. I remember you. This is my wife Eloise," Alasdair said, looking ashamed.

"Have you been Cleared from the land in Wick then?" Zahra asked.

"Aye, everybody has. It was a blood bath of mostly the women folk who were at home, and many were killed or beaten to a pulp," he replied.

"Who owns the land you lived on?" Zahra asked.

"The Laird of Ross, I imagine. We hardly had time to pick up all our belongings," Alasdair said.

"Is Lord Coinneach's grave still on that same property?" Zahra asked.

"Aye, it is. With a tombstone, not far from the house that they burned down," Alasdair said, and he gave her the address. "To enter it, you will need the permission of the Laird now, or the police," Alasdair added.

"Lord Coinneach was a Peer. I can demand access as a Peeress. How dare you throw my life and his into hell. You deserve what has been done to you, not to those poor women of Ross, but you do," Zahra said, and she finally got it off her chest.

Colm MacKenzie was a little shocked that she not only knew that he had been Cleared but had known the back story that involved her former husband and that bonny looking lad.

After they left the forge, Colm began asking inappropriate questions.

"How did you know that lad had been Cleared Mistress?" Colm asked.

"Good guess," Zahra answered.

Zahra now was not in the mood for his questions that didn't concern him or anyone else, except poor wee Coinneach. She put pen to paper immediately with her Peeress title, demanding access to the property where her Peer ex-husband, Lord Coinneach was buried and to remove his grave for the sake of his son, Lord Coinneach now that it was no longer in the hands of her husband's old friends. She wrote another letter to the paper expressing disgust at the Ross Massacre [5] which affected her ability to visit her husband, Lord Coinneach's grave, for his son, the current Lord Coinneach. There was already a public outcry over the Ross massacre resulting in many women becoming either insane because of their head injuries or who were shipped to the colonies to make way for sheep. Her letter at least balanced the London newspapers from painting those women as the perpetrators of the crimes and not the heavy handed, drunken and violent policemen.

At home, she was met with pride from Coinneach Og, but anger from both Hugh and Grigor who had been fully informed by the nosey Colm MacKenzie and then the newspapers and then Cinaed, asking her to explain herself. No-one, except wee Coinneach, took her side for involving herself in political matters in Ross Shire, of all places. She was quiet for a time, and heard them all out, but she was simmering underneath it all, as the injustices of the past, flooded into her mind, one after the other, and felt for those poor women, as well as herself.

"My son, Lord Coinneach MacAlpin, has the right to know where his father's grave is and where it can be relocated to now because of these Clearances in Ross Shire. [5] Alasdair did not own that land, the Laird still does, who I have written to also, using my Peeress. Lord Coinneach was a Peer, and his body cannot be left in a paddock full of bloody sheep," Zahra said in anger to them both.

"Look at wee Coinneach will you please. My son asked me if he could see his father's grave and that is what I discovered. Alasdair, the little swine, is back in Fraser Ville. Have I really committed a crime against this family, if I have defended a wee part of it, wee Coinneach, who is Lord Coinneach now?" Zahra asked.

They backed down seeing her rationale and her rare outburst of anger.

"Nae, I suppose not. Coinneach, I will help you get your father's grave from Ross Shire if I must dig it up myself," said Hugh.

"I will too," Grigor added unhappily. "Where is he going to be buried then Zahra, not here surely?" he asked.

"My place. Coinneach Og can visit him every week if he likes," Cinaed said.

"Don't you both love me as much as everyone else, because he was my father?" Coinneach Og asked both Grigor and Hugh.

"Of course, we do love you son, but your father was an asshole," Grigor said. "We know you are more like your

Mummy, thank God, without the evil that man had inside of him," he added.

"Och, did he Mummy?" Coinneach Og asked.

"He was a liar darling and many other bad things too, as you know, he hurt your big brother Hector, but he was not all bad, as Uncle Kenneth said, the other night. They were friends my darling. No-one is all bad, but it is lucky that you are more like me, as your Da said, and I replaced your real Da with these two good men, so you could have the best Da's ever, in the whole world. Look at how Da Hugh taught you about the carrots and Da Grigor taught you how to ride a pony and to drive the cart. That is a real father who kisses you goodnight and cares for you every minute of every day," Zahra said.

"I know Ma. I just need to know who I am, and why I am so big," Coinneach Og said.

"I can show you an old drawing that I did of what he used to look like, my son, before I knew that he was very evil," Zahra said. "You will get that big too son". Zahra showed him the only drawing she had sketched of him from very early in their relationship and she hadn't shown it to anyone. Now everyone crowded around Coinneach Og to see the drawing.

"He doesn't have many clothes on, Ma," Coinneach Og commented.

"It was bathing time, sweetheart," Zahra answered, not altogether truthfully.

"Thank you Cinaed for your kind offer. We accept. Do you know if he was buried in a coffin or a shroud at least, because we may need to go there? Although, I do need to wait for the letter from the Laird of Ross, with permission to enter first. It seems like a very serious situation that they don't want anybody to know the true facts about," Zahra added.

"A coffin sister," Cinaed said thoughtfully. "I wouldn't open it though, if I was you, it might be empty because of his sins,"

Cinaed added.

"Empty?" asked Coinneach Og.

"Aye it might be lad, but not because of his sins. If one of those people during the Clearances has disturbed his grave. He could turn up anywhere," Grigor added.

The twins were then listening in with great concern, as they always did and offered to take the Team to Wick, so a heavy headstone could go in the back, as well as the coffin. Hector offered to assist also on horseback and Coinneach Og wanted to go too, so that meant that they may need to sleep in the back at night with the coffin for two nights, unless they sat with the lads.

"I'm sitting up top with the lads and I'm going armed," Grigor said.

"Can we take it in turns?" asked Hugh, also anticipating being met with violence.

Zahra was looking distressed, as was young Coinneach, so Cinaed suggested he take them both up to her bed for a rest, which he did. That left the sitting room buzzing with questions from Hamish and Malcolm Og, as well as Flidas, while Isobel just sat and listened in. Colm MacKenzie was trying to absorb the family dynamics to fit in, but wasn't doing very well on that front, as both Hugh and Grigor answered questions that even Dihaoine and Causantin hadn't known.

Standing by the fire warming his hands, Hugh then burst out with, "What the feck?" he exclaimed. "It's him!" Hugh said.

Cinaed had since returned from upstairs and was then seated beside his wife, Isobel. He turned in the direction where the now, pale looking Hugh was staring. It was Cinaed's long-deceased brother, the former Lord Coinneach, dressed in nothing but an old cloth, covering only his genitalia. He was dirty, unkempt and smelled terrible. His expression was of confusion initially, as he looked around Zahra's mansion. The last time he had seen it, the décor was very different, and the spectre then began to speak, much to everyone's horror.

"What on earth has Zahra done to my place? What bloody awful décor," Lord Coinneach declared.

'At least we agree on one thing,' Grigor thought to himself, with a concealed smile. They had all just tolerated what Zahra thought was beautiful and they had thought was ugly. It made Zahra happy and that was all that mattered. Grigor concluded there must be a reason for the Turkish décor, other than its mere looks, like perhaps she had a grandparent who was Turkish.

No-one dared to speak to the undressed spectre, not even Mairi or her husband, Callum, never having seen him in such a dreadful state of undress and filth. Considering he had just been the subject of discussion, concerning his grave, Lord Coinneach was meant to be under the ground, why was he suddenly inside their loungeroom?

"Did someone summons me here? Those arseholes in that dreaded place, Wick or was it Strathcarron, broke open my bloody grave, but I just up and walked out of it. You should have seen the beggars flee at the sight of me, so I just grabbed a curtain from that burning wee croft to wrap around myself and came here. So where is Zahra and where is my son?" Lord Coinneach demanded. "And who are all of these people in my house?"

Cinaed then thought he had better say something.

"Hello brother. It's me Cinaed," he said.

"I can see that, you bloody ijit. Where is my wife and my son?" the spectre of Coinneach asked once again.

"I'll get your son, Coinneach brother," Cinaed said. Cinaed went back up to Zahra's bedroom where the lad lay sleeping peacefully beside his Mither.

"Coinneach, your real Da is here to see you, just like you wanted," Cinaed said as he picked him up and carried him downstairs, without disturbing Zahra.

He took him over to the spectre of Lord Coinneach, while the lad was still half asleep and thinking Cinaed had meant his other fathers. Handed into the smelly, hairy big arms of the spectre, wee Coinneach then opened his eyes fully, then screamed bloody murder and struggled to free himself then ran to Grigor and held tightly to his legs first. He tried to climb up him, as if Grigor was a tree, screaming all the while.

Coinneach MacAlpin, Grave

"Who's dat Da, who's dat dirty bad man? Da, Da. Hold me, hold me Da," poor Wee Coinneach kept repeating in sheer panic.

"It's alright son. I've got you. That is the spectre of the man that you were asking us about. Your real father who you wanted to see. Now you have seen him and smelled him," Grigor said.

"But he's not meant to be here. He's meant to be in a grave in the ground Da, not in our house," Coinneach Og screamed.

Zahra heard the commotion from her bedroom and despite sleep calling her to stay a while longer, she had to answer the call of her son's screams. Grigor's brain was ticking overtime, as to how to rid themselves safely this time of the spectre, without killing someone else.

As Zahra appeared, the spectre of Lord Coinneach was momentarily occupied with the sight of her loveliness, while Grigor spoke to his daughter, Isobel.

"Isobel, come here love. Do you still have some of those silver musket balls?" Grigor asked.

"Aye Da," she said, and Isobel took them from her apron pocket where she kept her musket too, surprisingly.

"Don't shoot anyone today, Isobel. Only we men will do the shooting, but you can keep your weapon," Grigor said.

Isobel then took all the younger women, like Flidas, Florence and Dihaoine, upstairs to where they had all of the wolf pups, who were now half grown. Isobel was teaching the lassies how to shoot after learning of the Ross Massacre from her Mither and she was going to kill anyone who entertained the idea of coming anywhere near her or her family, especially the wee ones and what Da Grigor said, she took with a grain of salt. If she had to shoot, so be it, she would shoot.

"Bloody hell," said Zahra upon seeing her ex-husband, semi naked in her loungeroom. "Why are you here?" Zahra asked.

"This is my home woman, is why I am here and who are all of these people?" he demanded once again.

"Husbands and wives. You've been gone a very long time," Zahra replied. "Go and wash. You are filthy, you smell awful and get dressed, there are bairns here," Zahra insisted.

Surprisingly he went to take a bath and put some clothes on. She then stood by the fire behind her two big husbands, who were discussing how to kill it with young Malcolm Og and Hamish, as well as Colm and Hector, all now armed with silver musket balls.

"Is this the man that harmed ye Hector?" Hamish asked seriously.

"Aye, it is, and I want to get the last shot into his brain," Hector said with a vengeance. All three young men were fired up to kill this beast of a man, not expecting what came next. Zahra heard his footsteps then change from a human being into a huge brown wolf. Cinaed must have helped his brother after all. Zahra took charge and commanded them all.

"Stop. Don't shoot yet. Put down your weapons. He has and is the new brown wolf," Zahra commanded. Coinneach wasn't supposed to have another wolf, but he had obviously been helped by his brother Cinaed after all, with an equally nasty wolf, like the one he once had. Cinaed had explained his position where he couldn't refuse his brother, both being Druids, but he could have told them that Coinneach was back on Beinn Coinneach and had made that request of him. She was disappointed in her son in law.

The Winter Wolf came out from inside of her, being able to smell the giant brown wolf, as Zahra began to shape shift into her own lovely grey wolf. Isobel could see that change taking place from the balcony above them and released Zahra's half-grown wolves, who could support her. Zahra's Winter Wolf met the spectre wolf of Lord Coinneach, meeting it at the bottom of the stairs and communicating through thought, the spectre wolf conveyed,

'What do we have here? An aged grey wolf and a little girlie wolf.' Then he immediately launched into an attack onto the female wolf of Zahra grabbing at her throat with his sharp lupine teeth. The Winter Wolf leapt onto him from behind, as the young wolves were all encircling them.

"What do we do?" asked Hamish.

"Wait," said Grigor. The Winter Wolf already had the brown wolf pinned down and was ripping out his throat, when he called upon his young wolves to attack also, so it became a frenzied attack on the one brown  wolf, while Zahra's lupine body lay motionless. Had the brown wolf pierced a vital artery? Blood was gushing from her lupine throat and her wolf's beautiful mane of grey hair was becoming soaked in blood, as was her beautiful Turkish rug. Upon realising their Mither's demise, many of her bairns began to cry out loud, even Isobel cried out for her Mither, thinking she had lost her.

The Fairy King then appeared urgently once more and pulled the lifeless body of Zahra's wolf aside, who was returning back into her human form, while her other wolves were doing their job well. The Fairy King tried his best, but Zahra's life was departing her, this time, and she asked to see her husbands. To anyone watching on, they had lost Zahra, as she was covered over carefully by the Fairy King

Upon seeing Hugh, she said, "My Celtic God Lugh."

34. The Celtic God Lugh

Hector was poised to end the brown wolf when he had the chance without killing either one of Zahra's own young wolves. They then stood back, as if to allow him to do his work and Hector ended the life finally of that spectre. However, Hector's Mither lay dying when another shock was to greet the family from Misty Mountain Ranch.

The Celtic God Lugh himself appeared, surrounded by a blinding bluish light, and was carrying a long spear, a sword and a sling shot at his waist belt. He had responded to being called upon. He carried Zahra upwards and back into her true and glorious human form, high up to the ceiling of her mansion where the two of them glowed in perfect health which only he could restore. She was wearing a shiny, bluish shimmering gown to the ankles and was calmly looking down upon them all lovingly.

The two of them lit up the mansion with a strange bluish light. His big voice boomed throughout the huge mansion, and it bounced off the walls, but no-one could quite remember what he had said. Some thought he had said that she was a Goddess of Auld, some thought that he said she was a Priestess, others said it was Irish, others said it must have been Pictish. Zahra's injuries were instantly healed, and she had no memory of being close to death yet again, however she never called her husband Hugh, that name Lugh, ever again nor her Celtic God. It was somewhere in Zahra's memory that she had called on, the actual Celtic God, Lugh and he was gorgeous looking with long blonde flowing hair with a blonde beard and moustache.

Balance was once again restored on Misty Mountain Ranch when Cinaed finally left with the old Lord Coinneach's remains to bury on his own property as he had promised. He also left with some shame at what could have happened to his Mother in Law. Zahra's two husbands, although desperately upset, were especially proud of their wife for taking on that dreaded,

enormous and vicious beast. The stories are told around the firesides to this day as to how the Celtic God Lugh himself, came to her rescue, as she lay dying.

The mystery of who Zahra truly was, having appeared in so many time periods like that of a young King Coinneach McAlpin in ancient Alba, seeing the death of his son King Causantin on a beach in Fife, watching over the massacre on Culloden Field in 1746 and knowing the things that she knew, were all a mystery to her husbands. She didn't mention many other things because it upset her too much. Who knows how long they would all be there in their Otherworlds together and apart, and how much more Zahra would tell them to prepare for, or the Beings that they would encounter, as the centuries passed?

But the most mysterious of all mysteries was the enduring love and devotion between Zahra and her husbands and Hugh and her Sweet Grigor.

THE END

Epilogue

Zahra's spirit wolf, Ulvy Stiorm, promised that he would fight to the death for her, and he did. Zahra buried him in the Craskie Farm cemetery the following day with the name "Ulvy Stiorm" on the headstone, "Great friend to Zahra and Hugh Chisholm."

Hamish and Cora Chisholm were also buried in the Craskie Farm cemetery following the severe storm on the mountain. Grigor Og MacGregor died shortly after Colm MacKenzie's wedding on Misty Mountain Ranch and was buried there too and

Craskie farm was then run by his great grandchildren. James Grant lived to an old age without remarrying, still running the hotel with his spectre guest, Padruig Dubh Grant. James had changed the business name from 'The Hart of the Highland Manor' to 'The Heart of the Highland Manor' because he had no one to take guests hunting anymore and there wasn't the level of interest either. It's heart, with Zarah's portrait, always hung above the front desk.

Marion MacDonald's land, known as 'New Farm', was inherited by both Malcolm and Kenneth MacNachten when she passed away and the two brothers in turn left it to both Ali and April

MacGregor. The homes on the loch, which were rented out to guests, were equally divided between all of both Kenneth and Malcolms' families as well as staff needing a holiday.

Malcolm MacNachten was aging and went to visit his twin sons, Malcolm Og, and Hamish on Misty Mountain Ranch, with his wife Ailsa, who was also aging fast. They all spent the weekend together and were all reunited with family. They talked about old times and all the things that they had been through. Kenneth had already passed away from his kidneys having failed him. Zahra still appeared young, even though Malcolm appeared now old and Zahra wondered then at the value of the Otherworld, with mixing the living with the unalive.

It could be in her next book. Missing Malcolm, unless he joined them too, would be too hard to endure. Malcolm's old farm was to be run jointly by his two youngest children with their industry, while the Old MacDonnell farm was inherited by the twins, although they sold it back to the MacDonnells and continued to live on Misty Mountain then later moved to Loch Insh. Ali and April sold their farm in Glengarry and went to live on New Farm and lived off rents from the other houses, until Padruig offered him work on the oat fields at the Heart of the Highland Manor, where they continued to live. Ali never quite restored his relationship with his Mither again due to his feelings of guilt over his ill treatment of her.

Druidic/ Celtic Photographs

The photographs are by Simone Garset, Chapter 30 in Book 3, of the Druid site and Celtic symbols are genuine but are in Dunino's Den, Fife, Scotland, as well as the old maps of the Highlands. Thanks to a local man, David Chambers in Stravithie Castle, revealing its location. According to David, the Celtic God, Bel from where Beltaine originates, was worshipped in Dunino's Den, Fife long before Christianity was introduced to the Picts. All other photographs in the novel are also attributed to Simone Garset of Spean Bridge, Scotland.

Early Kings of Alba

This book has taken licence in using the name similar to the first King of the first united country of Alba, once known as Pictland, later to become Scotland. Dal Riata was on the west coast, taken over by the Gaels/Irish with the introduction of the Gaelic language. The remainder of Scotland was still under the control of the indigenous peoples, the Picts. The Vikings from both Norway and Denmark were attacking both east and west coasts and it was decided to unite under the one King to combat a common enemy. The Picts had Kings going back centuries and the lists can be found in the National Museum of Scotland in Edinburgh, as well as current texts, that name each one. Dal Riata had a King named Kenneth MacAlpin, otherwise known as Cinaed MacAlpin, who invited the Picts, also known as Pechts (meaning the ancestors), to discuss unity and would then choose a King. All the Pictish Kings and Nobles attended. One account relates that to ensure that King Kenneth MacAlpin became the King over all of Pictland or Pictavia, that he had all the Pictish Kings and nobles killed, but there is no remaining evidence of that as fact. He became then the first King of Alba, but some historians prefer to refer to his son, King Constantine I, as the true first King who died at the hand of Danish Viking invaders and was left decapitated in a cave in Fife, which is still called King Constantin's cave. I visited his cave in September 2023 and was aided to do so by using a short cut to the cave, thanks to the Craile Golfing Society.

The Druidic Curse, was written by Zaynab El-Fatah

"May your cattle wander off at night,
May your chickens cease to lay,
May the wolves eat your sheep,
And your wife's face turn to mush...
by your violent hand....
Lost be your horses, your bairns and your life
Never again will love return to your marriage bed
Only a wolf like stranger can ....
Her face restore.
But love for you will be....
Never more – A Druidic Curse.

About The Author, Zaynab El-Fatah

I was born in a very small town in Western Australia and enjoyed a relatively ordinary life, good friends, a pony club, the swimming club and netball. Agriculture was a big part of my growing up, hence its inclusion in all my current four novels, with variations to include the Scottish farm varieties in both the animals and the crops. Horses appear throughout my writings also because of my continued love of horses.

My daughters and I moved to Queensland in 1992 to the city of Cairns, where frequent cyclones were a threat and the eventual reason for my departure from that lifestyle only to better improve life by living in Brisbane, with its greater amenities and closeness to everything, not to mention employment for my family. One by one the family have moved on, leaving just myself and one schoolteacher daughter and our three cats.

This past year of March 2023 finally saw the publication of my first novel, called 'Isobel of Glenmoriston', followed by 'Secrets of the Braes and Glens' in 2024. There are two more novels in the Isobel series, one named, 'Wolves and the Curse' and the final in the series being named, 'My Sweet Grigor'.

I visited Scotland in September 2023 to ensure that my facts were correct in 'Isobel of Glenmoriston' and to gain new inspiration for all my work, as well as to locate as many of the graves of the Seven Glenmoriston Men, as possible. I was fortunate to find a co-operative lady in the village of Drumnadrochit, in the Highlands who directed me to the grave of Padruig Dubh Grant. Our valued historian, Hugh Allison directed me to Hugh Chisholm's grave, the youngest of the Seven Glenmoriston Men. Donald Chisholm was buried in Canada after moving there, as was John Campbell aka MacDonald. I was unlucky to be unable to locate Grigor MacGregor, Alexander MacDonald or Alexander Chisholm.

I started writing with a greater emphasis on historical facts to include the events of 1745/46, also known as the last Rising in Scotland. I wanted to keep love alive in all the novels as well as history, then moving into fantasy with the inclusion of everyday violence in Scottish life of the period. Not wishing to part with certain characters, they remain as spectres, or ghosts who live alongside the living, without realising it, as time goes on. The emphasis focusses less on history, although it is ever present with the inclusion of fantasy and mythology for the reader with a strong imagination.

The characters are family and friends, who follow the books through until their own deaths at times, but our mysterious author Zahra, decides in the final novel of the four-book series, that will surprise, as the emphasis is even more on the 'Otherworld'. I hope you all enjoy following your favourite characters through these novels.

Zaynab El-Fatah,
Brisbane, Australia.

About the Artist, Claire Karger

Born in New South Wales, then growing up in Western Australia, before moving to Queensland with my family, I had once enjoyed escaping into the canvasses and sketches that I created, being drawn deep into the West Australian bush, or soaring out over the whitecaps of the deep blue ocean. Becoming a schoolteacher in Queensland, I was too busy for art at all. That all changed in 2023.

Portraits were very rarely something that I had painted, as there was no need for them, until my mother wrote 'Isobel of Glenmoriston', and then the need was born.

Starting with the main character of 'Isobel of Glenmoriston', herself, as a pencil and charcoal sketch, I then moved onto using other mediums, including acrylic paints.

My mother's novels moved into mythology and supernatural themes, wolves sprang from the pages and their lives became interconnected with the living and the unalive. Experimenting with painting a wolf one afternoon, Wolfie padded his way through the forest, his eyes looking directly back at me. I looked at him and saw my first beautiful Scottish wolf.

Waterfalls roared, highland coos lay in the grass and hares stood alert in the snow. Rugged men with their beautiful women and children, along with their attractive Celtic Gods, were depicted, from descriptions by the author, in the narratives. The Scottish Highlands became the backdrop for art imitating life.

I thank my mother for the encouragement that she has given me, from when I was a young student interested in art up until now, where I have been given the honour and privilege of contributing the work to her four beautiful novels.

I appreciate the contribution of Scottish based artist, Jonathan Grant and find inspiration in his work.

Claire Karger, Brisbane, Australia

Army of Old John– illegitimate sons, all born to Old John MacDonnell of Glengarry, who were loyal sharp shooters who followed orders from Old John.

Beaton, Ruth – Midwife in Glengarry. Delivers Malcolm Og and Hamish Og. Marries Hugh Mohr and he moves to Glengarry.

Cameron, Annabel – wife to Aonghus MacGregor. Trained nurse. Daughter of Donald and Janet Cameron. Commences the 'Gathering of the Bairns', on Craskie Farm each week. Mother to Hugh Cameron MacGregor. Works in law office after marrying Aonghus.

Cameron, Siobhan – young lady who marries Alexander Og Grant of Loch Garry Ranch in Glengarry. Very shy lady. Becomes Siobhan Grant and the bee lady on the farm.

Camerons, Lochiel of the – Charles 21st & Donald 22nd Lochiel, lived in Achnacarry, adjourning lands to MacDonald and Grant lands. Assisted Alexander Grant in purchasing a farm on MacDonald lands. Married.

Campbell, Lieutenant – From Fort William. Reports Cherry's death to Malcolm.

Chisholm, David – Father of Hamish and Hugh Og. Husband to Mary. Drowned in Loch Craskie.

Chisholm, David – son of Hamish and Cora Chisholm, brother of Donald and Mairi

Chisholm, Donald – one of the Seven Glenmoriston Men. Son of Paul Chisholm. Brother to Alexander and Hugh. Moves to Canada with wife and family until his death.

Chisholm, Donald Og – son of Hamish and Cora. First baby to be baptised in the new Chapel. Brother of David and Mairi, learns to fish at Loch Insh.

Chisholm, Ferne – only daughter of Meredith and Hugh Og Chisholm

Chisholm, Fleur – miscarried daughter of Hugh Chisholm and Isobel MacGregor Grant.

Chisholm, Hamish - one of the fisher lads. Brother to Hugh Og. Son of the widow Chisholm, later the widow MacDonald. Married Cora MacKinnon. Father to Donald Og and David. Employed on Craskie and Grant Farms and the Glenmoriston School as security. One of the men who go out fishing together with Malcolm and Kenneth. Becomes Craskie Farm manager, then builds a salmon farm for Zahra but dies in a freak storm on the mountain.

Chisholm, Hugh Mohr 🌿 – youngest of the Seven Glenmoriston Men. Son of Paul Chisholm. Brother to Alexander and Donald. Fathered a miscarried child with Isobel Grant, named Fleur. Lived and worked in Cannich. Married Isobel Grant after the death of Padruig Dubh Grant. Blamed for planning the theft of a portion of Marion Grants (MacDonalds) inheritance. In death, Hugh re-marries Zahra, and they have a son, Wee Hugh, but Hugh Mohr is killed once again on the day of their wedding. Later he is re-awakened miraculously, and Zahra has to live with two husbands on Misty Mountain.

Chisholm, Hugh Og – one of the fisher lads. Brother to Hamish. Son of the widow Chisholm, who was later the widow MacDonald. Married Meredith MacKenzie and father to Ferne. Employed on Craskie Farm as head groom then later runs and manages the team as head teamster. Moves team to Glengarry. Trains Malcolm's twins as teamsters

Chisholm, Mairi - daughter of Hamish and Cora Chisholm, sister of David and Donald

Chisholm, Meredith – daughter of Alexander and Ferne MacKenzie, wife of Hugh Og Chisholm. Employed in the house at Craskie Farm as well as wool waulking. Leaves Craskie job to work in Glengarry for Malcolm. Works temporarily for Zahra.

Chisholm, Paul – Father of Alexander, Donald and Hugh. Tenant at Blairie/Blame

Chisholm, Sakina- deceased, unborn child of Zahra, when she was married to Hugh Chisholm.

Chisholm, Wee Hugh – Son of Zahra and Hugh Chisholm in their second marriage. Born after Hugh's death and raised by Grigor until Hugh returns.

Colquhoun, Annie – Goat milker on MacNachten farm, fancies Colm MacKenzie, then prefers Iain who she hand fasts with.

Forbes, Bishop Robert ❧ – Bishop of Ross and Caithness, Episcopalian Church, Leith. Collector of witness statements of survivor's post Culloden battle through to 1775. Died before it was published.

78ᵗʰ Fraser Highlanders ❧ – formed by Simon Fraser, Master of Lovat. Fought and won in Quebec Campaigns against the French.

Fraser, Alasdair – Zahra's bodyguard and love interest of Coinneach MacAlpin. Coinneach's body was buried on his property in Wick/Strathcarron from which he was cleared.

Fraser, Anastacia – Middle aged widow and live in laundress at Beinn Coinneach for Zahra who marries Cinaed Fraser.

Fraser, Anndra MacDonald – child born to Isobel Fraser. Later adopted by Coinneach MacAlpin, adopted again by Cinaed MacAlpin jnr. Educated at Fraser Ville school then attends university at Cinaed's expense. Both him and his brother Domnhall remain close to Zahra and live close by after Cinaed marries their Mother.

Fraser, Charles – Accountant from Fraser Ville. Works with his Father Martin Fraser, on Zahra's house on Misty Mountain Ranch to formalise her inheritance along with Cinaed Og.

Fraser, Colin – Drunken brother to Ivy Fraser. Lives in the Beauly Firth. Wolf hunter.

Fraser, George – Drunken and dangerous brother of Ivy Fraser. Wolf hunter.

Fraser, Isobel – daughter of Zahra MacGregor with Hugh Chisholm. Marries John Fraser first and has two children, Anndra and Domhnall who are both sired by Alex MacDonald. She then has a daughter born to old Lord Cinaed then later marries the young Lord Cinaed MacAlpin after her divorce and has another daughter.

Fraser, Ivy Simone – Entomologist. Author of a book on insects, seeks out Kenneth MacNachten for illustrations for her book. She is hopeful for a romance and marries him secretly and becomes Ivy MacNachten. They have one child, April Marion MacNachten.

Fraser, John - Farmer in the Aird and husband of Isobel Fraser. Unable to sire children.

Fraser, Martin – Bookkeeper from Fraser Ville. Worked for Lord Coinneach in secret office. Reveals truths.

Fraser, Rabbie – groundsman for Misty Mountain. Son of Charles Fraser of Fraser Ville, Accountant of same.

Fraser, Lord Simon 🐝 – Husband of Elizabeth Grant. Fictionally, son of Anna and John Fraser of Stratherick. Became a politician and a Peer.

Fraser Simon Jnr- son of Simon Fraser who dies at the age of sixteen in horse riding accident. Becomes one of the unalive and lives in the Aird as the nephew of John Fraser and marries Fatma, temporarily.

Fraser, Simone-Anna – daughter of Beth and Simon Fraser

Fraser, Zahra Isobel MacAlpin – third child of Isobel Fraser, half-sister to Anndra and Domnhall and Cinaed Og. The father was Lord Cinaed MacAlpin who was not made aware Isobel was expecting his child. Isobel's unhappiness after the child's birth was partly attributed to the deception as well as the loss of her father, Hugh Chisholm.

Fraser, Rauri- Yardman, Beinn Coinneach

Grant, Alexander – son of Padruig and Isobel Grant. First married to Therese. Six children including being Jean and Alexander. Loses two children in Nova Scotia. Fictionally, marries Matilda MacMartin upon his return to Scotland and fathers two more children, Moses, and Sarah. Buys a new farm called Loch Garry Ranch and accommodates his twin Marion and her son Malcolm MacNachten.

Grant, Alexander Og – youngest son of Alex Grant. Fictionally moved to Scotland from Nova Scotia. A talented chef as well as competent farmer specialising in animal husbandry. Sensitive nature misunderstood by Malcolm. Marries Siobhan and inherits Loch Garry Ranch.

Grant, Beth – daughter of Patrick and Henrietta Grant. Married to Simon Fraser. Fictionally begins her own business breeding Highland Ponies. Mother of Simone-Anna. Known as a snob.

Grant, Freya – mother of Isobel Grant originally from Loch Insh. Wife of John Grant. Mother to Grigor MacGregor from a previous marriage. Also, Clan Gregor. Murdered by British troops in 1746.

Grant, Helen – daughter of Padruig and Isobel Grant. Fictionally, wife of Grigor Og MacGregor and artist. Mother of Isobel-Mairi, Aonghus Grigor and Morag-Freya. Grandmother to Nachtain and Bridei. Fails to succeed in running the farms after her Mither's death. Separates from Grigor. Commits suicide.

Grant, Henrietta – wife of Patrick Grant. Mother to Beth, James and Sarah. Lazy in business.

Grant, Henrietta Jnr – baby daughter of James and Susan Grant

Grant, Isobel 🌺 – b. 1702. Wife to Padruig Grant. Mother to Patrick, Helen, Marion and Alexander. Miscarries Fleur. Fictionally, Clan Gregor. Daughter of John and Freya Grant. Second cousin to Gillcrest MacNachten. d. 1788.

Grant, James 🌺 – son of Patrick and Henrietta Grant. Fictionally, married to Susan Chisholm. Assists Malcolm MacNachten in dressing correctly to propose to Cherry. First to see Zahra with new husband after the breakup with Grigor. Known as a gossip.

Grant, Jean – youngest linguist daughter of Alexander Grant, who fictionally moved to Scotland from Nova Scotia, wife of Dr. Benedict Browne, mother of Benedict Alexander Browne. Hand fasts with Duncan Mohr MacDonnell after her divorce from the Doctor has a child with him.

Grant, John 🌺 – father of Isobel Grant. Fictionally, husband of Freya Grant. Leaves an inheritance for Marion Grant, one of twins.

Grant, Moses - son and 8th child of Alexander Mohr Grant and son of Matilda MacMartin

Grant, Padruig – b. 1701 known as Padruig Dubh. Jacobite soldier and husband to Isobel Grant. Father to Patrick, Helen, Marion and Alexander. d. 1786. One of the Seven Glenmoriston Men. Rapes Zahra in his spectre form and known for making trouble.

Grant, Patrick – son of Padruig and Isobel Grant. Husband to Henrietta. Father to Beth, James and Sarah. Fictionally, inherits the Hart of the Highlands Manor House and succeeds in business but unpopular and dies after seeing his father as a ghost.

Grant, Sarah – daughter and 7th child of Alexander Mohr Grant and daughter of Matilda MacMartin

Grant, Susan – Clan Chisholm. Married James Grant, son of Patrick Grant. Divorces him. Has one child, Henrietta who later runs the hotel.

Hamilton, **Mr John Alexander**- Lawyer from Inverness.

Heath, Dr. Peter – Effeminate English doctor based in Inverness. Befriends both Alex MacDonald and Alexander Og Grant. Matilda Grant discovers that he was charged with assault with sodomitical intent in London which becomes headlines. He is called on by Coinneach MacAlpin, aware of his previous history, to treat Zahra's spine. He later lives with Zahra, before Hugh's death then he reignites his love affair with Alex MacDonald but is tortured by unknown assailants. Peter then goes to live with the Sidhe (Fairies).

Lugh, The Celtic God- Rescues Zahra after wolf attack.

MacAlpin, Annie Chisholm- daughter of Isobel and Cinaed MacAlpin. The youngest of Isobel's bairns following, Anndra, Domnhall and Zahra Og. Her first and only child born to Cinaed MacAlpin.

MacAlpin, Anndra– Brother to Lord Coinneach, son of Lord Cinaed. Suspected of gold heist. Disposed of by Grigor.

MacAlpin, Cinaed Og – Youngest brother to Lord Coinneach. Son to Lord Cinaed. Assists with Zahra's pregnancy. Last of the Druids. Marries Isobel and sires, a daughter with her.

MacAlpin, Cinaed Snr – Father to Lord Coinneach, Lord Cinaed Og, Lord Padraig, Lord Anndra and Lord Griogar. Head of MacAlpin Industries known to be corrupt.

MacAlpin, Coinneach – mysterious older man with whom Zahra meets, at the house of the old Crohn. He identifies Zahra who has regal ancestry. Marries Zahra MacGrigor after she is brutalised by her husband and they live on the top of a mountain, Beinn Coinneach. Artist and bi-sexual who later takes a male lover, Alisdair Fraser from Fraser Ville and the marriage with Zahra is annulled. Can shape shift into a nasty, big brown wolf which affects Zahra.

MacAlpin, Coinneach Og – baby born to Zahra and

Coinneach MacAlpin.

MacAlpin, Griogar Prince – half-brother to Lord Coinneach. War Lord and dangerous.

MacAlpin, Padraig – Brother to Lord Coinneach and Lord Cinaed and Prince Griogar. Son of Lord Cinaed.

MacAlpin, Ruari – red haired security guard for MacNachten Enterprises. Unrelated to the Beinn Coinneach family.

MacAlpin, Zahra – Becomes wife to Coinneach MacAlpin. Known then as Lady Zahra Coinneach. Formerly known as Zahra MacGregor, married to Grigor MacGregor who has six children. Delivers one more child with Coinneach who they name Coinneach Og. Later marries both Hugh and Grigor and has one more child with Hugh.

MacDonald, Bruce – childhood friend of Grigor Og MacGregor, moves to South Carolina in 1746, marries an Indian woman then returns to Scotland in adulthood after her death. Marries Marion MacNachten, Malcolm's Mother. Becomes close to Marion's sons, Malcolm and Kenneth and works on Malcolm's farm with the goats. Retires to Loch Garry. Passes away before Hamish Og's wedding to Fatma MacGregor.

MacDonald, Cameron – Drover from Craskie farm. Friend of Hector MacGregor.

MacDonald, Domhnall Og – Isobel Fraser's youngest son, born to Alexander MacDonald. Brother to Anndra Fraser.

MacDonald, Lillian – washer lady for MacNachten Farm three days a week.

MacDonnell, Donald – young hunter who attends the wolf hunt in the Aird and sketches the picture of the five deceased wolves, including the Alpha wolf and the MacDonalds, who killed them, with Malcolm MacNachten of Glengarry.

MacDonnell, Dougal – childhood friend of Grigor Og MacGregor, marries an heiress in Glengarry.

MacDonnell, Duncan Mohr – security man for Cherry Farms and Loch Garry, 30 years old, married with children, skilled with weaponry and fitness.

MacDonnell, Duncan Og– groomsman at Craskie Farm recommended by Killian MacDonnell.

MacDonnell, Duncan Snr. – marksman, hired as security for Glengarry farms. Grandfather of Duncan of Craskie. Has a love interest in Jean Grant after her divorce whom he later marries and has one child.

MacDonnell, Killian – door neighbour of Matilda and Alex Grant in Loch Garry. Formerly taught the Gaelic language to Matilda, whilst in London.

MacDonnell, Mairi – wife to Duncan Mohr MacDonnell, security guard to MacNachten Farms.

MacDonnell, Old John – elderly, cunning wolf killer from Glengarry. Led the group to kill the pack of wolves in the Aird. Known to have an army of bastards. Kills Cherry MacLean. Becomes Malcolm's surrogate father later in life before his own death. Leaves his property to Malcolm.

MacDougal, Dougal – Senior groomsman for the Clydesdales after Bruce MacKay moves to Inverness, brother to Milread. Marries the widow MacKichan taking on her two sons, Charles, and Henry. Live temporarily at Chisholm House.

MacDougal, Fergus – Aonghus' friend from university, member of Pict club. Travels to Loch Fyne with Gillcrest and Patrick Hamilton. Contemplating writing a joint paper on the Picts.

MacFie and the Black Dog- folk law of the Isles.

MacGregor, Ailsa – devoted second wife of Malcolm MacNachten, daughter of love interest of Grigor Mohr MacGregor. Finds raising twin boys difficult.

MacGregor, Ali – oldest twin son of Zahra MacGregor. Studies and works at Craskie farm while living with Hamish until his father returns, threatening his security. Returns to re-build the Aird. He is re-named Ali Gregor MacAlpin. Later re-sells farm back to his father and buys a farm neighbouring Malcolm in Glengarry.

MacGregor, Aonghus – son of Grigor MacGregor Og and Helen Grant MacGregor. Husband to Annabel Cameron. Became a lawyer in Inverness. Highly intelligent and shares an interest with Fergus about the Picts. Manages all legal matters for the family farms and new business.

MacGregor, Belle – widow from Inverness. Ailsa's Mother and love interest to Grigor Mohr MacGregor who leaves with him to go to the Americas. Is left behind in the Americas when Grigor returns home to Scotland.

MacGregor Bridghe- One of four children to Hector and Flidas MacGregor. Becomes a lady Doctor and works out of Fraser Ville with her other three siblings. Marries, the Celtic God Lugh, without knowing that he was a God.

MacGregor, Causantin – young son of Zahra MacGregor. Kidnapped also when Zahra is taken but left in the Aird, with his sister Dihaoine. Later reunited with Zahra to live on Misty Mountain Ranch. Loyal to his mother and becomes a jeweller by trade. Has a Spanish male lover for a short time, then later has an interest in Alex MacDonald.

MacGregor, Dihaoine Freya Dorothea – youngest daughter of Zahra and Grigor Mohr MacGregor in the Aird. Adopted by Coinneach MacAlpin, later returned to her father. Marries Malcolm Og MacNachten of Glengarry and lives with the twins and Zahra and Grigor on Beinn Coinneach.

MacGregor, Fatma – twin daughter to Ali of Zahra MacGregor and Grigor MacGregor who initially live in the Aird. Hand fasts with Simon Fraser Junior and is adopted by Coinneach MacAlpin when Grigor abandons the family. Later marries Hamish Og MacNachten and lives on Misty Mountain with the family and grows bees.

MacGregor, Grigor Mohr – One of the Seven Glenmoriston Men. Fictionally Father of Grigor MacGregor Og, husband of Morag, half-brother to Isobel Grant. In death becomes the husband of Zahra MacGregor. Has six children with Zahra while working the Aird until he strays to Belle MacGregor then moves to the Americas, but it doesn't work, and he returns. Remarries Zahra but upon Hugh returning to life must share her.

MacGregor, Grigor Og – husband of Helen Grant, son of Grigor MacGregor, Father to Isobel-Mairi, Aonghus-Grigor and Morag-Freya. Hard worker and soil perfectionist on the Cannich farm. Influenced adversely after Isobel's death. Retires from farm puts Hamish in charge then returns when Hamish leaves to build the salmon farm on Beinn Coinneach

MacGregor, Hector – second oldest son to Zahra and Grigor Mohr MacGregor. Briefly takes on the name Hector MacAlpin. Known to be wild but saves his Mither in snow. Raises highland ponies with his wife Flidas to pay for their four children's education.

MacGregor, Hugh-Cameron – baby son of Aonghus and Annabel MacGregor who attends the gatherings of the bairns each week until it ends.

MacGregor, Isobel-Mairi – daughter of Grigor MacGregor Og and Helen Grant MacGregor. Wife of the disliked Ewen MacNachten. Mother to Nachtain Grigor MacNachten. Leaves the farm to open a mill and tartan shop in Inverness during the year of the sheep. Causes trouble for her Mither, Helen and Cannich and borrows money from Helen which she is too slow to re-pay.

MacGregor, Zahra – Married to Grigor Mohr MacGregor. Becomes Grigor Og's temporary cook. Mother to eight children, first living on a farm in the Aird with husband Grigor Mohr MacGregor. Part of an eccentric family group who are no longer of the living. Becomes the wife of Coinneach MacAlpin, then re-marries Hugh then Grigor. Inherits the huge mountainous property on Beinn Coinneach as compensation.

MacKay, Iain – Adult teamster offsider who works for Malcolm Og and Hamish Og in Glengarry. Likes one of the goat milking lassies.

MacKay, Milread – born MacDougal. Wool waulker and spinner, sister to Dougal MacDougal, wife of Bruce MacKay and Mother of Robert. Moves to Inverness to work in new milling business spinning tartan for Isobel-Mairi MacNachten. Returns to Glenmoriston.

MacKenzie, Alexander – Father of Meredith from Kinlochewe. Husband of Ferne MacKenzie. Refused to attend the wedding of Hugh and Isobel.

MacKenzie, Angus – Offsider to Hugh Og, Teamster. Young and very handsome. Cousin to Meredith from Kinlochewe. Islay likes him then marries him and has two daughters and a son, Winnifred and Florence and Padraig, living in Malcolm's house in Glengarry.

MacKenzie, Callum – Farm manager on Misty Mountain, Beinn Coinneach. Mairi's husband.

MacKenzie, Colm – 40 year old security guard employed by Malcolm in Glengarry. Knows Meredith from Kinlochewe and unpopular with her. Love interest to a goat milker also. Later marries Florence MacNachten.

MacKenzie, Ferne – Mother of Meredith, wife of Alexander MacKenzie.

MacKenzie, Flidas Winnifred Isobel– First born daughter of Islay and Angus. Grandchild of Malcolm MacNachten. Marries Hector and becomes Flidas.

MacKenzie, Florence, Marion – Second daughter of Islay and Angus. Grandaughter of Malcolm MacNachten.

MacKenzie, George – Farm manager for the Aird.

MacKenzie, Mairi – cook to Coinneach MacAlpin, from the mountains.

MacKenzie, Padraig Nachtain- first child to Islay and Angus MacKenzie, Malcolm's grandson. Dies from emphysema at a young age.

MacKenzie, Rose – Farm manager's wife who cooks and cleans in the Aird.

MacKichan, Alexandria – mother of Charles and Henry. Cleared from her croft to live on Craskie Farm. Marries Groom Dougal MacDougal.

MacKichan, Charles – 16-year-old student. Son of the widow MacKichan. Apprentice soil specialist to Grigor Og for soil movement. Older brother to Henry MacKichan.

MacKichan, Henry – 12-year-old son of the widow MacKichan. Younger brother to Charles MacKichan. Assistant to Hugh Mohr.

MacKinnon, Dr Alicia – new head Scientist for the perfection of soil at Invermoriston Hospital, replacing Gillcrest MacLachlan as Head of Department

MacKinnon, Cora – daughter of Mairi and Donald MacKinnon (dcd), wife to Hamish Chisholm, mother to Donald Og, songstress, schoolteacher, and wool waulking. Dies tragically on Misty Mountain.

MacLachlan, Gillcrest Lachlan – Laird of Lachlan lands in Argyle. Husband of Morag-Freya Grant. Head scientist specialising in crop yields by perfecting soil. Father of Patricia Fleur. Lives in Invermoriston before they move back to Loch Fyne.

MacLachlan, Morag-Freya – daughter of Grigor MacGregor and Helen Grant MacGregor. Became a nurse at Invermoriston Hospital. Wife to Gillcrest Lachlan MacLachlan to be a Laird's wife. Mother to Patricia Fleur. Introduces Aonghus and Annabel Cameron who later marry.

MacLean, Joshua – Islander and farm hand on Cherry Farm in Glen Garry. Known as Joe. Uncle to Cherry, wife of Malcolm. He moves with his family to New Holland. Guilty of prostituting Cherry MacClean before her marriage to Malcolm MacNachten. Has her first unborn bairn to Old John MacDonnell terminated.

MacLean, Murdoch – farmworker cleared from the Islands. Friend of Joseph MacFie from Loch Garry Ranch, Glengarry. Helps Craskie Farm get back on track. Uncle to Cherry who marries Malcolm. Moves to New Holland after hurting Malcolm in a fight. Guilty of prostituting Cherry before her marriage with Malcolm.

MacMartin Grant, Matilda – adopted daughter of Hector and Elizabeth Menzies. Born to a crofter family on Craskie Farm. Educated in London. Degree in biology and botany. Marries Alexander Grant of Loch Garry Ranch and has two children. Creates issues for Dr Heath. Establishes old growth forest on the land.

MacNachten, Dr. Alexander – oldest son of Malcolm and Cherry MacNachten. Marries Mairi. Competent Doctor who delivers a few of Zahra's family's children. Runs medical centre in Glengarry.

MacNachten, Alexander Cinaed- second son to Dr Alexander MacNachten and Mairi MacNachten

MacNachten, April Marion- first and only child to Kenneth and Ivy MacNachten. Lived on MacNachten Farms with both of her parents. Fraser Grandparents begin to visit her. Marries Ali MacGregor and lives in Glengarry then Glenmoriston. Becomes April MacGregor and has one child.

MacNachten, Cherry – formerly MacLean of the Isles. Marries Malcolm MacNachten. Mother to Islay, Alexander and the twins Hamish-Hugh and Malcolm Marion. Niece of Joseph MacFie and Murdoch MacLean. Worked as a chef before marrying Malcolm. Divorces Malcolm to leave him for the colonies but returns. Found deceased in a forest. Shot in the head by Old John MacDonnell.

MacNachten, Eschina Isobel – youngest daughter to Malcolm and Ailsa MacNachten.

MacNachten, Ewen – born MacThreynfhir or Armstrong – adopted son of Gilcrest MacNachten. Husband to Isobel-Mairi. Father to Nachtain Grigor MacNachten. Blacksmith and farrier at Craskie Farm. Ventures into business with his wife in Inverness. Has a fight with Malcolm. In debt with Helen.

MacNachten, Gilcrest – adoptive Father to Ewen MacNachten, foster Father to Marion Grant, second cousin to Isobel Grant, Loch Insh, Foster Grandfather to both Malcolm and Kenneth MacNachten. Married off Marion to his nephew Nachtain MacNachten who dies from pneumonia when Malcolm is only four years old.

MacNachten, Gordon Padruig– youngest son of Malcolm and Ailsa MacNachten. Hopes that he will study law. But ends up in an engineering project on the farm which he inherits with his sister, Eschina.

MacNachten, Hamish-Hugh – handsome twin son of Malcolm MacNachten, Glengarry. Becomes a teamster with his twin brother. Marries Fatma MacGregor. Lives on Beinn Coinneach

MacNachten, Islay – daughter of Malcolm and Cherry MacNachten. Wife of Angus Mackenzie. Runs the goat farm. Moves briefly to Misty Mountain, then purchases what is left of Craskie Farm for her goats with her husband Angus MacKenzie.

MacNachten, Kenneth – Son of Marion and Nachtain MacNachten decd, younger brother of Malcolm, Grandson of Isobel and Padruig Grant, trained as a stonemason, becomes educated as an accountant paid for by John Fraser, takes up being an illustrator and an artist. Marries Ivy Fraser. Owns an Art gallery on MacNachten Farms with his brother. Has one child, April who marries Ali MacGregor. Kenneth dies young due to his ill health.

MacNachten, Mairi- Nurse and wife to Malcolm's oldest son Alexander, a Doctor in Invermoriston.

MacNachten, Malcolm Coinneach- oldest son of Dr Alexander MacNachten and Mairi MacNachten

MacNachten, Malcolm Mohr – Son of Marion MacNachten and Nachtain MacNachten decd, older brother to Kenneth, Grandson of Isobel and Padruig Grant, trained as a stonemason. Lived with Alex in Loch Garry Ranch. Marries lady from the Isles, Cherry MacLean. Had four children, Islay and Alexander, Hamish and Malcolm with first wife. Divorces Cherry and marries Ailsa MacGregor and had two more children, Gordon and Eschina. Inherits properties in Glengarry and is successful and well liked.

MacNachten, Malcolm-Marion – twin son Malcolm MacNachten, Glengarry. Teamster with his twin Hamish. Marries Dihaoine MacGregor. Moves the team to Misty Mountain. Later moves to Loch Insh to run a bed and breakfast.

MacNachten, Marion – Twin sister of Alex Grant. Concealed daughter of Isobel Grant. Raised in secret by Gilcrest MacNachten in Loch Insh. Is returned with her two sons, Malcolm and Kenneth to Craskie Farm and is re-united with her twin brother, Alex. Meets Padruig Dubh before his death. Is moved to Loch Garry Ranch due to the clearances and Helen disliking her. Marries Bruce MacDonald. Lives happily in Glengarry.

MacNachten, Nachtain [senior]– deceased beloved husband of Marion Grant MacNachten, father of Malcolm and Kenneth. Died from pneumonia when his children were very young in Loch Insh.

MacNeil, Iain – Groomsman and teamster on MacNachten Farms, Glengarry.

MacPherson, Carmel Juliann- Midwife in Cameron lands. Interested in meeting Grigor after the death of Helen, then successfully get together.

MacPherson, Ewen of Cluny – Laird of Clan Chattan and Clan MacPherson, contemporary of the gentle Donald Cameron of Lochiel.

Mathieson, David – Drover from Craskie farm and friend of Hector MacGregor. Stayed in Beinn Coinneach for one night playing music.

Menzies, Elizabeth – adoptive Mother to Matilda MacMartin later became Matilda Grant.

Menzies, Hector – adoptive Father to Matilda MacMartin later became Matilda Grant.

Menzies, Kenneth – The Editor, Inverness Times Newspaper, Scotland. Bought Clearance painting off Helen through John Fraser.

Ross, Frederick – husband to Lillian Ross

Ross, Iain - Groom from Craskie Farm, friend of Ali MacGregor.

Ross, Lillian – midwife from Inverness, connected with the Glenmoriston and Glengarry midwives who attends the birth of Zahra's daughter, Dihaoine Freya Dorothea

Shaw, Ann – housekeeper of Malcolm Law Rooms, Inverness

Wolves – two spirit wolves attached to Zahra MacAlpin were named Ulvy Stiorm and Winter Wolf. Zahra's actual pet wolf was named Wolfie until his release back into the wild.

Urquhart, Domnhall – Jeweller from outskirts of Inverness who teaches Zahra's son, Causantin, the trade of making fine jewellery.

Wool Waulking Women - Isobel (until retirement), Helen, Mairi MacKinnon (until dc'd), Cora, Meredith, Isobel-Mairi, Morag-Freya and Milread [until it moves into a mill in Inverness].

Bibliography

1. El-Fatah, Z. (2023) *Isobel of Glenmoriston*, Angel Key Publications, Brisbane, Australia.

2. El-Fatah, Z. (2024) *Secrets of the Braes and Glens, Isobel of Glenmoriston Series of Books*, Angel Key Publications, Brisbane, Australia.

3. Forbes, Rev. Robert (collected 1746-1775) (published 1895) *The Lyon in Mourning*, 1895 Vol. III, Edited from 1746-1775 Manuscript by Henry Paton MA, Forgotten Books, University Press, Scottish History Society, Edinburgh, UK.

4. Fraser, S. (2012) *The Last Highlander*, Harper Collins Publishers, London, U.K. pages 220, 324.

5. Gunn, Robert M. The Tragic Highland Clearances, Chapter 5: Murder of Ross women; Clearance mythology? www.skyelander.orgfree.com

6. Zaynab El-Fatah, 2023, Isobel of Glenmoriston, "This is Isobel's Story".

7. Zaynab El-Fatah, 2024, Isobel of Glenmoriston Series of Novels, "Secrets of the Braes and Glens".

8. Zaynab El-Fatah, 2024. Isobel of Glenmoriston Series of Novels "Wolves and the Curse".

9. Zaynab El-Fatah, 2025, yet to be published. Isobel of Glenmoriston Series of Novels "My Sweet Grigor".

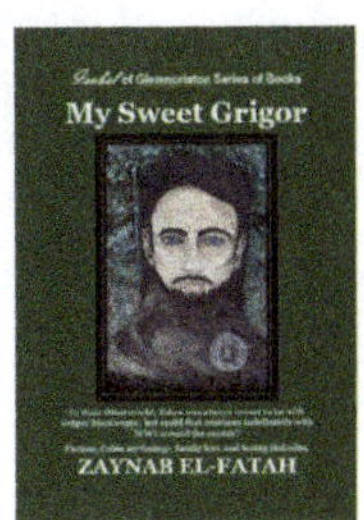

Acknowledgements

As a novelist, I rely in many ways, on family, friends, or connections throughout the world, to enhance the enjoyment for the reader of the work. I am constantly looking for ideas and correcting work that I have already written and for this, so many people I know need to be thanked and they know who they are, especially my family.

Many thanks to Broch Ridsale and Debbie Watt and their beautiful Irish Wolfhound, Niamh, who posed for her photograph to be taken in Brisbane at the Celtic Festival in 2024, and she has been included in this novel.

The second novel, 'Secrets of the Braes and Glens', introduced my artist daughter, Claire into the technical side in the world of book publishing, as well as her artistry and I thank Claire for both her lovely artwork as well as her technical work that she has stepped up to assist me with.

Naturally I thank my publishers: Alice our consultant, as well as Ian Lewis - CEO and Graphic Designer from Angel Key Publication,

Tracy and her husband from Carindale, for printing out the paintings so well, are to be thanked once again, as does one of my doctors for checking on some medical facts.

A special thankyou goes to the Cameron Clan at The Australian Celtic Festival in Glen Innes, who promoted the books on their stall and in their Scottish Museum in Scotland. Thank you to Clan Cameron.

I hope you all enjoy reading 'Wolves and the Curse'.

Zaynab El-Fatah
Brisbane, Australia.

www.ingramcontent.com/pod-product-compliance
Lightning Source LLC
Chambersburg PA
CBHW070311190726
48291CB00012B/2